That night, Jarom dreamed again of dragons and epic battles frightening in their clarity, where thousands perished and rivers of fire singed the air. He witnessed first-hand the euphoria that illuminated the faces of those called upon to wield the Swords of Asahiel—those marvelous talismans whose own internal fire could never be spent. He experienced their raw passion, their righteous fury, and knew in that moment that he too must one day partake of the endless exhilaration pouring from that cup.

THE CRIMSON SWORD
Book One of THE LEGEND OF ASAHIEL

"Eldon Thompson wields more than just a little magic in his debut novel . . . Don't fail to get in on the ground floor of what promises to be an exciting series."
Terry Brooks

"Thompson's first novel creates a richly detailed world of shadow assassins, demon queens, and magical swords. Jarom is a sympathetic and engaging hero . . . In the tradition of high fantasy, this book belongs in most fantasy collections."
Library Journal

"A fantastic adventure with fun characters and events that really aren't what they seem, and an intriguing twist on the epic quest."
Robert Newcomb, author of *The Scrolls of the Ancients*

Books by Eldon Thompson

The Legend of Asahiel

Book One
THE CRIMSON SWORD

Forthcoming
Book Two
THE OBSIDIAN KEY

ELDON THOMPSON

THE BOOK ONE OF THE
LEGEND OF ASAHIEL

CRIMSON SWORD

An Imprint of HarperCollinsPublishers

This is a work of fiction. The characters, incidents, and dialogue are products of the author's imagination and are not to be construed as real. Any resemblance to actual events or persons, living or dead, is entirely coincidental.

EOS
An Imprint of HarperCollins*Publishers*
10 East 53rd Street
New York, New York 10022-5299

Copyright © 2005 by Eldon Thompson
Map by David Cain
Excerpt from *The Obsidian Key* copyright © 2006 by Eldon Thompson
ISBN-13: 978-0-06-074151-8
ISBN-10: 0-06-074151-1
www.eosbooks.com

First Eos paperback printing: May 2006
First Eos hardcover printing: May 2005

HarperCollins® and Eos® are trademarks of HarperCollins Publishers Inc.

Printed in the U.S.A.

10 9 8 7 6 5 4 3 2

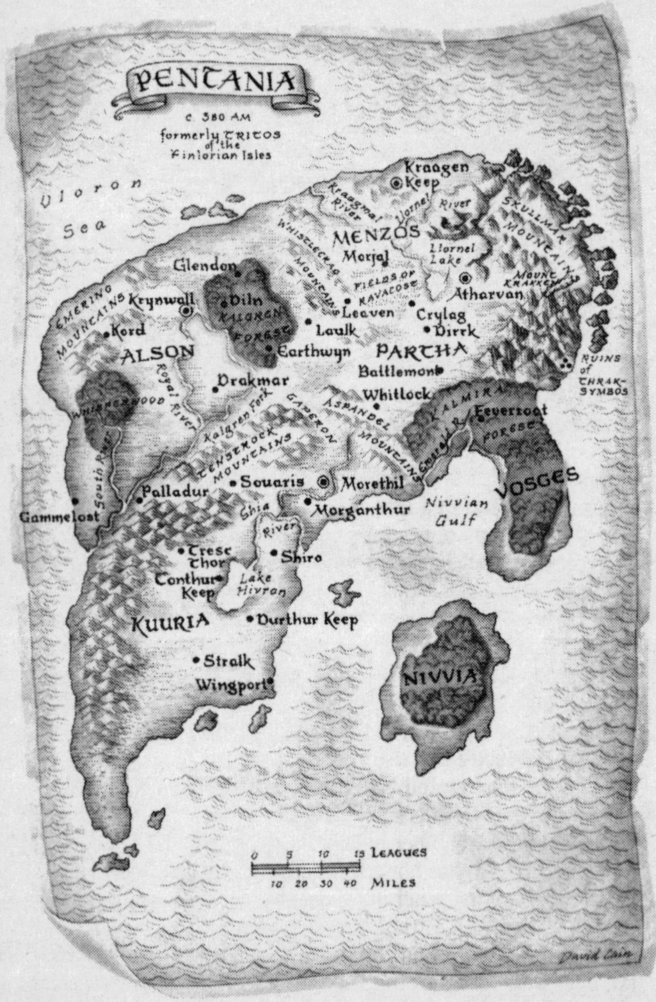
PENTANIA
c. 380 AM
formerly TRITOS of the Finlorian Isles
Uloron Sea
Kraagen Keep
Kraagmal River
Llornel River
SKULLMAR MOUNTAINS
MENZOS
WHISTLECRAG MOUNTAINS
Morjal
Llornel Lake
Glendon
FIELDS OF RAVACOSE
Mount Krakken
Atharvan
EMERING MOUNTAINS
Krynwall
Diln
KALGREN FOREST
Leaven
Crylag
Kord
Laulk
Dirrk
ALSON
Earthwyn
PARTHA
Royal River
RUINS of THRAK-SYMBOS
Drakmar
Battlemont
Whitlock
WHISPERWOOD
Kalgren Fork
GAPERON
ASPANDEL MOUNTAINS
KALMIRA
Feverroot
FOREST
TENSTROCK MOUNTAINS
South River
Souaris
Morethil
VOSGES
Palladur
Gammelost
Shia
Morganthur
Nivvian Gulf
River
Tresc Thor
Shiro
Conthur Keep
Lake Hivron
KUURIA
Durthur Keep
Stralk
NIVVIA
Wingport
0 5 10 15 LEAGUES
10 20 30 40 MILES

CHAPTER ONE

Midnight shadows filled the forest, spectral images born of moonlight filtering through a thicket of gnarled oak and shagbark hickory, of pine and spruce, of ferns and fronds and slithering ivy. Upon the ground, dark profiles weaved and merged, gathered over twigs and needles in a series of dry pools. Once puddled, the darkness shifted in silent ripples, mimicking the languid motion of branches and leaves swaying overhead in a late summer breeze.

At the edge of one such pool, standing just within the sifted radiance of a pale moon, a mouse lifted its head to sniff the scented air. Whiskers wriggled atop its nose, brushing the air with ceaseless anticipation. Its heart beat furiously within its chest. The creature glanced quickly to one side, then the other, then looked back to the small grain seed clutched in its paws. Once, twice, it nibbled experimentally, turning the morsel over, testing it from either end. Finally, it cast the seed aside and reached for another.

A sudden shadow fell over it. The mouse squealed as iron talons pierced its flesh, a sharp squeak of fear and surprise. Before it could draw another breath, its chest collapsed beneath a crushing grip as it was hoisted free of the earthen floor.

The owl bore its twitching meal skyward, winging its way through a labyrinth of dark trees.

The Shadow watched the owl's flight and remained hidden, eyes and ears probing the darkness. But the attack had been perfect. Almost immediately, the shrill echoes of the mouse's cry were lost to the wind, and what remained of life within the forest went about its business without notice or concern. The Shadow permitted itself a private smile. Perfect.

It detached itself from its concealment then, peeling from the trunk of a nearby birch like a strip of bark. It cast north and south, crouched low, searching for a response to its movement. Detecting none, it resumed course, a shimmer amid the trees. Like the owl, it flew upon wings of death, slipping through the foliage without a whisper to mark its passing. Rodents scurried from its path; trees shuddered in a gust of wind. Made anxious by its ghostly presence, nature recoiled, finding safe quarter from which to watch and wait out the trespasser's foul purpose.

It helped the Shadow to think in such exaggerated terms, to distance even itself from its true identity, to imagine itself a creature of supernatural origin and prowess. It fancied itself a fiend among children, pitiless, as inexorable as death itself.

Unhindered, it slid into a copse at the fringe of the forest. Less than a hundred paces to the south, down a gently sloping hill, loomed a forbidding shape, a wall outlined against the night by the pale wash of moon and stars. The Shadow's gaze swept the wall's surface, a skin ravaged by mosses and ivy and crumbling mortar seams. Despite its weathered appearance, the stone structure towered over the land. A trickle of a moat ringed its base, little more than a stream of sewage headed for the nearby Royal River. Most importantly, only a single sentinel stood watch upon this section of the rampart, one who, amazingly enough, appeared to be dozing while leaning upon his rusted pike.

Without further hesitation, the Shadow dashed from its cover, plunging into the knee-deep prairie grass that carpeted the hillside. It crossed the clearing in a crouch, leapt the putrid stream, and came to rest against the cold stone of the castle wall. With only a slight breeze to mark its passing, it need not have paused to ensure that it had not been spied. But the Shadow wore caution as a soldier would his heavy armor, a coat of arms enmeshed over limbs and joints, impossible to remove without concerted effort, and shed not a moment before the battle was won. Caution shielded against overconfidence, which often led to mistakes. And in a contest such as this, a single mistake could grant passage into death's domain. So the Shadow made none.

An army of crickets chirped in shrill cadence. Farther off, an owl hooted deep within the woods. Nearby, the waters of the moat lapped against their earthen banks. But the Shadow's presence, draped flat against the wall, remained undetected.

Secure in this thought, the Shadow turned to face the unyielding stone, producing a coiled length of slender rope from within its cloak. To one end was fastened a tiny, three-pronged grapnel, its metal hooks wrapped in cloth to help quiet any sound and guard against the reflection of light. With deft movements, the Shadow sent the hook hurtling to the top of the crenellated battlement some ninety feet overhead. The throw was true. A muffled clank echoed upon the wind as the hook swung around a crumbling merlon and bit like a serpent into the resisting stone.

Below, the Shadow waited, a tiny crossbow poised to bury its bolt into the unsuspecting face of any curious sentry. But once again, its caution proved unnecessary, as a sudden snore broke the near silence.

The crossbow vanished, and a pair of daggers appeared. After spinning them in its fingers, the Shadow placed the blades in its mouth. Seizing the threadlike rope, the invader tested its hold before beginning to climb.

The Shadow breezed up the monstrous structure, running skyward along the wall while pulling hand over hand upon the rope. Upon reaching the top, the Shadow swung skillfully between two moss-covered merlons, drew the daggers from its mouth, and buried each to its hilt in the throat of the oblivious guardsman. Slumping to the ground within a shadowed alcove, the sentry fell silently into a sleep from which he would never awake.

Pausing briefly to draw a breath, coil its rope, and retrieve its blades, the Shadow turned and raced along the battlement, down a flight of lichen-covered steps, and into the city below.

Closed shops stared with blank expressions as the Shadow passed through the slumbering marketplace. It knew well the route to take, racing through the empty business center while avoiding the areas infested at this hour with drunks, whores, thieves, and various other miscreants. Although more at home with their type than most others, on this night, the Shadow had other business with which to attend.

Overhead, scattered clouds hid the moon and stars as they tracked across the sky. Pools of lamplight were scarce in this sector of the city, and easily avoided. Though ever mindful of its surroundings and watchful of the darkened alleys through which it passed, the Shadow hastened its pace.

Within moments, the iron fence encircling the royal palace emerged from behind a slat-wood building. A pair of watchmen stood before the towering grillwork, laughing over some obscene gossip about their queen. As it studied the men and their surroundings, the hidden Shadow considered their raillery with wry interest. In other nations, speaking such words meant death, but in Alson, half the rumors about Queen Ellebe were started by King Sorl himself—by the sound of it, this one included.

Only in Alson, the Shadow thought, where the king's penchant for lurid tales and unrestrained revelry was the stuff of legend. It was said that no ruler in history knew better how to sate the base urges of himself and his exclusive guests than old King Sorl. His was a large and wealthy land, built on his father's efforts, and it was not in Sorl's nature to worry about cost or consequence. Though Alson fell into further ruin with each passing season, the king demanded that his treasury be kept full, his father's fortune supplemented from time to time with taxed and stolen treasures in order to fund his appetites.

A shame he reserved so little of that fortune for the commission of more-competent sentries.

When the pair of guards erupted into an uncontrollable fit of laughter, the Shadow stepped forward and slit their throats before they could register its presence. As it lowered the second guardsman softly to the ground, the Shadow found a confused expression on the man's stubbled face.

"You're dead," the killer said in a whisper, like that of a dry leaf scraping across the cobbled street.

The soldier's grunt fell from his throat with a choking splash of blood.

With that, the Shadow wiped its blade before scampering to the top of the gate and jumping lightly to the ground beyond. It hit the stone running, and within moments had reached a structure that dwarfed its surrounding companions.

Despite its size, the tower of King Sorl was by no means magnificent. Once upon a time, it had been the most splendid structure in Alson, a proud symbol of her lands and ruler. But now, it more rambled into the night sky than soared, and was so cracked and weathered that it seemed as if only the clinging ivy kept it standing.

Upon reaching the tower, the Shadow skulked alongside its circular outer wall, making for the servants' entrance. But the area was heavy with traffic, as the last of the revelers and food merchants and drug mixers from the night's festivities headed home or lingered about, not yet ready for the debauchery to end. Most were too inebriated to give the Shadow pause. Whores giggled and sighed, some teasing and demure, others open and inviting as they considered last-minute propositions. But others appeared more cognizant, such as scullery maids pushing out wagons of refuse and the whoremasters come to collect their fees. When a trio of guardsmen sauntered over to inspect and then join the commotion, the Shadow decided to seek another avenue.

Flitting away, the Shadow moved back toward the front of the building, where it considered the broad flight of steps leading up to the tower's main entrance. A murky collection of moon and lantern light washed down over the stone, taunting the Shadow with its ability to expose the darkness, daring it forward.

The Shadow cast an ear back toward the side of the tower. The risk, it had begun to realize, was minimal.

After mounting the steps, the Shadow pushed experimentally upon the enormous pair of doors fronting the structure. They knocked briefly against the crossbar locked within. Spinning away, the Shadow came to rest against a postern. Hearing nothing from within, it went to work on the keyhole of the wrought-iron gate that warded the wooden door beyond. Soon, the tumblers shifted and the latch released with a click. With the protective grillwork unlocked, the Shadow reached between its bars for the knocker clinging to the main door.

Carrus groaned. Realizing that the tapping was not a result of the dreams in his head, but of a spear butt against his helm, he came awake and slapped at the intrusion. "What in the Fiend's eye?"

Tehmin snorted and withdrew his spear. He offered a toothy grin as Carrus's thrashing did little more than knock askew his own helm. "We's got company."

"What?" Carrus finally centered his helm and glared at his fellow guardsman, who pointed to the receiving door of the main foyer. "Well, run them off already. What do you need to wake me for?"

"Procedures," Tehmin reminded him, although the man's smirk betrayed the fact that he had roused his companion for no other reason than to irritate him.

Chuckling at Carrus's muttered curses, Tehmin approached the door and drew back the viewing slat. His statement of dismissal caught, however, as he gazed past the bars of the security gate.

"What is it?" Carrus prompted.

"Bah, kids." Tehmin slammed shut the viewing slat and turned away. Before he had taken two steps, the knock sounded again. Spinning about, he tore open the slat. Someone on the other side of the door gave a low whistle.

Tehmin growled and threw back the locking bar. Behind him, Carrus chuckled.

"Now, now, Tehmin. Procedures."

Tehmin ignored him and yanked open the wooden door. As soon as he did, the security gate flew open as well, and Tehmin doubled over. Carrus stopped laughing long enough to squint at the shadow that came rushing forward. His eyes widened as they caught a flash of steel, but before he could so much as find his voice, Carrus felt his windpipe collapse beneath the shredding tips of twin daggers. He clutched at his assailant, but might as well have been grasping at the wind. He felt his muscles stiffen and convulse, heard blood splatter as he coughed, then watched the world fade.

The Shadow squinted against the torchlight. Ordinarily it would have shuddered at such a risk, but this mission had become a touch too easy, and having granted caution its due consideration, the Shadow did not mind adding some excitement to its task. Now, after positioning the pair of guards in a pretense of slumber and securing the portal, the Shadow slipped away from the reaches of the revealing chamber light to the base of a stairway fronting the main hall. Climbing to the top took a matter of heartbeats, at which point the Shadow chose one of several side passages and moved cautiously down its length toward a second set of stairs beyond.

With silent efficiency, the Shadow navigated the maze of corridors and stairs that crisscrossed the interior of the royal palace, winding its way skyward. Reaching the upper floors proved no difficult task; nor was there any challenge in locating Sorl's room. The passages were empty of life, and once it had reached the tower's apex, the Shadow followed the snore of a sentinel to the king's door. The fool lay on the ground in a drunken slumber, a half-filled mug of ale leaning dangerously upon his lap. Above his head, a torch burned gleefully, its light creating strange yet innocuous shadows that helped to make the lethal one invisible. There were no sounds from within.

The guard did not see the glint of steel as the killer's dagger slid from its sheath. Nor did he see how close the blade came to slitting his throat before the Shadow shifted and withdrew the weapon, deciding against the spilling of the man's blood. Let the man try to explain himself in the morning. Let him squirm before his captain and wish that he had been slain. Let him live to wonder at and to curse the Shadow's inexplicable mercy.

Smirking to itself, at its ability to play games with fear

and death the way others played with dice, the Shadow shoved the unlocked door fully open. Without a second glance at the dozing guardsman, the Shadow blew like a stray gust through the arched opening and into the chambers of Sorl, king of Alson.

The door closed silently. Inside, the Shadow found a comfortable sitting room, complete with a flaming hearth and padded chairs. Clothes and mugs and food trays littered the otherwise plush landscape. To the left, an empty doorway opened in on the king's bedchamber.

Sliding along the near wall, the Shadow sheathed its dagger and produced again its tiny crossbow. It could see the king's slumbering form clearly now, a mountain beneath rumpled sheets. Surprisingly, the man slept alone, sprawled upon his back beneath the awning that stretched across brass bedposts, their curtains drawn back.

Alone, save for his cat.

The animal lifted its head as the Shadow crossed the threshold of the bedchamber. One eye was missing, the scarred lid stretched tight and sewn shut against the hollow socket. Its good eye glittered while the cat hissed a slow, steady warning. When the Shadow eased forward, the animal bounded away, scampering across Sorl's chest before dropping to the floor and vanishing behind a dresser.

In its wake, the king woke with a start and jerked upright.

"Who's there?" he coughed.

Pieces of the man's evening feast still nested in his tangled black beard. His eyes were puffy and shaded. His garments appeared to be those he had worn that day, stained with gravy and drink and the stench of smoke from feast hall torches.

The Shadow offered no response. It stood motionless while Sorl blinked and rubbed his eyes and cast about for the source of his alarm. After a moment of searching, Sorl finally saw the Shadow, and he began to tremble as he spied its weapon, leveled already with deadly aim.

"What . . . whatever you want—"

"I shall have," the Shadow whispered.

Sorl's face went pale and he began to cast frantic glances

about the room. The Shadow watched him, reveling in the man's fear. Ironic, that the people of Alson might actually think the assassin had done their land a service.

People were, after all, shortsighted and foolish.

Realizing his doom, the wide-eyed Sorl finally shrieked a desperate cry for help. But it was cut short as the lethal bolt leapt from the assassin's instrument and buried itself in the king's throat, pinning him to his bed.

Awakened by his king's cry, the sentry from the outer hall scurried to his feet and rushed into the room. Inside, he found Sorl lying in his bed, and unaware of the small arrow sticking through his lord's bleeding throat, his eyes flew to the window, where he was certain he saw a man leaping over the stone sill.

His sense of duty lured him to the open window, where he poked his face into the warm night wind and scanned the vista below. After searching in vain for several moments, the sentry shook his head. Perhaps the old coot had had a nightmare. Or perhaps the entire episode had been of his own imagination.

The yawning guardsman closed the shutters, fumbling with the latch as he blinked away the odd dream, then wiping at his breeches where he'd spilled his unfinished ale in his haste to respond. As he stepped from the window, muttering to himself, the sleeping king behind him made a strange gurgling sound. The guardsman turned at once. Bowing respectfully as he backed toward the room's exit, he apologized for disturbing his lord's slumber, nightmare or no.

"Your pardon, my liege. 'Twas merely a shadow."

CHAPTER TWO

Thunder rumbled across the land, rolling forth in a single, endless peal. Beneath its advance, the earth quaked. Soil shifted, pebbles danced, trees shook. A scattering of farmers and tradesmen caught within the storm's path looked to the heavens in bewilderment. The day was warm and serene, the sky above cloudless and pure. But the roar and the tremors were unmistakable. A whirlwind of destruction drew near, and would soon be upon them.

From atop the battlements of Krynwall, stationed within a parapet facing to the southwest, Vagrimmel scanned the horizon in confusion. As the thunder intensified, confusion gave way to apprehension. On any ordinary day, he might not have been so quick to allow fear and misgivings to crowd to the forefront of his mind. But the news of Sorl's death had put everyone on edge. Regardless of one's personal feelings toward the man, Sorl had been their king, the foundation upon which their government, city, and lives were built. A single night had changed all that, shattering beliefs and routines and leaving once-steady futures suddenly vague and uncertain. Still reeling from the unexpected loss and what it might mean for his family and loved ones, the watchman was regarding everything this day with the utmost cynicism.

Shielding his eyes against the midday glare, he focused on a dark cloud approaching. The cloud hovered just above the ground, its shadow painting the earth beneath the color of spilled ink. The watchman scowled, squinting. Within moments, the stain took on a new form, not the shadow of a storm cloud, but an army of riders pouring across the slopes, driving toward the city.

Grimm turned, calling out, eyes wide in fear and disbelief. His cries were soon echoed by others, and as the alarm swept back along the established chain of communication, he spun back, praying that he had been deceived.

His second survey only confirmed what the first had suggested. Those few people who had dared and been allowed to conduct their business outside the city walls on this ominous day now scurried for cover, abandoning wagons and wares and racing for the safety of their homes. Their cries mixed with those spreading across the battlement, calls to arms giving way to the bark of military commanders and the steady thump of booted soldiers marching into position. But all were drowned out by the frenetic roar welling up from the invading horde. Their dark bodies churned over the land in waves, crested by the accompanying cloud of dust as though it were scud upon the sea, eclipsing both earth and light while drawing ever nearer to the city gates.

Ten thousand, Grimm determined. A sizable force, though hardly enough to send him forth screaming. Not when their own garrison numbered closer to fifteen, and had the walls of the city to protect it. On an open battlefield, he would not like their chances. Their infantry and cavalry were ill trained and ill equipped, a casualty of Sorl's reckless spending. But the heart of Krynwall's army had always been the Legion of the Arrow, a corps of bowmen, thousands strong, whose commander had convinced Sorl to keep them properly outfitted throughout his reign. As long as they held the battlement, the city was safe.

And yet the watchman could not deny the look of dread on the faces of those lining the ramparts of the capital city of Alson. A force this sizable should not have been able to appear upon the city's doorstep without warning. The enemy tide swelled before them, seemingly oblivious to the fact that it lacked ladders and towers and other weapons of siege. But for Grimm, it was more than this. It was a weight in the pit of his stomach, a tightness in the nape of his neck, the cold certainty that a fateful reckoning had come for them all.

He plucked a spyglass from his belt and, after wiping the lens, used it to scan the approaching horde, sweeping back and forth in search of that which had him so unnerved. It did not take him long. All at once, his tightened jaw went slack, and his anxious heart fell, as he found himself staring in mute horror at a single man surfing the tide's furious crest.

Riding a stallion of black mist, the man's very appearance promised death. Long ebony hair whipped in the gale created by his own forces, while narrowed eyes gleamed with both hatred and triumph. Winds tore at his body, which sat upright with rigid defiance, shielded in studded leather armor the color of night. Cords of sinewy muscle tensed as he clenched a gnarled ebony staff in a grip so fierce it appeared as though the wood must snap. Atop the staff's head was the carving of a serpent, hood wide and ready to strike, and from a long chain encircling the man's neck bounced an iron skull, its mocking sneer mirroring that of its wearer.

When Sorl's corpse had been discovered that morning, Queen Ellebe's first reaction had been one of relief, if not joy. The depraved tyrant who had controlled much of her life and driven her homeland into near ruin was finally gone, ending with a single dawn's arrival what seemed to the queen a lifetime of bitterness and sorrow. No longer would her countrymen be forced to endure the brute's oppressive arrogance and greed. No longer would she have to suffer the indignity of his scorn, the perpetual disrespect that had made her old before her time. After so many years of pleading, her prayers had at last been answered.

But a sobering realization had quickly tempered her jubilation. A land without its king became a target for every aspiring warlord in the known world. And though its wealth and resources had been diminished by the irresponsible, sometimes ruthless exploits of her mad husband, Alson remained one of the most fertile and treasured regions of the island continent of Pentania. In the absence of a recognized heir, it fell upon the duke of Kord to wear the crown. But Sorl's uncle was a feeble old man unlikely to accept the responsibility. Nor were any of the duke's daughters, as women and only indirect heirs, apt to have the people's support. If this proved true, then the throne of Alson would be up for grabs among the feuding barons of this land, a situation that would be viewed as an opportunity for expansion by the rulers of Pentania's other major kingdoms. It was but a matter of time before the claimants began to arrive.

Even more troubling was the nature of Sorl's death. The king had been murdered by an assassin, the kind whose expert services did not come cheaply in this corner of the world. Someone had gone to a great deal of trouble and expense to see it done. But who? With no one to whom the crown would clearly pass, it was difficult to finger any suspects. Aside from this, Sorl had no real enemies. Ellebe would have been hard-pressed to find anyone who actually cared for her husband, but she had to admit he had known how to keep those around him pleasured and contented. Who among Alson's nobility would have wanted the eternal string of orgies to end?

An outsider, then, and not someone within the land's hierarchy of power. But again, who? Or better yet, why? Had someone actually wanted to plunge the nation into civil war? Or perhaps an outside nation hoped to weaken and confuse Alson's forces before laying siege to her lands. Ellebe had scoffed at the notion. For despite the legends about Krynwall's battlement and the legion of archers who defended it, Alson was not known for the strength of its standing army. Nor was Sorl himself a warrior or tactician. An army of even moderate strength and discipline would likely sack Krynwall in an attempted siege, whether or not the city's monarch was in command of its forces. What truly kept Alson safe, more than anything, was the land's diplomatic ties with its southern neighbor, Kuuria. So, if the assassination was an invasion tactic, why the added expense?

Unless the invader was hoping to stamp out any challenges beforehand. Conquering a weak nation was one thing. Maintaining that hold against powerful neighbors apt to refute such a claim was another matter altogether. And if Sorl were to somehow escape an invader's sword, a challenge there would be. But if Sorl were not around, the neighboring kingdoms might be less apt to feud over who should rule, and Ellebe found it impossible to believe that Alson's barons would be able to combine under a common banner without tearing one another apart.

And yet, while Sorl's death might indeed serve to eliminate certain difficulties ahead of time, it remained an obvious assassination. Thus, anyone laying claim to the throne too quickly would be accused of orchestrating the entire affair. So why risk it?

It was a maddening chain of questions, a study of schemes and counterplots and machinations that could take weeks to unravel. In the meantime, they would have to prepare for all contingencies. While continuing to puzzle over the ramifications of her husband's death, Queen Ellebe had therefore called a meeting with the king's chief advisor of military operations, thinking to take things under control while the city ran without a monarch. But after a heated lecture concerning a woman's place in determining matters of a royal—let alone military—nature, the chief advisor had stormed off to oversee *himself* measures for what he considered an inevitable siege. Having half expected as much, Ellebe had promptly shifted her efforts to other matters— specifically, preparations for her personal escape.

That had been but hours ago, after which Ellebe had retired to her tower bedchamber to rest, her heart still swimming with conflicting emotions and her head pounding with the effort to make sense of it all. So when the thunder had reached her ears, Ellebe arose with genuine curiosity. Quietly, she slipped to the doors of a private balcony and passed through into the open air, squinting against the sun's radiance. Once beautiful, the tired queen looked now upon her world with a strained expression and saddened eyes. Beneath her feet, the city sprawled forth in ramshackle fashion. Sweeping the horizon beyond with dry and weary eyes, she caught sight of the distant army as it stormed near. The sight made her blood freeze.

With one glance, Ellebe understood that there would be no discussion, no talks with this army concerning its petition for the crown of Alson. The enemy below had come to seize the city of Krynwall by force, to stake its ruling claim through sheer brutality. Suddenly the only question that mattered was whether or not they could survive the onslaught.

Ellebe found herself oddly impassive as she inspected the formidable procession. With such a force driving toward her city, she should have felt remorse for her people, overwhelmed with sympathy for their plight. Perhaps she was merely suffering the effects of shock and fear. Perhaps she took comfort in the fact that they had been enslaved for some time and should be accustomed to it. Or perhaps she found exoneration in that they had never really been *her* people at all.

Regardless, Ellebe continued to gaze beyond the citizens and structures sprawling forth from the base of her tower toward the city's main gate. More curious than afraid, she watched the distant enemy's surging approach as she would watch a wave roll onto the beach. When the invaders churned to a dusty halt before the massive outer wall just as the drawbridge drew shut, she remained in mute silence, a passive observer to the events transpiring below.

Directed by their commanders, the forward battalions of archers lining the ramparts unleashed a hailstorm into the enemy ranks. Grimm nodded approvingly as he witnessed the act, taking pride in the defiance of his comrades. His expression of approval, however, melted into one of horror as he watched the black-clad leader swing his staff in a wide sweeping motion, causing the swarms of arrows to fall to the ground, well short of their targets.

Despite their obvious shock, the commanders repeated the order to attack, and a second flurry of iron-tipped missiles ripped through the air, arcing upward before cascading down in a shower of certain death. Although a few of the enemy cringed reflexively as the arrows neared, the reaction proved unnecessary. Once again, the entire volley was swept up and knocked astray by a hurricane gust, called forth by the narrow-eyed wizard below.

After that exchange, the city's principal defenders held their position, riveted with uncertainty. Rather than waste a third volley, they lowered their weapons and waited for the enemy to respond. At this, the wizard's pale lips drew taut as he dispelled the sorcerous mist serving as his mount and left himself standing upon the earth below, dark cape billowing in the breeze.

An unnatural silence settled over the field as all eyes focused upon the figure. Armor and weapons clanked and jostled as thousands of enemy horses fidgeted beneath their riders, whickering and snorting and pawing the dusty earth. The wizard's eyes had grown wide as he turned his attention upon the drawbridge that sealed the main city gate. Mumbling commands in some archaic language that echoed ominously upon the wind, he raised his staff, then slammed it butt-first to the ground.

Groaning in protest, the bridge began to drop forward while the portcullis behind it began to rise.

Somehow, the gatekeepers managed to respond. Under the direct command of their strong-willed captain, a team rushed forward with lock bars and levers, trying every method they knew and some they could only guess at to jam the mechanisms that controlled the portal gates. Their efforts were useless. Cogs kept turning, bending and snapping pry bars or flinging those who wielded them aside. One unfortunate man had his arm caught between the grinding spokes of an iron flywheel and torn off at the elbow. His wail did nothing to halt the pace of the machinery or the steady movement of chains.

As the bridge neared the end of its slow descent, the enemy glared at the assembled army of Krynwall, lodged in tight formation against the inner wall in order to seal off the city beyond. Having prepared to meet the onslaught, the city's cavalry and pikemen now stood in awe, their bodies as frozen as their hearts. Draped in eerie stillness, the entire spectacle seemed a nightmare that might yet be willed away. But as the drawbridge slammed into the earth with a reverberating thud, the horror became irrefutably real.

In shock, Grimm observed as wave after wave of the

mounted invaders poured into the city, mowing through its soldiers as a giant might wade through a grassy field. In a matter of moments, the enemy had split the defending army in two and begun circling back to crush the twin halves without mercy. Atop the battlements, the archers renewed their attacks upon the wizard and those still massed outside with proficiency and daring. But all training and skill was rendered useless by the smirking sorcerer, who simply reached up with an invisible hand and cast their projectiles to the earth. Foiled on that front, the archers turned one by one to the chaos carried inside the city, where they fired occasionally but mostly gaped uselessly, unable to distinguish friend from foe. When the enemy soldiers began to swarm the ramparts from within, the archers lost any chance to alter their decision and were cast screaming to their deaths below.

As the whirlwind approached his position, Grimm put away his spyglass and drew his shortsword. Soldiers and couriers raced all around him, wild-eyed and frantic, knocking into one another like pebbles in a rockslide, seeking retreat where none would be found. He did not think to join them, recognizing these to be his final moments and hoping that in making a stand, he might in some small way make his wife and daughter proud. Perhaps in doing so, the Ceilhigh would favor him, and reward him by keeping them safe. On this darkest of days, it was the only light he had to cling to.

The slaughter was so swift that it took a moment for Ellebe to fully comprehend it. Krynwall had fallen, conquered in the time it might take to draw water for a bath. Never before had she even heard of such terrible domination. If the strongest city in the land had fallen so easily, what of the lesser towns and holdfasts throughout Alson? And from there, how safe were the other kingdoms of Pentania?

Questions to be answered another day, shrieked some warning sense within her. She awoke from her musings with a start, searching immediately for the distant wizard. He stood now before the drawbridge, and upon finding him,

Ellebe shivered, feeling as though he had turned his sights directly upon her tower, the royal tower of Krynwall.

Shaking, she tore her gaze from the sorcerer's vile form and fled from her parapet through her private chambers, hair flying from its ties as she stumbled down a flight of steps and through a series of corridors toward the secret passage. The clamor of battle, the screams of her army, ushered her dizzying retreat. Her eyes stung, her heart raced. Her lungs burned with their inability to draw breath. But the private route offered her only escape. If she could reach it before the invaders sealed off the city, her waiting steed would bear her safely away within minutes.

She still had time to make the truth known.

If the gods were with her, perhaps that would be enough.

The muscles in his arm and shoulder tensed as Jarom drew the bowstring to his cheek. He held it there long enough to take careful aim, squinting against a streamer of sunlight that pierced the forest canopy. He held his breath, stilling himself within and without. When his movements had steadied, he released the string, sending the arrow whistling through the air until it struck a target crudely painted upon a monstrous oak some thirty paces away. Lowering the bow and lifting his free hand to shield against the sun, he looked to see what had become of his shot. Among the half-dozen arrows buried within the oak's coarse hide, he found the one that still shivered, its shaft protruding from the upper left region of the central ring.

He permitted himself a proud smile. "Almost as good as Allion himself."

A fit of laughter erupted from behind him, and he turned in annoyance.

"That's funny, Jarom," Allion remarked, scampering sideways down the needle-strewn slope that marked the southern edge of the small clearing. A ponytail bounced against his neck, and matching brown eyes twinkled with superior delight.

"Ah, Allion. I was hoping you'd come along." As his friend came up, Jarom tossed him the longbow. "Impress me."

Grinning rakishly, Allion bowed low. Jarom tossed an arrow at him as he did so. But with eyes in the back of his head, the hunter snapped upright, a pillar of concentration. With movements so fluid and quick that they appeared to be a single motion, he caught the arrow's shaft between two fingers, nocked it to the bowstring, drew the string to his cheek, and released it. The arrow sang through the air and buried itself in the direct center of the target.

As he watched the arrow's oscillations, Jarom's pride vanished, and he turned to regard his companion with renewed respect and admiration.

Allion grinned. "Stick to your blades, my friend. You haven't the grace for so refined a skill."

Jarom smiled sardonically at the taunt and searched quickly for a retort. It would have to be clever, something—

His opportunity was cut short by a sharp cry. He and Allion glanced at each other, smiles gone. The cry had been that of a horse, in and of itself a rarity in these parts. Of greater concern had been the urgency of the animal's call. For a moment, the two men stared into the woods, ears cocked, brows furrowed. In the sudden quiet, they heard plainly the pounding of hooves, not far from their position. The horse's squeal sounded again, followed by a woman's shout.

Jarom leapt into motion. A quiver lay at his feet, resting atop his discarded jerkin and waterskin. He reached for the quiver, scooped it up by its leather strap, and tossed it to Allion, who still held the longbow. Disregarding the remaining items, he and his friend dashed toward the disturbance.

Branches slapped at them as they raced through the foliage, and roots and underbrush sought to trip them up. But the young woodsmen were accustomed to swift forest travel, and they were more than familiar with this particular stretch of their homeland. Running with knees high, balanced upon their toes, they ducked the low-hanging branches, darted past clinging growth, and loped their way over the uneven terrain, skirting its obstacles.

In a matter of moments, they broke free of the thicker wood and skidded to a halt upon the sheltered roadway that afforded passage from the forest west or to their village east. Jarom cast about, Allion at his side. Riders barreled from the west toward the young woodsmen, perhaps a hundred paces off.

Swiftly, Jarom pushed his friend back into the concealment of the growth that sprouted out toward the edges of the roadway. There they crouched, sweat glistening upon their brows as they marked the riders' approach. Five in all, from what they could tell. A woman led, riding at a frantic pace, leaning over the head of a richly ornamented mare. The remaining four gave chase, bearing down on the woman. Soldiers, by the looks of them, though Jarom did not recognize the patterns or design of their black-and-silver uniforms. Beneath the foreign surcoats, chain mail shielded their legs and arms, weighing down their horses, which wore strategically positioned armor plates of their own.

Their greater burden notwithstanding, the soldiers' horses were making ground on the woman's mount. Though by all appearances winded and weary, the soldiers seemed invigorated to have their quarry so nearly at hand. They surged forward, growling their battle cries, jockeying for position. It was the woman's horse that had cried out, doing so again as she urged it on. The woman did not look back, but her face was wracked with despair.

And then they had her. Fanning out to either side, the soldiers worked in concert to bring the woman to bay. It happened suddenly, not more than a dozen paces from where Jarom and Allion crouched in the brush. The first pulled up and seized the reins to her mount. Another grabbed her hair in a gloved fist and yanked her from the saddle. The final two skidded to a stop, cutting off any chance at escape. The entire procession ground to a halt amid a shower of dust and debris and the woman's screams.

The soldier who had torn the woman from her saddle dismounted and stomped back to where she lay. With a sneer, he grabbed her again by the hair and pulled her to her knees.

"On your feet, wench."

The woman responded with a grimace, reaching for the hand tearing at her scalp. The other soldiers laughed at her cries, and her tormentor looked up to take in their praise. As he did so, the woman rose to a crouch, pulled his hand down to her mouth, and bit him. The soldier wrenched free, yowling in surprise, and slapped her across the face.

Jarom lunged from the trees, launching past the woman's collapsed form to tackle the bitten soldier. After a startled moment and hurried glances to one another, the remaining three soldiers drew their swords.

Upon the ground, Jarom grappled with the woman's assailant. He could tell that the man was stronger than he, but Jarom was no weakling, and by far the more agile of the two. And for the moment, he still enjoyed the element of surprise. The soldier rolled hard to one side, where he drew a long, scraping gasp. Jarom let him go, regaining his own footing and snatching up a broken tree branch to use as a weapon.

By then, the companions of the fallen soldier were coming to his rescue, charging forward on their mounts. Jarom faced them squarely, half-crouched, shifting in his stance while his first opponent remained writhing on the ground. Before any of the three came within six paces, the foremost in their wedge formation arched sharply in his saddle, grunting in pain and staring down at the bloody arrowhead protruding from his chest. By the time his comrades realized what had happened, a second arrow shot out from behind them, and the soldier in its path had a wound to match the first. Choking and clutching at the killing shafts, both riders tumbled from their mounts.

Meanwhile, Jarom's opponent had regained his feet. His heavy sword swung out in wide arcs meant to finish this fight with a single blow. Jarom backed away, then calmly held his ground, using his branch to parry the other's desperate strikes. This further enraged his assailant, who lunged at him with a powerful thrust. Jarom reacted instinctively. He sidestepped the attack, brought up his branch, and cracked the soldier across the side of his bearded face. The blow sent the man's helm flying free and his body spinning into a ditch. His heavy sword dropped at Jarom's feet.

At that moment, the last soldier from the mounted formation of three careened toward Jarom. Jarom ducked as the man's sword slashed at him in a wicked sweep that would have claimed his head. In the same movement, he discarded his branch and reached down to retrieve his first opponent's fallen blade. As the rider skidded to a halt and spun about, Jarom whirled to face him. Spurring his horse with a kick to the flanks and himself with an angry cry, the rider bore down on the young man, lining his target up to his right. Jarom held his ground, fighting to remain steady, allowing the rider to determine the alignment of impact. At the last possible instant, Jarom moved, spinning around in front of the charging horse to the rider's opposite flank, following through with a swing of his borrowed sword and hacking the soldier down from behind. The rider cried out, threw his hands up in pain, and fell back, pinwheeling over his horse's rump. The horse ran on.

As he peered down to inspect the fallen rider, Jarom felt a rush from behind. He spun about as the disarmed soldier, one side of his face smeared in blood, lunged at him with a dagger. Jarom danced aside, sucking in his torso just enough to avoid the dagger's tip as it raked past. At the same time, a whiplike sound signaled the release of a bowstring, and a muted thwack indicated an arrow striking home. The stricken assailant made no sound, but staggered about before pitching to the earth. He hit the ground staring, eyes wide in denial, an arrow lodged in his throat.

Jarom turned, looking for Allion. He found his friend a dozen paces off, stepping free of the trees, bow in hand. Strewn upon the roadway, the soldiers' bodies twitched and bled in the throes of new death. Their horses stood scattered in the sun-dappled shadows, snorting and whickering, catching their breath. The rescued woman knelt among the carnage.

Jarom and Allion glanced at each other, then went to her. The woman looked up, torn and disheveled, her breathing labored and her eyes haunted. The two men shared another glance. Neither recognized her, although her robes would suggest she was a person of some means. When Jarom looked back at the woman's face, he found her eyes fastened upon the sword in his hand, where a line of blood dripped from its edge.

He tossed the weapon aside and crouched down, drawing her gaze level with his own. Sweat glistened upon his face and arms, but his heart beat comfortably within his chest and his own breathing was smooth and controlled.

"Are you hurt?"

The woman stared at him, a stricken animal. For a moment, she did not seem to understand where she was or what had brought her there. Then, all at once, she gathered herself, looking briefly up at Allion, then back to Jarom.

"You are from Diln?" she asked.

Jarom hesitated only slightly. "Yes."

"You must take me to your village council."

Jarom regarded the woman with evident surprise. But she met his gaze evenly, as if no further explanation were required, seemingly certain that her wish was reasonable and would be fulfilled.

Jarom glanced once more at Allion, who shrugged, then back to the woman, and helped her to her feet.

CHAPTER THREE

Afternoon sunlight etched intricate patterns against the forest shadows, forming a blanket that lay across the village center like a moth-eaten shroud. Birdsong warbled on the shoulders of a light breeze, the birds themselves darting from branch to branch in sudden flashes of color. Squirrels rummaged about, scampering up and down trunks, across limbs, and over roots and woodland debris. A rabbit appeared briefly, foraging through the underbrush. All behaved as though they had not a care in the world, mindful of the activity around them while intent on their own business.

From his seated perch on the wooden steps fronting the council hall, Jarom peered about distractedly, taking in the familiar sights and sounds. He attuned himself to his surroundings because he had been trained to do so. In a wild world, it did not pay to let one's level of awareness drop too low or for too long. But his attention just now lay elsewhere, making it difficult to keep focus.

What could be taking so long? He turned briefly to regard the double doors that barred his entry into the village council hall, closed and locked from the inside. He had found it oddly discomfiting to be turned away by the Circle in a matter over which he would normally be presiding. After all, *he* had discovered the woman and helped to deliver her from her tormentors. At her behest, *he* had escorted her to the village and assembled its leadership. More importantly, he and no other wore the mantle of Fason, the Village Shield, guardian of Diln. It was upon his shoulders that the burden of safety for the village and its inhabitants rested, whether those inhabitants were permanent residents or temporary patrons and guests. Given that, he should have been one of the first called into any closed-door council meetings. To be purposely excluded seemed ridiculous.

Allion had felt the same, at first. As usual, however, he had been the quicker of the two to come to terms with things as they were. Then again, Allion rarely did anything to challenge those in a position of authority over him. Although he'd been as surprised as Jarom when they had been turned away after the Elders had received an overview of events and assembled in haste to meet with the woman, he had just as quickly shrugged his shoulders and agreed to wait until called upon.

In the meantime, the archer seemed perfectly content to share his account with any who would listen. He stood on a bench not ten paces away, making grand gestures as he related his recent adventure to a cluster of wide-eyed children gathered at his feet.

"Two against four?" pressed Coy, an enraptured eight-year-old with a smattering of freckles and tousled blond hair.

"And they were on horseback," Allion confirmed, drawing a collective gasp from his assembly. He hefted Jarom's bow and added, "Of course, I had to do most of the work."

Jarom smiled and said nothing. Allion had indeed shot down three of the four marauders. Then again, not even Allion could have brought them all down *and* prevented one of their band from slicing the woman's throat. It was Jarom who had offered himself up as the distraction that had saved her life. But Allion could tell the story as he saw fit. Jarom was no more interested in the adoration of youngsters than he was in the praise of adults. His pride was rooted not in the opinions of others, but in his own sense of fulfillment. In this instance, he was satisfied with his efforts and Allion's in a job well done.

Still, he shook his head in private amusement as Allion's tale wore on, filled with moments of action and danger and excitement that Jarom did not recall. The oration was largely for the children, Jarom knew, whose imaginations rarely found such fuel within the sheltered confines of their forest home. But Allion's recitation was for Allion as well. Whatever else, the hunter was here and now the center of attention, garnering recognition for his words and deeds, seeking approval like one half his age.

Jarom was more mature than that, or so he preferred to believe, a necessary side effect of his role as village peacekeeper. Granted, the position was largely ceremonial. In this tiny community, order was seldom threatened. Those who chose to live and work beneath the boughs of the western Kalgren did so with similar goals and ideals. Every resident was a neighbor, and every neighbor a brother or sister. Politics served no purpose and were virtually nonexistent. As with any family, disputes surfaced from time to time, but were resolved swiftly. Rarely was there a need to call upon Jarom to maintain order.

Nevertheless, it was his responsibility, entrusted to him more than a year ago at the age of eighteen—younger than any other who had held the position before. Jarom viewed it therefore as a trust to be taken seriously. He worked diligently to meet and exceed the expectations of those who had asked this of him, but mostly to meet and exceed the expectations he held for himself, which precluded the kind of grandiose behavior being displayed now by his friend.

Or perhaps it simply wasn't in his nature. While there was nothing shameful about Allion's display, it remained a public exhibition, which Jarom's disposition did not allow. In that regard, he wished himself more like his friend. Sure, he was open and affable enough in the company of a few close associates, but given a larger audience, Jarom generally shut down, became quiet and reserved, cautious not to say or do anything that would offend another or embarrass himself. Often, he wished he could just let loose and relax.

Perhaps that would allow him to be less concerned with circumstances that lay beyond his control.

Jarom sighed. He curled his toes within the tips of his soft leather boots, running out of ways in which to pass the time. The Elders had offered no reason for their actions, and Rigdon, who had given the order to wait outside, had been downright gruff. Jarom had immediately looked past the Second Elder to the First. He had found the man, his own father, standing in a far corner of the room, reassuring the strange woman in hushed tones. When the First Elder had looked up, he had been cool and evasive, offering nothing more than a shake of his head and a stern nod to Rigdon. Beyond that, Jarom had been out of luck. None of the others who milled about the gathering chamber would even meet his gaze.

It was uncharacteristic behavior from all of them, most of all his father, and Jarom could not conceive of what had brought it about.

He glanced past Allion to where the woman's horse had been tethered. The magnificent animal grazed on a patch of grass, seemingly recovered from its harrowing flight. Jarom marveled anew at the embroidered saddle blanket and the ornamentations that decorated its harness and traces, hung now from a railing, all of which reaffirmed that the beast could belong only to a wealthy owner.

But who, exactly? There was something peculiar about this woman, something that ate at him from inside, an animal he could not corner. It was more than just her sudden and alarming appearance, more than her tacit refusal to confide in either him or Allion anything about her person or situation, though they had perhaps just saved her life. It had to do with her look and bearing, with the way she had studied them both while he and Allion had escorted her into the village proper, stealing glances as if trying to determine their secrets. Certainly it had to do with the way in which the village leadership had responded to her presence, leaving even their Fason out to wither like unpicked fruit.

Jarom's gaze lifted past the woman's steed, and the carousel of his thoughts turned back to his surroundings. The village center spread before him in widening circles, a quiet hub of activity. In addition to the community gathering hall before which he sat, the central district of Diln consisted of a dozen lodges of various size, there to serve the common needs of the populace. The structures were plain and sturdy, built from logs that had been notched, cross-laid, and stacked atop one another, then sealed with pitch to protect against the elements. Among the humble enterprises were a leather shop, smithy, storehouse, schoolhouse, inn and tavern, and others. Some of the structures were used for more than one purpose, such as a pair of storerooms attached to the smithy's forge that doubled as stockade pens, the heat and noise of which served as strong inducement for prisoners kept there even for a short time to behave themselves in the future. Others among the clustered buildings were scarcely used at all, but well tended and preserved for when they were. Aside from these lodges, the center's main attraction was a marketplace where residents and visitors alike bartered their wares and services.

Beyond the center, trails snaked forth into the surrounding woods, paths worn smooth by feet and rutted by the wheels of carts, causing the natural undergrowth to pull back to nearby edges. These slender roadways fed outward to the various homes and harvesting plots scattered throughout the trees, clustered loosely about the village center. All was embraced and sheltered by the trees of the forest—cone-bearing evergreens such as fir, pine, spruce, and larch, alongside colorful hardwoods such as maple, oak, birch, and magnolia. Each grew in intermingled stands, a patchwork of groves and clearings that stretched for leagues in every direction, a quilt no man could weave.

It was a remarkable setting, made more so by the people who populated it. Some milled even now about the village center. Most were heading to or from the processing warehouse, toting their baskets of mushrooms, herbs, and spices, those rare foods and medicines for which their community was known. The strange woman's arrival had created little stir. Jarom was not surprised. It would have gone against the nature of his people to react with anything more than subtle curiosity. Instead, they continued to go about their normal routine, without hustle or gossip. These were quiet cultivators—men, women, and children who spent their time in the light and lucrative toil of harvesting and gathering, or in recreation. They were not the type to harbor cravings of excitement or intrigue. Those who did generally moved away, north to Glendon or south to Earthwyn, leaving behind a small, secluded, and self-sufficient population that had little use for the outside world.

A cardinal came dancing up to the base of the porch steps on which Jarom was seated, its movements sharp and wary as it cast about for food. Just before the bird reached him, Jarom heard the light scrape of a locking bar being lifted free. He turned as one of the double doors to the gathering hall opened and Rigdon, the Second Elder, poked his head free.

"Jarom."

The Fason of Diln rose at once, failing to read anything within the Elder's expression. The man might as well have been a stone, with his chiseled frown, gray hair, and flat gray eyes that peered out from beneath a craggy brow.

Jarom glanced at Allion, who was in the midst of disentangling himself from a trio of children with whom he had started to wrestle. Rigdon opened the door further, a clear summons. Jarom passed through, then looked back as Allion came up just a step behind, with one lone child still clinging to his leg. But as he moved to enter, Rigdon stopped him with a shake of his head. Allion scowled, but Rigdon only closed the door and locked it behind him.

Inside, Jarom waited for instruction. The interior of the community gathering house was little more than a spacious assembly hall, ringed by small offices whose doors were closed. A table of polished oak squatted in its center, around which the Circle of Elders and the strange, dark-haired woman were seated. Scores of additional chairs and tables, designed with hinges to be folded away, lay stacked on carts and stowed back within dark bays neatly hidden beneath a curtained stage—a platform used to showcase public entertainment. Whenever necessary, the hall could hold the entire population of the village, some three hundred souls, with room to spare.

As Jarom stood waiting, Rigdon moved to reclaim his seat, completing the eight-member Circle. The remainder curbed their hushed conversation and sat back, faces grim. Though he'd met with the Elders numerous times, the look they gave him now caused Jarom's stomach to tighten—the imaginary rodent that had been gnawing at him earlier beginning to stir. Doing his best to dispel the sudden nervousness, he directed his gaze toward the man who represented the head of the circular table, addressing the First Elder with a nod.

"Father."

It was his customary greeting. The Circle, and Esaias in particular, cared little for formalities, especially in private. Belatedly, Jarom remembered the woman visitor and wondered if he should not have chosen a more official salutation.

"Jarom," Esaias replied warmly, dismissing such concerns, "sit with us."

A callused hand motioned to a vacant seat beside the woman, who sat to the left of Esaias, as all eyes continued to bore into the young Fason. Jarom hesitated, searching those stares for hidden meanings, then moved to occupy the assigned chair. He began to feel a little more at ease until he realized that the woman, seated to his right, was trembling visibly, on the verge of tears. He turned to regard her, but as he did so she glanced away, wiping her eyes while pretending to brush aside a lock of hair. Knowing not what to say, Jarom frowned, studying the woman's careworn face until Esaias's firm voice broke the thickening silence.

"Young Jarom," the First Elder offered by way of preamble. Jarom turned, only to find his father chewing carefully upon his words, uncertain as to what he was about to say. Unusual, Jarom thought, as was the man's tone, gentle as always, yet failing to hide an underlying sense of urgency. "It is my hope that today you are mature enough to handle a tremendous surprise."

Unsure whether the words coming at him formed a statement or a question, and feeling all the more puzzled, Jarom nodded dumbly. Of course he was capable of handling a surprise.

"A grave matter has come to bear," Esaias continued, his words gathering strength and momentum. "The time has come to tell you the truth."

Once again, Jarom could only frown in puzzlement.

"Truth?" He glanced at the strange woman with suspicion. "What truth?"

"May I present to you our guest, Her Royal Highness, Queen Ellebe of Alson."

Jarom felt his eyes widen, reflecting his surprise and embarrassment. He regarded the woman anew, his mask of suspicion melting away beneath a sense of apology. Ellebe faced him squarely. Tears glistened in her eyes, and this time she made no attempt to hide them.

"Your Highness," he whispered, bowing his head deeply. "I had no idea. I meant no disrespect."

Ellebe gave a sharp little cry. A glint of amusement sparkled in her eye, even as a tear fell from her cheek.

Jarom turned his confusion back to Esaias, but it was the Second Elder, Rigdon, who came barreling to his aid.

"Those soldiers," the Elder growled impatiently, "were part of an army that has lain siege to Krynwall. King Sorl is dead."

"Blazes. Who would—"

"We do not know." It was Esaias's turn to intervene, fixing Rigdon with a stern gaze as he reassumed control. His gaze softened as he turned back to Jarom, yet his words maintained the more straightforward approach set forth by his companion. "What we do know is that our queen has asked for your help."

"*My* help? Why?"

"Because you have already proven yourself worthy," Queen Ellebe responded. Jarom found her visage kind and reassuring, and was calmed by the silence that ensued as everyone waited for her to resume. "And because you are heir to the throne."

Lulled by her first phrase, Jarom was slow to absorb the second. When the words finally struck him, they did so with the sudden power of a lightning bolt, complete with the blinding glare, paralyzing fury, and thunderous reverberations thereof.

Nevertheless, when the storm had passed, his first instinct was to laugh.

"But there are no heirs. We all know that." He glanced

about the table, at each of the faces staring back at him. "Prince Soric was banished, and Prince Torin died as an infant."

Only when he realized that none of the Elders were nodding in agreement did Jarom turn back to the strange woman who claimed to be Ellebe, queen of Alson.

"No, my son," she said quietly. "Not dead. A ruse. Secreted away so as to have an opportunity to become the king this land deserves."

She said no more, but regarded him with a strange, loving look in her eyes. For an instant, Jarom felt the stirrings of something within, a part of himself that he had never known, or had forgotten long ago. His gaze flew around the table in desperate escape, seeking help from any quarter.

The grim faces of the Elders—family, neighbors, and friends—made his smile vanish. Dizziness washed over him, and he gripped the table to steady himself.

"You mean to suggest . . ." he tried, but could not finish. His tongue felt thick and his throat dry. "I . . ."

The woman had become suddenly relentless. "You, my son, are Prince Torin, and in light of your father's death, king of Alson."

Jarom struggled to respond. The rat inside his stomach scratched and clawed, fighting to tear free. His father had been right. Already, this meeting was too much to grasp.

The First Elder looked to Ellebe. "Perhaps you should start from the beginning," he suggested, casting yet another pointed glare in Rigdon's direction. "We can answer his questions when you finish."

Jarom did not miss the fact that he had been reduced to a third party in this matter, as though he were no longer present. It seemed fitting, for the swirl of his thoughts made him light-headed, as though his spirit had lifted free of his body and made him no more than a casual observer to this most absurd council. For a moment, he thought he might simply float up through the rafters and skylights and disappear. Or perhaps he could slip back into a recess of his mind untouched by this dream, and hunker there until dawn. Even as he entertained the thought, however, he became painfully

aware of Ellebe's concerned gaze as she awaited some sign
to proceed. Dream or no, he was chained to this scene, and
if he did not allow it to continue, it might never end. Gathering enough of himself to reclaim physical control, he managed a wordless nod.

Ellebe paused, seemingly to collect her thoughts, as if
even she was unsure where to begin this particular tale. Several times she started to speak, only to swallow the words
and fish about for others. When at last she began, she did so
tentatively, as though deciding she would simply have to
work her way through it.

"I did the best I could," she explained, a defense and apology both. "With Soric, I mean. I was too young, perhaps. I
thought I was prepared . . ." She shook her head. "He was my
firstborn, and I loved him dearly. He lent a purpose to my life
that had long since gone missing. Ecstatic about becoming a
mother, I was determined to raise him to the best of my abilities. Someday, my child would be king, and I wanted him to
be the greatest king these lands had ever known."

She sighed heavily, and the fond delight that had begun to
enliven her tone was dispelled by a wistful melancholy.

"Alas, my best intentions were no match for Sorl's crude
and wicked ways. In the end, Soric fell sway to greed and
bitterness, to the lonely cravings that led to his treachery and
banishment. I was devastated, knowing in my heart that
there was nothing I could have done to prevent it, and yet
feeling as though the entire affair was my fault, mine alone,
that it was I who had failed."

Jarom's eyes bore into the center of the table, but he could
feel Ellebe's gaze heating the side of his face. If she was
looking for pity—or any other response—she was looking at
the wrong man.

"My grief consumed me. But I had a responsibility, to
myself, and to my people. Sorl cared nothing for his legacy
or the future of his subjects, and so it was left to me. As time
passed, I became determined not to allow Sorl to destroy
me, to take from me the last thing that held any meaning in
my life—helpless feelings at first, but over the course of
many months, they became a conviction forged of iron."

She leaned forward, fixing Jarom with her stare, trying to turn his gaze to hers. Jarom held himself like a statue.

"I was willing to do anything, *anything,* for a second chance. I prayed to the Ceilhigh that if they would bless me with another son, I would do whatever was required to ensure him the opportunity to fulfill his destiny as king. I swore that my failure with Soric would not be repeated, that I would not allow another child to be corrupted by Sorl's ways. To make certain of this, I knew that I would have to shield him from his father, utterly and completely. Only, I knew not how.

"At last, when the Red Death first began to cast its shadow of fear over all the land, I devised a desperate plan. I met with the Elders, here in the village in which I was raised. Once I had secured their pledge of support, I set about persuading Sorl to have another child. It required a measure of deceit on my part, and a healthy dose of herbal concoctions, but in the end, the effort proved a success."

Again she paused, awaiting reaction. The only one she received was from Rigdon, whose irritated cough urged her to proceed more quickly.

"Torin was born—and died just two months later, a victim of the Red Death. With the assistance of an apothecary whose father had been unjustly executed by royal order, I was able to convince Sorl and the rest of the kingdom that the dreaded plague had claimed the life of our son. The funeral was held, and the coffin brought forth, but the only body it contained was that of a slain pig. Once that evidence had been buried, I took the babe from hiding and brought him here, as arranged."

Finally, she turned her heavy gaze from Jarom, shifting it to Esaias. In that moment an understanding passed between the two of them, deep and profound. Jarom wondered what it could be, then decided just as quickly that he didn't care.

"I knew that here, my son would be sheltered from many of the vile influences of the outside world. Growing up in the unmolested peace of Diln, he would develop, I could dare hope, into a true man, kind and just. The village Elders assured me they would care for him and keep his identity a secret from all. And thus Torin, prince of Alson, became Jarom, child of Diln."

There it was again, the implication that he was not really a part of this, that they were all speaking of someone else in another time and place. Jarom wished it were so as Ellebe studied him with passionate eyes, begging, he thought, for his reaction.

He refused to give it, and his silence unnerved her. He could tell by the way she glanced again at the First Elder, a plea for assistance. Finally, she addressed Jarom directly, in a tone meant to be soothing but that sounded to him shrill and caustic.

"I vowed that if I lived to see Sorl's death, I would return to Diln to inform you of your heritage and birthright. If not, I knew I could trust the Elders to bear witness to . . ."

But Jarom was no longer listening. He refused to hear another word. Why hadn't he been told this before? Why had he been tricked into living out a lie? His bitterness engulfed the room and its occupants. This woman, Ellebe, who professed such care for him, was turning his life upside down in the same breath. And the village Elders, whom he had always respected, were contributing to his betrayal—even his father. Not only were they stripping from him the life he had grown to love, the only life he had ever known, but by the sound of it, they meant to dress him in a perilous new one, one whose folds would suffocate him like a burial shroud.

As Ellebe droned on, Jarom regarded these men and women, young and old, elected to serve as leaders of the community. Banon, who knew it better to listen than to speak; Leuk, whose foppish smile hid a rakish wit; Olenn, who had once saved him from a wild boar; Hidee, whom he had always found pretty though he had never been bold enough to tell her so; Taya, whose delicate tongue had never uttered a single curse; Vahl, who had been like a mother to him; Rigdon, whose obdurate manner was at times comforting in its reliability; and Esaias, who did nothing but give of his time and strength. They were all in on it, he realized. They had to have been. All except Hidee and Leuk and those in his age group, who would have grown up with the same false knowledge that had been imparted to him. But the generation before . . .

He could picture it now, the entire village gathered in secret council, plotting and swearing to take their machinations to the grave. How else could it be that among all he knew, the story was the same? Even among so small a population, this was no simple feat. His mother had died of a fever, they said, just a few short years after his birth. None really knew her. Esaias had brought her back from travels abroad, and she had been a shy and reclusive soul who kept close to home. Esaias had refused to speak of her, except to say that he loved her and would forever, forsaking all others. Jarom had never pressed the issue. Blazes, he had not even a single portrait. Too painful a reminder, Esaias had claimed. He had destroyed them all. A lie, Jarom now realized. Like everything else he had been given to believe. Layer upon layer of falsehoods, carefully crafted, fed to him since birth like so much porridge.

"My entire life is a hoax," Jarom mumbled. He looked up, fixing Ellebe with an accusing glare. "Is that what you're telling me?"

The woman choked on whatever words she had been uttering and fell back slightly. "My son, I . . ."

Jarom waited until her response died, then turned to the others in challenge. "This is absurd. I may be Fason, but I'm certainly no king."

"But you are, my son," Ellebe insisted. "You are." She reached out, as though to place a hand on his arm. Jarom sent her back with a withering scowl.

"It is your born responsibility," Rigdon added. "That you are learning of it only now makes it no less true."

Jarom focused on the Second Elder, incredulous. "And what is to convince the people?"

"My son—"

"Have you any proof of this tale?" Jarom demanded, whirling upon her. "Any evidence at all? What is to convince the people of Alson that I am their new king?"

Ellebe shook her head sadly. Jarom was hardly surprised.

"And this army," he continued, returning to Rigdon, armored now in the conviction that he was right, that this was all a terrible and ridiculous mistake. "I assume it has a leader. You expect me to send this warlord home simply by repeating to him the ludicrous tale you've just spat at me? Why? To give him a laugh before he hangs my body out for the vultures?"

Again, his outburst met with only silence. Unwilling to match his arguments, perhaps. Or unable. Jarom drew further fuel from their quiet stares.

"And if he agrees? If he packs up his weapons and soldiers and leaves? What then? What do I know about ruling a kingdom?"

The concern on Ellebe's face had been mounting, and she glanced at the First Elder in desperation. Esaias sat quietly, infuriatingly calm. The queen tried to speak, but could only stare helplessly.

"This . . . this can't be happening," Jarom stammered, the words stumbling over one another in their rush to escape the maelstrom of his thoughts.

"Torin, my son," Ellebe said at last, sending a shiver up Jarom's spine, "I know this is difficult, but—"

"Difficult? I can't believe I'm hearing this!"

"I never meant . . . I only wanted—"

"I don't care what you wanted. And I don't care what is expected of me. This isn't happening. This isn't . . ."

He surged to his feet, sending his chair skidding across the floor behind him.

"Jarom!" Rigdon snapped. "Sit and be the man you must!"

Jarom ignored the Second Elder, and instead aimed a final glare at the First. No one else said a word, frozen in their seats, following directions, in all likelihood, issued before his summons.

Jarom shook his head and stomped toward the exit. He threw the locking bar aside with a disgusted heave and flung wide the heavy doors. Allion, on his back in the dirt with children clambering all over him and shrieking with delight, looked up at once.

"Hey, what happened in there? I . . ."

Jarom spun away, thudding down the steps of the council

hall and marching past those gathered. He disregarded Allion and brushed aside the children that reached for him, making his way from the village center. A few residents stared after him with those looks of mild curiosity, but Jarom paid them no heed. Finding the nearest trail, he melted into the forest, leaving all that he could behind.

As he stormed from the room, Ellebe watched him go, concern creasing her wrinkled brow. Her baby was a man now, this the first time she had seen him in nineteen long years. He had obviously been raised according to her expectations, but with their first association, she had alienated herself from him utterly. Nothing had turned out as she had dreamed. Despite the circumstances, despite the shock and confusion she knew must result, she had hoped the reunion with her son would prove to be a joyful occasion. Now that it was over, there was little in which to take heart. She wanted to run after him, to tell him how sorry she was, that these revelations hurt her too, and that she loved him and wanted the chance to truly serve as his mother. But she did not. She let him go, and a piece of her died.

"You did not tell him of your suspicions," Rigdon observed, a distant voice.

Ellebe turned her attention from the vacant doorway when she realized that she had been addressed.

"The wizard," the Second Elder clarified. "He will have to be told."

Ellebe returned her wistful gaze to the doorway. "Will he?" she asked of no one in particular. "Or might it only hinder his resolve?"

"He will accept his fate," Esaias assured her.

But that was just it, Ellebe thought. Part of her wanted him to refuse it. Part of her wanted simply to chase after and run away with her son, far from the horrors of this land. But she had forced herself to put aside such selfish desires before she had arrived, knowing that more than her own life hung in the balance.

"Yes," she said, "I know."

With that, her strength crumbled, and she fell into tears. The Elders let her be. They sat in silence for some time, while the tears ran unchecked down her cheeks. When at last her crying stopped, she shook her head as if clearing away the remnants of a bad dream, and rose.

"I must go," she said, stiffening resolutely. A cold urgency replaced the weary longing in her tone. "I thank you for your assistance. For everything."

"You are returning to Krynwall?" Esaias presumed with evident alarm and dismay.

"I must know."

The First Elder scowled. "It could mean your death. And you would better serve this people and your son as an ambassador in their behalf."

The queen shook her head, scoffing at the notion.

"Are you sure?" Esaias asked, a plea for her to reconsider.

Ellebe paused, eyeing the man, then the doorway, and nodded.

CHAPTER FOUR

Jarom watched the stone skip across the stream until it disappeared into the shallow depths, then reached for another. He flung it with an angry grimace, arm low and to the side, out across the waters. It hopped along the smoothly rolling surface, tearing ripples in the shifting crystalline skin, long and slow, then short and quick. This one traveled farther than the last, and Jarom had the next in hand before it vanished.

In the trees overhead, a crow sounded its raucous call. Jarom did not even flinch at the cry. Behind him, Allion sat on the grassy bank, his back to a drooping willow, knees drawn to his chest. Jarom had given him no reason to remain. In fact, he had pointedly told his friend to leave him alone. Allion had refused, however, and rather than force the issue, had taken up his silent position nearby, figuring to wait out Jarom's frustration. Jarom had clenched his jaw and said nothing.

Already his meeting with Queen Ellebe and the Circle of Elders seemed a thing of the past, a memory that might have belonged to someone else entirely. With each stone's throw, Jarom felt himself further removed from the episode, released from its strain on his mind and soul and returned to the peaceful reality he had known mere hours ago. Here, in the shelter of his favorite place, he could pretend that none of the day's events had occurred.

He was deceiving himself of course. He did not believe for a moment that he had successfully avoided the issue simply by walking out on those who had raised it. This was not some minor ordinance he might disagree with, a village measure whose restrictions he was authorized to impose or ignore as he saw fit. This was his life.

And that was the misery of it.

He was no king. He had no desire to become one. He had dreamed of adventure, but not this, not now. He knew his place. He was a peasant, born and raised, a harvester of forest-grown delicacies, playing out his insignificant role in the great game of life. He needed nothing more than what he had, here and now.

Perhaps that was what truly bothered him. Call him what they wished—woodsman, Fason, king—it mattered not. What had pained him was to learn that his home was nothing more than some kind of staging ground, that those he believed to be his family and friends were in fact nothing to him. If what the Elders had told him was to be believed—and despite its incredible nature, he had no evidence with which to deny it—he was not one of them, but an outsider, a child cast off by his parents into a world in which he never belonged. Now, unable to go back, he belonged nowhere.

The brush behind him rustled with movement. Jarom turned, as did Allion, to find his onetime father, Esaias, approaching through the trees. With a subtle gesture, the First Elder dismissed Allion from their presence. To his credit, Allion refused at first, rising to his feet to stand with arms folded across his chest. Jarom recognized the look of frustration that crossed his friend's features. When was someone going to share with him just what in the Abyss was going on? Then Esaias scowled, a forbidding countenance that made Rigdon's fiercest grimace seem as warm as an infant's first smile. Allion glanced at Jarom, hung his head, and tramped away in disgust.

When the archer was gone, Jarom turned back to his stone throwing. Esaias drew up beside him. As he had with Allion, Jarom did his best to pretend that the other was not even there.

For many moments, neither man spoke. Jarom tried to lose himself in his activity, honing his mental focus through physical exercise. But at last he could stand it no longer.

"You lied to me. All these years."

He addressed the other without looking at him, chucking another stone at the ceaseless flow of water.

"It was necessary."

The First Elder's tone was compassionate, paternal, the same firm and steady timbre he used with everyone, and at all times. Jarom was incredulous. His bitterness and resentment toward this man who had betrayed him came roaring to the fore.

"Necessary? For what? For whom?" He held back a throw as he turned to rake the only father he had ever known with his bitter gaze.

"We did what was asked of us. We did what we believed was right."

Jarom's jaw hung open as he stared at the First Elder's profile. How could Esaias just stand there, as impassive as another might be in discussing the evening breeze? Jarom could see no reason for Queen Ellebe's elaborate scheme. And he was outraged that the man he trusted most, Esaias, had helped her to orchestrate it. The First Elder should be apologizing. He should be on hands and knees, begging Jarom's forgiveness for his part in the initial deception, and afterward, for refusing to trust his son with the truth.

"You could have told me. You should have told me." When Esaias refused to meet his gaze, Jarom turned back to the river. "Blazes," he swore, "the least you could have done was admit I was a ward. It might have made the rest of this nonsense easier to swallow."

Jarom had already reflected upon the irony. After all, it was an all too common fantasy among fosterlings, that they were really the children of royalty, heirs to glimmering kingdoms full of beautiful maidens and chests of gold and adoring supplicants—and that one day, it would all come to light. The ultimate dream of escape. Except that Jarom had no desire to escape his life. To him, these revelations were not a dream fulfilled, but an impossible nightmare, too incredible and undesirable to be true. A ridiculous fairy tale, rehashed for the thousandth time.

"That you were a ward was hidden because wards tend to become curious about their true lineage," Esaias explained. "In any case, the decision was not ours. Your mother felt—"

"Mother?" Jarom snorted, casting yet another stone. "I have no mother."

Finally, Esaias turned to him, and it was Jarom's turn to avert his gaze.

"She would be hurt to hear you say so. Think of the sacrifice—"

"Sacrifice?" Jarom whirled, and at last their eyes met. "You're asking me to sacrifice everything—my friends, my family, even my identity—for that of a complete stranger, someone I don't even care to know!"

"Jarom," Esaias urged quietly, looking down at him, "you are who you've always been. Your friends, your family, none of that has to change."

Though he had held up well beneath the considerable weight of the other's stare, Jarom was the first to blink. "Everything I've been told is a lie," he insisted, looking away.

"No, my son, not everything."

Jarom glanced back quickly, his expression challenging. "Oh?"

"My love for your mother, that was true." Something in the man's voice strangled the scoff that built reflexively in Jarom's throat, and though he had meant only to glance in the First Elder's direction, Jarom found his eyes ensnared. "It was as it always has been. Would you care to know the truth of how Ellebe became queen?"

Jarom swallowed, his interest piqued. This was indeed a tale he wanted to hear, even now—one seldom told, and then only by those who knew nothing more than the simple fact: Ellebe, a onetime resident of Diln, had been selected by Sorl to be his bride. Something of which the villagers *should* be proud. But Jarom knew better. For topics of civic pride were discussed openly and shared freely with any who would listen. Not so in the matter of the queen. Where Ellebe's history was concerned, those who knew more than the obvious kept those details to themselves.

At last, Jarom nodded.

"Thirty-seven years. Nearly twice the span of your life

have I loved your mother. I was seventeen, younger than you are now. Ellebe was one year my junior. With both our families among the original settlers of this village, we'd been friends all our lives. No one was surprised when we announced our intent to marry. Indeed, it seemed as though we were the last to know."

Esaias's gaze lifted, peering past Jarom as if the trees beyond framed a doorway into the past.

"And then Sorl entered our lives. He was prince then; his father, King Sirrus, still lived. He stormed into our village one day with a band of ruffian friends, weary after a long day's hunt. They stayed the night, and spent it reveling in a euphoria brought about by their own special blend of the forest's offerings. Earlier, he had taken an instant liking to Ellebe; most male visitors did. This was something I had learned to accept. Then again, most male visitors were not the firstborn son of a king.

"Sorl invited Ellebe to join him. And I, in my jealousy, left them alone. Late that evening, while most were asleep, I crept back out to spy upon them. Sorl had left the others, had taken Ellebe with him. In full thrall to his mind-numbing root, he forced himself upon her."

Esaias had tensed, his words slipping now through clenched teeth.

"I arrived in time to save her from all but a few bruises and a torn dress. Sorl fared not so well. Before Ellebe and others awakened by the struggle were able to pull me free, the crown prince of Alson had been beaten to within a few shades of death."

Esaias relaxed somewhat, as though the ancient act still provided him with some small measure of satisfaction.

"Dawn gave rise to a terrific mess. Our citizens were well respected. My father, and Ellebe's, were trusted merchant suppliers to King Sirrus himself. Few, I think, would have doubted our account of what had happened, and Sorl himself must have understood that he had landed in a sticky web. In order to avoid scandal and embarrassment, Sorl made the claim that on the previous night, Ellebe had agreed to be his bride. Their amorous interaction was simply youthful enthusiasm, and my assault but a terrible misunderstanding."

"But why didn't you—?"

"Before making this claim," Esaias continued, fixing Jarom with an ominous glare, "Sorl offered Ellebe a private proposal. Either she would agree to marry him so as to protect his honor, or he would see me hung for my attack and her slandered as a whore. He was still the prince, after all, and he had a troop full of witnesses. Given this choice, she departed for Krynwall. She said nothing to dispute Sorl's story of their betrothal, and for the longest time even I was left in the dark."

He sighed, his bitterness subsiding into resignation, a yoke so worn about his shoulders as to appear almost comfortable.

"Years later, she at last confided to me the truth. She had made the decision alone, and was sorry for it. This revelation came about following Soric's banishment, at the time in which she was contemplating your birth. She admitted to me that at first, while Sirrus still lived, her life had been tolerable. But Sirrus's hunting accident occurred just two short years following Ellebe's arrival at Krynwall. By then, Sorl had begun already to treat her as a discard. He would not allow her to leave, however, for that would be a disgrace. So he kept her as queen, a private conquest, even as he satisfied his cravings elsewhere. Ellebe's only goal in life became to bear an heir that would be nothing like Sorl. That would be her legacy and revenge. Then, after what happened with Soric . . .

"You were to be her last great hope. I could not refuse her that; nor would I allow the Circle to do so. And so I supported her in her cause, promising to raise the child as if it were the son we should have had together."

Jarom remained silent, waiting for more as Esaias fixed him with that smooth, expressionless look that could calm an approaching storm. Perhaps, Jarom thought, he had been too hasty. Thinking only of himself, he had given no thought to the feelings of others. Now, as he tried to imagine these events of which Esaias spoke, he thought he could fathom the depth and intensity of emotion that had culminated in the odd shaping of his life. How hard it must have been for a loving mother to surrender her son when that son was all she had in the world to call her own. And for Esaias, to have lost the woman he loved to misfortune and misunderstanding— a void he had never even attempted to fill—only to accept the charge of raising the child she had conceived with his loathsome rival as his own.

Still, Jarom felt only partially ashamed. It remained difficult for him to pity either his mother or foster father for the sacrifices they may have made or the pain they may have had to endure. For theirs had come about from their own choices, while his had been thrust like a dagger in his back by those who, despite their concern, had not trusted him enough to make the choice for himself.

"Listen to me, Jarom—Torin." The younger man shook his head at the name, but did not turn away. "I am your father, and I always will be. I could not be more proud of you if it were my own blood in your veins. You are as smart, as dedicated, as selfless as any man I've ever known. In heart, mind, and body, you are everything a king should be."

The words rolled off of Jarom's back like rainwater upon waterfowl. Still, they triggered the realization that the village Elders, especially Esaias, had been preparing him for this day all along. Lessons of honesty and fairness had been pressed upon him like brands from birth. Even as a youth, he had been placed in positions of leadership among his peers, not as subjugator, but as someone to whom others could come for guidance—much like the First Elder's role among the community at large. And his position as Fason, he now understood, had enabled him to practice the teachings of justice, pity, and order. He had even been encouraged in his efforts to teach himself swordplay, an exercise mostly eschewed by the peaceable members of his community. Never before had he given any of this a second thought, but now it all made sense. Although he did not necessarily agree with Esaias's assessment of his qualities, it was obvious that every effort had been made to instill them.

"But I don't want to be king," Jarom said dully, his voice weak and hollow. Even he was growing weary of the refrain.

"That is not your choice. As Rigdon said, you are born to

it. Your only choice lies in what you make of the fact, because you are king, whether you asked for it or not."

Jarom shook his head. "But it's not that simple, is it? Even if I am king, no one is going to let me serve as such."

Esaias sighed, another rare indication of emotion. How taxing must it have been, Jarom wondered, to safeguard this secret all these years?

"Jarom," the Elder replied at last, "the land of Alson depends on you. This village depends on you. Your friends and family depend on you. Who is to help them if not you?"

"I don't understand. You speak as though my birthright gives me some kind of leverage. But I don't see it. King or no, what can I possibly do?"

Esaias hesitated. "We did not foresee this," he admitted. "We were expecting a rather smooth transition. Ellebe was to introduce you as king. With her account, and ours, and that of the apothecary who assisted her, there would be but the small matter of exhuming your false remains. After some general confusion, we supposed the people would accept the truth."

And what about me? Jarom thought, but kept it to himself. Apparently, there had been no concern as to whether *he* would accept the truth. From the first, it had simply been assumed.

Esaias changed topics. "This morning's assault was led by a wizard."

Jarom lurched in surprise. The stone he threw plunked directly into the stream's waters with a deep-throated splash and did not reappear. "A wizard?"

Esaias shrugged. "That's how the queen described him. A practitioner of magic. We know not whether he acted alone, or if he is in service to another, but by your mother's account, his powers are formidable."

Jarom was speechless. The only magic-users he knew were those illusionists and tricksters encountered at city carnivals. The best, it was said, performed exclusively for the royal courts. But never had he heard of one to practice real sorcery, the kind spoken of in legends of the prior age.

"In any case," the First Elder continued, "you cannot drive back an army alone. The Circle's advice would be to journey south to Kuuria. Seek an audience with Emperor

Derreg and the Imperial Council. If our adversary is as powerful as our queen suggests, then you will need to petition the aid of a military force strong enough to combat him."

Jarom laughed. "And you expect the emperor to grant this request to a lowly mushroom farmer?"

"I expect you'll find a way to make him see the truth. If not, our lives and lands will be forfeit."

Jarom thought quickly through this new line of reasoning. It contained some merit, but he remained skeptical. "Would it not be better to send the duke of Kord or one of the barons to the south?" he asked. "The emperor might be more willing to listen to them."

"Perhaps," Esaias agreed. "I would assume that as the duke and barons receive word, they will be sending emissaries of their own in search of assistance. But who is to represent our interests? Would you truly trust any of them to do so?"

After a moment's hesitation, Jarom shook his head. "But if the emperor's forces were to free Alson, he would turn the crown over to one of them long before he gave it to me—if he were to relinquish it at all."

Esaias faced Jarom squarely. "Who shall wear the crown remains to be seen. We must first think to save our lives and lands before it's too late."

Fair enough, Jarom thought. So long as everyone understood the most likely outcome to all of this in advance, and tempered their expectations accordingly.

He blew his breath out in a long sigh. "Why me?"

He could feel his resistance crumbling. Nevertheless, his inner turmoil was unrelenting as self-doubts and fear of the unknown gripped him. Esaias must have read this in the contortions of his face, for the First Elder moved quickly to console him.

"Son, I dare not fathom why each of us is given the path we find laid out before us. There are few, if any, who can. But I have to believe that these paths are not placed upon our heads randomly, without purpose."

Jarom peered into the waters gliding silently before him, gleaming crimson as their mirrored surface reflected the light of the setting sun.

"And remember this. Ultimately, it is left to each man to choose where his own path leads. So before you cry to the gods for the injustice of your fate, realize that you have the final decision as to where that path will take you. Will you make it the path of Torin, king of Alson, or that of Jarom, now ward of Diln?"

Jarom knew what the Elder was saying, the message behind his words. Esaias had always preached and abided by two uncomplicated—and uncompromising—rules. The first was a simple creed of civility, which demanded that each man treat others the way he would wish to be treated. The second was his somewhat fatalistic belief that life was not about dictating circumstances and events, but one's own attitude in response to those conditions. It was in this manner, and no other, that a man was given control over his life's scroll. The first of these teachings, Jarom had taken to heart readily enough. The second was easier said than done.

Jarom looked up from the shallows before him. When his reluctant gaze met that of his father, his unswerving mentor and guide, he felt a surge of confidence, for he saw that whatever decision he made, he would have the full support of the Elders—and therefore, the entire village. Knowing this imbued him with a sense of calm, and for the first time, he began to consider his options in earnest.

"One caution," Esaias added. "Your path may in fact affect the lives of many around you. You will find that sometimes, your decisions weigh upon others as much as they weigh upon yourself."

So much for choices, Jarom thought dryly.

But his anger and resentment were spent. Despite his father's manipulations and subterfuge, Jarom could not deny that even now, he trusted the hardworking man who had raised him from infancy. Esaias had never asked him to do anything without honestly believing that he could handle the responsibility and deliver on the task. Thus far, Jarom had yet to betray that faith. Why should this be any different? If his father was asking him to do this, it was only because he had complete confidence in his judgment and abilities, even in this wild and unknown venture. So perhaps Jarom should allow himself the benefit of his own doubts. He was not, he realized, entirely unprepared for this. He merely needed to reach the necessary level of acceptance.

Because, he admitted dejectedly, although he had not asked for it, he was going to have to fight for it.

"The queen," Jarom said carefully, keeping his tone respectful. "I assume she would be traveling with me?"

Esaias shook his head. "She has already left. Back to Krynwall, to face her unknown usurper."

"And you let her go? Alone? Isn't that dangerous?"

The First Elder did not answer right away. "Son, your mother has known nothing but pain for so long, she embraces it, clings to it because she has nothing else to cling to."

Jarom flinched, expecting an accusation for the way in which he had reacted to Ellebe earlier. For it might very well have been his reaction that had driven her away. But the young man saw no such indictment in the other's face, just sadness and longing, barely evident beneath his father's polished veneer of implacable composure.

"I fear she is no longer capable of electing happiness, and that it will prove her undoing."

Jarom was silent a moment, his mind like the nearby stream, awhirl with an endless array of shifting reflections.

"Promise me this," he said finally. "If I agree to play queen's errand boy and things don't work out the way you've planned, promise that you'll allow me to return home and live in peace." He faced his father squarely, determined to secure that pledge.

"My son, if things don't work out the way we've planned, you may have no home to return to at all."

CHAPTER FIVE

The maw of the chasm loomed beneath her. Lyssa felt its stale breath as she lost her precarious grasp upon the rock wall. Gasping in terror, she clawed against the unyielding stone, desperate for a hold, for the purchase that would prevent her from plunging to her death. But the wall offered nothing to stall her momentum. Its callous disregard mocked her efforts, and she felt a scream welling within her constricted lungs.

Suddenly, her struggles were ended, the rigid fingers of her left hand wedged into an invisible crevice, while those of her right clutched a small protrusion farther up in a white-knuckled grip. Her left leg still dangled out over the abyss, but the footing seemed solid enough beneath her right. For many moments, she refused to breathe, despite her lungs' desperate cries for air. She simply held her position, frame stretched out, clinging to the cold wall.

Once her throbbing heart had slowed its frantic rhythm, Lyssa dared open her eyes. Not surprisingly, the glimmer of her brother's lantern was vanishing ahead, though she needed no illumination to feel the ravenous void beneath her as it seethed over its lost meal. Hurriedly, she thanked the Ceilhigh for watching over her, then drew her leg back up to the stone lip from which it had slid. After a steadying breath, she resumed her trek, seeking to negotiate the rocky ledge—more carefully this time—before being deprived of all light whatsoever.

Hampered by raw nerves and unsteady movements, not to

mention the difficult and unfamiliar terrain, her efforts
proved agonizingly slow. The absolute darkness consumed
her quickly.

Left with no other choice, she called to her brother.

"Rett," she cried meekly, cringing at the chasm's voice as
it mimicked her plea.

Her companion gave no response, so she called again,
louder. "Rett!"

"Hurry, Lyssa!" came the excited reply. "I've found something!" She listened to the words as they reverberated
against the cavern walls, but did not cower from them as she
had her own echo. She was more than a little relieved to find
that her elder brother had not abandoned her completely.

"I need light," she pleaded, fighting to sound calm.

In a moment, the rays of a lantern clenched in Rett's teeth
fell upon her, revealing the precipice upon which she stood.

"C'mon," Rett urged through his closed mouth. "Hurry."

Hurry? The echoing word rang incredulously in Lyssa's
mind as she inched her way along, praying that she would not
lose her footing a second time. On the other hand, she had no
wish to hear any more of her elder brother's remarks about
what a burden she was. Every time she insisted upon accompanying him, it was the same. She wasn't strong enough. She
wasn't agile enough. She would only slow him down. To be
fair, she often did. But they'd been exploring these caves together for years, ever since she could remember—just as
their father had, and his father before him. Given that, she
refused to be left behind simply because Rett had become
more adept at traversing the treacherous ledges and
precipices such as the one Lyssa negotiated now. In her
mind, they were still a team. And despite his complaints,
Rett appreciated her company as someone with whom to
share the danger and excitement of his subterranean explorations. He might argue otherwise, but the fact that he had
come back for her—now, as always—would seem to prove
her point.

After what seemed an eternity, Lyssa emerged from the
narrow ledge onto a broad, flat shelf. Rett was waiting, his
lantern held high in one hand. For a moment, as she began

brushing the dust and pebbles from her body, Lyssa thought to tell her brother that she was leaving, that her thrill at having discovered this new chain of tunnels had fallen into the chasm behind them. They had gone far enough for one day. She was tired and hungry and wanted to go home. As she looked ahead, she quickly changed her mind.

Before her stood the entrance to a cave. While at first glance unremarkable, something about it called to her. She studied it quietly, trying to discern just what it was that she found so striking. It was small in comparison to most of the caves through which they normally trekked, jagged and rough-hewn. But its shape was just a little too round, its edges too well formed. Lyssa had seen enough of the tunnels and caverns beneath her home to realize that something more than nature had helped to fashion this hole deep beneath the earth.

Forgotten was her brush with death. Forgotten was her discomfort, the scrapes and bruises and bone-numbing cold that permeated the vast, windless expanse of the subterranean cavern. Forgotten was her father's stern warning as to what would happen should they fail again to return home before sunset—never mind the fury they already would have to face at having once again given old Paladius, their guardian escort, the slip. Here was a discovery that wouldn't wait. She glanced at Rett and knew he was thinking the same. The cave stood openmouthed before them, teasing the young explorers behind its curtain of blackness, the only obstacle remaining between them and its secrets.

Garett and Elwonyssa Culmaril, prince and princess to the throne of Souaris, smiled at each other, unable to resist. In all of their many expeditions throughout these endless tunnels that bored their way through the Tenstrock Mountains behind their home, they had never before happened upon anything nearly as exciting as this—an underground den carved by mortal hands. Fashioned, no doubt, by one of the ancient races—by elves perhaps, or dwarves. In any case, they knew without speaking that they had stumbled upon an incredible find, and they meant to be the first to explore the promise of its mystery.

Rett plunged ahead recklessly. Lyssa followed on his heels and was enveloped in a darkness that seemed to suffocate both her and her brother—and the feeble glow of their outstretched lantern. Enough light escaped, however, to expose the walls of a rugged corridor. Upon closer examination, they were surprised to find very little dust or other signs of age, and the farther they traveled, the more captivated they became. The hollow within which they traveled was not merely a single passage, but part of an immense warren, a complex series of corridors that burrowed their way hundreds of paces into the surrounding earth.

It wasn't long before they found their path more clearly illuminated by a dim radiance, a muted glow with no apparent source. This was not the twinkle of minerals embedded in the rock, nor even the flicker of torchlight, but a steady wash the color of emeralds. Rett and Lyssa stumbled along in wonder, allowing themselves only cursory glances into the many passages that branched off to either side of the main tunnel. Soon after, they detected the slightest hint of a breeze, a current of wind warm and inviting. Lyssa slowed, glancing at her brother to see if he had felt it. The look on his face suggested he had, and that he too was confused. Where could such a draft be coming from? He smirked and hastened forward. Only one way to find out.

When at last the tunnel ended, Lyssa held her breath. The corridor opened into an immense cavern forested with razor-tipped rock formations rising up from below and hanging down from above, and which in many instances had grown together at their narrow tips. The ceiling soared into blackness overhead, and scores of statues lined the long, circular walls—sculptures of hideous, unknown creatures. Each figure faced the center of the room and a large, placid pool of water, from which the green luminescence seemed to emanate. A squat ring of stone contained the wide pool, its carven sides replicating on a smaller scale the ghastly hordes that rimmed the cavern's walls.

"Oh, Garett!" Lyssa gasped.

Her brother nodded beside her. Neither yet was able to

step forward, to cross the threshold between tunnel and chamber. It was too marvelous a sight, too spectacular to be disturbed until they had taken it all in.

But as her gaze swept the chamber and its contents, Lyssa spied something jarring. Against the far wall, beyond the jungle of rock formations and past the glowing pool, she saw what appeared to be a cocoon, suspended within a nest of webbing. It hung several hands above the jagged floor amid a cluster of the natural stone pillars, the supporting strands stretched across and tied to those columns so as to keep it aloft. The object reminded Lyssa of the withered insect husks she sometimes found trapped within a spider's web, and the mere correlation was enough to give her pause.

Her brother had either missed the nest or was not troubled by it. He stepped forward boldly, an eager grin in place as he moved to enter and explore more closely their find. Before she even realized what she was doing, Lyssa placed her hand on his arm in an effort to restrain him.

Rett turned in annoyance. "What?"

"Are you sure it's safe?" Lyssa felt suddenly foolish.

"Of course it's safe," Rett declared irritably, jerking free of his sister's grasp. "Don't be such a child."

Lyssa kept quiet, but made no move to follow as Rett took half a dozen strides into the chamber. The movement carried him to the first of the statues, a beaked monstrosity that looked like a falcon with arms, but was nearly twice her brother's height. Rett studied the sculpture for a moment, examining its angles and lines in the light of his lantern. Realizing that she had not moved, he glanced back at her.

"Are you coming?"

Lyssa opened her mouth, then clamped it shut. She shook her head.

"What are you afraid of?"

"I'm not," she objected, but when her brother laughed, she summoned no further defense. Her eyes darted about the cavern, marking with furtive glances each of its shadows, making sure none had moved. "It's late, Rett. We should come back tomorrow. Father will—"

Rett laughed again, harder this time. "Run along, then,

little Lyssa. But this is the last time I let you drag along behind me."

Lyssa frowned. She must have heard that threat at some point during each and every expedition they had ever undertaken. She was more concerned by his lack of reverence. This setting had much the same look and feel as the royal tombs buried beneath their city, tucked back within the tunnels closer to home. Despite the inexplicably warm air, a deep chill had settled within her stomach, and she felt queasy. She was beginning to get the impression that they had violated someone's sacred ground—an act that was never appreciated. Shouldn't her brother be more careful?

As if in response, Rett gave a sharp yelp of pain. Lyssa's heart stopped. Her gaze flew back to her brother, who had been tracing the statue of the birdman with his free hand. Now, he hunched tight, his torso curled over that hand, his features scrunched in pain and shock.

"Rett!" Lyssa squealed in fright.

Her brother laughed again and lifted his hand free to show that it was undamaged. His eyes glimmered with delight as he studied Lyssa's foul expression.

"Curse you, Garett."

Rett shook his head and turned away, snickering as he made his way around the room, pausing to inspect each of the statues that he passed. For a while, Lyssa marked his progress, watching as the globe of his lantern slipped farther and farther away, leaving her bathed in the faint green light emanating from the waters of the bizarre well. Perhaps she *was* being a child. She hated giving her brother the satisfaction of being right, but she could not escape her misgivings. She certainly could not bring herself to enter this forbidding place. Something held her back, kept her feet rooted securely to the stone floor. Good sense, perhaps, or maybe just fear. Either way, her father had taught her early and often to trust her instincts, and her mother had always encouraged her to be her own person and not to follow blindly after others—both of which she was doing now.

She allowed her eyes to drift, to roam once more about the chamber as she pondered its history and purpose. It must in-

deed have belonged to some lost civilization. But who?
There were no known histories of any of the forgotten races
having lived within these mountains. If this had been someone's home, then what manner of room was this? Who had
carved the statues? What was the origin and purpose of the
strange light? Was it a sort of enchantment? And what about
the rest of the complex? What remained to be found within
its unexplored depths?

As her gaze came back around to where Rett should have
been, Lyssa realized with sudden alarm that she had lost
sight of him. A quick panic seized her. Then she found him,
catching sight of the distant lantern. He was standing beneath the nest of webbing and the cocoon it held, looking up,
his mouth agape. Lyssa gave a startled gasp, but could only
watch helplessly as her brother drew near the ancient corpse,
lifting his lantern for a more thorough inspection.

"Rett!" she hissed. "What are you doing?"

Her brother paid her no attention. Instead, he reached up
and, to Lyssa's great distress, placed his free hand against
the side of the cocoon.

"Whoa." He turned to face her with a smile. "It's warm."

Lyssa sighed. For some reason, she had half expected the
ensnared carcass to come to life, to thrash free of its clinging shroud and pounce upon her impudent brother. Now that
it hadn't, and she realized how ridiculous the notion was,
she began to breathe a little easier, suspecting that indeed, all
her fears were unreasonable and unfounded.

In the next moment, those fears came rushing back. Without warning, Rett's smile vanished, and he turned to where
his hand was placed against the webbing, tugging softly at
first in an effort to break free. Held fast against the sticky
strands, he pulled harder, twisting and yanking as his anxiety mounted. The threads stretched and curled, but refused
to let go.

Gracious gods, Rett, Lyssa thought, her hand over her
mouth. *What have you done?*

Then the light appeared, a brilliant jade glow that spilled
from beneath Rett's entangled palm and spread outward
across the surface of the cocoon in narrow streams. Rett

ceased his struggles long enough to examine those streams as they raced throughout the webbing like veins through flesh, their trails broadening and brightening at the same time. In the next moment, he was thrashing uncontrollably, desperate now to tear himself away. He dropped his lantern, which shattered on the stone floor. The flame surged, spreading out to devour the spilled oil, then died abruptly as the fuel was consumed. By then, the entire cocoon was filled with the pulsating green light, flooding the room with its eerie glow.

In a blinding flash of green flames, the shroud of webs that had gripped the suspended carcass burned away. Lyssa closed her eyes to escape the glare. When she opened them again, she found her brother cringing upon the stone floor, freed from his snare. The cocoon was gone. In its place stood a woman, perfectly formed, naked save for a few tattered strands that remained of her cocoon webbing. Her dark-skinned body was tall and beautiful, by turns slender and voluptuous in all the right places. And her face . . . her face was stunning to behold, its youthful features perfect in shape and balance and dominated by pupilless gemstone eyes—pale rubies that flashed once before transforming into emeralds of infinite worth.

Lyssa dared not move. She doubted she could had she wished to. Across the chamber, the odd pair stood fully revealed by the now radiant light emanating from the central pool—her brother, paralyzed with wonder and fear, and the woman, who did not yet appear to understand where she was.

Then the woman's gaze fell upon Rett. For a moment, her incandescent eyes blinked steadily. She glanced down at her hands, her wrists, her arms. She looked back to Rett, and her delicate lips spread wide in a tender smile.

"Ackh chays ein vroagh!" the woman hissed exultantly, her voice pleasant and chilling at the same time.

Although she had never heard the language before, Lyssa understood the words as clearly as if they had been spoken in her own tongue, their meaning echoing within her thoughts: *At long last, I'm free!*

Rett was trembling. The woman saw this and reached down to grasp his quivering hands. Rett flinched, but made no effort to pull away. Gently, ever so gently, the woman drew him to his feet. When she spoke to him, the words were once again foreign, but, as if by magic, understandable at the same time.

"I must thank you," she whispered to the adventurous young prince. "I hid myself well, did I not? But you found me, yes, you found me."

The woman leaned over and pulled Rett close, nuzzling his forehead with motherly delight. A curtain of ebony hair draped them both, reaching almost to the cavern floor. Rett did not react. Whether her brother was frozen with fright, awe, or something else, Lyssa could not know, but the prince showed no signs of struggle as the woman leaned nearer, turning her mouth to his ear as if to share with him a special secret.

"I should like to kiss you."

The woman bent to Rett's neck, her mouth opening in a wide smile. Lyssa squinted, angling for a better view. Suddenly, Rett screamed, a terrible, bloodcurdling wail that erupted from his lungs and gathered strength as it echoed throughout the cavern. The initial blast caused Lyssa to rock back on her heels. The resounding peals were like needles in her ears and daggers in her heart.

With lustful jubilation, the woman tore free, leaving an exposed artery to spray blood as a fountain. Exhibiting a strength that belied her delicate form, the creature lifted Rett's convulsing body from the bloodstained earth and tossed it skyward as one might an infant. Before gravity could work its course, bolts of energy crackled from the woman's outstretched hands, accompanied by deafening blasts of thunder. The lightning struck Rett's body, a savage blast that could not be contained. Lyssa watched as her brother's form disintegrated in a shower of flesh and bone that cascaded to the floor. Beneath this spray, the woman's head snapped back, and a cackle rolled from her lips as she bathed in her victim's remains.

Driven by hysteria, Lyssa finally fled the wicked scene.

Spinning away from the chamber's glow, she stumbled
blindly back through the corridor, the woman's hair-
prickling cackle reverberating all about her. She wept uncontrollably as she groped along the wall, fighting through
the darkness. She knew that nothing she had just witnessed
had actually happened. She needed to get home. Her parents
were waiting for them, for her and for Rett. If they hurried,
they might arrive before sunset and thereby alleviate some
of the tongue-lashing to be received from both Paladius and
her father before dinner. "Wait for me, Rett," she called
ahead to her brother. *Wait for me.*

She scrambled heedlessly, her mind raked by denial and
terror. She was alone in the darkness. Her brother had taken
the light on ahead. Panic propelled her, driving her legs
without mental command. Rett had not heard her cries, or
was ignoring them as usual. But he would come back for
her. He always did. Perhaps she should call for him again.
No, she decided. She wasn't going to give him the satisfaction. She could make it home without him. She was almost
there. . . .

Beyond the lair's entrance, the hungry chasm waited.

Lyssa finally screamed as she plummeted to her death.

Jarom remained silent, awaiting Allion's response. In the
near twilight, insects chirped and hummed. Food smells
wafted on the air, the scents of roast and stew and bread, and
Jarom realized suddenly how hungry he was. For a moment,
he considered suggesting that they head back to the village
rather than continue to grapple with revelations for which
neither of them had any use. But Allion had not yet digested
the account that Jarom had finally shared with him and was
not going to let the other go anywhere until he had. Nor was
Jarom about to allow Allion to dodge his last question, the
one he knew would bring his friend around.

When Allion's silence persisted, Jarom looked away long
enough to watch a pair of water mosquitoes skim across the
surface of the stream. Since he could remember, this had
been the place to which he had come to make sense of

things, Allion at his side as he shared with his friend his dreams, his fears, or confessions regarding the latest girl to capture his attention. They must have wasted years on this forested bank, bantering about imagined adventures or devising the ultimate formula for future happiness. Now everything had changed. What should have seemed the most familiar of settings was instead foreign and unsettling. The scenery was untouched, and the characters the same. Yet this discussion bore no resemblance to those countless talks that had gone before. It was then Jarom realized that even without acting in any way upon his newfound charge, his life would never again be the same.

"You'll be no more than a glorified herald," Allion declared finally, "a messenger with an unsupported claim to the throne who is going to get himself killed."

In a reversal of their earlier positions, Allion stood near the ceaseless flow of water, while Jarom was seated on a patch of sponge grass beneath a fire poplar that he himself had planted as a young boy, a tree that now reached nearly sixty feet into the sky, with a slight lean toward the stream's edge. Jarom had not moved from his favorite location for nearly an hour, not while he had related to Allion what had happened within the council meeting, and not while debating with his friend the matter of his newly discovered responsibility. Allion had been seated, initially, but had leapt to his feet as he echoed nearly every argument that Jarom himself had uttered earlier. Some had been phrased differently, while others mimicked word for word those from his own mouth. How could this be true? King or no, what was he supposed to do about it? If he never expected to wear a crown, nor wished to, then why was he to become involved at all? And what was this about a wizard?

Jarom had listened patiently to each and every argument, nodding agreeably. Indeed, when he had first approached Allion, he had done so hoping that his friend would purge him of the notion to undertake this mission. He had found, however, that the harder Allion tried to do just that, the deeper his sense of responsibility grew, and the more rooted his resolve. He had not asked for this. But the matter wasn't going to go away. The words of his father were too sensible to ignore. It would be foolish to pretend the mysterious wizard's invasion had never happened, or leave it to others to see that the wizard's forces were vanquished. In the end, he was going to make the only decision he could.

Still, Allion had been every bit as relentless in his attack as Jarom had been, fueled by the raw sting of emotion. Finally, Jarom was forced to settle upon the one contention that he knew his friend would be unable to dispute. If their roles were reversed, if Allion were the one being asked to undertake the trek to Kuuria, what would he do?

Sure enough, this had prompted Allion's prolonged silence. At first, he had pretended not to hear it, then squirmed uneasily and turned away to collect his thoughts. Finally, he had offered up this latest remark, a capitulation, Jarom sensed, in meaning and tone.

"Who said anything about staking a claim to the throne?" Jarom replied. He shook his head, a sardonic grin twisting his features. "Besides, even if I stake this claim, all a rival has to do is challenge my story or lack of experience. No one is going to waste the effort required to kill me."

"They might," Allion warned, his expression dour.

Jarom stared at him, appreciating his friend's concern, but needing to resolve this now. After a moment, Allion turned his gaze outward, seeming to study the woodland features now hidden behind veils of evening shadow.

"I don't know," the archer admitted. "They're asking too much, having you put your neck out like this. But maybe you're right. It's just quite a shock, is all."

"How do you think I feel?" Jarom demanded. "But consider. To what am I really committing myself? If this wizard is truly all that ruthless and powerful, someone's got to warn the other kingdoms. It'll be their fight, not mine. I really don't see that my task is so terrible when compared to what's at stake."

"Oh yeah? And what is that?"

Jarom blinked. "Our lives, Allion. Our sleepy little lives. Or do you really think we're just going to continue our daily endeavors and not be affected in any way while our land and its people are ravaged by a malevolent monarch?"

"Shouldn't be much of a change, should it?"

Jarom's expression soured. Allion saw this, and Jarom could tell that the other was instantly ashamed, remembering suddenly that the man to whom he was referring, the man who had ruled Alson for their lives and longer, was in fact Jarom's father. In truth, Jarom cared nothing about a relationship that had never existed. His frustration was not with Allion's flippant attack on Sorl's character, but with his friend's stubborn denial of their new reality.

"Difference is, Sorl didn't care about us. Sorl didn't seem to care much about anything. Do you honestly believe that this invading warlord will treat us with similar apathy?"

"I didn't mean it."

Jarom brushed aside the apology, pressing his advantage. "I don't know about you, but if something were to happen here, to our homes, our families—something that I was given a chance to prevent and didn't—I'd never be able to forgive myself."

Allion studied him, grinding a ready retort between his teeth. Jarom braced himself, then relaxed as his friend blew out a long breath.

"You're right," Allion confessed. "If it was me being asked, I'd agree to play messenger awhile. Blazes, it's not like I've got much else going on. Besides, if living under this wizard's shadow is going to be that terrible, then the farther we go to escape it, the better."

"You'll go with me, then?" He hadn't intended for Allion to accompany him; he hadn't thought far enough ahead to even consider the possibility. Now that it lay before him, he was undeniably heartened by the prospect. There was no one he trusted more, no one with whom he would more willingly risk his life against any peril he might face.

"Of course. I'm not going to let you have this adventure to yourself." The archer managed a wry smile. "After all, this is just the sort of thing we used to dream of doing, isn't it?"

Jarom shook his head at the absurdity of it all. "When I was twelve, perhaps. Now that it's real, it's not so fun as I imagined."

"Nonsense. This makes it all the better."

Jarom managed a crooked smile.

"So," the archer asked, "when will you inform the Elders?"

"Now, I guess. No point in giving myself the chance to change my mind."

Allion nodded, then considered him quietly.

"What?" Jarom asked.

Allion continued to regard him curiously. "Torin, huh?" He mumbled the name repeatedly for a moment, testing its feel upon his lips.

"Don't worry," Jarom groaned, rising to his feet. "You won't hurt my feelings if you never call me by that name."

"Too late," Allion said with a smile. "Come, Torin. Let's go chat with your father, shall we?"

Htomah eased his way down the stark stone corridor, shoulders hunched, white robes sweeping the floor. His brow was furrowed, his head bowed in concentration. Leather sandals scraped softly on the smooth blocks beneath his feet. Gray hair formed a veil about his withered face, and as he arrived at the open door to the summoning chamber, he reached up with the gnarled fingers of one hand to comb the foremost strands aside.

Within the chamber, a horned pit fiend bellowed and cracked its flaming whip. A dozen of the aged man's peers encircled the creature, masters and students alike. As Htomah watched from the hall, the fiend lashed out at the nearest of its tormentors, a bare-chested youth. The youth threw up a single hand, deflecting the strike with a shield of glimmering white energy. With the other, he formed a rope of the same energy, and as the fiend withdrew for a second strike, he heaved it forward, lassoing the creature about the neck. Additional cords followed as the youth's companions joined the struggle. Within seconds, they had bound the creature about the arms and waist. The fiend thrashed and roared in response, foaming at the mouth, but failed to wrench free.

For a moment longer, Htomah studied the formation and

movements of his brethren, saying nothing. Then, with a subtle motion, he filled the doorway to the chamber with a wall of stone, muting the thunder of the creature's cries.

Farther down the corridor, he came to yet another portal, this one opening into one of the secondary celestial chambers. Again he stopped to peer inside. Barwn and Sovenson were occupied within, staring upward at a star-filled sky and discussing a black maelstrom that churned among the heavens. As Htomah paused, Sovenson glanced out into the hallway and gave a brief nod. Htomah returned the gesture and moved on.

When at last he reached the end of the corridor, Htomah paused before the closed portal that marked his destination. A quick wave caused the door of stone to vanish, and after a moment's hesitation, he stepped through.

"Well?"

Htomah ignored the greeting as he turned back to close the door. Once he had secured their privacy, he slipped toward the center of the chamber, where Maventhrowe sat before a massive drawing table, scribbling upon a thick sheet of parchment with a quill that required no ink. As he approached the other, Htomah stared down at Maventhrowe's flowing mane of white hair and considered the question. After a moment, he drew a deep breath of the stale keep air.

"Spithaera is unleashed, awakened as foreseen. And Torin?"

Maventhrowe stared intently at the page before which he was seated, his hands scratching across its length with a practiced flair. He did not look up as he responded. "Torin will soon set forth to visit with the emperor of Kuuria."

Htomah moved toward a side table. An empty chair slid free without his touch. The aged man claimed his seat and leaned forward, resting his arms upon a tabletop of polished hardwood. "Will Ranunculus reach Earthwyn in time?"

"If he hurries."

A moment of silence passed in which Maventhrowe continued to work beneath the weight of Htomah's contemplative frown. "Are you certain Torin will seek the Sword?" Htomah asked.

"He must. They've no other power with which to withstand the Queen."

"Ah, but that is not the true reason for this. If you were concerned about the Queen, it would have been easier to keep the Culmaril children away from Spithaera's lair. You've set upon a dangerous course, Maventhrowe."

At last, Maventhrowe set down his quill and peered up from his study, sapphire eyes glowing within their jagged, deep-set sockets. He met the anxious gaze of his fellow Entient with an almost mischievous smirk.

"Indeed. But you, Htomah, you wish to see the Sword as well as I. After all this time, we have found the one person with sufficient cause and determination to search it out and bring it to us—and with it, clues to the missing history we seek."

"And are you sure he's the one? From what you've said, he has yet to embrace his birthright."

"His birthright has little to do with it. It is his faith in the Sword itself, his passion, that must sustain him in this endeavor."

"In either case, I question the necessity," Htomah admitted quietly. "Spithaera? A Sword of Asahiel? These are powerful forces we are toying with. I wonder if this world can bear the strain of the inevitable conflict."

"If left to his own designs, man will destroy himself."

"Yes, but are we not simply hastening this fate?"

Maventhrowe pinched the bridge of his nose, rubbing gently at his eyes. When finished, he fixed his companion with a confident stare. "A common enemy is the best way to redirect the focus of the peoples of these lands, to bring them together and thus avert their premature extinction."

Htomah snorted. "A cause, I dare say, which may not warrant the risks we're taking."

"Yes, well, without man, we lose a great sense of our own purpose."

Htomah could not quite disagree. Of what use was a shepherd without his flock? He looked away, a profound sigh rattling from his lungs. "Nonetheless, I am unaccustomed to this ignorance of how it will all play out."

"Agreed. But you are not a pawn, and neither am I. We will continue to have a hand in this until it is finished."

"And if it escapes our control?" Htomah asked pointedly, arching one brow.

Maventhrowe merely smiled. He came to his feet, a whisper of movement, rolling his parchment and tucking it under one arm.

"Where are you going?" Htomah asked.

"To visit with our young king," the other replied. "To plant the seeds of this adventure within his mind."

"Then it is too late to change ours?"

"Spithaera will not return to her slumber quietly."

"No, but we might yet convince her."

"Let us allow mankind that opportunity," Maventhrowe challenged. "If we must, we shall deal with Spithaera ourselves at a later time."

"I shall remember you promised that," Htomah called after the swiftly departing Entient.

As he listened to the raspy echo of the man's footfalls, Htomah stared at the surface of the table in silence, slipping within his thoughts to determine what he could of the suddenly murky—yet undoubtedly volatile—future of Pentania.

CHAPTER SIX

Jarom spent a restless night tossing in his bed, thrashing his way through a violent landscape of thought and emotion. For much of the time, he lay awake, staring into the shadows of his room. The remainder was passed in fitful slumber, wracked with nightmares concerning the horrors of his unknown fate. Hopes and fears assailed him, often indistinguishable one from the other, and only the darkness remained steady. The throes of unwanted change had gripped him, leaving him to writhe in his blankets like a butterfly in its cocoon.

At times, while wading through the hours toward dawn, he understood clearly what had happened and what lay ahead. But most of the time, he could not even recall his name. An avalanche of truths and lies descended, suffocating him with their combined weight. Past, present, and future churned before him. One moment, he was praying to be inspired with a more complete course of action for the coming days. The next, he was sorting through his life's experiences among family and friends—the setting for all of which was this forest, this village, this home. But nothing of what had seemed real was true, and nothing of what was true could possibly be real.

At some point, as he wandered through dreams genuine and imagined, a recollection from the past came hard and fast, brushing aside all other thoughts and concerns. Its vivid lines were sharper, its colors more vibrant. Like an unannounced visitor, it demanded his full focus, and though he knew not what had spawned it, he had little choice but to welcome it.

It had been a chill winter evening when the travel-weary man who called himself Darinor had meandered into Diln seeking shelter. He had been greeted warmly, and that night, Jarom, at eight years of age, had found himself huddled around the village fire with all of the other children—and most of the adults—listening to the stranger's enchanting tales of heroes, dragons, and ancient talismans.

The visitor's focus had been on the Swords of Asahiel, a legend tied closely to the myths of creation. For it was in the beginning, when the Ceilhigh, the great creators, came together to shape this world and its inhabitants, that the Swords were forged—blessed by the elven gods, Darinor had said, after being fashioned by the Ha'Rasha, those avatars whose charge it was to assist in the creation process and in the herding of the earthly flocks. With their divine talismans and transcendent understanding of the natural energies by which all life was formed, these avatars carried out their role as overseers and caretakers of the world and its races.

Like their Olirian fathers, both the Ha'Rasha and their talismans were many and varied. But it was the Swords that found their way into mortal hands, seven thousand years ago, when the elves of ancient Finloria led a humanoid resistance against an onslaught of dragonkind. Although the Ceilhigh themselves were not involved in this great conflict, their avatars were, by passing down their talismans of divine nature for use as weapons in the struggle. Unable to withstand the matchless power of the Swords, the armies of the Dragon God were eradicated, bestowing victory upon the elves and their kind.

The enemy was vanquished, but the Swords remained. With them, the Finlorians ruled their empire for millennia, until they, as all great civilizations, eventually passed into legend. Likewise, the Swords gradually disappeared, one by one, until finally, the last of the mythical blades slipped mysteriously into the annals of history, three thousand years ago.

Young Jarom had been enthralled by the tale. When the narration had finished, he had approached the storyteller, asking him if any of the Crimson Swords still existed, or if they, like the elves of ancient Finloria, had vanished forever. Even now, he could remember his childish delight when Darinor had simply replied, "Yes, my boy, the power of the Crimson Sword remains."

The dream ended abruptly, and Jarom awoke with a start, bolting upright in his bed. He blinked uncertainly at the moonlight pouring through the windows of his room. Already, the memory was fading, its crisp, defined images seeping back into the wellspring of his subconscious. How real it had seemed! Had it truly been nothing more than a dream?

As he pondered the question, his eyes slipped over the many swords that hung from the walls of his loft, myriad weapons of iron and steel with hilts of wood and leather. Admittedly, the collection served no real purpose beyond decoration—although the act of gathering them had long been his favorite amusement. Some were exquisitely crafted and a beauty to behold, while others sacrificed appearance for function. At the moment, neither was of particular interest to Jarom. Instead, his gaze was held by a tapestry hung front and center amid the array, depicting a single sword whose blade was wreathed in flames. Even as embroidered cloth, the weapon outshone those of gleaming metal that flanked it. For it represented no mere hammered ore, but an artifact forged in the fires of Olirium. A shard of divinity.

A Sword of Asahiel.

Could it be? Jarom wondered. Could they possibly still exist? Could they still be found? Only in the tales of bards and minstrels, his father had warned following his conversation with Darinor—that was what the storyteller had meant. But it was too late. The seed was planted, and his fascination with the blades had grown ever since. Soon thereafter, the young Jarom had made it known to all that he would one day find the Swords of Asahiel and return them to the world of men. Everyone had laughed, of course, but none had challenged his newfound obsession. They understood it to be a child's fantasy, a young boy's desperate dream that could today withstand a dragon's fury, but would inevitably give way to reason and maturity.

They'd been right, of course, and yet wrong. After years of fruitless research and study, Jarom had long ago given up the notion of actually venturing forth to seek out the ancient weapons. But he had never once doubted their existence, clinging to his trust in the legend of the Swords—legend, not myth, as most would have him believe. He had refused to lay to rest entirely the idea that they could be found. If not by him, then by someone else. And if by someone else, then why not him?

In the twilight of his bedroom, Jarom shook his head. Odd, yes, that he should relive this memory now, but he had not the time to entertain such meaningless reveries.

With a heavy sigh, he fell back to his feather-stuffed pillow, hands locking behind his head. It was a long time before he slept.

When morning finally arrived in all of its stunning, late summer glory, Jarom awoke with a feeling of dread and an agonizing sense that his world had been uprooted. The night had done nothing to settle matters in his heart and mind or to prepare him for the upcoming adventure. If anything, what little confidence and conviction he had mustered had eroded completely, leaving him hollow with doubt. Almost without meaning to, he began rethinking the entire affair, hoping it was not too late.

With a groan, he slipped from his covers and stepped toward the window, there to bathe in the wash of early sunlight that poured through the dust- and pollen-streaked glass. He rubbed his bleary eyes and made an effort to stretch the stiffness from his neck and back. As he leaned this way and that, his gaze fell again upon the tapestry of the Crimson Sword that hung upon his wall, an artist's rendering. What had he been thinking of last night? He recalled his memory of Darinor, and of his subsequent lifelong dream to reclaim one of the fabled weapons. Jarom shook his head at the episode, a midnight flight of fancy that had seemed so relevant at the time, but which he now recognized as only so much foolishness.

After dressing in a loose-fitting tunic and breeches and a pair of stiff yet comfortable leather boots, he made his way down the ladder connecting his bedroom loft to the main floor of the house that he and his father shared. Upon the dining table, he found an apple and a note from Esaias. Jarom quickly read the note, munching on the apple as he did so. Next he gathered up the sack of supplies that had been furnished by the Elders the evening before. He had made few promises to the Circle, only that he would set forth for Kuuria as suggested and would do what he could to convince Emperor Derreg and the Imperial Council of the peril facing them all. The Elders had lauded his decision and Allion's to accompany him, and had quickly set about seeing to the companions' provisions while sending the adventurers themselves off to rest. Food, oil, medicinal herbs, and various other travel items now filled the knapsack that Jarom fitted to a strap and slung over his back.

Before he had finished, a knock sounded and Allion appeared in the cabin doorway, outfitted in alternating layers of wool and leather. His longbow and a quiver of arrows were slung over his shoulder, and a skinning knife was sheathed at his side. He might have been off on nothing more than another of his daily hunts.

"Morning," he offered, feigning a smile, "I trust you rested better than I."

Jarom finished off his apple and reached for the sheathed broadsword leaning against a wall of the entryway. While this particular weapon lacked the fanciful designs of some of those that hung from his walls, it was the one with which he felt most comfortable and effective.

"I doubt it," he replied.

Allion stared at his chosen blade. "Suppose we'll get to see how well you really know how to use one of those?"

Jarom held back a dismissive retort when he realized his friend was serious—and appropriately perceptive. Here he was, playing as adventurer and king while undertaking what could prove to be a very dangerous mission, without even knowing if he could truly defend himself. Throughout his years, he had worked long and hard to teach himself the fundamentals of swordplay. He had read and studied and interacted with all who visited his village that had any knowledge to share, and had spent countless hours in practice, learning by trial and error the basic techniques. But he also knew that when it came to a true confrontation, technique went only so far. Experience was what counted, and he had precious little to draw upon. His dedication and training may have made him far more skilled than anyone else in his village, but even that wasn't saying much.

Allion must have sensed Jarom's uneasiness, for he quickly changed topics. "Is your father still here?"

Jarom shook his head, recalling the note. "He left earlier this morning. But we're to stop by the council house and speak with him on our way out."

Allion nodded.

"Are we ready?" Jarom asked lamely after securing the last of his belongings.

Allion gave a snort and muttered some inaudible sarcasm, then headed out the door. Jarom shook his head and followed.

It was with a wistful sigh that Jarom turned to close the door behind them. The dawn's strengthening rays poured meekly upon him, and poignant memories of his life in Diln, many of them stirred throughout the night, suddenly washed over him.

"Come," Allion urged. "My parents are expecting you to stop by and bid them farewell, and I'm anxious to see what your father and the rest of the council have prepared by way of last-minute advice. Besides, we've got a lot of ground to cover."

Jarom turned, drawing a deep breath of the crisp morning air. Without another word, he stepped from his porch, and the two companions began their march toward the center of the woodland village.

Bloated bodies littered the bloodstained Fields of Ravacost. The corpses lay abandoned, frozen in the final throes of death, wearing masks of horror and incomprehension. They covered the land like a tattered quilt, a patchwork of colors that blanketed meadows, swept over hillocks, and filled ravines. Discarded weapons and severed appendages peppered the war-torn region, baking in the light of day.

All about, the battle raged. Those who might have tended to the dead or dying dared not, lest they fall themselves under an enemy sword. The time to take stock, to seek out one's comrades among the fallen and tend to the wounded, would come later. There would be burials and mourning and fresh oaths of vengeance before the new day. But right now, for those who remained, there was nothing but the continuing struggle.

From atop the ridge that served as his command position, Chief General Corathel of the Parthan West Legion lowered his spyglass and gazed upon the carnage spread before him. His forces had done well today, repelling a frenzied attempt by Menzo brigades to recapture a trench taken yesterday, and pushing forward to seize another. Of course, the advance had not succeeded without heavy casualties, and he knew that he was running the risk of wearing his units thin and opening himself up to a flanking maneuver. Today's gains might very well be tomorrow's losses. But in this back-and-forth struggle, he was not about to allow an opportunity to pass him by.

"Runner." He paused as a sweat-streaked herald snapped to attention at his side. "Convey my orders. General Ledryk is to cease his advance and hold position at Ferret Hill. General Jasyn is to shift one-third of his division to a reinforcement of the west slopes, and General Rynar is to move the Asp sling battalion and Wasp and Hornet arrow battalions to the eastern fore. Return with casualty reports from each."

"As you command, Chief General, sir," the herald replied with a sharp salute.

Corathel dismissed the man and squinted at the afternoon sky. "Water," he called, and his mess officer stepped forward with a ready skin. After two quick swallows, he handed back the container and licked his lips.

A brutal day to be on the front lines, he thought. Probably

why his men, better conditioned, had been able to make such progress. On the windless flats below, blood flowed in sticky streams, kept fluid by the sun. A putrid odor hung over the land, unstirred except by an occasional breeze. Worst of all were the tumultuous sounds that rang across the length and breadth of the plains, echoing sharp and shrill within the chief general's own ears, causing his head to swell with pain. The sudden screams of death, the incessant groans of the wounded, the endless clanging of iron and steel, the booming voices of the commanders—

And suddenly, in the distance, the terrible rumble of the inner earth.

The chief general dropped to a crouch as the ground beneath his feet shifted and rolled. Stores rattled within their housings, tent poles swayed, and animals cried out in fright. The men around him shouted, and arms began to point. Corathel turned, staring out upon the eastern horizon, and his breath caught in his throat.

On the battlefields below, the melee began to slow, then came to an unnatural halt. Enemies stood side by side without regard, all attention focused suddenly upon the ominous spectacle to the east.

For their lifetimes and longer, Mount Krakken had lain dormant. Not since a forgotten age, centuries before, had its wrath been displayed. Yet all knew that it was Krakken's fury that now erupted from the midst of the Skullmar Mountains. There was not a mountain in all of Pentania that rivaled Krakken in size, including those others of the mighty Skullmar range that cowered like supplicants at its feet. Across the eastern half of the island continent, from the Skullmars to the Whistlecrags, young and old alike beheld Krakken's power—the trembling earth, the rumbling roar, and the great black cloud erupting forth to blot out the sun.

For several moments, the mountain held its viewers in thrall, leaving them to marvel at its display and whatever omens it might portend. Then the tremors ceased, the roaring quieted, and only the mountain's ashen huff remained as evidence of Krakken's unrest.

Corathel straightened slowly and glanced about as others

did the same. Upon the fields below, a murmur swept through the ranks of his soldiers and those of the enemy, replacing the impossible stillness as combatants were reminded of what they were about. Gradually, battle resumed upon the Fields of Ravacost, rejuvenated by the force of the fiery spectacle. A common fury washed over all, breeding insanity upon ground already fertile for it, and the centuries-old war between Menzos and Partha raged as violently as ever before.

"What was that?" Jarom asked, looking to Allion to see if the archer, too, had felt the tremors that passed like waves beneath their feet.

Allion shrugged. "Quake of some kind. Nothing to get excited about."

Jarom wasn't so sure, but he kept the thought to himself. That was the difficulty with tremors. Light ones often meant nothing, as his friend had indicated. But for all they knew, an earth-splitting cataclysm had just buried the distant Gaperon beneath thousands of tons of rocks and debris, cutting off their only route to Kuuria. Or else that small tremor might be a precursor to a larger one soon to come.

But Allion was having none of it. And even Jarom realized there was nothing much to be done should either, more extreme scenario prove out. They couldn't turn around and go home without confirmation that their passage forward had been blocked; nor was there anywhere to seek cover should a massive tremor choose to ravage them out here in the open woods. Most likely, his reluctance was manifesting obstacles that did not exist.

By all signs, nature agreed. The forest shivered with activity, its wildlife unperturbed by the disruption. Autumn was fast approaching, and preparations had to be made. While foxes fashioned their winter dens, squirrels busied themselves harvesting nuts. A trio of white-tailed deer foraged as a group nearby, their loose formation and the lack of velvet on their antlers suggesting that mating season was not far off. The sun shone brilliantly, but even that lone reminder of summer was muted by the screen of branches enmeshed overhead. Beneath the cover of their taller, evergreen cousins, several of the smaller trees had begun already to lose their leaves, sewing into the earth the first threads of what was sure to become a thick and dazzling carpet of earthen hues.

Jarom absorbed the sights and smells of the woods as though for the first time, admiring their flavorful aroma with a dull ache in his breast. Even during these languid days of the dying season, the forest remained a cache of nature's treasures, rare and wonderful to behold.

As he finished the thought, Jarom snickered ruefully at his sudden appreciation for his surroundings. All these years, he had believed himself grateful for the quiet grandeur of his homeland. Only now did he realize how much he had taken for granted. This was his home, as it was meant to be. Of what consequence was the fact that he had been born the son of a king and queen? For he loved these natural surroundings more than any palace that might have sheltered him, and the kind and innocent people of Diln as much as any royal family he could have known.

His thoughts of family turned abruptly to his mother, Queen Ellebe, and a flush of anger returned. He was now thankful she had left the evening before, so that he'd not had to face her again before setting out. At the same time, he felt frustrated by a nagging twinge of guilt, as if it were he who had behaved unreasonably, his reaction alone that had chased her off. She was the one who had lied to him, not the other way around.

To ease this undeserved feeling of culpability, he had made an effort to smooth things over with Esaias. While carefully avoiding any apology, he offered his foster father the grudging acknowledgment that they had done what they thought was best for him. In any case, it was too late to un-make their decision.

Esaias had accepted the words without comment, a sign of forgiveness or complete lack thereof. So Jarom had gone on to suggest that perhaps the time had come for the First Elder and queen of Alson to resume the life together that they had been cheated out of so many years ago. To this, his father had nodded and forced a wan smile, then bid him on his way. As a result, Jarom had set forth without any sense of satisfaction, toting along with his possessions a gnawing regret that would not be reconciled.

Well, he thought, *at least I'm doing the right thing.*

The labors of a woodpecker scattered his reflections, sending them skittering away like the chips of wood beneath the bird's beak. Jarom let them go. What purpose did they serve? It didn't matter whether or not his mother would choose to forgive him, or he her. It didn't matter that all he cared for could be found within these woodlands, and that regardless of what was needed, he did not want to leave. All that mattered now was the path that lay stretched before his feet, a narrow trail of rutted soil and patched growth that served as the roadway from Diln to the southern city of Earthwyn. And so he marched without further complaint.

He marched because he had no horse. The villagers of Diln lacked any need for horses. The nearest outposts of civilization, Glendon to the north and Krynwall to the west, were no more than a day's trek afoot. Even Earthwyn was but two days away at a brisk pace. And the members of Jarom's community rarely strayed even this far. Trips to the city were generally reserved for the transportation of wares to market, and since it did not require a large amount of Diln's rare and lightweight foods to turn a tidy profit, horses were not needed as pack animals. If a villager was returning home with a load too heavy to carry, he or she could always rent a cart and team of horses from the city. Besides, the constricting confines of the northern Kalgren were not naturally amenable to the keeping of large animals, making the presence of horses within the village impractical as well as unnecessary.

The need for swift travel to Kuuria, however, had not been overlooked. Jarom and Allion each carried a sack of coins bouncing at his waist, plenty of money with which to purchase steeds and replenish supplies once they reached Earthwyn. Once accustomed to riding, they would quickly make up time in their journey to the southern reaches of Pentania, where . . .

Where what? Jarom asked himself suddenly, then just as quickly tossed the question aside. No sense in worrying about that now. He would carry out the task he'd been given, useless though it may seem, return home, and try as he might to put the entire episode behind him.

Even the slim hope that he might do so brought a welcome smile to his face.

That night, Jarom dreamed again of Darinor and the Crimson Swords, images of dragons and epic battles frightening in their clarity. Jarom saw in his mind's eye the grand struggle that had taken place between the winged titans and the elves of ancient Finloria, where thousands perished and rivers of fire singed the air. He witnessed firsthand the euphoria that illuminated the faces of those called upon to wield the Swords of Asahiel—those marvelous talismans whose own internal fires could never be spent. He experienced their raw passion, their righteous fury, and knew in that moment that he too must one day partake of the endless exhilaration pouring from that cup.

The dream lingered in his memory, both when he awoke in the morning and while he journeyed throughout the day. He said nothing to Allion about it, though. All in all, this day felt better than the last. The sun filtered radiantly through the forest's ceiling. Birds chirped and whistled, and rabbits and squirrels scurried frivolously through the underbrush. The familiar scents and sounds enveloped both Fason and hunter like a warm blanket and helped to ease the troubles of their minds.

But the dream would not go away, and after a time, Jarom grew frustrated with its nagging allure. Try as he might, he could not dismiss the fantasy in which he, like the Finlorians of old, possessed one of the legendary Crimson Swords. All he need do is recover the artifact, his thoughts teased. By that act alone, he would capture the respect of all. With such a talisman—and only with such a talisman—in his possession, he would be able to raise and command his own army, and would need no help from the emperor of Kuuria in claiming his birthright. He would then hold the power to flush the wizard's forces from Pentania's shores, and to forge a destiny of his own choosing. Whether a noble king or a humble villager, he would be at peace with himself, having made the choice on his own terms, and having earned the honor and admiration of all the land.

At some point during this flight of fancy, the notion that all of this might be feasible embedded itself as a genuine possibility in Jarom's consciousness. It must have happened gradually, for he could not recall a specific moment during which the seedling of promise had sprouted forth, breaking free of the good sense that kept it buried. And surely, had the idea appeared more suddenly, he would have immediately crushed it underfoot. Before he could think better of it, he had shared with Allion both the previous night's dream and his memory of Darinor from the night before, and had watched his friend's features scrunch up with suspicion.

"I thought it strange," Jarom admitted, "that I should relive that particular memory—two nights in a row."

Allion shrugged dismissively. "I relived a lot of memories last night."

"Okay, but this one has got me wondering."

"Yeah?"

"Well, consider. If the legends of the Swords are true, if the blades are even half as powerful as the stories tell . . ."

"They're just stories," Allion responded. "You're talking myths, my friend."

"But what if they're not? What if finding one actually gave me a stake in all of this?"

Allion turned to face him. "I don't understand. Now you *want* to be king?"

Jarom frowned. The question was ridiculous, and his friend knew it. Being king had nothing to do with this. The safety and liberation of his people was one thing. That much he was ready to commit to. Ruling them was another matter altogether, and one in which he would never be interested.

"I want this to be over. I want things to be like they were."

"And how is chasing after some mummer's tale going to help that?"

"Just because it's a mummer's tale doesn't mean it never happened," Jarom remarked stubbornly.

Allion laughed. "You're not serious." Then he looked over and saw the determination in Jarom's eyes. "You're mad, that's what you are. All these stories have damaged your head."

Jarom's voice raised defensively. "I'm not suggesting we abandon our course. All I'm asking is that when we get to Earthwyn, we visit the library, take another look at the histories. If there are clues that could lead to the recovery of a Sword of Asahiel, then it's worth our time to find them."

Again Allion laughed. "Jarom, you've combed that library a hundred times. You already know everything it has to reveal concerning the Swords. Blazes, don't you have those books and scrolls memorized by now?"

"There's got to be something I've missed. Or perhaps," he added excitedly, "there may be something new."

Allion was already shaking his head, laughing wryly to himself. "Fine," he agreed at last. "We'll take a look. Just so you know, I think the entire idea is absurd. What do you expect to find, exactly? You're not going to stumble across any treasure maps collecting dust in the vaults of a library. And even if you did, *and* it was accurate, how would you know someone hasn't already beaten you to the treasure?"

"No one has," Jarom asserted quickly. "Do you know of anyone said to have wielded a Crimson Sword during the last three thousand years?"

"I don't know of anyone to have wielded one before that," Allion countered.

Jarom didn't respond. His friend was taunting him, seeking to goad him into a fight. Allion knew the tales as well as he. Although steeped in mystery, there was a certain amount of lore widely accepted as truth concerning the Crimson Swords. Among this were the specific names of both the location and wielder of the last known Sword of Asahiel. It was held that three thousand years ago, the high king Sabaoth, lord of the Finlorian elves, had possessed one of the legendary blades while ruling at Thrak-Symbos, the capital city of Tritos. And Tritos, of course, was the name of ancient Pentania, largest of the island string known at that time as the Finlorian Isles. Still, nothing was known of Thrak-Symbos itself, save that the once magnificent city had been destroyed in some manner of cataclysm—a cataclysm that had presumably prompted the disappearance of the Finlorians from these lands once held as their own, and given rise to the wild, barbaric age that had existed for centuries upon these shores before the coming of man.

Assuming, then, that Sabaoth and the Sword had been buried within the elven city, all a person need do was search through the ruins of Thrak-Symbos and dig them up. Granted, this was no small challenge. For even if a Crimson Sword were to be found within those ruins, to Jarom's knowledge there remained no maps of ancient Tritos to finger the city's location. Save for perhaps the Entients, those mystical harborers of history and knowledge walled away in their hidden stronghold of Whitlock, all anyone knew was that Thrak-Symbos rested somewhere on this island continent, and a continent was a large place to search for a single city, regardless of its former majesty.

The clues were few and untested, as Jarom would be the first to admit. It would take a desperate individual indeed to begin scavenging for the legendary weapon based on these alone. But Jarom was convinced of at least three things. First, there had to have been those who had tried. The legends were too enticing, and three thousand years too long a time, to believe that none had undertaken the seemingly foolhardy quest. This led to Jarom's second conviction, that there had to be more information out there. If any had searched for the Sword, then surely some had made progress. And that progress would have been chronicled somehow, a trail left behind to be happened upon by others. Finally, Jarom had long been told by friends and family that his own fascination with the topic bordered on obsession. So be it. Obsession could be a source of strength, if directed properly. Should the opportunity arise, Jarom believed he was just the type of person who could succeed where others had either failed or dared not try.

With mixed spirits, the companions strolled along, each to his own thoughts, their boots plodding softly against the earth. Although bemused by Jarom's imagination, Allion was clearly beginning to experience the rush of excitement that always accompanied a grand undertaking. His strides were long, his pace energetic. A carefree tune whistled from his lips. Observing the man through the corner of his eye, Jarom had to wonder if they were in fact traveling the same road.

Still, Jarom could not deny his own sudden sense of relief, the feeling that had come over him upon sharing with Allion his plans and thus making them a reality. For the first time, he too was beginning to believe that this adventure might amount to something. A temporary sentiment, he was sure. He expected that by nightfall, when they reached Earthwyn, or by daybreak at the latest, his enthusiasm would have succumbed to the harsher realities of their situation. But until then, he fully intended to enjoy this unexpected reprieve.

It did help to have his best friend beside him. Even when speaking and acting in a manner contrary to his own—as was often the case—Allion was a steadying presence. They had been inseparable for much of their lives, to the point that many of the villagers and even their own parents had confused the pair from time to time. And it wasn't because of their appearance. Allion was clearly the taller of the two, and leaner, his musculature that of an experienced hunter. Due to his training with heavy swords, Jarom was stronger and more chiseled in form. His own hair was black and cropped close, not long and brown, and his eyes more closely matched the color of the sky than that of damp earth. Yes, he reassured himself, the differences between them were obvious with but a glance.

Less obvious, perhaps, were the similarities, such as the heartfelt dedication of each to his selected calling, and the dry wit with which each masked his earnest affection for the other. Earlier in their childhood, they had believed there was nothing they could not conquer together. Jarom had known then that no matter what lay ahead in life, with Allion as his ally he would make it through unscathed. But that time had been long ago. The responsibilities of adulthood had a way of dulling one's aspirations and muting such self-assurances, and Jarom would admit that the last few years had done much to temper their once youthful exuberance. If nothing else, perhaps this journey would help them to recover some of what they had once held dear.

If such were the case, he decided, then all of his fears and concerns would be worthwhile.

With a light heart and a spring to his step, Jarom cast his cares to the wind and proceeded along the sun-dappled roadway, marching without hesitation toward his uncertain future.

CHAPTER SEVEN

An array of stars speckled the night sky, robbing colors of their vibrancy and casting all in a bluish, metallic sheen. Hanging in the east, a corona encircled the moon, a ring of light like a nest among the heavens. Together, moon and stars offered a soft and comforting luminescence. For those who continued to carry out their business through the cooler, quieter hours following dusk, the daylight was hardly missed.

Upon reaching the northern outskirts of the city of Earthwyn, Jarom and Allion stopped at a well-respected livery stable. The liveryman there was an honest proprietor, a bald yet ageless fellow with whom the folk of Diln had done business for as long as Jarom could remember. Surprisingly, the stout man recognized both Jarom and his companion at once, greeting them with a congenial smile and a callused handshake. After inquiring briefly as to their welfare and needs, he brought forth a pair of horses—strong as they'd be able to handle, he claimed—that would bear them with swift assurance to their southern destination and beyond. When asked of their purpose in making such a long trek from their village, the adventurers were open and honest with news of the usurping wizard, keeping to themselves only the bizarre tale of Jarom's pedigree. Not surprisingly, the news had already spread, set loose by those who had managed to flee the slaughter at Krynwall, and carried forth by a network of couriers staged throughout the realms to operate day and night. When hearing that Jarom and Allion intended to speak with the emperor, the liveryman responded with a light-hearted chuckle.

"Rest easy, lads. Every city, town, and barony is sending emissaries south. The emperor will know of our troubles here in Alson soon enough."

Jarom nodded his agreement. He too saw little reason for their journey other than to do as they had been told. He thanked the man, handing over a bag of coins and a sampling of Diln's renowned harvest, which the fellow accepted with delight. After transferring their packs and weapons to the horses, the two woodsmen took their leave. With practiced courtesy, the cordial liveryman wished them luck and let them be on their way.

Within moments, the villagers had led their mounts along a clean, dusty road and into the city proper. Though nestled among the southern reaches of the same forest Jarom called home, there were few similarities between Earthwyn and its northern neighbor. Where Diln was a tiny, rural community of quiet folks and nature-loving farmers, Earthwyn was a sprawling commerce center bustling with activity. Unencumbered by walls of wood or stone, the city was comprised of a horseshoe-shaped marketplace that opened to the west. Within this ring of businesses lay the homes and public buildings of the inner city. Due to its location at almost the exact center of Pentania, where it bordered the four largest of the five recognized realms, Earthwyn had flourished throughout the years of Alson's oppression. Though larger and louder than Diln, it had remained a clean and beautiful city, and bore a reputation of warmth and hospitality well known throughout the lands.

Many of the market stalls were closed by now, the bulk of the artisans and traders having secured their goods for the evening and headed off toward home or their night's recreation. It took a while for the two visitors to find anyone peddling foodstuffs. When they did, they browsed quickly through the woman's wares. A selection of bread and cheese, fruits and nuts, and salted strips of dried meat was more than enough to replenish that which the companions had consumed over the past two days, and would be plenty to sustain them for several more.

It was with some regret that they passed through the remainder of the marketplace without slowing, as the night offered them little time to taste of the city's pleasures. Instead, they made their way toward the city center, passing by parks and schools and small flocks of children who raced from their parents in an effort to extend their gaming hours. More than once, Allion suggested that their time might be better spent in leisure, so as to revitalize themselves for the journey ahead. Fighting against his own desire to do just that, Jarom rejected his friend's urgings and kept to a well-known path—one that led to the best-kept library in northern Pentania.

Beneath the wash of light from moon and stars, Ranunculus made his way without haste along the deserted highway, listening to the dull thud of his mare's hooves plodding against the soft earth. The tomes he carried swung lightly against his steed's sides, tucked away in a pair of leather saddlebags. There were four books in all, selected for this journey by Maventhrowe himself. Inside their covers were the writings of his order, a compilation of history and prophecy, of knowledge and discovery, a record of assorted studies pertaining to the race of man and this land upon which he lived.

Wisdom that, in this Entient's mind, had no business leaving the vaults from which it had come.

Ranunculus scowled, the only expression his features knew. To the north, ahead through a series of pine groves, lights from dwellings clustered about the city of Earthwyn winked into view. The city itself remained some ways off, its still-distant clamor no more than a loose collection of echoes in his ears. With any luck, he would finish this business tonight and be on his way home before dawn. It had been a hundred years since an Entient had last stepped from the confines of Whitlock, and he remained none too pleased at having been the one selected to break that isolation. For more than two days he had been on the road, hunkered within his dirt-colored robes, doing what he could to ignore those he encountered while choking on the dust of their passing.

It might have helped had he believed there to be any purpose to his travels. He had been sent against his will, charged by his order to journey here to Earthwyn to meet with a certain young man who Maventhrowe claimed would be passing through. He was to pose as a scholar, one who could share with this young man, this Torin, a glimpse of the histories he carried. Just enough to make plausible the dreams that would by now be plaguing the lad. Enough to launch the poor fool upon the quest that Maventhrowe and some of the others had designed.

There were many who had disagreed with the decision, but ultimately their voices had gone unheard. Ranunculus himself had raged vociferously against both the plan and the idea that he be the one to see it all carried out. Never mind that he had better things to do. Never mind that the entire affair was a colossal misjudgment on numerous levels. Why should the Entients care if mankind destroyed itself? There were other races better suited to govern this world than those of man.

The wind shifted, blowing from the north. Ranunculus snorted. Although cleaner than most, the air of the approaching city was afoul with the sultry toil of man and his civilization. The stench of it caused the Entient to ponder the sense of his own existence. Back home, occupied with his studies, it was easy enough to forget much of that which he hated about mankind. But out here, among those he both served and directed—and with little more to engage his mind than to remember not to fall from his horse—it was difficult to deny the ultimate insignificance of his calling. How ridiculous it seemed to chronicle and even to dictate the affairs of this juvenile creature called man. For nine hundred years he and his forebears had done so upon these shores, having followed man from his nesting grounds across the seas, where they had watched over him since the time of his creation. And for what? To see him tame a savage wilderness and build up a mighty civilization, only to tear it down with those same hands. If not today, tomorrow. If not tomorrow, then soon.

It was a pattern that had been followed since the dawn of

time. The endless cycle of a world abandoned by its gods, with *his* kind left behind to oversee the futility of it all. A maddening fate. At times, Ranunculus wondered if it might not be better to stroll through life as one of his mortal charges, oblivious to all but his own hedonism while entwined in a web of self-importance.

It was this enigma that plagued Ranunculus as he hunched his shoulders against a sudden chill, the same enigma that had plagued his order from the beginning. One of the few questions, perhaps, that he and his brethren could not answer. Was their advanced knowledge and awareness a gift or a curse? A cursed gift, the Entient decided for neither the first nor the last time, then muttered an oath as his mount stumbled on a rut in the road. Whatever the real answer, it lay far from here.

High above, the stars dimmed, their light smothered by the darkness of a passing cloud and screened away by the thickening array of trunks and limbs that closed about as he entered the first of the pine groves. With his cowl drawn over his face, he neither saw nor heard the approaching danger. He didn't have to. For he felt the shadows as they descended upon him.

Suddenly alert, he probed the night with his senses. They were all around him, more than a dozen in number, dark forms crouched in the darkness. He maintained his pace, giving no indication that he was aware of their presence. He felt their eyes upon him, the tension in their muscles, and the nervous roiling in their stomachs. Experienced men, hard and feral, their formation that of a noose about to close. They were sizing up their prey while taking note of the Entient's bulging saddlebags. Ranunculus let them look, pressing forward. Perhaps good sense would prevail and they would let him pass without challenge.

Then one of them came forward, stepping free of the brush to block the roadway. Ranunculus pulled back on the reins, bringing his mare to a halt.

"Evening," the ruffian spat, his arms folded across his chest. "What be your business this night, old man?"

"None of yours, I assure you. Make way."

"Ah, but you must first pay the toll, old man," sneered the rogue, dropping his hand to rest on the pommel of his longsword.

"I see the impudence of youth has not changed in the past century," Ranunculus grumbled.

The bandit's smug smile dropped from his chin. "Are you refusing to pay? I don't think me boys'll take well to that."

As if on cue, the brush about began to rustle where the rogue's companions lay concealed, and the rasp of drawn steel hissed upon the air. The Entient bent lower to his steed, his brow furrowed in concentration.

Ranunculus waited, wondering just what it would take for this scoundrel to realize that he was not going to bargain. When it happened, it happened suddenly. The rogue gave his signal, a snap of his gloved fingers. Without hesitation, the brigands lunged from the trees in a coordinated attack, moving with a deftness and precision gleaned from experience. Only the leader held back, the smug grin returning to his greasy face.

As the bandits took their first strides, a splintering stream of lightning crackled down from an invisible cloud hovering in the night sky. In a heartbeat, eight bodies were blasted to the ground, where they writhed in pain and surprise. Cries rang out, followed by moans of anguish and accompanied by the stench of smoldering flesh. Ranunculus smirked to himself with grim delight, fully expecting the others to turn and flee at the frightening display.

They did not. The five remaining assailants barely paused in their rush, too quick and furious in their attack to have halted had they wanted to. They hammered into the Entient from all sides, clearly prepared to make short work of him, and Ranunculus knew in that instant that he was going to pay a price for underestimating their skill and tenacity.

He was yanked from his mount and thrown to the ground, where a cord was slipped about his neck. The remaining rogues struck at his horse. One wicked dagger slashed through the straps of the saddlebags, spilling food and books to the earth, while a second slit the jugular of the hapless mare.

When Ranunculus was securely bound by the cord cinched around his throat, the leader stepped forward, quickly inspecting those who had been struck by the Entient's magic. Already, they were rising to their feet, relatively unharmed, shaking their heads as trailers of smoke wafted from their clothes.

The rogue clapped his hands in mock salute. "A fine illusion. Street magic, no? My father used to perform a similar trick, though not nearly as well."

Ranunculus watched as a pair of bandits rummaged through his possessions before turning to their leader with books and rations—nothing of value.

The rogue fixed him with a glare of disapproval. "Well, old man, am I to believe you've no toll?"

Fire blazed in the Entient's eyes, flashing a brilliant, phosphorescent blue, forcing the brigand to step back. Before him, Ranunculus rasped and sputtered, the skin of his bearded face turning purple. The ruffian, regaining his composure as swiftly as he had lost it, merely sighed.

"Pity." He waved dismissively to the outlaw holding the cord, then turned to leave. The cord tightened. New lights appeared like fireflies before the Entient's eyes as Ranunculus felt the last of his breath begin to fail.

Suddenly, a shriek pierced the night sky, and each of the bandits turned to see their companion's horror-stricken visage. What had been a strangling cord was now a slithering serpent, its venomous fangs lodged deep within his hand. The unfortunate bandit saw his death reflected in the stares of his comrades as, in a matter of seconds, the poison streaked and sizzled through his body, its progress marked by the bulging and darkening of his veins. The doomed man began foaming at the mouth, and when his frame stiffened and convulsed sharply backwards, he managed a meager grunt, the last noise to ever escape his lungs.

"Die, sorcerer!" shrieked the wide-eyed ruffian leader as he hurled a gleaming object at the scrambling Entient. The knife buried itself to the hilt in the back of Ranunculus's neck, but not before lightning once again crackled from a thundercloud that was not even there and into the midst of the twelve outlaws who were huddled where the aged man had lain a moment before. This time it flashed with a blinding white brilliance, gouging a hole in the earth as it turned seven of the bandits to ash and blasted the limbs and lives from two more.

Ranunculus stumbled away from the battle, exhibiting a strength far beyond that of his gaunt frame as he clutched at the knife in his throat. Feeling the four remaining rogues rush him from behind, he turned to face them, but dropped to his knees. He might have been dead a moment later were it not for the spinning daggers that dropped two of the thieves in their tracks, causing the other two to spin and face the new threat.

"You!" hissed the leader of the decimated band.

"Aye, worm. Come fence with one who can stand."

The rogue hesitated, then rushed the mysterious new arrival with a curse upon his lips. The two clashed, and then the stranger slid away, with neither making any move to reengage. Ranunculus waited, confused, for it appeared that the stranger had simply stepped aside, dodging the initial assault. He had seen no other movement, no flash of a blade that would indicate a counterstrike. A moment later, the truth became clear as the rogue turned unsteadily, his chest a wash of blood seeping from his flayed throat. He coughed, glared at the other in helpless denial, then collapsed.

Ranunculus was not the only one stunned by the exchange. The remaining bandit stared incomprehensibly at his leader's body until the stranger slapped him with the narrow flat of one of his blades. Reflexively, as if uncertain of his own movements, the bandit lifted a shortsword to strike the other down. No sooner had he done so than he found himself slumping to the ground, hugging his entrails to prevent them from spilling out of his gruesomely grinning torso.

For a brief moment, the Entient's eyes met that of his rescuer. Then, with a swift yank, he pulled free the small knife buried in his neck. He felt the warm splash of blood that followed, swooned, then slipped into a deep blackness. The last thing he knew was the gentle touch of a youth's hands helping him from the ground.

Htomah sat before the crystalline mirror, observing the fall of his fellow Entient. When finally it ended, with Ranunculus lying unconscious in the middle of the road, he huffed bitterly and, with a wave of his hand, dismissed the image.

As he turned, there was Maventhrowe, the only one who could ever steal upon him like that. Htomah tried not to show his surprise, but made no attempt to mask his disgust.

"Looks as though your dreams will have to be enough," he grumbled.

Maventhrowe showed no concern. "Perhaps. Although this presents an interesting notion."

"The Kronus youth?"

"Can you imagine a better guide?"

Htomah shook his head. "We've discussed him before. He hasn't the conviction."

Maventhrowe's blue eyes sparkled. "We shall see."

"Well, this stop was of no help," muttered Jarom, slamming the dusty volume shut and dropping it to the table.

The noise woke Allion, who had been reclining openmouthed in a nearby chair. Startled, the archer scrambled for his bearings, nearly knocking himself to the floor in the process. A pile of books and scrolls lay scattered upon the table. Jarom shook his head as he swept them up and stuffed them back into place on the shelves.

Allion yawned. "No luck?"

Stowing the last of the books, Jarom reached for his belongings and stalked away.

"I warned you not to get your hopes up," Allion chided, rising to follow him.

Jarom gritted his teeth. He did not need Allion to remind him that this had been a fool's errand. He had allowed himself to get carried away, was all. He would have said so, but realized that he had no right to be angry with his friend. Allion had been good-natured enough to humor him, permitting a search that he could just as easily have argued off as a waste of time they could not allow. What had actually caused Jarom to believe he might find within this library any of the secrets that continued to elude him and the rest of the world remained a mystery, even to himself. He had simply let his dreams get the best of him. As he stormed past the front desk toward the exit, he vowed privately that he would not do so again.

Allion was more forgiving, coming up and placing a reassuring hand on his shoulder. "Remember, if it was going to be easy to find, it would have been recovered long ago."

Jarom nodded, then shook himself free.

A short while later, the two friends had left the cold silence of the library and were making their way once more through Earthwyn's outer quarter. The evening was alive with song and dance and flavorful aromas, an enticing blend of sound and color and fragrance. Jarom watched Allion carefully, fully aware of his friend's fondness for the city's amusements. He could see the other's face brightening as he absorbed the delightful mix that swirled to the steady rhythm of his horse's footfalls. With midnight drawing near, the last of the shops and markets had closed, but the taverns and pleasure dens were just beginning to reach the height of their festivities, and that was where anyone seeking enjoyment would want to be found.

Originally, they had planned to be camped well south of the city that night, but their stop at the library had taken longer than expected. So Jarom was not at all surprised when Allion suggested what he thought to be a sensible alternative.

"Hey," he said, leaning over to nudge Jarom as they passed an especially boisterous tavern, "perhaps we should stay the night here in town." He concocted a yawn for dramatic effect.

Jarom shook his head. "We're supposed to be saving our money. Besides, we don't have time to waste."

"We took time enough to search through your library," Allion reminded him pointedly.

"Which means we have even less than before."

Allion scowled. "Come on, live a little," he persisted, eyeing the tavern hungrily. "It may be our last chance."

Jarom chuckled. Allion faced him in annoyance.

"What?"

"Your thirst for excitement is never satisfied."

Allion turned back to the tavern, where some fool had just been thrown from the doorway. Together, the companions watched the man tumble down the steps and land in the dirt, where he lay mumbling to himself in a slurred voice.

"Looks like great fun," Jarom observed dryly. "Anyway, I wouldn't worry. I'm sure the sooner we get on our way, the sooner we'll come upon more thrills than even you can handle."

Allion was not really listening, but nodded absently as he focused on the road ahead. He turned back suddenly. "You know, we might overhear some news about the fall of Krynwall," he offered in a final attempt. "That could prove invaluable."

Jarom hesitated. The suggestion made sense.

"No," he decided finally, dashing his friend's hopes, "we've got enough to worry about with what we know to be true. No use in spreading what may be false rumors."

Allion groaned. "I see. Rumors of divine talismans, spread by mad storytellers, those must be true. But rumors of current events, shared at the local watering hole, that's just useless gossip."

Jarom was not amused. "The queen told us all we need to know about the wizard. Let's just hurry and deliver her account to those who will have to face him."

If Allion had any further disputes, he kept them to himself. Grateful for the silence, Jarom directed his own attention to the path ahead.

The city's dwellings thinned, then fell behind altogether. Moments later, all that remained was the road, the woods, and a handful of figures making their way from one place to another. Soon, the last of the citizens had disappeared, the lights and the clamor faded away, and Jarom and Allion found themselves alone in the starlit darkness. The land was quiet about them, save for the shrill chirping of what sounded to be thousands of crickets. Jarom lost himself in their song, his thoughts drifting aimlessly.

South of the city, they passed through a series of groves. Weathered boughs sheltered them in cool evening shadow, filtering out the most radiant beams from moon and stars. In the distance, a wash of light signaled the end of the sylvan tunnel, where the foliage thinned, then dropped away into the rolling grasslands of southern Alson. The companions rode toward it without comment, giving free rein to their mounts as they sauntered along at an easy pace.

Without warning, Jarom's horse snorted and reversed its direction. Eyes wide, Jarom clutched the reins, murmuring to calm the frightened beast. Remarkably, it responded to his protests and refrained from bolting back toward the city, but the animal continued to stamp the ground beneath its hooves and refused to swing about to the south.

"Whoa, boy," Jarom exclaimed, patting the horse's sleek neck with a reassuring hand. He glanced over to find Allion having similar troubles with his own steed.

"They smell something," Allion said. "Whatever it is, they don't like it."

"What do we do?" Jarom asked, jolting in his saddle as his mount continued to fidget roughly beneath him.

"Do you have any salves or ointments that we can rub in their nostrils?"

Jarom nodded. "Yeah, but is that such a good idea?"

"It'll block out whatever scent has got them spooked."

"I know, but if they're spooked, maybe we should be too."

"Should we head back, then?" Allion asked, annoyed.

Jarom responded by reaching into his saddlebag and rummaging blindly through its contents. When his hand grasped the item he was searching for, he carefully dismounted, keeping the horse's reins firmly gripped in one hand.

"Steady now," he soothed, stepping in front of the beast.

With the reins wrapped about his wrist and with that same hand pressed comfortingly against the creature's jaw, Jarom dipped into a tiny metal container and scooped forth a small amount of clear, mildly scented ointment. He whispered as he worked, gently smearing the lotion upon the inner rim of his horse's nostrils. The animal accepted the treatment without complaint, and stood sniffing the new air experimentally.

"Here," Jarom said, tossing the container to Allion.

Allion caught the vessel in the air and proceeded to treat his mount in the same fashion. Jarom continued to pat and rub his steed's neck while Allion worked, and after a moment or two, both beasts had calmed considerably.

"All right," Allion said when he had finished. He handed the container back to his friend, gave his horse another moment in which to relax, and then remounted. "I suggest we proceed with caution."

Jarom ignored the unnecessary remark, climbed into his own saddle, and turned his horse's head back to the south. The beast offered little struggle this time, expressing its discontent with a single snort. Jarom urged it forward at a walk. He glanced back once to ensure that Allion was following, then concentrated upon the shadowed road ahead.

The grove seemed now unnaturally still, and the two men scanned their path with intense concentration, probing not only the trodden earth but the bushes all around. Just before Jarom's imagination could begin lending life to his fears, Allion stopped and pointed with a whispered shout, indicating the outline of a shape in the road before them.

"It looks like a horse," he hissed.

They approached slowly, Jarom in the lead, his curiosity mounting with each iron-shod step. As they drew nearer, they began to make out several other forms that lay near the first. These they recognized as the bodies of men, and Jarom pulled up short, reaching for his blade.

It was soon evident, however, that this was a dispute that had already been settled, albeit recently. Thickening streams of blood oozed from the fresh wounds of the horse and four men while wisps of smoke drifted from the charred remains of nine others. Jarom studied the blackened corpses with disgust, marveling at the power that must have been called upon to inflict such damage.

"It's as if they were set afire by lightning," he gasped,

choking on the stench. Beneath him, his horse snorted, pawing anxiously.

Allion, meanwhile, had already dismounted. With one hand covering his nose and mouth, he conducted a quick examination.

"Bandits," he declared. His face contorted with revulsion as he inspected those who had been reduced to piles of ash. "Not much left of most of them."

While Allion bent for a closer look at one of the bleeding corpses, Jarom stepped down from his mount. "Why'd they kill the horse?" he wondered aloud, veering toward the slain animal.

A moment later, he turned as Allion grunted in surprise. "Whoever did them in didn't bother to take their money," his friend said.

Jarom saw that Allion was holding up a small leather purse filled with coin. He started toward the man when a flicker caught his eye from beneath the body of the unfortunate horse. Reaching down, he found a leather-bound tome protruding from a damaged saddlebag, and slid it free. Twilight glittered against the gold-leafed writing stamped upon the cover, markings he did not recognize.

"Allion, come look at this."

The other did not respond right away, intent on his own tasks. Jarom used the time to open the heavy book and to examine its ink-ridden parchment. The edges were frayed, but the binding was strong and certain. He began to browse the book's contents, the calligraphy and images that adorned its crinkled yellow pages. Some of it, he could read. Most, he could not.

Finally, Allion joined him, drawing near to peer over his shoulder. "Look at this," Jarom remarked again, continuing to leaf through the pages.

Allion kept silent, withholding judgment. The book was unlike any they had ever studied, intriguing in its archaic appearance. Whether that meant anything remained to be seen.

Then a drawing trapped Jarom's breath in his throat. He exchanged glances with Allion, and the solemn look mirrored in the other's face told him his friend had seen it too. He flipped back to the illustration of a marvelous sword. Its hilt was lavishly wrought, intricately carved and studded with gems. But it was the depiction of flames burning up and down the length of the blade that held him spellbound. Jarom knew at once that the picture was that of a Crimson Sword. Words accompanied the drawing, and finding that he understood them, Jarom began to read. It took but a moment to realize that the next few pages held priceless information about the weapon's powers, history—

And a map.

With barely bridled exhilaration, Jarom hurriedly examined the map of Tritos, the ancient world, this very land as it had appeared during a time no longer remembered. He practically yelped when he found the name of Thrak-Symbos scrawled upon the page at the southern expanse of the Skullmar mountain range. The ink was faded, the characters fancifully drawn in an archaic style. But there was no doubting that which the map revealed—Thrak-Symbos, seat of power of the Finlorian Empire, situated by the sea in the southeastern stretches of what today belonged to the kingdom of Partha.

Jarom trembled with excitement, blinking to make sure his eyes were not deceiving him. "Thrak-Symbos! Allion, it's Thrak-Symbos!"

Allion leaned closer, studying the region to which Jarom pointed.

"It's got the main road marked and everything!"

"Roads change," Allion reminded him, his tone doubting.

But Jarom's enthusiasm would not be tempered. He glanced about briefly, searching the shadows for any sign of the book's owner. After reassuring himself that they were alone, his eyes flew back to the treasure cradled in his arms. "I don't believe it. It's like a gift fallen from the heavens. Think of . . ."

He trailed off, suddenly bewildered. Upon finding the image of the Crimson Sword, his excitement had grown such that he did not even notice the gradual change in the script. Now that he did, Jarom assumed it to be a trick of his own eyes. In the seconds that followed, he watched in desperate horror as the writings faded, then vanished entirely. The map, the lore, the illustration—all of it was gone.

"No!" Jarom cried, bending to scrutinize the parchment.

"What sorcery is this?" Allion demanded as Jarom flipped through the pages in dismay.

Jarom paused, reining in his anxiety as he puzzled through the situation. Obviously, whoever the book had belonged to had wanted its secrets to remain protected. The ward had probably gone into effect as soon as the book had been opened, or perhaps even touched by unauthorized hands. His face brightened in recognition. "The Entients."

"What?" Allion asked. "Don't be a fool."

But the thought, at first a desperate reach for understanding, seemed to Jarom the only plausible explanation, and the more he considered it, the more he knew it to be right.

"Who else in this age could draw up such an account?" he challenged. "That map showed this land as it appeared in the time of the Finlorian elves!"

Allion shook his head. "Jarom, the Entients are as much a myth as the Swords themselves. And even if they do exist, what would they or their books be doing out here?"

Jarom had no specific answer, but his mind spun with possibilities. Certainly, the manner in which the book was protected would seem to suggest the involvement of the Entients, an order of men rumored to have descended from the Ha'Rasha, the first avatars themselves. Allion might argue that the book could belong to anyone—a scholar, a collector of antiquities, a wandering minstrel—but to Jarom, no other choice made sense. The more intriguing question was, indeed, if it belonged to the Entients, what was it doing here? Had it been stolen? Not likely, or Jarom would not have been the one to trigger the protective magic. Perhaps they had been delivering the tome to the library at Earthwyn. It seemed a reasonable explanation. But why would they bring a book whose contents no one else was allowed to view? And what about the timing? How extraordinary was it that such a history would be making its way to Earthwyn at the same time as he?

A sudden suspicion entered his mind, one he dared not voice. Instead, he looked once more upon his surroundings, at what remained of the frightening struggle that had taken place within the grove. If only they had arrived earlier, he thought. If only he had stumbled upon this grisly scene in time to question its participants. For as the many questions and possible answers blew past on tornado winds, there was one idea in particular that held fast and clear before him. An Entient. An Entient of Whitlock. Here, outside of Earthwyn. And they had just missed him!

Stepping beyond the tempest of his thoughts, he closed the tome and gripped it in his hands, forcing himself to recall what it had shown him, thinking on what that information might mean.

A moment later, he smiled. "This changes everything."

Allion's own wonder vanished. "Hold on," he demanded. "What are you thinking?"

Jarom said nothing, but fixed his friend with an assertive glare, his eyes gleaming with purpose.

"Oh no," Allion groaned. "We just got over this."

"Allion, you saw the map. A map!"

"I saw a useless sketch, a dot of ink buried within a mountain range on the far side of Pentania. A dot of ink that hasn't existed in three thousand years!"

But Jarom could not deny the fever welling within. "What if, Allion? What if? If we could find Thrak-Symbos, then we could find the Sword. And if we found the Sword . . . Allion, if we found the last of the Crimson Swords . . ."

He let the implications hang in the air, a tantalizing vision, but Allion only shook his head. "I don't buy it, Jarom. You're assuming way too much. *If* we can find the city. *If* the Sword is there. *If* we can find the Sword . . ."

"The Sword is there," Jarom insisted. "I know it's there, waiting to be found."

"How?" Allion asked incredulously. "How do you know? You claim this book must belong to the Entients. Fine. If they've had this information all along, what makes you think they didn't reclaim the Sword centuries ago?"

Jarom groped for a response. Allion was right. What he had could not be classified as knowledge, exactly. All he had were feelings, as ephemeral as smoke, and a child's faith and desire. With these alone, the very suggestion of searching for a Sword of Asahiel was preposterous. Still, as smoke was wont to do, those feelings clung to him, thick and acrid, and even with a strong breeze of reason would not easily be cleared away.

"Don't you see?" His desperation allowed a hint of his earlier suspicion to break free. "First the dreams, and now this." He shook the book for emphasis. "This can't be mere chance."

Allion hesitated, and Jarom saw that his friend was indeed unsettled by the alarming coincidence. They had just left the library where they had been in search of such an account. And now, here one was. Regardless of whom it belonged to or where it had come from, the improbability was disturbing. The most reasonable conclusion was that someone had intended for them to find it. But who? A friend, or an enemy? Allion betrayed his thoughts by casting about the grove with a scowl on his face, searching for whoever might be playing some kind of trick on them—or worse.

"Look," the archer decided finally. "Whatever the reason for that book being here, we'd be best off having nothing to do with it. Besides, with the way things stand, it's worthless."

Jarom frowned, his hopes slipping. Once again, he had absolutely nothing with which to defend his own curious beliefs, no argument that could possibly withstand the other's logical assessment. He looked up, allowing his plaintive gaze to meet Allion's harsh glare. His friend's features remained stern.

"Listen," Allion allowed calmly, "I know you've been made to feel responsible for doing something about all of this. But what you're suggesting is well beyond our power. We've got nothing to go on here, nothing but the task we've been given."

Jarom remained silent, genuinely contemplative as he opened the book and fingered its empty pages. "Perhaps you're right," he agreed finally.

Allion blew a sigh of relief. "Of course I'm right," he said, moving already to retrieve his restless mount. He secured the money he had gathered from the slain bandits, tossing the extra coin sacks in with his own, then stepped up and into his saddle. "Let's get moving," he added, glancing about guardedly. "I don't want to be here when the city authorities stumble onto this mess."

With a slow breath, Jarom closed the heavy book. He held it only a moment longer before dropping it to the ground at his feet. Allion nodded in satisfaction, then urged his steed ahead.

As his friend trotted off into the distance, Jarom reached for the reins to his own mount, pulling the animal near. He had only one foot in the stirrups before he stepped down again. Staring ruefully after Allion, he reached down, retrieved the book with its empty pages, and stuffed it into his saddlebag. In that moment, he was not even certain as to why. It might have been because some part of him, that part that was governed by intuition and not reason, still believed, making the act an irrational gesture of defiance and determination. Or it might have been because just a short time ago, he had promised not to let his dreams get the best of him, and had failed. Either way, perhaps clinging to this tome would serve some useful purpose—if not as a key to unlocking his dreams, then as a stark reminder to keep them in check.

A moment later, he sat astride his horse, bouncing in the saddle as he hurried to catch up with Allion on the road south to Kuuria.

CHAPTER EIGHT

*E*llebe, queen of Alson, rode tall in her saddle, shoulders thrust back in a practiced display of dignity. She felt the weight of the world upon those shoulders, the full burden of shame and sacrifice that the Ceilhigh had called upon her to bear. Any normal woman—or man, for that matter—would surely have crumbled long ago beneath the excessive load. But she was no normal woman. She was strong, a warrior who had survived every conceivable hardship life had to offer. Never had she bowed before those challenges, and she refused to do so now. Forsaken by her family, her friends, and the gods themselves, she was determined to face her destiny with head held high.

Even as she rode to her doom.

She had repeated such words over and over, girding herself for the task at hand. It was only fitting. She had lived her entire life, it seemed, in service to others. She had given of herself until there was nothing left to give. And yet, she was unrecognized, unpitied, unloved. No matter. If this was her calling, so be it. She would bear her burden without complaint, setting forth an example sure to be admired and followed once she was gone. If her just reward was not meant to be found in this life, then she would claim it in the next.

The decision had not been an easy one. It had been simple enough to leave Diln following her reunion with the Elders and her son Torin. The results of that meeting had left her weary and bitter and feeling like an unwanted castoff of humankind. Although the Elders—and especially Esaias—

had urged her to stay the night, to take at least that much time to rest and reconsider, she had flatly refused. Their concern, whether real or feigned, was of little use. They did not understand. No one did. And so she'd taken her leave, riding north and west through the darkened woodlands until she had reached the deserted hunting lodge that Sorl had kept at the edge of the forest, thinking to stay for but a single night before returning to her besieged city.

But with the coming of dawn, she had been unable to depart. Conflicting needs warred within her, splitting her head and her heart. She had resolved to carry out her duty to her people without protest. But it had finally occurred to her, long after she had departed Diln, that perhaps she was being too hard on herself. Sorl was dead. Her power as queen had been usurped by another. She was free, it seemed, to return to her former life, to Esaias, who had remained true to her all these years, and to Torin. It would be awkward at first. But with time, the joy that had been denied her for so long might at last be hers. Certainly, she owed herself the chance to find out.

For two full days, she had wrestled with the decision, lying about the cabin or taking short walks within the nearby woods. During this time, her moods swung back and forth like a pendulum. In moments of light and clarity, she knew the road to happiness lay open before her, and that she was deserving enough to take it. But then would come the darkness and doubt, borne upon foul winds that hissed of her life's true purpose as that of a victim, a martyr. Happiness for her was but a lie, a temptation she could ill afford if she wished to reap eternal salvation within the fields of Olirium.

Finally, on the third morning following her departure from Diln, she had made her choice. Fate would dictate her course. She would ride to Krynwall, doing what she believed was required, putting the needs of her people before her own. If destiny were to grant her a reprieve from death, then perhaps she would return to those with whom she had once belonged. At that point, she would be able to do so with a free conscience, absolved of any guilt. Until then, with unfinished business at hand, she intended to do as she must, not as she wished.

So it was that she had set forth with the coming of dawn, allowing the sun's rays to usher her journey westward. The lands about had lain deserted, curiously so, had she not already known the reason behind it. The swift and devastating capture of Krynwall had chased off all who lived within a dozen miles. The roads were littered with the debris of their exodus, left in the haste of departure. Farmsteads, communities, and roadside market stalls lay abandoned, as though the tenants had simply vanished. Of the land's citizens, all she saw were looters, feral-eyed bandits rummaging through the discards, men who disappeared like roaches upon spying her approach. Hers was a land stripped by plague, and all that remained were insects.

For a time, she kept her mind tightly focused, afraid that if she allowed her thoughts to wander, her body might follow. But as the hours passed, that focus drifted—though never far, an animal pacing in its cage. It began with a study of the land itself. Her flight of a few days ago along these same paths had allowed her little time to reflect on what she had seen. Now, as she and her mount retraced their steps with a slow, deliberate pace, she marveled disconsolately at how, even at breakneck speed, she had missed the obvious signs.

Barely a generation previous, Alson had been recognized far and wide as the most fertile region of Pentania, rich in mining, agricultural, and commercial resources. Nature had had a hand in this, but no more than King Sirrus, Sorl's father, a strong-willed man who had used his life to build an empire of material wealth. He had done so with hard labor and diligence, and without the money or influence of his royal father. Despite being born and raised as the first child of the ruling family of Alson, Sirrus had spent his teenage years serving in the royal military as an enlisted officer. Thereafter, he had begun his merchant career, amassing a private fortune with honest dealings at home and abroad. Upon ascending the throne, he had taken those same principles and tenets that had led to his success and applied them to the regulation of his kingdom. Chief among these had been his uncanny ability to discern and implement a perfect balance between growth and consumption. In the years that followed, Alson and its people had flourished, become a model for the other kingdoms of Pentania to envy.

Sorl, however, had never understood the adage that one could shear a sheep for life, but butcher it only once. This man wanted the feast, and so had indulged himself at the expense of his land and its citizens, taking what he wished and giving nothing in return. After just a few short decades, he had managed to almost completely ravage Alson's plentiful stores. Ellebe had known all along what was happening, but tucked away within her palace chambers had rarely imagined just how far things had gone. Out here, there was no denying the truth. Villages, once prosperous, hung now in rotting tatters, populated by the ghosts of the impoverished and starved. Mines lay stripped, forests leveled, fields barren. And as the land buckled beneath the strain, so did its citizens, turned to thieving and murder and, in rare, horrific circumstances, even cannibalism in order to survive. And yet, until the day he had died, Sorl had remained oblivious to it all, concerned only with his next meal and his next whore and enticing his personal guard to do the same, indulging their every fantasy in order to support his own.

Ellebe squeezed an angry tear from her eye. Even knowing as she did that Sorl had been replaced already by a marauding warlord, she wondered, could things get any worse?

At the same time, she actually felt sorry for the man. He had not been born a wicked despot. But he'd been given little chance to become anything else. His mother had died giving birth to him, and his father had mostly ignored him. Sirrus had wanted to be a loving father, but following his wife's death saw the boy as little more than a painful reminder of the woman he had loved and lost. Sorl's attempts to win his father's affection had ultimately fallen short. Eventually, Sorl had found companionship among a group of peers of the lower court, wayward thugs who befriended the prince because of his station and helped to mold him into the crass and selfish brute he had become.

Despite all of this, there had been a time during which Sorl had actually shown promise as a husband and king. It was two years after Sirrus's death that she had given birth to their first son, Soric. To Ellebe's great astonishment, Sorl was thrilled at the prospect of becoming a father, at the chance to show love to a child the way it had never been shown to him. For a brief while, the man had been nurturing and attentive to both child and mother—a period of several months that to this day Ellebe recalled as one of the happiest of her life.

The episode had turned out to be an aberration, and not the beginning of an altered course. As the novelty of having a child wore off, Sorl returned little by little to his selfish devices. Ellebe had tried to reason with the man, to explain to him the dangers of the example he was setting for their son, but Sorl would hear nothing of it. Rather, he seemed determined to grant the child's every whim, teaching the lad to follow his fancies and learn through experience, without the restraints of moral compunction. She, on the other hand, did her best to raise the boy to be more like his grandfather, imploring him to win the respect of his fellow man through means kind and just.

In the end, Sorl's influence won out. Soric, for all his intelligence and good nature, saw greater opportunity in the methods of instant gratification than in the slower and sometimes disappointing results of honest work. Before he ever reached manhood, Soric had fashioned himself in Sorl's spitting image, following and then building upon the precepts set forth by his father until that ill-fated day on which he proved himself to be even more ruthless and impatient.

Ellebe caught herself, shivering at the recollection. She would have brushed the memory aside, but it was too late. At the age of twelve, on the eve of the celebration to welcome him into manhood, Soric had tried to poison the king. When the treachery was revealed by the very apothecary who had helped the lad—and who, upon a change of heart, decided to confess—Sorl had the man put to death. He then gave his son every opportunity to deny the apothecary's charges. But Soric had proudly boasted that the entire affair was his idea. Sorl was an aging, overstuffed fool, and the prince had stood by long enough while watching his father squander his inheritance. It was his turn to rule.

Ellebe had pleaded with her husband to spare their son's life. Sorl had listened, but in the end made up his own mind to spare the lad, to send him into exile. Soric was sold to slavers, escorted from the shores of Pentania in irons, and shipped west across the Oloron Sea, never to be seen again.

That had been it. Following Soric's betrayal, the king had launched into a hedonistic frenzy like never before, and Ellebe, consumed with grief and guilt, had slipped into a depression from which she had never truly recovered.

As if attuned to her thoughts, the sky darkened abruptly. A mass of clouds gathered thickly on the horizon, and the sun, which had overtaken her on its own westward course, passed behind the bank. Ellebe shivered anew. The city lay ahead, somewhere beneath that dark gathering, hidden by a series of rolling hills and stunted ridgelines. If she was to turn back, now was the time. If not . . .

Ellebe closed her eyes and took a deep breath. It would all be over soon.

The stench of decaying flesh assaulted her suddenly as the wind changed. Ellebe almost swooned in her saddle. She grasped her mare's neck, to which the beast responded with an angry whicker. Ignoring its protests, she lay there, temples throbbing, before turning to root through her saddlebags. At last she drew forth a scented cloth, which she pressed to her mouth. She dared a few breaths, found them bearable, and used them to force back the bile that had risen to her throat. Only then did she open her eyes, to discover before her a small bridge that cut through a shallow gorge running north over a dry streambed. Hesitating for the first time since setting out that morning, she crossed the bridge and followed the torn dirt road as it wound past a weathered ridge. As she rounded the corner, she emerged onto the open grasslands, where a horrid panorama was revealed.

Ahead lay the city of Krynwall. It squatted atop its hill, a looming presence made ominous by the dark clouds clustered overhead, and by the thousands of bodies that littered the pocked and barren rise. Ellebe gasped and gripped her mount's reins more tightly. She wanted to cry. The bodies were those of her city's armies. Rather than being buried or burned, they had been cast out like refuse, carrion for scavengers, as if to serve as territorial markers for the enemy's new domain.

The former queen felt her stomach churn as she wound past the scattered corpses. Some had barely been touched, frozen in death and bloated by the sun. Others were nearly devoured by the motley gathering of vultures and crows, beetles and flies. At her approach, the foul birds danced away or took to the air, shrieking bitter cries and circling overhead. The insects skittered and buzzed about her in clinging swarms, unable, it seemed, to taste the difference between her flesh and that of the dead. Ellebe saw now that there were civilians among the soldiers—men, women, and even children who had resisted the invasion or simply been swept up in its foul tide. The queen gagged and forced herself to turn away, to keep her gaze fixed upon the city itself, and not upon its erstwhile inhabitants.

She could sense the evil will of what Krynwall had become as though it were a living force bent against her. She felt its whispered warning, but would not be cowed. Not now. Not by this or any other atrocity her enemy might flaunt. A condor watched her with gimlet eyes as she passed, blood dripping from its sharpened beak. Though she had hoped to find solace away from this land, and to never return to it again, she had been foolish to think she could escape into another life. She understood now that there had never been a choice but to stand with her people—those who now lay stiff and cold, prostrate upon the earth. . . .

The iron gate of the city's smaller, eastern portal appeared before her. Ellebe rode toward it in open defiance. She had considered entering the city in secret, to give herself the best chance for reaching her ultimate destination. But not now. Not after glimpsing Krynwall in its wretched and sullied form. Even if it threatened her chances of learning the truth, she would not be made to slither underground like some foul serpent. She was an angel of light, not a creature of shadow. She would not resort to their tactics.

She soon realized that the invaders' senseless exhibition of carnage had not been limited to the surrounding fields.

The city itself had been decorated, its crenellated walls adorned with a seemingly random selection of skins and skulls. Ellebe forced herself to scan the stripped and grotesque faces, hoping to discern whether there were any prominent citizens among them. If so, then she no longer recognized them.

Save one.

One whose body had been eviscerated, but whose face had been preserved, protected from insects and winged scavengers, she guessed, by perfumes and by the guardsman who stood post beside the remains. Atop the bearded face rested a crown—a crown worn in death, as in life, by Sorl, king of Alson.

Ellebe looked away and fought to slow her breathing. What had she been thinking? What was it she had hoped to accomplish by returning here? How had she become so deluded?

But it was too late now. The city gate stood just ahead, flanked by half a dozen soldiers like those who had chased her east three days ago. They marked her approach, some with faces gruff and threatening, others with bemused smirks. The chance to flee had abandoned her. She could only pray that the Ceilhigh had not.

Ellebe slowed her already measured pace, preparing to come to a halt in front of the lowered gate. But as she drew near, one of the sentinels signaled to the gatekeeper above, and a moment later, the portcullis began to rise. The commanding officer turned back and bowed, a study in mock civility. The others glared or grinned. But none moved to stop her. None said a word. Their ranks parted, and Ellebe, more disturbed than she cared to admit, rode through.

Once inside, the former queen met with a troubling sight. The city was deserted. Alone, she rode down the thoroughfare that sliced its way through the center of the city marketplace. Ordinarily, this zone was packed with merchants, peddlers, pickpockets, and all other manner of men as they went about their business, lawful or otherwise. On this occasion, however, she found herself listening to the solitary sound of her own steed's footfalls as they dropped against

the crumbling roadway and reverberated off the walls of the
vacant shops. Where were the vendors, the tradesmen, the
wandering entertainers? Where were the milling throngs of
beggars and buyers? Undoubtedly, they had locked themselves away in the relative security of their homes, uncertain
how to conduct themselves under the eye of this new regime,
but having wits enough to keep out of sight. If only she
could say the same.

Her question as to whether Alson had seen its worst days
seemed now ridiculous. Sorl's reign, marked by misuse and
neglect, had been a relatively passive affair. Even if this
usurper's reach extended no farther than the capital city,
peace and freedom were but a memory. For more than thirty
years, Ellebe had counted the uncertain number of days that
stood between Sorl's exploits and a return to normalcy for
the citizens of her kingdom. Her life's ambition had been to
make sure that day came about—her only hope that she
would live to see it. Those efforts had failed, and it was with
a profound sense of regret that, once and for all, she allowed
her hope to die.

Nevertheless, she continued on. Without hope, without
reason, she rode through the haunted aisles of the city. Trash
blew along the streets, caught up in swirling gusts of wind.
The silence was unnerving. At times, Ellebe felt as though
she was being watched, by the patrolling sentries, certainly,
but also by the people huddled in the homes and businesses
that she passed. She could feel the weight of those stares
adding to the burden she already bore, the massive load of
expectations that could not possibly be fulfilled. It was all
she could do to keep from shrieking out at them, at the un-
fairness of it all. Why should she be tested so?

Her wallowing harangue was cut short as the royal palace
came into view. The first glimpse struck her like a plunge
into icy waters. For a moment, she remained submerged,
desperate and disoriented. Then she managed to kick free,
fighting to the surface, where a fresh wave of nausea swept
over her.

The stone tower had been poisoned. In the few days since
she had abandoned her home, bricks and mortar had become

sheer walls of obsidian, seamless and smooth as they absorbed the weakened rays of the cloud-smothered sun. The walls were no longer of uniform circumference, but bent inward as they lifted skyward. Where before all manner of ivy and lichen had clung to the surface, now nothing lived, killed by a black tar that oozed down the sloping length. At the tower's base, a roiling mist shrouded the palace grounds, smelling of decay.

Ellebe went rigid in her saddle. A sweeping dread wracked her body. Once again, she recognized her mistake in returning. Had it not been real, she might have laughed at what was surely the wizard's handiwork, whether genuine or illusory. The landscaping of corpses, the array of skins and skulls, the alteration of the tower—such were the acts of a true villain, of the sort found not in life, but as a caricature in the tales of storytellers. How could such a fiend actually exist?

Her gaze, heavy lidded for want of sleep, was ripped from the tower only when her steed came to a halt. To her surprise, she found that she had passed already through the open palace gates and had reached the broad steps that fronted the base of the tower. Before her, upon bended knee, was another sentinel.

"Might I escort this beast to the stable, Highness?" he inquired, making no attempt to hide the mockery in his tone.

He grabbed the reins without waiting for a reply, drawing from the brave and obedient mare an angry whinny. But Ellebe knew that she wasn't being given a choice. She dismounted silently, refusing even to look at the other. The animal voiced again its discontent. Ellebe stroked the beast's neck, whispering in its ear, then fell back. The sentry snickered as he led the horse away.

She watched them go, bidding the mare a silent farewell, then looked back as another pair of guards approached. Ellebe straightened her robes before allowing herself to be escorted up the steps and to the black surface of the tower. Only then did she note that there did not appear to be any door. As the fact entered her mind, however, the wall began to shimmer before her, and a moment later she found herself, along with the guardsmen, facing an open archway that stretched away into blackness.

Ellebe peered into that opening as though it were the maw of a dragon, then took a deep breath. Whatever happened, at least she would know.

The two soldiers shoved her through the archway. She whirled back haughtily, but found herself separated from her tormentors, face-to-face with nothing more than the inside of the tower wall. She touched it to be sure. The wall was solid, appearing within very much as it did without, a smooth sheet of ebony glass that lacked only the oozing tar that coated the exterior. The former queen swallowed thickly.

She turned to view her surroundings. The interior of the tower had been altered as well, the once spacious entrance hall reduced to a cramped foyer. A single flight of steps was all that occupied the dank and shadowed chamber, beginning its ascent just a few paces ahead. The only lighting was an eerie, colorless glow that had no apparent source, yet seemed centered upon the stairwell. Ellebe quivered, feeling as though she had been sealed away in a tomb. She drew a deep breath for strength, but the heavy and humid air offered no comfort. For several moments, she didn't move, willing this nightmare to end. After a time, she realized there was but one way to make that happen. Slowly, stiffly, she began to ascend the ebony stairs.

At the top, the stairs opened into an empty room, which, strangely enough, appeared much larger than the hall below. Curious, she turned to face the staircase behind her, only to find a lightless chasm. An unnecessary reminder, she thought, that there was no turning back.

Facing forward again, Ellebe located the staircase across the room as it continued upward, illuminated by the unnatural, one-way light. Leaving the vacant chamber behind, and resolving not to be unnerved by the wizard's defensive tricks, she resumed her climb into the heart of the tower.

Six times, she reached an empty floor larger than the ones below it. Six times, she glanced back to find her return path swallowed in darkness. Finally, she came upon what she assumed to be the highest chamber in the wizard's tower. Like the others, this room was lit not by torches or candles, but by a dim, sorcerous glow hanging upon the air itself. Books and scrolls and vials filled with exotic solutions lay everywhere, scattered on desks and tables or tucked into place upon the numerous shelves that encircled the walls. A bronze bowl was seated upon an iron tripod in the center of the chamber, red wisps of smoke drifting from its shallow depths.

Ellebe had taken her first steps toward that bowl when a hiss raked her spine.

"Welcome, Mother."

The former queen turned slowly in an attempt to locate the voice. After a complete revolution, she gasped, finding the wizard directly before her, his yellow eyes piercing. The man stood tall, his muscled form wrapped in studded leathers and a black cape. One hand gripped a serpent staff of black walnut; the other was lifted forward, palm extended in greeting.

Ellebe recovered from her start, more quickly than she would have believed in the face of such perversion. "Your banishment was on pain of death."

"Dearest Mother," the wizard rasped through pale, taut lips, "is that any way to greet your long-lost son?"

Ellebe fought to remain steady. The voice crawled beneath her flesh, and her pulse raced to flush it from her system. "My son is dead."

The wizard's brow contorted with an unreadable mix of emotion. "So I've heard," he responded at last, lowering his arm and its unrequited welcome. "A victim of the Red Death, was he? I've paid my respects."

He gestured vaguely toward a far corner of the room. For a moment, Ellebe was confused, unsure as to what he was talking about, and afraid to see for herself. Finally, she risked a quick glance and felt her stomach lurch. A filthy coffin, much too small for a grown man, rested unceremoniously among a pile of refuse, its lid removed.

"Strange indeed," the wizard continued. "For the grave was marked that of Prince Torin, second son of Sorl. And yet, 'twas a pig's bones found in my brother's coffin. Tell me, Mother, to where did you flee upon my arrival?"

Ellebe dared not breathe. She could feel the wizard's eyes upon her, probing for a sign of confession. She refused to give it, and yet could think of no response with which to allay his suspicions.

"Ah yes," he hissed, divining from her silence that which he had all but confirmed already, "a clever ruse by a desperate mother. A means by which to shelter a child from the influence of a wicked father. And now you would have him steal my birthright, much as my father tried to keep it from me."

The former queen was frantic, stricken with horror at how easily her scheme had been uncovered. All she could think of was the need for escape, the need to warn Torin of the danger she had so foolishly brought upon him.

Before she could manage a reply, the wizard waved the issue aside. "No matter," he said, forcing a smile. "For I give you now a chance to rectify your betrayal, to prove your devotion to your firstborn."

Ellebe blinked. "What chance is that?"

"Proclaim my rule. Let the truth be known to the nations of this land that I am the rightful heir."

Despite the whirlwind of emotions tearing through her, Ellebe scoffed. "After what you've done?"

"What I've done," the wizard snapped, "is remove a blight from this land and set a people free."

"Free? Is that how you describe this . . . this slaughter of innocents?"

"Innocents? Please, Mother. We are all but animals, scratching and clawing for a place in this world. You should be proud to have seeded a dragon, rather than a mouse."

"I'm ashamed to have brought such evil into this world."

"Evil?" The wizard seemed amused. "Pray tell, is a lark evil? To you a creature of color and song. But let us ask the worm it feeds upon." He gritted his teeth. "Regardless, you are as much responsible for the deaths of these people as I, by not helping to overthrow my father when you had the chance."

The queen shook her head, fending off the potential truth

behind his words. "You do not belong here," she attempted, fighting for control. "By royal order, you were stripped—"

"I remember my father's words," the wizard interrupted. He stepped forward, eyes flashing dangerously. "Do you? 'If ever again I lay eyes on you, you shall be put to death.' Alas, my father died tragically before my return, thus negating the terms of my exile and legalizing my occupation of these lands."

Ellebe swallowed her words, recognizing them to be useless. She thought back suddenly to those first few hours following her discovery of Sorl's death, those wasted hours in which she had puzzled over the possible motives behind it. She realized now that it had been a futile endeavor. It was not for any military or diplomatic gain that Sorl had been assassinated, but to adhere, in one man's view, to the strict conditions of his own banishment. Ellebe could see that the wizard believed what he had just told her, that by making his return within the accords of Sorl's law, he had ensured the legitimacy of his ascension to the throne.

"The kingdoms of these shores," she managed finally, "will never recognize you as Alson's king."

A cruel smile broke over the wizard's features. "They will, one way or another," he vowed ominously. "Will you?"

For a long moment, they stood there, staring into each other's eyes. When the former queen failed to respond, the wizard stepped forward.

"Be honest, Mother, with yourself if not with me. You are grateful he is gone. No longer must you live in shame and fear. His death is my gift to you." Another step, and his lean shadow covered her like a shroud. "I can protect you, Mother. We can be a family again, as we might have been all along. You, me, even this child you would use to replace me. All I ask is that you grant me what is mine. Your treason might yet be forgiven. You need but ask."

Again the hand went up. Ellebe stared at it and felt her chin tremble. Was this not what she had always wanted? A life for her and her children, unfettered by any will but their own?

Instead, she once more shook her head. "Your father once spoke words to me sweeter than those. I will not be beguiled again, not even by my own blood."

The wizard paused, then gave a disgusted snort and turned away. He took no more than two paces toward the center of the room before he stopped, without looking back.

"Mother," he asked, as though it were an afterthought, "do you still love me?"

Ellebe hesitated, weighing the notion with a pang of regret that surprised her. She wanted to say yes. But try as she might, she could see nothing of the boy she had birthed and raised within the monstrous shell before her. She considered what he had done to her city, her people, and to Sorl—even Sorl, who might have deserved worse. How was she to reconcile with anyone who could commit such acts?

Holding back a heavy sigh of bitter longing, she replied with as much dignity as she could muster. "I could never love the beast you have become."

The wizard did not flinch. "I am what you made me, Mother. Now, as always." He squared his shoulders, then stepped away, waving his hand in dismissal.

As he marched toward the bronze bowl in the center of his chamber, Ellebe became strangely light-headed. A moment later, she dropped to her knees, clutching her head in a futile attempt to alleviate the sudden pain. She had no idea as to what he had done, but it felt as though all the fluid within her body was rushing suddenly toward her brain. She could feel the pressure building, swelling within her skull like a gathering swarm of bees. Her temples throbbed. Veins and arteries bulged beneath her skin. The suffering was so intense that she could neither scream nor control the spasms of her body. Blood ran down her face, streaming from ruptured vessels within her nose and ears. Finally, like a blister, her head bloated, then burst, soft tissue erupting from every cranial orifice in horrific gouts of flesh and blood.

All the while, the wizard stood bent over his smoking bowl, intent upon its depths while doing nothing to acknowledge his mother's agonized throes. Now, as the woman's remains scattered throughout the chamber, a stray piece of flesh slapped against the basin's outer surface.

"Bitch," he muttered, wiping it away.

CHAPTER NINE

Border's closed."

Jarom gave a polite nod, doing his best to appear cordial while making no move to act upon the man's warning. He and Allion had heard this already from scores of angry travelers being turned away by the Kuurian patrol encamped ahead. The closer the woodsmen from Diln got to the barricade, the more often they heard it, as citizens and refugees forced aside like waters before a dam spread word back along the lines. Most simply shared the news with those who asked and went on their way. Others, like this gruff fellow, seemed to want to satisfy their frustration by taking it out on any who would listen.

"Ya might as well turn around," he insisted, pushing his two young boys before him. "They's not letting anyone through."

Jarom gritted his teeth. He had no doubt as to the man's sincerity. After hours of sitting astride his horse within the dust-choked mountain corridor, he was near enough to hear not only from those being turned away, but from the soldiers riding up and down the lines encouraging people to head back to their own lands. Still, he had little choice. He hadn't come all this way to give up simply because others were doing so. He felt—and at this point probably smelled—like a sheep. But given his responsibility, he could ill afford to just follow the masses. Blockade or no, he had to find a way through.

"Bah," the man snorted. "Sit out here all night, then. Bunch of mules. Too good to listen to the likes of us, I see."

Predictably, Allion turned. Jarom reached up and caught his friend's arm, shaking his head. He looked back at the man and his boys, who were finally moving on, muttering all the way.

"I was just going to wish him a pleasant evening," Allion remarked innocently.

"Of course you were."

Jarom let go the other's arm and turned his gaze to the west. The man was right about one thing. The sun was on its downward arc, edging steadily toward dusk. If the pace didn't pick up, they were indeed liable to be stuck waiting out here all night.

They had set out that morning with surprisingly good spirits, the events of the previous night all but forgotten. Well, not forgotten, but strictly ignored. This despite the fact that Jarom had dreamed yet again of Darinor and the Crimson Swords—the third such dream in as many nights. But he was determined not to get sucked down that road again, and had thus made no mention of the dream to Allion. They were two days from the city of Morethil and, hopefully, an audience with Emperor Derreg. Focusing on this had helped Jarom to dispel much of the doubt and confusion otherwise attached to this venture. In two days' time, he would know better the details of their situation. He had resolved to set aside all other questions until then.

Neither Jarom nor Allion had ever been south of Earthwyn. Nevertheless, the roads to Kuuria were broad and well traveled and, barring ill fortune, sure to lead them steadily south until they reached the Tenstrock Mountains, which formed the natural border between Alson and her southern neighbor. For a time, they had stuck to the banks of the Kalgren Fork, where a breeze from the west propelled the mist of the river's waters across the land, keeping their bodies fresh and spirits high.

Eventually, they'd had to break from the river as it wound westward, and move onto the highway. They spoke incessantly, sharing memories, hopes, and dreams while keeping their fears carefully locked away. Although talk centered at times upon the future, they had been careful to skirt the more unpleasant possibilities of what that future might contain. Once or twice, Allion quipped about what life would be like once they had moved with their families into the palace at Krynwall, suggesting that at last he might fulfill his dream of becoming a commander in the Legion of the Arrow. Jarom had responded with assurances that there was no way he would allow Allion to accompany him to Krynwall, and that friend of the king or no, the archer would receive no such commission as long as his parents continued to balk at the idea.

So it went, back and forth between them, as they touched upon serious subjects without treating them as such, and alluded to harsher prospects without exploring the sharp and jagged edges. As the day wore on, their mood remained relaxed and agreeable, if only through conscious effort. By noon, the rugged peaks of the Tenstrock Mountains had filled the horizon, an immutable reminder of reality and their quest. They had therefore done their best to laugh and enjoy themselves as much as possible, not knowing when next they might have cause to do so.

They had passed few travelers heading north. Those whom they did encounter were curt with their greetings or offered none at all. Most were traveling south, some with all of their worldly possessions in tow. Every now and then, the Fason and hunter from Diln eased their pace in order to visit with these fellow citizens, to listen in on tales of strife, on the off chance they might learn something useful or lend some assistance or comfort. They tarried for various lengths of time, moving on quickly when happening upon those whose attitudes were rife with bitterness, and lingering with those whose demeanor was found to be more jovial and uplifting. Jarom was amazed by the range of responses to life's hardships. Often, those who had the most to complain or worry about spent the least amount of time doing so. Each time he came across someone who had known true suffering and yet refused to let it hold sway, his own wallowing made him feel guilty and foolish in comparison.

Except for a prolonged episode in which Jarom and Allion helped a young family to repair a busted wagon wheel,

the day had passed without event, save for the shifting of
sore muscles. By midafternoon, the companions had passed
into the mountainous draw known as the Gaperon. Unless
traveling by boat, this natural gateway between the inter-
secting ranges of the Tenstrock and Aspandel mountains
served as the only entrance to the lands of Kuuria. Trees and
boulders plugged ravines and dotted the arid landscape,
overgrown by sage and scrub and bits of broken rock.
Through this wound a wide and oft-traveled road, the principal artery between Kuuria and the other lands of Pentania.
Temperatures dropped within the pass, helping to cool both
Jarom and Allion from the labors of their day. It was also,
Jarom had noted, free of rockslides, proving his earlier concerns about a major earthquake unfounded.

More than three-quarters of the way through, however,
their passage had lurched to an unexpected halt. The southern mouth of the pass was blocked, packed with an estimated five miles' worth of congested people and animals,
wagons and carts, and belongings of all kind. Allion had
suggested they force their way through, but Jarom had argued for patience. These others had arrived first. He and Allion would await their turn.

It seemed now a poor choice. The lines were longer than
either of them could have anticipated, and the wait had cost
them precious hours. Assuming they made it through the border guard, tomorrow's would be a hard ride. Not only that,
but sitting there for so long, being jostled to and fro, fighting
back others who had tried to crowd forward, reeking of their
own sweat and assailed by the stench of those around them,
had made them both irritable. Whatever patience Jarom had
started with was wearing thin. He was afraid that if he had to
wait much longer, or encountered one more fellow such as
the one who had just harassed him, he was liable to draw his
sword and lop off someone's head.

His was not the only set of wits reaching its end. All around
him, tempers flared, especially as they neared the blockade
and people learned for themselves that there was no getting
through. Many refused to leave, shouting at the guards about
how they had nowhere else to go. Inevitably, protests grew vi-

olent. Jarom had witnessed more than one man hauled off forcibly by Kuurian infantry. Of special concern, it seemed, was the safety of merchant caravans bringing food and supplies into the lands south. After careful inspection, these were being waved on through. Some, however, were having difficulty making it that far, as hungry refugees took to helping themselves to the plentiful wares. The Kuurian military was quick to respond, and had set up special escorts, but even these were of only moderate determent.

And all of this on only the third day since the wizard's siege.

At long last, the crowds parted, sloshing off like breakers to either side, and Jarom found himself within a few paces of the main cordon. A host of guardsmen were strung out along the line, directing people one way or another, but mostly back the way they had come. Jarom motioned to Allion and urged his horse into a trot, finding a break in the guard line and pushing deeper into the military encampment. He needed to find an officer, one who held greater decision-making authority than the grunts set out front.

Though unfamiliar with the uniform markings of Kuurian military, Jarom zeroed in quickly enough on a clean-shaven youth giving orders to a half-dozen men working to erect a schilltron. The youth seemed confident, but not overzealous in his command—a captain, perhaps—and was lending physical help now and then to his subordinates, rather than simply barking at them. While it was impossible to tell for sure, he appeared to be of fair judgment and even temperament—just the kind of man Jarom needed.

"Pardon me, sir," Jarom greeted. "I was wondering who we might talk to about—"

"The border is closed," the captain replied as he lashed together a pair of sharpened stakes.

Jarom hesitated. The man had not even bothered to look at him. "We are emissaries from Alson," he explained, "sent to visit with the emperor."

Again the captain replied without looking up. "The emperor has word of your troubles, and has taken them under advisement."

Jarom frowned. So much for his judge of character. He may as well have singled out a boulder with which to parlay.

Allion was equally frustrated. "Would it make any difference if I told you my friend here is the king of Alson?"

That at least got the captain to look up. If he was amused, or even moderately curious, he didn't show it. "I don't care if he's my own grandmother. I have my orders. Unless you wish to spend a night in the stocks, you'll turn around at once!"

The men under the captain's command had stopped what they were doing in order to stand ready. For a fleeting moment, Jarom considered the odds. By his estimation, there were at least two score soldiers currently assigned to this northern border patrol. More were undoubtedly en route. Even if he made it past the barricade, it was unlikely he could outrace fresh riders dispatched by the patrol's senior officer all the way to Morethil. And even if he did that, he was certain to be thrown in prison the moment he arrived. Neither option afforded him much of a chance to complete his assigned task.

"We will pay for passage," he offered in a final bid to get through.

"Sergeant!" the captain spat. A muscled soldier snapped to attention. "It seems these men wish to be taken into custody."

The sergeant grinned. "Yes, sir!"

"Stand down, Sergeant," Jarom sighed in defeat. He glared at the captain. "We were just leaving."

Allion followed as he turned his horse about. For a moment, Jarom half expected to be rushed from behind in response to his defiance. But when he glanced back, the captain and his men had returned already to the more immediate task before them.

"Now what?" Allion asked.

Jarom shook his head. Finding no other alternative, he began working his way north, along with masses of others, back the way he had come.

That night, Jarom sat beside the fire after Allion had gone to sleep, pondering his options. He did not have many. The way south was closed, at least for now. Allion had suggested they strike a bargain with one of the merchant caravans, offering protection as private escorts in exchange for entry into Kuuria. But even if that worked, how were they to get in to see the emperor? Clearly, the man had heard all he cared to about the wizard's invasion. And in truth, unless he chose to speak of the incredible story of his birthright, Jarom had nothing to say beyond that which the emperor had listened to already. Allion's advice had been to cross one bridge at a time. Get through the pass, and worry about the emperor once they reached Morethil. But Jarom knew a dead end when he saw it. Any further attempt at reaching the Imperial Council would be a futile endeavor and a waste of precious time.

Which left them to do what, exactly? Return home? Allion had claimed that to be a reasonable alternative—the more sensible of the two, in fact. They had done what was asked of them. They had made the required effort. They could not be expected to work miracles. Jarom hadn't argued the point. But he couldn't quite bring himself to agree. Turning back at this juncture would accomplish nothing. And despite his own feelings and reservations, he knew that to be unacceptable.

And so, while his friend slept beneath the boughs of an aged sycamore several hundred paces off the main highway, Jarom sat nearby in silence, alone with the wind and the flames, afraid to do the same. He knew what sleep would bring. Another dream. Another false vision stirred by his imagination—whose only purpose was to tease and torment, offering him a glimpse of strength and achievement he would never know. The answer to all his troubles, summoned by his subconscious out of fear and need. A lie.

Or was it?

He found his gaze drifting to his saddlebags, wherein lay the tome he had found outside of Earthwyn—the strange tome he had decided must belong to the Entients. After a time, he moved over to retrieve the book, watching Allion all the while as he slipped it free of the concealing leather pouch. He shifted then to the opposite side of the tree against which his friend slept and opened the book upon his lap. The blank pages spread before him, and he leafed through them quietly, reflecting upon information no longer written there. A map of Tritos, and of the ancient Finlorian city, Thrak-Symbos. A record of the Crimson Swords and of the last one's final resting place. And all of it just lying there in the mud, beneath that dead horse, waiting to be found, mere moments after he had surrendered his search for just such an account within the library at Earthwyn.

A secret suspicion, which he had first felt upon finding the tome but had not dared contemplate, demanded now to be addressed. Was it possible that the legendary Entients were somehow behind the strange happenings of the last few days? The incessant dreams, so clear and lifelike. The book. Could it be there was more to all of this than private fancy and extraordinary coincidence? Did the Entients wish for him to find the Sword? Or could there be an even greater force behind it all? Just how strong was destiny's pull?

His path, it seemed, was predetermined. By this line of thinking, he had but one road to follow, a road east, through the dangers of southern Partha, to the foothills of the Skullmar Mountains. A road that led to the ruins of an ancient city and the divine artifact rumored to be buried there. And yet, if heading south to visit with the emperor was a futile endeavor and a waste of time, then how was he to classify this, exactly? How could he even consider the prospect?

There had to be some other answer. He was close to it, he knew. He could feel it, a shiver in his bones. His true path lay not south to Kuuria, north to Diln, or east to Partha. Rather, it lay somewhere in between, an alternative just waiting to be uncovered. Nothing so impractical as forcing an audience with a ruler who did not wish to be seen, returning home empty-handed, or sallying forth to comb the uncharted depths of a ruined city. Something that was within his power to carry out. Something that would lead to a resolution of this conflict, or at least provide the answers that would enable him to—

Jarom stopped short, fingering the blank page before him, staring at its empty contents as if seeing something he had missed before. The solution was obvious. He should have known almost from the start. Had he just taken a moment to step back and review the situation, he would have figured it all out much sooner and saved himself a day's worth of standing in line and an evening's disappointment. Allion might disagree, but then again . . .

Jarom glanced up at the stars of the heavens, at the sparkling dome of the night sky, and found its clarity to be a reflection of his own—a forgotten feeling that caused him to smile.

Allion woke to a cacophony of invisible birds hidden among the trees. For several moments, he tossed from side to side in his makeshift bedding. Even with his eyes closed, he could tell it was not yet dawn, but he could take the warbling no longer. With a disgruntled huff, he sat up, rubbing at his puffy eyes.

When he had wiped away enough of his sleep to clear his vision, the hunter considered his surroundings. Dawn wasn't so far off after all, he determined. He might as well wake Jarom and decide upon a course for the new day. Although he'd promised to think about what they should do while resting for but a moment, he had fallen asleep too quickly, and was as empty of ideas as he had been the night before. He sighed. Perhaps Jarom had thought of something.

He stretched briefly beside the smoldering fire pit, gazing westward toward the little stream by which they had set camp. Through a scattering of trees, he watched his horse stretch against its tether to graze upon a patch of sun-dried grasses beneath its feet. He considered the scene without interest, until it struck him that his horse had not been tethered alone.

"Jarom?"

Allion frowned, wide awake now. His belongings were stashed where he had left them, against the sycamore under which he'd slept. His friend's, however, were missing. In addition to his horse, Jarom's bedroll, supplies, and the man himself were nowhere to be found.

"Jarom!"

Soric, king of Alson by right of birth and power, sat among a pile of cushions upon the floor of his tower chambers. His eyes were closed, his arms and legs crossed. An array of candles burned in a circle around him, each of a different color and giving off a different smoke. He inhaled deeply, breathing a potpourri of carefully mixed fragrances, and slipped deeper within himself, attuning himself to the energies, both internal and universal, that gave him his strength. The spheres of magic opened before him, and one by one, he examined that which they had to offer, that which had brought and would continue to bring him everything he desired.

Malkuth, sephira of earth, of body. Constancy of form. That which can be made to tremble or break . . .

Although it had been nearly twenty years, it felt like only yesterday that he had uttered his first incantation, a minor dweomer that had left him unconscious for days before he awoke in a pool of vomit there in the deepest crypt of the keep—his home following the storm and shipwreck that had sent his slavers to the bottom of the Oloron Sea and left him marooned on that forsaken isle.

Chilkuth, sephira of water, of blood. Fluidity of form. That which can be made to morph or swell . . .

He had found the keep abandoned, a holdover from ancient times, from an age in which mankind had been driven to unlock the secrets of the Ha'Rasha—having learned that he too could tap into the natural energies by which all was formed, to manipulate these energies and use them to rule over his fellow man. It was within the vaults of this stronghold that he had discovered, along with the remains of its former occupants, the crypt and its trove of scrolls and tomes, relics and artifacts, upon which a wealth of this knowledge was contained.

Nezwah, sephira of air, of breath. Shaper of form. That which can be made to mold and chisel . . .

It had taken years to translate the languages in which this knowledge had been recorded, and nearly two decades beyond—two decades of unbearable solitude—to master its use. Even now, he had much to learn, so much more beyond these, the elemental spheres, the lowermost branches on the Carafix of Life.

Retwah, sephira of fire, of spirit. Consciousness of form, of thought and passion. That which can be made to bring to light or cast into darkness, to temper or destroy . . .

But all of the insufferable agonies, both mental and physical, had been well worth it, for through them he had at last found the means by which to return and claim that which should have rightfully been his long ago. His lands. His freedom. The fear and respect of all.

"Ah, Xarius Talyzar," he rasped.

The wizard opened his eyes, looking at once toward the entrance to his chamber, where a shadow detached itself from the darkness and slid across the threshold.

"You summoned?" the Shadow inquired, a voiceless whisper.

The wizard smirked. After all this time, the Shadow clung to its own aura of mystery, refusing, even in the presence of he who had become its master, to offer up the slightest revelation of form. Loose-fitting garb the color of midnight disguised size and shape. A cowl hid his features. Gloves trapped the prints and oils that might otherwise reveal the passage of his hands. Even his speech was cloaked by that substanceless hiss. Home? Possessions? Save for his weapons, the man kept nothing in terms of material attachments. All so as to maintain himself as an unidentifiable wraith.

Not a bad idea, the wizard supposed, when your own life was devoted entirely to stealing that of others.

"Track down the younger son of Sorl and bring him to me."

"Alive or dead?" A strong emphasis accompanied the latter condition, indicating the assassin's preference.

"Alive, if possible." Sensing the smirk at the corner of the Shadow's lips, the wizard added, "If at all possible. A contingent stands ready to accompany you."

A foul wind brushed against the wizard's consciousness. "I work alone."

"When it is my coin, you do my bidding. Now go. I wish you away before the dew has melted."

The Shadow nodded before slipping away like mist into darkness. Once he had gone, the wizard returned to his meditations, wasting no more thought concerning his mysterious brother. The assassin would see that all went according to his desires. There was no better tracker than Xarius Talyzar, and no deadlier a man. Unless Torin shared the wizard's own powers of heightened awareness, he wouldn't even see the Shadow coming. Like a great owl, the man flew upon wings of death. . . .

CHAPTER TEN

Jarom yawned, wearied clear through, while stretching the stiffness from his legs. After a moment, he looked up to find the red sunrise like a river of molten rock swimming sluggishly through the sky. The clear night had surrendered to yet another glorious morning, one that would lend strength to body and soul.

That strength would be much needed, Jarom admitted. His decision of the night before to search for the secret stronghold of the Entients was his first understanding. But whereas the notion had filled him with such hope and exhilaration the previous evening, he now found the idea sputtering in the pit of his stomach like a poorly digested meal. What had he been thinking? Did he truly intend to spend the next weeks, months, or even years scavenging through the caves and dens of an entire mountain range in search of a place believed by some not to exist at all?

As he pulled himself into a sitting position, Jarom's eyes fell upon a bulge in one of the leather saddlebags resting upon the ground beside him. At once, the young Fason began forcing the uneasy feeling from his gut. He had to know for certain whether the book had been left for him intentionally. It still seemed the best explanation as to why he had found it when he did. Any other explanation relied too heavily on freakish happenstance. In any case, the best way to find out was to take the book in search of Whitlock, return it to its owners, and learn from them the truth, once and for all.

He was further encouraged by last night's dream. As expected, it had come unbidden, as crisp and clear as those before. In it, he had found himself marching through jungles and forests, en route to the ruins of Thrak-Symbos and the Crimson Sword. Allion had been with him, as had some other figure he hadn't recognized, a fluid, faceless stranger in loose-fitting garments. Whatever the dream's purpose, he took it as a sign that he had indeed selected the right path.

The only path, he reminded himself, that did not lead to certain defeat. This one alone offered hope, and was not completely lacking in common sense. Whitlock was fabled to lie within the eastern slopes of the Aspandel Mountains, not all that far from here. If the book truly belonged to the Entients, and if the Entients were indeed guiding him in this endeavor, then it seemed logical enough to assume that as he neared their general location, they would seek him out. Although a cruel possibility, he did not foresee himself wandering blindly through the mountains forever. He had to believe that the Entients—or destiny, or whatever forces controlled his future—would not allow that.

Rising to his feet, he breathed deeply of the morning air. He felt guilty for having ridden off without a word to Allion, but he hadn't felt like arguing. His friend would never have agreed with his decision. Rather, he would have convinced him that it was all part of the same self-inspired delusion, that the only real solution was to head home to consult with the others of their village. That was what Allion would say, because Allion always did what his parents would have him do, even to the point of putting aside his own dreams. It was only natural for him to encourage others to do the same.

In any event, Allion would be smart enough to realize what had happened, and after an initial round of oaths and curses, was sure to settle down and head back to Diln with the news of all that had transpired. Of the two of them, Allion's was bound to be the safer road.

After running through the list of self-reassurances, Jarom felt appropriately satisfied with his reasoning. He also knew that, to be honest, much of it was a lie. There was really only one reason he had to do this. After finding this tome that had suddenly become his most prized possession, he owed it to himself to discover whether his longtime fantasy of retrieving a Crimson Sword could prove true. If he were to stumble across a once-in-a-lifetime treasure like this and do nothing, failing to utilize it in a concerted effort to search for the last known Sword of Asahiel, then by the gods, he might as well surrender the dream of doing so forever.

His midnight travels had carried him just beyond the northern mouth of the Gaperon, a four-hour advance on Allion's position. Plenty of time, should he make use of it. The archer was apt to set a mean pace initially, in an effort to catch up to his friend—something Jarom was determined to avoid. One more reason to get moving.

Around midmorning, he hooked up with a merchant caravan bold enough to be heading north, making for Earthwyn. After buying some of their wares, he rode with them, sharing fresh stories so as to pass the hours more quickly. Caught up in the amusement of their company, Jarom lingered longer than he had intended. They did not separate until noon, when they passed a smaller road forking to the southeast. The caravan leader suggested to Jarom that if heading to the Aspandel Mountains, he should follow that road winding through the local farmlands rather than continuing along the main highway from Kuuria, which would mean having to cut east across the plains later. At that point, Jarom thanked the party for its hospitality, bid them caution in their travels and good fortune at the northern markets, and veered off alone.

He found the road onto which he had been directed mostly deserted. As promised, it cut a meandering path through rural communities and open grasslands, keeping a southeasterly course as it traversed the highlands north of the Aspandel Mountains, a region that marked the loose boundary between Alson to the west and Partha to the east. Jarom found the scenery beautiful, if a bit rugged, especially in those areas overlooking panoramic vistas that stretched for leagues before fading into the horizon. They served to remind him of just how big the world really was—a notion that filled him with a yearning for home. The world might

well be a marvelous place, full of riches waiting to be discovered. But he had found already most of that which he
needed. If life was a search for contentment, well then, were
it up to him, he would gladly sacrifice any of the treasures
he might find for the chance to reclaim and preserve those
that were already his.

As he rounded a high bend hours later, he caught sight of a
humble village nestled within a shallow valley. Oceans of
prairie grass surrounded the clustered dwellings, topped with
cresting waves blown by the wind. It was then that he came
across a family's covered wagon, working its way out of the
lowland farming community. The wagon was steered by a
blunt-faced man with a knotted beard. A striking young
woman, the kind whose unembellished beauty made her all the
more enticing, sat up front at the man's side, presumably his
daughter. Jarom slowed his horse's canter to a walk. As he rode
past, he could not take his eyes from the girl, whose soft brown
hair and enchanting smile stole his breath. When he nodded to
her in greeting, thinking they might all stop for a brief visit, the
father frowned at the smiling girl, then turned his glare upon
Jarom. With a sharp command and snap of his reins, the man
urged his wagon team onward.

Undaunted, Jarom allowed his gaze to turn and follow
after, hoping that the girl would glance back one last time.
She did, peering around the side of the wagon's canvas and
offering a blushing grin. A jab from her father caused her to
scowl and turn away, leaving Jarom to view nothing more
than the jostle of the wagon as it pitched and wobbled on up
the hill. Still, the picture of her face remained with him,
causing him to envision how—with the Crimson Sword in
his hand and the crown of Alson upon his head—their encounter might have been different.

He had no sooner regained his focus than he was turned
about by the whinny of a team of horses and a string of
angry shouts. A single rider was barreling down the road in
Jarom's direction, scrabbling past the girl's wagon, which
leaned dangerously as it rounded the bend, fighting to stay
upright. The rider cut in sharply and looked back in apology,
but spying Jarom caused him to dismiss the disgruntled

wagon owner quickly enough. Instead, he continued down the hill, finally skidding to a halt in a swirling cloud of dust.

Allion.

The archer sat there for several moments, seething in his saddle as he paused to catch his breath. Jarom glared past him to the girl's wagon, where the father shook an angry fist before urging his team forward once more. Jarom watched them until they had disappeared safely around the bend, just about the same time Allion found his voice.

"You missed the north fork back there."

Jarom scowled at the man and said nothing, furious at himself for having underestimated his friend's tenacity.

"I ran into your friend Garm. He said I'd find you headed this way. Care to tell me what's going on?"

Jarom shook his head. He hadn't thought to tell Garm, the leader of the merchant caravan with whom he'd spent most of the morning, about Allion. He hadn't told the group much of anything, allowing its members to believe he was traveling alone, journeying with herbal medicines toward a remote mountain village situated upon the eastern slopes of the Aspandel range. It was close enough to the truth. Now that he thought about it, however, he should have said something about others who might be following him, and asked Garm and his comrades to remain silent. Instead of helping to hide his tracks, they had led Allion right to him.

Jarom turned his gaze southward to where the peaks of the Aspandels loomed on the horizon. "Go home, Allion. By the time you arrive with news of the emperor's blockade, I'll have found Whitlock."

"Whitlock!" Allion grappled momentarily with the notion. "Wait, I've a better idea. Why don't you simply find some elven avatars and have them forge you a new Crimson Sword, one for your very own!"

With an exasperation to match that of his friend, Jarom tore into his saddlebag and yanked free the tome, holding it up for Allion to see. "This belongs to the Entients. What better key could one have for gaining entrance to their stronghold?"

Allion shook his head, a demeaning gesture, as though he

should have suspected that Jarom had kept the book. "This obsession of yours is going to get you killed."

"Well then, I'll just be saving this wizard the trouble, won't I?"

Jarom felt the lines of his forehead deepen, even as he watched those of his friend smooth ever so slightly. Allion wiped at the sweat and dirt streaming down the sides of his face. Despite his softened expression, the hunter refused to give ground.

"Gallivanting off in search of mythical weapons or hidden strongholds is not going to bring any of this to an end."

"Then tell me what will!"

Allion stopped short, disarmed by the ferocity of Jarom's assault. But Jarom could read that which flashed in the other's eyes. He was crazy, Allion wanted to say, as mad as the stranger from whom he had first inherited these wild imaginings. But that was just it. The more Jarom struggled with the enormity of the task before him, the more his memory of Darinor instilled in him a sense of fate and his only glimmer of hope. For the legends held that one who wielded the power of a Crimson Sword was invincible. Only with such a talisman in his possession would he be able to raise an army and drive the wizard's forces from his land. Only with such a talisman would the people of Alson come to accept him as their king, should he be forced to it. While it was possible the Swords were merely the invention of some ancient bard's imagination, he was tired of feeling helpless. He was tired of feeling as though nothing he could possibly do would matter when there were those who expected otherwise. Allion thought he was mad. But Allion was wrong. He had thought long and hard, considering his options with a clear and rational mind. In light of all that had occurred, his proposed course of action seemed to him sensible enough.

Jarom looked down at the tome gripped in his hands, then gazed northward, picturing in his mind the now distant wagon girl. "Listen. You have a choice in this. I don't."

"Jarom—"

"If I'm meant to find the Sword, I intend to do so. If not, I'll be no worse off than I am now."

"What about Kuuria?"

"What about it?" Jarom echoed. "The emperor knows about the wizard. Nothing we say or do is going to have any effect upon his decision. What sense does it make for us to go there?"

"Because that's what we set out to do."

"Yeah, well, things have changed." Jarom wished again that he could have avoided this argument altogether. "I'm telling you now that with this book, I think I can find Whitlock. I believe it's my destiny to at least try. With or without you, that's where I'm headed."

"If I agree to this," Allion haggled, "promise me that if we don't find Whitlock, that will be the end of this madness."

Jarom smiled inwardly as he saw that his friend realized—now that he had overcome the initial shock—that this was not a course to be easily dismissed. Or maybe it was just Allion's adventuresome spirit taking over. The thought of meeting the Entients or recovering an artifact such as the Crimson Sword was about as promising an adventure as one could hope to undertake.

Outwardly, Jarom's scowl displayed his reluctance to make any concessions. Failure was not an option he cared to consider. Nor did he believe there to be any point in fighting to reach Morethil or returning to Diln, regardless of whether or not he was able to return the abandoned tome to the Entients.

"Oh, come," Allion moaned. "If I can agree to what you're suggesting, then you can agree to this. If we don't find Whitlock, or if we discover that the book does not belong to the Entients, we end this ridiculous quest and head straight to Kuuria—or back home."

Jarom ran his fingers across the leather skin of the mysterious tome. "All right," he said at last.

"Good," Allion exhaled in a loud burst, visibly relieved at having salvaged something from the argument. He waited for a response from Jarom, who offered none. Finally, the archer shook his head, forcing a meager smile. "We may as well get moving. It's only a matter of time before I regain my senses and knock you over the head until you regain yours."

Jarom grinned in spite of himself, hiding his feelings of self-doubt while cherishing his friend's loyalty. Even in such a desperate, potentially foolish matter, Allion was willing to exhibit the complete confidence that he held in his longtime friend. If nothing else, Jarom could be comfortable in the knowledge that he would not be alone.

"All right," he said again, sliding the book back into his saddlebag and cinching down the cover flap. "Together, then."

Nevik, heir to the barony of Drakmar, slumped wearily in his high-backed chair, letting himself sink into the velvet padding that lined its seat. It had been an arduous discussion thus far, endless hours of one argument circling after another but deciding nothing. Four full days had passed since the news of Krynwall's fall to the wizard, and the barons of Drakmar and Palladur, corresponding via staged messengers that rode night and day, had hastily assembled to discuss the grave matter of defending their lands. The duke of Kord, first claimant to the throne of Alson now that Sorl was dead, had been invited to the assembly as well, but the messenger sent to him had returned alone.

Kord had already fallen.

The council had begun in a state of emergency. It was obvious that if both Kord and Krynwall had fallen within days, then neither Drakmar nor Palladur could hope to repel the imminent attacks that would be launched against them. And if the four walled cities of Alson fell so easily, then the remaining villages and townships would be mere fodder for the invading forces. It was Nevik's father, Nohr, who had suggested what he thought to be their only chance.

A siege, he had explained, launched against Krynwall. Strike down the wizard's bastion before he could extend his reach. To some, the idea seemed preposterous. Most, however, had agreed that it was their only logical option. Before long, talk had turned from *whether* they should do it to *how,* exactly, a siege could be carried out.

Recruiting outside help was vital. If Alson could convince its neighbors of the danger to their own lands, it would be able to assemble a considerably larger assault force. But this seemed unlikely. Baron Nohr had flatly refused to accept help from either Menzos or Partha. The only reason these nations had not invaded Alson before was that each was too involved in its struggle against the other. Even if they were able to tear the two from each other's throats long enough to drive off the wizard's forces, the two kingdoms would end up battling over Alson as they did their own lands, like two hounds tearing at a single blood-red steak. Others were adamant that to attempt a siege without the two mighty powers would be suicide, and argued that concessions would have to be made, if necessary, to enlist their aid.

Naturally, all agreed that Kuuria would be able to provide the most formidable force, and must be asked to do so. The Imperial Army was the largest in Pentania. The garrison of any one of its three greatest cities—Morethil, Souaris, or Stralk—might be sufficient to reclaim the throne. But the Imperial Council would be slow to answer any such call. Geographically sheltered, and weary from the wars fought to secure a fledgling mankind's place among the wild races that had once dominated these shores, the Kuurians had long ago adopted a policy of isolation, confident in their own defensive strength and reluctant to involve themselves in the struggles of their neighbors. Still, Kuuria was Alson's closest ally, and heralds had been sent immediately to approach the emperor. Baron Nohr, however, insisted that there was no time to waste trading emissaries before the battle. If a siege was to transpire, it would have to be initiated immediately, trusting to the fact that help would arrive once the campaign was under way.

It was at this juncture that the makeshift council stagnated. Its wrangling was pointless, as best as Nevik could tell. Either they perpetrated a mass exodus into some foreign land, or they carried out the siege as his father suggested. He did not understand why the others spent so much time trying to discredit Nohr and his strategies. He was a warmonger, they snarled, too anxious for battle. Nevertheless, the man had steadfastly maintained his position, and it now seemed that he would win the support of his compatriots after all.

Nevik gazed distractedly at the shafts of twilight pouring through the tall council room windows of his home castle, at the way their radiance gleamed upon the chain mail of his fellow noblemen of Drakmar and reflected off the plate armor of the visiting lords of Palladur. All of a sudden, he realized that the room was locked in silence, and he looked up to find all eyes boring into him impatiently.

"We await your vote, young Nevik," sneered Satallion, the self-titled high lord of Palladur.

Nevik snapped to attention, facing the other with a scowl. Despite the man's trim and polish, Satallion had always seemed to him a bit of a weasel. "I ride with my father," he replied firmly, drawing strength from his father's nod.

"Then it is settled," Nohr announced in a booming voice as he rose from his chair. "Satallion," he began, "return to your stronghold and prepare your forces—"

A dismissing wave of Satallion's gauntleted hand caused the dark-bearded giant to cut short his order.

"Save your breath, my fellow baron," the other said without a hint of respect. "I agreed to abide by the majority decision of this council, but a siege upon the wizard's fortress would be suicide, and I will not be bullied into thinking otherwise. If a worthy solution cannot be reached, then my lords and I shall simply return to Palladur and prepare its defenses."

A murmur arose from those lords of Palladur who had voted for the siege.

"If they wish to remain as lords of Palladur," Satallion snarled.

An unnerving silence ensued, and a roomful of gazes shifted to Nohr, whose glare looked to tear Satallion asunder.

"You and your private council of lords," he grumbled. "Very well. Leave my castle. Take shelter within your feeble walls, and may you die like the dog that you are!"

Satallion's hand flew to the pommel of his sword, and in an instant, the entire room bristled with steel and iron. Nevik stood with the others, mace in hand, his heart racing. Only his father remained inert, deathly still, as though realizing that if he allowed any measure of himself to explode, there would be no hindering his rage. Satallion seemed to sense this and, after a moment, to recall that he was deep within the fortified home of his rival. After an agonizing pause, he sheathed his gleaming broadsword, a smirk playing about his lips.

"As you wish, Lord Baron."

He wheeled about and strode toward the chamber doors, flocked by his entourage of lords, whose weapons were still drawn protectively. Upon reaching the exit, he turned to face Nohr, his expression suddenly sincere.

"When this is over, one of us will be king of Alson."

The smirk returned, and he spun from the room, leaving Nohr to smolder in his rage.

CHAPTER ELEVEN

Dusk settled like a weary traveler across the land, slumping over hillocks and into valleys and pulling the covers of night up about its slow-breathing form. The sun's glow dimmed over the western horizon, taking with it the heat of the day and leaving the world dark and ashen, awash in shades of gray. A blanket of near silence hung upon the air, broken only by the steady thrum of insects and the occasional call of a waking predator set to begin its evening hunt. Within this vast stretch of rugged wilderness, the world seemed at peace.

Jarom knew otherwise. Nevertheless, he marked the sense of calm that had descended over the foothills of the northern Aspandels with a private sigh of relief. They had encountered no one upon the road since the afternoon, nor anything else that might be construed as an obstacle to their endeavors. Even the weather had remained pleasant.

Allion, however, had been relentless. From the moment they had resumed their journey, he demanded to know precisely what Jarom intended, as though seeking to find a flaw of reasoning that, when exposed, would bring the entire notion of their search for Whitlock crumbling down to earth. While neither had visited this region before, the hunter had been quick to predict that there would be no clear trails along which to travel, and certainly none that would mark the route to the Entients' secret fortress. They might spend years combing the mountainous region and still come up empty.

But Jarom was quick to remind the other that he was not relying on the hope that they could somehow discover a place it was said no outsider had ever found. Rather, he was betting on the chance that the Entients would know of their missing book and would be out searching for it. In doing so, *they* would find *him,* at which point, he would learn just what was expected of him. All he and Allion need do was skirt the eastern slopes from north to south until contact was made, one way or another.

He had done his best to sound self-assured, hiding his own doubts while responding patiently to Allion's every claim. He believed so firmly in the dreams, in the book, in the Sword, that he did not want to confront the likelihood that he was wasting everyone's time. His ultimate destination, he still hoped, was the Skullmar Mountains to the east, a journey to which he was already giving some thought. Assuming that the Sword was in fact buried there in the ruins of Thrak-Symbos, and that those ruins could be found, there was no easy way to reach them. Central Partha was a war zone through which he had no desire to march. Nor did he care to swing through southern Partha and risk an encounter with the savages living in the jungles of Vosges. If he never made it far enough to find the buried city, how could he expect to recover a thing?

The Entients. The Entients would provide the answers to his questions. They would guide him past whatever perils lay between here and his goal. He had to believe that. And if that were true, then he had no cause to concern himself now.

Still, Allion's shallowly disguised complaining was a thorn underfoot, and Jarom had found that by keeping his mind occupied, he was able to ignore the man's presence somewhat. Even so, his head ached by the time night fell and brought with it an unexpected hush to the archer's taxing assessments. Whether Allion drew his strength from the sun, or had simply tired of his own protests, the end result gave Jarom a much-needed respite. Before long, they would set camp for the night. Perhaps by morning the air between them would have cleared.

For tomorrow, their search would begin.

The assassin's gloved hand shot into the air, signaling a halt. At once the men in the company froze, grinding to a stop behind their leader. Twigs snapped; foliage whipped and swayed. The Shadow frowned. Thus far, the mercenaries sent to accompany him had been responsive and obedient. All, he imagined, would serve well enough as battlefield fodder. But they lacked grace, balance, and cunning, requisite skills for an operation such as this. Cursing the wizard for the burden of their presence, Xarius Talyzar slid silently from his mount. Like marionettes, the soldiers in tow moved to follow. The assassin spun, sniping at them with a venomous glare from beneath his drawn cowl. Their puppet strings severed, the men collapsed in place, becoming bundles of sticks within their saddles. With an unmistakable gesture, the Shadow commanded the clods to remain where they were in silence, then vanished into the forest gloom.

Alone among the shadows, he began to feel more at ease, at home in purpose and attuned to his surroundings. Following the trail of Queen Ellebe, they had come upon this forest village—Diln, according to the maps. Her former Majesty had done nothing to disguise her frantic passage. And this setting was too remote to have been an accidental stop. Without a doubt, this had been Ellebe's destination. Thus, it was here that he must begin to learn something about this Prince Torin.

With perfect efficiency, the Shadow slipped through the various natural and man-made corridors of the night-cloaked village. Activity was at a minimum. The hour was late, and only a handful of lights shone from dwelling windows, the rest as cold and dark as empty eye sockets. There appeared to be no sentries or guardsmen, no patrols of any kind wandering the woods. Every now and then, a stray villager was seen making his way along a starlit pathway, humming or whistling, oblivious to the Shadow's presence. The world remained quiet and still, the assassin's private and well-stocked hunting ground.

He had learned early on about the pointlessness of life. The aunt and uncle who had raised him had been poor, disgruntled folk who had sought escape in root and drink, animal lust and violent bickering. By the age of fourteen, Xarius had tired of watching this, and of taking the brunt of their abuse. He had killed them not out of anger, but disgust.

What he could not have anticipated was the exhilaration that ending their lives had brought him. It was in this that he had found his calling, a means by which to elevate himself above the rabble of his fellow man. He would outlive them all through his deeds, leaving behind a legacy of fear and mystery—a legend of the kind used by parents to keep their children in check. Men and their names, no matter how great, were eventually forgotten. So he would become a living myth.

One kill at a time.

After tracing a broad perimeter with his movements, Xarius worked his way inward toward the heart of the village. Before long, he came upon a clearing, a plaza of sorts occupied by a dozen or so commercial lodges. Like the smaller, more secluded homes he had passed, these buildings appeared mostly deserted, abandoned for the evening or filled with resting inhabitants. Even what looked to be an inn and tavern was locked down. A more richly boring existence the assassin could not imagine.

His sight was quickly drawn to the centermost building, whose windows were awash with torchlight. The lodge was by far the largest in the clearing, some kind of gathering hall. For several moments, he examined the structure, marking the complete lack of comings and goings. At last, the Shadow made his move. Keeping as always to the concealing darkness, he crept across a carpet of woodland needles to reach the dark side of the central hall. After casting about one last time, he leapt up to catch a low rooftop overhang and began his ascent, slinking toward a skylight open to the cool evening air and whatever breezes might find their way through. . . .

"I grow weary of these midnight meetings, Esaias," a stone-faced man complained. "We've wasted enough time already."

"On that we are agreed, Rigdon," Esaias responded with a weary sigh. "But we can do little else until we resolve ourselves to a course of action."

The Shadow slipped carefully through the open skylight, coming to rest, unnoticed, on one of the narrow rafters. Across the room, more than twenty feet below, a gathering of citizens continued their discussions. Eight in all, the assassin noted, young and old, male and female.

"Then let us decide the issue once and for all," the one called Rigdon pressed. "We should already be moving our folk south to Drakmar or Palladur. We won't have forever to do so."

"No, we won't," Esaias concurred. "But do you think for a moment that either will stand where Krynwall did not?"

"Then we continue south, or turn east. Either way, we cannot just sit here, patiently awaiting Jarom's return."

A third council member, an older woman with thick dark hair, tried to intervene. "Rigdon—"

"You're all behaving as though he's some great savior sent by the gods," Rigdon barreled on. "Jarom—or Torin, or whatever we're calling him now—is a fine young man, I grant you. I wish my own sons were more like him. But we've no reason to believe the emperor will grant his request, whether or not Derreg believes him to be heir to the throne."

The woman was shaking her head. "The danger to our village is not immediate. We are not that important."

"We're too close to escape the wizard's attention," Rigdon argued. "Neither can we hope to defend this village."

"It would be safer for us to remain here, out of the way of the conflict, than to go traipsing out into the middle of it."

Several of the others nodded and murmured their concordance with the woman's appraisal. As their grunts died away, the room quieted. One by one, each set of eyes began working its way to Esaias, clearly the leader among those in attendance.

"Vahl is right," he offered at last. "Let us give Torin and Allion the time they need to return from Kuuria. There's no need for us to make a move until the emperor makes his."

"But—" Rigdon began.

"Upon their return, we'll be better able to gauge this crisis and more properly determine our future here in Alson."

"We have no future in Alson," Rigdon huffed. "If we wish to survive at all, we must leave now."

Esaias closed his eyes and sighed again. "And you are free to do so, my friend. I for one am not yet prepared to surrender all I've built here simply because of a vague fear that has yet to manifest itself as a direct threat."

A number of heads bobbed in agreement. The assassin, perched atop his beam, watched the stone-faced Rigdon settle back in his seat, an admission of defeat in what the intruder imagined had become a nightly ritual.

Just when it seemed the proceedings might come to a close, a man who appeared much too young to be seated on a governing council cleared his throat. "It might be wise to establish a time after which we'll wait no longer. I mean, Rigdon is right. If Torin should return too late, or not at all . . ."

The assassin did not wait to hear anything further. He could sense this debate, like most, circling back on itself. In any case, he'd learned all that he would here. This heir to the throne, Torin, who also went by the name of Jarom, had headed south to Kuuria, traveling with a companion named Allion. That was what he needed to know. He cared not about Alson's plans to defend itself against the wizard's conquest. To the Abyss with both parties. His concern lay only in finding those with the wealth and need for his particular services. Loyalty was a burden, a commodity to be bought and sold like swine at market. It so happened that for now the wizard Soric held his, but only as befit specific tasks. With regards to his current undertaking, the rest was only so much distraction.

At one with the shadows of the night, Xarius Talyzar exited through the skylight, slid down the rooftop, and dropped to the earthen floor below, just in time to see the torches and hear the bloodthirsty cries.

"Fools!" he cursed to himself, then melted away as the sixteen mounted mercenaries came thundering into view, the flame of their torches bouncing in the darkness.

Esaias froze in his seat. He glanced at the others, and at Rigdon in particular. They had heard it, too, a terrible commotion, punctuated by shouts of death and cries of alarm. A lump of dread clogged Esaias's throat. The stone shelf of Rigdon's brow crumbled like an avalanche, the eyes beneath flashing with grim warning. All at once, the Circle broke, its members scampering from their seats. The First Elder pulled his gaze away from that of the Second in order to follow. In a knot, they spilled out of the council hall, only to skid to a halt on the porch outside in disbelief.

The village was ablaze. A band of soldiers was tearing through the forest in a wild stampede, flinging their torches at homes and sheds and anything else that might burn. Given the dry, late summer season, the fires caught easily. Shrieks of confusion rent the serene night, followed by those of death and mourning. With howls of bloodlust, the marauders swarmed the village, laying waste to the forested plots where men worked, the tiny glens where children played, and the homes where all lived. They slaughtered men, women, and children, most before the victims had rolled from their beds. As those living farther out emerged to see what was happening, the soldiers scattered through the nearby woods in pursuit. A few of the villagers tried to fight, most tried to flee, but caught so unawares in the middle of the night, nearly all perished.

Esaias remained a statue upon the porch of the council hall, observing the slaughter as though it were a nightmare existing only in his mind. The wizard had come for them. Just as Rigdon had warned, only faster and harsher than they could have imagined. All they had worked for, everything he had dedicated his life to achieve, was turning to ash before him. The fire's breath stung his eyes, causing them to bleed cleansing tears. He watched as the younger Elders tried to act, dashing forth to find their families, only to be cut down or burned alive. Rigdon and Vahl, who had lived here since Diln's founding, remained beside him. They, too, could only gape at the devastation, recognizing full well what it meant. Their place was among their people, and their people could not be saved. Death's shade had come for them all.

As screaming citizens stumbled or rolled about in flames, one of the armed riders spied the trio of Elders upon the front porch of the council house. Shouting to a nearby comrade, he galloped toward them with a bloodied broadsword. Esaias stood tall, refusing to move, refusing to respond. He heard himself grunt as the cold steel split his flesh, and watched his blood spatter upon a patch of mushrooms to one side at the base of the stairs. Beside him, Rigdon grappled with the second assailant. Esaias slumped to his knees. An arm fell to the wooden planking that rushed to meet him, an arm he recognized as his own. What had Ellebe brought upon them? he wondered suddenly. What could Torin do for them now? A warm explosion exposed his brains to the cool night wind, and he realized nothing more.

Almost before the groans of those first slain had died in the wind, the job was finished and Diln destroyed. Xarius Talyzar surveyed the damage from the center of the village, where the roaring flames soared into the night and the lingering screams echoed against the burning walls of the central lodges. The wizard's mercenaries had been remarkably efficient, given their clumsy assault. Doubtless there were those who had escaped the slaughter. The assassin could sense them, huddled deep within the cold forest, hearts aflame, minds whirring, understanding and sorrow swallowed by the night. But the vast majority had been slain. The parched earth was soaked with their blood and littered with their charred forms. And, the assassin noted, as the killers began to regroup, it appeared the wizard's soldiers had not suffered a single casualty.

Looking up from the corpses of Esaias, Rigdon, and Vahl, the mercenary captain noted this as well. A smirk of grim pleasure spread up one cheek as he counted his men. A moment later, the soldier caught sight of the assassin, who had made himself visible against the backdrop of the flaming council hall. Sneering in triumph, the captain urged his mount forward.

"Now that's more like it. Better than all of your sneakin' around, eh?" He looked to his gathering men for approval and was rewarded with a chorus of jubilant shouts.

Xarius waited for the man's confident smile to thin. "And what did you learn about Ellebe's son?"

The captain frowned as he fumbled for an answer. As his men continued to close ranks, one or two of them snickered. After a moment in which his entire body grew tense with anger, the man dismounted and marched close, where he lifted his sword and ran a gloved finger down the length of the bloodied blade. Glaring down at the smaller assassin, he licked his finger.

"He's dead."

The gathered mercenaries roared their approval, and a fierce grin split the captain's scarred features.

As always, the assassin's voice was a whisper. "Then who is that?"

The captain turned. In that same moment, Xarius drew a slender shortsword from his belt. Without hesitation, he slid the blade up through a seam of the captain's chain mail and deep into the man's groin. The captain howled, drawing the attention of the others back to Xarius. A host of horror-stricken visages faced him as the doomed mercenary cupped his hands in a futile attempt to quell the blood flow. A moment later, he slumped to the ground with a dull thud.

"Was it he who gave the order to attack?"

Not one of the mercenaries stirred, their expressions as ghostly and rigid as that of their dead captain.

"Lieutenant!" the assassin hissed.

One of the men looked up, his lips quivering in apology. "You . . . you were gone so long. We . . . we didn't know—"

"Was it he who gave the order?"

"Y-yes, sir."

Xarius wiped the blood from his weapon with a square of

cloth, which he then dropped upon the captain's twitching body.

"Very well," he whispered, returning his shortsword to its concealed sheath. "You, Lieutenant, are now captain. I trust that in the coming days, you will display better sense than he."

The mercenary gulped, then nodded.

Satisfied by the response, the assassin added, "Bring me my horse." He then set off in search of the southern road, that which would lead him along Torin's trail to Kuuria.

It did not take him long to find it.

Jarom awoke with a start, facing a black, cloudless night. A cool wind blew across the rocky trail, freezing the beads of sweat that clung to his body. The fearsome images haunted his mind a moment longer and then were gone. He took a deep breath and held it. As realistically horrifying as it had been, the nightmare had still been only his imagination. And yet, he dared not move, convinced that the monstrous howl that had chased that nightmare and all semblance of sleep from his head had been very real.

Several moments passed. After a time, he began to wonder if the feral cry had in fact been but a part of his foul dream. He was about to lie back when suddenly there was movement. His heart skipped a beat, then quickened pace as if to make up for it. As silently as he could manage, he slid his sword from its sheath and roused Allion.

"What is it?" the hunter asked in annoyance.

"There's something out there," Jarom whispered as loudly as he dared, "over behind those rocks."

"I hope it's your sanity," Allion muttered, squinting in the direction Jarom indicated.

For a moment, everything seemed as it should, the two of them alone in a mostly barren wilderness. They heard it first, then saw it, an immense shadow shifting and snorting among the distant boulders.

"It's a mountain wolf," Allion surmised. "A big one."

Jarom swallowed hard as he observed the colossal shadow slinking about in the distance. A sheen of sweat gathered between his palms and the hilt of his sword, threatening his grip. "Well, what do we do?"

"I'm not sure," Allion admitted. "I doubt he'll bother us. I don't see any others, although they normally run in packs."

Jarom cast about, startled by the possibility. "Should we kill it, then? Run? What?" He heard the apprehension in his own voice, and was troubled by it. He should not have been so afraid of a mere wolf, especially when he knew Allion could slay the creature before it came within fifty strides of them.

"Calm down. A single wolf is not going to hurt us, but I don't want to be taking on a score of them."

"Not so loud!" Jarom hissed. "It might hear you."

Allion failed to contain a sharp laugh. "Man, what's got you so spooked?"

Jarom responded with a start as the wolf pricked its ears and turned to face them. It sniffed the air once, then came bounding toward them, snarling.

Jarom leapt to his feet, sword in hand. "Shoot it!"

This time, the hunter didn't argue. Instead, he scrambled for his bow. A moment later, the string was loaded and drawn back to his ear. But instead of firing, the archer dropped his aim, muttering an astonished oath. "Sacred blazes . . ."

Jarom understood why as the beast came into full view. This was no ordinary mountain wolf, but rather some freakish monster unleashed from a child's nightmare. Bony spikes ran the length of its spine. Muscles bulged beneath its sleek black coat. It stood nearly four feet off the ground from paw to shoulder. And its pupilless eyes, set deep in their sockets, were not those of an animal, but glowed a fierce, unearthly green.

Allion's fingers released the bowstring. Once, then twice he fired, each bolt burying itself deeply into the beast's tough fur. The creature roared its displeasure, a sound no wolf could make, then reared back on its haunches.

And continued to run toward them on two legs.

Jarom froze. The monster's arms slashed at the night air some six to eight feet above the earth. Even on two legs, its bounding pace failed to slow. It was close enough now that Jarom could see its curled lips and the saliva strings that stretched between its gleaming teeth.

A third arrow finally dropped the beast, no more than ten paces away, as it entered through the creature's rib cage and pierced its heart. With a hacking yelp, the beast settled into a motionless heap. Just to be sure, Allion launched a fourth arrow, this one into the top of its skull. The beast didn't move. The archer glanced back, drawing forth a hunting knife. It was Jarom's turn. Nodding slowly, the swordsman moved cautiously toward the apparent kill, while Allion followed on his heels.

As they neared the slain monster, the companions viewed a beast more horrifying in death than it had been in life. Its hair was too short for that of a wolf, and huge scars that had not been visible before ripped across the coarse black hide. Its arms and legs were too long—thin and sinewy rather than short and stocky. Its front paws were fully formed hands, each containing a thumb and three clawed fingers. A head too big for its body lay within a rapidly enlarging pool of the thick black blood oozing from its wounds. Its tongue, wrapped in slaver, convulsed in its mouth as if refusing to die, and the eyes . . . green no longer, the solid eyes now shone a dull red.

Jarom's mind raced. Not in all the legends he had ever heard had he come across an animal such as this. It couldn't possibly be real. Just looking at it filled him with a sense of dread. Perhaps he'd been wrong in coming here. Perhaps this was a warning not to disturb a race of men whose dealings were said to be beyond mortal understanding. Perhaps he was to turn around now, before it was too late.

Overcome with loathing, Jarom attacked the beast's corded neck with his broadsword. It took four strokes to finally sever the head from its body. As it rolled away, Jarom spun around to vomit.

Allion turned with him, his own disgust writhing in the muscles of his face. He placed a hand on Jarom's shoulder, as though to comfort his friend and to steady himself.

"Where do you suppose it came from?" Jarom asked when the heaves had diminished.

Allion started to speak, then closed his mouth and just shook his head.

"I'm sorry," Jarom panted.

Allion nodded, then braced himself and turned back to the carcass. Jarom remained where he was, hands on knees, until he heard the other gasp.

He spun about quickly, fearful of what his friend had seen, thinking at once that it must be another of the wolf-creatures. Prepared as he was for that horror, the truth stole his breath.

He glanced about, peering into the night, searching for some sign that his eyes were deceiving him. Finding none, he looked back to where the carcass had been.

Where all that remained was a tarlike pool of its blood.

As its glow brightened, Spithaera rose from her nest and approached the pool in the center of her cavern. Dressed in a gown of transparent silk, she leaned over the stone edge and peered into the foaming waters. She smiled consolingly at the wolf statue lying within.

"My dear Lobac," she crooned. "What has happened to you?"

The waters calmed. Their glow dimmed. With a mother's caress, Spithaera reached her slender hands into the pool and withdrew the massive statue of her demon wolf. As she held the stone form in her arms, she took a moment to study the fresh scratches marring its surface, paying special attention to the one that encircled its neck.

"Dear Lobac," she sighed. "Who would show such cruelty to a darling such as you?"

With noble grace, Spithaera carried the sculpted figure to its position within the ring of statues that encircled her chamber, and replaced it carefully. She then stood before it, stroking with long, delicate fingers the polished stone of its inert head.

"Tell me, my dear," she whispered in their shared tongue, "what have you seen?"

CHAPTER TWELVE

Jarom saw Allion wince as the hunter turned his ankle upon yet another loose stone. While his friend drew a painful breath, Jarom braced for the inevitable outburst.

"How in the Abyss did I let you talk me into this?"

Jarom said nothing, understanding that his friend's bitterness would pass more swiftly if he kept silent. He would only spark an argument with any words that he might summon, and neither man had the energy to waste.

"There's nothing up here but wolf dens and rockslides. Yet here we are, marching through a deserted wasteland in search of a place that doesn't exist!"

Jarom slapped at one of the tiny insects that buzzed about his head, smearing its flesh against that of his own sweaty neck. Put to it, his own assessment would not have been all that different. Upon awaking that morning, he'd been of a mind to rethink the entire affair. As had been the pattern of late, his courage and conviction had escaped him during the night, seeped back into the chambers of his heart like water through sand. Only this time, it was not just the lack of confidence that came with the disorientation of a new day. This time, he had real cause to consider abandoning their quest.

First and foremost was the inexplicable encounter with the monster wolf. Following the attack, neither man had been able to sleep. Dangers of the wild, they had agreed after a lengthy discussion, a holdover from ancient times that predated the coming of man. Jarom was as convinced of that as he was of the claim that the strange tome discovered outside of Earthwyn had nothing to do with them, but he kept the thought to himself. It would not do, he realized, to waver and give Allion a chance to reopen discussions as to whether they should be out here.

Second was the nightmare with which he had wrestled before the monster's coming. For the first time since they had begun back in Diln, his dreams had taken on a threatening cast. In it, he'd been lost in a black woodland, hunted by a sinister wraith. He'd found no familiar faces or landmarks, just an unmistakable threat of danger. Meaningless, perhaps. But considering the role his recent dreams had played in bringing him here, he felt it unwise to dismiss this one out of hand.

They had agreed to take turns sleeping so that at least one of them was on watch at all times. But neither man had been able to find rest and had begun the day gruff and irritable, disheartened and wary. They spoke sparingly during breakfast, concealing from each other their private fears. Despite his doubts, Jarom convinced himself that they must keep following their present course. Action would choke out hesitation, and once their misgivings had withered and turned to dust, all would be as it should. On this day, the road would be their ally.

Nature had wasted little time in proving him wrong. The sun, once a strengthening friend, betrayed them. All that day, its burning rays had scorched the earth and the two men as they marched along the lower paths of the Aspandels, dragging their mounts after. The refreshing breezes of the plains had deserted them as well, leaving them to face the heat without defense, and to fall prey to the swarms of insects intent on sucking what life juices were available from their parched bodies.

Under such conditions, their trek had quickly become an ordeal. The companions trudged doggedly through the foothills, following the trails south and always searching. They explored every cave, probed every crevice, scoured every crack and defile they came across. Thus far, their most exciting discovery had been the den of a mother wolf and her pups, a chance confrontation they had only narrowly escaped without a fight, and which had served as an unnecessary reminder of the previous night's encounter. Beyond this, as Allion noted, they had found only dead ends, barren trails, and the occasional rockslide.

The hour had not yet passed during which Jarom was not required to explain yet again his rationale in coming here. Kuuria was just over these mountains to the west, Allion would remind him. It was there that they should be. They might have reached Morethil by now. With any luck, the emperor would already be preparing to send his army north, to reclaim Alson from the invading wizard. Certainly, that was more likely than uncovering the entrance to a place that existed only in drunken tales and legends.

Jarom agreed. He acquiesced to Allion on every point. Logically, their hunt was ridiculous. But he was not thinking in strictly logical terms. Although he could not explain the forces at work inside him, he knew that what he was doing now had a far greater potential for setting aright their lives, for salvaging the future of their land and homes. In essence, he was because he felt compelled by fate, persuaded by every inner sense and emotion that this was where he belonged.

So he simply accepted it—both the challenge and the responsibility that went with it. He accepted Allion's complaints as he accepted his own doubts. He nodded, shrugged, cowed to every grievance, and kept marching. With the first day behind them and an unknown number ahead, he pressed forward with twisted joints, bruised limbs, parched throat, and swollen tongue, praying each time he rounded a bend, crested a bluff, or probed a defile that Whitlock would be revealed, or that the Entients would discover them—that in some way, this journey would come to a merciful and constructive end.

For the harder he fought, the greater became his need for success. With every step, every strained muscle, every drop of sweat, the more precious became the ultimate prize. He was too proud, too confident, too unwilling to admit defeat. The more he struggled, the brighter his determination burned.

And so, once again, Jarom met his friend with respectful silence as the man cursed and muttered and kicked at the dry, loose earth. Although he dared not say so at this moment, he remained optimistic that they were close—close to Whitlock, close to fulfilling this quest. They couldn't bloody well expect to have found the ancient stronghold on their first day. Glancing at the tome that bounced in the bag at his horse's side, Jarom envisioned their eventual achievement. To find Whitlock and visit with the Entients. To gather from the mystic order information that would lead to the recovery of a Sword of Asahiel. All of it was within reach. Riches such as they could scarcely imagine would be theirs, if only they had the heart to complete this journey.

But it was not to happen on this day. They marched until the sun went down, then by starlight a mile more. Fearful of missing some clue in the dark, they then stopped and made camp in a patch of scrub. Baked and blistered one moment by the windless daylight, they shivered in the next, blasted as if by wailing banshees—frigid breezes that pierced cloak and tunic and gooseflesh to claw at weary bones. Their sweat dried; their muscles stiffened. Too tired to make a fire, they wasted few words as they tended to their mounts, then ate a tasteless meal of bread and cheese and tiny berries gathered along the way. As the first full day of futile search settled over them with the weight of iron chains, Jarom wrapped himself in his bedroll, curled up on the mountain floor, and whispered mental encouragement to himself, promising a new and fantastic future to be discovered on the morrow.

Despite the cold, despite his aches and pains, he soon felt himself drifting to the stars. The sparse grass, the mountains, their horses—all fell away as his dreams came unbidden.

Lemm stopped what he was doing as the company of riders pulled up before his stable. A quick count revealed sixteen men, some kind of military patrol by the looks of them—save one, a man cloaked head to foot in loose-fitting garb as black as pitch. The liveryman frowned, but set down his grooming brush on a nearby stool, patted the horse to which he had been tending, and marched forth to greet the stern gathering.

"Evening. Something I can help you sirs with?"

"We're looking for someone," the cloaked stranger replied.

"Yeah?"

"A pair of men from a village north of here. Came on foot, but would have needed horses to complete their journey south."

Lemm scowled. Why was the man speaking in whispers? He ran a hand over his head, wiping the sweat from his bald pate. "A lot of folks pass through here. Know where they was headed?"

"Kuuria."

The liveryman chuckled. "All, it seems, are headed to Kuuria these days."

"It would have been about three days ago. Young men. One calls himself Allion. The other goes by Jarom or Torin. Do you remember them?"

"Can't say I do."

"Perhaps you'd be good enough to check your log, see if their names are there."

"I don't keep a log," Lemm lied. He tapped a finger to the side of his head. "I've got a good memory."

"And yet you don't remember two men from Diln, on the long road south to Kuuria."

"Must not have come this way."

The stranger sat perfectly still within his saddle, his tightly drawn cowl hiding his expression from view.

"Your mounts look tired," Lemm observed. "I don't have room for the half of you, but old man Farron, I imagine he'd be happy to put your beasts up for the night."

"Farron?"

"Just follow the road into town. He's on Farthing Street. Massive outfit. Can't miss him. Perhaps that's where your boys went."

The stranger looked as though he was about to say something more, then nodded instead. Without a word to his company, he turned his horse about and urged it into a canter.

One or two of the others gave Lemm a hard look as they moved to follow. The liveryman met their stares evenly, then addressed the last in their train.

"These boys you're looking for, they in some kind of trouble?"

The soldier glared. "We've a message for them."

Lemm nodded as the man trotted after the others. When they had gone, the liveryman shook his head. Dangerous men, those. A minor miracle that he'd been able to dismiss them so easily. Of course he knew Jarom and Allion. Strange, he thought, that Jarom might be using another name. Had the lad gone and done something foolish? Regardless, he wasn't about to turn them over to ruffians such as these, not without knowing who they were or what was going on. They were not of any legitimate authority he recognized; nor had he cared for their gruff tone. And that whisper, why, it was enough to rake a man's bones. Sixteen armed men to deliver a message? Not bloody likely.

Retrieving his brush, he went back to grooming a stallion whose master was set to depart in the morning. The moments slipped by, and as he fell into the rhythm of his duties, he managed to push all thoughts of the strange company to the back of his mind. It was none of his concern. He'd done what he could to buy the lads some time. Jarom and Allion were capable young men. With any luck, their pursuers would never find them. Otherwise, he was confident they could fend for themselves.

A shadow filled the open doorway, clouds brushing past the evening sun. Lemm leaned forward, preparing to give the animal its final rubdown. Only when he heard the latch to the stall scrape against its housing did he turn to see who it was that had come. Before he could respond, a black form fell over him. A hand covered his mouth. He sucked in deeply, fighting for breath. Too late, he caught scent of a smothering perfume. Then his legs buckled, and the lights went out.

When he awoke, it was to an agony such as he had never before experienced. He heard himself scream, but the sound was muffled, the bulk of it echoing within his own mind. An instant later, the searing pressure subsided, and only a throbbing ache remained. Unclenching his eyes, Lemm realized quickly enough what had happened.

The liveryman was trapped in his own stable, bound and gagged like a trussed pig. He was seated on a bench in the back of a corner stall, the farthest from anyone who might hear his struggles. The stable door was closed, its interior guarded by a circle of armed soldiers, men he recognized from his earlier encounter. Lemm's stomach churned. The smell of blood mixed with that of sweat and manure. His eyes fell. The hay covering the floor beneath his feet was spattered red. He looked up, fearful of what he might find. His horror was complete when he saw his hands, roped before him to a block of wood, save the thumb of his right hand, which lay in a sticky pool.

Lemm screamed. Again the sound traveled mostly within his head. His breath quickened, fighting past the clog in his mouth. As he continued to stare at his thumb, a hooded face leaned into view, fronted by a gleaming dagger whose bloody edge played with the faint light streaming in through filthy windows.

"Now," the stranger whispered, "about these two men from Diln . . ."

Jarom peered into the darkness, one hand pressed against the stone for balance as he leaned forward at the mouth of the cave. Shaded by a natural overhang and a cluster of surrounding boulders, the fissure revealed little of what lay within. Nevertheless, it remained the most encouraging discovery thus far in their search for Whitlock. If early indications held true, then this cleft was not just another shallow defile, but a tunnel to an inhabitable cavern, and if that were so . . .

Despite his many hopes and assurances of the previous night, it had not taken long for Jarom to come crashing back to reality. Though he'd fallen quickly to sleep, it had been a long, fitful evening during which he'd wrestled with cold breezes, the hard mountain floor, and, as usual of late, the demons in his head. He had awakened not refreshed, but more haggard than when he'd started out.

His disposition had improved only slightly throughout the day. As cold midnight doubts were burned away by the morning sun, he was able to persuade himself anew that this was where he belonged. Physically, however, he was already showing signs of wear. His eyes burned, scratched by dust and wind and lack of sleep. His muscles ached, and would only get worse. Blisters had begun to form on the balls of his feet. He said little to Allion, his tongue swollen with thirst. His friend appeared no better off than he, and on this day, mimicked his silence. All that morning, they had gone about their business with long faces and heavy hearts.

Much of that had changed the moment they found the footprints. Up until then, they had encountered few signs of life among the barren reaches, and none of those human. But the prints had changed all that, depressions most definitely made by a man. Or men, as Allion had quickly corrected, for the tracks were not those of a single human, but a band of three or four.

With a mix of eagerness and caution, they had followed the trail. The task was difficult, for in many areas, the ground was solid stone, its surface swept free of the softer soils or vegetation that best captured signs of passage. But the clues remained, as Allion, the experienced hunter, had pointed out—a discoloration here, a scuff mark there. And although there were few breaks in the terrain that could be considered paths, they had begun after all this time to discern natural patterns in the rugged landscape that were more amenable than others to the passage of two-legged beings. The tracks, they discovered, seemed to follow the same natural flow of the land.

As the hours wore on, the trail led them higher into the mountains, weaving a southwesterly course. After a time, the prints were joined by others, seeming to support the theory of the existence of a tribe of men whose members would disperse and wander down out of the higher elevations in small groups. It all made perfect sense to Jarom, who for a while had forgotten his discomfort, forgotten his fears. They were onto something here. He could sense it.

Eventually, the tracks had ended, disappearing into the mouth of the cave before which the woodsmen now stood. The threshold was well worn, leading Jarom to believe the opening must lead to a semipermanent dwelling at the very least.

"Well?"

Jarom bit his lip, urging himself to keep his enthusiasm under control. "I can't see much from out here," he replied. "We'll have to go in and take a look." He turned to face his companion. "Time to find a torch."

They did so quickly, locating a suitable piece of dead-wood from a fallen tree and igniting it with a bit of pitch, flint, and steel. Within moments, they had returned to the suspicious cleft, Jarom leading, the smoke of his torch wafting skyward.

Allion drew his hunting knife. "Be careful."

Jarom nodded and unsheathed his sword.

A pocket of cool air greeted them as they plunged into the opening. Jarom welcomed its brush. The flame of his torch reflected in the blade of his sword and cast the shadow of their creeping forms upon the pitted cavern wall. The way was crooked and narrow, the floor hard and uneven. Even with the light, Jarom felt more than spied his way through. Should it prove to be a tunnel into Whitlock, he doubted it could be the front door.

Just when he was beginning to fear that the corridor was without end, he slid between a pair of jutting crags and found himself in a pocket-sized cavern. The ceiling hung low, forcing him to duck slightly. Numerous clefts and fissures lined the walls, natural burrows along the floor in which a man could curl up to sleep. The footprints were everywhere, a scraping and pushing around of the siltlike deposit that carpeted the stone floor. There were no other signs of life, no rations or tools or cooking implements. Whoever's home this may have been, it appeared to be abandoned.

"Look here."

Jarom shifted to find Allion bent near one of the burrows.

To one side was a small mound of loose stones and gravel, piled beside a shallow hole. His brow furrowed, and he looked to his friend for an explanation.

"Thieves," the hunter explained. "Holes for burying loot. Look, there are others."

Jarom wasn't sure how exactly Allion knew this, but as he examined the other hollows, he spied more cavities such as that which the hunter had found.

Allion snickered, more derision than mirth. "A dead end, my friend."

Jarom shook his head. They hadn't come all this way to have it end like this. "There might be another path," he suggested hopefully, "a passage farther in."

Allion, however, had already made up his mind. While Jarom searched, he took a seat on a flat stone shelf, removed his boots, and proceeded to rub the soreness from his feet.

Jarom pretended not to notice, gritting his teeth and persisting in his explorations. After several moments, he came up empty, and at last turned around to face his friend.

"Are you finished?" the hunter asked.

Jarom spun away, the sudden motion drawing a whooshing sound from his torch. He didn't bother to check on whether Allion was following as he stormed back the way they had come. Though loath to admit another defeat, and reluctant to return to the dry heat awaiting them outside, he was anxious to put this episode behind them. They were wasting daylight. With each passing moment, their chances of finding Whitlock before sunset decreased. Allion could sit and rub his feet until his toes fell off. If the hunter was happier making light of their situation and pausing to rest, so be it. Until their search was successful, Jarom had no intention of doing the same.

The assassin's head throbbed within the folds of his cowl, an echo of the pounding he had listened to throughout the day as his hunting party raced southward. The difficulties of the previous evening had set them back a bit. They had set forth straightaway following their visit with the liveryman who had sold Jarom and Allion their horses. Leaving Earthwyn, however, had proven no easy task. The authorities had all but sealed off the southern road, aggressively hunting for anyone who might have been involved in a recent murder that had taken place just south of the city. Had he been alone, the assassin could have slipped through with little effort. But extricating the wizard's soldiers had required extensive negotiations, part of which had involved the payment of a small personal fortune that—when this was over—the assassin meant to recoup.

Once they had freed themselves, Xarius Talyzar and his mercenary band had followed the flow of the Kalgren Fork along the trail of Prince Torin and his companion. The ride had been swift and furious in an effort to make up for lost time. Since he knew where the pair was headed, the assassin was not concerned with missing any signs. Thus, after just half a day, they found themselves here, among the southern stretches of the Gaperon, scratching at the threshold to the lands of Kuuria.

As were legions of others. Their stench filled the assassin's nostrils, thousands upon thousands of refugees, huddled like rats within their containment camps. The emperor, it seemed, wanted no part of these starving masses. The border was sealed tight, a blockade reinforced by what looked to be an entire battalion of soldiers. These troops had done their job well, driving away those seeking entry and regulating the formation of the various camps. A limited effort had been made to provide food and provisions, but it seemed clear the Council was hoping these people would eventually tire of the conditions and go home. As the assassin led his men toward the lines of the blockade, drawing stares of hunger and curiosity from the dirt-faced hordes, he found himself hoping that if and when the wizard launched an offensive into Kuuria, the battle would take place right here, where the collision between forces of north and south would grind up these people like gnats.

"Hold!" shouted one of the patrolmen before the assassin's party had made it anywhere near the front lines. "Where are you headed?"

Xarius pulled to a stop. The mercenaries behind him shifted in their saddles, seeking to relieve cramped muscles. "We seek passage into Kuuria."

The patrolman shook his head. "All passage is disallowed by order of the emperor."

"All?"

"Without exception."

The assassin craned his neck, peering past the patrolman to make a further study of the barricade beyond. "How long?"

"Pardon?"

"How long has the border been sealed?"

"None have entered the empire of Kuuria in the past two days."

The assassin frowned. By his estimation, Jarom and Allion enjoyed a lead on his position of closer to three days. "And prior to that?"

The patrolman paused to shoo a ragged wanderer back the way he had come. "What was that?"

"Three days ago. Any chance a man might have made it through then?"

"Not unless he was a member of an authorized merchant guild." The patrolman stopped to address the stray refugee a second time, threatening force if the man did not return to his assigned camp.

"You're certain?"

Between the stubborn refugee and the assassin's questions, the patrolman seemed to be fast losing any pretense of civility. "'Tis our duty to make certain," he snapped. "Whomever you seek, chances are he was turned away like everyone else. I would suggest you do the same before I'm forced to—"

The remainder of the man's threat was lost as the assassin reined his horse about so that its tail swatted the patrolman in the face. Xarius coiled, hoping for a retaliation. Sure enough, the patrolman sputtered in angry defiance. But as he prepared to rush after his offender, the stray refugee made a dash for the barricade. Ranking duty above the need for redress against personal insult, the patrolman spun about and chased after the foolish refugee, tackling him to the earth and unleashing his frustrations thereupon.

The assassin continued northward, his departure heralded by the beaten man's howls. He gave no command to the wizard's mercenaries to follow, riding past them without acknowledgment. He had ceased giving unnecessary orders. Since their raid on the village Diln and the execution of their original captain, the soldiers had been perfectly behaved, keeping their mouths closed and doing exactly as Xarius desired. As he rode past, they turned to follow, a private pack of well-trained dogs.

Unfortunately, he was now forced to make a decision. Despite the patrolman's confidence, there remained a window of opportunity for Jarom and Allion to have slipped past the blockade before it had gone into full effect. The fact that his party had not encountered the two men heading north on a return trip to Diln seemed to support that possibility. The question was, where might they have gone if they had failed to get through? Would they necessarily have returned home, or might they have taken their cause elsewhere?

In his haste to reach Kuuria, the assassin had completely lost his quarry's trail. That he had done so made matters more difficult. Still, it seemed he had few options. The simplest answer was most often the correct one. Even if this Jarom had managed to enter Kuuria or gone elsewhere, he would eventually return north with the news. Thus, until he had evidence to the contrary, Xarius would follow that route, retracing his own steps—more carefully this time—all the way back to Diln, if necessary. As he had already proven, there were other, easier ways to track a man than by his steed's print in the dirt.

Leaving the stinking masses of human vermin in his wake, the assassin led his dogs northward, resuming the hunt.

For the remainder of the afternoon, they kept to that trail, the wind at their backs. The sun was well overhead, its stinging glare draped over shoulder and out of their eyes. They made good time, even pausing to interrogate each traveler with whom they came in contact along the main highway.

Traffic was lighter than before. It seemed that most of those who intended to flee the war-torn lands of northern Alson had already done so, while the remainder of her citizenry hunkered down close to home. Few were those brave or foolish enough to be conducting their normal business on the open road.

Few, but not lacking altogether. With the scales of the day leaning heavily toward dusk, the assassin and his band encountered a rather large caravan of merchants headed south on a return trip from northern markets. As with all others, Xarius took the time to question the company's members about the two men for whom he was searching. In a refreshing departure from the norm, he found these men to be of a free-spirited nature, remarkably friendly and unsuspicious. He was introduced quickly enough to their leader, who proved decidedly less guarded with his information than others with whom the assassin had come in contact, such as the liveryman back in Earthwyn.

"Sure, I know them boys. Rode half a day with Jarom. He went east in search of some village. Delivering medicines, as I recall. That Allion, he came after, looking for his friend. Don't know whether or not he ever caught up to him. Nice young lads. You find them, be sure to tell them they both owe old Garm here a drink. Speaking of which, your men look thirsty. What say we share a few rounds of my own award-winning ale? I've a selection to choose from. I'll sell it to you at near my own price. Hah! It's like I'm inviting thieves to dinner. Just promise you won't tell no one what you paid for it. My missus would never forgive me. Hah! If I had one! Think I want to be shackled to some stinking cottage somewhere, mending fences, painting shutters, that sort of thing? No, thank you!"

And on and on it went, bringing a rare smirk of genuine amusement to the assassin's face. So, Jarom and his friend had failed to enter Kuuria and had veered east toward the Aspandels. Medicines? That didn't sound likely. Then again, if Jarom had half the wits that his elders back in Diln had credited him with, it seemed sensible that he would have come up with a false excuse to hide his true purpose from a garrulous fool such as this. But what might that purpose be? And why would Allion be chasing after him? Had they had a disagreement? The assassin's smirk widened. Dissension in the ranks. Excellent.

His amusement was short-lived. As the minutes dragged by, he began to fear he would have to cut the wind from Garm's lungs in order to stop the man's speech. And if he were to do that, he would have to slaughter the entire caravan. Not a task he wished to undertake while his quarry slipped farther from his grasp with each passing moment. Finally, he managed to break free, faking a cough while Garm paused for breath. When the merchant leader inquired as to his state, the assassin admitted that he was terribly ill, in need of the medicine Jarom carried. The lad was to have returned with it by now. Desperate, he had come out in search. That caused Garm to put a measure of distance between them, a distance that widened considerably once Xarius confessed that the illness was highly catching. Offering thanks and begging forgiveness, the assassin and his company swung around to the south, and rode off ahead of Garm's gang.

Back to business.

A short time later, the wizard's hunting party turned east. The assassin knew the road that the merchant claimed Jarom had taken. He also knew an even quicker route. Using this, he would intercept rather than follow Jarom's trail. He had wasted enough time already.

And so, as the second night out from Diln settled, it found the assassin weary of travel and anxious for sport. With each galloping stride, he had to fight the urge to leave the wizard's soldiers behind and to carry out the remainder of this task the way it should have started—alone. Nevertheless, he had not attained his level of proficiency without having first learned patience. Now that he had their scent, success was all but assured. The end was coming. He could wait.

They continued together well into the evening. When at last his company reached the road, the assassin called a halt. Dropping soundlessly from his mount, he bent to examine the earth. Without a word of explanation, he slid from view, a stray patch returned to the fabric of night.

Those whom the assassin had left behind on the deserted roadway stayed where they were in an accepting stupor. They had come to expect this of the scoundrel, and dared not speak against him. For all they knew, he was mounted behind one of them, ready to slice any rebellious tongue from its mouth. As a result, the mercenaries remained motionless for several minutes, swaying with exhaustion within their saddles, keeping to the safety of their silence as they awaited the assassin's return.

"Their trail turns off the road and into the mountains not far ahead."

To a man, the soldiers felt their neck skin crawl. Only after hearing the utterance could they make out the form of the assassin, a shadow in the dim twilight, mounted upon his steed as if he had been with them the entire time.

"They're leading their mounts afoot, as though searching for something."

The soldiers glanced at one another, unsure as to whether they should respond. The assassin seemed to be sharing the news with no one in particular, whispering aloud only to himself. He stared forward, chewing mentally upon a private thought, then spoke forcefully to all.

"We camp for the night. The tracks are just two days old. If they continue to march, we should take them on the morrow—the day after, at most."

The villain's excitement was evident as he delivered this final piece of information, and each man in the company silently reminded himself to make a point, when this was over, to steer as far as possible from this creature's path, especially if traveling in an opposing direction.

Jarom reached up with the back of his arm to wipe the sweat from his brow. Despite the heat, he still wore his tunic as protection from skin burns. He wasted no effort in scanning his sleeve for a dry spot, but simply ran the soaked cloth across his forehead. The act did little to relieve his uncomfortable state. Still, it diverted the stinging sweat from his eyes long enough for him to look up and take stock of their situation.

After nearly three days, they were fast closing on the Kalmira Forest, a sprawling woodland of old-growth conifers that, as far as he and Allion were concerned, marked the southernmost boundary of their search through the Aspandel Mountains. The range traveled farther, of course, all the way to the Nivvian Gulf. But by all accounts, Whitlock lay north of the Kalmira tree line. That was the word of the select trappers and miners who claimed to have seen the Entients coming and going from their secret stronghold, and from the even rarer individuals who now and then claimed to have been given shelter within during the passing of some great storm. Granted, any man who made such a claim was laughed off as delusional. And the fact that none had ever succeeded in leading a party back to the purported site seemed to support that theory. But these legends and tall tales were all that Jarom had to go on.

Unfortunately, reaching the Kalmira was a mark of failure more than a checkpoint of success. For if they had not located Whitlock by the time they reached the forest, they would have little choice but to retrace their steps northward, scouring the higher mountain trails for the elusive path that would lead them to Whitlock's front door. Either that, or Jarom would have to succumb to Allion's demand that they abandon this foolhardy quest and return home. Neither prospect was particularly encouraging.

Several paces ahead, Allion trudged along, munching sour-faced on some tiny berries plucked from a dusty trail bush. The two had spoken even less today than the day before. Given what he believed his friend must be thinking, Jarom was grateful. With each step, the Fason was made increasingly aware that this may have been a mistake. He didn't need the other to remind him.

He was about to lower his eyes to the trail before him when Allion stumbled. Twisting to spit out a rancid berry, the hunter had stepped too close to the ledge along which they marched, a sheer drop of several hundred feet. First one foot, and then the other, slipped out from under the man, sliding upon a carpet of loose stone. Almost before Jarom realized what was happening, Allion fell, drawn by natural forces over the edge.

Jarom released the reins of his trailing mount and bolted forward. Allion had somehow managed to hold on to his. As Jarom reached him, the hunter was scrabbling against the cliff, his look frantic as he grasped his steed's reins. The animal whinnied and snorted as it tugged against the other, its neck bent low and its hooves braced against the ledge. With each yank of the horse's head, however, Allion slipped farther down the leather lines, his sweaty palms unable to maintain their grip.

"Hang on!" Jarom shouted, an instinctive command as he reached down to seize the back of his friend's tunic.

Allion gasped and sputtered, but was in no position to articulate a response. He simply focused on his hold and fought to steady his churning legs long enough to let Jarom help him. After a moment, the combined pull proved sufficient to reel the unfortunate hunter back to a position of relative safety, where he lay on his back in a startled daze, his chest heaving from the exertion and fright.

Jarom sat back, closing his eyes against what might have been. For several moments, neither man moved. When at last he looked again to reassure himself that his friend had survived, Jarom started to speak, but couldn't. A reprimand? A jest? Neither seemed appropriate. Not when this entire episode was his fault.

He braced instead for his friend's response. Whatever Allion had to say, it was well deserved. He should never have allowed the hunter to accompany him. More to the point, he himself should not have come. They were risking their very lives, it now seemed, and all for some frivolous belief and yearning that Jarom could not even explain.

Finally, Allion rolled over and lurched to his feet. He did not so much as glance at Jarom. He merely took a moment to inspect the fresh scrapes and bruises, then seized his horse and started forward once more, this time keeping safely away from the ledge.

Jarom shook his head, feeling somewhat cheated. He hadn't expected a display of gratitude. But a reaction of some kind was in order, even if it was just an angry outburst. Perhaps Allion had come to realize that such a response served no purpose. Perhaps the hunter realized that to argue with him was a waste of effort. Perhaps Jarom, too, would be best off pressing forward in silence until this ordeal was brought to a close.

The swordsman took to his feet with a weary sigh, dusted himself off as best he could, retrieved his lagging mount, and resumed the now senseless march.

They continued throughout the remainder of the afternoon, their hearts leaden, their bodies dragging. Although there remained miles of territory before them in which to search for clues, virtually no effort was made to do so. Allion's near calamity had sapped even Jarom of what desire remained in him to spy out the Entients' warren. It was not to be found, and at this point, he was too tired and too dejected to care. All he wanted was to reach the relative comfort of the Kalmira before he settled down for the evening. He knew without consulting his companion that neither of them wished to spend another night sleeping within the barren region, and that a night within the cool confines of the forest—and perhaps a nice dinner of rabbit or venison—was about the only thing that might do them some good.

Their crawling pace, however, made it well after nightfall before they finally left behind the mountain foothills and slipped down into the hazy warmth of the night-cloaked woods. The forest was thick and green, an army of aged sentinels weary of standing guard. Their trunks twisted and leaned; their limbs interlocked for support. Jarom and Allion stumbled through the foliage, trampling the undergrowth. By now, Whitlock lay behind them for certain. Jarom's hope that the Entients would sense the closeness of their missing tome had proven vain. Or perhaps they had chosen not to come for it. Jarom had no way of knowing. What he did know was that they would gain no more information that would support a quest for the Crimson Sword, no further aid in their task to discover a means by which to protect themselves and their homeland. After all he had caused them to endure, he had nothing more than when they had started out.

They came to a ragged stop within what seemed the closest they might find to a clearing. Tending to their mounts was a hurried and haphazard affair. As Jarom tossed his saddlebags to the earth, a strap loosened and the book found outside of Earthwyn slid free. He considered it briefly. Had he the opportunity, he might have heaved it into the nearest well. Instead, he kicked it aside and moved to retrieve his bedroll.

Across the way, Allion didn't bother to do that much. He simply slumped to his seat against a huge tree and closed his eyes, as though to shut out the trials of the day. Jarom was quick to follow, easing himself into his blankets, feeling the welcome coolness of the needle-strewn floor beneath his body. On this night, weariness overcame worries, and a deep slumber stole swiftly upon him.

CHAPTER THIRTEEN

Dragons filled the afternoon sky, riding its currents like ships at sea. They circled and wheeled in endless swarms, caught in a tempest of their own making, spewing flames and causing the earth beneath to tremble with the echo of their roars. Their dark forms were etched in stark relief against a backdrop of crimson and gold. Indeed, it appeared as though the very heavens had caught fire, bathing all the world in a scarlet flame.

On the ground below, an army of Finlorian elves scattered and fled the onslaught. Their own numbers filled the mountainside, wedged into crevasses and defiles, blanketing the slopes, bristling upon the ridgelines. Some fired arrows or hurled spears at the winged titans above. Others could do little more than scream as billowing flame melted skin from bones and turned bones to ash, or as gnashing teeth and slashing claws raked and pierced both armor and flesh, as though they were one and the same.

From his distant vantage point across the rugged and pitted valley, Allion crouched low behind a boulder, seeking cover from a struggle he could not escape. Although the elves fought bravely, it was clear that theirs was a battle doomed to failure. The scale of slaughter was incomparable to anything the hunter had ever witnessed. The closest he could come was to imagine a flock of hunting birds—hawks or falcons—descending upon a hill of ants. To suggest the Finlorians were outmatched would be like suggesting that winter might follow autumn in the course of changing seasons. It was undeniable. They were utterly helpless, at the mercy of an enemy that knew nothing of pity or remorse. Given the horrific stench of charred corpses and the endless cacophony of screams, even a blind man could discern as much.

Then, suddenly, shouts of another sort rose up among the Finlorian ranks, a common cry that surged and swelled until it drowned out all others. The sound drew Allion out from his cover. Peeking carefully over the top of his boulder, the hunter gasped at what he saw. From a ledge high upon the far slope, a line of crimson fire streaked skyward, rocketing forth to ensnare a dragon that had veered too close. The beast was engulfed, its armored flesh ablaze. Within seconds, it was reduced to a flaming ember that fell shrieking from the sky.

Additional lines of fire shot forth. Each struck a dragon as if drawn to it. And in each instance, the result was the same. The winged creatures, impervious to all previous assaults, lit up like fireflies before plummeting to their deaths. None, it seemed, could withstand the stinging threads of fire for more than an instant.

Allion could scarcely believe his eyes. Already, the tides of battle were shifting. Undaunted, the dragons massed for an assault on the new threat. But as one after another they were blasted from the heavens, they began to hesitate. First one, then another swung about, turning tail to the hateful lines of fire and winging away as fast as the winds would carry them.

The elves continued to cheer, an uproar of jubilation. Allion looked closer, scanning the distant ledge for the source of the strange fire threads. Scattered about the ledge stood nine Finlorian generals, each wielding one of the legendary Swords of Asahiel, from which the streaks of crimson fire poured forth in steady streams. Saviors all, they focused as one on forcing the beasts into retreat, annihilating those that refused. The power of the Swords appeared boundless, an endless supply of divine strength that seemed in that moment capable of forging an entire world, as the myths had claimed.

Caught up in the euphoria, Allion came to his feet. As he

searched the faces of those who had arrived to save the day, he caught his breath. Jarom! One of them was Jarom! His friend's face was unmistakable alongside those of his elven comrades. As Allion watched, Jarom's weapon brought yet another dragon down from the sky. Triumphant, the young man searched quickly for another. So intent was he that he did not sense the shadow that descended from behind. Nor did any of the others. Only Allion, from his unique position, seemed aware of the vengeful beast. As it closed in for the kill, the dragon snarled, its bloody claws glinting in the sun. . . .

Jarom glanced up as Allion lurched awake. His friend wore a wide-eyed expression turned suddenly curious, as though fearful of something that he now realized wasn't there. The hunter blinked uncertainly, searching for his bearings.

"Bad dream?"

Allion looked at him, then shook his head. "I'm not sure."

Jarom saw no need to press the issue. He went back to his business, tending to the pair of quail that he was roasting over a small spit.

"Care for some breakfast?"

Allion hesitated, then hauled himself over to the fire. Jarom removed the spit and used his dagger to hand one of the wild fowls to his friend. The two of them remained quiet for several moments as they picked carefully at the steaming bird carcasses. It was Allion who finally broke the heavy silence.

"How are you feeling this morning?"

Jarom glanced at the hunter through the corner of his eye. "All right," he said with a shrug, chewing his words along with his food and finding the former harder to swallow. "You?"

"I've been better."

"Sore?"

"Yeah. It'll pass."

Jarom grew quiet again, uncertain as to how to proceed. He was in no rush to resume the discussion and where next it must take them. Then again, if he waited, he gave Allion the chance to dictate the course of that discussion, something he could ill afford. He finished chewing the meat in his mouth, swallowed, and cleared his throat.

"I don't understand," he confessed. "Why would they deliver the book, only to then deny me an audience?"

Allion shook his head, answering between mouthfuls. "You still don't even know the book belongs to them, let alone that they intended for you to have it."

Jarom hid the mild sense of satisfaction he felt at having set his friend up so easily.

"Then it must be fate."

"Fate?"

"What else? If the Entients meant for me to have the knowledge shown in this book, then they would have come for us. They didn't. So I have to assume that there's some other force behind all of this—the book, the dreams. I refuse to accept that it's all nothing more than sheer coincidence."

Allion seemed strangely subdued, more thoughtful than usual. "I agree," he said finally, causing the other's jaw to drop. "If it's all coincidence, then it's the most alarming one I've ever heard of. But I still say it could be any number of things."

"Like what?"

"I don't know," the hunter admitted. "But I think you're seeing what you want to see. You want to believe now that destiny, rather than the Entients, is driving all of it? Fine. What I'm trying to figure out is *why*."

He looked up, studying Jarom's visage as he chewed. Jarom lowered his eyes.

"You're not going back." The hunter knew him well enough to make it a statement. "You mean to find Thrak-Symbos on your own."

Jarom stirred the coals with a stick. "I'm not asking you to go with me."

Allion sighed, as weary as Jarom had ever seen him, despite the long, uninterrupted slumber. "Blazes, someone has to. Otherwise, we'll never know what became of you."

Jarom felt the look of surprise that swept across his features. Recovering quickly, he fixed the other with a caution-ary stare. "Allion, if something should happen to you be-cause of me—"

"Don't you think I'm capable of taking responsibility for my own choices?"

"But you wouldn't even be thinking about this if it wasn't for me."

"No, I wouldn't," Allion agreed. "But you're not going to change your mind, so that's beside the point here, isn't it?"

Jarom hesitated. "Are you sure?"

Allion gave a burst of a laugh. "No, I'm not sure. Truth is, I still think you're mad. I think you're so mad that now you're making *me* mad." He shook his head, then fixed his gaze as if struggling to recognize Jarom after a long ab-sence. "Then again, if I'm wrong about you, then maybe, just maybe, you have a chance to do what no one else has even dreamed of doing for hundreds, perhaps thousands of years. At this point, I'd say it's worth the risk."

Jarom's own gaze took on a suspicious cast. "What about Kuuria? What about returning to Diln and your family?"

"Ah, my family can take care of itself."

"Allion—"

"So long as the worst that happens is that we don't find Thrak-Symbos, or the Sword, I'll be happy."

Unable to squeeze a word in edgewise, Jarom just stared at his friend with a look of guarded skepticism.

"Look, we're halfway there. There's nothing to be gained in us doing anything else at the moment, so why not con-tinue on? Besides, I can tell you're never going to forget this ridiculous legend until you see firsthand that it's false."

"And if it turns out to be true?" Jarom challenged.

"Then something tells me our lives are going to change dramatically, my friend."

Jarom was stunned. He had expected Allion to put up much more of a fight. He had expected his friend to wage a furious campaign against this, the most foolish in a length-ening string of foolish decisions. He could not conceive of what might have caused the other's thinking to change so easily. He had been fully prepared to explain and defend the rationale with which he had awakened that morning with any one of a dozen impassioned pleas. And yet, all had gone unspoken. A miracle, of sorts; another coincidence. Another sign, perhaps, that he was indeed destined to follow this unlikely course.

The two considered each other for a moment more, each man keeping to his own thoughts. Without another word, the decision was made.

They finished their meal in silence, resting within the tiny glade, in no rush to set forth. The wooded surroundings filled them with a longing for home that they could not hope to appease. Despite this bittersweet reminder, the forest offered a welcome change from the harsh mountain trails, and Jarom found himself almost anxious for the journey that lay ahead through the shadowed tangle of leaves, trees, and blossoms.

When at last they set out, they did so with blessed conditions—light underbrush, alternating patches of warmth and shade, and a gentle breeze to push them along. Jarom felt invigorated. The long night's rest and hearty morning meal had dispelled the fatigue from the previous day's trek, and the excitement of their new undertaking could barely be contained. Now that the decision was made to seek out the Sword, he no longer felt the need to batter himself over it. Doubtless, the opportunity to do so would come. For now, however, he felt as if a weight had been lifted from his shoulders, as though, at long last, he was doing something worthwhile. That unexpected confidence, along with the ease with which they now journeyed, cleansed him of any and all disheartening concerns.

Of which there were many. Too many, in fact, to sort through all at once. The course of their journey no longer lay clearly before them. It was a matter they had yet to discuss, and which Jarom feared would bring an end to their truce. They would make better progress using the roadways to the north. But with the perpetual war between Partha and Menzos, any traveler caught without excuse in either land was assumed to be an agent of espionage, and had little chance of escaping a painful death. Jarom could always tell them the truth, but when the truth was unbelievable even to himself, he doubted it would convince a suspicious Parthan tribunal of his innocence.

The only alternative to slinking through Partha, however, was to keep to their current course, a low, sweeping route through the southern stretches of the Kalmira Forest. In doing so, they would not only add days to their journey as the untamed growth thickened, but they would also pass uncomfortably close to the southeastern peninsula of Vosges, a region of swamps and marshes inhabited only by the Mookla'ayans, an aboriginal race known for its cannibalistic rites. Having not the slightest desire to be eaten alive, Jarom had already decided it best that they have nothing whatsoever to do with the southern jungle inhabitants.

Which left no safe answer. He could try chartering a boat to ferry him around the Vosges peninsula, but he knew without even fully considering the notion that he could not afford the cost or the time—assuming he could find someone crazy enough to try to land him anywhere near the ragged Skullmar coastline. The more he thought about it, the more he came to realize that his only path to the east cut through the Kalmira, pinched by the warring Parthans to the north and the Mookla'ayan savages to the south. A narrow line to skirt, which promised to be the most harrowing trek he had ever undertaken.

So be it. His true journey had finally begun, and wherever its path led, he was determined to see it through, regardless of those perils to be encountered along the way.

Xarius Talyzar knelt upon the forest earth, perfectly balanced and ready to defend himself, even crouched as he was upon one knee. His dogs were where he had left them, huddled somewhere back in the trees. He had not wanted their presence to jeopardize his investigation, now that he was closing in on the kill.

He was surprised, actually, that one of the wizard's mercenary soldiers had not yet tried to eliminate him. Fear only went so far when it came to keeping subordinates in line.

Eventually, that fear would lead to desperation. A knife as he slept, perhaps, or an arrow in the back. Thus, even now, alone in a tranquil woodland, the assassin was fully aware of every sight, sound, and scent around him.

The campsite was deserted. He had made sure of that much before he had crept into the open. But a campsite it was. The brush was matted and torn. Separate tree trunks bore the light scrapes of tether lines. Here, a small fire pit was marked by blackened earth and a makeshift ring of stones. The remains of roasted fowl lay scattered nearby, feathers and bones and cooking-related discards. Of interest to the assassin, however, was not what his quarry had eaten, but when.

He held his hand over the fire pit, then jammed a gloved finger into the pile of ashes. Deep down, it was still warm, the once-bright coals simmering in recent death. He sifted through them while making a final survey of the overall site. Locating the trail of departure, he rose to take his leave.

This hunt was coming to an end. Tonight.

The companions from Diln took their time that day, keeping alert for any sign of unwanted attention. The forest was quiet, a refuge showing no sign of man's invasive presence. There were no trails, so Jarom and Allion forged their own, pushing through the shadowed undergrowth. A profusion of life surrounded them, woodland creatures large and small seen flitting from limb to limb, skittering along trunks and branches, or burrowing beneath the lush vegetation. Apparently curious, the animals and insects ushered the companions at all times, though they were heard more often than seen, and did nothing to disturb the pair's progress.

By late afternoon, they had forded the western fork of the Emerald River and found themselves in a more aged region of the forest. Here, shrubs and hardwoods gave way to a proliferation of fir and spruce, towering giants that stretched skyward in fierce competition, in a race to touch the sun. The thickening shadows cast by interwoven branches and leaves covered nearly every inch of ground, lowering the temperature. Shallow roots bulged and stretched in all directions, and cones and needles lay scattered upon mosses and ferns like a child's crumbs. A potpourri of rich scents seasoned the air, the smell of spores and pitch and woodland decay.

Despite their leisurely pace, the pair had covered several leagues by twilight, when sunset transformed the sky above into a blazing dome of color, then left it to the cool darkness of nightfall. Having started out late that morning, and still feeling well rested, the friends agreed to press on despite the lengthening hour. They traveled well into the night, until they came upon the eastern fork of the mighty Emerald. Deciding to put off a crossing of the chilly waters until the warmth of daylight, they stopped for the evening. They located a glade beside the rushing river, larger and clearer than the one they had occupied the previous night, and resolved to enjoy a pleasant rest beneath the hidden stars.

"I'll make a fire," Jarom announced almost as soon as he had dismounted. "You go catch us some dinner."

Allion nodded. Stringing his bow, he disappeared into the woods before Jarom knew he had gone.

Xarius Talyzar peered intently into the night, his eyes glimmering with anticipation. A fire illuminated the clearing that lay just ahead through a copse of trees, revealing a lone figure bending to add fuel to the flame. The figure's companion was nowhere in sight. The assassin frowned. Should he wait? He had been traveling for five days now, riding quickly enough to gain three days on his quarry. From the time he had rediscovered Jarom's trail in the northern Aspandels, when he had thought himself only a day behind, it had taken him two full days to finally reach his goal. The dawn would mark a full eight days since Jarom had set out from his forest home. The assassin's patience was all but used up.

At the same time, he had no way of knowing which man was standing before him, Jarom or Allion. The only sure way would be to capture both, and snatching one might alert the other.

The assassin weighed his options. That the wizard wished for Torin to be delivered alive complicated matters. Xarius didn't care for confrontations in which his hands were tied. One of the easiest mistakes for a young assassin to make was to pick a fight with a man whose combat skills were unknown, and whom he was not allowed to kill. Such was the situation here. Although he considered them to be unreliable allies at best, perhaps it was time to put the wizard's soldiers to the test. And that only widened the range of potential outcomes.

Within moments, Xarius had made his decision.

Leaving their steeds behind, the mercenaries quietly encircled the glade, following the assassin's instructions. Xarius watched them through the concealing wall of brush, sensing their progress, allowing them the time they needed to secure their positions. When content that all was set, he strode into the camp to greet his victim.

The young man—Jarom or Allion—was gathering firewood, his back to the assassin. Xarius did nothing to alert him, allowing him to continue. It would be harder for him to draw a blade with his hands already full. The assassin paused beside the campfire, waiting for the other to turn. When finally he swung about with his armload of branches, the young man gasped.

"Are you the one called Torin, prince of Alson?"

For a moment, the young man gaped at him. "Who are you?" he inquired guardedly. It was difficult to tell which startled him more, the assassin's knowledge or his mere appearance.

Then the soldiers were upon him, bursting from the surrounding thicket. Eyes wide, the victim dropped his bundle and fumbled for his sword. But before he had the chance to draw his weapon, he was beaten face-first to the ground, where he kicked and struggled while his hands were bound painfully behind his back.

The assassin stepped forward, kneeling beside his captive. "Your name."

The young man spat dirt from his mouth, thrashing against his assailants' hold.

Xarius placed a booted foot upon the other's throat. He produced a dagger whose polish reflected the firelight, and stabbed its tip into the flesh atop of the young man's left cheekbone. "If I ask again, you lose an eye."

"Jarom!" the man wheezed, his struggles all but ceased. "I don't know anyone named Torin!"

"And where is your friend?"

"I travel alone," Jarom grunted. "Who in the Abyss do you think you are?"

Xarius dismissed the retort. He stood, watching a trickle of blood spill from his victim's face. Jarom. Torin. Whatever he called himself, the young prince was his. The assassin's quest was finished, it seemed. The wizard had made no mention concerning any of the young man's companions. And since Allion had not been here to witness Jarom's abduction, there was no real sense in seeking him out.

Or was there? First, the assassin didn't like the idea of leaving anyone alive who might find cause to give chase as he headed back to Krynwall. And second, this hunt had been too long for Xarius to settle for such a swift and easy end. The assassin hungered for sport, which could only be provided now by the missing half of the duo. The wizard might not care for the time wasted to seek the other out, but how was he to know?

He would know, the assassin quickly corrected himself. He was a wizard after all, a genuine magic-user not to be trusted. Nor were his soldiers, who were sure to deliver their own report of the hunt when this business was finished—unless the assassin took it upon himself to slay them all, which would again require a greater amount of explaining than he wished to provide. Whatever his actions, he needed a legitimate reason for them.

Xarius looked down at Jarom. The man denied even having a companion, which the assassin knew to be false. As he reconsidered the lie, Xarius smirked within the shadow of his cowl. In truth, he had no way of knowing this man was Jarom. He believed him to be, but it might be Allion, lying in order to protect his friend, and it wouldn't pay to wait until returning to Krynwall to discover the deception.

But why spend his time tracking the other down? Clearly, there existed some degree of loyalty between the two. And if he was to believe that, then the assassin could rest assured that Jarom's friend would be along soon. Rather than race back to Krynwall, fighting to stay ahead of any pursuit, Xarius would go at his own pace, waiting for the man to catch up with them.

"Silence him."

The soldiers obeyed, producing a gag, which they lashed into Jarom's mouth against only a single, moderate protest. With a wave of his hand, the assassin then slid from the clearing. His dogs followed, hauling Jarom after.

CHAPTER FOURTEEN

Allion trudged through the tangle of undergrowth that hugged the forest floor, mindful of the roots and vines that sought to trip him up. He led his mount afoot, its bridle become a halter. Dragging behind was the carcass of a young elk, packed with more meat than he and Jarom would be able to eat before it spoiled. Though not one to waste such an animal, the hunter and his friend needed something more sustaining than roots and berries if they were to continue on this mad quest, and he'd had little choice but to take what the forest offered. It was cool enough within the shaded woodland that with the proper salts, they could dry and preserve enough meat to last them several days. That which would not keep would be left to the forest scavengers.

Despite the lunacy that had caused him to agree to this course, and the folly that kept him on it, the hunter found himself in good spirits. There was something refreshing about trekking through an unknown wilderness, where survival depended upon little more than his training and instincts. For whatever reason, he felt better tonight than he had in days, less anxious and more alive, and although he couldn't justify the feeling, he knew himself well enough to trust and accept it.

Whistling cheerfully, he continued to guide his horse and its heavy load through the brush, marching back along the narrow animal trail that had led to his kill. Starlight filtered down through woodland rafters, a pale wash that staved off the utter darkness. Though he couldn't see it beyond the screen of trees, the river was a constant and reassuring presence marked by a steady growl of rushing waters. Moments later, as he looked up from his path, he made out a flicker of light amid the forest tangle, a sure sign of the clearing in which Jarom waited with a roasting fire. Hastening his pace, Allion angled toward it.

He broke through the clearing wall with a triumphant shout, gesturing proudly at the elk carcass as it was hauled into view.

"I hope you're hungry, my friend, 'cause I—"

The figure waiting beside the fire glanced up. Allion froze, his smile forgotten. Whoever was tending the flames was not Jarom. After a sweeping glance, the hunter slipped his bow from his shoulder while reaching for an arrow.

Before he could complete the movement, a hurtling stone struck the arrow from his grasp, leaving him to gape in astonishment at the stranger before him.

"Now, now," the other chided, seemingly unconcerned by the exchange, "if'n ya want to see your friend again, you'd best get to know me 'fore ya go sticking me full o' arrows."

As he shook the pain from his fingers, Allion glared at the suspicious figure, but made no further threat on his life. The stranger, wrapped in a greenish-gray cloak, sat back confidently against the trunk of a giant fir, unmoving. Finally, after a time in which he seemed to be measuring the hunter's response, he lifted his hands to draw back his cowl, revealing a slender, sun-browned face. Dirt-blond hair ran an unruly course about his head and shoulders, while plain brown eyes found Allion's, glinting with amusement as they awaited the archer's reaction.

Allion was stunned. This was a mere boy! He couldn't be more than sixteen years old, yet he had just taken a stone and . . . The archer had to fight back a sudden urge to send a bolt hurtling through the lad's smug face. He dared not. Not after their initial exchange, and not until he had learned something more about what was happening here.

"Nice beast ya gots there. Might I share it with ya?"

Allion could scarcely believe his ears. Who did this lad think he was? "Where's Jarom?" he demanded.

"Jarom? Ah, yes, your friend. They made off with him just a bit ago."

"Who?"

The youth shrugged. "Don't know yet. Figured I'd learn more 'bout the whole mess 'fore I did anything rash."

"Then how do you know he was taken?"

"I stumbled 'cross a pair o' soldiers over there," the boy revealed, nodding toward a small thicket across the glade. Allion followed the youth's glance, but could see nothing of interest. "They was waiting for ya. Said they had orders to take ya to where they have your friend."

Allion considered the claim with a suspicious glare, trying to piece it all together. Obviously, whoever the youth was referring to was not there now. "And who are you, if not one of them, that they should share this information?"

"Who I am had little to do with it," the youth admitted. "I had to kill one and threaten to cut the other's tongue out."

Allion glanced anew at the thicket the lad had indicated, his interest piqued. "What did you do with the one who spoke?"

"Killed him. Left him his tongue, though. You're welcome to go over and takes a look."

Allion shook his head. "Which way did they go?" he asked instead, anxious to rid himself of the brash youth and set out after his friend.

"Ya know, ya seem to have more questions than answers," the lad observed. "I'd hoped you'd be able to tell *me* a thing or two."

"Which way?" Allion repeated.

"West. But from what I was told, there's fourteen o' them, give or take the two I killed. Either way, you're not going to defeat a dozen armed men with a single bow."

Allion's first reflex was to show the impertinent youth just how deadly his bow was, but he managed to wade past the taunt to find the admonition in the lad's words. The boy spoke truthfully—if indeed he spoke any truth at all.

"I'd be willing to help ya, however, if'n you'd promise me some o' that meat when we gets back."

"And why should I trust you?"

The youth chuckled. " 'Cause if'n I was interested in killing you or your friend, you'd both be dead already."

Allion's scowl deepened. By all appearances, the lad was serious in his claim.

"So? What do ya say?"

"I say I'm not wasting any more time," the hunter growled. "I'd appreciate your help, and can only hope you're half as good as you think you are."

The youth grinned and hopped soundlessly to his feet, a motion so quick and effortless that it caused Allion to rock back on his heels in reflex.

"Kylac Kronus," the youth offered, "a mere sojourner by trade. Pleased to make your acquaintance, Sir . . ."

"Allion," the hunter replied, suddenly unsure of himself.

Kylac's smile was encouraging. "Let's have some fun, shall we?"

Together, the newly formed duo slipped from the campsite, following the trail that a large company had left behind just a short while ago and that its members had made no effort to hide. They traveled beneath a blanket of silence, having left Allion's mount behind, and the hunter, who had always been proud of his capacity for stealth, found himself awestruck by that of the impudent youth. It seemed to him that his own shadow rustled more leaves, snapped more twigs, and pressed more needles than Kylac's physical form. Further astonishing was the fact that the boy would disappear entirely if he drew more than a few paces ahead, his green-gray cloak blending into the foliage about him like the skin of a chameleon.

They had not traveled far before Kylac motioned for Allion to be still. The man obeyed, peering through the tangle. No more than twenty paces from their position stood a man armored in black chain mail, spit-polishing a nasty, four-finned cudgel. Allion turned his attention back to where Kylac had crouched beside him, but found the undisturbed leaves of a sword fern to be his only companion. The hunter started, certain he had been betrayed. He cast about quickly, anxiously, seeking escape. In the next moment, his gaze fell upon the oblivious mercenary once again, who buckled suddenly to his knees, blood pulsing from his throat. With rapidly mounting respect, Allion watched as Kylac laid the corpse silently upon the earth and, in the next moment, was crouched once again beside him. The boy said nothing, but grinned roguishly as he used a small black cloth to wipe the blood from his slender shortsword.

Allion turned away in order to conceal an impressed smile. When he did so, he spied a second sentry off to his right some thirty paces. Instead of waiting to be dazzled further by the youth, he drew an arrow and nocked it to his bowstring.

"No!" Kylac hissed as he realized Allion's intent.

But there was no stopping the arrow as it leapt from the archer's bow. With a subtle thwack, it lanced into the victim's neck, lodging in his windpipe. His only scream was a muffled gargle as he fell to the earth. Allion turned to face Kylac and smiled in spite of himself when the boy nodded deferentially.

In similar fashion, the two circled the area and dispatched the four remaining members of the watch. By the time they had completed the perimeter slaughter, each had acquired a respect for the other. Kylac had never met anyone whose proficiency with a bow was as precise and accurate as Allion's, as the archer learned when at one point the boy asked the man to teach him this skill. Allion, on the other hand, observed Kylac's work with avid enthusiasm. The youth was an instrument of flawless precision. Not once could his movements be traced as he slithered off time and again to escort another man to the eternal afterlife. His agility and dexterity were uncanny, beyond belief had Allion not witnessed them firsthand, and the hunter yearned to learn these ways.

But first, he would rescue Jarom.

With its ring of defense decimated, the camp of the unknown enemy lay open, and the two companions slipped in unmolested. Seven more soldiers slept around a dying fire. Their horses were tethered in a line nearby. Upon inspection, Allion found Jarom's steed among them. His friend, however, was nowhere in sight.

"Jarom?" Allion whispered despairingly.

Kylac shrugged, then pointed to the circle of slumbering mercenaries. He didn't know, but he knew whom to ask.

Allion continued to glance about, a strange warning twisting in his gut, then followed Kylac. After twirling his rapier-thin shortsword in the air, the youth flashed Allion a playful smile and bent to his task. But as he leaned over his first victim, he had to dance back to narrowly miss the gleaming tip of the sleeping soldier's swinging broadsword.

"Damned assassin!" the soldier bellowed. "I knew we couldn't trust you!"

The man leapt to his feet, then paused in bewilderment as he gazed upon his assailant. Kylac, meanwhile, had flung his cloak from his frame and now faced his opponent with a sparkle in his eye. He wore loosely fitting breeches and shirt, their color matching that of his discarded cloak. A longsword appeared in his right hand to complement the shortsword gripped in his left. Both were of the same exotic fashion, slender and slightly curved with an odd, disc-shaped crosspiece.

The soldier overcame his initial surprise, charging forward behind the tip of his blade. Kylac sidestepped the thrust at the last moment, spinning about with his own weapons. Once, twice, as quick as raindrops, the blades bit through the links of armor as easily as they would bare flesh, the long blade finding the man's heart from behind. The soldier gaped in confusion when his legs gave way beneath him as he turned to face his slippery opponent. His corpse was already cooling by the time Kylac spun to greet the remaining six soldiers, who were scrambling for their weapons.

"Behind me!" he ordered sharply.

Without quite knowing why, Allion obeyed. One boy against six men? Nevertheless, he positioned himself safely behind the young warrior and loaded his bow, thinking to get off a couple of shots before—

The soldiers, having oriented themselves, wasted no time in pressing the attack. These were experienced men, and charged as one—three broadswords, two pikes, and an axe readied to take the boy's life. But Kylac held his ground, eyeing the two pikemen, and before he took his first step in retreat, a pair of fluid motions left both men down. Again, the protective armor did nothing to deflect the boy's blades, nor to discourage the youth from his task.

Back Kylac danced, then forward again, his motions a blur. The blades slashed upward, whirring relentlessly. Two more men fell and another howled as he watched his weapon drop to the earth, still clutched by his dismembered hand. The remaining soldier lunged recklessly. Adrenaline lent him new strength as he raised his blade again and again against the skilled youth. Each time it withdrew unstained. Kylac's defenses were perfect. Regardless of the angle from which the soldier attacked, a blade stood ready to slap the encroaching weapon aside, while the other would slip in a playful counter, pricking the man here and there to further fuel his rage. After a time, the man slumped to the ground, gasping for breath and bleeding from a hundred tiny cuts that fed into a rapidly filling pool beneath him.

Kylac turned to face the stunned Allion. "So much for that little threat," he smirked, barely winded.

"Well done," came the whispering response.

Allion spun and had to take a second look to confirm that the shadow contained physical form. The man's black clothes were of the same loose style as Kylac's and rendered him invisible to the oblivious eye. But there he knelt, on the opposite side of the dying fire, crouched over Jarom, who lay securely bound upon his belly. The man was using the tip of a dagger to delicately trace the line of his prisoner's spine. Allion trained his bow upon him.

"Release him, Talyzar," Kylac demanded calmly, his gaze narrowing. Allion did not miss the change in tone and posture. The previously untroubled youth stilled with dour recognition, as though resigning himself to some grim task.

"This is none of your concern, Kronus," the assassin whispered. Retaining Kylac under his watchful gaze, he then addressed Allion. "I've seen your skill, archer, as you dispatched the clods about this camp. If you so much as twitch, your friend here will die."

Allion tensed. Jarom squirmed beneath the assassin's knee, staring at him and shouting. But whatever warning his friend was trying to convey was smothered by the gag

roped tight in his mouth. Allion hesitated, then slowly lowered his bow.

"Fool," the hunter spat. "How do you intend to get away
without your pack of soldiers?"

"On the contrary, I thank you for sparing me the trouble."

"Let him go," Kylac repeated, "and be on your way."

The assassin, Talyzar, never blinked. "These men are
mine, Kronus. It would be better for you if you did not in-
terfere."

Allion glanced from one man to the other. Neither moved.
Neither blinked. By the look and sound of it, these two had
squared off before. Although morbidly curious, Allion
sensed that it was a conflict he would rather not witness.

The hunter's gaze shifted, and his eyes widened in shock.
At some point during the course of his struggles, Jarom had
managed to slip free of the binds that lashed his wrists.
Now, as the assassin and his counterpart faced off, it appeared as though the forgotten Fason was about to try
something foolish.

Jarom! No!

Perhaps the assassin heard Allion's thoughts. More likely,
he simply felt his captive's movement. Or maybe he was
aware of Jarom's state all along. Regardless, the moment
Jarom made a twisting move for the assassin's dagger,
Talyzar responded by shoving that dagger into Jarom's back.
Kylac Kronus, however, seemed to sense the movement as
quickly as the assassin, and launched himself at his opponent in that very moment. Disallowed the time to ensure an
instant kill, Talyzar was forced instead to draw a pair of
rapiers with which to meet Kylac's assault.

"No!" Allion shrieked, raising his bow to strike down the
assassin. But he responded too late. For as the two warriors
clashed, they became entwined in a sadistic dance that left
one fighter indistinguishable from the other.

"No!" he cried again. Thrusting aside his useless weapon,
he turned toward Jarom, who was writhing untended on the
ground and clawing at the knife in his back.

Allion rushed to his friend's side, grimacing at the sight
of the dagger and the man's spasms. "Hold still!"

Hesitating for but an instant, he tore the dagger free. Jarom grunted, his lungs choking on fluid. Allion cut away the gag, but it was too late. Jarom's eyes rolled back in their sockets. His entire body shuddered and went still.

Groping for a pulse, Allion felt his own heart plummet as he bent to examine the wound. Blood oozed freely, filling the hole left in the wake of the dagger's removal. The wound bled slower than he might have expected, but was deep enough to have punctured a lung, perhaps even nicking Jarom's heart from behind. While he might control the surface bleeding, there was no way for him to quell the internal flow.

Dizzy with fear and denial, Allion pressed firmly against the wound, his only thought to prevent the death of his friend.

Within the corner of one eye, a mesmerizing battle raged, one that Allion sensed again to be the renewal of a conflict rather than the inception. Neither warrior seemed to be gaining an advantage. Each seemed as much an instrument as a man, incapable of deviating from his designed purpose. A blur of motion, they pressed each other relentlessly, and as the battle progressed, its fury intensified rather than slackened, as though each clash served as fuel being added to a fire. As the moments passed, those flames drew higher, the dancers settling into a rhythm that only gained momentum as they exchanged a seemingly endless flurry of slashes, parries, and thrusts.

Through enraged eyes, Allion sought to follow the course of the conflict, savoring a vision of Kylac's blades stabbing through the assassin's chest. But he soon gave it up, unable to determine which swords among those in the whirring maelstrom belonged to his companion. He took comfort in knowing that his bow was at the ready. Should the outcome favor the assassin, it would be but a small distraction to put an arrow through the man's skull. Such an act would not save Jarom, but Allion would be damned to the Abyss before he allowed his friend's murderer to go unpunished.

He started to turn away, when suddenly, the battle was over, ended as abruptly as it had begun. Talyzar was on his back, clutching the slim hilt of a shattered rapier. Before he even hit the ground, Kylac was upon him, kicking the remaining weapon from the other's left hand while pointing his longer blade against the assassin's throat.

"You're beaten, Talyzar!" he cried out, his chest heaving in triumph.

"I still breathe," the assassin spat, denying defeat.

Kylac hesitated, as if unsure how to proceed.

"Kill him!" Allion commanded, aghast that the youth had not done so already.

Kylac ignored the outburst, his eyes pinned to the fallen assassin, whose gaze locked with his own. In that instant, a tacit understanding passed between the two. While the youth's features twisted in frustration, the assassin smiled, and a sinister gleam cooled the inferno raging within his eyes.

"Your father would not be pleased," the assassin sneered. "Until next time?"

Kylac frowned. His gaze seemed to pierce the other's body, as though assessing the man's character. Without warning, the blade at the assassin's throat leapt to the man's arm, where it sliced a deep gash from elbow to wrist. Talyzar winced, but did not cry out, and scrambled to his feet while dropping his shattered blade. Kylac stepped back, swords ready.

"When next we meet," Talyzar hissed, his eyes smoldering, "the outcome will not be decided by the strength of a weapon!" He spat this oath as a curse, before vanishing into the trees.

A hastily fired arrow whizzed after him, then another, lancing through the darkness. Allion nocked a third when Kylac wrenched the bow from his trembling hands.

"You let him escape!" Allion howled.

"The damage is done," Kylac reminded him, looking past the hunter to the motionless Jarom. "Is he alive?"

"Less so than that accursed killer," Allion spat, fighting to hold back the tears he felt welling up inside.

Kylac bent to examine the dagger that Allion had plucked from Jarom's bleeding back.

"The blade's likely poisoned," the youth said slowly.

"What?"

"The man knows his business."

Allion quivered, fighting back waves of despair. Poison or no, Jarom's destiny would be decided in the next few minutes.

He put aside his anger to grope for a solution. "What can we do? I can't even stop the bleeding, let alone any poison."

"There's a place nearby," said Kylac. He glanced over at the line of horses. "We must move him, now."

Without pausing to ask questions, Allion rushed to pick out the strongest of the tethered mounts. Kylac worked to plug and wrap Jarom's wound, with an expertise that surprised the hunter. When he had finished, the two of them hoisted the unconscious Jarom onto the broad back of the animal that Allion had selected. The hunter then mounted up behind his friend, while Kylac set the remaining animals loose. He saved one for himself, vaulting into its saddle. With a pair of urgent cries, the two riders bolted from the clearing.

Nearly blind, they raced through the darkness. As best as Allion could tell, they followed no trail, and his fears weighed upon him as heavily as Jarom's limp body hung about the horse's neck. Even now, though, he found himself trusting in the youth. He had to. With both mind and body, he urged his steed onward, following the boy who guided his own steed through the brush with precision and confidence, as if he had traveled this route a thousand times in the past.

But Allion's despair grew worse with each fleeting moment. Before him, Jarom twitched and moaned, slipping in and out of fevered consciousness. Memories filled the hunter's mind, bits of a life in which Jarom had always been there to play a part. The fact that his childhood friend might die didn't seem real. It had all happened too quickly, too unexpectedly. He didn't even know who was behind it. Now, as he tried to imagine what life would be like in his friend's absence, he found that he couldn't do so. And yet, it was happening. Jarom was slipping away. Whether or not he could imagine it would do nothing to prevent it.

Despite his best efforts, he could not seem to keep such

morbid thoughts from the forefront of his mind. So he focused on the figure before him, peering past the whipping branches and clinging brush to stare at Kylac's fleeting form. The youth's cloak billowed behind him, caught in the wind of his passage. Who was this boy? Where had he come from? Why had he chosen to help them? He had not hesitated to kill those soldiers. Why hadn't he slain Talyzar?

The forest opened abruptly, and Allion found himself on the banks of the Emerald River. Kylac did not slow, so neither did he before skidding down the muddy embankment and plunging into the icy waters. The river swallowed him almost immediately, its powerful current bearing him swiftly downstream. He could feel the muscles of his steed flex and bulge as it fought the river's flow, straining for the far shore. Jarom groaned. Allion reached down and seized the man's collar in order to keep his head above water. Ahead of him, Kylac was pulling away, the youth's mount making steady progress while Allion's bucked and snorted against its heavier burden. At once, the hunter realized that the two horses would not make it across anywhere near each other. He could feel his animal losing its strength as they slid steadily downriver. Already, it was beginning to founder, easing into the frigid depths. The waters rushed higher and higher, rising toward Allion's chest. When Jarom's body nearly slipped under, the hunter shrieked a startled cry.

"Kylac! Help!"

The youth whipped his head about, and it was apparent that he too recognized their peril. Turning around once more, Kylac bore down on his mount, urging the beast forward. It seemed the youth was hoping to gain the far bank before throwing him a lifeline. Allion gulped in alarm. The distance between the two would soon become too great to span with any rope. There wasn't time.

He was about to call out again when Kylac appeared to come to the same conclusion. Reaching down, the youth unlashed the coil of rope from his saddle, slipped a loop in one end over his saddle horn, and slid with the remaining length into the churning waters. Swept by the current, the youth swam quickly toward them. It was all Allion could do to hang on, the river growing rapid as they neared one of the many forks that lay in its path to the Nivvian Gulf. In addition, the cold had begun already to work its will upon his numbing limbs, weakening his muscles and slowing their response. By the time Kylac reached him, he had to clench his teeth to halt their chatter.

"Cinch it up!" Kylac yelled above the rush of water.

Allion obeyed, his movements stiff and awkward as he took the free end of Kylac's rope and wrapped it about his failing steed's saddle horn. A moment later, the rope drew taut as the youth's horse continued to swim toward shore at the other end of the makeshift towline. The added measure of strength helped to draw Allion's mount from the murky depths not a moment too soon. Reinvigorated, the animal renewed its struggle. Allion held tight, both to his horse and to his friend's semiconscious form, while Kylac swam beside them. Doggedly, they worked their way across the river, and after what seemed an eternity, Kylac's steed, and then his own, lurched and staggered onto dry land.

Allion stopped, waiting for Kylac to pull himself ashore. The hunter closed his eyes, shivering with cold and exhaustion, then opened them to check on Jarom. He was still moaning—a good sign, as far as Allion was concerned. Quickly, he untied the dripping tow rope and looked to see what had become of Kylac, who was just now dragging himself from the river.

It was then that he saw the creature.

"Behind you!" he cried.

Kylac must have seen his face before he heard the warning, so fast was his response. Standing in knee-deep waters, he whipped about, shortsword in hand as a hooked tentacle reached for him. A reflexive strike swatted the appendage to one side, causing it to recoil. Allion drew a sharp breath and waited for the youth to break for his mount. Rather than scurry away, however, Kylac drew his second sword, waiting to see what it was that had come for them. Although alarmed by the youth's battle-ready stance, Allion could do little more than gawk as the impossible sight emerged before them.

Looming fifteen feet above the surface of the river was the most horrifying beast Allion had ever seen. Thick, slime-coated scales armored an immense, wormlike body. Rows of dark hair scarred the giant torso, lining the mid of its back and neck and cresting its monstrous, lizardlike head. Acid dripped from a tongueless maw into the water below, causing it to hiss and boil. Its nostrils flared, its pointed ears pricked up, and devoid of pupils, its eyes glowed a fiery green. As it reared from the water, four thick tentacles were revealed, each capped with a miniature maw warded by three snapping hooks. Two dragonlike legs hefted the beast into the air with the strength of ancient sequoias, and a short, clubbed tail whipped behind them, creating geysers whenever it struck the water.

Allion blanched. Despite the creature's fully revealed horror, Kylac stood his ground at the river's edge.

"Move!" Kylac ordered him.

The spooked horse needed no urging from its rider to flee the unnatural monstrosity, and thankfully so. For as they lunged up the river's embankment, Allion watched with fear and revulsion as another of the long, tentacled arms lashed out for the animal's driving legs. But just as suddenly, Kylac was there, his blade arcing down with lethal speed and precision, opening a deep gash that squirted black fluid into the water. Wailing in agony, the beast recoiled its injured appendage while Allion gasped in disbelief. The same blade that had pierced chain mail like warm butter had barely scratched this demon! He looked to Kylac, waiting once again for the boy to come scampering up behind him. But the young master swordsman was holding his position as if preparing to fight the thing!

"Run!" Allion screamed as he fought to bring his terrified beast under control.

Kylac whirled to face him, eyes wide with excitement. An eager smile spread across his boyish face.

"Go!" he shouted back. "The road lies east! Follow it south! Tell 'em I sent you!"

Allion started to protest, but Jarom's low moan reminded him of his priorities. Resisting the urge to look back, he turned his mount eastward and plunged into the forest's depths.

Once he had seen Allion disappear safely, Kylac Kronus returned his attention to his enemy. He was too late. Before he could leap out of harm's way, the monster's clubbed tail smashed into him. Wind and weapons flew from him as he sailed backwards to land roughly in a clump of tall grasses. He felt himself reeling, and nearly succumbed to the wave of blackness that crashed over him. As if sensing a swift and easy victory, the creature waded toward him.

Kylac rolled to his feet, drawing another shortsword from his waist. Once again, a hooked tentacle reached out hungrily, groping for the youth. This time, at the last moment, Kylac plunged his blade deep into the center of the snapping hooks, ripping upward as he did so. The creature howled as its blood poured from the wound, and again it reared back protectively. Relentless, Kylac whipped a tiny dagger from his soft boot and hurled it at the demon's head. A sickening pop accompanied the blade's entry into the creature's left eyeball, which burst in a splash of gore.

By the time the blade had slammed home, Kylac was at the water's edge, retrieving his lost weapons and clearing the last of the cobwebs from his head. Confident and controlled, he awaited the beast's next move, reminding himself that he could defeat any opponent driven by blind fury.

He stared intently as the beast stopped its howling to draw a deep breath. An instant later, a thick stream of acid spewed forth. Fortunately for the youth, the creature was off its mark, unused to just one eye, and Kylac was able to leap aside. Where the acid hit, all vegetation swiftly burned away, leaving only a charred patch of lifeless earth.

Undaunted, Kylac's mind raced for a strategy with which to combat this beast. He could not dodge the lethal acid forever. Eventually the demon would adjust its aim, or would simply get lucky, and that would be the end. If he was to have any hope of defeating this creature, he would first have to find a way to neutralize this weapon.

A second sharp intake of breath warned Kylac of another acid attack. Reflexively, the youth whipped a dagger from his belt and hurled it at the beast's throat. The blade buried itself to the hilt just below the creature's mouth. A monstrous bellow deteriorated into a gargled scream as the demon spewed forth acid in an undirected shower. Everything the drops touched sizzled and burned away, including the beast's own filthy hide.

Kylac moved immediately to take advantage of the surprising discovery. As the creature thrashed and howled in unbridled fury, the youth rushed in. At such close range, the demon's breath weapon would be useless, for it could not hope to strike its adversary without harming itself in the process. While this reasoning proved true, it did nothing to hamper the beast's resolve. Summoning every available appendage, the monster thrashed recklessly, bent on smashing the life from its assailant.

But Kylac, calling upon every bit of technique and training he had ever learned, had different plans. In an almost artistic fashion, he danced nimbly about the beast, his weapons whirring and stabbing with deadly precision while he ducked and dodged his way around the flailing tentacles, snapping jaws, and slashing tail. Kicking forth mud and froth at the river's edge, the youth became a human tempest, slipping, sliding, hacking, diving—using any and all means to bring his opponent down.

Within moments, the tarlike blood oozed from a myriad of wounds, and while the demon's assaults began to slow and become less intense, Kylac's dance gained momentum and vigor. At last, with a triumphant shout, he launched his longsword deep into a gash he had struck several times, severing the club from its tail. The demon reared back, but without its tail for support, toppled over into the bloodstained river. As soon as it struck the water, Kylac was upon it, thrusting his blades deep into its neck. The foul blood sprayed like geysers, and Kylac leapt back to avoid its touch, watching from a safe distance the creature's sickening convulsions. It tried to rise, but its strength had deserted it. Before long, its death throes ceased, and only its twitching tentacles gave any indication that it had once lived.

For a moment after, Kylac Kronus knelt at the bank of the river, observing the waters that lapped at the motionless demon. The adrenaline seeped from his veins, and a sudden shiver raced through him, rattling his bones like those of a wooden puppet. Moonlight washed down from the heavens, pouring through the gap in the forest carved by the river's passage. Its dim radiance cast the already unnatural scene in an eerie light. Where in the Abyss had such a creature come from? he wondered. And what was it doing here in the Emerald?

It was then, without warning, that the water about the body began to churn and boil, and Kylac realized that the corpse was sinking into the river! With the fluidity of one of the river's own currents, the youth waded out to the beast's head and yanked his daggers from its throat and eye, just before they vanished beneath the rushing waters.

The last thing he witnessed before it winked away was the pale red glow emanating from its remaining eye.

CHAPTER FIFTEEN

Jarom felt his eyelids crack and flutter before they opened anew to the world of men. A bright light greeted him, forcing him to squint until his sight could adjust. When it did, he assumed for a moment that he was dead. This was not the world he knew, but some celestial existence far beyond that of his wildest imaginings.

Hovering over him was one of the most attractive faces he had ever beheld—the countenance of a goddess, or of an avatar at the very least. Crystalline blue eyes gazed upon him affectionately, gleaming against a backdrop of soft white flesh. Curling wisps of golden hair flowed over her head and shoulders and splashed against her back, catching the light in such a way as to shine around the edges. Jarom's eyes traced the delicate curvature of her nose, her jaw, and stared at a pair of lips that were drawn in a teasing smile.

The lips parted, and words poured forth. "Welcome back."

The dulcet tones danced in Jarom's ears like the sweetest birdsong. He felt her light touch upon his chest and his heart fluttered with longing. He sat up, but as he did so, a sharp pain stabbed at him from behind, lancing up and down his spine. He fell back.

"Careful," the voice said while tender hands eased him into a lying position. "You're in no condition to be up and about."

Jarom grimaced, eyes clenched against this harsh reality. After a moment, the pain subsided until only a dull throb remained, centered beneath his left shoulder blade.

"Your friends have been worried."

All of a sudden, Jarom's memory rushed upon him, inundating his weary mind with forgotten knowledge. His identity . . . his quest . . . his abduction . . . his struggle against the black-garbed man . . .

"Where am I?" he asked slowly. His own voice was dry and hoarse, grating against his ears.

"You're in the Lewellyn community of Feverroot," the woman replied, "in the home of Master Nimbrus himself."

Jarom's brow furrowed in puzzlement. Lewellyn. Feverroot. Nimbrus. None of these names were familiar to him. The woman recognized his confusion, and did not seem surprised.

"Not many know of us," she explained, bringing a cup of foul-smelling broth to his lips. "We're a reclusive group, dedicated more to the study of healing than the commercial practice of it." She tipped the cup, and he sipped at its contents. "You're fortunate you ran into Kylac."

Jarom swallowed the liquid. It tasted worse than it smelled.

"Kylac?"

"A dear friend of the Lewellyns. He found your companion and guided you both here after you were wounded. But then, they can tell you more about that than I."

She placed the empty cup upon a small wooden table beside Jarom's bed, then rose and slipped gracefully toward the door.

"I'll get your friends," she offered. "They'll be excited to see you."

"Wait."

The woman paused, turning to face him.

"Who are you?" he asked, embarrassed by her accommodating manner.

"Marisha Valour, apprentice Lewellyn."

"Did you heal me?"

"No," she replied quickly, dismissing the question with a lilting laugh. "I'm merely an apprentice. Your wound demanded the attention of the most skilled healers in Feverroot, and even then, we were all left holding our breath for a while." She smiled comfortingly at him. "You gave us quite a scare, but you'll be fine now if you just relax and get some rest."

Jarom nodded, and Marisha exited, leaving him to gather his thoughts. Strange, but he had no awareness of the time of which Marisha spoke, the time in which his healing had taken place. His last clear memory was of the showdown in the forest, when he had tried to warn Allion to flee, and when he had made his own desperate attempt to secure their escape. How long had it been? Hours? Days? Regardless, it seemed he should have some knowledge of the time in between. All he had were fragmented dreams, disorienting recollections of pain and strife. He remembered a sensation of drowning, as well as alternating feelings of burning warmth and frigid cold. If he had nearly left this world, where had he gone? And either way, why couldn't he remember?

Frustrated by these musings, Jarom chased them away. Whatever had happened, he was alive now, aware of himself and his surroundings once more. Better to concentrate on that than on questions that could not be answered.

His eyes shifted. The room in which he found himself was quaint—small yet cozy, clean and polished. The walls reminded him of those that had sheltered him back home. They supported a slanted ceiling of lacquered wood slats—a reflection of the floor below. His bed lay in a corner, next to an open window through which the now comforting sunlight streamed. This and the table beside it were the room's only furnishings.

A breeze pushed its way through the window, rustling the curtains and bearing with it the scents of pine and juniper. Somewhere among the trees, a bird twittered. Jarom eased his hands up behind his neck, locking his fingers to keep them in place. All in all, it was as pleasant a setting as he could imagine. If he couldn't be at home, he suspected that this was perhaps the next best thing.

A knock drew his attention from the window and to the door. It burst open, and Allion strode into the room, an exuberant smile splayed across his face. Behind him, with a relaxed grin and a gleam in his eye, strolled the young stranger who had accompanied Allion during their attempt to rescue him from the enemy soldiers.

"Well, well, it's about time!" Allion greeted. He reached out, clasping the hand that Jarom offered in return, and shook it vigorously. Jarom winced at the other's enthusiasm.

"I thought you'd be halfway home by now."

"Just waiting to see whether or not I was going to have to bury you first," the other responded, smiling.

A moment passed before Allion introduced his companion, whom he seemed to remember suddenly. "Oh, Jarom, this is Kylac Kronus."

Now that he looked more closely, Jarom found the youth strangely familiar, as if he already knew him from somewhere. Though it didn't seem right, he brushed the feeling aside as a residual memory from that night in the forest. When Jarom continued to stare at the tanned face and wild hair, the youth winked in acknowledgment.

"I hear I owe you my life," Jarom said finally.

"Nonsense. I's gots my hands full looking after my own."

Jarom grinned inwardly at the unassuming response, and found himself liking the young adventurer immediately.

"Interesting accent," he noted. "Where are you from?"

"Here and there." Kylac shrugged.

Allion interrupted them then, seemingly unable to contain himself. "I've a lot to tell you," he beamed, pushing aside the cup and a vase of flowers in order to seat himself upon the bedside table. "You feeling well enough to talk? Or at least listen for a while?"

"Fine," Jarom assured him.

"You ought to be," Allion teased, "with all the constant nursing you've received this past week."

"What?" Jarom gasped, suddenly alarmed. "A week?"

"Five days," Allion amended, as if that should appease him.

"Five days?"

"Now, don't go getting all riled up about it," his friend scolded. "There isn't a thing you can do now but to get well as soon as possible, which won't happen if you start fretting over lost time."

"But Alson—"

"May belong entirely to the wizard by now," Allion finished for him, "and there's nothing we can do to change that. Anyway, by all reports, our lands are safe, for the moment. It seems the barons are holding their own. Either that or the wizard has chosen to cool his heels. Regardless, we've heard nothing to indicate that the greater portion of Alson has been overrun."

Jarom continued to protest silently. Five days? How could he have lost five days without even realizing it? Although he didn't know exactly where he was, he suspected that five days would have been enough time to finish trekking through the Kalmira, perhaps even to have reached the Skullmars. Regardless, given the current state of affairs, he didn't have time to waste. Five days!

He leaned upward, but stopped himself halfway, reminded by a spasm of pain what the price would be for doing so. Allion was right. As angry and sick as it made him to admit it, he was helpless in his present condition. His eyes fell upon Kylac, who had not shifted in his stance or changed the easygoing expression that he wore. A sudden question entered Jarom's mind, and he looked back to Allion, who recognized his concern and answered it aloud.

"There's no reason to hide anything from him or anyone else here," he said. "Everyone knows who you are and what our quest is. Although it's only fair to warn you, they all think you're as mad as I do. Even Kylac, though he's offered to go with us."

"Man owes me an elk," the youth added, as if no other explanation were necessary.

Jarom's scowl only deepened. He wasn't pleased that Allion had decided to share everything there was to know about him with a bunch of strangers. Then again, he hadn't been there, so he had no idea as to what may have prompted the man to do so. In any case, once again, he was helpless to change matters. Rather than waste energy fighting the results of a lost battle, he might as well accept them and move on.

"What other good news do you have for me?" he groaned.

Allion paused, as though unsure where to begin. "Well, to

start with, I thought we should discuss the night you were stabbed."

Jarom nodded, surprised that the topic hadn't entered his mind from the first. There was indeed a lot that he wished to know, not only in regards to what had happened, but also why.

Off Jarom's look, Allion proceeded to relate the events of that ill-fated evening, now six nights past. He began with the surprise encounter with Kylac in the riverside glade and wrapped up with their arrival at Feverroot. The assassin's dagger, as it turned out, had not been poisoned, and Allion did not refrain from telling his friend that had it been otherwise, they would not be here discussing the matter with him now.

Kylac remained silent until the time came to speak of the river monster. Even then, he tried to shrug the matter aside as just another confrontation with one of nature's more ferocious denizens. At Allion's urging, however, the youth finally delivered a full account of the struggle, sharing with Jarom all of the twists and turns of battle as they had unfolded. As incredible as the story seemed, Jarom drank up every word. Though he could scarcely imagine such a beast or the skills required to defeat it, he found himself in awe of the courage and prowess this boy claimed to possess. Despite the inherent horror of the incident, he wished he had been there to see it.

"It seems to me," Allion said, cutting in, "that the wizard must have heard of you, and that the soldiers and creatures that we've encountered were sent by him."

Jarom nodded slowly. He had already come to the same conclusion, based on the fact that the uniforms of his attackers matched those of the soldiers he had fought back in Diln.

"But how?" he wondered aloud. "How could the wizard have learned . . ." He trailed off, his thoughts and suspicions clicking into place. "Ellebe."

"What?"

"Ellebe. My father said that Queen Ellebe was returning to Krynwall. The man who attacked me, this assassin, knew me as Torin. As far as I know, Ellebe's the only one, other than the Elders, who knows the truth." A sudden fear constricted his throat. He forced a deep breath in order to continue. "Allion, if they tracked me, they might have made their way through Diln."

Allion waved both hands in a placating motion, as though trying to put Jarom at ease. "There are many ways in which the wizard might have discovered the truth. Anyway, the Lewellyns were kind enough to send a courier west to see what they could learn. Your father is wise and resourceful. I'm sure he and the others are fine."

Allion's response was encouraging, but Jarom could tell by looking into his friend's eyes that he too was worried for their home, their families, their friends.

Jarom's head spun. The mere thought of his existence having endangered the peaceful folk of his home village was more than he could bear. Had he been able, he might have lurched from the sheets then and there and begun making his way back, crawling if he had to. If the wizard's forces had been through there . . . He shook his head. He was assuming too much. What was he to do, race back and deliver himself straight into the wizard's hands? If it would save even a single soul, then yes. But there was just too much he didn't know. Before he did anything, he should wait for the courier's report. Bedridden as he was, did he have any choice?

"Anyway, things have been quiet since. It may be that after dealing with Kylac here, he's lost interest."

"Why would he bother?" Jarom asked finally, his mind still sorting through the myriad ramifications of Allion's suggestion that the wizard was after him. "I'm no threat to him."

"Not yet," Allion agreed, "but there's a chance that you soon will be."

"He doesn't know that."

"We can only guess as to what he does or doesn't know, Jarom. And we have no idea whatsoever as to how he might feel about it."

Jarom heaved a sigh of frustration. Once again, his friend was right, and he shuddered inwardly at the thought of being hunted by a man whose minions included the likes of that demon wolf, that river creature, that assassin . . .

"What about the assassin?" Jarom blurted. He turned his gaze so that the question was directed at Kylac. "Why didn't you kill him?"

Allion frowned, giving Jarom the impression that the hunter and youth had already had this discussion, and that his friend had been less than pleased with the result.

Kylac hesitated, as though determining how much he wished to share. "Xarius Talyzar is a product of my father's assassins guild—"

"Assassins *guild*?" Jarom echoed, his surprise evident.

"It's not a guild in the truest sense, but more akin to one than you'd expect. The order has been around for centuries. My father just happens to be the ruling guildmaster."

Jarom glanced at Allion, who shook his head. "You're an assassin, then?" he asked, doing his best to withhold judgment.

"I kill when necessary, but never for money."

"And yet, that's what you were raised to do."

"I's been raised from birth to fight," Kylac corrected. "And I'm better at it than anyone you'll ever meet. But my aims are my own. I serve no man's bidding. Not my father's, no one's."

Jarom nodded slowly, trying to understand. "And Talyzar?"

"Xarius Talyzar was my father's best pupil, his pride and joy. We spent nearly a decade training together, fighting each other, every hour of every day."

"So you were friends."

Kylac laughed. "Hardly. The man—if'n a man he is— cares nothing at all for no one. I was never like that, no matter what my father wanted. Mind ya, I gots no qualms with cutting a villain in two, but I don't believe that a man should profit from another's death. One o' the reasons I left. Set out on my own three years ago, after I'd learned all I could—or at least, all I cared to. Haven't been back since."

Jarom took a moment to digest everything he'd heard so far, then returned to his original question. "So, if you weren't friends, why let him go?"

The youth appeared untroubled by Jarom's scrutiny. "First off, Talyzar is like a spider; he preys on insects. The rest of us are usually well served by the removal o' those Talyzar and folks like him are commissioned to kill."

Jarom squinted. "And?"

"You'll laugh, but since leaving the guild, no one has come close to testing me the way Talyzar once did. He made me into what I am. If'n I was to kill him, I wouldn't know how to measure myself—physically or morally."

Jarom considered the words, thinking he understood, then realizing he didn't. He looked to Allion, who shrugged. "I won't laugh," Jarom decided. "I just hope your choice doesn't cause anyone else unnecessary harm."

Kylac nodded. "Agreed. Rest assured, if'n I ever catch Talyzar troubling someone like yourself again, I'll have more to say about it."

Jarom sighed. "In any case, I'm glad you were there and did what you did for me. If it's ever within my power to repay you—"

"Show him your swords," Allion urged Kylac suddenly.

Jarom flashed the man a puzzled expression.

"His blades. You've got to see them."

Jarom looked back to Kylac, who had silently produced a gleaming weapon about three feet in length. It was obviously a sword, but unlike any Jarom had ever seen before, with a slim blade sharpened on only one side, a makeshift hilt wrapped in cross-threaded leather, and a tiny, disc-shaped crosspiece.

"Interesting," Jarom offered. "Looks kind of flimsy, though."

"Show him," Allion urged the youth, his eyes sparkling with enthusiasm.

Kylac shook his head. "I don't thinks it'd show proper appreciation for what the Lewellyns have done to go hacking their bedposts into firewood."

Jarom regarded the thick bedpost at his feet, then looked to Allion, who frowned in disappointment. "Is he serious?"

Allion grinned. "Absolutely. Those blades of his slice through armor like it's not even there."

"What's it made of?"

"Don't know," Kylac confessed. "And no smith I's asked has been able to tell me."

"Where'd you get them?"

"I found 'em."

"You found them?"

"More than two years ago. In a cove in the northern Skullmars."

"You know what they remind me of?" Allion interjected. "The quills of a saber rat."

Kylac glanced at him, incredulous. "You ever seen a saber rat that big?"

Jarom kept his eye on Kylac. "The northern Skullmars?" he asked, his tone doubtful. "On the coast?"

"That's right."

"But I've always heard that travel up there is impossible."

"So they says. But I's explored for myself places the rest o' ya have only heard about."

Jarom continued to scowl, but lacked any evidence with which to argue the point. "They were just lying around like that? How many were there?"

"Thousands, some the size o' spears. And no, they weren't quite like this when I found 'em. I had to polish 'em up and fashion hilts for 'em. Sharp as sunlight, though. Made me a nice collection o' swords and daggers that I's been wielding ever since. The amazing thing is, I's never even chipped one, never even nicked the edge of a blade."

Jarom studied the weapon. Its flawless appearance seemed to substantiate the youth's claim. Still, Jarom's skepticism shone through his tightly guarded visage.

"Thinks what ya want." Kylac shrugged, slipping the blade into a void within his loose-fitting clothing. "I'll keep these over a broadsword any day."

"What do you think?" Allion pressed Jarom eagerly. "As good as any Crimson Sword, eh?"

"Against a single opponent, perhaps," Jarom conceded. "But one man with an armor-piercing weapon is not going to overthrow an army—or a wizard."

"Then what are you thinking in going after this Sword of Asahiel?"

"Come, Allion, you know the legends. With the power of the Sword—"

"I know, I know," Allion said, waving him off. "I was only trying to see how close you are to having your strength back. By the look of things, we'll be out of here before long."

Jarom let go his harangue with a slow puff of air. "I hope you're right."

Allion nodded, then brightened with yet another recollection. "Oh, here's something else. Remember that scene outside of Earthwyn, where we found the book?"

"How could I forget?" Jarom asked, his interest piqued.

"It seems Kylac was there. The dead horse belonged to an old man who was jumped by some brigands. Kylac helped to dispatch the assailants, then brought the man and his belongings here to have his wounds tended to."

"An Entient?" Jarom could hardly contain his excitement.

"We don't know for sure. But from what Kylac saw of him, he seemed something more than your ordinary man."

"His wound should have killed him," the youth acknowledged. "But he was nearly healed by the time we arrived. Slept the entire way. When he woke, he took to raising a storm 'bout one o' his books missing—the one you found."

"I don't believe it," Jarom huffed. "That would be twice that we've just missed the guy!"

"Entient or no, if'n you're planning to hold on to that book o' his, be expecting a visit from him eventually."

Jarom grinned at the prospect. He had been right all along. An Entient! Then again, Kylac said the man had been angry. If he was still upset by the time he finally caught up to them . . . Jarom recalled an image of the nine charred heaps that he and Allion had discovered within the pine grove south of Earthwyn—heaps of flesh that had once been men with whom the Entient had been displeased. Perhaps running into this legend of a man would not be so pleasant after all.

"Well," Allion sighed after a collective silence, "they asked us not to trouble you for too long. Is there anything I can ask them to get for you?"

"Actually, yes. Now that you mention it, I'm famished."

"Nothing to it," Allion promised, hopping to his feet and turning to follow Kylac to the doorway.

"Allion."

The man swiveled back attentively.

"Thank you. To you and Kylac, to these Lewellyns . . . for everything."

Allion smiled, then strode from the room on the silent heels of the young Kylac Kronus. Once they had gone, Jarom worked to sort through all that he had learned during their brief visit. Before anyone could return with the requested meal, however, he had once again fallen fast asleep to dream peacefully—despite all his many concerns—of a pair of crystalline blue eyes gazing down at him through cascading wisps of gold-tinted hair.

"Where is the boy prince?"

Xarius Talyzar clenched his jaw, biting back no less than a dozen antagonistic responses that scampered through his head. He stood in the wizard's chamber, in the highest room of the man's private tower, come to report his most humiliating defeat. It was a meeting he had put off for nearly two days—and this after he had taken his time returning to the wizard's home city. In the fiery hours following his unlikely encounter with Kylac Kronus, he had thought about setting off after the whelp straightaway. But in the end, reason had prevailed. He could not defeat the youth in his current condition. And he did not dare keep the wizard waiting for as long as it would take to patch himself up and secure a new set of blades worthy of the task. Nevertheless, he had been in no rush to face the wizard with his failure, and had put it off as long as possible.

He wished now that he had put it off just a little longer.

"The lad is likely dead."

"Likely?" The wizard glanced up from his smoking bowl, meeting the assassin's glare at last. Despite his proclivity toward shadow and obscurity, Xarius hated that the wizard disdained to even look at him, as though he was not worthy of the man's full attention.

"I mean to make sure."

"I ask you to return him to me alive. Not only do you fail at that, but you cannot even assure me that he is dead? You disappoint me, assassin."

Xarius bit his tongue, holding his anger and excuses in check. The wizard continued to stare at him as he might a wayward child, then sniffed suddenly.

"You are wounded. Show me."

Xarius hesitated. He was pleased that the wizard seemed genuinely surprised, as though the notion of his prized assassin being fallible had never occurred to him. Nonetheless, it was bad enough having to divulge his failure vocally. He had no desire to share the physical proof.

"Show me!" the wizard repeated, his yellow eyes flashing in the near darkness.

Xarius obeyed, rolling up the sleeve that covered his right arm. He kept his gaze on the wizard, noting the man's reaction as the hideous gash—crudely stitched by a physician who now lay dead in a gutter—was revealed.

The wizard gasped ever so slightly. "Is that not a sight? I did not believe there to be a man alive who could best you."

Xarius dropped his sleeve, covering the inflamed line of scarred flesh. "There isn't."

But the wizard wasn't listening. "Perhaps I have underestimated this upstart brother of mine."

"It wasn't him. He had help, from one of my order."

"One of your order? But I thought you the best of their breed."

"I need but a new blade," the assassin hissed between clenched teeth.

"It will have to wait," the wizard said, waving the issue aside. "I've another matter for you to tend to—a more 'likely' threat, you might say."

For a moment, the assassin's shame was forgotten. "The demons?"

"I need to know if the rumors are true, and if so, the cause."

The assassin nodded. He had heard of little else during his return trip. Across the countryside, word was spreading as to the existence of foul and unnatural creatures, demons and devils, denizens of the Abyss, come to haunt the surface of Pentania. Talk ranged from guarded whispers in homes and taverns to outright proclamations of doom on the city streets. It was a portent, a harbinger of some great evil set to befall them all. Some attributed their appearance to that of the vile magic-user who had so quickly and thoroughly usurped the throne of Alson. Others claimed that there were darker forces at work, forces beyond that of mortal men, while still others dismissed the reports altogether as the latest fireside drivel.

The assassin was skeptical, having encountered no such monsters in the course of his own recent travels. Still, he knew enough about hearsay to understand that more often than not, there was a kernel of truth at its core. Stories this widespread could not be so readily dismissed. Judging by the wizard's reaction, he too understood this. The assassin could reject, then, at least one of the prevailing beliefs. If the wizard was curious about these creatures, then it was unlikely he was responsible for them.

Outwardly, the assassin bowed in acknowledgment of his new orders. Inwardly, he smirked, feeling a little more himself than he had in days. The wizard was more than interested, he was concerned. Why else would he have delayed his conquest? The assassin had learned before ever arriving back at the ghost city of Krynwall that the wizard's forces had stalled, making no move to widen their sphere of influence. Drakmar to the south and Glendon to the north, Palladur to the west and Earthwyn to the east—all lay untouched. Cities of Alson, not those of a fellow kingdom that the wizard might wisely consider inviolable until he was prepared to launch a full-scale assault on their ruling territories. The assassin had wondered why. Now it appeared he knew.

The wizard returned to his bowl, and Xarius Talyzar took his leave. Perhaps he would investigate these matters. Perhaps not. With a commission such as this, he had plenty of time to decide.

Plenty of time to heal.
Plenty of time to plot his revenge.

"Your pardon, my lord, but perhaps Nohr is right—"

"He's an oafish lout!" Satallion cut in sharply. "His only desire is to rule Alson, or to have us all die in the 'glory' of one last battle! I'll not be made a part of his madness!"

"But we cannot hope to defeat the wizard here."

Satallion halted his march down the corridor of his home castle, stopping at one of the floor-length windows that lined the ornamented walls. The portal afforded him an unmolested view of the western grasslands. Through its arched opening, he gazed upon a patchwork of fields and flowers, farmsteads and livestock, all of which stretched unbroken toward the distant coastline, bathed in a reddish hue cast by the setting sun.

After nine full days of preparation following the emergency council at Drakmar, Nohr and his armies had set forth that very morning with the intent to lay siege to Krynwall. Satallion, high lord of Palladur, had received word earlier that afternoon, and still could not believe his fellow baron's stubbornness. It was a fool's errand, one that guaranteed only death and suffering. Thus far, the wizard's forces had made no move to attack either Drakmar or Palladur. Why rush to join a fight that was not yet theirs?

Granted, war had been visited upon Alson. There was no mistaking that. And Satallion was not so naive as to believe that his lands would somehow be able to avoid the continuing conflict. After the same nine days in which Nohr had readied for an assault, Satallion's own armies had done as the high lord had promised; they had been outfitted and assembled and now stood ready to defend his keep. The prospect of having to do so, however, was only slightly more appealing than the proposed siege—a truth that even the high lord was quick to admit again.

"Indeed, Palladur's gates will never hold where Krynwall's gates did not."

"Then what choice do we have?" his advisor pressed. "There remain those among your own council who feel that Krynwall fell only because Sorl was dead and the wizard's forces had the element of surprise. With our help, Baron Nohr might actually succeed in recapturing the city."

Satallion clawed at the perfectly groomed goatee sprouting from his pointed chin, and continued to gaze upon the horizon. He had accomplished much in his life. Under his direction, Palladur had become more than a simple barony. Krynwall's standing had long been degenerating, even before the wizard's arrival. Having grown in strength and status to rival Drakmar, Palladur was poised to lay claim to the monarchy and carry its high lord to the throne of Alson. Now Satallion could feel his grasp slipping, at the pinnacle of his success. If he wasn't careful, he would be left with nothing.

"My lord, if he recaptures Krynwall without our help, the people will make him king."

Satallion grunted. There had to be a way out of this, some means by which to salvage his wealth and position. Nohr was risking too much, willing to throw everything away. If that was what the bleeding fool wanted, so be it. Ascending to the throne would be that much easier if the baron of Drakmar were not around to challenge him. But how was he to make himself king when a more powerful rival had already staked that claim?

"My lord?"

Even as his advisor spoke, Satallion realized the truth. There was one way to survive this war, and one way alone. That he had not considered it earlier made him laugh. The laugh was short-lived, but its residue settled upon his lips in the form of a grin.

"Your pardon, my lord, but I fear I don't see cause for your amusement."

The high lord turned to his advisor, his blood tingling, stirred by the newfound possibility. He placed a hand on the other's robed shoulder. The man stared at him, eyes clouded with disquiet and confusion.

"Fear nothing, my friend. For I know what must be done."

CHAPTER SIXTEEN

The morning after his revival within the Lewellyn community of Feverroot, Jarom found himself in much the same position as before—in bed, with Kylac and Allion hovering
over him. But he was sitting up now, at least, and without a
great deal of pain. How much of this could be attributed to
his body's own healing powers as opposed to the Lewellyns'
pain-relieving brews, he could not be sure. Either way, he
took it as a sign that he was on the mend.

Unlike the day before, he had done most of the talking
this morning, while Allion and Kylac listened attentively.
Although he had been open with both Kylac and the
Lewellyns about their purpose, Allion had done Jarom the
courtesy of withholding most of the details concerning their
quest. The hunter had shared already the improbable truth
concerning Jarom's upbringing, what they had learned from
Queen Ellebe of the wizard's invasion, and Jarom's determination to reclaim the last known Sword of Asahiel, a talisman with which he might be able to fulfill his unlikely
calling as liberator of the peoples of Alson. He had left it to
Jarom, however, to share the specifics of that decision—
namely, what had led him to believe he could, and should.

Jarom was not entirely certain of Allion's motives for
doing so. Whether it was simply because the hunter could
not properly explain his fantasy, or because the other hoped
that he would realize with a fresh telling how ridiculous it all
seemed, he couldn't say. But with Kylac's rapt attention and
Allion looking on, the Fason-turned-reluctant-king went on

to explain to the youth all about Darinor and the legend of the Swords, his yearning since that day to find one, and the recent, recurring dreams that seemed to be prompting him to do so. Combined with the wizard's invasion, the charge he'd been given to raise an army in Alson's defense, the discovery of the Entients' tome, and the lack of a better option, he had fashioned a foolish flight of fancy into a clear and valid resolution.

He had feared the recitation might hamper his resolve, as he attempted to explain the inexplicable. Surprisingly, however, his confidence had been bolstered. Even after his near death, it still seemed right. Despite fresh fears about the safety of his loved ones, he could scarcely imagine turning around. He could do this. He had to do this. The path had already been laid out for him, and nothing else made sense.

Now that he had finished, Jarom waited breathlessly for Kylac's response. In the throes of his narration, he had felt as though he could infect his listeners with his own enthusiasm. He could make them see what it was he saw, understand what it was he understood. But all he received was silence.

Jarom's thoughts raced. Was there something else he should say? Anything else he could do to make them see? He glanced at Allion, who sat with a lopsided smirk on the bedside table, staring at Kylac while waiting for the youth to pass judgment. Kylac sat in a borrowed chair at the foot of the bed, slumped back, his arms crossed before him. His tanned face might have been carved from wood. One half was marked with shadow, while hazy sunlight streaming from the open window lit the other like a midsummer day. Jarom could read nothing from either side.

Just when he thought he might scream from the lack of response, the lovely Marisha came to his rescue. She entered the room with a food tray, upon which was perched a bowl of fresh fruit and a cup of steaming liquid. Jarom looked up to receive her smile, then followed her with his eyes as she scooted Allion aside in order to set the tray upon his table. She did nothing to interrupt, but kept to herself as she stirred herbs from a pouch into the cup. Jarom stared at her profile a moment longer, then shifted his gaze reluctantly back to Kylac.

"That's some tale," the pensive youth offered at last. "Gods, dragons, a weapon with the power to forge a world . . ." He lifted a finger to tap lightly at his lower lip.

Jarom resisted the urge to glance at Marisha. "Are you sure you want to be a part of this?"

"Do ya honestly believe ya can find it?"

Yes, Jarom wanted to say. He had to. For without the Sword, he was nothing, powerless to help those who depended upon him to do so.

Instead, he merely nodded.

"Well then," Kylac said, flashing him a roguish grin, "I wouldn't miss it."

Marisha came forward then, blowing gently at the steam wafting from Jarom's cup.

"All right, boys. That's enough for now. He'll be up and chasing monsters with you soon enough."

She leaned over, handing Jarom the cup. Jarom took it, his fingers brushing lightly against hers during the exchange.

"Thank you."

"You're welcome," she said with a smile.

When she continued to stare at him, Jarom became suddenly self-conscious, and glanced over her shoulder at his departing friends. As they made their way from the room, whispering among themselves, both Allion and Kylac looked back, teasing him with a pair of knowing smirks.

Jarom flushed. Mercifully, Marisha had turned away and had apparently missed the unspoken banter. The young man took a quick sip of his drink as Marisha turned back to him, the bowl of fruit in hand.

"Are they done making faces at my expense?"

Jarom nearly choked. Marisha merely smiled.

"Don't be embarrassed," she said. "Kylac's forever trying to find a nice man for me to fall in love with. Hungry?"

Jarom coughed, then nodded. Ignoring the chair vacated by Kylac, Marisha sat upon the side of his bed. Using her fingers, she pulled a piece of melon from the bowl, which Jarom opened his mouth to accept.

After swallowing it down, he asked, "And that doesn't interest you?"

"Perhaps. Someday, when I have more time. My studies here are consuming." She fed him another piece of fruit. "And you?"

"I suppose I too am rather busy for that."

She smirked, causing Jarom to wonder if that wasn't what she had meant. "This Crimson Sword," she said, "what makes you think you can find it?"

Jarom frowned. "Because I have no choice."

"You believe in it that strongly?"

"You must think I'm foolish," he said, looking away.

"Everyone else does," she reminded him. "But that doesn't matter to you, does it?"

"No," he realized. His gaze found hers once more, and he was surprised by what he saw. Curiosity? Need?

She lowered her eyes to the fruit bowl. When she came back up with another slice, the strange look was gone. "I find that admirable," she admitted.

Jarom searched her face for signs of jest. After all, the woman had a way of keeping him off balance. Though he wanted to believe her, he wasn't sure that he could.

Nevertheless, as he gulped down a bite of melon, Jarom decided that perhaps he should not try to mend too quickly.

Nevik trudged wearily through the lines of tents and scattered bedrolls, boots sloshing and sliding on the sodden, trampled earth. As he passed the physicians' tents, moans of the dying echoed throughout the chill evening air, an ominous chord droning in his ears and hovering over the exhausted encampment. A shelf of clouds hung low in the sky, a ledge threatening to crumble and descend.

This had been but the fourth day of Drakmar's siege against Krynwall, and already, Nohr's army was losing heart. After all this time, they had yet to glimpse any sign of the wizard whom they had come to kill, giving Nevik and those with him cause for increasing concern. What was the vile conqueror waiting for? Why was he allowing them to

sever his city from the outside world? Was he even here, or
were they wasting time and effort while he was off ravaging
their defenseless homes?

Much of this frustration, Nevik sensed, stemmed from
unexpected inactivity. Nohr's troops had marched with a
cold determination in their hearts and a half-crazed gleam
in their eyes, anticipating battle such as they had never
seen. But thus far, there had been very little actual fighting.
Despite being the aggressor, the army of Drakmar had taken
no offensive against the wizard's forces penned within the
walls of the city. For the moment, Nohr was content to cut
off supply lines, allowing time for his troops to build additional siege engines and for any help that might be on its
way to arrive. Meanwhile, the enemy had barely taken notice of their presence, seemingly unconcerned with the
army encamped at its doorstep. Small skirmishes had broken out on occasion when the enemy had decided to relieve
its boredom with live sessions of archery practice, but aside
from these short-lived forays and Drakmar's ongoing
preparations, all was quiet. After four days, the anxiety had
begun to gnaw at the brave men of Drakmar, and its effects
were starting to show.

Nevik continued to stroll among his comrades, head bowed
beneath the weight of leaden skies and the dark shadow cast by
Krynwall's blackened battlements. He offered and received little more than grunts and nods from his fellow soldiers, who
huddled around their fires, cloaks pulled tight against the wind
and the rain. Wishing he could think of an encouraging word to
share with them, he plodded along until he reached the largest
tent in the camp. Above the shelter, his family's standard
twisted in the breeze, a boar's head upon the blade of a mighty
battle-axe. Without slowing his stride, he stepped through the
rain-slicked entrance flaps.

"Ah," Nohr grunted. He indicated a vacancy in the ring of
men upon the earthen floor. Nevik nodded a silent greeting
to the assembly of commanders, then claimed his seat, noting that his own distress was mirrored in the gathering's collective visage. As the cold damp of the floor began to soak
through, his father rose to initiate the meeting.

"The last of our messengers has returned. The Imperial Council wishes to remain aloof. No help is forthcoming."

He gazed heavily upon those gathered, permitting the implications of his statement to sink into the minds of his listeners. "Our time is come. We strike now or never."

A common murmur rumbled among those assembled.

"Without reinforcement?" It was Captain Eames, the highest-ranking officer in Drakmar's military, who sought clarification.

Nohr looked to his captain and nodded. "We gain nothing in waiting for help that will not arrive."

"But without reinforcement . . . perhaps we should not attack at all," suggested Lieutenant Heman.

Nohr fixed his glare upon the soldier and his opinion. "We came here with a purpose. That purpose was not merely to camp outside the wizard's walls for a few days as targets for their archers. Our plan was to take the wizard before he strengthens himself further and comes to take us."

Eames was quick to draw Nohr's ire away from the overmatched lieutenant. "With all due respect, Lord Baron, we believed at the time we would have aid once the siege was under way."

"Well, Captain," Nohr grunted, his voice deep and full of warning, "it is clear now we will not. So, do we turn and head home, having accomplished nothing? Or do we make a stand here and now? I for one do not feel we've reaped adequate reward for the blood we've lost these past four days."

"And what of our families if we fail here?" dared Eames.

"The surest way to fail is to not try," came Nohr's rebuff.

Nevik's gaze lifted from the floor to quietly examine the faces of his fellow soldiers. Truth be known, he had no desire to persist with this hopeless assault, and he recognized at once that he was not alone. And yet none, it seemed, were willing to refuse the baron outright. As the members of the council stared at the floor in common silence, Nevik glanced up and found his father glaring at him. Unable to break away from that glare, Nevik reacted with what he hoped would be the quickest form of escape.

"We attack," he said.

Eames, Heman, and the others fixed their stares upon him, but Nohr, with a triumphant grin, shifted his. Despite the fear and bitterness now aimed his way, Nevik felt much relieved. He faced his captain evenly, trying not to interpret what he saw in the man's expression.

"That's two in favor of a siege," Nohr pressed the others. His gaze fell squarely upon Eames.

"Aye," the captain agreed at last, still staring at Nevik. "Aye, we attack."

"Then it's settled. At first light, while their dreams are still thick upon them. Let us make those dreams their last!"

He said it with a smile, in a manner meant to rouse the spirits of those assembled. A few grunted reluctantly at first, then with more fervor, as if needing to convince themselves that they were up for this—as apparently, there was no avoiding it.

And so, while the ring of men challenged one another with a crescendo of shouts, Nevik looked away from Eames's persistent stare, rubbing at his beard while fighting down a growing uneasiness within the pit of his stomach.

His feeling was that they were making a foolish decision. Eames knew it. Nevik knew it. Only Nohr, it seemed, did not.

For Jarom, the six days that followed his initial awakening lasted an eternity. Thanks to the kind and capable Lewellyns, he regained his strength rapidly. This, along with the relentless intensity of his dreams, made him anxious to be on his way. But Allion strictly prohibited him from going anywhere until the Lewellyns pronounced him fit for travel, convincing him that any premature activity would only hamper his recovery and delay their departure. Thus, Jarom spent day and night confined to his quarters, where he mostly lay abed, coiled and restless.

Being bedridden, however, was not without its advantages. His friends made sure to stop in and visit him now and then, to say hello and to measure his progress, but mostly they let him be. That left Marisha to keep him company, and though far too bashful to admit it, Jarom found this much to his liking.

That he found her easy to look upon was only one small part of it. After all, he'd met many a maiden about whom he could say the same. It had more to do with her kind attention, an inquisitive nature that bordered on intimacy. With each visit, she asked him to tell her more about himself and the Swords. Little by little, he felt a kinship grow between them. Only natural, he supposed, given the nature of their relationship and the time spent together. But there was more to it than that, even. There was the urgency he sensed in her, hidden beneath her playful personality. He could not explain it, and whenever he looked for it, it went skittering out of reach. For all her probing questions, she remained shy and evasive when it came to matters of her own. Time and again it seemed as if she was on the verge of revealing some painful secret, only to tuck it away again and dismiss his concerns with a laugh.

He wasn't sure what to make of it, except that it couldn't possibly have anything to do with him. What he did know was that she was the only one who believed in him. Though she did not come out and say so, not once did she suggest he was mad, or that he should reexamine his plan. Her unspoken faith fulfilled a need in him he did not realize he'd had, and he felt a strange ache whenever he thought of leaving her—an ache, he was sure, that had nothing to do with the assassin's wound.

He did his best to put aside the feeling as an unnecessary distraction. Now was not the time to pursue such fantasies. Nevertheless, with every passing moment spent with her, he gave more and more thought to the idea that somehow, someday, they might end up together. There was so much he wanted to share with her—his home, his family—and so much more he would like to learn about hers. If only circumstances would permit him to do so.

That evening, the sixth since his revival, Master Nimbrus paid him a visit and quickly pronounced him well enough to leave, whenever he and his companions should deem themselves ready.

The news was bittersweet. Jarom felt as though he was ready to scale the summit of Mount Krakken, should his journey require it, so anxious was he to set forth. And yet, he found the notice painfully abrupt. After a hurried meeting with Allion, it was agreed that they would depart at first light. No reason to tarry longer, he himself had suggested. But when Allion had left, and Marisha had returned, he was made all too aware that these were perhaps the last moments he would ever spend with her.

"Seen Kylac today?" he asked.

Marisha sat with him at the edge of his bed, working to unwrap the bandages from his bare chest and back. As they so often had in the previous days, they found themselves alone. Always before, Jarom had enjoyed these moments. Now, suddenly, he was in a cold sweat, nervous for reasons he could not begin to define.

If the woman sensed his awkwardness, she was kind enough not to point it out. "He went exploring again this morning. I'm sure he'll be back soon."

"Protecting, you mean."

Over the past few days, he had seen very little of Kylac Kronus. Whenever he inquired as to the whereabouts of the youth who had saved his life, the answer was the same. And there was no real secret as to why. Although the boy seemed calm enough, the appearance of the creature in the Emerald River had clearly rattled his sense of what was proper in nature. While Jarom had agreed with Allion that the demon must have been sent after them by the wizard, the youth remained more circumspect. Whatever the beast's origin, Kylac had taken it upon himself to patrol the surrounding region. And while the stillness of the passing days had made such threats seem diminished, Kylac Kronus, despite his relaxed front, remained ever vigilant, ready for action at an instant's notice.

Indeed, Jarom had known the answer to his question even before it was asked. Still, he had needed to say something to dismiss the quiet and to ease his tensions.

"Yes, well, he cares for you," Marisha said.

She glanced up from her work. Jarom caught his breath,

feeling a rush of warmth as he realized her closeness. He stared into her eyes and wondered at what lay behind them.

"For all of us, I mean."

Jarom gulped and nodded. Marisha went back to work, a little too hurriedly, he thought. Or was it his imagination? He closed his eyes and took in the fragrance of her hair.

"What do you know of him?" he asked.

"Not much," Marisha admitted. "It's hard to get him to speak about himself."

"Maybe he's shy."

"Maybe."

Marisha continued to slip the bandages free of his torso. The task caused her to nearly embrace him, again and again, as she passed the coiled wrappings from one hand to the next behind his back. With each revolution, Jarom secretly hoped that she would lean in and complete the movement. She worked slowly, and he savored every close encounter, knowing that it would all be over—and all too soon.

"He's not convinced that those creatures were sent by the wizard, is he?"

"No," Marisha confessed. "Word is, such creatures have been spotted elsewhere, in other lands. They appear and vanish, but rarely threaten. It's like they're scouting, observing, wondering what we're all about."

"Looking for someone in particular, perhaps."

"Perhaps. But Kylac feels the appearances are too random and widespread. The wizard must know how close he was to you. So why not a more focused search?"

"But who else but a sorcerer could command such creatures?" Jarom wondered aloud.

"I'm not sure I even want to know."

The last of the dressings fell free. The cool air felt good; that she was finished with him did not.

She surprised him, though, by remaining seated, pulling him close as she leaned over to inspect the scar on his back.

"How does it look?"

"Master Nimbrus and the others did a wonderful job," she responded evasively, touching the wounded area lightly.

Jarom laughed. "In other words, not good."

"It'll improve with time," she assured him.

She withdrew, and Jarom let his wry grin fade into seriousness. "When we're gone, will you be safe?"

"Oh yes, I'll be fine. We all will be. And you, sir, had best take better care of yourself out there. Come back to visit when this business is done, will you?"

The thought pleased him. "I will."

They continued to smile at each other until it became awkward. Marisha was the first to blink.

"I'd best be going," she said, scooping up the roll of swathes and rising to her feet. "You've preparations to make."

She turned to take her leave. Jarom stood, feeling as though he wanted to chase after her.

"Marisha, I . . ."

She swung back to face him, her expression unreadable. Curious? Hopeful?

"I don't know how to thank you."

"You don't have to. It was a pleasure to meet you, Jarom. I'm glad Kylac brought you here."

Jarom's mind raced for a fitting response, but came up empty. Marisha moved to the door, and his stomach fell. He dropped to his seat upon the bed, his eyes trailing after her.

When she reached the doorway, however, she paused, turning his way once more.

"Don't ever give up," she offered with a final smile. "What you seek exists."

His thoughts already a jumble, Jarom gaped in confusion. Before he could muster a reply, she was gone.

As planned, the time to depart finally arrived that very next morning, a full week since Jarom's first awakening, and twelve days since his arrival. His back was still tender, but the Lewellyns were convinced that there was scant risk of recurring injury, so long as he was careful. With the breaking of the forest dawn, the three adventurers found themselves bidding their final farewells to their friends of Feverroot.

The embrace for which Jarom had hoped came quickly on this occasion. He tried not to appear too eager as Marisha stepped forward and welcomed him into her arms.

"Believe," she said to him. That was what she had said to him last night when at last he had managed to catch up to her after their initial parting. That was all she had meant by her seem-ingly cryptic reference to the Crimson Sword. If he wanted it as badly as he did, and truly believed in it, then it would be his. Jarom had eyed her with a measure of suspicion. But as he'd struggled to formulate a specific question, she had flashed him that effer-vescent smile, and the matter was forgotten.

"I do," he assured her now, enjoying the way she felt in his arms.

She gave him an encouraging squeeze, then moved on to hug Allion and Kylac in turn.

The remaining farewells were just as brief. Jarom sin-cerely thanked each and every Lewellyn who had worked to preserve his life. Once again, he offered payment for their services and was refused. Whatever Kylac had done for these people, it was such that Master Nimbrus and the oth-ers would accept no compensation for aid rendered to one of his friends. Helpless to do otherwise, Jarom nodded gra-ciously and expressed once more his appreciation. Once Al-lion and Kylac had done the same, there remained nothing for the trio to do but mount their steeds and take their leave, waving their last good-byes.

Moments later, the community of Feverroot disappeared behind a tangle of forest growth, and the companions turned their attention to the raveled path ahead.

Long after Jarom and his companions had gone, and she herself had returned to her duties, Marisha wondered whether she had done the right thing. She had come so close to telling him, to showing him. Closer than she had with anyone ever before. But she was glad she hadn't. Though a certain ache still filled her within, a hunger unsatisfied, she had done what her father would have wanted. She had kept their secret safe.

Still, she worried that it might turn out to have been a missed opportunity. Not for herself, for she had sought what answers she could, and had found his knowledge to be less than her own. But perhaps she had been meant to do more than simply encourage him in his quest. At long last, here was someone who believed, appearing under such extraordinary circumstances. While she did not share Jarom's faith in destiny, she could not help but marvel that their paths had crossed. And here they each had so little to show for it.

She shook her head. History and common sense suggested that countless souls had gone in search of the Sword of Asahiel before Jarom. He only seemed special in that he was the first she'd met. That he seemed so selfless and determined in his pursuit was endearing to her. That he could stand alone, ignoring the ridicule of all around him, was even more so. But unless he were to actually succeed in his quest, he was not the one who could help her.

If he found the Sword, she assured herself, she would know otherwise. Perhaps then she would tell him. Perhaps then they could help each other to understand.

Setting aside the linens she was folding, Marisha moved to the window of the empty room, where she gazed out upon the wind-stirred forest. When certain no one was about, she put her hand to her chest and gripped the pendant that hung hidden beneath the folds of her dress, wondering if she might ever see this Jarom again.

Peering through the incessant rain, Nevik watched in dismay as the iron portal once again withstood the blow of his army's battering ram. After a dozen such impacts, the door's blackened surface had yet to be marred. Again the armies exchanged a flurry of flaming arrows. Men from both sides pitched to the earth, grunting or wailing, faces and bodies twisting strangely as their souls fled the horrible scene. Nevik observed it all as he stood by his father's side as commanded, just back of the main force, the wind howling in his ears. Again the ram drove forward, smashing into the

seam of the double doors that sealed the southern gate, but
with no greater success than before.

"Away!" Nohr bellowed over the din. "The gate is
cursed!"

The men pushing the ram were quick to obey, abandoning
the massive war wagon and rushing to rally about their
baron.

"Man the siege towers!" Nohr roared. "Use the ladders!
We'll scale the walls!"

The ponderous towers rolled forward, four in all, their
wheels digging trenches in the mud, their axles screeching
under their own massive weight. Soldiers scaled their
heights, climbing ropes and footholds, anxious to lead this
fight in the defense of their homelands now that battle had
begun. Ladders struck up against the city walls, and men
scurried up the rungs, under cover of fire by their comrades
below. Their actions made Nevik proud, and he felt his
blood stir.

But their enemy welcomed the charge. Nevik shivered,
not from the wind and the rain, but with a rage that continued to build. He wanted to be up there on the front lines. The
carnage, mostly one-sided, sickened him, but did nothing to
diminish his fever. He did his best to count the number of
fallen, intending to repay the wizard's forces double just as
soon as his father set him loose. How any single man, let
alone a legion of them, could be persuaded that all the world
was theirs for the taking, and to show such lack of remorse
in doing so, was beyond his understanding. These men deserved to die. And he meant to make sure it happened.

For the better part of an hour, the two sides tore at one another. Invariably, as the invaders crested the walls, they were
forced back once again. Cauldrons of oil and tar rained
down from the battlements, hindering the ascent of Drakmar's forces. First one, then another of the siege towers was
set aflame and reduced to cinders. Charred and mutilated
corpses began to pile up about the city walls. The thin, shallow moat turned red with blood.

But Nohr would not let his men rest. The baron was an
unyielding taskmaster who with but a glance could yank a

withering man from the mud and force him to his feet. Nevik observed his father with unbridled admiration, and hoped to one day be half the man that he was. Men feared Nohr, but were also enthralled by him. His passion and temper had cowed many an adversary, but these same traits were sources from which his friends and soldiers drew strength. Nohr believed he could do anything, and that belief was infectious. He was a leader, a champion, the type of man who won battles that could not be won.

So it was on this occasion. Despite being foiled time and again in their efforts to breach the line of mercenary defenders entrenched atop the battlements, Nohr's soldiers at last found a way through. A fresh contingent, led by Lieutenant Heman, had forced an opening from atop one of the remaining siege towers. Although the wizard's soldiers struggled to plug the rift, it appeared that Drakmar's passion was finally beginning to win out. If they could just manage to get the bulk of their forces inside the city walls, Nevik thought that perhaps they stood a chance. He had yet to witness any sign of the wizard, and without the man's black arts to bolster them, he had to believe that the mercenary defenders would prove inadequate to the task in the end. But they had to do it soon. They had to hold and secure this opening. If they were thrown back even once more, the day would be lost.

His father must have sensed this as well, for when Nevik turned to him for what must have been the hundredth time, the baron nodded.

"Nevik. Take two reserve squads and reinforce Lieutenant Heman. He is to make for the gatehouse."

And that was it. No words of parting. No wishes for success—much less a farewell hug or handclasp. In the next breath, his father turned away, barking orders to another of his couriers as he had all day, directing every aspect of the battle from his command position. That was soon to change. For the baron's very next order was for his personal command to form up and prepare to rush the main gate, just as soon as Heman had opened it from inside.

"Nevik," his father snapped a moment later, as though

surprised to find him still standing there. "You have your orders. Move out."

"Yes, Lord Baron," Nevik said with a sharp salute.

The next few moments were but a daze, a series of reactions born of training. Men fell into line, weapons at the ready. Nevik issued a command, then rushed forward at the front of his column, up the ravaged hillside, toward the base of Heman's siege tower. The next thing he knew, he was scurrying up the central rope, pausing at each level to regroup with his men. When reality came back into focus, he was standing within the walls of the third tier, one floor beneath the battlement. There, the baron's son braced himself, listening to the heavy concentration of fighting that thundered upon the boards just above his head—wondering suddenly what he had gotten himself into.

He closed his eyes, steeling himself for the fray, and those crowding this level of the tower did so with him. Though well trained in the techniques and strategies of war, the young heir had never participated in anything more than mock combat. And what he was about to face was not wooden swords and padded lances. His stomach churned, muscles and organs all knotted together. In that moment, he gripped the haft of his mace, still sheathed at his belt, and growled away his fears. The only way to learn if he was prepared for this was to do it. Grinding his teeth in challenge to his comrades, he snatched up the rope that hung down through the center of the tower and prepared to hoist himself up to the tumult above.

It was then, through the open side of the tower facing the land southward, that he spotted the approaching army.

"Father!" he cried out, realizing even as he did so that there was no way for Nohr to hear him. He hesitated, then turned to one of his companions. "Corporal," he snapped, flush with excitement. "Follow through with our orders. I'll catch up."

Without waiting for a response, Nevik dropped back through the tower, sliding down the length of rope so swiftly that the skin of his palms burned away. He grimaced but did not slow. His feet were moving before they touched the ground, and doing his best to avoid the slush of flesh and blood, mud and tar that had accumulated at the base of the wall, he half slid, half sprinted back to where his father stood bellowing commands and encouragement.

"Father!" he gasped. "Reinforcements . . . from the southwest . . . the army of Palladur!"

Nohr snapped his gaze in the direction Nevik indicated, and his brow furrowed. Even over the tumult of battle, he could hear the pounding of several hundred horses' hooves upon the earth, and he did not seem thrilled about it.

"What's wrong?" Nevik asked.

"Pull back," his father replied grimly. "Order them to pull back."

Nevik fought to quell the sense of dread rising within as he rushed off to relay the order. Pull back? Why should they surrender their progress? If anything, now that help had arrived, should they not be pressing their advantage? He kept these questions to himself, however, trusting in his father's judgment. Within minutes, Drakmar's forces had initiated a gradual retreat. As Nevik returned to his father's side, Captain Eames came rushing up to them.

"What is it?"

Nevik kept quiet, watching the exchange between baron and captain with increasing concern.

"Satallion approaches."

Eames's mud-streaked face took on an ashen hue. "Shall we prepare a two-front defense?"

Nevik's jaw dropped, his heart settling deep within his chest. It couldn't be.

"I think we must. We cannot afford to take any chances."

Eames nodded and reeled about, shouting commands.

Despite the wet and slippery conditions, Trask took the stone steps two at a time as he descended his command post and came up alongside the forward battlement. A crowd of mercenary soldiers, battered and weary, stepped aside at his approach. Some clutched at grotesque wounds, leaning upon or begging help from their comrades. Commander Trask ignored these and the scattered salutes he received as he bulled his way through to see for himself the sudden change of events.

"What's happening? Why have they pulled back?"

"A force approaches from the southwest, Commander. Judging by our friends' defensive positioning, it's an enemy to them."

Trask rubbed his chin with an oiled glove. His brows knotted, his eyes closing in a discerning squint. For the most part, the wizard had been right. The peoples of these lands were scarcely capable of putting up a fight, making this realm ripe for plunder. The wizard had promised Trask and his soldiers an easy conquest, and in the beginning, all had gone according to plan. They had landed their ships to the north, far from any port. From there, they had left their supply trains to follow after, and had ridden swiftly south, mostly under cover of darkness, bribing, killing, or outrunning any encountered along the way who might raise an alarm. With the wizard's command over wind and earth, nothing had been able to stand in their way.

Lately, however, Trask and some of the other senior officers had become disenchanted. First had been the unexpected stay of their invasion, a sudden shift in strategy that remained unexplained. Then there was this siege, a nuisance at first, but which had now grown rather serious. The commander could not understand it. A few well-placed spells might have ended this thing days earlier. But aside from the wards placed upon the city gates, the wizard had refused to involve himself. Rather, he remained tucked away in that cocoon of a tower, preoccupied with matters that Trask and the others dared not guess at.

The commander was fast growing weary of the entire mess. At this point, he wanted little more than to collect the balance of his payment and return home, a king's ransom in hand. But that would not happen until they had quashed what remained of Alson's resistance, including these worms below. Now it appeared as though final victory was indeed theirs, despite the wizard's lack of involvement, and the commander was anxious to make it so. Still, he'd been a soldier for far too long to allow eagerness to waylay prudence. The wizard didn't tolerate mistakes. If this force proved as cunning as it had stubborn . . .

"We cannot be too hasty," he determined finally. "It could be a trap. Ready two cavalry battalions and await my signal."

"Yes, sir."

Nevik stood shoulder to shoulder with his father, mace in hand. On the opposite flank stood Captain Eames, his bloodless countenance that of a man preparing to face his execution with forced dignity. Planted between them like an ancient oak, Nohr hefted his huge axe in his muscle-wrapped arms and scowled at the trio of riders that pulled up before them. The center of the three rode forward by half a length. Satallion, with an imposing air, removed his helm to reveal his lean face and that ever present smirk.

"Greetings, my fellow baron. How goes the battle?"

The baron of Drakmar gave no response. Nevik glanced over. His father's chest heaved with slow, deliberate breaths, like a bull about to charge.

"Why have you come, Satallion?" Eames asked wearily.

"Why, Captain, you seem in rather foul spirits."

"Do you fight with or against us?" the other demanded.

A chill gust blew across the battlefield. Nevik studied the high lord of Palladur as though awaiting his own death sentence, searching the man's visage for the slightest clue.

It was Satallion's turn to scowl as he surveyed the carnage before him—the heaps of bodies, the smoldering towers, the blood-soaked fields. His gaze lifted to take in the lines of enemy soldiers waiting atop Krynwall's scarred battlements.

"I fight for my life and the lives of those I rule," he said finally.

The rival barons, Nohr and Satallion, stared into each other's eyes. Behind each, several thousand men shifted and tensed, awaiting some sign.

"You're a fool," Nohr snorted finally.

"I can accept the fate of this land. You cannot. It is you who are the fool."

"Today you die," Nohr growled, rubbing a meaty finger along the notched blade of his axe. "By my hand, your treachery shall be repaid in full."

Satallion sneered, tearing his sword from its scabbard. He brought it down, and his army surged forward, shouting their battle cries.

Within moments, Commander Trask was convinced. The conflict below was no ruse. There was genuine animosity between the two armies, with the newly arrived forces clearly determined to put an end to the other's aggression. For what purpose, the commander could only guess. In all likelihood, it was an attempt by one of the Alsonian baronies to curry favor with his master, for the wizard had no allies that he was aware of. Trask smiled. If that was the case, then whoever led this new army should be congratulated for his survivalist way of thinking.

As a ray of sun lanced through the thick clouds, the commander of the wizard's mercenary forces gave his signal. The front gates of Krynwall were flung wide, unleashing a wave of mounted soldiers onto the battlefield. The commander's smirk widened. He would be counting his treasure and making his way home soon enough.

The worms below didn't stand a chance.

CHAPTER SEVENTEEN

*T*hey rode eastward at a leisurely pace, screened from the sun's harsh rays by the thick forest canopy. The paths were choked with underbrush, free to grow where men so seldom roamed. Faint breezes rustled the surrounding foliage, stirring the scents of cedar, fir, and countless other varieties of woodland vegetation into an aromatic blend. The calls and movements of wildlife were all around them, but the animals themselves remained mostly invisible, revealed only occasionally while stealing glimpses from afar of these strange creatures that had wandered unbidden into their domain. Jarom felt their eyes upon him, and thought of himself as a trespasser in this unspoiled wilderness. As he and his companions wound their way among the aged conifers that had ruled for hundreds, perhaps thousands of years over the north-central Kalmira, he couldn't help but scoff at the fleeting and ultimately meaningless struggles of man.

Despite his convictions concerning the Sword—based as they were on preternatural dreams and a growing determination to make those dreams manifest—the decision to ride east had not been an easy one to make. Both he and Allion remained more than a little worried about those they had left behind, now that it was believed the wizard was after them. When the Lewellyns' courier had failed to return from Diln by the time the companions were ready to depart, they had debated whether they should make for home instead. In the end, however, they had agreed there were too many reasons not to. The wizard's forces might not have visited Diln at all.

If Ellebe had betrayed him, willingly or otherwise, then it was possible she had also revealed Jarom's plan to head south to Kuuria. And if so, there would be no need to ransack his home in search of him. If his village *had* been targeted, then in all terrible likelihood, whatever damage might be done had been done already. There was no cause to believe the wizard would harm Jarom's people for harm's sake. Most likely, they would be held captive, in which case it was unlikely Jarom could secure their release by turning himself over. Besides, they might have escaped before any attack had taken place. And as for any future danger, the Circle would be warned by the courier already sent forth.

Rationalizations, to be sure, intended to make him feel better about his decision and the accompanying sense of betrayal. But that didn't mean they lacked sense.

The final determination was that they had come too far already. The best Jarom could do was continue on, trust in the Elders to keep their people safe, and work to empower himself so that when he did return, he could liberate or avenge those who might have been made to suffer on his behalf. Looking back, Jarom realized that the choice had been made the moment he'd turned east in search of Whitlock. Whatever consequences were to come of that decision would be faced in time. Until then, such concerns served only as anchors to weigh him down, so he did his best to cast them aside.

It was a refreshing change, actually. For the first time, Jarom no longer felt as though he was pulling the full weight of this undertaking on his own. Even following their failure in the Aspandels, when Allion had agreed to search for the ruins of Thrak-Symbos, it still seemed as though the full burden of the task was his to bear. With Kylac, things were different. The youth was genuinely enthused about the challenge that stood before them, and that excitement had improved Allion's attitude as well. Together, the two of them had actually encouraged Jarom to carry on when raw fear and guilt had made him believe he must turn around. With Kylac's guidance, Allion's support, and his own mounting determination, he was beginning to believe not only that he would see this crazy adventure through, but that they might actually succeed.

From his position at the rear of their procession, Jarom was able to observe unnoticed the budding friendship between his two companions. Although their journey had resumed, things remained much as they had back in Feverroot, when Jarom had been unable to participate in his friends' activities. When the pair had not been out scouting for demons in order to ensure the safety of the Lewellyns' community—both during and after their stay—they could often be found, Jarom had been told, practicing each other's respective skills. Kylac was eager to learn what he could about the finer points of archery, and by all reports was fast becoming Allion's equal. In exchange, the archer had been taught more in one week concerning swordplay, he claimed, than Jarom had pieced together throughout all his years growing up in Diln. Jarom had smiled at the news, certain his friend was exaggerating, but felt a little left out nonetheless.

It was the same now. Up ahead, Kylac led them along the hidden forest trails, alert at all times. Allion was behind him, as close as the youth's own shadow. The two were laughing and talking as though they'd been doing so for years, relaxed and comfortable in each other's presence. Jarom, on the other hand, had yet to even get a straight answer from the youth concerning their course. Back in Feverroot, Kylac had assured him that their journey, at least to the Skullmars, was a straightforward matter that required no action on Jarom's part beyond a speedy recovery. Though it bothered him to be excluded from the plotting of his own adventure, Jarom saw as yet no reason to challenge the youth.

So Jarom hung back from the others as they rode, listening in on their mostly irrelevant exchanges and making no effort to involve himself. In truth, he was not altogether uncomfortable with the arrangement. The Lewellyns had cautioned him to avoid any agitation. And Jarom had always been more at peace within his own thoughts than among the company of others. In any case, he was not alone. As in Feverroot, he had Marisha to keep him company. The woman was ever present in his thoughts. Despite all his many concerns—past, present, and future—pertaining to this quest, it took a sharp mental focus to concentrate on these and not on the touch, the smile, or the encouraging words of the apprentice healer who had so enchanted him. Like a dream or some faerie spirit, she had ingrained herself in his awareness, so that every thought, feeling, and sensation led to a memory or fantasy involving her. There was no escape. Or if there was, Jarom was not inclined to seek it.

Oddly enough, no one mentioned the wizard as they wound their way through the lush woodland. Hovering like a dark cloud in Jarom's mind was the fear that at any moment they might stumble across another of the wizard's demons. And he was certain that the ever vigilant Kylac and even Allion had to be thinking the same thing. But none gave voice to the concern. Perhaps they did in fact feel safe after going for so long without an encounter. Or perhaps they had truly buried this fear along with all others in order to better concentrate on what lay before them. Or perhaps there was nothing more that needed to be said.

As the hours wore on, weariness began to drag upon Jarom's mind and body, and the enthusiasm with which he had greeted the renewal of this venture wore off. By midafternoon, he felt as though he'd spent the last two weeks as he had—languishing in bed. His back ached, tender tissues throbbing in annoyance. He began to wheeze, coughing as his breath scraped against a sharp itch upon the wall of his healing lung. A cool sweat soaked his underarms and chest and clung to his face and brow. Now and again, he considered stopping to take some rest, at least long enough to heat some water for a cup of the pain-relieving tea with which the Lewellyns had provided him. But his pride would not allow him to do so. He was not going to hold back their progress any longer than he had already. The best way to break down the walls of fatigue was simply to push through them.

With the approach of evening, Jarom found himself lagging several dozen paces back of the others. The forest was a maze, unchanging in shape and form, with nothing to distinguish where they had been from where they were going.

He glanced up at the shifting flashes of red light that burned their way through the cracks in the forest's shield—cast by the setting sun over his right shoulder. If not for this, he would have had no idea as to how much time had passed. Instead, he squinted against the glare of each thin shaft and smiled. Nightfall was approaching. The close of their day's journey couldn't be far behind.

As he faced forward with renewed energy, a startling realization struck him. The last of his daze vanished like flaming cobwebs, and he kicked his steed ahead to catch up with his companions. Sure enough, the sun's rays were streaming down upon the right side of his face, which meant one of two things. Either the sun had changed its arc so that it no longer set in the west, or . . .

"Why are we heading south?"

Allion glanced back as though he had forgotten Jarom was there, then peered skyward to confirm his friend's claim. Apparently, the hunter hadn't yet noticed it on his own. He turned to Kylac, his own gaze questioning.

The youth didn't bother to look at either of them. "Don't worry. It's all part o' the plan."

Jarom and Allion shared another look. Kylac had deliberately shifted their course so subtly it had been unnoticeable. What wasn't he telling them?

"I thought the Skullmars lay east and north."

"Aye, but first we needs to make a detour into Vosges."

Jarom fought past a sudden shiver. The very name of Pentania's southeastern peninsula conjured up images of flesh-painted cannibals and their unspeakably barbaric rites.

"Dare I ask why?"

Kylac shrugged. "If'n ya thinks knowing now is going to make ya feel any better, ask away."

Again, the two men from Diln shared a less-than-comfortable glance, then stared at their suddenly tight-lipped guide.

"Well?"

"Do ya truly believe that some divine favor is going to show us the front door o' these ruins and carry us right to the Sword?" Kylac snickered. "No offense, but I's a better idea."

"That's wonderful," Jarom agreed. "What is it?"

At last, the youth turned to face him, a mischievous smirk strung across his lightly freckled cheeks. "As it happens, I know someone who's been there."

The wizard Soric sat undisturbed in the highest chamber of his private tower. He was seated comfortably, his body cradled by a cushioned chair, his senses dulled by a pleasurable incense that hovered thickly in the air.

He was anything but content.

A pile of scrolls lay upon the table before him, dredged up from the bowels of an archive kept by a monastic order within this very city. Much of the information had proven useless, filled with superstitions and the pedantic admonitions of holy men. In the last few moments, however, he had stumbled across a passage that intrigued him, a historical account whose accuracy he might have scoffed at under normal circumstances, but in light of recent events, read to him like gospel truth.

It spoke of an avatar, the handmaiden of a demon god, drawn into this realm by those seeking to use her as a weapon against their enemies. But one such as she would not be bound. Like a wild animal, she had broken free, turning her fury upon her captors and any other who opposed her will. Driven by vengeful urges and primal instincts the likes of which no mortal could comprehend, she and her minions had very nearly claimed the distant land of Sekulon as her own almost a thousand years ago. In the end, however, she had been vanquished, killed or forced into hiding—it wasn't clear which—by a sect of human avatars. She had not been heard from since, but the account here seemed to represent, as religious chronicles usually did, a cautionary tale whose conclusion was yet to be writ in stone.

According to the scripted legend, this creature had a

name. And as he came across it, the wizard ignored the ridiculous warning scribbled in preface and uttered it aloud.

"Spithaera."

The Demon Queen.

Satallion limped up the black steps of the wizard's tower, relishing the smirk that hung upon his lips. His tongue licked at a cracked corner of his mouth and came away with the taste of blood. The rest of him was lathered in grime. His entire body ached. But he was alive. He had survived the day. He had seen himself and his men through the battle of their lives. All in all, he could not have hoped for a better outcome. There was nothing left to do now but collect his reward.

A stifled chuckle escaped as he envisioned once more the "glory" of Nohr's final stand. A knife in the back—oh yes, the bards would sing of it forever. Of course, had it not been for Lord Augelot, Nohr's oath would have been fulfilled. Lying weaponless upon the earth, Satallion had had no prayer of deflecting the descent of that huge axe. Even now, the high lord cringed as the blade flashed again in his mind's eye. But as fate would have it, his fellow lord had arrived in time to skewer the baron of Drakmar from behind, and it was Nohr's blood that had been spilled, not his own.

As he finished congratulating himself on his good fortune, Satallion's journey came to an end. He had barely noticed his surroundings while climbing the near-lightless corridor of the wizard's home, but he took notice now. The wizard's quarters lay before him, a meticulous array of books and furnishings and alchemic solutions. A stench assaulted his nostrils, foreign and pungent, and he tried not to breathe too deeply. Tables were abundant, and at one sat the wizard himself, a scroll in hand. Satallion blanched at the sight, for as he entered, the creature before him lowered the crinkled parchment with a scowl that chilled him to the bone. Whether by what he had just read or by the intrusion, the wizard was not pleased, and with but a glance from the usurper-king, the high lord was made keenly aware of his own mortality.

"You must be Satallion."

The high lord dropped to one knee, his eyes scraping the floor and avoiding the sneering features, hollow cheekbones, and yellow eyes of his new master. "I am, my lord, come to serve and pledge allegiance to the king."

"Then the opposition has been crushed?"

"Yes. Their leader is slain, his armies scattered."

"And pray, what do I owe you for your services?"

"Nothing, my lord," Satallion assured him, feigning surprise at the notion. "My armies are at your command."

"Indeed," the wizard agreed, his tone of civility slipping somewhat. "But I would be remiss if I did not offer you just compensation for your contributions."

"Not necessary, my lord," Satallion reiterated hastily, concealing a smile.

"Oh, but I insist. It seems I owe you my kingdom. The least I can do is offer half of it to you."

"My lord!" Satallion gasped, meeting the wizard's gaze squarely for the first time. "You have my most humble gratitude!"

"Think on it no more," the wizard snorted with a wave of his hand.

Satallion grunted, then fell to the floor, clutching at the unseen pressures swelling within his head.

"As I said," the sorcerer mumbled, returning to his scroll, "'tis the least I can do."

Jarom felt his blood stir. Aside from the Entients, the very notion of finding someone with actual knowledge of the ruins of Thrak-Symbos was more than he had dared consider. "What?" he offered in response to Kylac's claim. "That's incredible!"

Allion agreed. "Why didn't you say something before?"

"I didn't want to debate the issue," Kylac responded with his customary shrug. "Besides, ya never knows who might be tracking us. I thought it best that everyone believe we was heading east. We only began to veer south an hour ago."

Jarom's thoughts raced, his mounting excitement flushing

away the anger he might have felt at the youth's one-sided decision. "*You* haven't been there, have you?"

"No."

"But you know someone who has."

Kylac nodded.

"And this person lives in Vosges?" Allion questioned, his surprise evident.

"Last I heard."

"How far south do we have to go?" Jarom asked.

"'Til we finds him."

Allion frowned. "What about the savages?"

"Savages? I assume ya mean the Mookla'ayans."

"Don't they inhabit these parts?"

"Since the time o' the Finlorian Empire."

Jarom cast a nervous glance right and left, and watched as Allion did the same. "Will we encounter any?"

"I hope so, since the man we're looking for is one o' them."

Jarom nearly gagged. In a flash, everything he had ever heard about the natives of Vosges rushed through his mind. As tavern tales had it, the Mookla'ayans were a clan of elves who hailed from the earliest annals of recorded time. In recent centuries, they had lived throughout the Kalmira, even after the Finlorian elves had gone and the men of Partha had come to power. They were fiercely territorial, by all reports, and said to revel in human butchery. Driven largely by fear and mistrust, the Parthan army had soon begun a systematic extermination of the forest cannibals. Unlike their Finlorian cousins, however, the Mookla'ayans had refused to vanish quietly, and it had taken Partha more than a hundred years to force them as far south into the jungles as they had. As it stood, they had been unable to eradicate the stubborn savages entirely, and had been forced to abandon the attempt when war to the north against Menzos had intensified, becoming too severe to allow for their divided military forces.

How much of this popular mythology was true, Jarom had no idea. But given the horrific stories of abduction and murder used to describe this people, he was not at all anxious to risk even the half of it. The Parthans might very well have

learned to live with the threat of the occasional Mookla'ayan
hunting party that strayed northward, but to head south with
the intent of actually finding one seemed to him patently
absurd.

"What makes you think they won't skin us on sight?"

"Despite all the gruesome stories ya's heard, not all
Mookla'ayan tribes are bloodthirsty marauders preying on
innocent women and children."

"But they do eat men."

"And they's been doing it a long time 'fore we came
along. Who's to say it ain't right?"

Jarom saw his own disgust mirrored in Allion's features,
and groaned. "Please don't tell me you've eaten with them."

Kylac turned on him with a roguish grin, the kind meant to
leave him to his own conclusions. "I should think that one
such as yourself would have more sympathy for a people
forced from their homes for no reason. The Mookla'ayans
lived for centuries without bothering anyone, until the
Parthans started pushing into their territories. It's man who
can't seems to share the land, not the other way around."

"Sorry," Jarom offered halfheartedly. "I guess we've
never heard the story told that way."

"Yeah, well, if'n ya sat around a Mookla'ayan campfire
half as often as ya sat on a tavern stool listening to money-
grubbing tale-tellers or those terrified by what they don't understand, you'd know the truth."

"Well, if I'm hearing you correctly, sounds as though
we'll have that chance."

Kylac gave him a wink. "Trust me."

Allion turned, his face inquisitive. Jarom shrugged. Did
they have any choice?

"Tell us more about this native, the one who's been there."

"Cwingen Grawl, chieftain o' the Powaii."

"Powaii?"

"The largest remaining tribe o' Mookla'ayans."

"How'd you meet?"

"Rescued his daughter from the gullet of a rival chieftain,
the A'awari. They're the ones ya's mostly heard about. Cruel
ones, they are."

"Is there anyone you've met whose life or friend's life you haven't saved?"

"Those I's killed."

Allion laughed. Jarom shook his head, sorry he had asked.

"And this man, this Cwingen Grawl. What was he doing in the Skullmars?"

"He was asked to lead an expedition not unlike yours, some seventy, eighty-odd years ago. Some treasure hunters thought an elf might have a better understanding of an ancient elven city."

Despite his fascination, Jarom couldn't help but feel a twinge of suspicion and resentment. Not once during the course of their discussions had Kylac hinted of any prior knowledge concerning the Sword or the ruins in which it was rumored to be buried. If the youth had known all of this, why hadn't he said something before?

"What happened?"

"The way Grawl tells it, the expedition was a failure. They found the city, and made their way through it. Then something happened. He never told me what, exactly, but he claims to be the only one to have returned."

"Perhaps he ate them," Allion quipped.

"Hold on," Jarom pressed. "You say all this happened nearly a hundred years ago?"

Kylac nodded. "Elves live a good deal longer than us humans. Grawl's an old man, but spry enough to provide us with some much-needed information. My hope is that he'll even agree to join us."

On the one hand, it was an encouraging thought. On the other, Jarom was uncomfortable with surrounding himself with complete strangers, and dangerous ones at that. Kylac had already saved his life, and was a risk he was willing to take. But taking on a Mookla'ayan chieftain, even at the youth's suggestion, was another matter altogether.

"And do you think he will?"

Kylac shrugged. "Hard to say. That's why we have to ask."

Jarom took a series of shallow breaths. He had learned already, for the sake of his lung, not to take any deep ones. "Is there anything else you'd care to share with us?"

"How do ya mean?"

"Now that we're out here, and we've agreed not to debate your plan. Are you holding any more surprises in store?"

"Ya wants to know what to expect," Kylac surmised.

"I would like to, yes."

"Even if those expectations were to work against ya?"

Jarom frowned. "What are you talking about?"

"Sometimes, it's best not to overthink what you're getting yourself into," the youth explained. "Plans are good, but what happens when they goes awry? If'n ya wants to survive, ya's gots to learn how to react."

"Fine," Jarom moaned. "All I ask is that you let us know when our lives are to be placed in jeopardy."

"In that case," Kylac said, "consider yourself warned."

They journeyed a while longer, until the sun had set in full. Without its light, the forest was as black as a cold cellar, and even the supremely confident Kylac Kronus did not wish to risk stumbling off course in the dark. With little ado, they created their own clearing by chopping down an area of underbrush beside a fallen sequoia and set camp for the evening. Gathered around a small fire, they ate their fill from plentiful food supplies, stretching weary muscles and tired minds. During that time, and in the waning hours that followed, conversation focused on plans for the morrow—despite Kylac's earlier criticism. Jarom learned more about the obscure, aboriginal people said to inhabit the region into which they would venture, stories that did nothing to allay his fears. Kylac told them what to expect as far as basic appearance and customs, then reassured them that they need not worry. If they kept quiet and followed the youth's lead, they would all do fine.

The woodland air had become chill with the setting of the sun, and Jarom found himself huddling near the warmth of the flames. Their crackle, a constant background to the companions' occasional chatter, drowned out many of the faint and twittering noises of the nighttime forest and helped to fashion a pocket of stillness. With his muscles relaxed, his hunger sated, and his aches numbed by the Lewellyns' medicines, Jarom lay back in his bedroll and found his eyelids heavy. The soft drone of Allion and Kylac's continued conversation lulled him quickly to sleep.

They set out early the next morning, just as soon as color had returned to the forest. For Jarom, it was an inauspicious beginning. He had risen earlier than the others, awakened by a nightmare that had him drowning in a shrouded bog. His friends had stood somewhere onshore, but had remained invisible, and had done nothing to aid him. Meanwhile, somewhere in the deep waters, a monstrous creature hunted him. . . .

He had escaped the dream, only to find himself in a cold, dew-soaked forest, wrapped in morning brume. His body ached in a hundred places, beset by sore muscles where he hadn't realized he had any. The recollection of where he was and what he was about hissed at him like a caged animal.

Not daring to risk further sleep, he set about rekindling their campfire and mixing himself a healing drink. By the time they were ready to depart, he felt marginally better. But his uneasiness remained. He still could not quite fathom the truth of this day's objective, to trek deep into the untamed wilderness of Vosges in search of man-eating tribesmen who might or might not be able to help him. He had not even decided as of yet which outcome he preferred, that this Cwingen Grawl accompany them, or opt to remain behind. He hoped to have a better idea when the time came.

By midmorning, the forest began exhibiting the first signs of change. The ground became soft, the air thick and moist. Trees thinned, their trunks grown scraggly, even as the undergrowth burgeoned around them. Scents changed from those of a dry and seasoned timberland to those of damp and decay.

Jarom kept close to his companions, forced in part by his inability to see past the profusion of towering, broad-leafed plants, and in part by a mounting sense of dread. A more uninviting stretch of land he could not have imagined. The earth slurped at his steed's hooves with every step, and as the day wore on, they were forced with increasing regularity to turn right or left or backtrack altogether, sometimes for several miles, in order to skirt the bogs and quagmires that spotted the salty marshlands. How Kylac maintained any sense of direction was beyond him. The sun had vanished, cocooned in a thick haze that clouded all around them.

Of the Mookla'ayans, they saw no sign. Or at least, Jarom didn't, and if the others did, they kept it to themselves. They were already much farther south than any informed traveler dared roam. It might have helped, Jarom supposed, if he knew what he should be looking for. What sort of markings might the natives use to distinguish their territory from the surrounding wilderness? Theirs was a nomadic existence, Kylac had explained. They lived not in homes of pitch and wood, but in dens and burrows. Any village they were to come across would as likely be set up at the edge of a swamp as in any jungle glen. In any case, the youth assured him, they would never get that close before being spotted by a sentry patrol. It was the natives who would discover them, not the other way around.

It all sounded to Jarom a reckless and haphazard approach, and the serpents writhing in his stomach seemed to agree. How did Kylac intend to locate a people whose very existence was built upon the aim that they not be found? And yet the youth exuded nothing but confidence, as always. Due to rivalries among the tribes, he told them, each usually confined itself to specific regions of the jungle. He remembered the areas in which the Powaii were inclined to roam, and knew of those which they were apt to avoid. It was merely a matter of traipsing through the one while steering clear of the other.

They stopped for lunch, then continued on. The afternoon came and went, bringing with it a sweltering heat that lingered until dusk. Jarom suffered through it, as did Allion, while Kylac seemed entirely unaffected.

In the last hour before sunset, Jarom began to sense that he was being watched. His back shivered, and his neck itched. On occasion, he would steal glances into the surrounding brush, and would often think that he saw the foliage move. Curious, he thought, since there was no wind, and few signs of wildlife other than insects and birds. He finally decided to question Kylac about it.

"I think someone's following us," he whispered out of the corner of his mouth.

The youth's nod was barely perceptible. "They's been shadowing us for some time."

Jarom frowned. "Why don't we go and meet them?"

"Because these ain't the ones we're looking for."

Jarom felt his skin go cold. He caught his breath and re- sisted the urge to cast fretful glances every which way. "A'awari?" he hissed.

Again Kylac nodded.

Jarom looked at Allion, and saw that each of them had come to the same conclusion. While the archer stretched back for his bow, Jarom reached casually for the hilt of his sword.

"I wouldn't do that if'n I was you," Kylac chided softly.

The two men eased away from their weapons.

"What do we do?" Allion asked.

"What we came here to do."

Jarom's eyes danced from corner to corner. "I thought you said they stayed out of each other's lands."

"Ordinarily, yes."

"Ordinarily?"

"'Cept in times o' war."

Jarom watched the last of the color drain from Allion's face. "When was it that you came through here?"

"Five, maybe six seasons ago."

A year and a half, Jarom thought. Time enough for any number of changes. Geographical boundaries could have shifted dramatically. One tribe or the other—the Powaii, it would seem—could have been wiped out entirely. These were the sort of omissions he had been talking about with Kylac in terms of sharing information. The kind of knowledge that might have made them decide not to come.

A forewarning that might have saved them from a terrible mistake.

But it was too late for that. Too late for questions about what might have been. Here they were, deep within a forbidden wilderness, surrounded by a race whose members were bred—or learned from experience—to hate man. The only question left to them was what precisely they intended to do about it.

As the last traces of brightness drained from the jungle dome, Kylac led them through a wall of reeds and vines and onto a barren stretch of mud. A vast swamp stretched before them, its placid surface undisturbed save for the ripples of spider-legged water skimmers. The knot in Jarom's stomach fell. They had stumbled out onto a tiny peninsula. Now there was nowhere left to turn. It seemed their journey had come to an end. A dead end.

"Here they come."

Jarom whirled instinctively. Sure enough, now that they had their prey cornered, the savages were making their move. They slipped from the brush like animals, their hairless, olive-skinned bodies bristling with sharp edges. Ignoring Kylac's earlier admonition, Jarom reached for his sword. At once, a volley of darts struck him in the arm and shoulder. Jarom snarled away the pricks as he might a series of bee stings and pulled his weapon free. But by the time he moved to raise it overhead, both the sword and his arm felt impossibly heavy. A moment later, he watched in horror as his blade dropped from his nerveless fingers to land in the mud at his horse's feet.

Allion fared no better. Somehow, the archer managed to fire off a shot before he too was struck by the paralyzing darts, but even that single arrow missed its target. Or rather, the target avoided being hit—not only by dodging the missile, but by reaching up and snatching it by the shaft, swifter than thought. By the time the hunter could register the act, he was sliding like a rag from his mount, a dozen darts sticking from his chest.

The same happened to Jarom. He saw the bald heads bobbing and thrusting from all angles. He saw the blowguns, the wide eyes, and the puffed cheeks. He knew what was happening, but could do nothing to stop it. They had targeted his sword arm first. Now Jarom felt the stings across his face and neck, then felt nothing at all as he slumped forward and pitched to the earth.

He landed on his side, his feet pinwheeling outward to splash into the stagnant waters of the surrounding swamp. His neck twisted so that he found himself staring at Kylac. The youth remained seated upon his horse, arms stretched above his head and crossed at the wrists in what Jarom could only imagine was a gesture of submission. Apparently, it was working, for he could find no indication that the youth had been attacked. The savages, however, were swarming all around the lad, clucking and chirping in their own language. Whatever they were saying, it wasn't pleasant. As Jarom waited to see what would happen, a sneering, tattooed face thrust into view. Sharpened teeth clicked together, in triumph more than hostility, he thought, although it didn't seem to matter. Slivers of bone protruded from either side of the elf's nose, running up and down its length like the terraced lines of a hillside defense. If the man's appearance was meant even in part to strike fear into the hearts of his victims, the goal had been accomplished.

He tried to speak, but his mouth wouldn't form the words. A wooden pole was brought forth, to which he was trussed at the wrists and ankles with leather bindings. He was then hoisted into the air on the shoulders of a pair of savages. As his head lolled around of its own accord, he saw that Allion had received the same treatment. Kylac was bound as well, but was on his feet at least, the pole draped as a yoke behind his neck and his arms lashed in place at the ends. Moments later, the trio's captors led them away, horses and all.

They would eat the horses also, Jarom supposed, then wondered which of them—he or his horse—would taste better.

CHAPTER EIGHTEEN

The effects of the poison were short-lived, but that was of small consolation to those taken captive by its sting. Jarom was almost disappointed when feeling returned to his limbs just moments after the Mookla'ayan party set forth from the edge of the swamp. Without the toxin to shield him, pain and discomfort were his to endure. There were the fresh bruises from his fall, the chafing of the leather bindings against his wrists and ankles, and the angry throb of his healing stab wound. But what truly frightened him was the unknown suffering that lay ahead. Whether he was to be skinned and gutted, roasted over an open flame, or submersed in a boiling cauldron, his death promised to be an ordeal throughout which he would have much rather remained numb.

The moment this realization struck him, he began searching for escape. His eyes roved in their sockets, his gaze probing the shadows. Kylac, marching beside him, was the nearest of his companions. Jarom called to him, meaning to ask the youth just how in the Abyss they were to get out of this mess. Almost before he could assemble the idea, however, he was rapped on the skull with the butt of a spear. A voice shrieked at him in a language he did not begin to comprehend, but the message was clear. Jarom swallowed hard and glanced at Kylac, who had been wise enough to keep his eyes forward and his mouth shut the entire time—and who continued to do so now.

After that, Jarom forced himself to be more rational. Kylac seemed relaxed enough. The youth could just as eas-

ily have been on his way to a festival as his own death. Then
again, Kylac was always like that. From his upside-down
position, he peered past Kylac's legs and those of half a
dozen A'awari to glimpse Allion. The hunter was tugging at
his bindings, only to receive his own stern reprimand for
doing so. Allion sagged back, defeated. Jarom looked away.

He closed his eyes for a moment, willing away his panic
and despair. There had to be a way out of this. Perhaps they
could reason with their Mookla'ayan captors, offer them
something of value in exchange for their release. He shook
his head at the thought. These did not seem to him the type
of people who had any interest in coin or jewels or any other
material possession that he might be carrying—and he
wasn't carrying much. Judging by their appearance, theirs
was a modest existence, focused on meeting the most basic
animal needs. Besides, how was he to communicate such an
offer? And even if he could, what was to keep them from
eating him once they had taken that which he possessed?

In an eye-opening reversal of natural roles, he and his
companions had become the huntsman's game. Their only
hope for survival lay in the mercy of their captors—or escape. And at the moment, neither seemed very likely.

As he continued to wrack his thoughts for anything that
might help to secure their freedom, Jarom made a more calculated study of those who had taken his life in hand. He
took no comfort in what he saw. Their olive-skinned bodies
were completely hairless and tattooed from head to foot—
wicked designs full of sharp and serrated edges. The markings twisted like snakes around torso and limbs, resulting in
the perfect camouflage. He recalled how they had appeared
to bristle when emerging from the undergrowth, and realized
it to be because of the piercings. Their flesh was riddled with
them, hooks and spines and barbed ridges like those that
might be found on some armored creature. Even their
clothes, scant strips of hide and cloth, were pinned to their
skin with more of the bone slivers. Jarom did not even want
to imagine the process by which an unspoiled A'awari infant
was transformed into an adult like those before him, and he
nearly laughed when he thought of Kylac's urging that he be

tolerant and understanding of the ways of this ancient race. It seemed to him now that the terrible stories he had heard barely began to do these savages justice.

His captors seldom spoke among themselves. When they did, it was with coarse chirps and angry gestures. They kept to their purpose, proceeding at a brisk pace through the sweaty marshland. Even at night, the air was thick and sultry. Jarom tried to discern the direction in which they were headed. East, he thought, although it might have been north. Not that it mattered. The jungle lay in every direction. Even if they were to break free, they would never escape this land before its natives tracked them down.

How much time did they have? he wondered. Never before had he felt so helpless. He twisted uncomfortably in his bindings. His neck ached from the weight of his dangling head, which throbbed from the increased blood flow. Spots and swirls weaved before his eyes. He felt every bump and scrape as they worked their way through the clutching tangle of jungle growth. The sooner they reached their goal, the sooner this torture would come to an end.

He thought suddenly of Marisha. He had not done so since they had entered Vosges, preoccupied with the perils they faced. Now that those perils had claimed him, his thoughts turned to what he would leave behind. Strangely enough, it was not his home, his father, his friends. It was Marisha, that wonderfully captivating girl who had nursed him back to health. A young woman about whom he knew so little, and about whom he would learn nothing more.

Jarom gritted his teeth. He was supposed to be thinking of a way by which they might save themselves. Here their very lives depended on his ability to do so, and he couldn't even keep his mind focused on the question at hand. He was too busy giving in to fear and depression. Why couldn't he think of anything? He wondered if Allion or Kylac was having any better luck. He hoped that they weren't relying on him.

The reminder that it was not just his own life at stake caused Jarom to redouble his efforts. He was going about this all wrong. Instead of trying to envision their ultimate escape from the jungle borders, he ought to be taking one

problem at a time. First things first. What exactly were they
up against? He began counting weapons, frightening shapes
in the sifted light of a now radiant moon. Spears mostly, the
primitive kind, little more than sharpened stakes. And the
blowguns. He saw a few bows and slings, and maybe half a
dozen knives that looked more like hand-axes, each a half-
moon blade with a wooden handle along the back edge and
finger holes in the middle. Then again, he could not even get
an exact count on how many members were in the party.
Their thin and sinewy forms continued to weave in and out
of the surrounding brush like vines twisting in the wind.
None would remain in place long enough to be counted,
save for the separate pairs that carried him and Allion and
the lone warrior guarding Kylac. But he kept at it. At least a
dozen, he decided. No more than a dozen and a half.

That meant four to six savages for each of them. Jarom
shivered at the odds, especially when he recalled the lightning reflexes of the one targeted by Allion's arrow. He wondered if even Kylac would be able to stand against these
elves in combat. The youth still wore his weapons. Only
Jarom's and Allion's had been confiscated, shoved back in
place with their other belongings upon their saddled mounts.
If they could manage to free themselves, they could make a
break for it. Not that he suspected their horses could move
any faster than the natives within this suffocating wilderness. If anything, they would be hampered by their bulk. No,
he decided, the Mookla'ayans, with their knowledge of the
jungle, their undoubtedly advanced eyesight, and their lithe
forms, would be much more suited to a chase through these
lowlands than they.

No matter how he examined it, survival in this instance
was a puzzle he couldn't solve. Although counting enemies
and weapons and envisioning various scenarios helped to
occupy his mind and make him feel as though he was doing
something useful, the harsh truth remained. They were all
going to die.

Their steady pace had been sustained for so long that it
startled Jarom when they came to a sudden halt. Three of the
A'awari had gathered ahead, and were now arguing. Or per-

haps not; it all sounded like arguing to him. Jarom did what he could to follow their gestures as he made a quick study of their surroundings. A thin hollow knifed its way across the uneven terrain before them, bathed in patchy starlight. It seemed there was a debate as to whether they should cross it or work their way around. When discussions became more heated, a ray of hope worked its way through the darkness of Jarom's mind. Perhaps the savages would become so enraged that they would kill one another and enable their quarry to escape.

It was too much to hope for. A moment later, their path was decided. The trio involved in the dispute split up. Two slithered off to either side of the procession, melting into the foliage, while the last remained at the point. He signaled back to the others and grimaced. The shifting column moved forward. They were going through.

Their formation tightened. The prisoners were gathered close in the center of the group. Jarom forced himself to remain alert. Something had happened, or was about to. His captors were displaying signs of unease. They sniffed at the air like animals, and their muscles drew taut with expectation. Jarom glanced around, but could discern nothing unusual as they marched down the slope toward the floor of the hollow. He looked over at Allion, whose head was turned away, then up at Kylac. He was surprised to find the youth staring at him from the corner of his eye. When their gazes met, Kylac spared him a barely perceptible nod.

Then it happened. As the point man of their company reached the angled floor of the hollow, he disappeared. The ground gave way beneath him, and with a sharp yelp and a scrabbling of limbs, he followed. Vines and dirt and brush rained after, pouring into whatever foul nest the unfortunate man had discovered. His cry echoed as he fell, then ended abruptly with an audible thwack. Jarom cringed. Whatever lay at the bottom of the concealed pit, it wasn't a bed of leaves.

A strange warbling filled the air. Jarom turned toward the sound and found it coming from Kylac's lips. An instant later, the youth pitched forward, sliding face-first down the side of the ravine. For a split second, a confused Jarom thought that the youth's guard had pushed him. But then came the arrow, a shaft nearly six feet in length that sang through the trees, passed right through the spot where Kylac had been standing, and punched clear though the chest of the startled A'awari guard. The native's eyes went wide, staring at the length of the missile protruding from his ruined torso. He then toppled forward, a ghost before his body hit the ground.

Everything that followed seemed to happen at once. Jarom crashed to the earth, cast aside by his handlers, and felt himself sliding. He came to a stop not far from where Kylac lay, just a few paces up from the edge of the exposed pit. All around him, missiles ripped through the air. The A'awari scattered like rats before a sudden flame, clawing for cover. A host of forms appeared in the trees, Mookla'ayans wrapped in vines and wielding massive longbows. Jarom recognized them from Kylac's description. Powaii!

"Keep down!" the youth hissed as a dart flew over his head. Jarom obeyed, hugging the ground. "There's a dagger on my left leg. Can ya reach it?"

Jarom wriggled and squirmed among the dirt and ivy, swinging his weight about. "I think so," he said, scratching at the youth's leg with his bound hands. He groped downward toward the soft boot. There it was, tucked inside just above the ankle. He grasped it by the handle and yanked it free.

"Cut me loose," Kylac ordered him. "Quickly!"

A rush of panic and exhilaration caused Jarom to juggle the dagger and nearly lose it altogether. He settled himself and took firm hold. He began to inch his way down toward Kylac's tethered hands when the roots of the ground cover in which he was tangled tore free, causing him to slide right to the edge of the pit. His head actually cleared the lip, granting him a moonlit view of the body splattered nearly twenty feet below upon a pile of jagged rocks. Blood filled a shallow pool of swamp water that had seeped up from below, creating a ghastly dark foam that outlined the victim's corpse and painted the surrounding stones.

"Hurry!"

Jarom closed his eyes and took a deep breath, punctured lung or no. With agonizing care, he righted himself and turned back toward Kylac. Slithering like a serpent upon the ground, he reached the youth and shifted into a position from which he could saw through the lad's bindings. Before he could so much as touch metal to twine, however, one of the savages was there. Howling with feral rage, the A'awari tribesman lifted his spear high over the exposed back of Kylac Kronus.

Jarom didn't think. He simply reacted. Hollering a denial, he cast himself as a shield over the youth's body. He could only hope the spear wouldn't skewer them both.

He waited for the end to come. When it didn't, he glanced up, peeking through one raised eye. The A'awari warrior teetered upon his knees, a wash of blood spilling over his chin like a waterfall. A pair of the spear-length arrows had caught him, one through the side, another through the heart. The shafts lay now in such a way as to prop the doomed elf in a kneeling position upon the slope, as though to prevent him from ever knowing the peace of death.

Jarom was still gaping at the blasted corpse when a Powaii danced up to him. With the speed and dexterity of a cat, the savage plucked the knife from Jarom's hand and, with a measured flick, ripped the blade through the bindings—first his, then Kylac's. The elf then yanked the youth to his knees and shrieked into his ear before dropping Kylac's dagger point-first toward the youth's face. Kylac reached up and snatched the falling weapon by the handle, with the blade no more than an inch from his nose. The youth glanced back at the Powaii tribesman, who shrieked again and clapped him on the back before spinning around to rejoin the fray.

"What was that?" Jarom asked, rubbing at the torn circles around his wrists.

"Stay here," the youth responded, glaring upward at the lip of the hollow.

Before he could think to protest, Jarom gaped as the lad shot through the foliage, dodging past a hailstorm of darts and ar-

rows to climb back toward the area in which the main battle
was taking place. A pair of blades flashed in his hands, one
long, one short. They whipped back and forth and from side to
side, like the folds of a pennant snapping in a strong breeze. A
pair of A'awari turned to meet his charge. Kylac ignored them,
slipping past to engage another. Or so Jarom thought. But by
the time the youth pulled his blades from the body of the third,
the first two toppled to the earth, blood sloshing from their severed throats.

Although fascinated by the continuing struggle, Jarom
pulled his gaze away long enough to spot Allion, still bound
in a helpless heap nearby. Keeping low as Kylac had instructed, he worked his way over to his struggling friend,
mindful of the hollow floor. He didn't know how far along
its length the pit stretched, and he wasn't about to discover
the hard way.

"Hold still," he told the hunter, who was writhing in an
effort to free himself.

"Jarom! How'd you get loose?"

"Hold still," Jarom repeated. He pulled his own hunting
knife from his belt and sawed at the ropes securing Allion's
hands and feet. A moment later, the hunter was free, kicking at
the pole to which he had been tied and scrambling to his feet.

"Let's get out of here," he spat.

"Wait."

"Wait? For what?" Allion was incredulous. He cast about
sharply, surveying the action. "We've got to make a run for
it while we can. Where's Kylac?"

Jarom pointed in the general direction in which he had
last seen the youth. Kylac had moved on, but remained
nearby, engaged now with a lone A'awari spearman. The two
men from Diln watched openmouthed as the young master
swordsman diced the native's weapon into kindling with a
flurry of strokes and, with a double thrust, plunged his
blades into the elf's chest.

"What is he doing?" Allion croaked.

"I think these others are his friends."

"Friends or no, I've had enough of this. He's going to get
us killed."

Jarom wasn't inclined to disagree. But even as the words left his friend's mouth, battle tapered off. Jarom took a quick count. Nearly a dozen A'awari lay dead upon the hollow slopes, and by their screams, he sensed that those who had escaped were swiftly being hunted down. The air was now free of darts and arrows. The only Mookla'ayans he saw were those dressed in ropes of ivy, whose tattoos were round and artistic in nature, and whose only piercings consisted of horn-shaped woodchips hung from earlobes and lower lips. A pair approached them, massive longbows loaded with those javelin-sized arrows.

Allion held up his hands in surrender. Before Jarom thought to do likewise, Kylac came skittering down the slope, making a series of weird noises. The Powaii turned, and Jarom realized that the youth was speaking to them. Even more surprising, the natives seemed to understand him, lowering their bows and nodding in acknowledgment. One of them responded with a series of chirps, then pointed toward the rim of the hollow.

"Come," Kylac said to his companions, turning to follow his Powaii escorts.

Jarom did his best to ignore the mutilated bodies that he passed. Strangely enough, he took no satisfaction in the demise of these savages who but moments before had meant to inflict untold suffering upon him. Powaii tribesmen were now swarming about the slope, inspecting the corpses and doing who knew what else with them. Few paid any attention to the former prisoners. As they reached the top of the ravine, Kylac headed toward a Powaii who was taller than the rest, around whom several others had gathered.

Looking back, he told his friends, "Check the horses."

Jarom and Allion obeyed, quick to duck aside from the growing assembly. Nevertheless, Jarom kept one eye fixed upon his young friend, even as he worked with Allion to calm their terrified mounts. Amazingly enough, the beasts had escaped injury, kept as they were at the rear of the column and away from the fighting. At last, a minor miracle in their favor. Perhaps their death-defying expedition into this forbidden jungle would prove worthwhile after all.

Gazing past the nearly three dozen Powaii who now milled about at the rim of the hollow, Jarom continued to watch Kylac's conversation with the native leader. The hopeful feeling that had begun to well up inside him ebbed somewhat when he saw the youth frown. After a couple more exchanges, Kylac turned and, flocked by no less than a dozen Powaii, came up to him.

"Sorry, boys," he said. "Looks like this may have been a waste o' time after all."

Jarom's hope plummeted. "Why?"

"Cwingen Grawl is dead."

CHAPTER NINETEEN

Their journey through the marshlands was only slightly less dispiriting than before. Although they were no longer trussed up like roasted boar, exhaustion had set in. They had been on the move now for a day and a half, and Jarom was in dire need of rest. Sloshing through the jungle with his mount in tow, his legs felt awkward and heavy. His shoulders sagged; his eyelids drooped. Most disheartening was the knowledge that all of it—the time, the effort, and their hair-raising brush with death—had been for nothing.

Kylac claimed they had never truly been in danger. The Powaii, he explained, had been marking their progress all along, even before they had been discovered by the A'awari. It was because of the latter's presence that the more hospitable natives had not ventured forth earlier. But the Powaii would never have allowed their rivals to complete a successful foray into their territory without putting up a fight.

The argument seemed thin to Jarom. Kylac had no way of knowing that the Powaii would intervene on their behalf. The natives might have chosen to wait until it was too late. Or the A'awari might have elected to kill them much earlier. In either case, he was once again miffed that the youth had said nothing beforehand.

He remained uncomfortable even now, surrounded as he was by a ring of the mysterious Mookla'ayans—a ring whose numbers appeared to be growing the farther they went along. Although they seemed well intentioned, he had no idea what their true motives might be. These Powaii might simply be marching them toward the same fate they had so narrowly avoided at the hands of the A'awari, only willingly. After all, why drag them along kicking and screaming if they were happy to carry the burden of their own weight?

That thought, of course, was more sinister than the Powaii deserved. Despite their harsh manners and appearance, these people had saved his life, and Jarom was being unreasonable to remain so critical. As he was with Kylac. He had agreed to put his faith in the lad as his guide and protector. So far, so good. They were alive, relatively unharmed, and there remained the slim possibility that they might learn something of value once they'd had a chance to meet with the chieftains of the Powaii clan. Instead of dwelling on their near losses, perhaps he should be grateful that the youth had seen them through.

At that moment Kylac sidled up to him, reaching up to place a hand on his shoulder before Jarom realized the youth was there.

"Kylac. You startled me."

The youth fixed him with a meaningful stare. "Don't think I's forgotten what ya did for me back there."

Jarom's brow furrowed in puzzlement.

"In the hollow. Against the A'awari."

"What are you talking about?"

"Ya saved my life," Kylac explained.

Jarom thought back to the incident to which the youth referred. That wasn't exactly the way he remembered it. Had it not been for the perfectly timed strike of the Powaii warriors, it was likely they both would have died.

He shrugged. "I guess it wasn't your time."

"I owe ya one," Kylac insisted.

Jarom shook his head. "You saved my life first, remember?"

"That was different."

"I'll say. Your actions actually affected the outcome. Mine didn't."

"My life was never at risk. Had things gone south against Talyzar, I could've slipped away with none the wiser."

Jarom's puzzled expression returned. What was the youth getting at?

"Ya offered up your life to save mine. No one's ever done that for me."

Jarom laughed. "I find it hard to believe anyone has ever had the opportunity."

"I intend to repay ya for it."

Jarom held back another friendly gibe. He could see that the youth was serious. "Kylac, that's a nice gesture, really. But there's no need—"

"We're here."

Jarom's gaze snapped forward, his unspoken words already forgotten. The Powaii at the head of their column were ducking beneath the interwoven boughs of a pair of trees—some kind of fig or banyan—gnarled and draped with hanging vines. Another of the natives pulled up short before the curious threshold and chirped instructions at Kylac.

"The horses stay," the youth translated for his companions.

Jarom and Allion glanced at each other, then turned to find trunks or branches to which they could tether the animals.

"Leave 'em. They'll be fine."

Jarom shrugged, as he so often seemed to do around the enigmatic youth, and let go his steed's lead rope. He then stepped up to the archway, a pace back of Kylac and a pace ahead of Allion.

"Careful," the youth warned them. "Many o' the plants around the camp will be poisonous."

Jarom glanced about fretfully. "Which ones?"

"You'll know it when ya touch one," Kylac said. "Just keep your hands close and follow me."

He may as well have been a blind beggar being led around by a dog, Jarom thought, but kept it to himself. He considered himself lucky to have received any warning at all. With his hands thrust deep into the pockets of his breeches, he did as Kylac bade and followed the youth up to the natural archway. With a quick glance at the Powaii natives who had taken up guard positions on either side, he ducked through.

Beyond the strange portal lay a sprawling collection of rivers and sinkholes, spread across an uneven floor of flowering plants and ground cover. What Jarom assumed to be dwellings looked more like beaver dams, nests of sticks piled about the water's edge. Others were simply holes burrowed into the earth or the trunk of one of the larger trees. Few looked capable of surviving even a moderate storm. Then again, if what Kylac had told him was true, the Mookla'ayans would tear it all down deliberately before nature ever could, and rebuild it elsewhere.

The natives themselves were everywhere. On the ground, in the rivers, in the trees. Some he could see. Many others he could not. And not just men. Women and children stopped what they were doing to look at him, the former with barely bridled disgust, the latter with intense curiosity. Jarom stopped where he was to take it all in. If ever there was a place humans were not meant to tread, it was here, within the sacred confines of a Mookla'ayan village.

A shrill cry startled him from his reverie. The leader of their company stood front and center, announcing their arrival. Women gathered up their children and disappeared inside their various hovels. A trio of men stepped forth from the only structure that could be called a hut—a dome-shaped frame draped in animal skins that rested atop a small rise. As best as Jarom could tell, the rise itself was the most elevated plot of land in the village. The men approached the lead Powaii who had brought the outsiders. These were older tribesmen, Jarom realized, their skin leathery, their tattoos faded. The guide lowered himself in respect, coming to rest on both knees before bowing his forehead all the way to the earth. There he remained until commanded to rise, at which point it seemed to Jarom that he endured a stern tongue-lashing from his elders. When allowed to speak, the guide did so hastily, chattering and grunting and pointing wildly at Kylac. When he had finished, the three elders scowled and stared in Jarom's direction. At last, one of them groaned, then all three turned away.

The guide bowed again, and waited until the elders had reentered their hut. Once they had, he picked himself off the ground and jogged back toward the new arrivals. He said something to Kylac, then squawked and gestured at the nearest guards, who closed about the three outsiders.

"What did he say?" Jarom asked the youth.

Kylac flashed him that roguish grin. "The tribune will see us now."

Flanked on all sides by Powaii bowmen, Jarom and his companions marched toward the hut from which the three elders had come and into which they had disappeared. Jarom did his best to keep his eyes forward and his step in line with Kylac's. Despite the youth's typical assurance, it was obvious that the natives were less than thrilled about their presence, and that any deviation from the assigned path would not be tolerated. He could only hope that this meeting would pass swiftly.

Upon reaching the hut, the company leader stopped and addressed Kylac with what Jarom presumed were last-minute instructions. Sure enough, when the native had finished, the youth turned back to his companions.

"Remove your boots. We goes in backwards. When asked to do so, we turns around and kneels before the assembly. We stay that way until granted our leave."

Jarom and Allion nodded dumbly. Strange, Jarom thought, that such a crude and primitive people should practice such pointed civility. Without even pretending to understand why, Jarom did as he was told, removing both boots and stockings until he stood upon the wet grass in his bare feet. Since no one offered to take the articles from him, he left them where they lay.

"One last thing," Kylac briefed them. "If'n ya should open your mouth, take care not to look at the chieftain whiles doing so. Do not address him directly. Don't even look his way, if'n ya can avoid it. Speak to the tribune, or to me. Or better yet, say nothing at all. Understand?"

Again Jarom nodded. He wasn't following any of this, but he knew how to keep his mouth shut.

With that, their Powaii guide pulled aside one of the many overlapping animal hides, revealing an opening in the wall of the tiny hut. Kylac ducked inside, leading with his back. Jarom followed, glancing at Allion and swallowing against his nervousness. The hunter entered right behind him, after which the door slapped shut.

They were met with silence. It lasted for several moments, until Jarom began to suspect that he had been deceived, that they were in fact the only ones inside the tent. Remembering what he'd been told, however, he resisted the urge to turn about, staring instead at the wooden poles that framed the inside of the hut, leaving his back exposed. Finally, he heard a clap, and felt Kylac shift beside him. After glancing over to make sure, he followed the youth's lead and turned around to face their hosts.

Despite Kylac's warning on how to show deference to the Powaii chieftain, Jarom's gaze focused on the man straightaway. The esteemed elf was seated on a pedestal of some sort—the stump of a tree, it appeared. He was tattooed and pierced like the rest of his tribe, except that instead of a wooden horn hung below his jaw, he wore a pair of sharpened sticks thrust up through his bottom lip like tusks. A series of smaller sticks encircled the crown of his bald head, jutting forth like a phalanx of spearmen. As best as Jarom could tell, they had been driven into his skull like stakes, after which the heads had been sharpened. His forehead had been branded, his cheeks scarred—and all of it in a designed manner. Jarom was reminded suddenly of his own birthright and of what little desire he had for the trappings of power.

The chieftain's gaze met his own. Jarom looked away, made quickly self-conscious. To his left—the chieftain's right—sat the three elders who had come forth to meet them. The tribune, Kylac had called them. Jarom could not have imagined a more openly hostile set of stares. Were it not too late, he might have called off the meeting then and there, so certain was he that he and his companions were wasting their time. Help was not to be found, or at least, not here.

One of the elders gestured. Kylac knelt, facing the chieftain, but with his head turned so that his gaze was locked upon the tribune. Jarom and Allion followed his lead. There they sat, in that tiny hut devoid of furnishings, upon a carpet of animal skins, waiting yet again.

At last, one of the elders pointed at Kylac and issued a series of sharp and angry grunts. The youth nodded, but said nothing in response. A moment later, a second of the elders did the same as the first. Again, Kylac nodded. Predictably, the third member of the tribune followed suit. The youth reacted as he had to the elf's comrades, accepting of whatever it was they had said. Then silence.

Jarom squirmed. He wasn't sure how much more of this he could take. Already his knees ached. He was tired and hungry and sore. He wished he was asleep somewhere, preferably back in Feverroot, where he could look forward to Marisha's morning arrival, with her tray of bread and fruits. They would eat and laugh and trade stories about their lives. He almost smiled at the thought.

That smile vanished when the chieftain spoke. He glanced instinctively toward the voice, then turned quickly away, recalling Kylac's warning. He focused his eyes on the ground, then peeked up at the tribune. One of the elders was looking at the chieftain—they, apparently, were allowed to do so. Another was watching Kylac. The third was staring heatedly at him.

When the chieftain had finished speaking, the elder who had received the message relayed it to Kylac. As soon as the elf was done, Allion leaned over to whisper in Kylac's ear.

"What are they saying?"

"They wants to know why we're looking for Cwingen Grawl."

So Kylac told them. Or so Jarom assumed. The youth was allowed to speak unchallenged for several minutes. His narration was quite animated, full of the quick and harsh gestures with which this people seemed to communicate. Several times, he made those gestures in Jarom's direction. At one point, the youth waved a hand over his head. On more than one occasion, he jabbed him in the ribs. Not once did the youth look at anyone but those to whom he was responding, the Powaii tribune. Jarom, however, did. For almost as soon as the telling had begun, he had felt the weight of the chieftain's gaze shift in his direction. He had worked hard to ignore it at first, stealing an occasional glance before looking quickly away. But his attention was drawn by the intensity of the high elf's gaze. By the time Kylac had finished, he was returning the chieftain's stare in full, and only when the elders of the tribune began to confer among themselves did Jarom turn away.

"Now what?" he asked the youth.

"They know something," Kylac said. "They're debating whether to share it with us."

"About the city?"

Kylac nodded. "And the Sword. Something about a prophecy. I'm not sure if—"

The youth stopped short, interrupted by a fit of chirps and growls from one of the elders. Jarom looked over as the one on his far left waved as though brushing them all aside.

"They's asked us to leave."

Jarom stiffened. "What? Why?"

Kylac bowed to the tribune. "We's worn our welcome."

"Just like that?"

"Two have agreed. That's how it works." The youth rose to his feet and turned toward the exit.

"No," Jarom insisted. "No, they have to tell us."

"Let it go," Kylac warned him, raising an arm to stop him as he spun back toward the tribune.

"Please," Jarom begged.

But the elders ignored him, glaring at him with unflinching animosity. Before he could think better of it, Jarom turned his gaze on the silent chieftain and offered up a desperate plea.

"If you know something, you must tell us!"

Only then did Jarom recall that under no circumstances was he to address the chieftain directly. The shrieking of the tribune reminded him, as well as Kylac's suddenly urgent tug. But it was too late to turn aside and depart quietly. There was a flurry of movement as the sentries positioned outside entered the hut. Jarom felt their arms wrap about his waist and neck. He fought against their pull, but found their grip like that of hardy bramble stalks, sharp and unbreakable as they forced him to his stomach. He stared again at the chieftain.

"Please!"

But the chieftain was no longer looking at him. The elf

was watching Kylac, who had been beaten to the ground without struggle or complaint. As had Allion. Jarom felt a pang of remorse. It was not for him that his friends should be made to suffer. His eyes went wide as a spear was raised to the back of Kylac's head. An image of their battle in the hollow flashed in his mind. Only this time, he was powerless to help.

"No!"

It was not his cry that halted the spear's thrust, but that of the chieftain, whose sudden and ferocious bark brought all commotion to an immediate halt. The elders of the tribune turned to their master, chirping out protests. The chieftain stood, and the elders withered in apology. He spoke then to the guards, who, after a moment's hesitation, finally relented. Taking their weapons with them, they exited the hut like water spilled from a bucket. When they had gone, the chieftain came forward, speaking to Kylac directly. Again, the elders of the tribune complained, and again, the chieftain silenced them with a glare. The chieftain resumed his words with Kylac, reaching forth to help the youth to his feet.

Kylac replied in the native's tongue, his tone questioning. The chieftain responded with an affirming gesture.

"Well, wouldn't ya know it?"

"What's happening?" Jarom asked, rising slowly, carefully to his feet.

"This here is Cwingen U'uyen, grandson of Cwingen Grawl. It seems that Grawl's daughter, the one I saved, is U'uyen's mother."

Jarom blinked slowly, making sure that he understood. "So, he'll tell us what he knows?"

Cwingen U'uyen spoke, and all in the room listened. Even Jarom, who understood not a word but did not want to wait for a translation, strained to decipher the elf's meaning.

"He has agreed to help," Kylac confirmed, "should ya prove yourself worthy."

Jarom gazed upward at the towering U'uyen. "And how do I do that?"

"Ya pass their test."

"Test?" Jarom asked with suspicion. "What test?"

Midnight brume hung thick about the marshland. Clammy
brush clung to Jarom's arms and legs as he tromped through
the misty darkness, encircled by yet another Powaii patrol.
This time, in addition to a troop of warriors more than two
score in number, he was accompanied by the elders of the
tribune and the Powaii chieftain, Cwingen U'uyen himself.
A phalanx of scouts led the way. Jarom followed, flanked by
Allion and Kylac. The highest-ranking Mookla'ayans hung
farther back, protected by a ring of personal guard. In the
trees beyond, additional natives from the village kept pace,
following the procession with evident curiosity. Once again,
even women and children were among them. Jarom found
this odd, especially given the late hour, and wondered when,
if ever, these people slept.

Along the way, Kylac explained the rest of what had
been gleaned during their visit with the tribune. U'uyen,
Jarom was told, knew everything they wished to learn,
everything concerning his grandfather's expedition to
Thrak-Symbos, made nearly a century ago. All of it had
been passed down to him orally, a time-honored practice of
the Mookla'ayan people. This tale was of particular interest. As Kylac had suspected from the whispers of the elders, the Mookla'ayans had a long-standing prophecy
concerning the recovery of a Sword of Asahiel. It was to
happen, they believed, achieved by an outsider with their
help. It was for this reason that Cwingen Grawl had led the
previous expedition. Others had occurred before that. Thus
far, all had ended in tragedy or failure, and there were
those among the Mookla'ayans who no longer believed in
the prophecy at all. Compounding fears was the heightened
state of war between the Powaii and the A'awari. The tribune, therefore, was dead set against the idea of their chieftain abandoning them, if even for a little while, to oversee
this doomed venture.

Nevertheless, Kylac said, U'uyen had given his pledge.

Should Jarom prove himself in a test of courage and fate, the chieftain would join them in their quest.

It all sounded well and good. But there was still the matter of the test, and no small matter at that. Whatever this trial turned out to be, it was not one he was looking forward to.

And yet, he had no choice. To turn away at the possibility of failure would be to live ever after a life of doubt. Better that he should fail than surrender to the fear that he might.

Their company finally came to a halt at the edge of a lake whose borders stretched away into hazy darkness and whose far shore was shrouded in oblivion. Jarom snorted. The smell of rot and decay befouled the air. A fear of the unknown began to gnaw upon his entrails, a feeling with which he was growing all too accustomed.

The tribal leaders came forward, still surrounded within their circle of protection. When they reached Jarom's position, Cwingen U'uyen issued a command and a pair of guards parted. The chieftain stepped through the breach, gripping a ceremonial spear. For a moment, the high elf just stood there, staring at Jarom, who did his best to match the other's gaze. Then, up came a rawboned finger, pointing at him. Jarom flinched, but did not move, and remained quiet as U'uyen chirped at him in typical Mookla'ayan fashion.

"He says to remove your weapons and clothes."

Jarom broke eye contact with the Powaii chieftain long enough to scowl at his young interpreter. "Did he say why?"

"I suspect he will once ya do as he says."

Jarom glanced at Allion, who frowned.

U'uyen grunted and spoke again. Jarom turned to the chieftain, then to Kylac.

"He wishes to remind ya that it was us who came to him."

Jarom nodded. Without further complaint, he unbuckled his weapons belt and proceeded to undress. Moments later, he stood beside a rumpled pile of his belongings, and although keenly aware of his naked state in front of countless sets of eyes, remained calm and patient as he awaited additional instruction.

The chieftain held his gaze for what seemed like several minutes before speaking again. When he did, his words projected farther than before. Jarom had the distinct sense that this was not so much a personal address as a proclamation. When at last U'uyen had finished, Jarom was forced to wait yet again as Kylac contemplated what he had heard and worked to formulate an accurate translation.

"They wants ya to swim the lake," the youth said finally. "From here to the other side."

"That's it?" Jarom had expected something far more frightening. While growing up, he had spent his fair share of time in the lakes and rivers beyond the borders of the Kalgren, and fancied himself a strong swimmer. Then again, he wasn't exactly in swimming shape. As he peered out over the mist-shrouded waters in search of the far shore and failed to find it, he had to wonder if what the Powaii had asked of him would be beyond his present strength.

Cwingen U'uyen resumed his speech, and again, Jarom was forced to wait for Kylac to make sense of the words.

"If ya drown, ya fail. If you are devoured by the Nieten, ya fail."

"The Nieten?"

"A creature o' some kind. Lives within the lake."

Jarom gulped and looked again out over the waters. They looked placid enough, making it hard for him to imagine that a creature hunted their murky depths. Then again, he'd known from the beginning this would not be easy. A swim, no matter the distance, was too simple. A swim through the domain of a monstrous creature against which he had no defense—now *that* was more along the lines of what he had expected.

"I don't suppose he'll tell me how to avoid this thing."

Kylac relayed the thought to U'uyen and the others. Within their ring of guards, the elders of the tribune seemed to snicker. Their chieftain's answer, delivered by Kylac, was not much more encouraging.

"That is for fate to decide."

Jarom continued to stare out at the quiet lake. "Anything else?" he asked tentatively.

Once again, Kylac swapped words with the Powaii chieftain.

"He says if'n you are the one, ya's nothing to fear."

"This is ridiculous," Allion snapped. "Don't do it, Jarom. We'll make do without their help."

Jarom looked at his friend, then turned a questioning gaze upon Kylac.

"I'd not have brought us if'n I didn't think it necessary."

"It's not worth dying for," Allion insisted.

Jarom smiled. His friend was partly right. It was not worth the hunter's life. It was not worth Kylac's life. But therein lay the crux of this challenge. The Mookla'ayans' test was meant to challenge *his* strength, *his* will, *his* destiny. If he were to fail, no one but he would suffer the consequences. Should he die, he would do so alone. It was the best he could have hoped for. It was what he had wanted all along.

"Watch my things, will you?"

Allion heaved a mighty sigh and shook his head. Jarom faced Kylac, then Cwingen U'uyen, and nodded resolutely. The chieftain swung a single arm out toward the edge of the swamp.

"We'll be waiting for ya on the other side."

Lest any hesitation cost him his resolve, Jarom turned and made his way alone through the sedges and cattails that grew along the lakeshore. Mud oozed between his toes as the spongy earth gave way to stagnant waters. His eyes shifted left and right, scanning for some sign of the Nieten. But he saw nothing beneath the black surface of the lake. He waded forward, his feet sinking into the silt below. The water was colder than he had expected, and his body shuddered in an effort to adjust. The waters reached his waist before he felt the ground angle sharply away from him. Pausing just long enough to close his eyes and take a deep breath—and to remind himself that he could do this—he lunged forward, kicking his legs out behind him and casting the whole of his body into the lake.

The initial shock of the chill waters stole his breath and chased away his weariness. Forgotten were the hours of lost sleep, his hunger, and his wounds. None of that mattered now. Unless he managed to make it to the other side in one piece, nothing else would ever matter again.

He swam with overhead strokes, pulling the majority of his weight with his shoulders, kicking with his legs to provide that extra thrust. The water tasted foul, but there was no help for it. Time and again he lifted his mouth to one side for a gulping breath, which he would then hold for as long as possible so as to concentrate on speed. Within moments, he had settled into an easy rhythm, one that he prayed would carry him swiftly to the other side.

It wasn't long, however, before his shoulders began to ache with the unfamiliar strain. He tried at first to ignore their burn, hesitant to switch to a slower, more comfortable stroke so early on in this endeavor. Then it occurred to him that all of his thrashing was bound to attract the Nieten. The thought startled him and he stopped at once. He bobbed in place, waiting for the noise of his passage to die down into quiet ripples. Glancing about, he saw no sign of danger. With a deep breath, he started forward once more.

He swam this time more like a frog, kicking his arms and legs out to either side before swishing them back behind him. By keeping his limbs beneath the surface, he was able to proceed much more quietly. It also enabled him to keep his head above water, where he could scan for signs of trouble. Although his progress would be slower, it would be much safer.

Unfortunately, he found it impossible to hold this form for any length of time as well. His muscles simply couldn't handle the endless repetitions. Again he switched styles, turning sideways in the form of cutting shears, then over on his back. When he did so, he risked a backwards glance. He had made it far enough out that he could no longer see the shore from which he had started. Or perhaps it was just that the mist had thickened. Either way, there was no going back.

He continued on for several minutes, turning this way and that within the water whenever his muscles begged for a change. All the while, he kept his eyes and ears alert. The jungle haze hung like clouds just above the water, obscuring his vision. The only sounds were those of his sloshing limbs and his own labored breathing. Once or twice he thought he heard something large splash down into the lake, at which point his heart beat a little faster while his pace slowed. But nothing approached him. Nothing threatened. He took comfort in the knowledge that it was a large lake. Perhaps the Nieten, whatever manner of creature it might be, was occupied elsewhere.

That thought vanished in the instant that something large bumped his leg. Jarom kicked out, sputtering swamp water. He spun frantically, swimming in place, his task momentarily forgotten. The only ripples appeared to be his own. Neither fin nor scale broke the water's surface. His eyes wide, Jarom continued to scan his surroundings, fearful that at any moment, a monstrous pair of jaws would scoop him up from below. But none did, and after several empty moments, Jarom relaxed slightly, telling himself that it had been nothing more than a piece of debris—a sunken log, perhaps—or some small animal that had in all likelihood been even more startled than he.

Though unconvinced, he had little choice but to continue. He was cold and tired and his strength was fading fast. But as he went to right himself, he realized suddenly that he was no longer certain as to the direction in which he was supposed to be heading. He cast about, searching for the nearest shoreline. He could find none. It all looked the same in every direction, mist-shrouded waters stretching away into nothingness.

Again, something bumped him, and again, Jarom kicked out, whimpering instinctively as he fought down a rising sense of panic. He was struck by the recollection of a recent nightmare, a dream in which he had been hunted in a swamp such as this by some unseen creature while his friends waited onshore. If only he could blink it all away now as he had then.

Interesting, he thought, that he should dream of his death before it happened. But what then of his other dreams? Many had been mere recollections of times come and gone. But had there not been others linked to his future? He wished he could remember. Was there any chance he would live to see them come about?

Not if he didn't get moving, he reminded himself. He could

do nothing about the Nieten. He could not even see the beast. Nor did he have any weapons with which to fight it. He had but one option, to swim the lake as U'uyen had charged, to trust in fate to deliver him. The thought gave him hope. After all, he could not imagine that destiny had carried him this far only to abandon him now.

Once again, he made a quick study of the surrounding waters, fighting to regain his bearings. Although subtle and listless, no body of water this large was without its natural currents, driven by wind, weather, and yes, the movements of creatures locked within. Jarom steadied himself, searching for the ripples of his prior passage. In the end, he made up his mind, selected a direction, and continued to swim.

He pressed on for some time, doing what he could to concentrate on his course and not on whatever invisible terrors lurked beneath. Was it possible that the Nieten did not exist at all? Could it be that Cwingen U'uyen had made mention of the creature simply to test his resolve? Jarom had no way of knowing, but he thought it at least as likely as the notion that a singular monster lived within a forbidding bog such as this, feeding off whatever smaller animals made their way through. And in the end, the idea gave him hope, which was all he had to cling to.

He changed strokes so many times that he might have been swimming in circles. But he kept going. Fighting numbness and exhaustion, he continued through the darkness, one stroke, one kick, one pull at a time. He felt as though he would be forced to do so forever. But if that was the case, then he still had a long way to go.

It was without warning that he spied his goal at last. While switching from a lazy backstroke to his forward-facing frogstroke, he caught sight of a host of dark forms huddled on the shoreline. Jarom paused, wiping the water from his eyes and blinking to be sure. The forms remained, as did the mist-choked backdrop of jungle growth. He could scarcely believe the scene was real. Yet there they stood, just a few dozen lengths ahead of him. Had he the energy to spare, he might have cried out to them. He was almost there.

He pushed forward, more relieved than invigorated. The

image ahead came into focus. The dark forms were those of the Powaii. Oddly enough, they did not appear to be especially concerned with his arrival. Allion alone gazed back at him, standing apart from the others upon the bank. The main group, Kylac included, was huddled at the water's edge among a stand of rushes, as though inspecting something of interest. Jarom did not bother to wonder what it might be, but continued to concern himself with only one thing, making it to shore.

His knee struck something soft, and his heart sank. The Nieten, he realized, come to snatch him up at the last possible moment, having lain in wait all along, if for no other reason than to torment him with a false hope of escape. Now, with the end in sight, the beast would finish him.

Once more, it proved to be his imagination run amok. His other knee hit, then so too did an elbow. Not the slime of an animal's skin, he realized, but that of earth and mud. He had made it.

He crawled forward on hands and knees, splashing through the lily-strewn waters. Allion, recognizing his condition, came forward to help him to his feet. He shivered in the cold air, his teeth chattering. Weeds and grasses clung to his skin, which in the darkness appeared to have turned varying shades of purple and blue.

"I was beginning to think you'd drowned out there," his friend offered in heartfelt greeting. "Looks like I was right."

Jarom managed a quivering smile, then looked to where the others were gathered. "What's happening?"

The hunter shook his head, as though he didn't believe it enough to speak the words. "See for yourself."

Jarom eyed the man quizzically before staggering through the lakeside muck. The Powaii turned to stare at him with what seemed to Jarom a mixture of awe and suspicion. He shrugged their gazes aside, assuming them to stem from the fact that they had not expected him to make it.

Then he saw the creature.

Or what was left of it. Its half-eaten carcass lay in a twisted heap among the concealing rushes, chewed upon as though by a thousand tiny mouths. Where it had not been eaten, its smooth brown skin was lacerated and torn in the manner of whips and barbs. Where it had, sharp and slender bones peeked through layers of mangled flesh. The beast was huge, easily a dozen feet in length, and looked to Jarom to be some sort of cross between a fish and a salamander.

"Is that—"

"The Nieten," Kylac finished for him.

Jarom swallowed hard and shivered through a fresh wave of fear. So much for the Nieten being just a ploy to frighten him. He stared at its unbroken rows of teeth and the socket from which it was now missing an eye, and shuddered at what might have been.

Allion stepped up behind him, offering him his breeches, which he gratefully accepted. He put them on without ever taking his eyes off the remains in front of him.

"What could have killed this thing?"

"No one knows. They says the Nieten has lived unchallenged within this bog for better than fifty years."

Jarom glanced uneasily at Cwingen U'uyen, the elders of the tribune, and the dozens of Powaii who had turned their stern and disbelieving gazes from the Nieten to his shivering form.

"What does this mean?" he asked Kylac.

"The Mookla'ayans are a superstitious folk. They're not certain what to make o' this, but the prevailing opinion seems to be that whatever killed this thing did so that ya might swim across safely."

Jarom blinked in the darkness. Was he to be punished for this twist of fate? He watched as Kylac looked to the Powaii chieftain, then back to him.

"What it means," the youth explained with a wink, "is that ya's won yourself a guide."

CHAPTER TWENTY

They slept for about three hours before setting forth once more. Following his successful swim, Jarom and his companions had returned to the Powaii village among a steady murmur of guarded whispers. After a while, Jarom did not need Kylac's help in order to understand what the Mookla'ayan people were saying. After all this time, he had come. He who would reclaim the Sword of Asahiel from the gullet of history. He who would be led by one of their own into the ruins of another age to take hold of the ancient artifact and return it to this one. He who would plunge the world into darkness before delivering it once more to the light.

When translated, much of it sounded to Jarom like a lunatic's raving. Nevertheless, the overall discussion was music to his ears. With their coarse words and guttural speech patterns, the Mookla'ayans were singing the praise of his accomplishments. And though he had yet to achieve any of that which they were hailing as truth preordained, Jarom found it to be a welcome change from all of the desperation and uncertainty that had marked his journey thus far.

"If'n ya were to ask me," Kylac offered quietly at one point, "I'd say it stumbled 'cross one o' those prowling demons. Lucky for you. Unlucky for it."

But Jarom would not be discouraged. Regardless of how it had happened, if ever he'd needed further sign that he was treading a destined path, the Nieten's death was it.

Of course, not all were pleased. While it could be said that the general populace was thrilled by the prospect of the long-standing prophecy coming to pass during their life-times, the tribune remained anything but. Throughout the entire trek back to the village, the elders had urged their chieftain to reconsider. Jarom was not the chosen one of the prophecy, they said, but an imposter. U'uyen would be wasting his time and risking his life—risking all of their lives—if he were to leave his people. Tell Jarom what he should know and let him be on his way, they pleaded. Upon returning to the village, they had continued the debate. Jarom could hear them arguing outside the hut in which he and his companions took their rest. Despite U'uyen's assurances that they would set forth at dawn, Jarom had lain awake for some time, fearful that by the time he awoke, the chieftain would have changed his mind.

But Cwingen U'uyen remained true to his word. When Jarom was roused from a much-needed slumber, the chief-tain stood armed and ready alongside the companions' trio of fresh and well-stocked horses. Final preparations and instructions concerning the welfare of the tribe while U'uyen was away had been made during the predawn hours. All that remained was for Jarom and his friends to mount their steeds and follow the Powaii native north. With a small amount of fanfare exhibited by the people despite the scowls of the elders, the company did just that.

For the rest of the morning, the three outsiders rode their mounts in a slow trot behind the nimble Cwingen U'uyen, who jogged afoot. Notwithstanding some nagging reservations concerning the Powaii chieftain's presence, Jarom continued to be amazed by the elf's stamina and apparent dedication. As of yet, U'uyen had shared nothing concerning what he knew. Nor would he, he had explained to Kylac, until they were safely beyond the borders of Vosges and within the confines of the Kalmira Forest. The A'awari were everywhere, he claimed. Speed and silence would be required in healthy doses in order to see them through. Until then, they would have to settle for the company of their private thoughts and trust him to reveal what was needed when the time was right.

At this, Jarom had looked at Allion and rolled his eyes,

wondering when it was he would find a guide that would be good enough to discuss matters at *his* convenience. First Kylac, now U'uyen. At times, it was as though he was not even there.

Jarom was grateful, however, when the first day of travel passed without incident. By noon, they had left behind much of the swelter and stink of the jungle. By dusk, not a trace remained. The ground hardened, the vegetation changed, and the more familiar birds and animals of the Kalmira reappeared. Jarom wondered in passing how U'uyen must feel to leave his homeland, then decided he didn't much care. What mattered was that he was free of the deadly swamps and back among the familiar wilds of the more civilized world. He had survived the Mookla'ayans' land. Let them see if U'uyen would survive his.

They were permitted a small fire, and so ate well that evening of warm stew. Jarom mixed himself the last of the tea provided him by the Lewellyns, and sat back as his aches and pains faded away. Kylac and U'uyen spoke quietly among themselves, away from their companions from Diln. Both Jarom and Allion had grown weary of asking to be included, and thus didn't bother. Perhaps they would do so in the morning.

"Show him the map."

Jarom paused between mouthfuls of porridge, confused by Kylac's request. "What map?"

"The one in the book."

"You mean the one that's no longer there?" Allion clarified.

The four of them were seated around the campfire, reignited from the previous night to heat their breakfast. While Jarom and Allion ate, Kylac and U'uyen sat as before, debating matters without interference. Now, all of a sudden, the youth had asked for their involvement in what Jarom thought a peculiar fashion.

"What makes him think we even have one?"

"Because I told him so. Back before we left the village."

"Why?"

Kylac gave an impatient sigh. "Because their prophecy says we would. Like those led by his grandfather. So I told 'em the truth, that we had one, but that we couldn't read it."

"You tricked him?" Jarom coughed, somewhat aghast. He did not want to start out by making an enemy of he who was to lead them through the ruins.

Kylac shook his head. "I's been trying to explain to him about the book. But the Mookla'ayans don't seem to have a word for magic. I thought it'd be easier to shows him."

"Why not?" Allion shrugged. "Who knows? Maybe he'll be able to read it."

Jarom hadn't thought of that. The Mookla'ayans, and U'uyen in particular, seemed to be full of surprises. Perhaps the native would know of a way to make the faded writings reappear.

Setting aside his bowl, Jarom moved over to his stash of belongings. It didn't take him long to retrieve the massive tome that had played such a pivotal role in his decision to undertake this quest. Removing the book from his saddle-bags, he hefted it thoughtfully, then marched across the campsite in U'uyen's direction.

"What does he need a map for?" Jarom asked Kylac as he approached. "He knows how to get us there, doesn't he?"

The youth nodded. "He just wants to compare information."

"Shouldn't take long," Allion scoffed.

Jarom smirked as he cracked open the tome. Sure enough, its pages remained completely empty. He turned it about and held the blank pages forth as he extended the book to U'uyen.

"Gone," he said, waving his hand over the parchment.

The native glanced up, brow furrowed, then reached for the book. But as soon as he touched its covers, he recoiled as if burned, giving off a frightful howl as the book dropped to the earth. Jarom was so startled that he stumbled backwards, nearly into the fire. He managed instead to pitch sideways into a clump of brush, where he turned quickly to see what had happened. Allion and Kylac appeared equally stunned. The hunter had dropped his food bowl and sat frozen in place. Kylac crouched in a fighting position, swords drawn.

Cwingen U'uyen ignored them all, staring at his palms as if blighted. He then lunged forward. For a moment, Jarom thought that the elf meant to attack him. But he dove right past to plunge his hands into the fire. Jarom cried out in shock, Allion fell backwards over his log, and Kylac, sheathing his blades, leapt forth to drag the chieftain away. U'uyen shrugged the youth aside, grimacing in pain that Jarom could only imagine as he pressed his palms against the fire's coals.

A moment later, the Mookla'ayan pulled free his ruined hands. Smoke curled upward from blackened flesh, and a terrible stench filled the air. Beads of sweat simmered upon the native's forehead, and tears spilled down his ashen cheeks. From their various positions, Jarom, Allion, and Kylac gaped at the elf in horrified awe.

When finally the Mookla'ayan spoke, he did so quietly, addressing his hands as though in prayer or incantation. He then glared at Jarom, who cringed, before turning on Kylac. The youth bowed, offering apology before seeking an explanation. U'uyen responded, kicking dirt upon the discarded tome and hissing in fury before turning and stalking from their midst.

Once he had gone, both Jarom and Allion worked themselves tentatively to their feet. Kylac ignored them, staring after the departing U'uyen.

"Seems the Mookla'ayans have a term for magic after all." He turned to Jarom. "They calls it 'devil's bite.'"

Despite all appearances, Cwingen U'uyen did not leave them altogether. Kylac explained to them as they broke camp that the reaction with the fire had been some sort of purification rite. He wasn't sure what exactly had happened with the book, but it seemed clear enough that the Mookla'ayan people could sense a sorcerer's spell when they encountered it, and that the experience was less than pleasant. But Kylac assured him that all was well. U'uyen realized that they had tried to tell him of the strange ward upon the tome. The Powaii chieftain did not blame any of them, Jarom included, for the unfortunate misunderstanding.

Jarom remained skeptical, but trusted the youth's judgment. Sure enough, by the time the three of them caught up with U'uyen less than an hour later, it seemed the matter had been all but forgotten. Aside from the charred and blistered state of his hands and a surly detachment from those who followed him—including Kylac—the elf showed no ill effects from the incident. They remained on course, with the outright hostility that Jarom had expected nowhere to be found. And thankfully, the native made no further mention of any maps.

Nevertheless, a strained silence persisted throughout the day. While all tried to pretend nothing unusual had happened, Jarom could not stop thinking about it. The chieftain's conduct troubled him. Why was he not more upset? Why hadn't he decided to just turn around and have nothing further to do with any of them? The elf remained unapproachable as he led them northward through the dense maze of trees, but that seemed to Jarom a mild reaction given what he knew of human behavior. Then again, as he was forced to remind himself, Cwingen U'uyen was not exactly human.

Such thoughts, harmless at first, only led to deeper, more sinister ones. In all actuality, what did they know about this elf? Was it possible the native harbored some plot unknown to the rest of them? Did he mean perhaps to betray them and steal the Sword for himself? Why not? Why surrender it to a man who had no more right to it than he, especially when its power might be used to defend his tribe against the savage A'awari? His grandfather, Cwingen Grawl, had been the only one to return from the previous expedition. U'uyen had yet to tell any of them why. What was it he was hiding?

Jarom shook his head. There was no way to know. Not yet, at least. And until he had a better idea, he intended to keep his eyes open.

By the following day, all had been forgiven. Kylac and U'uyen resumed conversation as before, bantering back and forth like old friends. They even managed to make light of the previous day's incident, with U'uyen suggesting that Jarom should perhaps consider carrying something less harmful in his bags, like a nest of vipers or a hive of angry bees.

They set forth at a leisurely pace, with Kylac and U'uyen leading side by side through the virgin undergrowth. It was important that they keep the horses fresh, the youth claimed, for the trek through the Skullmars. Cool winds rustled loose needles from the surrounding brush, and the spread of overhead limbs diced up the sun until there was nothing left. Once more, Jarom felt grateful to be back in the forest and clear of the southern swamplands. If he never again set foot within the land of Vosges, it would be too soon.

Conversation was led that day by an unlikely source. The Mookla'ayan native, Cwingen U'uyen, took advantage of Kylac's language skills to share with his companions extensive knowledge about the sights, smells, and flavors of these lands. He began by pointing out certain plants and animals overlooked by the others, rare and wondrous species that could only be encountered here, where man and his kind were strangers. These gestures soon led to talk of Pentania, both past and present day. The elf spoke of those who had inhabited these shores throughout the ages, of their myths and legends, of their civilizations come and gone. Jarom was especially excited to learn of the ancient Finlorians, the elven peoples who had ruled these islands for untold centuries before surrendering their homelands to the harsher, younger races. Whether or not the Finlorians still existed, U'uyen could not say, but the native assured him that if they did, theirs was but a thin shadow of their former majesty.

Of the Swords of Asahiel, the elf knew little. He recited the common legends easily enough, of how they were forged by elven avatars and blessed by their gods for use in the creation of the earth, of their role in the Dragon Wars to vanquish entire armies of the winged titans, and of their gradual disappearance thereafter. But he knew nothing concerning the particular blade they sought, that wielded by the Finlorian high king, Sabaoth, other than that it was said to be the last.

Much the same was true concerning Thrak-Symbos. While the Mookla'ayan was well versed in the city's layout and day-to-day workings, he knew nothing about the cataclysm rumored to have destroyed it. As far as he had been told, no one did. The fall of the Finlorian Empire had formed a void in the annals of history, both oral and written. Aside from the Mookla'ayan prophecy that it would one day be recovered, the Sword and all that surrounded it remained a mystery. Whatever history was to be told would have to be discovered anew.

Jarom took the other at his word. He would have felt better had U'uyen chosen to share with them some of the details of his grandfather's expedition, but the Mookla'ayan did not volunteer that information, and Jarom was not yet bold or desperate enough to ask for it. As long as Kylac continued to trust the native, he would try to do the same.

Immersing himself in talk of the past, Jarom was able to backtrack through the centuries, to journey within his mind to another place and time. Locked within the shadowed vaults of this alien forest, he felt that his life and home to the west were a world removed. No rays of the sun touched them here; only its faint glow filtered through the tightly interwoven boughs overhead. They were strangers in a new land, or an ancient land, rather. He rode now among the elves and dwarves, orcs and trolls of the untamed world. Just beyond the walls of this forest lay the sprawling civilizations of these ancient races. At any moment, he half expected to break through the foliage and spy the gleaming ramparts and whipping banners of Thrak-Symbos, whose king could offer him a long-sought look at the very real Crimson Sword.

The trance came and went throughout the day, interspersed with various thoughts that circled constantly through his mind. Some did so like vultures waiting for him to fall—haunting whispers concerning U'uyen's motives, the darkening nature of his nightly dreams, and the safety of loved ones left behind. Others were more like eagles spiraling toward the sun—soaring visions of finding the Sword, raising an army, and chasing the wizard from his lands. He imagined visiting Feverroot when this was over, returning to Marisha Valour triumphant. What might she say to him? What might she feel for him?

Midday came and went, and with the rise of the afternoon, Jarom became aware of a distant rumbling, a faint sound he could feel as well as hear. The sound and quaking increased at times, then abated. The travelers made no mention of it. All knew that it was the throes of the agitated Mount Krakken, more than thirty leagues to the north. For those who had not seen or heard for themselves Krakken's awakening, the news had spread. Jarom and Allion had heard rumor while on the road south from Earthwyn that the dormant volcano had come alive. It startled Jarom even now to realize that he would soon have his first view of the monstrous mountain, and likely at a much closer proximity than would make him comfortable.

That thought triggered in Jarom another concern, which he called out to Kylac. "Are you sure we don't have to worry about the Parthans?"

The youth glanced back at him and quickly shook his head. "They're heavily engaged these days with Menzos to the north. Their patrols seldom travel this far south."

"Looks as though no one does," Allion observed.

"We're nearing the Skullmar Mountains. Not one man in a thousand has any business there. Rest assured it'll be a lonely trip."

Despite that assurance, Jarom noted that Kylac, as always, offered a study in concentration. To an untrained observer, the youth was as indifferent to their surroundings as a tree to the moss growing upon its side. But Jarom had been around Kylac long enough to recognize the truth. Nothing went unnoticed. The youth remained focused at all times on the five physical senses and maybe more, twitching at every new scent, every rustling leaf, every lengthening shadow. Whether due to his training or to a lack of conviction in their safety, Kylac Kronus was very much alert, and Jarom felt the better for it.

As he marked the youth's sure and steady movements,

Jarom was overcome with a sudden twinge of excitement. He remembered this scene. It had been in his dreams some time ago, back when he had separated from Allion in order to search for Whitlock. It wasn't exactly the same now as it had been then, but he now recognized Kylac as the faceless stranger in loose-fitting garb with whom he and Allion had journeyed through an aged forest. Like the vision he'd had concerning his swim through the jungle lake, he had seen this moment before it had come to pass. Another indication, perhaps, that he was on the path to his true destiny. The thought made him smile, then frown. He could only hope that not all of the dreams he'd had of late would prove as real.

Spithaera lay back in her glowing pool, watching its emerald light play in ripples upon the cavern ceiling. Her veins tingled, a sign of energies stirring to life. After nearly a thousand years of slumber, her strength was returning.

Even so, she was not yet prepared to venture forth blindly, recklessly. Contrary to the beliefs of those mortals inhabiting this realm, she was not some raving creature of chaos. She let them think her such because their fear suited her purpose. For her, death and mayhem were not cravings, merely the surest way to see that her needs were met.

That the natural order of this world had been upset by her presence was not her fault. It was man who had summoned her, believing her a tool to be used. Though she had broken the bonds of his enslavement, still she remained trapped. Such was the trouble with passing between worlds. Even one as strong in nature's energies as she could not simply open a portal and stroll through. One had to be pushed or pulled. And there were none she trusted to return her to her realm of origin.

In any case, she liked what she had found here—a world of comforts and sensory delight. She had thus decided to make the best of it, for herself and for her brood. In man's eyes, an invasive species. Still, she was an avatar, a daughter

of the Cythraul, beholden to no one in this realm of the Ceilhigh. Did she not have the right to seek her own survival? To
ensure the safety of her children and provide for them both
luxury and amusement?

She may have been born of those whose beliefs had
caused them long ago to split from the creators of this particular earth, but that did not make her any less deserving
of life's pursuits. She wanted what any creature wanted,
and would use any and all means to obtain it. A thousand
years ago, she had failed in her attempts. Thus, she had
emerged carefully this time, sending forth her minions to
see what was out there, to learn how the world had
changed. Most had returned to her unscathed, with reports
that this land, a wilderness at the time of her self-imposed
exile, had since been overrun by man. Man's strength,
however, appeared to have diminished from that which she
had faced centuries ago. Her children had seen little that
might stand in her way.

But much of that might have been their own enthusiasm.
So she had maintained her relative silence, gathering inner
powers that had lain dormant for too long, while enlisting
the aid of another to build for her an army. With the bargain
she had struck, there wasn't much in any world that would
be able to stop her.

As if the gods she served were listening to her thoughts,
there came a gentle flapping from the ancient corridor leading to her lair. Spithaera arose at once from the waters of her
pool to greet the new arrival.

The imp entered her cavern in a rush, hoisting itself skyward with a triumphant flap of leathery wings, soaring high
among the hanging stalactites. It dodged past the wicked
rock formations in a display of agility that brought a smile
to her face, then swooped down to land upon her shoulder.

"Welcome home, Mitzb."

The little demon purred as she stroked the hair beneath its
chin. It nuzzled her finger, then leaned close and chittered
wildly in her ear. Its chest puffed with pride as she warmed
with delight.

Spithaera smiled and turned to her sculpted minions. "Our armies are assembled. Our time is at hand."

In single file, Jarom and Allion led their mounts along the narrow, freshly hewn path, twigs and branches snapping beneath their feet. Up ahead, Kylac's shortswords whirred ceaselessly, clearing a route by which the company could proceed through the thick wall of brush. Not even the adventuresome youth claimed to have ever trekked through this stretch of the Kalmira. The twisting growth, predominantly dry and dead, smothered every inch of the region, offering no indication that life had ever disrupted its dominance.

For Jarom, the journey had fast become an ordeal. Shoving at every step past the boughs and brambles that blocked his path, dragging at the steed laboring behind him, fighting for breath within the dust-choked corridor, he had fallen farther and farther back from Kylac's lead. Whipping vines and slashing thorns tore at his flesh and clothing, causing him to itch and bleed without reprieve. A vicious throb in his back had become a constant companion, and he had been forced to stop more than once already in order to treat it with a poultice.

He was not the only one suffering. Allion's stride had slowed as well, becoming more deliberate with each step through the slapping, clinging, stinging growth. But the man remained silent, bearing his aches and pains and doing nothing to discourage Jarom's belief in this undertaking. For that, Jarom was grateful, and it left him to wonder how he was to ever repay the man for his support.

Cwingen U'uyen, on the other hand, glided through the brambles and deadwood like a fish through water, untroubled by the thorns and splinters crushed beneath his bare feet. While Jarom and Allion dripped sweat from every channel, the native's skin was marked with only a thin sheen. It seemed impossible that he should proceed as he did, with nary a grunt or grimace, especially given that Jarom had yet to catch the Mookla'ayan taking any form of sleep. Elf or no, it seemed to him most unnatural.

The same could be said of Kylac. As finely tuned as any machine, he withstood the hours and elements without shortening his stride. Either he was immune to the weariness that numbed the others of his race with each step, or he had discovered a way to neutralize its effects. In either case, Jarom had never seen the likes of him before, and remained anxious to learn more about the remarkable youth.

But the companions exchanged few words as they traversed the land, each lost in the labyrinth of his own mind. Drawing ever nearer to his goal—or so he hoped—Jarom focused now upon the artifact for which he had already suffered much and would unquestionably suffer more. Licking at the salty paste upon his lips, coughing on the dust and splinters lodged in his throat and lungs, stubbornly placing one foot before the other, he attempted to recall everything he had learned about the Swords of Asahiel. In reality, he knew virtually nothing, and Allion's challenge back in Feverroot concerning what the Sword might do for him had summoned within Jarom's imagination a flurry of grim speculations. What had led him to believe he would be able to wield the thing? If the weapon did not consume him upon touch, what caused him to think he would be able to unlock its power? If he could not unlock its power, how was he supposed to use it against the wizard?

With these and other doubts plaguing his mind, he wondered whether or not the talisman would prove sufficient reparation for his sacrifices—let alone the weapon that would enable him to save his people and free the land.

A sudden shout interrupted the agitation of his musings. Jarom glanced up, and a shaft of light stabbed at his eyes. At last, Kylac had breached the suffocating wall of vegetation, and now the blushing rays of the evening sun stole through to greet them. To Jarom, it offered a warm welcome, ushering them from their world of shadow back into a realm of light and discovery. With a surge of renewed strength, he and Allion hurried, scraped and haggard, into the promising world beyond the dark forest.

They were disappointed by the sight. Directly before them loomed the harsh, domineering peaks of the Skullmar

Mountains. The colossal formations seemed to mock their diminutive forms, pointedly reminding them of their insignificance. Jagged peaks jutted skyward, piercing the clouds and bearing the scars of their age for all to witness. An awestruck Jarom allowed his gaze to trace their rugged outlines, scraping over the crags and crevasses, outcroppings and defiles that marred their weathered slopes. Such marvels of creation, he thought, marvels risen up to challenge the very heavens for dominion over the earth.

Reigning over all, within the heart of the range, surged mighty Mount Krakken.

The mountain seethed, trembling with tumultuous life, and Jarom froze, entranced by the distant spectacle. A cloud of gaseous fumes puffed skyward like the breath from a dragon's nostrils, its sulfurous stench piercing their senses. Thin red lines streamed from the mountain's summit, crawling rivers of molten rock that bubbled forth from a hidden cauldron before burning their way over ice and stone into the valleys below. A low rumble reverberated both above and below the earth, the snore of a giant not to be disturbed.

"Krakken," Kylac acknowledged respectfully. "Thank your history books we don't have to go there."

The youth turned then for a hurried conference with U'uyen, leaving Jarom and Allion to gape at the display. Jarom tried to imagine the forces that yet remained locked within the volcano and found that he could not. To a tiny mortal such as he, the magnitude of the mountain's power was unfathomable.

"We'd best be going," Kylac prompted when he had finished with U'uyen, loosening Jarom's concentration on the spectacle. "We don't have long 'fore dark."

Another solemn moment passed before Jarom and Allion turned and, following Kylac's lead, mounted their steeds, barely able to haul themselves into their saddles. The group headed eastward.

"We're at the southern tip o' the range," Kylac explained as they went, "where ya says ya saw Thrak-Symbos on your map. U'uyen claims the entrance we want is on the coast, a couple o' days in. We'll be heading northeast, keeping to the foothills. If'n we can keep our feet, we should be able to find it."

Jarom nodded, not really paying attention, fighting to keep his gaze from Mount Krakken and upon the perilous path ahead.

The new terrain offered little respite. Within moments, the sun's warmth, so well received at first, grew unbearable. It beat upon the company without mercy, and their glistening bodies were soon stripped to the waist in search of relief. Worse, the paths, even down at the base of the mountains, were narrow and hazardous, full of clefts and fissures hidden beneath the scrub pines and grasses that struggled for life, forcing the companions to move slowly and to study every step. Except for the distant rumble that served as a constant reminder of its presence, Jarom forgot about Krakken and refocused his efforts on keeping his feet as Kylac had warned. Despite its wondrous powers, Jarom had never heard anything about a Sword of Asahiel being able to heal a broken neck.

They proceeded until nightfall and for two days thereafter, following U'uyen's lead. Hours churned by in slow succession as the fatigued travelers traversed the barren slopes and steep valleys in perpetual cycle. They burned during the days and froze during the nights—all save U'uyen, who despite his lack of dress seemed not to notice the swinging temperatures. Strong winds lashed at them, driven from the east and bearing with them the brackish scents of salt and sea. The landscape remained bleak and forbidding, less hospitable than even the choking forests and sweltering jungles through which they had trekked to reach this point. All was arid and stark and hinted of a world that might exist if mankind were to destroy itself utterly. To Jarom, it felt as though the journey would never end.

Eventually, it did. On the eve of their second full day within the Skullmars, Jarom found his company navigating a particularly treacherous defile, its winding course stretched over a chasm and buffeted on all sides by a biting wind. As before, U'uyen guided them through with painstaking care and precision. Upon reaching the other

side, they caught their first unobstructed glimpse of the
ocean. From high upon a ridgeline, Jarom gazed out over its
expanse, at dark waves that stretched into infinity across the
horizon. Below them lay a sprawling coastal valley open to
the east, its lower slopes angling down gently to meet the
vast panorama of the Oloron Sea.

U'uyen spoke to Kylac.

"This is it."

Nightfall enveloped them in its cool cloak as they worked
their way to the valley floor, coming off the high and rugged
slopes that jutted skyward in sharp ascent. They stopped beside a meltwater stream wending its way from the ice-
capped peaks far above. There they drank their fill of the
fresh runoff, and allowed their horses to do the same.
U'uyen left them at that point, urging them to take their rest
and promising to return before dawn. The three who remained then washed themselves as best they could, using
their shirts as sponges. None felt like traipsing a mile down
to bathe in the saltwater breakers; nor could they hope to im-
merse themselves in the stream's shallow depths. They
washed their steeds as well, fed them some of the oats they
carried, then hobbled the beasts among a few of the larger
rocks that littered the arid ground.

"Why is everything so barren?" Jarom asked when the
three had settled into their evening meal of dried meats and
fruits. "I would think that being by the sea, there'd be more
growth."

None answered right away, leaving his question to twist in
the wind.

"Can't ya smells it?" Kylac replied finally.

Jarom and Allion glanced at each other in shared confusion.

"Smell what?" Allion asked.

"It wasn't nature alone gave birth to these accursed peaks.
One sidelong glance at Krakken should tell ya that. These
mountains were shaped by some power that lingers even
today, making them a place o' death."

The ocean's roar seemed suddenly eerie as it echoed off
the nearby bluffs, a restless call. Jarom's gaze played about
the region, and he sniffed at the salty air. Struck with a sud-

den itch, he reached up over his shoulder to scratch at the healing scar upon his back.

"Why do you suppose Cwingen Grawl never told you what happened to the others in his party?"

Kylac shrugged. "None o' my concern, I guess."

"It doesn't bother you that he kept it secret?"

"All men keep secrets. Even elves." The youth tilted his head in an expression of curiosity. "What's troubling ya?"

"U'uyen," Jarom admitted. "Are you certain we can trust him?"

Kylac laughed. "Are ya certain ya can trust me?"

Jarom scowled, letting the youth know that he was serious.

"There are shiploads o' folks out there ya can't trust, but if'n ya treat everyone ya meet as such, ya ain't going to make it very far. I lived for six months with Grawl and his kin. The Powaii are as honest as they come."

Ordinarily perhaps, Jarom thought. But since they seemed to be dealing now with prophecies and magic, how could the youth be assured that there weren't greater allegiances at play here than those to one's fellow man?

"What if it's all an elaborate cross?"

"Suppose it is. Ain't ya gots enough trust in yourself to believe you'll overcome it?"

"Out here?" Jarom shook his head. "I'm not sure."

"Then let me says it like this. What choice have ya got?"

Jarom let the matter lie. Penned between the ocean to the east and the Skullmars to the west, he felt slight and insignificant, keenly aware of his own mortality. To disturb this ground with hollow chatter seemed almost blasphemous. So he sat in brooding silence, not wishing to irritate the immortal mountains with the echo of his words. In a short while, he had finished his supper, and proceeded then to curl up in his blankets to endure a restless night's sleep.

He awoke the next morning in a panic. Allion and Kylac were gone. He scoured his surroundings, searching desperately for some sign of where his companions might have disappeared to. He soon found it, a trail of dusty footprints leading from their vacant bedrolls. Jarom heaved a sigh of relief. In the next moment, his anxiety returned. They had abandoned him, left him alone in this strange and desolate place. But why? To do what? He traced their path of departure in the pale light of early dawn. Evidently, the answers to his questions awaited him at the end of that trail.

He was on his feet in an instant, slipping into his boots and buckling his sword to his waist. He noticed then that the horses were gone as well, even his. He was alone, forsaken by his friends, stranded in the foothills of the most inaccessible mountain range in all the land. There was no indication of another's passing—nothing to suggest that his friends had been forced somewhere against their will. It made no sense.

Tortured by evil possibilities, Jarom raced across the valley floor. The route he followed sped northward, twisting around the rocks and ravines that scarred the base of these ancient mountains. Oblivious to the perils of the path, he ran on until he rounded the eastern slope of the valley's northernmost peak. What he found there flushed the apprehension from his soul and infused him with awe.

As the sun crested the eastern horizon, a wash of red light spilled over upon a monumental structure hunkered against the valley's west wall. Ivy and moss wrapped the ancient building, clinging to its pillars and walls, sprouting through its cracks and seams. Gray marble slabs stubbornly defied the buffeting of the coastal winds as they had throughout the ages. It was the most wondrous sight Jarom had ever beheld, for he knew at once that it was the legendary palace of Thrak-Symbos.

For a fleeting instant, he wondered if it was merely a dream.

The trail blazed by his friends continued on ahead, leading directly into the palace. Slowly now, reflecting upon the great history behind the venerable structure, Jarom stumbled forward, coming at length to a set of time-ravaged steps that invited him to become a participant in that legacy. As his friends must have sometime earlier, he harkened to that call and slipped past two monstrous pillars standing guard like ageless sentinels at the entrance to their home.

Within, Jarom found himself at the edge of a courtyard, bathed in shadows cast by the walls about him. Fallen pillars and bits of debris cluttered the otherwise barren ground, and the dust of their decay stirred in the wind. Jarom located the trail of his friends once again and followed it with his eyes across the enclosure, into the depths of a building beyond. Awe gave way to dread, and he became suddenly determined to locate his companions as swiftly as possible so that he could leave this place to its ghosts. He knew not what it was that tugged at him in warning, but he knew better than to ignore it.

Keeping to the patches of early light, Jarom slunk across the yard. Around him, shadows seemed to move, swirling and shifting as if to measure his progress. It was with relief that he finally reached the dimly lit foyer into which his friends' path bled.

He could not determine the hall's dimensions, for it was enveloped in darkness. Ahead, however, he could make out a flickering beacon, and he hastened toward it. A torch burned within a bracket on the wall, its flame dancing mischievously upon its charred head. Its faint light revealed very little, but did illuminate the tracks of Jarom's quarry. Anxious to bring an end to this pursuit, he stepped forward, pried the torch from its sconce, and proceeded down the passage.

As he persisted, Jarom became acutely aware of the tomb-like stillness that enshrouded his path. Nothing stirred in the darkness—not a rat or even the smallest insect. The silence pressed in on him, broken only by the misplaced echo of his soft footfalls. He suppressed a tension-relieving shout, fearing it might awaken some demon lurking in the depths. The torch was nearly expended, and the tunnel did not appear to end. Despair closed about him with the blackness, and he began jogging in an attempt to escape its grasp. Up ahead, the tunnel curved to the right at a spiked gate. Jarom twisted about this corner and froze.

His hunt concluded here, in a broken heap of blood and bones. A surge of nausea threatened to erupt from his stomach as he forced himself to examine the mutilated remains scattered before him. The neck had been snapped back, partially severed, and the eyes and ears were gone. Only the tattered clothes and shattered blades prevented the corpse from being unidentifiable. It was Kylac Kronus.

Jarom spun away, unable to gaze longer upon the lifeless body that had been his companion but hours before. Then he remembered Allion. He cast about frantically, hunting for some sign that would reveal his childhood friend. An icy claw hooked the heart from his chest as he spied a new trail of blood that had been smeared down the length of the passage. Blinded by denial, he raced down the hall. He did not have far to go. Just a couple dozen paces away, the path of gore ended, and there lay Allion.

Jarom could not even find the strength to scream, to share with the world his torment. All he could manage was to fall to his knees in agony. Allion was dead. The bloody pulp did not even resemble a human form, but there was no denying the truth. Grief swelled over him in everlasting torrents, beating him into a hapless, sobbing mass, oblivious to all but his sorrow. He simply lay there, wishing he was dead, unsure that he was not. Only a remote piece of him registered the howl that echoed around him, piercing the innermost reaches of his torn soul.

He understood at once that the source of that howl was responsible for his anguish. Whatever beast it was that issued it had murdered his friends, and unless he hurried, would claim him as well.

Something beyond conscious will hauled Jarom to his feet. Discarding the smoldering torch, he began to run. The monster scurried to take up pursuit. He heard its claws scrabbling upon the marble flooring. An angry snarl cut through the air, and within moments, Jarom felt its fetid breath upon his heels. He urged himself forward, somehow willing his legs to move faster, and the stink of the animal that chased him fell behind. Perhaps the creature's hunger had been sated. Perhaps he would escape after all.

Blind in the absolute darkness, Jarom did not see the wall before him, and plowed into it headlong.

He struck the ground amid a shower of bricks and dust,

his senses spinning. The wall had collapsed and left him in a small chamber lit by a crimson glow. He shook his head. Suddenly all vertigo fled from him. Upon an altar in the center of the chamber lay the artifact for which his friends had died. The Sword of Asahiel, gleaming brilliantly, was more beautiful than he had imagined. Its power radiated out to him, blessing his soul, infusing him with life. Shaking away the pain, blinking away his tears, he reached for it.

Jarom screamed as a frigid claw seized his ankle.

CHAPTER TWENTY-ONE

Jarom thrashed and squirmed, arching his back and crying out against the monster's grasp. But its grip upon his ankle was like iron. He reached forward with one hand, clawing the air in a desperate attempt to seize the glimmering talisman before him. . . .

"Jarom!" a voice yelled. "Jarom, wake up!"

His eyelids snapped open and he was awake again, staring at a star-filled sky. The roar of the Oloron Sea filled his ears, reminding him of his whereabouts. He managed to shift his gaze. There was Allion, looking over at him with evident concern, one hand wrapped firmly about his ankle.

"Blazes. Calm down."

Jarom blinked in relief as realization settled in. Allion released him.

"Are you all right?"

Jarom nodded, not yet certain. He stared down the beach at the moonlit breakers crashing upon the rocky shoreline.

"I've never seen you so worked up," the hunter remarked. "What happened?"

Jarom didn't answer right away. The horrible details of the nightmare were still too vivid in his mind. High above, stars glinted like needles in the pincushion of the sky. A steady breeze continued to blow in off the coast, filling the air with a touch of mist and the stench of brine. He could hear their horses whickering nearby, awakened by the disturbance. As his breathing began to slow, so too did the frantic drumming of his heart. After a moment, the maelstrom of images swirling in his head began to fade as reality took control of his senses.

"Maybe this wasn't such a good idea."

Allion groaned and lay back on his rumpled bedroll. "Now he realizes it."

Jarom sat up, picking at the remaining images of his nightmare as he would strands of clinging cobwebs. He looked around.

"Where's Kylac?"

Allion shrugged. "Went looking for our Mookla'ayan friend, I suppose."

"Should we go and find them?"

"Go back to sleep, will you? The sun's not even up yet."

"So?"

The hunter shook his head, grumbling as though to himself. "We've an entire lifetime of fruitless searching ahead of us, and he wants to get an early start."

Jarom couldn't help but smile. Allion wasn't nearly as upset as he pretended to be. Although he was probably right: They would need all the strength they could muster for the long days of searching that lay ahead—first for the ruins and then for the Sword. Recognizing this, Jarom acquiesced to Allion's demands and lay back, determined to get some rest.

It was a futile endeavor. Each time he began to drift off, he found himself awaited by the broken heaps of his friends' bodies. He could dispel the images by forcing himself awake, but it seemed as though they were painted upon the insides of his eyelids. Inevitably, those lids would grow heavy once more, and the nightmare would resume. At last he surrendered to his insomnia, propping himself upon an elbow to overlook the eternal expanse of the ocean to the east.

"Can't you sleep?"

Jarom looked to Allion, who lay unmoving, his eyes closed. "No."

"Neither can I." The hunter's eyes opened, glancing over briefly before turning toward the sea as well.

They lay for several moments without speaking, basking in the quiet of the waning night. It all seemed unreal there in the witching hours of dawn. Their surroundings, their quest,

their lives—once so steady and predictable—turned upside
down. What were they doing here? How had they made it
this far? And what beneath the heavens was to happen next?
Together, they watched as the sun's first rays peeked over
the horizon, painting the ocean's dark surface with a shimmering stain of silver and gold. Jarom welcomed the new
day, trusting it to offer a much-needed reprieve from the bitter night.

"How long do you think it will take us to find this place?"
Jarom asked, rubbing his swollen eyes uncomfortably.

"I couldn't guess," replied Allion, his tone surprisingly
optimistic. "But we've been lucky so far. Perhaps that luck
will continue."

Jarom shivered and pulled his blankets up tighter. Lucky?
The tome discovered outside of Earthwyn had proven
worthless, and they had failed to find Whitlock. He had
nearly been slain by the wizard's assassin, and they had lost
weeks in Feverroot. Their trek through Vosges had yielded
them nothing more than an up-close look at cannibalism and
a guide whose grandfather may or may not have been responsible for the deaths of those last foolish enough to venture here in search of the Sword. If through all of that they
were to be considered lucky, then Jarom did not want to be
around when their fortunes changed.

"Anyway," Allion yawned, "as anxious as I am to be done
with this business, I'm in no hurry to trudge back along the
trail that brought us here."

Again, Jarom silently disagreed. Scouring the rugged terrain about them was certain to be even less enjoyable than
their previous march. Even at these lower elevations, the
slopes were twisting and jagged, fraught with rockslides and
pitfalls. Thinking back, it seemed to Jarom only yesterday
that he and Allion had been traversing similar ground in the
Aspandels while hunting for the Entients' stronghold. As
difficult and discouraging as that effort had been, this one
promised to be even worse.

His stomach churned at the thought, poisoned with cruel
understanding. Time was running out. Soon he would have
to face the fact that his lifelong dream was simply that, a

child's dream. Within a few days or weeks, he and his companions would run short of determination or supplies or both. He would then be forced to make his return trek, a journey rife with self-loathing and disappointment. An immediate return to the horrible truth that had led him on this odyssey to begin with, without the slightest hope of setting things aright.

The wizard would still rule Alson. The only question was how far his forces would have spread. Would Menzos or Partha or Kuuria have been threatened? And what of Diln? He and Allion had deliberately avoided the subject, but what were they to do if they had no homes to return to?

If he perceived Jarom's inner anguish, Allion gave no indication. Nor did he offer any clues as to his own musings. Wishing that he hadn't broached the topic, Jarom said nothing more, but marked the approaching dawn in quiet reflection of nature, of time, of anything and everything except for the senseless dreams that had carried him here. Somewhere in that period, weariness stole upon him, and before he could think better of it, he fell back and drifted off to sleep.

When next he awoke, the morning sun was high overhead, encapsulating the shadow that hovered over him. Jarom jerked within his covers, startled by the sight of sharpened stakes embedded in a man's head and the tusklike sticks that covered his grinning lips.

A moment later, his fear was dismissed by the excited command of a familiar voice.

"Get your gear," Kylac said with a sparkle in his eye. "We're going searching for a Crimson Sword."

Jarom could barely control his exhilaration as he gazed down at the small hole in the earth before him. It appeared unremarkable enough, a black fissure in the mountain floor, hidden among a smattering of rocks and boulders half a mile to the west of their camp. As U'uyen knelt upon one knee and brushed at its edges, however, Jarom saw the speckle of granite, of polished stone lining the inner rim, buried by the dust and pebbles of ages gone. They were indeed staring at an entrance to the ruins of Thrak-Symbos, which meant that the ancient city had lain beneath them the entire night!

"Is this the only entrance?" Allion asked guardedly.

Kylac shook his head. "There are holes like this up and down the mountainside, most too small for a man, which drop somewhere into the ruins below."

"So how do we know this is the one we want?"

U'uyen grunted. Kylac nodded and began uncoiling a length of rope looped over his shoulder.

"Because our guide says it is."

Allion remained skeptical. "But how can he be sure? How do we even know this is Thrak-Symbos?"

"Do ya know o' any other cities buried 'round these parts? If'n so, ya might've mentioned it by now."

"This is it," Jarom agreed, breathless with anticipation.

Allion frowned. On the one hand, Jarom understood his friend's hesitation. Even with U'uyen to lead them, neither of them had expected it to be this easy. That it had taken the native less than a day's time to locate the entrance used by his grandfather to enter Thrak-Symbos eighty-three years ago was somewhat hard to swallow. Had U'uyen himself been here before, perhaps? But the Mookla'ayan had not, meaning that he was relying on description alone, a set of markers unseen by the rest of them. Jarom imagined that for his friend the hunter, it was unnerving not to be able to recognize those same signs.

But once again, Jarom was beginning to believe. Something more than Mookla'ayan memory and mapping skills had led them here. The same fate that had planted the seeds of this dream within his mind was now watering those seeds into reality. While it might appear that he had simply stumbled to this point, he had in truth been guided by a power beyond his limited understanding, beyond his ability to define or even describe. He was beginning to believe that he could not have fought this quest had he wanted to. And if destiny had carried him this far, then it would see him through to the reclaiming of the Sword of Asahiel. For only with that final achievement would the rest have any meaning.

And yet, as Kylac busied himself with the rope by which they would lower themselves into the ruins below, even Jarom remained somewhat guarded, frightened to surrender entirely to his convictions, understanding how severe would be his fall should his faith prove unfounded. Cwingen Grawl had reached this same point and beyond, only to come away empty-handed. The true challenge, and any potential vindication for their troubles, resided somewhere in the darkness below.

Kylac formed a double loop in one end of the rope and slipped it around one of the many boulders that lay strewn about the hole. He tugged against the anchor, testing its hold, then held the free end up to Allion.

"If'n you're that anxious to see whether this hole will lead us to where we needs to go, you're welcome to go first."

Allion shook his head. "Try not to stub your toe on the way down."

"I'll go," Jarom offered. This was his quest, after all. If there was any danger to be faced, he should be the first to do so.

Kylac bowed, presenting the rope with one hand. Trembling with nervousness, Jarom took it, feeling its corded thickness in his callused palms. He looked in turn at each of his companions—at U'uyen, so stoic and certain, at Allion, who scowled in warning, and at Kylac, who winked in encouragement.

"Here we go."

He lingered a moment, then dropped into the cavity. He gripped the rope beneath him with his ankles, keeping it steady as he lowered himself hand by hand, easing into the deepening folds of darkness. The light was sufficient at first, slipping through several sievelike holes in the ceiling, but was quickly choked out by the deeper chamber shadows. Before long, he was moving by feel and instinct. He slowed his descent, wary of what lay beneath, inching gradually toward the earth below with a probing toe. Just as he was beginning to wonder whether there was a floor to be

found, his foot struck something solid, firm and flat and unyielding. Convinced that he had reached steady ground, he
released his hold on the rope and drew a torch from the sack
slung across his back.

Upon igniting it, he caught his breath, his aches and pains
forgotten. Shivers traced his spine as he strolled back and
forth, surveying his surroundings. He stood in the midst of a
spacious chamber, its tiled floor broken and littered with
iron braziers and bits of shattered pottery, as well as fragments of marble and other loose stone. The windowless
walls were covered with molded metal sconces and decorative trappings—weapons, banners, and tapestries weathered
beyond repair. What had once been a magnificent corridor
punctured both the north and south ends of the hall and
trailed from view. Several smaller doorways, most of them
collapsed, lined the walls around these central exits. From
the various cracks in the ceiling, rays of sun dribbled down,
threads of light too feeble to reach the distant floor. They tethered the chamber by its ceiling to the world above, frail life-
lines against its descent into history.

"It's safe," he called up to his friends.

Kylac was the first to join him, scampering down the
length of rope with barely a whisper of motion. Allion came
next, followed by U'uyen. In a matter of moments, the company was reunited upon the floor of the rubble-strewn room,
their gazes casting about in wonder.

"Where are we?" Jarom asked. His voice echoed eerily in
the stillness.

Kylac was already asking U'uyen the same thing. "Feast
hall," the youth replied, translating.

Jarom recognized then the shattered pieces of crockery
and cookware at rest beneath a damp carpet of dust and cobwebs.

"Where are the tables?" Allion wanted to know.

Kylac responded without looking at him. "Would've long
since rotted, by my guess. Three thousand years?" He shook
his head.

The three of them remained quiet then as U'uyen inspected the chamber, checking the walls, gazing up at the

ceiling, and kneeling now and then to examine the floor. Jarom took note that the Mookla'ayan didn't use a torch. Nor did he seem to need one, disappearing at times in the utter darkness before returning safely again.

"Where do we go from here?" Jarom whispered to Kylac, his eyes continuing to probe the many intricate details of the vast room.

"U'uyen says that the Finlorians honored their rulers in the manner o' gods. Unless he was the last to perish, this Sabaoth was likely given a proper burial by the survivors." The youth studied their surroundings, plain brown eyes searching. "With any luck, the Sword was buried with him."

Jarom shook his head. "A Sword of Asahiel would have been much more significant to the Finlorians than any single man. Had they found it after the cataclysm, they would have taken it away with them."

"Ya said yourself that the Sword never left these ruins, else we wouldn't be here," Kylac argued.

"If anyone had wielded the Sword after Sabaoth, the legends would tell of it," Jarom agreed.

"The Mookla'ayans believe the same. But the Finlorians did not die out all at once. U'uyen's people insist that Sabaoth was likely found, either by those who survived, or those who came later to view the devastation."

"But why go through the trouble of digging him up?" Allion asked. "Why not leave the entire city as a natural tomb?"

"And trust any who came after to keep it sacred?" The youth eyed them pointedly, as though their very presence could be taken as the answer to his challenge. "A Finlorian's place in the next life was determined by how well he performed his duties in this one. If'n chief among those duties was to show honor to his king, then there's no way Sabaoth would've been left to rot in the rubble. And if'n he died without a worthy heir, it's quite possible his blade stayed with him."

"So we're to search the catacombs," Allion surmised.

"That's where Grawl and the others ended up," Kylac acknowledged, "and U'uyen has reason to believe they was on the right track."

Jarom mulled it over, trying to decide whether or not the reasoning made sense. "I just can't imagine anyone leaving a talisman like that behind, especially if left accessible to the outside world."

"They may have warded it," Allion suggested. "Left some kind of trap for would-be thieves."

"Almost anything is possible," Kylac allowed. "But until we find something to suggest they's been separated, U'uyen is going to treat the man and the Sword as one and the same. We can only hope that finding the one will leads us to the other."

At last Jarom nodded. After all, the Mookla'ayans knew much more about the Finlorians and their ways than he did. He had assumed all along that the Sword was still with Sabaoth's remains. For some reason, he had expected both to be hidden in some undiscovered pocket of the ruins. But what Kylac said made sense. Before they went rummaging through every collapsed pile of rubble, as so many before them must surely have done, they should indeed seek out some of the more likely resting places for clues.

"If we know where we're going," he asked, "what's taking our guide so long?"

"Searching for his grandfather's trail, I would guess. It took Grawl six months to make his way to the catacombs. No need for us to mimic the effort."

They waited in silence awhile longer, each giving thought to the challenge that lay ahead. As he studied again his surroundings, Jarom imagined how Thrak-Symbos must have appeared in its ancient days of regal splendor. Tattered banners and tarnished weapons became in his mind a lavish array of ornaments hung upon gleaming walls of polished granite. Shadows cast by the torchlight were transformed into noble lords and ladies sitting before teeming platefuls of roast and vegetables and pastry treats, all part of the evening feast. Jarom smiled in private wonder. He had glimpsed the shattered remains of only one room, and already he could envision how majestic this city must have been. And with that came the urgent need to learn more of its unknown history and destruction.

U'uyen returned then, materializing out of the darkness at the edges of Jarom's torchlight. The native spoke briefly, his harsh grunts violating the stillness.

"We's found the proper entrance, but there are no markers in this room as to which way to go."

Allion snickered. "We're lost already?"

Kylac shook his head. "There are only two ways to go from here. If'n we guess wrong, we're liable to lose the rest o' the day. U'uyen wants to know if'n ya'll want to follow now, or wait for him to find our path."

"We'll follow," Jarom said at once. "No need to lose that time should he guess right. Besides, destiny is on our side, remember?"

Kylac looked to Allion. The hunter shrugged. "We've come this far, haven't we?"

The youth flashed a grim smile. "Watch your step."

They journeyed to the south, initially, ignoring the many alcoves and doorways that lined the hall as they headed toward the main corridor. They treaded slowly, silently, eyes sweeping in all directions, marveling at the vaulted ceiling, at the cracked and weathered walls, and at the intricate tiled floor coated in dust. While the holes and ducts designed for ventilation were clogged with mud and stone, the air permeating the room was stale but plentiful, further evidence that the breach in the surface was but one of many such entrances into the ruins, exposed over the years by the erosive elements of wind and rain. How long had it been? Jarom wondered. How many centuries had passed since this ancient citadel had last seen visitors? Aside from those led by Cwingen Grawl, might theirs be the first footprints to defile these halls in three thousand years?

They reached the archway that marked the room's entrance and plunged into its murky shadow. The light from Jarom's torch crackled and danced and filled his nostrils with the acrid stench of smoke. The corridor's broken walls leaned toward them; the ceiling sagged. All was held at bay just beyond the flickering light of their beacon, and Jarom felt as though they were violating hallowed ground.

The corridor folded and turned through a series of adjoin-

ing passageways. They passed through chamber after chamber, some large, others small, all stark and empty, lacking
the clues that might otherwise have revealed their onetime
purpose. U'uyen seemed confident enough in where he was
leading them, although Jarom had lost already his sense of
direction. The elf was skilled in ways that he could scarcely
imagine, Jarom reminded himself, and had the benefit of his
grandfather's experience. While he continued to privately
doubt the elf's motivations, he had faith enough that U'uyen
would not allow them to become lost.

Through hallways and chambers and antechambers they
twisted and wound, slipping at length from a side passage into
a room that even Jarom could recognize. It was the largest
they had encountered thus far. At its center, great pillars lifted
skyward, columns to support a domed ceiling that looked as
if it might once have been painted. The bases of these
columns were ringed with statues, pedestals, and decorative
busts, most toppled and scattered, some still standing. But it
was the dais off to his right that caught and seized Jarom's attention. A collection of chairs rested upon it, ornately crafted
seats wrought of marble and gold. One among them stood
taller and more pronounced than the rest, its opulent majesty
unrivaled by the others. A deep shiver wracked Jarom's body.
The throne of Sabaoth, high king of Tritos and the Finlorian Empire.

Jarom gaped, struck with the full truth of where he stood,
and why. He was a trespasser in time, slipped into history to
steal from a ghost who in life could have slain him with but
a word, a gesture, a glance. He did not belong here. He never
would.

U'uyen spoke, and Jarom cringed at the sound.

"He wishes to apologize. He guessed wrong."

No one moved.

"We may as well turn back."

Jarom nodded. The movement finally enabled him to
wrest his gaze away from the royal dais. In doing so, he
caught sight of several features that he had missed before.
The walls of the throne room were lined with shattered windows. Dirt and debris had poured through, knocking aside

exotic suits of armor and forming mounds that clogged from view any light of day. The dust here was the thickest they had yet encountered. Having billowed up beneath their feet, it now scratched at eyes and throat like a sentient creature. At the end of the vast hall, he saw a massive pair of iron doors, bent and flung wide, smashed inward by yet another landslide of boulders and earth.

Jarom was reminded of the discussion they'd had with U'uyen back within the forests of the Kalmira. The native claimed to have no knowledge of the cataclysm that had ended the Finlorians' reign. But he did know that Thrak-Symbos had been buried by a landslide so vast that not a trace of the city remained aboveground, triggered in all likelihood by an earthquake so devastating as to have sheared off half the mountain. So where was the mystery? U'uyen had claimed that mighty as it was, Thrak-Symbos was but a single city. Its destruction did not warrant the collapse of an entire civilization. Not even a series of such quakes would do so. Seeing the devastation firsthand, Jarom was not so sure. It appeared obvious to him in that moment that the Finlorians had been driven from these shores by a power not even the Crimson Sword could withstand. The awesome fury of the land itself.

An elbow nudged him. Jarom pulled his stare from the blasted portal to meet Kylac's questioning gaze.

"Are ya all right?"

"We shouldn't be here," he croaked.

"Then we'd best get going," the youth responded, indicating their companions, U'uyen and Allion, who were already moving away. With Kylac on his heels, Jarom gave chase, slithering back into the side portal from which they had entered the royal audience chamber. Doing his best not to even glance at the empty throne, Jarom scurried from the room and all of its tyrannical splendor.

CHAPTER TWENTY-TWO

They exited the ruins at dusk, having retraced their steps through the cavernous bowels of the city's palace to the feast hall through which they had entered. There seemed little reason to sleep within the ruins when they could just as easily make camp outside and resume their trek at dawn. Jarom was thankful for the decision. Only when he had climbed the rope and returned to the outside world did he begin to recover from the oppressive weight that had settled over him upon finding Sabaoth's ghostly throne. Back among the cool coastal breezes, he was able to breathe a little easier. After an evening in quiet conversation with his companions around a tiny campfire, he gradually came around to feeling himself once more, freed of the haunting doubts that had claimed him below.

For the first time since the fateful visit of Queen Ellebe to his village, he did not dream about the Sword. As far as he could remember, he did not dream at all. It was his initial realization upon waking, and though grateful for the first night of uninterrupted slumber in a month, he was unnerved by what it might mean. Had the dreams abandoned him? And if so, why? Was it because, having come this far, they were no longer needed? Or had he been too slow in answering their call?

He tried not to let it bother him as he went about his morning preparations. Misgivings aside, he was indeed lucky, as Allion had claimed—lucky to have encountered Kylac, whose blades would help keep them safe, and Cwingen U'uyen, whose knowledge had already proven invaluable. Given their combined experience and his own staunch determination, Jarom refused to see how they could possibly fail.

Allion, however, would not be so easily convinced. He didn't say as much, but Jarom could read it in his friend's rigid movements and worried eyes. Once or twice, he thought to offer a word of encouragement, but changed his mind. The hunter's reservations were only natural, reservations that he himself shared but had chosen to ignore. Any attempt to reassure his friend might just as easily cause his own confidence to sway.

By sunrise, the companions were clustered about the hole offering passage into the ruined city, equipped with weapons, torches, and shoulder sacks full of provisions. Moments later, they stood again within the feast hall. This time, there was no discussion. Without comment or delay, U'uyen led them across the debris-littered floor and into the northbound half of the immense corridor. The lack of hesitation marked this day's journey with a different flavor—more intent and purposeful—than that of yesterday's exploration. Jarom's nerves tingled with anticipation. The trek through Thrak-Symbos had begun.

The northbound passage ran unobstructed for several dozen paces before ending at an archway from which a pair of massive doors hung askew on rusted hinges. Beyond lay another vast chamber, in which a pair of matching marble staircases, one beside the other, ascended to a terrace above. The terrace itself wrapped about the entire room. The floor, as in most of the rooms they had seen yesterday, was devoid of furnishings but layered with the settling debris of passing ages. The air, trapped by an unbroken ceiling, reeked of decay.

U'uyen chirped at Kylac, gesturing with his fire-blackened fingers.

"Entertainment hall," the youth translated. "For dances and such. We wants to go there."

With an outstretched arm, he indicated the stone balcony above, and followed U'uyen toward it. Jarom and Allion had just begun to move, when suddenly Kylac stopped, listening intently, a scowl upon his face. U'uyen, sensing the youth's hesitation, turned back, while the woodsmen from Diln glanced at each other with expressions of ignorance and concern.

"What is it?" Allion whispered.

Kylac kept silent, still listening. After a moment, he spoke to U'uyen in the Mookla'ayan tongue and received a curt reply.

"Forget it," the youth said. "Let's go."

Again Jarom and Allion looked at each other. The youth had dismissed the matter far too easily. But neither cared to challenge the frown that remained on Kylac's face. U'uyen started ahead and Kylac followed. Keeping pace, Jarom and Allion resumed their silent march, scared to breathe, ears pricked and wary.

U'uyen led them to the right-hand staircase, where he raised a halting hand as he studied the unsupported structure. Dropping to one knee, the elf rubbed a blistered finger over the top of the marble, the surface of which came away at his touch. He must have been satisfied, though, for he vaulted forward, dancing nimbly to the terrace above. After a cursory glance, he turned and motioned for the others to follow. Kylac obeyed, an arrow of perfect motion. Allion went next, easing his way up the decaying flight.

When it was his turn, Jarom eyed the disintegrating stone distrustfully before mounting the first step. Slowly he placed one foot above the other, watching the ancient marble grind into sand beneath his feet. As he neared the top, he quickened his pace. It was then, without warning, that the step beneath him vanished in a shower of chunks and powder. Jarom's heart plummeted with the cascading debris. He dropped his torch to claw at the musty air.

His fall was halted as suddenly as it began by a firm hand clasped about his forearm. Jarom glanced up into the plain brown eyes of Kylac Kronus. One foot remained perched upon the shattered stone, but the youth's hold was all that was keeping him from pitching backward amid a pile of rubble. His discarded torch hissed and spat as it tumbled to the floor. Jarom caught his breath as Allion moved to assist the struggling youth. At that moment, the remaining lip crumbled and Jarom's second foot fell into the void. But Allion was there, taking hold of Jarom's other arm and working with Kylac to haul him up to the terrace. Jarom held his breath the entire time, until he lay sprawled upon the dust-covered floor. There he remained, eyes closed, while his heart settled into a normal rhythm.

"Guess that makes us even," Allion said, hands upon knees while catching his own breath.

Jarom nodded, thinking back to the hunter's scare within the Aspandels. He pushed himself up into a kneeling position and turned to regard Kylac.

"Are we even as well?"

The youth held out a hand. "Is that all my life is worth, a few broken bones?"

"Of course not."

"Then I reckon I still owe ya."

Jarom took the youth's hand and allowed Kylac to help him to his feet. He glanced back at the shattered staircase, whose dying breaths puffed forth in gritty clouds. Looking down at the jagged bits of marble, Jarom wasn't so sure that he would have survived the fall. Nevertheless, he wasn't going to argue. Although he disagreed with the youth's perceived life debt, he felt much safer with Kylac on his guard.

Turning back, he found U'uyen regarding him curiously. Jarom nodded, slipping a fresh torch from his sack and using the flame atop Kylac's to light it. The elf studied him a moment longer, then twisted about and crossed the gallery floor, passing through an open doorway beyond.

The adjoining room appeared to be some manner of foyer, a reception chamber for guests, perhaps. As in the feast hall, the ceiling here was dotted with tiny holes connecting it to the outside world. From their vantage point atop the terrace, the companions gazed down upon the contents of this new chamber, seeing little of interest. The balcony continued to either side of them, encircling the perimeter of the hall, and at the far end, two more flights of stairs offered access to the floor below. Doorways were abundant throughout, both above and below, empty sockets that seemed to stare apathetically at the newcomers.

U'uyen led them around, pausing at each archway just long enough to peer within. Each time, an obscure corridor was revealed, and each time, the elf passed it by without a word of explanation. At last they reached the far end of the chamber, where a portal slightly larger than the others offered them passage. Nodding approvingly, U'uyen plunged into the darkness, silently bidding his companions to do the same.

"Pardon my asking," Jarom whispered to Kylac after a few paces, "but does he have any idea where he's leading us?"

"Some."

"Any more than yesterday?" Allion scoffed.

Kylac smirked. "Go it alone, if'n you'd rather. Just don't expect us to come looking for ya once ya gets lost."

Allion frowned, but bit back his retort. He looked instead at Jarom, who could only shrug noncommittally.

U'uyen proceeded to guide them with confidence through a labyrinth of halls and chambers. For a time, Jarom tried to commit their path to memory, deciding it wise should they hit another dead end or become separated. But he was soon forced to surrender the attempt. Few rooms offered enough to distinguish themselves from those that had gone before. To heighten his confusion, the elf redirected them more than once, retracing their steps in order to skirt a collapsed passageway, select a corridor they had missed, or, at times, only to turn them right back around to the original path. Jarom was turned inside out in no time, with no idea as to where they were or where they were going. He wondered, if forced to it alone, whether he would be able to follow the muddled trails of their dusty passage back to freedom, and decided he very well might not.

Upon realizing this, Jarom gritted his teeth, frustrated at his helplessness. He knew not whether he should be grateful for U'uyen's guidance or suspicious of it. Without it—assuming they had managed to make it this far—they would have been left to wander for months or years and likely would have become irretrievably lost. And yet, he couldn't help but wonder if that wasn't the native's precise intent.

Recognizing such thoughts as useless at best, he tried to refocus on his surroundings, which had begun to show certain consistencies. At every corner, the walls were scarred not only with age, but with the evidence of a fierce battle. Stairways, chambers, and corridors alike were chipped and pitted and scorched by fire. The threads of banners and tapestries hung limply about the vacant doorways that lined nearly every passage. Although there were no signs of skeletal remains, a battle had clearly occurred here. Of that much Jarom was certain, even if he couldn't begin to guess as to who or what had caused such a conflict within the confines of the royal palace.

At some point, after hours of travel through the ruins, U'uyen led them into yet another vaulted chamber. The contents of this room, however, were remarkable enough to make Jarom's breath catch in surprise. For among the dust and stone and shattered glass were benches and chairs whose lacquered hardwood, broken and half-rotted, was nonetheless amazingly preserved and hinted still at its once exquisite craftsmanship. A plush material that resembled felt was hammered to this wood with pins of brass, and as Jarom's gaze slipped beyond the useless benches to the altar and statuary at the far end of the room, he knew precisely where they were even before Kylac spoke.

"A chapel," the youth remarked. "The royal prayer room. It should adjoin the main cathedral."

"And if it does?" Allion asked.

"We's found our entry to the royal catacombs."

"How is it that all of this is connected?" Jarom ventured. As far as they had come, he couldn't conceive of how they might remain within a single set of castle buildings.

"The royals kept their own private passages for getting around the city," Kylac replied, "particularly here within the palace complex. Have ya seen how we keep having to submerge before we come out again?"

Jarom nodded. He hadn't really noticed, but he saw no reason to admit that.

"All these routes were tunneled underground to avoid having to travel among the general populace above," Kylac continued. "When the city was buried, the passages remained mostly intact."

The enormity of the implication was not lost on Jarom. No doubt Thrak-Symbos, like most cities, had been a sprawling collection of shops and homes, parks and cathedrals, palaces and outbuildings, most of which would have been effectively cut off from one another by the tons of dirt and stone that had claimed them. Thus, the entrance uncovered by Cwingen Grawl's company all those years ago might indeed be one of the few—if not the only—such entrance into the ruins by which one could tunnel his way through the royal sector. Jarom had been utterly naive to think that finding the city would be enough to allow him to search for the Sword. Allion's concerns as to whether even this entrance would lead them to where they needed to go had proven far more valid. The thought weighed heavily upon Jarom as they pressed forward, causing him to wonder if the task he'd set for himself was beyond the strength of even destiny to accomplish.

U'uyen guided them up past the altar to an alcove beyond. Sure enough, they found a latched doorway, except that the unpreserved wood had rotted away, leaving only iron locks and bindings and hinges, piled upon the floor or hanging against the stone jamb. Past these, the company crossed through yet another series of rooms—the priest's personal chambers, according to U'uyen. Here they found another doorway, gated in iron but bolted from the inside. Giving sign that the elf did indeed feel the pain of his ravaged hands, U'uyen had Kylac lift the locking bar and turn the latch, after which the Mookla'ayan used his shoulder to shove the gate open. Ears ringing with the shrill echo of grating iron, the companions pushed through.

They proceeded down a narrow corridor, passing by a series of antechambers. The end of the hall was not far, marked by a curtain of some exotic fabric drawn to one side. They slipped by the shredded, shimmering weave and into the next room, which appeared to have served as the royal cathedral. Here they stood upon a riser overlooking a vast floor where a measure of the nobility had once congregated to worship. A rotting carpet ran down the center toward what had once been a pulpit. Behind this stood an assortment of statues and altars, while the windows were like those seen in the throne room—thin and towering, their colored glass shattered by the weight of sliding earth that now lay piled up about the side walls.

When their fascination had abated, U'uyen took them down to the floor and led them to the entrance at the back of the chapel. Once again, all that remained of the main doors were hinges and latches and bands of useless iron, knocked aside by those who had come before. Passing these by, the company made its way into yet another foyer, which branched off into three different halls. Choosing one, U'uyen beckoned his companions to keep close.

Coughing and sweating and covered in grime, the three men followed their elven guide down a featureless corridor. The flame atop Jarom's torch was burning low, allowing the darkness to creep closer. Without losing step, he wrapped a strip of cloth around the head. With the new light, he could now view the passage walls, dotted by vacant doorways and empty sconces. As they passed these doors, Jarom peered inside, discerning what he could of the secrets that lay hidden within. U'uyen's pace was relentless, and Jarom found himself falling behind the group. Still, he could not simply saunter by, ignoring the many mysteries lurking just a pace or two to either side. . . .

His curiosity kept his eyes from the path ahead, and before he knew it, he had marched blindly into a solid form. Glancing up, he found Allion glaring irritably.

Jarom mumbled a quick apology, then looked past his friend to where U'uyen stood facing a sizable opening. Fragments of what used to be thick iron gates were strewn about the hollow archway, which marked the end of the extended corridor through which they had just passed. Shattered weapons, cracked helms, and a dented shield littered the floor. Once again, the walls were scarred and scorched by fire. It was a ghostly scene, in which Jarom found no indication of another company having passed this way. He wondered briefly about Grawl and the others before deciding that their footprints would have been covered up by now, nearly a century later. He turned his head from side to side. The hallway stretched into darkness, but U'uyen seemed interested only in what lay beyond this once-protected portal.

Kylac went to the elf. The pair held a hurried conference, after which the youth returned to Jarom and Allion, motioning them together and bending close.

"This is the entrance we seek," Kylac explained in a faint voice. "Silence and caution from now on. There's something else within these ruins, man or animal, I can't says which."

Jarom waited anxiously for further explanation. Instead, Kylac turned and dipped across the threshold, following U'uyen. Jarom and Allion glanced at each other in stunned silence. Neither lingered for an instant.

As the company marched down the passage, Jarom felt an eerie apprehension welling up within. He thought back to those led by U'uyen's grandfather, all of whom had made it this far, but none of whom had returned. There must have been others who had come before. If the Sword of Asahiel remained undisturbed after all these centuries, then it was either well hidden or strongly protected—or both. What creatures or traps were they delivering themselves into?

He recalled his final dream, in which he had found the Sword, only to have been snatched from behind by the creature that had slaughtered his companions. Had that been a vision, then its meaning was unmistakable. What then could they do to protect themselves?

The question scarcely scratched the surface of his fears, but in doing so, a cloud of others billowed before him. What if there was no Crimson Sword to be found? What if he was leading his friends to their graves because of his belief in a child's tale? If the Sword was real, what evidence did he have that it rested here? And assuming it rested here, what suggested that they would be able to discover it in this immense labyrinth? And even if they could find it, who was he to wield it? If possessed of all the power attributed to it through legend, how was he to control it?

Choking on the stagnant air, Jarom felt suddenly helpless. His sweating palm gripped the hilt of his sword. It was far too late for such misgivings. His companions were too engrossed in this adventure to abandon it now. Besides, he felt responsible for ensuring that the trials through which they had already passed did not go for naught.

It was all the solace Jarom could muster as he trudged down the solid stone steps before him, regaining focus. If nothing else, he had to be alert.

The walls of the stairwell were rough-hewn, lacking the cut and polish found elsewhere throughout their journey. Jarom released his sword hilt and reached out to touch the coarse stone. He found it to be that of the earth itself, a mountain's skin, and not that erected by man or elf. U'uyen was leading them into the lowermost bowels of the ancient Finlorian city, into tunnels reserved for the dead. A chill raked Jarom's spine at the thought.

The flight of steps ended abruptly, emptying the members of the company upon a rock landing sanded down into rough humps. Before them stood an open archway. There, U'uyen stopped so suddenly that all three companions bumped into his arms, held outstretched to stop them. The Mookla'ayan stood quivering, eyes pinched as though in pain. When all had come to a halt, the elf reached up and pointed with a charred finger at a set of runes etched into the keystone frame of the empty portal. He grunted, and Jarom thought that he recognized the word.

Kylac turned to them. "Devil's bite."

Jarom swallowed, his throat tight. U'uyen chirped softly, gesturing at a frantic pace. Kylac struggled to keep up.

"This is it. This is where his grandfather left the others. Devil's bite . . . all around. He refused to pass through. The others went in . . . and never came back."

Jarom cocked his head. "That's not such a terrible secret. If that's all that happened, why guard the truth?"

Before Jarom could stop him, Kylac relayed the message to U'uyen. The elf listened, then turned on Jarom with a withering look.

"His grandfather was disgraced," Kylac said, making

sense of the elf's chirps and signs. "It was his duty to lead the others. Had he gone with 'em, or gone in after 'em, he might've been able to save 'em."

Jarom spared the elf a deferential nod, but made no apology.

"So here we are," Allion remarked. The strain in his features was exaggerated by the shadowy torchlight. "Does he mean to lead us through?"

Kylac repeated the question, at which U'uyen stared up at the markings on the doorway and shrank back against the stairs.

"He meant to. He meant to follow through where his grandfather did not. But he says now that he can't. The devil's bite is too strong."

Jarom studied the proud elf, whose normally stoic features writhed in personal torment.

"Fine," he said, drawing a deep breath. "U'uyen waits here. I'm going in."

Allion immediately shook his head. "What about the magic? You have no idea what you might be up against here."

"What would you have me do, turn around and go back?"

The two friends stared at each other in challenge.

"Whoever went through the trouble to ward this passage did so for a reason," Kylac observed.

"To protect those buried within," Allion argued dismissively. "Not necessarily to hide a Crimson Sword."

Jarom didn't blink. "There's only one way to find out."

A moment slipped by in tense silence.

"We're wasting torchlight. Ya wants to do this, or not?"

Jarom turned to the youth. "You don't have to go with me."

"And you didn't have to take that A'awari spear in the back."

"Kylac—"

"He's right," Allion snapped. "Let's get this over with."

Jarom regarded the man, his lifelong friend, and felt a pang of guilt. He wasn't sure which would have made him feel better, leaving Allion behind in relative safety, or having him by his side as they went beyond to face the unknown.

As he considered the hunter's clenched jaw and squared shoulders, however, he recognized that the choice was not his to make.

"After you," Allion beckoned.

Jarom nodded. He glanced back at U'uyen. The elf sat now upon the steps, hands clasped about his bald head, his fingers interlaced with the spokes of his embedded crown.

Jarom hesitated. "It might be best if more than one of us stayed behind."

"He'll be fine," Kylac assured him.

Jarom locked gazes with the youth and hoped that Kylac couldn't read what was in his thoughts. It wasn't for the Mookla'ayan that he was worried, but rather, whether or not they were being foolish to trust the elf to watch their backs.

Kylac looked past him to offer the native some words of parting. U'uyen grunted in response and waved them along. Before lowering his head, the elf stared at Jarom and addressed him directly. Jarom frowned and glanced at Kylac. But the youth just placed a reassuring hand upon his shoulder, then turned toward the open portal.

Jarom and Allion turned with him, peering through to try to catch a glimpse of what lay within. But there was a bend in the short hall. They saw a curving wall of stone and the slit of an opening beyond, but the angle and distance prevented their lights from exposing anything more.

The youth grinned. "Shall we?"

Neither man responded, but both followed upon Kylac's heels as the youth slipped into the shadows beyond, shadows that were dismissed by the light of twin torches. At the end of the hall, a cavernous, dome-shaped chamber was revealed, smelling sweetly of perfume. Almost immediately, Jarom felt his eyes go wide.

The chamber was filled with treasure, mounds of coins and jewels that sparkled in the torchlight. Polished suits of plate armor lined the walls, standing vigil over the riches and—situated in the exact center of the crypt—a massive slab of gem-studded gold. Upon the slab lay a robed skeleton, its skull wreathed in a crown of silver, its bony fingers clutching—

A sword.

Jarom caught his breath. The skeleton's hands were wrapped low about the blade, revealing the exquisite nature of the weapon's hilt. It was large, fashioned for two hands, and appeared to be made of pure silver. Nine sparkling red gems were encrusted within an intricately carved pattern of webbing, and several smaller green gems gleamed amid these. The blade itself was perfectly crafted and emanated a divine crimson glow. In light of its holy brilliance, all other splendors in the room ceased to exist.

For several moments no one moved. Jarom gaped, unblinking. There it lay, unspoiled before them, the talisman for which they had come in search. An artifact that left no question as to its divine origins. Its aura was that of perfection, the ultimate culmination of strength and wisdom. By all appearances, it was his for the taking. A dream for as long as he could remember. A fantasy come true.

"It . . . it can't be," he stammered, breathless.

But it was. As plain as the sun. As real as those who stood speechless to either side of him.

The Sword of Asahiel.

He thought to turn away, to confer with his companions. Deep within, something felt not quite right. Could the Sword really be just sitting here like this, waiting for them? What had happened to the others who had come through here? Why hadn't they taken it?

Even as the thoughts began to take hold, the Sword called to him. Not words, but feelings, smooth and reassuring. He was the one, his own thoughts whispered, the one for whom the blade was meant. The others had realized this and let it be. He need but reach forth and claim it.

Jarom started forward, blind to all but the Sword's allure, enraptured by its holy summons. A moment later, he stood before it, bathing in its radiance. Slowly, he reached forth a trembling hand.

But as his eyes locked with the empty stare of the robed skeleton, his fears returned like floodwaters to wash him back.

"I can't," he whispered, recoiling from the blade as if bitten. He had no right. The Sword would strike him dead the instant it sensed his weakness.

Even as the childish words escaped his lips, he realized how ridiculous they sounded. A wash of comfort overcame him, emanating from the Sword. With new resolution, he stared at the glimmering weapon. Deliberately, he stretched forth and peeled the yielding hands of High King Sabaoth from the blade, noting only in passing the lack of dust and cobwebs that one might have expected to blanket the corpse. Having freed the talisman from any restraint, he recoiled once again, his features contorting in disgust, his hands brushing away the cold touch of decayed bone.

The warmth of the Sword called to him. Despite its encouragement, his heart quickened until he could feel it pounding within his chest. Beads of perspiration rolled down his face and arms, making his skin clammy. His jaw tightened, and fighting down waves of nausea, he extended his arms yet again. His fists clenched and unclenched just inches from the polished hilt.

This time, a new and irrational fear took hold. A fear of success. A fear of the uncertain changes that would be wrought upon his life. He was frightened of the consequences and unworthy of the rewards. He was nothing, no one, an imposter among ghosts and talismans whose powers he could not begin to fathom. The achievement for which he had striven for so long was within his grasp, and yet, he did not deserve to take hold.

Once more, he drew away, wallowing in shame.

"This is what you came for, remember?" Allion coaxed.

The sound startled Jarom, and he whirled to gape at his friend. But as he peered into the man's glazed eyes, he found warmth and reassurance like that from the Sword, a lending of strength to do that which was needed—not only for himself, but for so many others as well.

"Claim the Sword, King Torin," Allion urged him, "for every citizen of Pentania."

Jarom smiled, a determined spark catching fire in his eyes. He turned back to the waiting talisman. A final collection of warnings gathered in his mind. Might the blade be

poisoned? Was it all just a trap? But such doubts, like those
that had gone before, could find no purchase in his thoughts,
blowing past like dry leaves. Without further hesitation, he
grasped the Sword by its hilt and hoisted it from its resting
place of three thousand years.

As soon as he did so, the crimson glow shimmered once
and flicked out. The jewels upon the hilt vanished, and the
silver degenerated into ordinary, leather-bound wood. Jarom
gaped in horrified astonishment. At his touch, the last of the
Crimson Swords had become no more than a rusted piece of
hammered iron.

"No!" he cried.

He turned to his companions, who stood shaking their
heads in stunned disbelief.

"It . . . it can't be," Allion exclaimed, blinking away the
effects of the spell that had gripped them all.

Kylac bent to scoop up a handful of gems from the nearest glittering mound. When he uncapped his hand, he found
only dust and pebbles. As swiftly as the treasure in his palm
had vanished, he cast the debris aside, looking up as the rest
of the illusion faded from view.

Together, the three glanced about as if seeing the chamber
for the first time. And in a way, they were. The central slab
was of stone. The treasure was of earthen debris. What had
appeared to be the skeletal remains of King Sabaoth was in
fact a pile of empty rags. The suits of armor that watched
over the crypt lost their polish; some no longer even stood
erect. The chamber itself was all that remained, vast and
rugged. Dozens of tunnels, invisible before, punctured the
rotunda's perimeter, as though it were the hub of an enormous complex. Even the smell had changed, perfume giving
way to must.

A quiet crackle, like that of a dying fire, drew their attention toward the entrance through which they had passed. Instead of an open archway, they found themselves facing a
monolithic door of granite. Its surface was intricately carved
with figures and runes, unblemished by latch or pull ring. A
faint blue glow illuminated its edges.

A pair of skeletons sat slumped on either side of the door,

clothed in rotting furs and leathers. Weapons and pouches hung from their bones. One of them clutched a weathered parchment as might a desert wanderer his last skin of water.

Kylac shook his head in disgust. "Lads," he said, "I thinks we're in trouble."

CHAPTER TWENTY-THREE

Jarom stood frozen, fighting back a sudden queasiness as Kylac moved toward the massive stone slab that had materialized within the archway to block their exit. The youth studied the door, then pushed experimentally against it. It didn't budge. Ducking low, leaning sideways for greater leverage, he thrust against it with all the might he could summon. He may as well have been pushing against the mountain wall.

He called out to U'uyen, somewhere on the other side, with a series of chirps that echoed throughout the cavern. He then waited, ear cocked to the glowing door. The Mook-la'ayan did not respond.

Not yet finished, the youth produced his slender short-sword and slashed at the portal's surface. Sparks of blue flame ignited and winked out. But after bending to inspect the damage, he came away shaking his head.

Kylac next considered the skeletons that framed the door-way and bent toward the one, pulling the parchment from its chalky grasp. He unrolled it slowly, bits and pieces flaking away.

"A map."

Jarom turned back to the weapon in his hand, running his gaze along its nicked and rusting edge, noting the sweat of his palm soaking into the leather wrappings. He was only vaguely aware of Kylac moving to rejoin him, and was caught off guard when the youth swatted the sword from his grasp.

"Forget the damn blade!" Kylac snapped.

The battered iron actually broke as it struck the floor, its pieces sent skittering across the uneven stone.

"If'n we're to find a way out o' here, we haven't time to waste."

Jarom lifted his gaze from the shattered sword and stared at the youth, disbelief over what had happened giving way to understanding and fear. They were trapped, having ignored the many warnings and suspicions to become ensnared by a magical ruse they should have anticipated from the first. Even Kylac was obviously unsettled.

"What are we to do?" Allion asked, the strain of despair in his voice.

Kylac studied the map, his features grim. "U'uyen claimed that the catacombs had but one entrance."

"U'uyen," Allion snorted. "Who's to say we can believe anything he said?"

The youth looked up, his expression dangerous.

"Does the map show us anything?" Jarom asked, recognizing the tension growing between his companions.

"Not that I can sees. Dead ends, mostly. And unexplored routes."

Kylac handed the map to Jarom, who examined its crude and faded markings. It was a sketch of the catacombs, all right, the last effort of those trapped before them who had sought to work their way free.

"Had they found a way out, they wouldn't have died here," Allion remarked pointedly.

Jarom had to agree. The longer he studied the map, the more the chasm in his stomach widened. These had been experienced men, veteran explorers. If they had failed to escape, how could he and his friends hope to do so?

"Perhaps we can dig our way out," Allion suggested hopefully, desperately.

"Dig?" Jarom echoed, dubious.

"Through the walls."

"With what?" Kylac scoffed.

The hunter scowled at the young master swordsman. "You're so proud of your blades. Why don't you give them a try?"

Kylac laughed at the prospect. "I'm not going to spend my last days like some rat trying to claw from its cage."

Jarom didn't doubt that Kylac's weapons, though ineffectual against the magical door, could chip away at the mountain stone. But the youth was right. To tunnel around to the corridor that had brought them in would take months. If they were lucky, they would survive a week down here without supplies. If they were lucky.

"You'd rather just give up?" Allion contested.

"If'n you're set on scraping through tons o' rock in a mad panic," Kylac said, gesturing toward the shattered blade that but moments ago had been the marvelous Crimson Sword, "then don't let me stop ya."

The heat of Allion's glare might have melted steel. He thumbed the bowstring strung across his chest, which held the weapon in place upon his back. "If it's a slow death you're worried about, I'd be willing to end it for you quickly."

Kylac smirked, one arm holding aloft his torch, the other hanging loosely at his side. "Try it," he urged, unwilling to back down. "With your carcass to feed on, I might find time enough to free myself o' this trap."

Jarom cleared his throat, stepping between the two verbal combatants before their frustrations could escalate. "We do what we came here to do," he said, recalling Kylac's words back in the jungle of Vosges when it was discovered that the A'awari were tracking them. He looked first at Kylac, then at Allion. "We find the Sword."

"You still believe the Crimson Sword is down here?" Allion asked, incredulous.

Jarom stared at his friend. Normally the more laid back of the two, the hunter had grown increasingly worrisome over the past weeks, and seemed now uncharacteristically fearful and frantic. Jarom, on the other hand, felt curiously numb, resigned and determined all at once. That which had brought them here could not be helped. All that mattered was what they intended to do about it.

"I don't know," he admitted. "What I do know is that that pile of shards over there isn't it."

Allion heaved a sigh of complete aggravation. He looked back to Kylac, who was still staring at him. He refocused on the youth, glowering.

"Let's go," Jarom demanded with surprising authority. "We don't have an eternity to spend down here."

"Do we have a choice?" Allion piped. "Suppose we do find the Sword. How will that get us out?"

"We'll worry about that when we come to it," Jarom replied with false confidence. He turned to Kylac, who stared at him in challenge. "We're not going to die down here."

Kylac's gaze remained steady. "We'll see."

Jarom kept quiet, locking his jaw in harsh assurance.

"One torch," Kylac ordered, stamping the head of his fiery brand to the stone floor and grinding its flame into trailers of smoke. "We save the rest."

Jarom coughed. The cavern darkness grew bolder, pressing about him. When at last Kylac's torch was extinguished, the youth faced him squarely once more.

"Lead the way."

Jarom nodded. Spinning on his heels, he surveyed the plethora of open passages, trying to align them with those scribbled upon the parchment before him. He realized, as did his friends, that it scarcely mattered which one they took. Determined to show only confidence, however, he deliberately selected one a bit off to his right and strode toward it. Upon reaching the tunnel's mouth, he paused long enough to turn and face his companions.

"Are you coming or not?" he asked, then plunged into the blackness.

Although its ceiling hung several feet above his head, Jarom found the tunnel stifling. The air was cold and musty and reeked of time itself, ancient and enduring. In the shadowy light, the floor and walls appeared relatively smooth. But what struck Jarom more than anything was the pervasive, choking silence. Having been raised in a lush woodland, the onetime Fason was accustomed to being surrounded by the ubiquitous sounds of nature, from the hum of insects and the songs of birds to the trickle of water and the rustle of wind. Down here, within the depths of the earth, the only sounds he could detect were those of their soft breathing and gentle footfalls. Magnified by the still-ness, these only made him feel more isolated and alone.

They came quickly enough to the first intersection, a crosswise passage lined with niches and alcoves in stacked formation. Jarom recognized them as deathbeds, hollowed in stone. He paused, letting his torch play about the area. The beds were empty, devoid of bones, shroud, armor—any-thing that might indicate the remains of a once-living crea-ture. Although surprised, Jarom spared the matter little thought. There were perhaps dozens of reasons as to why these forward graves might be empty, none of which would be of any help in securing their escape.

He started to ask his companions what direction they should take from there, then decided against it. Better to keep them moving and avoid further discussion until tem-pers had cooled—hoping, of course, that they wouldn't come across anything that would cause dispositions to sour along the way. Turning from the corridor of graves, he headed deeper into the warren of elven dead.

They wandered throughout the remainder of the afternoon and evening. The complex was far larger than Jarom had en-visioned, based on the map. The tunnel stretched for miles, running outward through ring after ring of elven graves. The crescent-shaped burial rings were spaced every dozen paces or so, and were connected not only by the main tunnel, but by various service passages. Some of these tied together as few as two rings, while others ran through the entire com-plex, but all served to create an intricate web of corridors to be explored.

Along the way, they continued to stumble across the re-mains of those foolish enough to have come here in the past. They lay in scattered clusters, slumped against the walls, the skeletons of previous treasure hunters who had at last ad-mitted defeat. Humans, mostly, although in many cases the bones were so badly decomposed that it was difficult to tell. It made sense, Jarom realized, given the age of the cata-combs, that they should also find members of the older races, who might have come here in earlier centuries, before their kind had been driven from Pentanian shores. But the common fact remained: All who had made it this far had died. And though few in number, each served as an unpleasant reminder of what fate held in store.

Oddly enough, they continued to find the wall graves empty throughout, leaving the trio to assume that the Finlorians had been buried without armor or weapons, and that elven bones decomposed more swiftly than a man's. It seemed strange that within such a vast complex, not a trace should remain of those it had been built to house, even after three thousand years. Yet the fate of elves long dead was of passing concern to men still clinging to life.

Every so often, they came across a crypt like that through which they had entered, filled with a central slab and ruined decor, reserved, Jarom supposed, for the highest-ranking Finlorian nobility. Some even contained one or more adjoining antechambers, although these secondary rooms appeared to have been long since stripped of whatever valuables they had been designed to cache. A new set of tunnels branched forth from each of these central crypts to begin the process anew. While some of the primary passages did indeed come to an end, when taken as a whole, the burial ground was without boundaries, a sprawling series of interconnecting wheels and spokes.

By the time they stopped to rest for the evening, Jarom knew that they would never live to explore the entire stretch of catacombs. It was therefore agreed that they would concentrate on completing those portions of the map left unexplored by the original artists. Although they were fearful of missing something that the previous adventurers had overlooked, it made little sense to redouble those efforts when so much remained undone.

When Allion had drifted off to sleep, Jarom spoke with Kylac. It would seem that rather than attempt to safeguard the catacombs against the scores of treasure hunters who they suspected would descend upon their ruined city like vultures, the Finlorians had devised a means to ensure that any who ventured too close would be denied the opportunity to share their knowledge with others. Like those that had come before, Jarom and his companions had sealed their fate the moment they had stepped through the empty doorway. No one on the other side would have any idea as to what had happened to them. As a result, those left behind would enter as unsuspecting as they, or better yet, would be deterred altogether by stories of their strange disappearance.

And yet, the elaborate deception made Jarom believe that they still had a chance of discovering the Sword. Granted, such a trap may have been set up to draw attention from the Sword's true resting place, somewhere else within the ruins. But given all they knew, it seemed to him they were in the right place, and on the right path. They just needed to figure out where that path led, unravel the mystery, and make their escape.

In the end, their efforts proved as futile as expected. Day after day, they awoke from the cold, rugged earth to resume their exploration. With a determination that did little more than ward off insanity, they trudged through the maze of tunnels that burrowed relentlessly through the stone earth. They marked their trail so as to avoid getting lost, filling in areas on the map and relying heavily upon Kylac's perfect memory and sense of direction. Still, not a trace of an exit could be found, nor a single clue that might lead them to the treasure they sought. Each night, Jarom hoped for a return of the dreams that had led him here in the first place, a vision to light the way. But his mind was as stark and barren as the tunnels through which they delved, a dark and twisting void.

Torches burned to stubs and were discarded. Food and water, though carefully rationed, vanished swiftly. They had entered the ruins with the expectation that they would spend no more than a day or two at a time within its depths before returning to the surface for fresh food and water. Of an estimated six weeks of supplies, they had carried with them two days' worth. They had stretched that over five, but now they were down to their last torch, their last waterskin, and a single strip of jerky. They would not be able to stretch much further.

On the fifth day, as Kylac and Allion took this inventory

within the chamber through which they had first entered the catacombs, Jarom made his way down one of the central passages, unable to face his companions, needing to be alone with his thoughts. As he moved away from the light of Kylac's torch, the darkness enveloped him. He welcomed it. Cut and scraped from his many trips and falls to the jagged earth, throat and eyes sore from breathing the dust and squinting in the darkness, battered and weary from the countless hours and miles of hopeless travel, he was at last at his wit's end. Kylac had been right. There was no escape from these tunnels. If the Sword was down here somewhere, then it was hidden deep within the stone floor or walls. They might have had a better chance, Jarom realized, had they taken Allion's suggestion and spent all of their time fighting to dig through the mountain itself.

He felt guilty, remembering how he had been the one to rush every decision, to lead them recklessly onward, thinking himself bold and stalwart to do so. He had fancied himself a courageous leader, pressing forward when U'uyen, Allion, and even Kylac had hesitated. He realized now that the worries of his companions in passing through the mysterious archway and in scouring the catacombs in search of an exit had not been born of cowardice or a lack of conviction, but of an intelligent, less naive understanding. He alone had acted impulsively, vainly, and ultimately, foolishly.

He wondered again whether U'uyen had had anything to do with their entrapment. The elf had tried to warn them, hadn't he? And yet, he had brought them here, and was the only one now with any hope of returning to the surface. Perhaps he already had. Regardless, Jarom was no longer surprised by the relative ease with which they had come this far. The Finlorians had needed but one safeguard. For what purpose such a trap had been laid, he no longer cared to guess. But he could admit now, if only to himself, that he had in fact met his end.

He thought suddenly of their horses, left tethered beside the stream above. By now, they likely would have devoured the supply of oats left with them. Once they did, the animals would have nothing to eat but the sparse scrub that grew here and there in baked, salted patches upon the barren earth. Tethered as they were, the beasts would have to break free or would soon starve. Yet another set of deaths for which he was responsible. The worst, he supposed, since the helpless animals had not been given a choice in the matter.

An image of Marisha displaced those of the skeletal mounts in his mind's eye. Jarom stopped in his tracks, closing his eyes against a pang of regret. Her memory had sustained him throughout this ordeal, fueling his determination to break free. *Don't ever give up,* she had said. Now the image of her face was fading, its lines and colors bleeding together in a hazy smear. She was lost to him, along with all else, never to be found again. He wondered whether or not she thought of him, and found that he preferred she didn't.

His eyes opened. He glanced to one side of the ancient hallway and found himself staring at a shallow alcove, an ornamental inlay of bricks and mortar. They had seen similar alcoves throughout the catacombs, spaced at regular intervals within the tunnels. On some they had found messages scrawled by previous adventurers, final accounts left behind for family and loved ones. The bricks and mortar, shaped by mortal hands, provided a softer tablet, Jarom imagined, easier to carve than the mountain's flesh. He recalled having scoffed at these self-serving eulogies, having wondered why anyone would waste the effort. It was a final act of failure, marking the moment in which the individual writing it had surrendered to despair. At the time, he had been unable to fathom the emotions that might drive someone to such a fruitless end. Now, with nothing left to do but die, it seemed to him the most logical act he could ever perform.

He knelt before the empty wall, pulling a dagger from his belt. Scarcely able to see in the diminished halo of Kylac's torch, he began to carve.

In the nearby crypt—that which they had believed to be the burial chamber of King Sabaoth but which would now serve as their own—Allion looked up, alerted by a faint scraping sound from the tunnel into which Jarom had wandered.

"We've passed through that tunnel a dozen times," he muttered. "What is it he expects to find?"

Kylac continued to study the tattered parchment they had used to map their journey through the catacombs. "Ya's got to admire his spirit."

"That's what got us into this mess," Allion groaned.

He bit down on their final strip of salted meat, trying to ignore the rancid taste. Kylac took a swig from the nearly empty waterskin.

"Any passages we haven't searched?"

"Several. But I can tells ya right now where they lead."

Nowhere, Allion thought dryly, and continued to chew.

Jarom paused to wipe the sweat from his brow. He had begun his work slowly, unsure that he actually had anything to say. But what started as a simple grave marker had turned quickly into a tribute to his companions, and from there, an apology. To Allion and Kylac, to his father, to all he had ever wronged or disappointed throughout his brief life. Even Ellebe, the name of his birth mother, made his list. For he understood now that it had been unfair of him to lash out at her, to so thoroughly reject one who had sacrificed so much on his behalf. Though he might never have cared to mend their relationship, he knew deep down that he had hurt her, and done so unnecessarily. For that, he wanted to apologize, and it seemed this would be his only opportunity to do so.

He had etched his characters carefully at first. Now he was chiseling away like a man possessed, stabbing and gouging, sending chunks of mortar flying free.

So fierce was his attack that without warning, the wall buckled, crumpling inward at the point of impact. Jarom fell back in surprise. He breathed heavily for a moment, then leaned forward, using his dagger to punch through the broken seam. His fingers played about the small hole. Could it be? He chipped away at its edges. The puncture widened into a gap. These alcoves, he realized, weren't decoration.

They were doors.

Jarom felt an undue rush of exhilaration. He had no

cause to believe that his discovery would amount to anything positive. And yet, he knew in his heart that he had done it. Would the Finlorians truly build such a massive complex with only a single entrance? Each alcove was in fact a passage to the surface, an access route through which bodies, tools, and the like could be transported. When no longer needed, the passages had been sealed. By opening them up, he and his companions could work their way free.

The more he considered it, the more certain he became. He held his hopes in check, however, resisting the urge to call to his friends until he had made sure. Forgetting his eulogy, he continued to chip away at the wall until the individual bricks began to fall free. Peering past, he saw only darkness. But that didn't stop him. Before long, he put aside his dagger and began kicking the base of the weakened structure. As he did so, bricks from above rattled loose and fell about his legs and feet, a shower of debris.

Jarom pulled back, coughing on a cloud of dust. He took his feet, standing before the ruined portal. He envisioned himself on the other side of the open archway, at the base of a flight of steps leading to the palace above. Grimacing determinedly, he leaned into the upper portion of the door with his shoulder, cautiously at first, then with greater confidence and force. Bits and pieces continued to fall in heavy chunks. A few nicked his shins as they bounced away, but he didn't much care. Just a few more hits—

All of a sudden, the remainder of the barrier collapsed. He pitched forward as expected, running through to gather his weight beneath him. What he had not expected was for the floor beyond to slope sharply downward. Setting his feet in anticipation of level ground, he was caught swiftly off balance and was unable to recover.

He cried out as he felt himself falling, sliding, and then nothing at all.

"What in the Abyss?" Allion croaked, his voice laced with apprehension. He was already standing, urged by Kylac to go check on the commotion, when his friend's cry cut through the stillness.

Before the echo of that cry could be swallowed by the labyrinth, Kylac was on his feet, slender longsword in hand. Allion drew his dagger, and the two raced down the corridor. They had gone only a short distance when they came across the rubble of the collapsed alcove. Glancing uncertainly at each other, they bent to inspect the fresh cavity.

"Jarom!" Allion shouted into the hidden passage.

Kylac thrust his torch through the opening, shifting it left and right to reveal the chiseled walls of a narrow tunnel. He bent low, sweeping the floor, which angled downward into impenetrable blackness. In the dancing glow, they found a glistening streak of blood smeared upon the rugged ground.

Allion started forward until a hand on his shoulder pulled him back. He spun about, more frightened than curious.

Kylac sniffed the foul air, his nose crinkled in disgust. "There's something down there."

"We can't leave him!" Allion protested, fearing the youth's words to be an indication of his intentions.

"O' course not," Kylac agreed. The youth stared at him reassuringly.

"All right," Allion said, forcing his senses to calm, "so let's go get him."

Kylac remained pensive, then shook his head. "I'll go. Stay here till I call for ya."

"What? Why?"

"In case I needs your voice to guide me out again."

Before Allion could protest further, Kylac ducked through the shattered opening, scurrying agilely into the void.

Alone in the darkness, Allion waited.

CHAPTER TWENTY-FOUR

When finally he came to a skidding halt, Jarom lay still, unable to move. His mind spun while he fought to stay alert against a chorus of pains.

From somewhere above, someone called his name. The voice was filled with urgency, but Jarom didn't recognize it. He waited for it to repeat its call, but it did not. Perhaps it had been his imagination.

He reached a hand toward the back of his head, feeling something warm and wet. He tried to process this information, but could not overcome the turbulent sensation of being tossed and pounded by a roiling surf.

Carefully, he rolled over onto his hands and knees. The movement helped to steady him. Fragments of his recollection returned, his drowsiness began to dissipate, and the rolling within his skull settled into an acute throb. The remainder of his body ached in rhythm, droves of pain running the length of his limbs. He rested there a moment, feeling the jagged earth that dug at the palms of his hands and the caps of his knees. He blinked repeatedly, his eyes useless.

A familiar voice reached his ears, softly calling his name.

Jarom lifted his head. "Kylac?" he said slowly. "Kylac, is that you?"

"It's me."

Jarom turned, slumping to his seat upon the earthen floor. He saw at once a faint light easing toward him through the folds of gloom, and watched it grow brighter as it bounced from side to side within his narrowing vision. A moment later, Kylac's face slipped into view behind the flame of a small torch.

The youth strode swiftly to his side. "Are ya hurt?"

"I don't know yet."

"I sees ya gashed yourself."

Jarom felt again the back of his head and recognized this time the wetness upon it. "I thought it might be a way out."

They looked around. The escape route he had uncovered was anything but. He had indeed found another access tunnel—one that led not to the surface, but to a deeper level of the catacombs. A burial corridor stretched away to either side, its line of hollow death beds as empty and changeless as the thousands seen above.

"Where's Allion?"

"Waiting atop, so as to mark our exit. Ya might wants to head back up there."

Jarom glanced back at the sharply slanted tunnel through which he had fallen, its opening to the level above lost in the darkness. "What about you?"

"I wants to have a quick look around first," the youth replied, peering sideways into the gloom. He sniffed, and for the first time, Jarom became aware of a rank odor trapped within the passageway.

"I still think—"

"Shh!" Kylac hissed, his attention focused down the passage opposite from where they had come.

Jarom bit his tongue, alarmed by the other's intensity. He strained his ears for any sound, but heard nothing over the thrumming of his own heart.

After a moment, Kylac leaned toward him and whispered, "Did ya hear it?"

Jarom shook his head, knowing that Kylac would sense the motion without looking at him. The youth reached down to help him to his feet. Jarom stood slowly, gingerly. But while his flesh was battered, nothing appeared to be broken.

Breathing a quiet sigh that did nothing to alleviate his apprehension, he set his gaze forward, forgetting all but that which lay ahead.

Kylac started slowly down the tunnel. Jarom limped along

close behind, struggling to keep his imagination in check. He found it difficult to concentrate, sucking mouthfuls of the dank air that had coagulated at these depths, feeling threatened by the darkness. He wondered what it was they were heading toward. Try as he might, he could not shake the vision of the shapeless creature that had hunted him in his dreams.

After a short distance, Kylac stopped beside a hole in the wall, small and jagged, at floor level. Kneeling closer, they found that it was in fact another tunnel, too small for a man to pass through except on his belly. Beyond the aura of their torchlight, it wound away into blackness. Jarom had no idea who or what had carved it, but he was fairly certain that it was not part of the catacombs' design. He glanced at Kylac. The youth just shook his head.

They moved on, finding more of the strange holes as they went. This lower level was filled with them, winding tunnels that crisscrossed randomly through passages, burial rings, and crypts alike. Like those a worm might make through soft earth, Jarom decided, then shivered at the thought. He had no desire to meet a worm of that size, especially one that could chew through solid rock.

As they passed ring after ring of graves and central burial chambers, Jarom marveled anew at the size of the city's catacombs. As massive as the upper level had been, it would seem now they had but scratched the surface of the complex. Just how deep did these tunnels go? Was there any end to their labyrinthine passage through the mountain's core?

The pair traipsed aimlessly through the ancient warren. Although they maintained their silence, Jarom couldn't hear what had alerted the supersensitive youth. Nor could he discern whether they were any nearer to the source of the rank odor. He supposed Kylac was following one or the other or both. And yet, the youth led them along without hesitation, as if tracking footprints through fresh snow.

Jarom did not bother to question why. Although pursuing the unknown entity didn't seem like the wisest course, he recognized that it didn't matter. Barring some unforeseen turn of events, they would be dead within a few days. Their search for the Sword had failed, and it was highly unlikely at this point that they were going to stumble across some miracle escape that had gone unnoticed by all those trapped before. That they were doing anything other than sitting around waiting for the inevitable was what counted. If they kept themselves occupied long enough, they might yet find death's approach mercifully sudden rather than agonizingly slow.

It was for this reason that Jarom continued to examine the stone walls of the endless tunnel as they went along, imagining against all hope that he might yet spy a clue as to the location of the Crimson Sword. For some time now, he and his companions had thought only of survival, of their pressing need for escape. But if they were to escape without finding the Sword, what then? What options would he have should the quest that had brought him here end in vain?

With a conscious effort, he thrust the thoughts from his mind. He was done wallowing in the fear of death and failure. No one had forced him to come here. He had met with compelling circumstances, but everything he had done had been of his own accord, every decision made of his own free will. If death was to come, Jarom was determined that it would find him with a measure of dignity.

And so he marched, without hope, but without sorrow. The darkness was smothering, the stillness suffocating. What waited beyond? The air was thick, increasingly dank. When this life was ended, was he to spend eternity in Olirium as a servant of the Ceilhigh? Or would he suffer in the Abyss as a demon's plaything?

The infernal darkness pressed ever closer, vast and inexorable, fringed with gray at the edges of their torchlight. That light was dying, Jarom realized, unable to withstand the pressures of the deep. After that, they would be lost, their sight claimed by the blackness, followed soon after by their bodies and souls.

He suddenly remembered Allion, and wished now that they had brought the hunter with them. So much for a quick look. Of what use was it to guard an exit to nowhere anyway? If they were to die, they should at least do so together.

He was about to suggest as much when light tore him from

his musings—not the smothered gleam from Kylac's torch, but a dull, bluish haze that hung in the distance. Untrusting of his own eyes, Jarom glanced at the youth, who must have noticed, but who gave no sign. They continued to ease their way down the corridor, approaching what appeared to be yet another of the central crypts. By now, Jarom was certain. A blue radiance emanated from within the chamber, much like that which had welcomed them upon every return to the crypt in which they had first become trapped. For a moment, Jarom wondered if indeed they had managed to wander back to the beginning of the labyrinth, marveling at how they could have done so without his realizing it.

The thought vanished as he stepped from the end of the corridor and into the chamber beyond. It was perhaps the largest he had seen thus far, with more than a dozen open archways, some of which fed into egress passages and others of which led no farther than the rear wall of a hollow antechamber. One archway was blocked by a slab of stone exactly like that which sealed their exit above, with ancient designs and figures etched upon its surface. The familiar blue light emanated from its unyielding form, filling the chamber with its glow.

Jarom looked about slowly, uncertainly, refusing to blink lest the discovery prove a trick of his imagination. He felt a twinge in the back of his neck, a feeling he did not recognize. Hope? It was too soon for that, too soon for anything more than a calculated study of their find.

Or rather, it was too late.

He glanced at Kylac, whose brow furrowed, dimly illuminated by the pale glow.

"What's wrong?" Jarom asked.

The youth responded by tossing aside his torch and unsheathing his blades. Jarom stumbled back a step in surprise. He shifted his gaze so that it fell in line with Kylac's, focusing on yet another of the mysterious worm holes, this one set at the base of the chamber wall a pace or two to the right of the glowing door. Then he heard it, a sudden rasping, as though of metal sliding against stone, coming from that very same hole. A moment later, he watched an enormous ser-

pentine beast slither from the breach. Tufts of coarse gray
hair crested the top of its lizard head and lined its back. Its
nostrils flared, while its steel gray eyes gleamed with feral
anticipation. Bathed in the unnatural blue light, the silver
scales that sheltered the fully twelve-foot-long body glinted
like freshly polished metal. A row of stubby, reptilian legs
was pressed up against each side of the elongated torso so
that the bottom of the feet faced skyward, their wriggling
claws raking the air.

"What manner of beast is this?" Jarom gasped as he found
his voice and drew his sword.

"A dead one," Kylac replied, his voice eager.

Jarom glanced again at the young master swordsman, recognizing the anxious gleam that flickered in the boy's eyes.
Here at last was an enemy they could fight, unlike the faceless horrors of entrapment and starvation. Jarom marked the
youth's unyielding posture and confident poise. In his calculating gaze, the comfort of his stance, the balance with
which he held his blades, Kylac Kronus was an instrument
of death itching to be unleashed. Though nervous and frightened, Jarom felt a surge of excitement at the thought of
fighting—at long last fighting rather than slowly rotting—
beside a warrior of such skill.

The moment of exhilaration was brief, forgotten the instant the creature unleashed a guttural snarl that crackled
through its gullet and throat and shook Jarom like a peal of
thunder. His fingers fidgeted upon his sword hilt while
Kylac remained motionless, coiled to strike. As if sensing
the youth to be its more dangerous adversary, the beast's
eyes narrowed in a glare that sought to pierce the barrier of
courage and discipline that shielded Kylac at all times. But
Kylac refused to falter, confronting the threatening look
with a discerning stare of his own, probing his foe's
strengths—and weaknesses.

For Jarom, the face-off seemed to last forever. If not for
the nervous switch of the beast's tail and the flare of its nostrils, the scene might have been sculpted in granite. Kylac
didn't blink, unwilling to surrender even that split-instant of
vulnerability. The creature, remarkably restrained, seemed

to weigh its options as it sized up its opponent. At last, just as Jarom had determined to leap upon the unholy reptile in order to relieve the tension, the stillness was shattered.

The creature whipped its head around to face him. Jarom was already moving, ducking instinctively as the rearing serpent lashed out. He closed his eyes against a sharp flash coming from the beast's sizzling maw, then cringed as the wall behind him exploded in a shower of loose stone.

He might have been finished before he opened his eyes but for the swift action of Kylac Kronus. Setting aside the shorter of his thin swords, the youth produced a tiny knife and sent it hurtling end over end toward the beast's head. Jarom looked up in time to see the creature leap to its feet, unfolding its sixteen legs and hoisting its frame upon them like that of a lizard. In doing so, it dodged Kylac's whirling blade and, with its serpentine tail, swatted it to the ground.

If Kylac was surprised, he didn't take the time to show it. He merely crouched lower, a determined grin spreading across his youthful features.

"Let's see what ya gots, ya mutated worm."

The beast snarled again, then threw back its head and lashed forward, launching a brilliant bolt of concentrated energy at Kylac. The youth did not drop to the earth as Jarom had, but slid to one side, leaving the thin stroke of lightning to hammer harmlessly against the chamber wall. The blast rocked the crypt, its concussion reverberating through the stone floor. Chips of rock flew every which way, leaving behind a shallow and smoking crater. But Kylac remained on his feet, ready to defend himself. Jarom climbed slowly to his, preparing to do the same.

By now, the creature had worked its way to the middle of the room, where, as in many of the crypts, the central burial slab was missing. Kylac began to work his way around the perimeter, motioning for Jarom to do likewise. Jarom obeyed, relieved that the beast continued to concentrate upon the youth as they did so. For several moments, they circled slowly, wary of any sudden move their enemy might make. Then, without warning, Kylac shot toward the beast, swords reaching for its throat. He had to alter his momentum mid-leap, however, to avoid the whiplike tail that sought to swat him as it would a fly. Dropping somehow into a crouch, he rolled forward and whirled, prepared to draw first blood from the beast's defenseless flank. But the creature's tail was once again swifter than he had anticipated, forcing him to scramble away from its downward slap before he was able to strike.

Jarom held himself in check as the beast spun to face Kylac with its lips turned up in a raging snarl, clearly frustrated that its prey had twice been able to escape unscathed. The youth appeared similarly disgruntled, scowling, Jarom guessed, at his own inability to land a blow. Nonetheless, the fire that consumed Kylac's eyes seemed to burn away any doubt that victory would be theirs.

Now it was the beast's turn to initiate the attack. With a strength and speed belying their size, the stubby legs propelled the creature forward. As it scurried, the energy sizzled forth. Leaping upward to avoid the lethal impact, Kylac entered the direct path of the monster's slashing tail. It slapped against him, and the bold youth was sent hurtling across the chamber.

Jarom seized the opening, hacking downward and tearing a shallow gash in the creature's neck. The metal blade rang in his hands as though he had struck iron. He dodged a tail swat, then struck again, leaving behind a second gash that barely cleaved the armored skin. As he lifted his arms for a third strike, the beast's tail caught him in the ribs, flinging him against the chamber wall, where he collapsed in a rumpled heap.

Fighting against an avalanche of darkness, Jarom kept his eyes focused on the battle. The reptilian worm spun back to find Kylac already on his feet. Rows of teeth became visible above and below the curled lines of its lips. The youth ignored these, focusing instead on the beast's tail as it switched back and forth, stirring the dank air. Jarom did likewise, noting that while any attack on the creature's flanks brought them within easy range, the lashing weapon was too short to reach in front of the beast's head. If the youth was to be effective, that was where he would have to concentrate his assault.

Without hesitation, Kylac darted forward. As expected, the creature rotated its body in order to bring its tail within range for a strike. But the youth was too quick. As agile as a hunting cat, he danced around the shifting beast, maintaining a position in front of its lizard head and safely away from its thrashing tail. In response, the creature began to twist back and forth at irregular intervals, seeking to catch the youth going the wrong way. But Kylac's dance was flawless. With his legs reacting to the beast's jerks and jolts the instant his eyes perceived them, he invariably kept the head before him—a head that was now quite vulnerable to his attacks.

In a blur of motion that kept Jarom mesmerized, the whirring blades slashed, jabbed, and hacked through the beast's tough hide with uncanny accuracy and lethal precision. As though recognizing that its survival hinged upon an immediate change in strategy, the creature prepared to launch another bolt of lightning. But the beast could not seem to recoil from the stinging blades long enough to initiate its desperate counterattack. Sensing victory, Kylac pressed his advantage.

In mere moments, the outcome was all but assured. The creature had thrashed itself into a hysterical rage, blinded and mortally wounded. In evident agony, the lurching beast tossed back its head, exposing its throat to Kylac's slashing blades. The youth saw the opening and took it, unable to suspect what was to happen next.

As Kylac's longsword slit its throat, the creature launched a burst of lightning skyward, where it crashed into the vaulted chamber ceiling. It was a reaction to the pain, an act of sheer desperation. But as the blast of energy struck the ceiling, the earth shuddered and relinquished its hold on hundreds of pieces of rock. They cascaded downward, pulverizing the ground beneath. Jarom cried out a weak warning from his vantage point, safely away from the shower of debris, but Kylac didn't have a chance. The youth sprinted from the rocky shower, but failed to clear its pounding wake. A moment later, he lay motionless, half buried amid a shifting pile of silt and rubble.

As the final stones bounced and skittered away and the dust cleared, Jarom found the lizard a serpent once again, its legs tucked up into their folded position. The thing was still alive, amazingly so considering the wounds it had suffered.

Smeared and splattered in its own blood and oozing more with every twist of its body, it slid forward, probing the blue-lit darkness. Even blinded, it found Kylac's senseless form almost immediately. Jarom watched as it slithered around Kylac, wrapping, coiling.

With a desperate growl, Jarom struggled to his feet. He limped forward, his weapon dragging after. The entire room wobbled before him, rocking like a ship at sea. As he neared the creature, he raised his sword overhead, then brought it down with an angry howl.

The beast hissed at him in vengeful defiance. Jarom ignored it and brought the blade up for another strike. As he did so, he lost his footing, slipping upon a loose stone kicked free by the serpent's thrashing. He dropped his sword and hit the earth, where he lay drifting in and out of consciousness. With blurred vision, he watched the beast finish wrapping its elongated torso around his friend and begin to squeeze.

Even as its life flowed from its wounds in thick streams, the creature hissed contentedly. Kylac jerked awake, roused by the pressures being applied to his body, only to find himself helpless, bound in a crushing grip. He arched his neck in silent agony, unable to breathe. Jarom moaned but failed in his efforts to rise. They were both about to die. There was nothing left to stop it.

As he closed his eyes in acceptance, he was startled by a hair-prickling yowl. Jarom looked up at the sound of an arrow embedding itself within the creature's hide. Another followed, then another, humming through the air, striking with lethal precision. Jarom cringed at the reverberations of the beast's death cry. A dozen arrows, some the size of spears, protruded from its skull. At last, the beast abandoned the fight. With a gurgling grunt, it slumped into the unseen void that had been widening beneath it.

Jarom grinned weakly, then did the same.

Stop shaking me, he demanded. *Let me sleep.* . . .

Jarom's eyes popped open. Alternating flashes of light and dark danced before his vision.

"Allion?"

Relief flooded the other's concerned countenance. Still, the hunter shook him once more for good measure.

"What . . . How did you—"

"U'uyen," Allion answered, saving him the trouble. "He came through the door and led me down here. And by the looks of it, not a moment too soon."

The archer twisted to one side, allowing Jarom to gaze groggily past him to where Cwingen U'uyen leaned over the recovering Kylac Kronus, helping the youth to examine his wounds. Beside them lay the corpse of the serpentine lizard, a twitching heap of ruined flesh.

Brushing aside Allion's protests, Jarom struggled to his feet. Torrents of agony welcomed his return to consciousness, lancing through his head and his side and causing him to slump back against his friend. Doing his best to ignore the shooting pains, he stumbled through the haze to join his companions.

Kylac looked up as he drew near, and offered a grim nod. "Well fought."

Jarom shook his head, unable to recall just then whether he had actually been of any assistance to the youth in his battle against the earth-dwelling creature. All he could think about was how miraculous it seemed, given the nature of the beast, that they had managed to evade more-serious injury.

He looked then at U'uyen, who glanced over long enough to accept his appreciative nod. He knew not what he should feel toward the courageous Mookla'ayan, but guilt was certainly a part of it. The elf appeared physically unscathed as a result of his passing through the magical door that had separated them in the tunnels above; however, if the tormented look in his eyes was any indication, then the native was suffering far more than Jarom could imagine.

"Lord, you two took a beating," Allion berated. "But I suppose you deserve it for leaving me behind like that."

Kylac brushed the scolding aside with a simple gesture, and a grim silence settled over the group. For a moment, their eyes drifted from face to face and about the chamber, each man taking quiet measure of his companions and surroundings. Their final torch smoldered upon the floor, having burned itself out during the struggle. All that remained was the eerie blue light.

"The door," Jarom remembered suddenly, casting his gaze in the direction of the enchanted portal.

"What about it?" Allion asked, dubious.

"We never tried it," Jarom said, moving already toward its glowing surface.

"It looks exactly like the one above," Allion observed.

Jarom knew what his friend was thinking. They were never going to be able to open it. And perhaps the hunter was right. But they had come this far, and had nowhere left to go. It only made sense to try.

He stopped before the massive slab, letting his eyes and then his fingers play about the sculpted surface. Glancing back at his companions, he saw only doubts and resignation. Ignoring their bleak stares, he muttered a silent prayer and pressed his shoulder against the unyielding stone. As before, it refused to budge. Rather than abandon what hope remained for them, he pushed and shoved at all angles, willing the slab to slide free. But the effort was indeed useless. It was more like a wall than a door, a permanent fixture wedged in place by the Ceilhigh themselves. After a moment, he pulled away, slumping in defeat.

He looked back at the others. Allion shook his head, as though in reprimand of Jarom's continued devotion to a lost cause. U'uyen stared blankly, peering at him with that haunted look in his eyes. Kylac, however, stood slowly, rising from his kneeling position and moving toward him, an intense expression upon his face.

"Allion's right," Jarom breathed as the youth approached. "It won't open."

"It may not matter," Kylac said.

Because they were dead anyway, Jarom thought. Because it was too late to make any difference.

He realized then that Kylac was not studying the door, but the hole at the base of the wall, the jagged cleft through which the creature that now lay dead in the middle of the chamber had emerged. Jarom's departing hopes lodged in his throat as Kylac stopped and knelt beside the forgotten fissure, then glanced up at him questioningly.

"It may only lead to a nest o' those things," the youth remarked, eyeing him in fair warning.

"And it may be our only way out."

Kylac nodded, and the decision was made. Dropping to his stomach, the youth peered into the tunnel's depths. "There's light ahead."

That brought Allion over, and when all three were gathered, U'uyen joined them. Kylac went first, swallowed quickly from view. Behind the youth, Jarom eased his injured body down to the floor. Kylac was right. Beyond the youth's squirming form, a blue light glowed—yet another door, most likely. Whatever it was, it lay not far beyond. Even from here he could see the end of the tunnel, just a few paces away. Already Kylac was pulling free on the other side.

Jarom crawled forward, scurrying after as swiftly as his injuries would allow. The hole was dank and fetid, coated with slimy growth and silver scales. He held his breath as he wormed his way along, ignoring his discomfort, digging into the stone with his elbows and wriggling from side to side. A moment later, he was through, where Kylac helped him to his feet.

He did not believe his eyes.

In keeping with the size of the crypt, the antechamber was probably twenty paces across, among the largest they had seen. The blue light stemmed not from another door, but from the opposite side of the same door they had just worked their way around. The room was apparently sealed from both sides, with little question as to why. For in the very center stood a circular altar, mounted atop a small dais. Mystical runes were etched upon its sides, and a polished dome—an orb—shone atop it like a giant black pearl embedded in the altar's surface. Jarom stood openmouthed beside his awestruck companion. Thrust blade-down through the center of the display was the Crimson Sword.

He felt the truth before his eyes could discern it. For while the hilt matched that of the illusory weapon encountered days earlier—a silver webbing encrusted with a crutch of nine red gems and peppered with smaller green ones—the blade before him was not crimson, but obsidian, and emanated no light, but merely gleamed in the faint blue glow of the sealed portal. But the aura . . . the aura of the Sword convinced him, kept him from registering even a moment's doubt. He basked in its warmth as he might the rising sun on a frosty morning, partaking of a strength and serenity such as he had never known. It washed through him in endless torrents of life and peace and power. Just standing within the talisman's presence suffused his soul with a perfect rapture. Its emanating touch was wondrous, omnipotent, divine. The Sword of Asahiel. Nothing less could ever hold such sway. Lost for centuries, this was it, a vessel containing the most potent forces ever conjured by Olirian hands. This was no illusion, but the instrument he sought, that for which he had nearly died. And in that moment, had his life been deemed the price of this discovery, he would have gladly made the sacrifice.

And yet, improbably, impossibly, here he stood, in the resting place of the last known Sword of Asahiel. He had done it. Survived every maze, every trap, every doubt. Now the legendary talisman was within his grasp.

Jarom stepped toward it, powerless to resist its allure. He felt no fear, no hesitation. His only desire was to draw it, to unleash its wisdom and power—divine influences too long absent from this world. Enthralled, he climbed the lone step of the dais to stand before the altar, where a warm sweat pooled upon his brow. He reached forward . . .

A familiar rasping echoed suddenly throughout the room, growing louder. Startled from his reverie, Jarom cast about, noticing for the first time the many other worm holes marring the chamber walls. Through these holes slithered one after another of the serpentine lizards. They poured forth in nightmare fashion, dozens in all, their sound and stench overwhelming. Joined now by Allion and U'uyen, Kylac fell back toward the enchanted slab, blades drawn, crouched and ready. His eyes danced from side to side, taking in the odds, measuring their chances.

"Let this be another illusion," he groaned.

Jarom did not wait to see what would happen. He whirled, grasping the gem-studded hilt before him. Its holy force hammered throughout his body, melding with his blood and fusing with his spirit. He felt its energy pulsing with the rhythm of his heart, entreating him to release its strength to all the world. He drew a sharp breath, then pulled the weapon free.

As the blade slipped from their grasp, the orb and altar crumbled, falling away into an exposed pit beneath. From that cavity, a frigid gust ripped through the chamber, a stagnant wind that pierced Jarom's nostrils and clawed at his face—the icy brush of age-old death.

The massing lizards shrieked and spun about, heading back into the holes from which they had emerged. They did so in a mad panic, scraping and clawing at one another in order to be the first to escape. Jarom's companions pressed even closer together, shielding themselves from the vile wind and fighting to keep clear of the thrashing lizards.

Within moments, the breeze had passed and the last tail had slipped from view. What remained of the foul sensation vanished in an instant, dispelled by the radiance of the Sword—which, freed from its prison, now burned a flaming red. Jarom gaped in wonder. Beneath the polished surface of the blade swirled the tendrils of an eternal fire. The same blaze burned within the ruby gems that adorned the hilt. Together, their crimson glow filled the chamber and the heart of their wielder.

Jarom looked to his companions. All three were staring at him. Or at the blade, rather, losing themselves in the immortal peace of that unquenchable inferno. Behind them, Jarom noted with some surprise, the magically sealed portal was now open. The slab had vanished, its blue glow no more.

"Look," he managed to say, and the others turned, one by one, to view the empty archway.

It was too much to grasp all at once. And yet, it all made sense. The Sword's power was the key to everything. It had frightened off the lizards. It had opened the door. Already, it had done the impossible. Jarom could not yet imagine what more it held in store.

U'uyen spoke, a harsh sound given the sanctity of the moment. Kylac nodded with seeming difficulty.

"Well then, I suppose ya should sheathe that thing so we can makes our way out o' here."

Jarom refused. He would do so later. Once it had led them from these ruins, he would place the blade in his scabbard, discarding his old sword like so much useless iron. For now, he needed to hold it before him, to feel its heft and bask in its glow.

As he turned from the room, Jarom's gaze lingered, straying toward the pit into which the fragments of orb and altar had plunged. Allowing himself a moment's curiosity, he glanced down into that well. As he did so, his throat tightened, and his stomach dropped. In that instant, he felt as though he were staring directly into the Abyss, into that absolute cauldron of death and torment and sin, and the dread inherent in such a notion strangled the essence within him.

But as he turned away, he was welcomed by the pacifying warmth of the talisman before him. He drew a deep, purifying breath, closed his eyes, and rested his forehead against the radiant blade. Its power permeated his soul, dismissing all horrors, and he considered them no more.

He looked up, his eyes agleam, and found his friends. He felt himself quivering, trembling with disbelief and a joy that was staggering. His friends nodded, as though they too were beginning to grasp the magnitude of what they had accomplished—when in truth, Jarom wondered if any of them ever would.

With a contented nod to mirror theirs, and without looking back, Jarom strode reverently from the chamber, cradling in his palms the wondrous Crimson Sword.

CHAPTER TWENTY-FIVE

Dawn crept furtively from the east, stealing over the horizon through a thick cover of clouds. Its dim reflection rode within the troughs of scud-crested waves, borne ever nearer to the craggy shoreline. It reached land upon the surf, deposited there along with the foam and driftwood, seaweed and brine carried by the ocean's runaway wavelets. Riches in hand, these chained ripples rushed from the sea before being yanked back again, sputtering and seething at leaving their hoard behind with the glistening slap of their passing.

Despite its stealthy approach and his own fatigue, Jarom lurched from his slumber at the daylight's first innocent brush. For an instant, he panicked, gripped by the horrid realization that he had been dreaming. His eyes, though glued and unseeing, flew at once to his chest, to the treasure he had envisioned finding the night before.

All at once, his breath returned, and a controlled ecstasy burned through his veins. The hilt rested still within his palms. He blinked, squeezed his hands, and still the talisman remained. He felt himself tremble at the impossible notion. The recovery of the Sword of Asahiel had not been a dream, but an all-too-perfect reality. How, he could not be sure. Though the memories of his recent journey were real enough, the result seemed too marvelous to be true. The Sword his? Again he squeezed the hilt, needing the reassurance of its gem-studded silver pressed against his skin, half expecting the talisman to vanish in a sudden waft of ethereal mist.

With every step back through the ruins, Jarom had remained vigilant against just such a likelihood. He had hardly allowed himself to blink, to remove his eyes for one instant from the talisman clutched in his hands, as though his will alone was keeping it aglow. Its crimson radiance had paved their way through the darkness, just behind their guide, Cwingen U'uyen, who needed no such light to mark their path. When finally they had crawled free, hauling themselves one by one up the rope that had brought them in, Jarom had still refused to sheathe the blade, choosing instead to strap it to his back with belts of leather so he could continue to bask in its glow. As soon as he'd reached the surface, he had pulled it free once more, where it only flared brighter in the light of moon and stars.

He had emerged hungry, thirsty, and footsore—yet feeling better than he ever had before. While Allion and Kylac had slept, he had lain awake, the Sword clutched to his chest. U'uyen had left them, scurrying down to the ocean's edge to cleanse himself in the salty breakers—thankfully choosing that over immersion in fire. Alone in the vast emptiness of the night, with the heavens opened above and the sea stretching away at his feet, Jarom had continued to marvel. While tracing the weapon's intricate design with his fingertips, reveling in the caress of its life flowing within him, he had told himself that any lingering apprehensions were trivial and misplaced. The Sword was perfect, divine. There could be no doubt. It was the Crimson Sword, and it belonged to him at last.

Nevertheless, he had determined to remain alert until dawn, until he could assure himself that the weapon remained unchanged by the light of day. And though he had failed to stay awake, it would seem there had been no need.

He sat up. His body was punished for doing so, beaten from all angles, assaulted in waves. He didn't care. He simply closed his eyes and pulled the weapon up before him. All of it, he decided again, all of the pain and anguish and fear, had been worth the result—all and much more. He had always been obsessed with the legends. But he'd had no idea, no inkling of the truth. Had he known from his birth what he knew now, he never would have waited this long. He would have crawled over mountains of fire, through rivers of ice, past hordes of cannibals—anything and everything that got in his way. For the Sword was an elixir more potent and necessary than breath or blood. The Sword was life—not only that which pumped through his veins, but a transcendent, immortal power that gave meaning to creation, existence, all that was, had been, or ever would be. The Sword was all of this and more in the shimmer of its blade, the luster of its hilt, the dance of its flames. It calmed its wielder while triggering an unmistakable sense of the strength within, an anticipation of the unmatched power that was the wielder's to command.

His to command.

"Can't gets enough of it, can ya?"

Ordinarily, the sudden voice might have caused his heart to skip a beat. But in his current state of euphoria, he barely heard it, and he gave it not even a glancing regard.

"Can you?" he responded, still staring at the blade.

"It's the most marvelous thing I's ever beheld," the youth admitted. "Can I sees it?"

Jarom scowled. Both Kylac and Allion had made the same request the previous night as they had journeyed back through the bowels of Thrak-Symbos, and Jarom had refused. Perhaps because to relinquish the talisman for even a moment might have shattered the dream. Perhaps because the weapon's allure was such that he feared that either the one or the other of his companions might never give it back. Whatever the reason, Jarom understood it now to be born of his own avarice. Even now, the idea of sharing the blade was a difficult one. But Jarom could feel the discord that his fear and greed caused within himself and the Sword, the ripples such emotions generated within the placid river of the weapon's life force. The talisman was not his, but an instrument of gods and avatars, given not to subjugate one man to another, but to sow among all hearts and minds a matchless harmony, an immaculate strength and peace.

"Come," Kylac insisted, "for just a moment."

"Forgive me," Jarom said. He came to his feet as the youth stepped forward, extending the weapon with due grace. "You've as much a right to it as I have. Maybe more."

"Why do ya say that?" Kylac asked as he accepted the gleaming blade.

Jarom ached the instant the talisman left his hands, but continued to bask in its nurturing glow. "Because," he answered at length, "were it not for you, I'd have died three or four times over before ever laying eyes on it."

Kylac's eyes swept the length of the blade as he tested its heft and balance. "Nah, you'd have found it. This quest o' yours was too easy to be some quirk o' fortune. Some higher power intended for ya to have this."

Jarom smiled inwardly, both thrilled and frightened by the thought.

"Quirk of fortune?" Allion echoed, squirming within his bedroll. "You're suggesting this was easy?"

The youth handed the Sword back to Jarom, who tried not to appear too eager in reclaiming it. The two nodded at each other in common appreciation.

Allion groaned. "Have you forgotten how close we came to starving down there? Have you forgotten the past week of marching or your fight with that unholy serpent? Or maybe you've forgotten already that without horses, we'll be walking all the way home."

Jarom wasn't sure what to think. In some respects, it did indeed seem that they had earned this prize through ample trial and tribulation. One might say that for each turn of luck, they had paid a legitimate price, matching hardship to fortune. One might make such a claim, however, only until he looked at the culmination of their efforts, the ultimate prize for which they should have been required to lay down their lives and still come up laughably short.

"We walked most o' the way here anyhow," Kylac said.

Allion rose, gave a powerful yawn, then stumbled over to join them. "So, do I get to hold it now too?"

This time, Jarom didn't hesitate, but offered the weapon to his friend. Allion, looking somewhat surprised and suddenly solemn, accepted the blade gingerly, his eyes drawn to the flames swirling within its depths. Almost immediately, those eyes lit up, and for a moment, he did not draw breath.

"Ceilhigh!" he whispered at last, a quiver in his voice. His eyes were the size of moons, shimmering in the early light.

"All right, pass it back," Kylac urged, as if fearing they might remain paralyzed with amazement all day.

Allion surrendered the talisman. "What will it do?"

Kylac looked to Jarom. "Let's find out," he suggested.

Jarom nodded, somewhat nervous as Kylac led him over to a waist-high boulder nearby. He settled into position, the youth on one side, Allion on the other. U'uyen came up to join them, returned from the beach after having spent the entire night washing away the taint of the devil's bite. Strangely enough, the Mookla'ayan did not seem to fear the Sword, did not shy away in the least. He, like the others, waited on Jarom with bated breath, ready to bear witness to the Sword's strength.

Still, Jarom hesitated. This was to be the first test—not of the Sword, but of his ability to use it. There was no question as to the blade's authenticity. His residual doubts were nothing more than irrational fears. Between its effect on the serpent lizards, its dismissal of the enchanted doors behind which they had been trapped, and the way it made him feel, the truth was confirmed, no matter how absurd it seemed.

But plenty of questions remained, questions that Jarom wasn't quite ready to answer. In and of itself, the Sword was a miraculous find, its recovery a triumph that could only have come about with the will of destiny. What truly mattered, however, was whether he could wield it.

He continued to stall, studying the weapon as though for the first time. He marked again the principal stones adorning its hilt—heartstones, as the legends referred to them—in whose faceted depths burned the same crimson tendrils that swirled within the blade. Three adorned the crosspiece, while the remaining six traveled the length of the hilt toward the pommel. The smaller green stones, like emeralds, lay sprinkled among the larger, their facets agleam. All in all, the hilt nestled perfectly within the grip of his palms. If necessary, he could hold it for an eternity without tiring.

The morning sun slipped through a break in the clouds to warm his face and arms. From out over the ocean came the cry of a hunting bird as it dove toward the glistening waters. The anticipation of his companions was palpable. Inwardly, Jarom sighed. One way or another, he had to know. The longer he put it off, the more disappointed he stood to become.

Before he could reconsider, he thrust the blade tip-first into the boulder that lay before them. As it pierced the stone, scarlet flames erupted forth to sheathe the blade, which sank easily into the rock. Kylac gasped, Allion fell back, and all four men gaped in astonishment. Jarom quickly yanked the weapon free. The blade slid effortlessly from the stone, and as it escaped, the protective flames vanished, drawing back to resume their dance within the crystalline metal.

Pacified by the weapon's touch, Jarom was the first to recover from his start. Alarm gave way to fresh wonder as he inspected the blade's surface. Not a scratch marred its perfect gleam. Nor was the weapon warmed by the sudden conflagration. The talisman remained untarnished, pristine.

He looked to his companions, who had not yet recovered. Smirking at their stunned features, he swiped downward at the same midsized boulder. As expected, the blade cleaved the stone as if it were water, protected the entire time by a sheath of flames. Once the weapon pulled free of the target, the flames withdrew and the scorched halves of the rock fell away.

Long after the echoes of both the ripping flames and the crumbling stones had died into stillness, the members of the company stood silent, marveling at what they had just witnessed. Jarom held the weapon aloft with one hand, using the other to stroke the blade's unblemished surface. He allowed his eyes to lose focus, peering into the depthless inferno that raged within. The Sword's power was indeed his to command. Only, that wasn't right; he was the slave, not the master. In time, perhaps that would change. As he studied the Sword's nature, as he uncovered its mysteries and unlocked its further capabilities, he might actually become its wielder and not just its bearer. In time. Until then, he was but an instrument, a device for transporting the talisman where it willed—and happy to serve as such.

He stooped to the ground to pick up the scabbard that contained his old broadsword. Glancing at each of his companions, he tipped the case upside down, allowing the steel weapon to clang to the earth. After gauging the Sword's width in relation to the scabbard's throat, he proceeded to insert the volatile weapon carefully into the shadowed opening. To his delight, it rasped down the length of the protective hollow without erupting in protest, and settled to the hilt within its new case. At this, Jarom grinned roguishly. With growing confidence, he lowered the sheathed weapon point-first to the earth, then leaned upon it like a cane.

"Kylac, my young friend, you can keep your blades." He shifted his gaze to Allion, beaming. "Time to raise an army."

A reverent silence ended at last with shared smiles and congratulations. Afterward, the famished companions fished from the sea a meager breakfast, then went about the business of breaking camp. As Allion had been quick to remind them, and as Jarom had feared, their horses had at some point during their weeklong imprisonment broken tether, raided their stores, and gone off in search of additional food, leaving the companions to pack their own belongings. Electing which provisions to carry and which to leave behind was no small task. But with all that could still go wrong between here and Feverroot, and between Feverroot and Kuuria— where they would now head to petition the Imperial Council to rally behind the Crimson Sword—they thought it best to leave nothing of value behind.

It was for this reason that Jarom finally decided to keep the tome of the Entients. Considering the book's weight, and in view of the fact that they no longer needed it to find Whitlock or to recover the Sword, it seemed senseless to Allion that they continue to lug it around. On the one hand, Jarom agreed. But he also felt a strange sense of obligation to preserve the artifact. Although the tome might not have helped them as much as he had hoped, and seemed now useless, he hadn't forgotten how instrumental the book had been in convincing him to make this absurd journey. If nothing else, it would make a wonderful keepsake. Kylac, however, raised the most convincing argument, reminding them that there was still an aged man out there who was none too pleased with having found one of his books turned up missing. If that man was an Entient, as they suspected, then it was quite likely he would one day catch up with them. After sharing a memory of the charred bodies discovered outside of Earth-wyn, Jarom and Allion agreed that it would behoove them to be able to return to the man his property, should such a day ever arrive.

And so it was, an hour later, that the friends set forth, with just about everything remaining to them strapped in place. Jarom refused even to leave behind his old broadsword, claiming that if nothing else, it would fetch a good value at market. For two or three days, he decided, he could bear the extra weight. Thus, despite being laden like pack animals, they took to the mountain trails with light steps and even lighter hearts, awed by their own accomplishments and once again hopeful for what the future might bring.

Jarom, especially, could barely contain his newfound ex-hilaration. The journey home, regardless of the road or their mode of transport, would be nothing less than a wonderful experience, giving him all the time he would need to bask in the glory of their accomplishment. Up until now, he had dreaded all thoughts of the return trip, for try as he might, he had not been able to envision one in which he traveled tri-umphant, carrying the last known Crimson Sword back to the civilized world. But against all reason, that which he'd come for he had found. The next stage of his mission was no longer merely childish fantasy. Despite the army he had yet to raise, the wizard he had yet to face, and the horror he had yet to vanquish, it was, yet again, an all-too-perfect reality.

The clouds, still thick, darkened and descended, a sponge that soaked up all but the faint glow of the morning sun. The path was as treacherous as Jarom remembered, thin and winding and surrounded on all sides by drops and defiles, sharp crags and secret crevasses. The earth was slick with dew and mist. But none of this bothered Jarom. He was un-fazed, infused with a confident tranquillity. He kept one hand at all times upon the hilt of the Sword that hung at his waist, swaying with the newfound swagger in his stride. Marveling at the waves of power pulsing at his fingertips, he continued to reflect upon their impossible success.

For even now, he could scarcely believe it. The more he relived the adventure in his head, the less likely it seemed. Though enraptured by the Sword's touch, Jarom busied himself with thoughts of how easily their quest might have failed. What if he had not dreamed of the weapon incessantly since the night before his departure from Diln? What if Allion had not allowed him to stop at the library in Earthwyn, or what if they had decided to stay that night at an inn? In either case, they never would have stumbled across the Entients' book outside the city. And if they hadn't found the book, Jarom would never have thought to look for the Sword in the east. And Kylac? Had they not found him, Jarom would be dead by now. If the assassin had refrained from killing him, his master the wizard certainly would have wasted no time before seeing the would-be king drawn and quartered, disemboweled, peeled from his skin like a potato, or worse.

But no, Kylac had saved him from all of that, had seen him healed at Feverroot, and had led them ultimately to Cwingen U'uyen. They had survived capture at the hands of the A'awari, and Jarom had successfully swum the Nieten's lake. With U'uyen, they had traversed the Kalmira and passed through the lower Skullmars to the ruins of Thrak-Symbos. The elf had then guided them like no one else could, taking them clear to the catacombs of the ancient city. Even then, what if Jarom had not stumbled through the hidden doorway leading to the lower level? What if Allion and U'uyen had been a moment later in their arrival? What if Kylac had not thought to pass through the serpent lizard's hole? What if . . .

Jarom closed his eyes, fighting to quell the rushing flow. The questions were limitless. But the doubts they cast and the logic they challenged could not undermine the truth. They had recovered the Sword, and would now bear it to Kuuria, to display before Emperor Derreg and the Imperial

Council. By now, surely the emperor had been convinced of the danger to his own lands. Assembling a liberation force, even laying claim to Alson's throne, should Jarom choose to do so, had become little more than a formality. He was the first man in three thousand years to wield a Sword of Asahiel, and once witness to the weapon's power, no one would challenge his claim. They would honor him, respect him, follow him as they had the ancient kings of Finloria. For his was now an Olirian hand, his touch a divine stroke of power. Once he realized his full potential, there would be no one to deny him his wishes.

He opened his eyes, alarmed at how quickly he was getting carried away. He would use those wishes wisely, he determined. He would not be consumed by the addictive throes of power, but would serve those who needed his help. First, he would chase away the wizard, saving his village and all of Alson. With time and patience, he would then work to restore the land to its former splendor. The people would have him as their king, and he would accept the charge. Though it still appealed to him in many ways, he understood that he could not simply return to Diln as a cultivator of mushrooms and spices, nor even as Fason. So be it. He would be uncomfortable at first, but his fear of the crown, which had arisen because he did not recognize his own worth or see how he could convince others of it, was a concern of the past. He knew now who he was and of what he was capable. The rest of the world would realize it soon, and once it did, he would have nothing more to worry about.

Despite the foul weather and perilous landscape, Jarom could not recall a more brilliant day. His companions seemed to agree. The sun may have been missing above, but only because it had risen in their hearts. For a time, they spoke and joked and laughed as they marched, too excited to do otherwise. How great it would be, Allion told Jarom, when they rode into Diln. How marvelous would be the homecoming, how loud the cheers. And yet, how all of that would pale, Jarom countered, to the reception they would find at Krynwall, where they would be greeted by throngs of grateful citizens, men and women falling over one another with pledges of devotion. Especially the women, Allion had smirked, and Jarom had agreed. From here on out, whatever they desired in life would be theirs.

It was then that Jarom remembered Marisha. Would this achievement make him any more attractive in her eyes? The thought embarrassed him. But the lovely and mysterious apprentice was the most fascinating woman he had ever met, with her staunch dedication, her intimate smile, her tender embrace. If he was to become king, he would eventually need a queen. What might Marisha think of such a proposition?

Jarom forced the ridiculous notion from his mind. Despite the time they had spent together, they remained strangers in many respects. In any case, it was too early for him to be thinking of women and betrothals. There was yet battle to be waged, a war to be won. Before that was settled, he felt foolish to be contemplating any fantasy that might lay beyond.

Inevitably, the companions' adrenaline drained away. As it did, they grew quiet, settling into the rhythm of their travels. They seldom paused, pulling up only now and then to drink some water and catch their breath. No one wanted this journey to last any longer than it had to. Bowed by the weight of their packs, sweating through their ragged clothes, they trudged onward. A variety of wounds plagued Jarom with every step. Though diminished by the touch of his hand upon the Sword's hilt, they were like ticks under his skin, burrowing deep to find purchase. He bore them with grim determination, even smiled at their attempts to weaken his resolve. Nothing could make him wish he were anywhere but here, returning the Crimson Sword from the mists of legend to the world of men.

Two days later, the Kalmira Forest finally came into view, a dark, fog-shrouded blanket laid out to the southwest. That same chill fog swirled about them as they perched above the woodland, broken only by the hazy drizzle that had finally begun to drip from the clouds above. But they knew the Kalmira for what it was, and found it a welcome sight when compared to the bleak monotony of the Skullmar foothills.

Jarom inhaled deeply of the crisp evening air, grateful for

the rest and for this view, which marked the end of one leg of their journey.

"Quite a sight," Allion offered, kicking some pebbles from the ridge upon which they stood.

"Come," Jarom urged, glancing uneasily at the menacing sky. "Let's get down into the woods before the rains find us."

"Something's wrong."

They looked to Kylac, who was staring intently to the southwest.

"What is it?" Jarom asked.

Kylac did not answer right away, turning instead to U'uyen, with whom he exchanged words. "Smoke," the youth explained.

"All I see is fog," Allion confessed. "Are you sure?"

"There's been a fire," Kylac insisted. "A big one."

His tone chilled their hearts, and it was with a deepening anxiety that they began their descent into the forest below.

They beat the rains, barely. As the first stark boughs stretched forth to shelter their heads, the storm struck with rare fury. The ominous clouds churned in displeasure, loosing torrents of rain to the ground below. Fortunately, Kylac was able to guide them into the tunnel of brush he had carved while traveling north. All about the members of the company, the wind raged. The walls of thick and tangled deadwood held it somewhat at bay; nevertheless, it battered the damp forms of both Jarom and Allion, numbing their bones and hampering their effort to keep pace.

As he had too often already, Jarom could only marvel at Kylac, who appeared completely immune to the effects of the assailing storm. The winds whipped about his cloaked frame with fiendish glee, sneaking somehow through the tight-knit walls of brush to pelt him with dirt and debris. But he pressed onward, driven by whatever apprehensions haunted him. U'uyen alone was able to match his pace, and while the others slowed and dropped farther back, the youth only moved faster, obsessed with reaching Feverroot as quickly as possible.

They did stop, eventually, well after nightfall had descended and the winds had relented. As if grown weary of battering itself against the thick trunks and leafy mesh, the storm had passed on, continuing to the south. Having already reached the lusher region of the forest, Kylac finally gave heed to their need for rest and lay down beneath a towering pine in a bed of needles that was sufficiently dry when stirred. Jarom and Allion followed his lead, gobbled their dinner, and encouraged the youth to be more open with his concerns. Kylac answered with little more than shrugs and grunts, saying that it was probably nothing. He then set himself to sleep with an admonition that they do the same. Thoroughly exhausted, Jarom obeyed, taking but a moment to admire the Crimson Sword before lying down beside it for the night.

The next morning, Cwingen U'uyen was gone. Jarom noticed the absence at once, so accustomed was he to casting about their little company and seeing the olive-skinned, tattooed native with the crown of thorns and penetrating eyes. Sure enough, the Mookla'ayan had slipped away in the middle of the night without so much as a farewell to anyone but Kylac. The elf had wished them luck, Kylac said, with a message for Jarom. *Remain strong. Fear not the embrace of darkness. Like the stars at night, we need the shadow to see the light.*

As with the whispers of the Powaii people outside their village, Jarom was oblivious as to what that was supposed to mean. At the same time, he discovered with surprise that he was going to miss the elf and his unassuming manner. The Mookla'ayan had given everything he had, made every sacrifice—including that which his grandfather had refused—and had asked for nothing in return. Jarom doubted that he would ever be able to repay his debt to the elf, and to the Powaii people. And yet, he felt cheated at being denied the opportunity to say good-bye.

The discovery of U'uyen's departure was made before dawn, when Kylac had shaken them from a deep slumber and bid them gather their things. Neither Jarom nor Allion had bothered to argue, but had struggled dutifully out from under the weight of his dreams, shivering against an early morning drizzle. After their discussion concerning the

Powaii chieftain, they'd done as Kylac had asked and packed their belongings, ready for yet another day of hard travel.

The day commenced as the previous night had ended, with Kylac pushing a relentless pace that had his companions sucking for breath and begging silently for a reprieve. To them, the ordeal seemed endless. Allion appeared to be aging years as the hours drudged by, and only the perpetual reassurance of the Crimson Sword prevented Jarom from experiencing the same. After a while, however, the two men began to share the youth's anxiety. A foul odor permeated the air—the ominous stench of smoke—and the nearer they drew to Feverroot, the more pungent and prevailing that fetor became. Their uneasiness gave them new energy, with which they actually quickened their pace and lengthened their stride.

Soon thereafter, they came across blackened trees and scattered flames, the remains of a forest fire extinguished by the recent rains. Smoke and steam rose up all around them, choking them as they went. As they continued westward, they found the region through which the fire had blazed. Charred stumps jutted skyward, misshapen and lifeless. The earth about them smoldered, carpeted in ash and fallen boughs, disfigured beyond recognition. There were no birds, no animals or insects of any kind. The forest had become a tomb.

They hastened a few miles more, their concern mounting with every step. Perhaps it had been a natural blaze, a strike of lightning that had ignited and spread throughout the late summer land. Even so, had those in Feverroot been driven from their homes? Had the blaze stretched far enough west to have threatened them? If so, where would they have gone?

With such questions gnawing at him, Jarom stumbled with his companions some time later across an even more disturbing scene. Marching from the east, the trio found itself suddenly within an immense swath, a burned and trampled trail running south through the forest. The path, stripped of all but the larger trees, was more than a mile wide, and stretched in either direction farther than their eyes could see. Judging by the devastation, it was along here that the blaze had originated.

"An army's been through here. From the north."

Jarom gaped at the smashed and blistered earth, stepping carefully over fallen trees and broken boughs, all of it black with soot and slick with rain. "Parthans?"

"No," the youth replied immediately. "These tracks ain't human. See?"

Jarom moved with Allion over to where Kylac knelt examining the ashen earth. When they reached him, the youth traced for them an alien print consisting of three clawed toes, lizardlike, only far too large to belong to any reptile they knew.

Jarom shook his head. "Where did they come from?"

Kylac looked around, his gaze searching. Jarom found his own eyes drifting skyward, peering to the north through the charred trunks of those few trees still standing. Through this leafless cover, he spied the dark outline of the now distant Skullmars and, among them, the steaming pyre of Mount Krakken.

"From the mountains," the youth claimed. "From the western Skullmars."

"You know that?"

Kylac shrugged. "We'd have to backtrack along their trail to be sure. But if not from there, then they would've come from Partha. And a foreign army could not have come through Partha so quickly."

"Where could such a force be headed, traveling south?" Allion interjected.

The youth was silent for a moment, reflective. His brow furrowed beneath his cowl, his skin smeared with rain and soot. The sun emerged momentarily, peeking through a fissure in the clouds. As if disliking what it saw, it ducked away again.

"I don't know," Kylac admitted. "It might be they're just continuing in the direction from which they left the mountains."

Jarom frowned. "An army on the march that doesn't know where it's going?"

"But if that's the case," Allion reasoned, "then it would not be long before they ran into the southern marshes and would have probably turned around. And this trail looks to be several days old."

Kylac nodded. "We'd best hurry."

Jarom coughed, fighting against the lump in his throat. He looked to Allion, then to Kylac. No one said anything more. Together they picked their way across the devastation, reentering the charred forest to the west and making their way with fresh urgency toward Feverroot.

CHAPTER TWENTY-SIX

Through the felt of night they straggled, draped in drizzly darkness, led by torches through a scarred labyrinth of gloom and decay. The stark trees leaned over them, withered stalks in an abandoned field. Soot covered their faces, grime painted upon a canvas of dismay. Their limbs hung, their feet dragged, boots clumped with ash and mud. Overhead, a new moon hid within the clouds, clinging to its light like a miser to his gold.

Had the companions recognized where they were, fatigue might have melted away beneath the heat of their trepidation, the fervent desire to know what had become of their friends. But the land about was a solid stain, a crisp blanket of baked and sodden deadwood, an indistinguishable jumble of ash and boughs steeped in inky shadow. The recent conflagration had consumed all scents, trails, and markers; the land was as strange and new to Kylac as it was to Jarom and Allion. So they proceeded glumly, stooped by their despair, slogging along and wondering if they would ever escape this persistent nightmare.

Then Kylac found the stream. Trickling through the matted debris, glittering faintly beneath their torchlight, it wound out of the north before meandering westward. With a shout, he dashed forward. All brooding gone, the three young men scampered through the snapping woodland ruin. At last, with aching hearts and lungs, Jarom and then Allion caught up with Kylac, bursting through a scorched stand of fir and into a familiar glen, where they could only gape in horrified bewilderment at the devastated remains of Feverroot.

A cold wind swept past, strafing Jarom's heart and raking at his face before slipping beyond with a banshee's wail. The entire village had been reduced to smoldering heaps of ash, bricks, and boards, crushed together and left in misshapen mounds of rubble. Sweeping northward for as far as he could see through the haze, the vegetation had been annihilated, all of it burned and trampled save for the largest trees, which themselves were but husks of blistered bark. Not a living thing remained. Much like they had seen earlier that afternoon, leagues to the east, the breadth of the destruction covered several hundred paces from east to west. The only sound was the soft plodding of rain upon the bemired earth. Some vile force had simply eradicated Feverroot and all else in its path. Only desolation, accentuated by the odor of burnt timber, lingered in its wake.

A churning wrenched Jarom's stomach as he thought of all that had been destroyed. The homes, the trees, the animals, the Lewellyns who had saved his life—*Marisha!* The shock froze his blood, which was melted just as suddenly by the rage erupting from his heart.

"No!" he bellowed, tearing the Crimson Sword from its sheath.

But in the instant he pulled the weapon free, its soothing warmth washed through his veins, quenching the vengeful fire that had exploded within. The blade's light flared, as if sensing his excitement, but would not sustain his mindless fury. Engulfed by the talisman's reassuring power, Jarom felt only a gentle pang of grief as he surveyed the ruin about him.

Dolefully silent, he and Allion watched as Kylac drifted amid the devastation, sullenly seeking an explanation. With his hood drawn, it was impossible to see the youth's face, but Jarom could sense his sorrow as he picked his way through the debris. For many moments, he inspected the damage, searching for clues as to Feverroot's fate. Wrapped in his green-gray cloak, made ethereal by the mists, he seemed a ghost.

"Look here," Allion said.

Jarom crouched with the hunter to the muddy earth. Based upon the prints at their feet, the army had come this time from the south on a northwesterly course. But the marks told him nothing as to how, or why.

Finally, Kylac returned to them, sulking on silent feet.

"I's never seen such total destruction," he admitted, his voice strained. Despite his efforts, it seemed he could make no more sense of this madness than they.

"The wizard?" Allion suggested.

Jarom nodded, seething with anger once more. "His demons must have found our trail after we left."

"But this was an army," Kylac reminded him. "These are the same tracks we came across this morning." He looked to Allion. "They got themselves turned around all right."

"An army commanded by the wizard," Jarom maintained. "They're not human. You said so yourself."

The youth shook his head, a gesture of frustration more than argument. "I don't know. I just can't imagine any man commanding such a force."

"He sent those creatures after us," Allion reminded him.

The youth looked away, staring off into the haze. "Maybe."

Allion glanced at Jarom, then back again. "What are you saying? If not the wizard, then who?"

Kylac did not respond, continuing his silent study of the lifeless swath that now scarred the once-verdant landscape.

"Did you . . . find anyone?" Jarom managed, forcing the words past the lump in his throat.

"No one."

"Then they're alive?" Jarom asked, not daring to hope.

Kylac turned to him, eyes burning behind a cold stare. "Let's find out."

They set forth at once, wasting no more time on discussion. All of a sudden, Kuuria and the Imperial Council were forgotten. It was too late for audiences and petitions. The larger war had already commenced, and it appeared they would have to hurry if they wished to join it. Jarom, however, allowed his gaze to slide over the ruins of Feverroot once more before turning northward. He wanted to ensure that the scene would remain vivid in his mind, emotional fuel for the journey that lay ahead. Sheathing the Crimson Sword, he chased after his friends—puzzled, furious, and set on vengeance.

They marched on past midnight, fording the north fork of the Emerald River and continuing beyond, following the enemy's wake through the dripping forest. Their fury drove them. Black clouds roiled overhead, enveloping the land in an absolute, chilling darkness. A drizzle continued to fall, adding to their discomfort. They had been traveling without rest for more than twenty hours now, and were it not for their determination to overcome those who had ravaged Feverroot, they would have dropped hours earlier. But Jarom could not have slept had he wanted to. Not after what he had seen. Not now, knowing that Marisha was either dead or in the clutches of some unspeakable enemy. He would march all night if he had to, all week.

But Kylac, who was better conditioned than either of his companions for such a trek, understood the folly in ignoring their bodies' need for rest. What use would they be to their friends if they were too spent to raise a weapon in defense when they found them? Although the ache in his heart outweighed that of legs and lungs, Jarom reluctantly agreed. Kylac estimated they were yet a full day or more behind their quarry, and they couldn't expect to make up that ground in a single night. At this point, they were simply borrowing hours against the morrow.

The youth led them into a stand of spruce that lined the western edge of the enemy's trail. More and more, they were seeing sodden growth that, while scorched, had largely escaped the flames set by the passing army. Apparently the enemy had grown weary of igniting everything in its wake. Or perhaps the land had simply been too wet.

It was clear they were to see some heavy rains that night, so they spent several minutes fashioning a more worthy shelter, a meshed wall of logs and branches thatched over with smaller brush. When satisfied, they wiped off their hands, ate from a stash of roots and moldy cheese, and hunkered down to await the rising sun.

In his dreams, Jarom marched throughout the predawn hours. Part of his mind realized it was time to rest, and that he had only a brief amount of time in which to do so. That part tried desperately to relax him, to force him to cease his struggles. But another part refused to relent. It had toiled so diligently to keep his body going throughout the day that even now, it could not stop. Images crowded his mind, visions and memories jostling with one another until all had become a frenetic blur.

At last he opened his eyes, exhausted and aching. It took him a moment to orient himself. He was lying on his side, facing the inner wall of a makeshift hut. Tiny rivulets dripped here and there around the edges. But while the roof of their shelter was pelted by a steady rain, the ground beneath was only slightly damp.

It was still cold, however, and he shivered as he sat up from his bedroll. His muscles screamed in protest, and it was then that he recalled what it was that had brought him to this place in time. Growling away his soreness, he cast about the cramped shelter. Allion slept nearby, hunched close against the side wall. Beside him, Kylac's gear sat in a rumpled heap, but of the youth himself, there was no sign.

Jarom rubbed his eyes, grabbed only the Sword and his blanket, then groped his way toward the small, slanted breach left open to the night. A gust of wind greeted him, and he tightened the blanket about his shoulders. Once outside, he blinked against the falling rain, searching.

He made his way around their hut and down out of the copse in which it was set, making toward the swath of devastation that marked their enemy's trail. The sun had not yet risen, and the light of moon and stars was made murky by the churning cover of clouds. The wet earth chilled his bare feet, but felt good against his blisters. Picking his way carefully among the sharper sticks and thorny brush, he wound down toward a fallen tree and the cloaked figure who stood upon it.

Kylac heard him coming, he knew, but did not turn at his approach. Instead, the youth continued to stare northward along the river of blasted trees.

"If'n they don't change course, their path will carry them through Battlemont."

Jarom stopped beside his young friend, his own eyes locked on the horizon. "A city?"

Kylac shook his head. "An outpost. Military. Just large enough to maintain control o' the southland."

"Military? Any chance it's still standing?"

"It's got a better chance than Feverroot did." The youth paused, then faced him before continuing. "Our journey does not end tonight, my friend."

Jarom nodded in grim understanding. The thought of another full day of marching, followed only by another, did not appeal to him in any way. And yet, he owed Marisha and her people at least that much.

"However long it takes, we'll catch them," Jarom assured the youth.

It was a hollow declaration, its weight and strength seeming to evaporate as soon as it escaped his mouth. Kylac turned to him, hooded against the rain, eyes hollow and dark from lack of sleep.

"I envy you, ya know."

Jarom blinked. "Me?"

"Your sense o' purpose. The sure knowledge o' what it is ya were born to do. Three years now I's been in search o' mine. Longer than that, even. And here I stand, barely more than a wastrel."

"You're the most accomplished wastrel I've ever met," Jarom laughed.

The youth looked as if he was about to respond, then shook his head.

Jarom frowned. "Is there something you know that you're not telling us?"

"I wish there was," the youth sighed, peering ahead once more. "There's something unnatural 'bout all o' this. That's part o' why I'm here. I just wish I could unravel it. Had I done so sooner, Feverroot might've been spared."

The thought struck home with Jarom, who throughout this quest had spent too much time with thoughts of what might be or could have been. This entire affair had been marked by such sudden turns of events—from his rescue of Queen Ellebe in the woods outside his home to his tumble into the lower levels of the catacombs that led to his finding of the Sword. Now this. Yesterday, they had been swept up by their emotions, scarcely considering the ramifications of their actions in chasing north after an unknown scourge. Now, for the first time, he began to wonder just what it was they were up against. Could it be that this threat was in addition to that of the wizard? Or was the wizard truly powerful enough to command an entire army of demons? Either truth was terrifying. But just as frustrating was their ignorance. Regardless, they were doing all they could, and he hated to see Kylac tormenting himself over a situation none of them could have foreseen.

"Sometimes it's best not to overthink what you're getting yourself into," Jarom reminded him, recalling the youth's admonition upon their journey south into Vosges. "If you want to survive, you've got to learn how to react."

A bemused smirk played about the boy's lips. "You's been listening."

"I've a lot to learn." Jarom shrugged, scratching at the stubble growing in on his chin.

Kylac sighed again, and nodded. "Come, then. I suppose we'll unravel this one together."

They went back and woke Allion, who did not become alert until after he had put together his things. Leaving their shelter to whatever animals might brave a return to the scarred region, they embarked once again. They traveled in silence for the most part, avoiding the heavy topic at hand. Once again, Kylac set a brutal pace, and by the time dawn arrived, with the sun glaring red over the eastern horizon, they slid from the boundaries of the Kalmira and onto the warmer plains of southern Partha. Where the earth met the sky to the north, soiled clouds hunched like a set of distant, snowcapped mountain peaks, draped already in a silver blanket of early light. Otherwise, the travelers found the morning sky clear and agreeable, with a fresh breeze sweeping the region.

They pressed on without pause, ignoring the discomforts of hunger, wet clothes, and weariness. Jarom knew that as long as they kept moving, their muscles wouldn't stiffen. They would pay a price in the days ahead for pushing themselves thus, but only if they survived that long. Considering what lay ahead, it was possible they would not.

A sea of fog rose up about them as the sun continued to lift into the sky. It wrapped them in its swirling arms, hugging them close in a chill embrace. Like the spirits of those whose bodies had no doubt been trampled along this trail, Jarom thought, and he pulled his cloak tighter in response.

The light of day revealed little that they had not already determined. The devastation was complete and unending. From time to time, they paused to inspect the earth, searching desperately for some sign or print that would convince them that Marisha and the others were being herded north alive. But the sheer number of the enemy had washed away any such marker. The ground they followed was as torn and frothed as the choppiest sea. All that could be distinguished was the now familiar three-toed footprint, the only identifying mark by which they recognized their faceless adversary.

Eventually, the fog began to thin and lift, revealing in its stead a towering pillar of dark smoke that blotted out the northern horizon. By midmorning they had reached the smoldering ruins of Battlemont. A mountain of rubble awaited them, eerie in the hazy light and pervaded by a horrid stench. Jarom found himself in sudden peril of losing that day's nourishment. He could not have anticipated such thorough destruction; nor had he accustomed himself to the absolute putrescence of burning flesh. Oddly enough, there were no bodies to be found. The enemy must have carried them away or consumed them on the spot, for surely, many had fallen. All was in ruin, reeking of death. As far as Jarom and Allion were concerned, Kylac could not finish sifting through the ashes too soon.

"They tried to fight," the youth informed them, his brow pinched in disgust. "There are weapons everywhere." He paused to regard his companions, whose mouths and noses were covered. "Come."

They resumed their march, eager to put behind them the place of horror. To Jarom's dismay, it was more than an hour before they had extricated themselves from the stench. Even then, they were unable to escape it fully. Long after Battlemont was nothing more than a memory, the carnage and devastation remained. Hilltop ranch homes lay in embers, their fields stripped of livestock. Fences lay broken. Creeks and ponds were stained with blood. And over all of it hung the ghastly pall of death, thinned at times by wind and distance, sometimes thick enough to taste.

They did not stop for meals or water. They had exhausted their food stores for the most part, and had found nothing with which to replenish them. Nor would they have stopped to do so. Their desire to discover the truth drove them onward without protest.

For Jarom, not a moment passed without thinking of Marisha. Strange how time had elapsed so slowly while he had been with her in Feverroot, anxious to be off, whereas now it seemed he had hardly been there at all. With each flitting memory, he missed her more and more. If she was alive, he would find her. If she was dead . . . The thought filled him with anguish, and he gripped the hilt of the blade now slung over his shoulder. If she was dead, he would avenge her.

Remarkable, he realized, that he never tired of the Sword's weight, despite marching mile after mile, league after league. Contrary to the tome of the Entients that he and Allion shared responsibility for, whose weight and awkwardness seemed to double with every step, the large Sword was never a burden. Instead, it existed as a third, comforting companion, whose presence filled him with hope and fueled the fires of his conviction.

After a time, he hardly noticed the desolation. The ravaged land slipped by in endless monotony, dark and smoking and deathly silent. Although startled by what he'd seen at Battlemont, he was no longer awed by the unbroken carpet of blackened earth that stretched before them. What continued to trouble him and his companions was *why*. By all appearances, the enemy was sweeping northward with reckless abandon, annihilating any settlement they came across, as indiscriminate as nature's wrath. Given the lack of victims' remains, those caught within the path of the storm were being eaten or enslaved. As to what manner of creature was capable of such atrocities, none could guess. And until they could figure out who this enemy was or where it had come from, it remained all but impossible to speculate upon its ultimate purpose.

At times, Jarom continued to wonder whether or not Kylac knew more than he was revealing. The youth had a history of hiding his suspicions, after all. And it seemed strange that he should persistently reject Jarom's assertion that this army was but another of the wizard's weapons, yet refuse to offer an alternate explanation. More than once, Jarom caught the youth staring toward the Skullmar Mountains and a faint red glimmer against the eastern sky— Mount Krakken. When pressed, Kylac would shrug the issue aside, admitting only that he was trying to make the pieces fit. His guess was no better than their own. Such replies were too simple for Jarom's taste, and it was obvious that Allion felt the same. Nevertheless, it was pointless to force the issue. If Kylac had something to share with them, he would do so in his own time.

Until then, he could keep his secrets, Jarom decided. As long as they followed this path, they would discover the truth soon enough.

The remainder of the afternoon passed in a blur of pain and exhaustion, anger and dismay. The path continued northward, cutting through fields and farmlands, townships and baronies, a scarred trail that chewed up the soft earth only to spit it out again. The companions followed it over hills and through wetlands, running until it felt their legs must fall off, or trudging without complaint under a cloud-choked sky that continually threatened rain. They spoke sparingly, choosing to concentrate their full focus upon the task at hand.

With the approach of yet another midnight, they had left the ravaged city of Dirrk far behind and come to stand before the broken gates of Crylag. Despite all they had seen, none had expected this. The massive stronghold lay in ruin, razed by the unknown force, the strength and power of which seemed without end. Jarom shook his head in horrified wonder. *This cannot have happened.* He whispered it to himself over and over, a litany against the impossible, even as he gazed upon the fallen fortress in helpless awe.

For even he, raised in the west, knew of Crylag and Morjal, two cities whose only purpose was that of dealing war one against the other. It was here that the nations of Partha and Menzos concentrated their assaults upon each other's lands. A half day's ride across the Fields of Ravacost separated the two, each a fortress kept stocked with weapons and warriors who rarely saw a month's passing before charging forth once more to do battle with their detested rivals. Begun as a civil war nearly three centuries ago with the Menzo declaration of secession, the conflict between these two nations—and these two citadels in particular—persisted now simply for the joy of destroying one another.

But now Crylag had fallen, its rugged battlements burned and smashed and trampled like all else in the enemy's wake. As he skirted his way around the maze of ruined walls, coughing from the smoke and gagging at the stench, Jarom wondered how even the Crimson Sword could quash this rising horror.

"Who could have done this?" Allion asked in exasperation.

Kylac turned to the west, away from the black river of destruction that continued to swim northward. "Perhaps we can soon finds out."

Jarom, having expected no response, looked to the youth questioningly.

"At Leaven," Kylac explained. "Looks as if they's passed her by."

"Which means it's out of the way," Jarom reminded him. He wasn't about to relinquish the ground they had struggled so valiantly to gain. "What about Marisha and the others?"

"Look around, lad. This here is one o' the most defensible cities in Partha, and the enemy marched through her without breaking stride." He shook his head. "It's time we learned what we're chasing 'fore we have the misfortune o' finding it."

Jarom ignored the youth, staring northward along the trail of death, peering into the darkness of night as though he could make Marisha appear from within its folds.

But Allion agreed with Kylac. "We won't be doing any good by leaping headfirst into a wolf's den."

"There's bound to be someone at Leaven who can tells us what we're up against. If nothing else, we need horses if'n we're to ever catch up."

Jarom inhaled slowly, unable yet to avert his longing gaze. The idea made sense. Why didn't that seem to matter?

"I suppose you're right."

Kylac grunted and turned away, leading Allion westward. After a silent oath and a lingering glance at the demolished fortress, Jarom followed their tramping heels.

CHAPTER TWENTY-SEVEN

In the witching hours before dawn, Jarom and his companions approached the city of Leaven. Having marched all night, they were more than a little relieved when at last the watch fires upon her guard towers flickered into view. They were also concerned. The land about was deserted, empty of all but a handful of rodents that kept watch from the edges of the highway and a nightbird that circled the skies above. Even at this early hour, the slopes should have been astir with activity in preparation for the new day. Leaven was one of the largest, busiest, most populous cities in Pentania. To find her outskirts abandoned was ominous.

The companions reached the base of the hill and continued along the principal thoroughfare that stretched up to the city's main gate. A narrow moon peered through a hole in the cloud cover, squinting at the earth below. The city lay sprawled in an eastern basin of the Whistlecrag Mountains, whose humpbacked forms loomed in silent backdrop. An imposing bulwark of stone encircled its markets and homes, cold and uninviting. They had expected to be met long ago by patrolling sentries, welcomed as bearers of news regarding the recent onslaught, or at least as refugees. But the journey west had revealed to them not another living soul. They should not have been surprised, then, to find Leaven tightly sealed, a reclusive giant casting her forbidding glare upon the land. Indeed, were it not for the lights within the towers that straddled either side of its primary entrance, the city itself might have been deserted.

Trudging side by side, the members of the little company climbed the hill, bleary eyes shifting back and forth with caution. At last they came to stand before the mammoth entry doors, set deep within an alcove beneath the gatehouse. Having been on the move for countless hours, the sudden stop made Jarom dizzy. He closed his eyes, swaying unsteadily.

Beside him, Allion muttered, "They don't seem to have noticed our arrival."

Jarom nodded, his lids heavy. "Perhaps there's no one on duty. We could . . ." He stopped short, casting about in bewilderment. "Kylac?"

Allion glanced over both shoulders, then turned a complete circle. "Where'd he go?"

Jarom wondered if his own sense of alarm showed as clearly as that of his friend. As best as he could recall, the youth had been at his side all the way up the hill.

"Ho there!" a gruff voice shouted from above. "What be your business?"

Jarom scanned the ramparts, where he could hear archers jostling with ready bows. He felt suddenly naked, as though all the world was watching him. "We've come from Feverroot in the south," he began, then paused, probing the shadows for a glimpse of the gatekeeper. He did not want to reveal too much; nor did he dare lie or share too little. When he realized that no reply was forthcoming, he continued. "We've been following a trail of destruction for days now. We seek information concerning this enemy that has taken our friends."

"Feverroot? Where is this Feverroot?"

Before Jarom could reply, an access door at the base of one of the guard towers swung inward. Understanding that to move was to incur their deaths, the companions stood fast as a party of armored men rushed to greet them, clanking and rustling, confiscating their weapons and wrapping thick cords around their wrists.

"Rather well armed for refugees, I should think," remarked one of the burly soldiers.

The senior officer agreed. "Hold them for interrogation."

"We're not enemies," Allion tried to explain.

"Tell it to the general," the other snapped.

Neither prisoner voiced objection after that as the orders were executed. Jarom cringed when the Crimson Sword was taken from him, but remained silent, staring at the ground. Biting his lip to help hold himself in check, he reassured himself that this was no more than a minor setback.

Kylac Kronus was on the loose.

They were taken through the guardhouse and along torch-lit backstreets being used as a military staging ground. Hundreds of soldiers milled about, perfecting drills and constructing implements to be used in defense of the city. The troops paid scant attention to the pair of bound strangers as they shuffled past. Those who acknowledged Jarom's stare did so with grim glares. He could only guess how many more remained tucked away in the comfort of their barracks.

They were herded down a series of narrow, winding roads that crossed through dank alleys and slithered between dirty stone walls. Jarom kept his eye out for civilians—couriers, collectors, and others whose business might be conducted in the predawn hours—but saw none. If any still resided within the city, it would seem they had been stashed away for safe-keeping.

They arrived quickly enough at a two-story structure with pocked stone walls. A jailhouse presumably, for it contained only one, floor-level window. Spying their approach, a sentry posted beside the door knocked twice with his pike. A moment later, a brawny man with a bloated belly emerged to meet them. He hefted in one hand a seasoned cudgel stained dark with past use, while a ring of keys jingled from the other.

"Mornin'," he grumbled. "First catch o' the day, eh?"

"Found 'em admiring the main gate," one of the soldiers muttered in reply. "The general has been sent notice."

The jailor yawned. "Bah, let me question 'em. They look harmless enough."

"The general gave strict orders. He wishes to interrogate all prisoners himself."

The jailor belched. "If that's his wish." The man spied

Jarom's distrustful gaze and flashed him a toothless smile. "They'll enjoy their stay just fine."

The lead soldier nodded and led his troops away, leaving Jarom and Allion alone with the jailor and his lone sentry.

"Well now," the podgy man grunted as he eyed the squad's departure. His breath reeked, as did the sweat dried upon his body. "The two o' ya can step right this way." With his stained cudgel, he indicated the open door before them.

Jarom and Allion complied, and with a nod to the sentry, the jailor followed them in.

They entered through a cramped receiving office, furnished with a single desk and chair shoved into a niche on one side. Upon the desk rested a keg of foul-smelling liquid, a measure of which occupied a tankard set within the barrel's shadow. Beside this sat an oil lantern and a sheaf of papers.

The jailor let loose another yawn as he unlocked a second door. "Through here."

Again Jarom and Allion did as they were bid. This time, they stepped into a dark room containing a small table in the midst of four chairs. To their left, a short flight of steps descended to a barred door, while to their right, yet another led to the level above. The single window seen from outside was set high within the far wall, its filthy, crosshatched panes clouding further the faint moonlight that streamed through.

"Have a seat."

None too gently, the jailor shoved them into two of the chairs. At the base of each, anchored to the floor, was a rusted holding ring, to which he shackled them with leg irons. He then double-checked the cords that bound their wrists behind their backs, making sure they were secure.

"Sit quiet, ya hear? 'Less you'd rather be made carrion for the rats in the cells."

The jailor turned from them, rubbing at the bulbous nape of his neck as he tramped from the room. The door shut, and a key scraped within the lock, which slid into place. Behind the heavy door, they could hear the man as he slumped into his creaking chair.

"He could have warned us," Allion groaned.

It took Jarom a moment to realize his friend was talking about Kylac. "Maybe he didn't want to waste time listening to our protests."

Allion started to respond before shaking his head in quiet concession.

They passed the time in idle conversation. Despite the conditions, Jarom was almost content to be sitting there in the darkness, bound like a criminal. He was thirsty, hungry, and sore. Nevertheless, it was an opportunity to rest at last, to sit rather than march, and thus recuperate somewhat from the hardships of running and hiking for days on end. All in all, a welcome change.

But he soon found his mind wandering, drifting to distant and meaningless places. His head began to nod, falling forward and then back, too heavy for his neck to balance. Somewhere in the middle of Allion's words—or maybe his own—he fell asleep.

The sharp click of a lock being released startled Jarom from his repose. He awoke groggy and disoriented. He shifted in his chair, feeling the weight of the chain affixed to his ankle, and recalled what had happened. When he did, he sat up expectantly, waiting for Kylac to slide into the room. Instead, the door swung wide, and light poured in on him from a lantern. Jarom squinted and shied away from the glare, but not before recognizing the shape and smell of their unkempt jailor.

"Wake up, lads," the man chuckled, revealing again that mouthful of missing teeth.

Jarom blinked as his eyes adjusted and forced his gaze back to the door. While the jailor wiggled his key from the lock, a second man entered, holding the lantern. This other man, obviously a high-ranking soldier, was dressed in green tunic and breeches over which he wore a fine cuirass, bracers, and greaves of bronze. Beady brown eyes peered at them from a weathered face, above which grew a meticulously groomed head of brown hair. Under one arm, the man clutched their weapons—Allion's bow and hunting knife,

Jarom's daggers, and the Crimson Sword, still carefully sheathed in its worn leather scabbard.

"Take these and wait out front," he commanded the jailor, handing him their articles. His voice was deep and authoritative, yet lacked the harshness common among the veteran soldiers whom Jarom had encountered over the years.

The jailor accepted the small stash. "Holler if ya need anything," he replied before leaving. He disappeared behind the closed door, leaving them to the richly armored stranger.

For a moment, the man remained where he stood, examining them within the light of his lantern. Jarom did his best to match that calculating stare, though his eyes had not yet fully adjusted to the light the other carried. Finally, with a confident gait, the man strode to the table, set the lantern down upon it, and sat himself in a chair across from them.

"I know neither of you," he began, scowling. "I expect that to change."

Jarom said nothing and Allion glanced at him, awaiting his lead.

"It's said you are refugees from the south."

Again, Jarom remained silent, contemplating his response.

"Come now, have you something to hide?"

Then, without warning, the man stiffened, gasping slightly as a slender blade pressed against his throat.

"Nothing they mights have to say concerns ya, Corathel."

The man's features tightened, then relaxed. A smile eased across his clean-shaven face. "Kylac Kronus."

A shadow behind the man shifted, taking tangible form, and sat down comfortably beside him. Kylac sheathed his blade, which had left only the slightest welt upon the other's throat.

"This is a surprise," Kylac said, grinning roguishly from ear to ear.

"To say the least," Corathel agreed, rubbing at the soft flesh beneath his chin. "It's been too long."

The youth nodded, clasping the man's hand in greeting.

"So, these two are with you?"

"He's with us, yes," Jarom interjected, still somewhat puzzled by the scene unfolding before him.

Corathel chuckled. "Indeed." He turned to Kylac, arching a single eyebrow in question. The youth merely shrugged.

"I hate to interrupt this little reunion," Allion remarked, "but would someone mind untying us?"

"I beg your pardon," Kylac apologized. He came to his feet, dagger in hand. A moment later, Jarom felt the cords fall free, and he moved at once to rub the soreness from his wrists.

"You'll have to see the jailor for a key to those shackles," Corathel observed.

"No need," Kylac assured him, sheathing his dagger and producing his longsword. "You lads might wants to pull back."

Jarom did as suggested, scooting aside and stretching the length of chain along the stone floor. He cringed reflexively as Kylac slashed, a lightning strike that appeared certain to remove his foot. Instead, when Jarom opened his eyes and looked down, the chain binding him to the floor had been cleanly severed, leaving only the iron cuff attached to his ankle. The youth freed Allion in similar fashion, then winked at each of them in turn.

Corathel leaned back in his chair, clapping his hands in mock applause. "Masterful work, my young friend. Don't worry about the cost of the chains. I'll reimburse the city myself."

Kylac bowed before taking his seat.

"Well then," Corathel declared, smirking now with genuine amusement. "Why don't we start this little interrogation over again. I'd very much like to meet this duo."

"Jarom and Allion of Alson," Kylac announced, indicating each of his friends in turn.

"I'm honored. Any friend of Kylac's is a friend of mine."

Jarom reached across the table to accept the man's outstretched hand. He found the other's grip to be strong and solid, without exaggerated force.

"Chief General Corathel, commander of the Parthan West Legion."

"Chief general, huh?" Kylac echoed. He gave a low whistle. "Why, when last I saws ya, you were a mere field corporal."

"Yes, well, promotions occur fairly frequently when your

superiors are fighting all day on the Fields of Ravacost. Rare is the night that sees them all return home alive."

"How is it you know each other?" Jarom asked. Not only did he feel the need to catch up, he sensed here an opportunity to learn something new about his enigmatic young friend.

"Let's see," Corathel said, tapping a finger to his lower lip in thought. "What was it, three, four years ago?"

Kylac shrugged. "Something like that."

"Anyway, the squad to which I was assigned at the time was stationed at Dirrk, and we were out on patrol one day when we came across this little kid, all of twelve, thirteen years old." The general chuckled. "I remember it vividly. We were in the midst of helping ourselves to a lady merchant's wares—highway tax, you see—when Kylac showed up. The little piece of dung told us to give it all back, and when the matter escalated, he demanded the surrender of our patrol. Ten men! Sweet Olirium, this one lad was demanding the surrender of ten highly trained soldiers! Our squad commander told him to run off and play, but Kylac here refused. When it became evident he was serious, we were ordered to teach the bastard some respect. So we attacked, and I'll be damned if the boy didn't kill seven of us before we captured him. Seven!"

Jarom exchanged a knowing smirk with Allion.

"As you might imagine, our commander was furious. He took Kylac to Dirrk, and had him scheduled for public execution. The local magistrate wasn't about to allow a bunch of child rogues to start running rampant through his territory. I guess I felt sorry for the lad. Or maybe I was just intrigued by his skills. Anyway, I freed him. There's a bit more to it than that, but, well . . . let me just add that soon thereafter, Kylac helped me to attain my first major promotion."

Jarom glanced at the youth, who shook his head as though to disavow the entire story.

"We became friends. To repay my kindness, he taught me somewhat in his ways of combat—which probably best explains why it is I'm still here and not rotting away beneath some cairn. But he up and left one day, several weeks later, and that was the last I'd seen of him until now."

"Wonderful oration," Kylac said, "although I thinks your many battles have affected your memory."

"I think not," Corathel growled before flashing his friend another smile.

A moment later, the general seemed to recall why he had come. His smile vanished, his genial manner grown suddenly somber. "But enough of that. Tell me your story and we'll get back to matters at hand, which, I must warn, are grave indeed."

The general looked to Kylac, who turned instead to Jarom. Before he drew another breath, all eyes were upon him, and Jarom shifted awkwardly beneath the weight of their expectant gazes. He was reminded suddenly of his last meeting with the Circle of Elders, where he had first learned the improbable truth that had led to all of this madness.

Uncertain as to whether he should trust fully this General Corathel, he waited for Kylac's encouraging nod before clearing his throat. "It all started—I guess it'd be several weeks ago now—when our village in the Kalgren Forest was visited by Ellebe, queen of Alson. . . ."

In the adjoining office, the jailor sat back in his chair, pudgy fingers locked behind his head, listening without interest to the muffled conversation next door. He came forward for a swig of ale, after which his gaze fell upon the array of weapons piled on the desk before him. He thumbed through them, his attention drawn by the jeweled hilt of a sword that protruded from the end of a worn scabbard. Lifting the sheathed weapon close, he squinted carefully at the fine gems, marveling at those aswirl with some kind of fire.

He took another drink. What manner of stone shimmered as though filled with flames?

His eyes narrowed as he looked to the heavy oaken door behind which the prisoners and the general spoke.

In abbreviated fashion, Jarom proceeded to relate his adventures since the coming of Queen Ellebe, with Kylac and

Allion interjecting, occasionally, certain details that had escaped his memory. He felt strange at the telling, marveling at how much had transpired in such a short amount of time, thinking how little of it seemed real. He gathered speed and enthusiasm as he went, however, exhilarated by the truth of their recovery of the Sword of Asahiel, last of the Crimson Swords. By the time he and his companions had finished with the account of their expedition through the ruins of Thrak-Symbos, Chief General Corathel was leaning halfway across the table, fascinated by the narration.

"So this . . . Crimson Sword," he said at last, "is on your person?"

"Yes. Well, it's with the jailor."

"We shall fetch it at once," Corathel declared, rising to his feet. "I should very much like to take a closer look at it."

Jarom nodded eagerly, and the four men strode to the unlocked door, which Corathel flung open.

To Jarom's surprise and dismay, they found the jailor sitting at his desk, tongue between his lips as he pried with his dagger at one of the heartstones encrusting the Sword's hilt. The wretch glanced up as they entered, his face flushed, his dagger stabbing fiercely with his start. Jarom scowled, but before he could react, the blade's scabbard burst into writhing flames of crimson. The helpless jailor screamed as the fire engulfed him—searing away flesh and bone. Hearing the cry, the sentry posted outside the main door burst into the room, just in time to witness the inferno expiring into ashes. An instant later, these, too, had disappeared in a wash of heat. The jailor, along with his prying dagger and Jarom's scabbard, was gone.

For an agonizing moment, those who had observed the awesome spectacle stood paralyzed, left to gape at the shimmering air. Finally, Jarom broke the unnerving stillness, stepping forward to hoist the Sword from the table, which had been blackened by the flames. He grimaced as he did so, half expecting to be incinerated himself. But as before, the divine talisman was not even warm, and appeared otherwise unaffected by its assault. Jarom gazed into the swirling depths of the blade, enthralled by its secrets.

"Notify the city authorities," Corathel said to the wild-eyed sentry. His voice was a choked whisper, his gaze fixed upon the mystical weapon.

When the soldier didn't flinch, the general snapped out of his trance and spun on him angrily. "Go! Say nothing of the Sword! I'll speak with the governor myself."

With his visage twisted into a mask of terror and mistrust, the sentry wheeled away, scurrying to fulfill the general's request.

"And leave the door open!" Corathel added, covering his mouth against the stench.

Those who remained continued to stare in helpless wonder, as if expecting something more to happen.

"It appears to me," the chief general grumbled, "that you know little more about this blade's power than I."

Allion nodded.

"I knows enough to keep my hands off them stones," Kylac breathed.

"It was defending itself."

Jarom had not actually intended to speak the words aloud. When he realized that he had, he looked up to find the others regarding him with quizzical expressions. None seemed quite ready, however, to challenge his claim.

"Come," Corathel urged. "I've yet to tell you of these hordes that ravage our lands without mercy."

While Jarom and Allion gathered their possessions, the general snatched up the ring of keys hanging on a peg to one side of the jailor's desk. After thumbing through and trying more than one, he managed to unlock the broken leg cuffs still clinging to their ankles. With that accomplished, he ushered them through the jailhouse front door and into the gray and misty morning outside.

He took them down an empty road, away from the site and stench of the jailor's stunning demise. Along the way, he answered Jarom's question concerning the ghostly state of the city, explaining that his armies had arrived just thirty-two hours before. In that time, Leaven had been evacuated under emergency conditions, her inhabitants sent through the passes west to Laulk, a sister city situated on the other side of the Whistlecrag.

Jarom marveled. "You cleaned out the entire city?"

"Some had to be evacuated forcibly, a handful of whom have yet to be rooted out. And we've allowed the governor and his aides to remain. But for all intents, the city belongs to the army now."

Jarom shook his head. He was less concerned with the logistics of the mass departure than with the idea of sending some two hundred thousand people into enemy-controlled territory. "But the wizard—"

"Has been holed up at Krynwall for weeks, according to our scouts," Corathel reassured him. "Almost since his initial invasion. He is of no concern when compared to the threat that faces us."

Jarom started to argue, to remind the general of how quickly the wizard's forces had conquered Krynwall, and to reaffirm his suspicion that the wizard was behind this newest threat from the east. But he held his objections in check, reminding himself of how long he had been away and of what little he actually knew. Better to wait and listen before he began second-guessing the general's decisions.

"You sound as if you're all doomed already," Allion noted. "Why remain if there's no hope?"

"Desperation," the general replied. "Thus far, we've done little more than run. Shades, we fled Crylag—Crylag! A city that has flourished for centuries and withstood countless enemy assaults. We simply abandoned it in terror!" He stopped to shake his head, as if shamed by the memory. When he resumed, his tone was one of angry determination. "We realize well enough that we cannot run forever. And we'd all prefer to die in combat than be hunted down like frightened animals."

Jarom found neither solace nor inspiration in the general's words, but was forced to respect the man's fighting spirit.

"How did ya escape without the enemy following ya here?"

"I led a mounted diversion north, drawing the fiends

across the Fields of Ravacost toward Morjal. They took to attacking the Menzo lines, and we were able to sneak away."

"What kind of beasts?" Jarom asked, expecting at long last to receive a response to everyone's question.

But the general just shook his head as they arrived at an abandoned inn, reopened as a storehouse when the military had assumed control of the city. Corathel led them inside, where he sat them around a dirty table and served each of them a mug of cold ale. Finally, he settled down to join them, fixing Jarom with a warning glare.

"Dragons," he said.

For a moment, Jarom wasn't sure he had heard correctly. He blinked uncertainly, then looked to his companions. Allion had gone pale. Kylac's brow was furrowed. *Dragons?*

"Not the beasts as you know them in legends," the general added hastily, "but I don't know another name for this foe. It's an army of fire-spitting serpents, black-scaled brutes that do not fly, but carry themselves upright like men. Although their numbers are not overwhelming, each is as strong as half a dozen soldiers. Their skin is as tough as any plate I've encountered, and I watched them decapitate my men with bare-handed swipes!"

Jarom gawked, the general's words having slashed the air from his lungs. He gripped the Sword, held in his lap, until its gems dug into his palms. Having witnessed the devastation at Crylag, he had little trouble envisioning the slaughter as it must have unfolded. An army of humanoid dragons, just as Corathel described them, tearing through the ranks of men like lions, leaping about, biting and clawing, scattering the weaker prey. He imagined the horror of those who had tried to fight, those whose weapons had barely scratched an enemy's skin before their heads went rolling away. He could almost taste the horror and smell the stench as the city and its occupants burned, while amid the chaos, Corathel and his officers fought to organize a retreat. . . .

"Where did they come from?" he asked, struggling to repel the nightmare taking form. Had the wizard discovered them? Created them? Man-sized or not, what could be done against such an army?

"We don't yet know," the general confessed, his eyes dark and weary. "I should add, however, that your encounters with demons are not the first to malign my ears. Such tales have been as rampant as these man-dragons—dragonspawn, as we've come to call them. I've not seen enough to know whether they serve the will of another. Perhaps, indeed, your wizard is to blame."

"We's been through Crylag," Kylac said, his features twisting pensively. "We found no bodies."

Jarom was amazed by the youth's sense of calm. While he and Allion wrestled with emotions of dread and disbelief, Kylac remained as stoic and pragmatic as ever.

Corathel nodded. "They eat their dead. And ours."

Jarom blanched, a great chasm opening within the pit of his stomach.

"Ya were able to slay some?"

"No more than a handful," the general admitted. "In truth, we scarcely stopped to try. I'm one of maybe a dozen men who took a swipe at one of those things and is alive to tell of it. We saw what they were capable of and we ran. Those who didn't run fast enough were killed." He shook his head. "I mean, we had no notice. They moved faster than any warning that may have been sent. Had we been able to brace for the assault, to anticipate—"

"Then ya knows o' the southlands?"

"I sent scouts out to comb the enemy's trail the moment we arrived. The first reports have just begun to trickle in."

"Dirrk and Battlemont have been razed," Kylac said, "along with every other settlement south along that line, deep into the Kalmira. We had us some friends there we believes were taken hostage."

The general put a hand to his chin. "I'm not sure about any hostages, although they would not likely have been on the front lines. In either case, I'm glad the assault on Crylag came at a time of high conflict with Menzos, when our civilian populace was low."

"We means to rescue them," Kylac pressed.

The furrows in Corathel's brow deepened. "I understand your concern. These are my countrymen, the people I'm sworn to protect. But I'm not sure you understand. They are most likely dead already. And you too will die if caught trying to infiltrate—"

"We're not here to debate the matter," Jarom interrupted, startled by the strength of his own conviction. He glanced at Kylac, then continued. "My companions and I will follow the enemy until we've done all we can to save our friends."

Corathel eyed him squarely. "That's an extremely dangerous proposition."

"Compared to what? Waiting for them to attack you here? Tell me, what happens to the rest of your lands while you remain locked within these walls?"

The general's face took on a stern cast. "What are you saying?"

"That we needs to go after 'em," Kylac said bluntly. "All of us."

Corathel was incredulous. "You want us to assault?"

"As Jarom said, what is it ya thinks you're doing here?"

For a moment, the chief general appeared to be at a loss for words. Those that he found sounded less than convincing. "We're providing ourselves with the best chance for survival, by fortifying our position and bracing for the enemy onslaught."

"Like seasons in the Abyss," Kylac contested calmly. "If'n ya were interested in maintaining your best defensive position, you'd never have left Crylag."

"Sweet Olirium, Kylac, that was different. We'd never faced an army of monsters before. We were flushed like cowards, I admit, but next time we'll be prepared, and might even have a chance—*if* we seize every advantage available to us."

Kylac's continued poise offered sharp contrast to the general's mounting agitation. Though quiet, his words were staunch and uncompromising, sheathed in certainty. "These creatures have already passed Leaven by once. Who's to say they won't do it again? It can't be in the way o' any particular objective if'n they're out for all o' Pentania. What threat do ya pose them here? They can scoop up all the world whiles you're locked in your stinking hole, then deal with ya later."

Corathel kept silent, so Kylac continued. "Jarom's right. Even if ya secure Leaven for a while, you're doing nothing to defend the rest o' your lands or destroy this enemy. With her people away, all you're really protecting are empty homes."

It was with some effort that Jarom nodded as the youth looked to him. That had indeed been his thought when the general had challenged his resolve to rescue his friends. He hadn't meant it, however, as an invitation for Corathel to join them in an all-out raid, which, to his thinking, would be like using a pick-axe to dig for truffles. His words had been a reaction, a defensive taunt meant to question the wisdom of the general's strategy as Corathel was questioning his. Somehow, that simple criticism had spread like wildfire into a course from which he did not dare back down.

The general sighed, then rubbed his eyes with his fists. "I might agree," he confessed, "*if* we were hunting down human marauders. But damn it, these creatures are not mortal men! The very thought of meeting them on even terms scares the living fury out of me. Any lack of advantage for us becomes an advantage for them—we can't hope to win."

"Ya said their chief advantage before was your own fear. Next time, that won't be the case, especially if'n the men are stirred by a march rather than asked to wait around like caged animals."

The general took a long swig of his ale. "I understand how a soldier's heart works, my friend. But trust me when I tell you that a boost in morale is not going to change the outcome of this war. We need something more."

"How 'bout the divine power of a Crimson Sword?"

Corathel's gaze shifted to the gleaming weapon held in Jarom's lap, the glow of its fires weak but steady in the shadowed room. An ensuing silence persisted for several long moments. Jarom found himself holding his breath, uncertain as to what he hoped the general's response would be.

"I don't know," Corathel grumbled at last. "I'd just as soon let the Menzoes deal with them."

"They'll be back," Kylac reassured him. "You and I both know that a Menzo will never stand where a Parthan could not."

Corathel scowled, telling Jarom that Kylac had struck a nerve within the proud general.

"Are you actually suggesting we can defeat this horror?"

"I'm saying no one's tried, and that I too would rather die fighting than be hunted down like vermin. Besides," he added, producing his dagger and running a fingernail along its edge, "ya already know my thoughts 'bout any enemy."

Corathel smirked in spite of himself, and looked as though he had been relieved of a grievous burden.

"Kylac Kronus, my adventuring friend, we may yet win this little war."

Kylac nodded, but a crestfallen Jarom was not so sure.

CHAPTER TWENTY-EIGHT

*F*eeling refreshed, if not rested, Jarom marched unmolested alongside Allion and Kylac as they made their way through the streets of Leaven. Summer, it seemed, had come again, steeling itself one last time against winter's onslaught. The midmorning sun burned away the last of the early mist and glinted off the weapons and armor of the soldiers they passed. A breeze ushered them along, stale and used within the city walls, but nonetheless brisk and stimulating. Sounds echoed around them, the reverberating steps of shod horses and booted men, of creaking wheels and pounding hammers, of shouts and jostling and all manner of general military commotion.

Despite the weather and surroundings—a welcome change from the lonely, sodden, war-torn plains of western Partha—Jarom remained emotionally subdued, wary and watchful. Not only did he remain troubled by Corathel's account of their unimaginable enemy, but his presence, it seemed, had come to draw unwanted notice. Upon their arrival, Jarom recalled, he and Allion had attracted little more than indifference from these men-at-arms. Now it seemed that nary a soldier was too busy to look up from his work to regard the trio with a distrusting glance or harsh whisper. Apparently, the story of the jailor's demise had leaked, for the apprehensive gazes were always directed at the silver, gem-studded hilt protruding from the freshly acquired scabbard that swung at Jarom's side.

"I don't like this," he admitted as they passed a large company of soldiers. From the corner of his eye, he watched the stares that stretched after him as though he had just walked through a wall of cobwebs.

Corathel had left them nearly two hours ago to conduct a preliminary consultation with his chief officers about Kylac's proposed attack against the dragonspawn. Left at the inn with food and water, fresh clothes and a bath, the weary travelers had urged the chief general to take as much time as needed. Now, as the companions neared the rendezvous at the appointed council house, where they would lend what support they could to the dubious proposition, they found themselves thronged by the skittish soldiers, causing Jarom to wonder how he had ever gotten himself into this situation.

"Don't worry," Kylac offered reassuringly. "None o' these louts will lay a finger on ya." He pushed back his cloak until Jarom caught a glimpse of his leather-wrapped sword hilts. "Besides, I doubt a one o' them would risk being burned to ashes just to hassle ya and your cursed sword."

The youth spared him a wink, and reminded of their own formidable strength, Jarom relaxed considerably.

He did his best to put the matter out of mind after that, occupying himself with a study of their surroundings. Save for Krynwall, which he had visited only a handful of times, Leaven was by far the largest city he had ever seen and a minor marvel to behold. Its area covered more than five times the breadth and span of Earthwyn, its structures piled one atop the other, stretching skyward until they blotted out the sun. Neighboring districts were divided by thick bulwarks and sharp fences, particularly those whose splendor—from homes and orchards to parks and roadways—outshone those that lay crammed below. All in all, Jarom found it to be a sordid den in which nature played slave to man's needs. The people may have fled, but not without leaving signs of their passing. Across wide, brick-laid avenues and in narrow alleys filled with refuse, Jarom saw little more than filth and pollution. A perfect setting, he imagined, for the many tales of death and disease, crime and corruption, for which the major cities were known. Ironically, the same walls that kept Leaven secure from the outer world served as a barrier inside which these man-made horrors were bred. For all its wonders, the city seemed to Jarom a cesspool. How anyone could grow accustomed to such conditions, especially when surrounded invariably by war, was beyond his comprehension.

They cut across an open plaza framed by tall, weathered buildings that served as tenement housing. Jarom recognized it by Corathel's description. Personal articles—flowerpots and clothes and trinkets—clogged tiny, windowed balconies overlooking the plaza's uneven floor. In the middle of the square stood a fountain whose bed had gone dry and whose center was adorned with the statue of a man, painted in grime and the droppings of birds. A monument of some kind, although Corathel did not know the tale—a tribute to a man whose story and cause were now forgotten. Jarom studied the neglected sculpture as he marched by, peering up at the cracked visage and lifeless eyes, and wondered just how long it had taken for the man and his achievements to slip into the void of unremembered history.

A pair of roadways led out from the opposite side of the plaza. They chose the one on the left, then followed it south for several minutes, arriving at last at a gated compound. A guardsman posted out front nodded at their approach, and moved hurriedly to swing wide a hinged portion of the wrought-iron gate. He said nothing, and kept back as far as he could while they entered, his dark eyes riveted upon the exposed hilt of the Sword. Jarom only shook his head as he shuffled past.

Within the compound, a wide path lined with stone benches carried them past gardens and shade trees and up the steps of the appointed council house. A pair of sentinels posted in front of the tall double doors parted immediately upon the company's approach, allowing its members to enter the structure unimpeded.

Eyes forward, Jarom made his way through a foyer, up a short flight of stairs, and down a hall that led to a great door wreathed in brass. A cacophony of shouts could be heard from behind the door, causing Jarom to slow. Kylac, however, did not hesitate, but shoved the door ajar and led his companions into the room.

Corathel and the five men who sat with him around a solid table all turned to acknowledge the trio's arrival. Three empty chairs remained, interspersed among the members of the assembly. Following Kylac's lead, Jarom and Allion each settled into one, the former finding himself wedged between a giant of a man whose gaze was grim but without accusation, and a brawny, bearded man with a face full of scars who glared at him as if he were some form of plague. The commotion had ceased, and Jarom noticed quickly enough that every other eye in the room was also trained upon him. Somehow, he managed not to recoil under the mass of appraising stares, though already he found himself thinking of ways in which he might bring this meeting to a close.

Sounding a bit disgruntled, Corathel was the first to speak. "I suppose that a brief introduction would be in order. Gentlemen," he said, addressing the new arrivals, "these are my division commanders, lieutenant generals all." He held forth an outstretched arm, presenting in turn each of his compatriots.

"Fourth General Lar," he began, indicating the barrel-chested giant beside Jarom. Rusty blond hair sprouted from the man's head in curling clumps, and he apparently had not shaven that morning, for stubble peeked from the skin of his cheeks and chin. He nodded politely toward the newcomers.

"Third General Maltyk," the chief general continued, gesturing toward a baby-faced man with mischievous blue eyes and a cropped, corn-silk beard. He too nodded, seemingly without interest.

"Second General Jasyn," Corathel proceeded, indicating a raven-haired man with freckled features and a wiry frame. A sleeveless shirt exposed his arms and shoulders and much of his chest, all of which were etched with muscle beneath a stretched skin. He offered a disarming smirk.

"Fifth General Rynar, my chief strategist and engineer . . ." The small man wore his brown hair without style over a pinched face tanned by the sun. He nodded, his expression intense.

". . . and First General Ledryk," the chief general sighed, indicating the burly, scar-faced man fuming beside Jarom.

Though he did not hope to remember their names beyond this meeting, Jarom was taken aback by the age of those seated before him, none of whom looked much older than he. In fact, Jasyn, with his freckled cheeks, and Maltyk, despite his beard, looked to be his own age. That such young men could have advanced themselves to such a station intrigued the village Fason. At the same time, it seemed odd, in both a sad and frightening way. Like their chief general, who was himself in the prime of life, it was unlikely they had attained their rank through proficiency alone. Jarom knew not whom to pity more, the many superiors who must have perished to make room, or these young men whose entire lives had been centered around war.

"As for the rest of you," Corathel continued, addressing his advisors almost without pause, "this is Jarom, guardian of the village Diln—and, if his story is to be believed, Torin, son of Sorl and heir to the throne of Alson."

Jarom reddened as the introduction was made, and though he kept perfectly still, his eyes glanced quickly from face to face to gauge their reactions. But the proclamation did nothing to alter their level of attention. Apparently, Corathel had already shared with his lieutenant generals this otherwise surprising information and given them time to digest it. Or perhaps they simply didn't care.

"The others are his companions, Kylac Kronus and—"

"Yes, yes," growled Ledryk, cutting him short. "Let's get back to the matter at hand."

"Easy, Ledryk," Rynar groaned. "Unless you've got some new argument to add, I'd rather save my ears the beating."

Ledryk whirled upon the slight man with a glare that might have turned a dragon's gaze, but Rynar didn't flinch. "How about this?" he snarled, leaning in toward the center of the table, balancing his weight on a pair of forearms thicker than any Jarom had seen before. "Take a look at whose scheme this was to begin with—a boy's!" He pointed an accusing finger at Kylac, who offered no reaction whatsoever.

"What would it matter if the plan was coughed up by an infant? It is sound, whatever its origin."

"And you," Ledryk spat, regarding Jarom with a smoldering eye. "What is it you guard your village against? Gophers?"

Corathel frowned. "Ledryk—"

"We have not the strength to defeat them in the field!" the First General roared, pounding the table in emphasis.

"I still share Ledryk's skepticism," Jasyn confessed, then quickly added, "though not so vehemently."

Maltyk nodded. "I've seen nothing to convince me that we'll fare any better than before. A war on the open plains would be suicide."

"Perhaps it's time for Jarom of Alson to change our minds," Lar prompted. His gentle tone sounded strange, given the rumble of his voice.

Again, Jarom found himself swimming within the waves of expectancy created by others, barely able to keep afloat. Confidence, he reminded himself, was needed here, the kind of certainty and determination that had led to his recovery of the Sword. To hesitate was to show his fear and reveal his own self-doubts. He could not allow that. This was what he had been called to do in the beginning, to gather an army with which to combat the sinister forces come to plague these lands. The lives of Marisha Valour and countless others depended upon his strength or lack thereof. Assuming, of course, as he had with Marisha, that they were not, the whole of them, doomed already.

Setting aside his own misgivings, Jarom rose from his chair with what he hoped was the strength and grace of self-assurance. Putting forth an air of nobility that felt to him stiff and unnatural, he drew the Crimson Sword, flooding the room with its radiance. Those unfamiliar with the talisman sat dumb with awe, while those growing accustomed to it admired anew its flawless elegance.

"It is truly beautiful," Ledryk admitted, noticeably mollified. "But what power does it hold?"

"Ask Leaven's jailor," Kylac suggested dryly.

Ledryk scowled, as if to say he hadn't invited the youth to speak. "But Corathel says that no one has drawn this . . . fire from the blade except for the jailor," he countered, regaining his conviction. His gestures and tone made it clear that he was speaking only to his fellow Parthans. "So let me restate: What power does it hold that we can use?"

Rather than lash out with a spoken retort, Jarom raised the Sword overhead and sliced down upon the table. When the Sword struck, the red flames from within billowed out to envelop the blade. And once the weapon had slid effortlessly through the wood, the flames vanished. The only evidence of their existence lay on either side of the gash in the table, where the smoking wood had been seared in the wake of the blade's passing.

Despite the gasps and grunts of those around him, Jarom was no longer awed by the display. He now felt something closer to triumph, reveling in his ability to exhibit such power at will, to startle others with the strength he possessed. Satisfied, he turned to confront Ledryk and any other who would challenge him.

"An impressive display, but—"

"Come now, Ledryk," Lar cut in. "With power such as that on your side, you can't tell me of an enemy you would fear!"

"I fear no enemy now," Ledryk boasted. "But I will not risk the lives of my men on a lost cause. If I possessed a hundred such weapons, I might like our chances. But what is one such blade going to accomplish against an army of these dragonspawn?"

"Aside from its ability to cut one of those fiends in half? Hope, confidence for all," Jasyn submitted, suddenly a believer. "Everything that stirs a warrior's soul. If this man was able to retrieve the thing, why then can't he lead our forces to victory?" The lieutenant general's eyes were wide, his teeth gritted, his chest heaving with a sudden fire.

"We've debated long enough," Corathel decided, rising to stand with Jarom. "The longer we wait to retaliate, the more precarious our position will become. Already our people have been scattered or killed. And knowing nothing of this enemy, we have to assume that there may be more on the way. So I put the matter to a vote. Who elects that we march forth and destroy this scourge before it destroys us?"

Kylac, Allion, Rynar, and Jasyn rose in a united body. Lar came to his feet soon thereafter, burying Jarom in his shadow, and Maltyk contemplated the matter only a moment longer before standing to join them. In the entire room, only Ledryk remained seated.

"This assembly has decided by a majority to march, Ledryk," Corathel proclaimed. "Will you abide by the decision?"

The seething Ledryk scowled disapprovingly, but nodded. "We march," he agreed bitterly, regarding Jarom and the Sword with a caustic glare.

The remaining hours of that day were exhausted in preparation for the army's exodus. Corathel and his lieutenants had unanimously decided to set forth by the following daybreak. The chief general met first with the city governor and his aides, encouraging them to depart west in pursuit of their people. Immediately afterward, he turned his attention to informing the soldiers and procuring their collective reaction.

Entertaining hopes of igniting a fire within the hearts of his men as Jasyn had suggested, Corathel assembled his divisions and addressed them from the top of a battlement, entreating them to vaunt their courage in an active fight to free the land. He spoke of their struggle as a pivotal moment in the shaping of human history, promising glory and remembrances the likes of which they had never known. He suggested that theirs was a calling sent down by the Ceilhigh themselves, and after vowing that the Crimson Sword would be at the vanguard of their assault, he had Jarom present the talisman for all to behold.

As it turned out, those of the Parthan West Legion were eager to take up the fight. Inspired by their chief general's words and the sense of power that emanated from the breathtaking blade, the soldiers below scraped the fear from their hearts and brushed their spirits clean with fresh hope and desire. The rally climaxed in a state of euphoric frenzy, with close to thirty thousand men pledging to wage war to the death against the dragonspawn. Their battle cries trumpeted skyward, spilling over the city's walls to ring across the land. When at last the furor abated, the general ordered his troops to disperse and prepare.

"Shades of mercy," Corathel sighed in a strained voice once the ordeal had concluded. "That went better than I had dared hope."

Jarom nodded. The results had indeed been gratifying. For the Sword to have had such a dramatic effect over so many seemed to him miraculous, divine.

"Something wrong?" Corathel asked. "You seem troubled."

"No," Jarom assured him. "Just tired."

The chief general was not convinced, and the suspicious eye with which he fixed Jarom said so.

"Well," Jarom admitted slowly, "I *am* a bit concerned. It's not important, but . . . I'm worried about Ledryk."

Corathel nodded as Jarom continued.

"He just . . . seems so angry. Can he be trusted?"

"Thoroughly," Corathel assured him. "Don't let his nasty disposition scare you. Above all else, the man's loyal, and as good an ally on the field of battle as you'll find. He did not achieve the rank of lieutenant general of the First Division by charm and good looks. You just have to get to know him."

It was now Jarom's turn to appear skeptical. "But at that meeting," he insisted, "he was so fiercely opposed to the idea."

"It's impossible in war to propose a strategy without resistance. You'll always find at least one cynic to contend with. A necessary evil, I might add, because without someone to expose the flaws in its plan of attack, an army will soon make a critical mistake. Ledryk hunts for these flaws like no man I've ever known, but don't condemn him for it. His attitude may win him few friends, but it saves many soldiers their lives."

Jarom started to protest. "But—"

"And I can assure you," the general finished unequivocally, "that once a course of action has been decided upon, you'll find nary a man more devoted to carrying it through."

Jarom found this to be true over the next few days. The army departed Leaven without fanfare, with but a handful of scouts left behind. As it crawled northward, following the

swath of devastation across the Fields of Ravacost to the ruined husk of Morjal and beyond, Jarom could always find
Ledryk riding throughout the ranks, bellowing encouragement and ensuring that no one faltered. It became evident as
well that of all the divisions, Ledryk's was the most disciplined and the most determined, giving the First General
every right to his title as Corathel's second-in-command.

The entire army, however, operated like a well-oiled machine. Had he not seen it for himself, Jarom would not have
believed it possible to guide this immense procession of men
and wagons and engines of war as though it were a single-
bodied creature. But Corathel proved to be an extraordinary
leader, impressing Jarom with the ways by which he directed the affairs of his fighting force with precision and
competence. Each man, from the legion commander to the
lowliest rank-and-file soldier, had his place and performed
his duty without protest. It was a simple matter, really, or so
Corathel claimed. Establish a set of rules and enforce them
without prejudice. Engender within each man a sense of
pride and accountability in something larger than himself.
Most important was to surround oneself with good leaders,
be they captains of a squad or commanders of a division.
Men will obey orders, Corathel explained, but follow an
example.

Jarom was wise enough to understand that none of it was
quite so easy or played out quite so smoothly as the general
suggested. But whatever Corathel's formula, it worked. For
his part, Jarom mingled among the various regiments, doing
what he could to keep their spirits up and their hearts focused. He was only too happy to do so, as it helped to free
his mind of the impending conflict—his first on a field of
battle. Doubts and fears plagued him. Was he ready? Would
the mysterious power of the Sword be enough? When all
was said and done, would any of what he had set forth to do
matter?

Of particular help against such fears were the lieutenant
generals who had agreed to this course. Watching them in
action, it did not take Jarom long to realize that these were
men whose experience he could draw upon.

At six and a half feet and more than three hundred pounds, Lar was the largest man Jarom had ever met. The man possessed the strength of a stallion, and toiled twice as hard as anyone else without pausing to complain. He went about his tasks with quiet determination, and despite his size and power, treated everyone as his equal.

Then there was Jasyn, who treated Jarom and anyone else who came within shouting distance as though they were best friends sharing drinks in a crowded tavern. He was pleasant enough, but never tired of hearing himself speak, loud and long and usually about the numerous feats of glory he had performed throughout his young life. The stories were interesting enough, especially once Jarom learned from others who knew the man that all were true. Still, the Second General would speak until Jarom's ears ached, and only his congeniality made this bearable.

In Maltyk, Jarom found a man who could make him laugh like no one else ever had, readily and uncontrollably—especially when Jasyn came anywhere near. Together, the lieutenant generals of the Second and Third divisions formed a riotous pair. Were it not for the thousands of others with whom he marched or the trail of destruction they followed—all of which served to remind him of their true purpose—Jarom might have thought he traveled with fools and minstrels rather than an immense army heading toward battle.

In sharp contrast stood Rynar, whose grim focus was matched only by his vast-ranging knowledge. From science to alchemy to military tactics, he seemed to understand quite a lot about everything. In just the short time they spent together, the man introduced to Jarom a good deal he didn't know, particularly with regard to engineering. This oft-overlooked aspect of war amazed Jarom, who grasped well enough how these complex mechanisms worked, but marveled at the minds that had conceived them.

Unfortunately, there wasn't time for more than a glimpse into this or any other of the military's workings. By midafternoon on the second full day of travel, the army had forded the raging Kraagmal River, just a day's march from the Menzo capital of Kraagen Keep. As before, the trail they followed was scarred and rutted, plowed under by the invaders' assault, empty of life or any sign thereof. Somewhat shocking to Jarom, the Parthans actually enjoyed seeing these northern lands devastated, lands claimed for their lifetimes and longer by the Menzoes. Why Partha had not long ago accepted Menzos's independence and relinquished its own claim was none of Jarom's business. Nor was he fool enough to make it otherwise among this biased group. Nevertheless, it seemed ridiculous to him that they should take joy in their neighbors' ruin, or that they should have to worry themselves over a potential Menzo retaliation for their presence here when both nations were faced with this common enemy.

Yet worry they did. As a matter of procedure, the entire army was ringed with a network of scouts, outriders who probed the surrounding region for two reasons. One of these was to keep an eye out for the hated Menzoes. The second was to ensure that the force of dragonspawn they followed had not altered course and swung around to head southward once more. The last thing they needed was to waste time tracking a winding path north and south across the eastern Pentanian landscape. Thus far, the answer to this concern had been the same with each report. There was no indication that the enemy swarm had deviated from its northward trek.

When this same news reached them on the eve of the second day out from Leaven, Corathel summoned his lieutenants along with Kylac, Jarom, and Allion.

"It appears that the Menzoes," he began, spitting the name as he would a curse, "have done well in stalling the advance of the dragonspawn, fighting to the death for every last league of this land. The trackers inform me that the trail is less than a day old now, so it's possible that the beasts battle even now at Kraagen Keep."

Rynar nodded. No one else stirred. Jarom marked the anxiety upon the faces of those in attendance, etched beneath ridges made shadowy by the firelight.

"Then tomorrow we join them," Ledryk snarled at last, "and commence the spilling of dragon blood."

"And should any Menzoes happen to get in the way . . ." Maltyk added, then let the thought hang.

The comment drew harsh laughter from the ring of Parthan generals. Jarom glanced at Kylac, finding the youth's features unreadable, and at Allion, whose frown reflected his own concern. His stomach knotted and wrung, and he reached reflexively for the hilt of the Sword, hoping to ward off a sudden chill.

"Drink up, lads," Corathel bade them, raising a tankard, "for we dance tomorrow with devils of an unholy ilk."

Jarom stared into his cup as the others drank, searching for grace in the company of madmen, wondering how in the Abyss he was to keep the next dawn from being his last.

CHAPTER TWENTY-NINE

The demon Gravlith tromped down the granite-laid corridor, his stone feet scraping against the tiled flooring. Every now and then, a tile would crunch beneath the monstrous weight of his footfalls, the ruined pieces splaying in all directions around the shallow crater. Gravlith did not care.

Filled with the Queen's filthy dragonborn, the hall was cramped and narrow. Most had the good sense to turn at his approach and clear a path, pressing themselves into one of the many alcoves that lined the pillared walls, bowing in deference to the Queen's appointed general. A scant few were too occupied with matters of their own to take note, and had to be knocked aside. As the demon neared the end of the corridor, he came upon a pack huddled close about an arched entryway, set there as guards, but ringed now around a pair who were at each other's throats in the manner of fighting dogs.

Gravlith didn't slow, breaking through the ring of armor-scaled bodies as easily as a stone hurled through parchment. A few hissed and growled at him as they fell aside, but none dared a direct challenge, and the demon ignored them. The combatants, however, remained in his path, locked in their power struggle. One of them spied his approach, and tried to break away. At this, the other lunged ravenously, driving its opponent back, pressing the advantage. Unfortunately, its attack brought its own body squarely in line with Gravlith's knee, bent forward to take a step. The collision spun the weaker creature about, and it lashed out in response.

It was a reflexive act, one that the beast never would have considered in a rational state. That didn't matter to Gravlith. Realizing its mistake, the enraged creature was instantly cowed, its claws raking and scrabbling against the stone floor in desperate retreat. Too late. The demon reached out a single craggy hand, seizing the dragonborn by the face, his fingers wrapped over the top of its forehead and around to the back of its skull. With an effortless squeeze, Gravlith caused the creature's head to rupture in his hand, bits of soft flesh oozing out between the seams of his clenched fist. A muffled grunt was all the beast managed in protest before the demon released it, dropping its twitching carcass to the floor.

Gravlith marched on through the open archway, head scraping against the keystone rise.

Once inside, the demon cast about the open-air solar, ignoring the sounds of the dragonborn behind him as they feasted upon their dead comrade. He found what he was searching for, outlined by the stars as it perched upon the sill of an open window, across the spacious bathchamber to the west. The tiny creature had its head buried beneath its wing, digging with its beak at the soft fur that grew upon its lavender-skinned body. Gravlith turned and made his way toward it at once.

The little demon glanced up at his approach, ceasing its preening long enough to take in the other's expressionless features, and looking as though it might flee. Gravlith gave it no reason to do so, his heavy gait slow and steady as it carried him around the bathing pool and up a pair of steps that cracked underfoot. A moment later, he was across the room and standing over his skittish companion, a shiny, adamantine giant as dark as his own shadow.

Mitzb.

The imp nodded at the unspoken greeting, tiny ears flattening against its batlike skull, green eyes glittering in the moonlight.

The keep is secure. We await her coming.

Again, Mitzb nodded. The little demon spread its wings, its body wet where it had been licking itself. With a cursory flap and a grin of its needlelike teeth, it leapt from the stone sill and into the night. Gravlith leaned out to watch its fall from the tower heights. The imp plummeted for a long moment, then caught a current of wind and swept skyward, winging south with message in tow.

When satisfied that the creature was on its way, Gravlith, with preparations still to make, turned on his heels and headed for the solar entry, wondering idly if he would have to kill anything on his way out.

"The keep is fallen," the scout reported matter-of-factly, "yet the dragonspawn remain."

Jarom had just about gone off to bed, having given up hope that any of the northern trackers would return before dawn. Though he had desperately wanted to be there for the debriefing and subsequent strategy meeting, he was worn out. The Parthan West Legion, under Corathel's command, had traveled for more than eighteen hours over each of the last two days, and while horses had been provided for Jarom and his companions, the fact remained that they had covered four days' worth of travel in just two. He had sat with the others as long as he could around their fire, eyes dry, lids heavy, catching snatches of conversation while doing what he could to dispel the weight that had settled within the pit of his stomach like a block of ice. Between the soothing crackle of the flames and the hushed murmurs of his comrades, it had been all he could do to keep from falling asleep where he sat.

Now he leaned close, his weariness all but forgotten, replaced by the nervous anticipation of a condemned man awaiting sentence.

"How many?" Corathel asked, his bronze skin stripped of color in the pale light of moon and stars.

The scout, a boy of no more than fifteen years, shook his head, his eyes darting from face to face before fixing once more on that of his legion commander. "We counted between four and five thousand clustered about the city walls. There looked to be perhaps another thousand or more within."

"Any prisoners?" Jarom was unable to help the desperation in his voice. Corathel looked at him before nodding for
the scout to answer.

The boy shook his head. "We found no sign. If there are
any, then they're being held somewhere within the city."

"Why aren't they on the move?" General Jasyn asked of no
one in particular.

Corathel waved him off, pressing the young scout. "You
say the city is intact?"

"Mostly," the boy confirmed. "Compared to the others
we've come across. It appears as if they've made it their
home."

"Why would they do that?" Jasyn demanded.

"And for how long?" Maltyk added.

"It doesn't matter," Ledryk growled. "They've stopped.
They've gone as far north as they're able. They're sitting
right in front of us should we choose to strike."

Lar frowned. "But if they are up to something, we might
at least—"

"Ledryk is right," Corathel intervened, keeping the meeting on course. "We can't be concerned with why or whether.
If we're going to do this, we do it now."

"Surely you don't mean to lay siege to the city," Rynar
observed rather pointedly. "Fighting them on the open mesa
would seem challenge enough."

Corathel offered no indication that he heard the man, rubbing his chin thoughtfully. Jarom's worry was beginning to
deepen when the chief general turned back to the scout.

"You say they are encamped primarily outside the city?"

"Yes, sir."

"And the draw?"

"Clear, sir. Ridgelines and all."

Again, General Jasyn scowled. "They've not taken the
high ground?"

"What good would it do them?" Rynar realized. "They've
no range weapons, no capacity for launching an attack from
afar."

"Still, to surrender such an advantage . . ." He left the
thought to complete itself in the minds of his listeners.

"They don't know we're here," Kylac reminded the lieutenant general. The youth lay comfortably against a fallen
log, ankles crossed, hands clasped before him. His hood was
drawn so close and his form was so still that it appeared he
might be sleeping. "They certainly have no reason to suspect
an attack."

At this, a few of the generals seemed to smile. Lines of
tension released, and one or two even sat back. As usual
when he felt as if he was missing something, Jarom looked
to Allion. Judging by the other's expression, the hunter was
as in the dark as he was.

Corathel bent forward, eyes glinting with determination.
"Tomorrow," he said, picking up a stick with which to draw
in the dirt. "Before first light. This is what we do."

As a new sun crested the eastern horizon, Jarom found himself astride his horse between Chief General Corathel and
Kylac Kronus, staring down the rugged throat of Bane Draw.
A little more than a league to the north, he could just make
out the stark edges of Kraagen Keep, his eyes beginning at
last to separate shadow from solid form. Named for the
citadel at its center, the city was built atop a plateau deep
within the broken hill country of northeast Pentania. A single causeway climbed to the top of the mesa, visible at the
far end of the draw. Haakon's Arch, they called it, a natural
rock formation that spanned the canyon below, of stronger
strata than that which had been etched out from underneath
eons ago by a once-tunneling river. There had been numerous such archways, Jarom had been told, bridging the gap
between the stretch of ground upon which he stood and that
which rose above. All but one, however, had been destroyed,
dropped into the chasm below, their rare beauty cast aside
for the sake of defense. Peering now at the landscape before
him, it was not hard to understand why.

By preserving only Haakon's Arch, the defenders had left
just one approach to their city. And that approach was
through Bane Draw, a deep and narrow cleft that gutted its
way between a pair of rugged hills fronting the keep. The

hills themselves were thickly forested with mountain scrub, dry and sharp, grown over steep climbs and jagged pitfalls, hairline fissures, and secret crevasses plugged with break-away carpets of loose stone. Shattered and twisted throughout the ages by earthquakes, landslides, and high winds, it was a nightmare landscape no sizable force could cross. And even if one were to do so, it would find itself trapped on the other side by the sheer drops of Dagger Canyon, which ran beneath Haakon's Arch and formed the plateau upon which the city rested. The canyon had been described to Jarom as a deep and sharply slanted gorge carved by an ancient tributary of the Llornel River. Its bed was dry now, the river having been rerouted at some point in ages past by the re-formation of the earth, due yet again to a slow series of catastrophic quakes. Regardless, the canyon was impassable except by way of Haakon's Arch and the draw that fed into it.

And the draw was death. Its name was a derivative of Iskin's Bane, so given back in the earliest days of Menzo secession, some ninety years before the League of Man had recognized formally its independence as a nation. It was then, nearly three hundred years ago, that King Iskin of Partha had led his invasion into the northern lands, intent on reclaiming them from the Menzo king, Haakon. His armies had met with great success until they had arrived at this very draw, upon the threshold of what was then a fledgling castle. Determined to press forward and lay siege to the seat of Menzo power, Iskin had waged war for three months in the dead of winter, but failed to navigate the narrow draw. Bombarded by Menzo troops entrenched upon the slopes above, moving over rough and unfamiliar terrain, fighting at the same time to protect his supply trains from harrying Menzo forces in the south, the overzealous king had never really stood a chance. In the end, he surrendered the attempt and headed home with losses too numerous to count, having forged his way no more than a few hundred paces into the three-mile-long passage. He had vowed to return in the spring, but had died of exposure on the way home. In all the years since, no Parthan force had come within twenty leagues of the draw.

A tale of encouragement, Corathel had claimed, under the circumstances. The trick to the draw was to use it to their advantage, and the chief general had devised a plan to do just that. For the dragonspawn, intelligent though they were, had disdained to secure the hazardous stretch of land by manning its heights. The draw's slopes and ridges had been left empty, its trenches and bunkers theirs for the taking. This time, it would be they, and not their enemy, who held the position of supreme advantage. Such advantage had evidently done the Menzoes little good against the dragonspawn, Jarom had observed darkly, but Corathel had been quick to explain.

It was a basic strategy, really. Though revolutionary when first conceived, it had been borrowed and used throughout the ensuing ages until it had become standard practice when called for. Despite being outnumbered by a margin of more than four to one, the dragonspawn were the superior force. They were also less disciplined and in all likelihood could be made to surrender their strength advantage by stringing them out through the draw. Once that happened, Corathel's divisions, having secured their positions on the slopes under cover of darkness, would stream down from their places of concealment to close upon the enemy from either side. Archers would be used as cover only. Raking the enemy lines with arrows first would likely do little more than annoy the dragonspawn and alert the beasts to the presence of the infantry. Judging by the amount of broken arrows and spears littering the draw, that had been the Menzoes' mistake. It was more important to make sure that the enemy lines remained thin, and that they, as the attackers, did not give up the element of surprise. If they could make that happen, Corathel claimed, then their force would be upon the beasts before they realized it.

And given that, they might just stand a chance.

Drawn up with care and precision the night before, greeted mostly with enthusiastic nods and a grunt of approval even from First General Ledryk, the plan had looked sound enough—so much so that Jarom had slept undisturbed during the few hours he had been allowed. Now, in the cold and mist of early dawn, gazing not at a map or diagram but at the living truth of things, he was not so sure. An ominous mass of roiling black clouds hung over Kraagen Keep, refusing to be pushed aside by the sun's rays. Although the bodies of the dead—and maybe the living—had already been devoured, their blood stained the earth red. An expectant hush, deep and soulful, lay stagnant upon the land, unstirred by wind or breeze. Jarom could not help but reflect on the fact that this stage, with its history as a site of human slaughter both ancient and day-old, was set to serve so again.

With the strengthening of the light, Jarom could now see movement atop the mesa. Dragonspawn, he realized. The hordes swarmed the city within and without the broken outer wall, their dark forms like flies upon a half-eaten carcass. The air reeked with the stench of their greasy, black-scaled bodies, like that of decaying human flesh. Jarom crinkled his nose in disgust and gripped the hilt of the Sword in search of much-needed strength.

"Easy, my friend," came a voice from beside him. Jarom only half turned, but Kylac's eyes held his and would not let go. The youth spared him a wink and a smile. "I won't leave your side."

Jarom nodded, managing a display of outward resolve, while on the inside his guts were a steaming, roiling mess.

"Colonel."

Jarom nearly jumped from his skin at the sound of the chief general's voice, a gentle summons for the battalion commander of the Ninth Cavalry, who had been selected to lead the initial foray across Haakon's Arch and to lure the enemy south through Bane Draw. The colonel, a blunt-faced veteran with a receding hairline and gray in his beard, urged his mount forward, one of the many who to Jarom remained nameless.

"Ready, sir."

"On my signal."

The colonel nodded. Jarom studied the older man's rugged profile, searching for some sign of human emotion. He found none, and wondered what to make of it.

They continued to peer northward from their position of relative concealment at the mouth of the draw. The Fifth Division was at their backs, tucked away behind a screen of rocks and trees clustered about the shaggy hillside, their war machines oiled and ready. Jarom searched the slopes of the draw farther in for sign of the four forward divisions, but saw none. All was quiet, projecting a false and unsettling sense of calm given what he knew of the circumstances. At last, as the first rays of filtered sunlight began to spread over the heights of the eastern hill and spill down into the draw, Corathel gave the signal to commence the first stage of attack.

The battalion commander obeyed, motioning his corps of riders ahead. Jarom watched them file past at a steady trot, mounted men-at-arms of varying age and rank, a mobile attack unit of more than twelve hundred souls. Enough to lure the enemy from its encampment, but small and fast enough to evade pursuers. They forged their way deep into the draw with timing and precision, holding formation over and around random obstacles and uneven terrain. Normally a smooth and well-traveled highway, the floor of the draw was littered now with debris cast down from the weathered heights, a jumble of boulders and deadwood that had been intended, no doubt, to slow the dragonspawn assault. The Ninth Cavalry, however, moved ahead with ease. Coughing against a light cloud of dust kicked up in their wake, Jarom turned to watch Corathel, who observed his troops with unconcealed pride.

Before the battalion had made it halfway through the draw, the dragonspawn greeted its coming with shrieks of surprise and hungry anticipation. Their primal call rose up in a hissing wail that poured down off the heights and echoed across Dagger Canyon, as the hordes shook off their common lethargy and began their descent with unmistakable eagerness.

To Jarom's horror and amazement, the Ninth Cavalry did not turn at the sight of the black wave cresting before them, but continued toward it, their pace unbroken. The dragonspawn surged across the span of Haakon's Arch like floodwaters spilled from a dam. They frothed about at the entrance to the draw before funneling in, a tide gathering in size and strength. Flames spouted from their throats in quick, unsustained bursts, setting fire to weeds and grasses already charred, scorching the blackened stone. Smoke drifted skyward, the breath of small fires they could only hope would not become a blaze. Though the description rang hollow with overuse in the legends of bards and storytellers, Jarom could not deny that the approaching army had the look of a thunderous sea, with the dragonspawn—capped by their smoke and fire—like swelling waves beneath the charcoal and lightning of billowing storm clouds.

Still, the Ninth Cavalry pressed forward, a line of ants beneath a crushing tide about to descend. They continued on as if unaware of their fate, as if somehow blind to its shadow and deaf to its roar. Jarom wanted to scream at them, to wave his arms overhead, to do something to turn them around and quickly, before it was too late. Only the unflappable composure of those around him—Corathel, Rynar and his charges, and Kylac Kronus—kept him from acting upon his most desperate urges. Instead, he held his tongue and himself in check, a marble statue set to shatter from within.

When it appeared from his vantage that the dragonspawn were already atop them, when it seemed that surely it was too late for escape, the veteran colonel and his cavalrymen put spur to flank and charged right into the approaching horde. A terrible battle cry arose from their throats, feeble compared to that of the dragonspawn, and yet one that filled Jarom's heart with rage and defiance. The collision of the forward waves sounded to him like the crack of a mountain being torn asunder, and had his eyes not been riveted upon the unimaginable spectacle, he might have looked around to make sure that was not the case. As it was, he hunkered in his saddle, tensed to the core.

Then came the howls of agony and death, from human and dragonspawn alike. Jarom wasn't sure which sounded worse. One such cry would have been bad enough, but once they began, they continued to pierce the morning air, one after another until they had formed an endless chain of lightning, each ragged stream a quicksilver chariot upon which a single soul flew to the fields of Olirium or slid into the bowels of the Abyss. Their thunder became a monstrous, earsplitting roar from which there was no escape, the shrieking wind of a funnel cloud that would destroy whatever it touched and scar forever those who survived the rake of its passing.

Helpless, Jarom watched the struggle, forced to wait and see whether the storm would consume him. And it would, quickly enough it seemed. Already, the Parthan battalion was being borne back by the crush, shoved southward in his direction. For a moment, Jarom was startled by the realization. Though hemmed in by the slopes of Bane Draw, the dragonspawn were more than a match for the swords and lances of the Ninth Cavalry. As many dragonspawn died under claw and foot of their own trampling kind as at the hands of the brave Parthan soldiers. The cavalrymen, too, seemed to realize this. Already, the flanks were peeling away and the rear guard turning about in defeat. They would flee, as Jarom had silently urged them. But in so doing, they would be bringing the threat to him.

Then Jarom remembered that their charge had been meant to do just that. As the initial shock gave way to self-awareness and understanding, he recalled what it was they had come to do.

And it was working perfectly.

"Make ready, lads."

This time, the chief general's voice was strangely soothing. Jarom actually glanced away from the battle to regard the man, whose posture and expression was unchanged from when this day's conflict had begun. As resilient as a mountain stone, Jarom thought, accepting of the scars to be inflicted by lightning and winds, braced to weather their storm. He looked to Kylac. The youth, like the general, was peering ahead, keeping an eye at all times on the danger that faced them. Even now, his face was relaxed, his smooth skin showing nothing of concern. He shared with Corathel a natural immunity, perhaps, or a calculated resolve. Whichever, Jarom admired their strength and focus, raised like a shield in spite of their hidden fears.

Jarom turned back to the battle then, closing his eyes and

concentrating on the power of the Sword. Though it was sheathed, he could feel the power's flow as his hand gripped tightly its gem-studded handle, swirling in anxious tendrils of crimson fire, waiting to be unleashed. If those around him could face down this horror *without* the comfort of such a blade, then what was his excuse for failing to do so *with* it?

He opened his eyes. Much of the Ninth Cavalry was in full retreat now, bearing down the length of draw, steeds and riders alike wide-eyed with terror and exhilaration. A measure of the forward ranks, now the rear guard, held up, poking and prodding at the trailing hordes just enough to ensure continued pursuit. The entire procession was perhaps halfway through the draw already, and closing fast. As Corathel had hoped, the dragonspawn were strung out in narrow lines, rushing ahead heedlessly. General Rynar, with his battalions of catapults and ballistae, was ready and waiting to seal up the south end, to make sure that the enemy remained trapped within the draw, where the forward divisions would hack the beasts into so much pig feed. All were set to play their part, the enemy included, in Corathel's design.

Jarom steadied his grip, steeled his resolve, and waited for them to come.

The demon Gravlith stood upon a rampart of the citadel he had prepared for his queen and gazed out over the land below. That a human force had rallied against them hardly came as a surprise. This entire phase had been designed to do little more than just that, to draw out what strengths this apparently weak civilization might be holding in reserve, to give fair warning to his queen and any she brought with her. Thus far, after a week of wholesale slaughter, nothing of what he had seen was cause for concern.

What seemed strange was that the humans would choose to retaliate with such a small and pathetic party. Alerted by the initial thunder of their approach and the response of his army, he had gone at once to seek out the source of the disturbance. Almost by the time he had spied them, tearing through the cleft in the hills stretching south across the canyon, they were turning around, giving way to fear and to the press of the Queen's dragonborn. An act of sheer desperation, perhaps. But in his experience, an animal desperate enough to make such a strike was also too desperate to simply turn around and flee. To flee, or to fight, was a natural response. This appeared to be an unnatural combination of both, and something about it did not feel right.

He took a moment to survey the so-called battle. The Queen's dragonborn were racing south after the invaders, rabid wolves unleashed upon a wounded animal. The humans, however, seemed not to be pulling away as quickly as their horses should have allowed them. In fact, many looked to be hanging back, engaging still, but without any real threat of force. For all their strength and intelligence—and that of their creator—the dragonborn were driven by primal urges that even Gravlith, at times, had found difficult to control. For the moment, it would appear they were simply being led along by the nose.

Gravlith, despite his capacity for mayhem, was a more rational creature, far more cunning than the earthen material he resembled and less prone to letting his judgment be clouded over by primordial instinct. He scanned the horizon, seeking signs of danger cloaked upon the high ridgelines, but found none. Tracing ahead along the combatants' current path, however, he spied shimmers of movement amid the rocks and trees that spread beyond the south edge of the draw, still miles out from the focus of battle. He could discern nothing specific, but enough to confirm that his armies were being led into a trap. Whether or not that trap would prove harmful to them remained in doubt, but Gravlith was not about to take a chance, not when his queen would soon be receiving word that all was well.

Communicating as easily as these humans did with tongue and voice, Gravlith focused his thoughts into mental words and reached out to the forward lines, ordering his dragonborn back.

"What's wrong?" Jarom asked.

Without warning, the dragonspawn had slowed their

chase, then stopped altogether, their front lines still a mile
north of his position at the south end of the draw.

Jarom searched for Corathel's response, repeating the
question on everyone's mind. "Why have they stopped?"

But the chief general could only frown. The beasts had not
come far enough through for him to call down his forward divisions. There was no reason for it, no apparent explanation,
but the ramifications were clear. Already the enemy lines
were thickening as reinforcements filled in the gaps left by
the first frenetic rush, a crush of reserve dragon bodies that
made no effort to move their comrades forward, but instead
held up behind those that formed the front.

Then, even as Jarom fought to reconcile what he was seeing, the beasts began to recede. They did so hesitantly, backing away rather than turning about, hissing and snarling in
anger. A scant few continued on, ignoring the rest, lunging
ahead into the trailing midst of the Ninth Cavalry, whose
soldiers swarmed in to hack them apart. But the vast bulk of
the enemy horde was drawing back as though caught in a
riptide, their pursuit—and Corathel's plan—finished as
quickly as it had begun.

The surviving members of the Ninth Cavalry glanced at
one another in confusion. Sensing the danger, they wheeled
about, company by company, to reengage the enemy. The
dragonspawn, however, would not be drawn in a second
time. They fought and they killed, but only enough to keep
their antagonists at bay.

"They must have caught wind of us," Corathel said, peering through his spyglass in search of something the rest of
them hadn't seen.

Kylac scowled. "Even so, why would they turn back?"

By now, a handful of dragonspawn located around the
fringe were heading up the slopes to either side, prowling
and sniffing about. Jarom's heart thrashed in his chest as
though caught in a pool of quicksand.

"If they find our forward divisions, we're finished," Kylac remarked pointedly.

"General!" Corathel snapped, drawing Rynar's attention.
"Can we hit them from here?"

The Fifth General spat in disgust. "From a mile off? With the engines we brought? Not a chance, sir."

Corathel growled, marking again the failure of his chosen cavalry battalion to lure the dragonspawn from their defensive posture. "We need something to attract their attention. Anything to draw them on!"

"Perhaps this will work."

The words escaped Jarom's mouth before the thought they shaped was fully formed. By the time the chief general looked at him, he held the Crimson Sword aloft, bathing in its glow.

Corathel did not look pleased. "That weapon is to be our standard. We can't have you running forward and getting yourself killed."

Jarom cast his eyes northward toward the departing storm front, inclined in no small measure to agree. Instead, he said, "It seems to me, I'm the only bait you've got left."

Corathel's thoughts raced behind his steely gaze. He too glanced northward, measuring the distance between the searching dragonspawn and the approximate positions of his concealed troops.

"We go together," the chief general agreed at last. "Kylac?"

"Just give the order, General," the youth replied. His eyes were at last filled with that familiar fire, his features set.

Corathel turned to Rynar. "Your orders remain the same. Ready your battalions to cover our retreat." He turned to his personal cavalry regiment, a company of two hundred and fifty men. "Valor Sergeant, on my command."

The company commander nodded smartly, and echoed the order back through his ranks. Jarom's heart settled, but his stomach was alive with the flutter of butterfly wings. Despite the soothing assurances of the Sword, he could not seem to control his fearful anticipation. He wished Allion were here and not tucked away with a squad of archers high on the west ridge. As matters stood, there was no one to save him from his own decision.

Corathel must have read this in his face, or at least a portion thereof, for the chief general turned to him in angry concern. "Can you do this?"

Jarom flashed the man his most fearsome grimace, his body a puppet, it seemed, to a will not quite his own. "We're wasting time, General," he said.

"Then let's bring these monsters to us," Corathel muttered. "Hook and reel," he shouted to all in his booming commander's voice. "On my signal." He looked back for his valor sergeant's sign of readiness, which was quickly given. He then lifted his sword, drew a deep breath, and bellowed an unending cry.

"Parthans, *raaage*!"

With that, he spurred his mount forward, setting the pace for all to follow. For a harrowing instant, Jarom was nearly swallowed by the crush of riders surging from behind. Somehow, he managed instead to set heel to his horse's flanks. The animal responded like an arrow released, and in a mind-numbing rush of adrenaline, Jarom rode it northward, on a collision course with destiny.

CHAPTER THIRTY

To Jarom, the next few moments seemed a dream from which he might never awake. He clung to his horse with a white-knuckled grip as it barreled through the draw, dodging ruts and debris with sharp turns and sudden twists, lurching this way and that at breakneck speed. The world to either side disappeared in a smear of hazy lines, colorless and indistinct. Somehow, his mount bore him to the front, side by side with that of the chief general. Gaining balance and stability, he sat tall in the saddle, swept up like the foam of a cresting wave. The Crimson Sword flared in his hand, its intense glow heightened by his passion. It sensed his need, his desire, and made them its own, each fueling the other in an endless circle. Its light cleaved the darkness, both the shadows that draped the land and the doubts that clouded his thoughts. He felt nothing beyond the surging warmth of its radiant fire.

A black wall appeared before him. It hissed at him, a sound like steam erupting from the earth. He responded with a feral cry, growling in defiance, and drew strength when the echo of that cry became a roar taken up by those around him. His vision cleared, etching sharp focus against the surface of the wall, revealing scales and teeth and claws. . . .

He drove into their ranks before he could think to slow. He could hear the beasts scream. Only then did he register his own movements, hacking and slashing in wide arcs. The Sword was ablaze, crimson flames erupting in short bursts—all the time that was needed to sever a dragonspawn body and vanquish the life that inhabited it. He drove a wedge deep into their ranks, scattering them like roaches before an unexpected light. The passion with which he did so was raw and unrestrained, a euphoria the likes of which he had never known. He churned ahead, an unstoppable presence.

A strange hush settled over the draw. Though the shriek and clamor of fighting continued around him, Jarom found himself wrapped in a pocket of stillness—not of peace, but of dreadful anticipation. It lasted only an instant, but in that time, Jarom felt the shift of unseen forces, titanic in scale, like the cracking of a dam or tearing of a bridge.

As quickly as they had scattered, the dragonspawn were upon him. They rose together as one, it seemed, a black wall once more without crack or blemish. They attacked with such fury and hatred that Jarom simply sat astride his mount, unable to move, scarcely able to comprehend what was about to happen.

His horse gave a cry and reared back on two legs, flailing at the dark beasts closing in. Jarom clung to the reins with one hand, refusing to fall. The other whipped out as the enemy drew near, seemingly of its own accord. He cut a dragonspawn in half, then another, sweeping them aside as they lunged at him with maddened eyes. He wasn't sure how, in that moment. Instinct, perhaps, or the endless hours of self-training. Whether natural or learned, his impulses saved him, enabling him to fend off his attackers while his horse turned around to flee.

He was startled to find that the way back was already cut off. Corathel and the others were trapped behind a wall of black-scaled bodies. Their charge, Jarom recalled belatedly, was to have been a raking maneuver. He alone had made it something more, allowing himself to get carried away, to press recklessly forward. It seemed now that he had delved too deep, separating himself from his comrades, even Kylac. He was alone on a battered atoll, and the tide was closing in.

Once again, instinct drove him where rational thought could not. Despite being surrounded by the enemy, he urged his steed forward, south toward Kylac and the others. His sword arm worked furiously, driven with relentless purpose.

Though they tried, the dragonspawn could not reach him. Their fires singed the air, turning it thick with smoke and a sulfurous stench. But none escaped his focus and that of the Sword. They came at him in waves and died as swiftly.

Then, suddenly, he was free, breaking through the lines that had cut off his retreat. He was staring at a familiar face, a boyish countenance set with determination and tinged with wonderment at the fact that he was still alive. They exchanged no words. Already the youth was turning, whipping his horse about. Jarom spurred his mount to follow.

The dragonspawn came after, drawn to the Sword like flies to a corpse. Jarom glanced about as he rode alongside Corathel's cavalry company. Remnants of the Ninth were at their flanks, their faces sweat-streaked and ashen. Dragonspawn scrambled down from the heights, abandoning their search for the army's forward divisions and concentrating their fury upon him. Jarom could not quite believe what had happened; nor could he have explained it beyond the obvious. The Sword had proven to be the lure they needed. Despite their initial shock and dismay at its approach, the dragonspawn were once again charging south on the army's heels, desperate to catch up, stringing themselves out through the draw. Corathel's plan was going to work.

Whether or not they would survive to participate in the main battle remained in doubt. Jarom could feel his mount tiring beneath him, and could hear the enemy closing in. The fury of their rush was staggering. They were charging twice as fast as before, far more determined to catch him and his comrades than they had been in pursuit of the Ninth Cavalry. A matter of perspective, perhaps, but while the Ninth had been almost casual with its retreat, holding up enough to make sure the enemy followed, Jarom was fleeing for his life at full speed and was yet losing ground with every stride.

He stayed low, crouched in the stirrups, his weight forward to urge his horse on. The mouth of the draw lay just ahead. If only he could reach it, he would have the protection of the Fifth Division. Time enough to collect himself and regroup. Time enough to prepare—

The thought skittered out of reach as his horse went

down, its ankle twisted in a deep rut. Jarom flew forward, over its head. He crashed against the back of a retreating rider and crumpled to the earth, the Crimson Sword slipping from his grasp. He spun at once to retrieve it, choking on a mouthful of dirt. His horse cried out in pain and terror. Glancing up, he watched as the dragonspawn ripped the animal apart. Horrifying and yet mesmerizing, the display very nearly cost him his life. For as he watched, crouched on hands and knees, a pair of dragonspawn vaulted the doomed beast and came for him. He found the Sword, but it remained just out of reach. . . .

He lunged for it anyway, knowing he was too late, seeing his doom in the gleeful eyes of his assailants. But suddenly, Kylac was there, leaping from his own mount so that he could bring two blades to bear—one long, one short. The dragonspawn could not have known what hit them, for the youth's weapons tore at them in a manner that iron and steel could not, shredding them in a spray of black blood.

However, this only strengthened the resolve of those who came after. And Jarom harbored no delusions as to what that meant. The youth would stand over him as he'd said he would, no matter the cost, shielding the woodsman with his own life if necessary, as Jarom had shielded the other with his.

Refusing to accept such a sacrifice, Jarom retrieved the Sword with a growl. He was on his feet in an instant, the talisman's fire surging through him with fresh force. Standing side by side, they faced the end together.

A gust of wind blew overhead, followed swiftly by a thunderous explosion that rocked the battlefield. Fresh screams went up as Jarom recoiled from a raking cloud of dust and earthen debris. Another blast sounded, then another, each preceded by an overhead gust. Once again startled and confused, the dragonspawn hesitated.

Kylac shouted at him, "Let's go!"

The youth's features were taut, but the glimmer in his eyes revealed his excitement. Jarom glanced skyward as he spun about. Massive boulders and thick wooden spears were arcing through the sky, hurtling northward into the dragonspawn, decimating their forward ranks. Farther south, the Fifth Division's hulking war engines cast their shadows in defiance of the cresting sun. Jarom almost smiled as he imagined Rynar and the savage grin that must be splayed by now across the Fifth General's intense face.

Before he and Kylac had run ten paces, Corathel was there, his cavalry company forming a defensive line by which to guard their escape. All was a flurry of motion and shouts. A pair of horses whose riders had been felled were brought forth, and both Jarom and Kylac clambered into the empty saddles. The bulk of the company formed up at the mouth of the draw, filing into place with the remainder of the waiting battalions, preparing to meet the onslaught. Jarom and Kylac pulled into position alongside Corathel, who shouted triumphantly, "Now we'll see!"

The chief general pointed, and Jarom turned northward to follow the line of his outstretched finger. The forward divisions were already slipping from their trenches and bunkers and setting their charge. Signaled by Rynar's assault, they poured down from the slopes, four separate wedges in staggered formation, two on each side of the draw, like the teeth of an iron bear trap. To Jarom's surprise, each wedge was led by its division commander—Ledryk and Maltyk to the west, Jasyn and Lar to the east—with the First Division set to the far north and the Fourth set closest to Jarom's position in the south.

Corathel must have seen his expression. "We lead by example, remember?"

Jarom nodded, not really paying attention, his thoughts and sensations a whirlwind in his head. That he was able to think at all was a testament to the Sword, which even now held sway with a calming effect. Were it not for its soothing comfort, he had no doubt but that his emotions would already have forced him to make a costly mistake. His survival thus far was a miracle, and he entertained no illusions as to that miracle's source.

He was given little time to dwell on it. Corathel was barking orders, the Fifth Division was pressing its advantage, and the forward divisions were descending. The army of dragonspawn waited in the center of the trap, stretched across the mountainous passage like the body of a serpent. There was no time for reflection, no time for wonder, no time for congratulations on a job well done.

The battle for Kraagen Keep had begun.

When Gravlith saw the Sword, he thought that surely he must be mistaken. The Swords of Asahiel were legend. The last was said to have vanished with the Finlorian elves more than three millennia ago. Even at the advent of his queen into this realm, a thousand years prior to her awakening in this age, the talismans were but forgotten relics of an ancient history. Mankind had lost so much over the past centuries in terms of strength and knowledge—seemingly all of that which had driven his queen into exile so many years ago. It seemed terribly unlikely, then, that a member of its race would have come to possess an artifact of such matchless power—or if one had, that the Queen's minions had not heard or seen rumor of it before now.

But there could be no mistaking the reaction of the Queen's dragonborn, who had lashed out with an instinctive hatred beyond even his control when set upon by the Sword. Snapping the chains of his mental commands, the beasts had taken up once again their reckless chase. It would seem they recognized that blade as anathema to their kind, if only at a primordial level. It was all he could do to hold back a portion of those stationed inside the city.

Impassive atop his rampart, Gravlith had watched events unfold. At first it appeared the dragonborn would slaughter the Sword's wielder. But the man had somehow managed to withstand and then escape their rabid fury. Now the human invaders had sprung their trap. Before they knew what was happening, the dragonborn were under siege, pelted by a lethal hail of sticks and stones unleashed from afar by machines that resembled great beasts. Unnerved by the sudden explosions, those that were not slain were quickly scattered, sent roaring and shrieking every which way. From the slopes east and west, the others Gravlith had suspected of hiding revealed themselves, spilling from caves and burrows and massing swiftly to attack. By the looks of things, the dragonborn were hopelessly ensnared.

Regardless, Gravlith remained focused on the Sword. Here at last was a force of opposition with which to be concerned, and by that token, a trophy in which his queen would hold great interest. Were he to deliver unto her a Sword of Asahiel, she would likely forgive him the fall of the city and the loss of its prisoners. She might not even care that he had allowed her dragonborn to be slaughtered.

He needed to act swiftly. And yet, he remained where he stood, observing what he could of the battle without issuing further commands to his forces. The dragonborn could see easily enough at this point the untenable position in which they had placed themselves. If they were to be saved, it would be through strength alone, not any tactical maneuvering. Gravlith was less concerned with their strength, however, than with that of he who bore the Sword of Asahiel. Given what the demon had witnessed thus far, there was no reason to believe he possessed anything near full command of the Sword's legendary power. For if he did, there might be nothing left of the dragonborn by now. As it was, he seemed, as humans often did, to be toying with a power he could not possibly comprehend.

Moments later, Gravlith had seen enough. Though prepared to do so, he had no intention of surrendering anything—not his armies, his prisoners, or this keep, carefully selected as the Queen's new seat of power. He could either trust in the dragonborn to deliver all that he desired, or he could see to the matter himself.

Gravlith turned from the tower wall. Swatting aside a clutch of dragonborn sentries, he made for the nearest staircase, grinding stone and mortar to sand beneath his feet.

It became clear in just a handful of minutes that the Fifth Division, despite the force and precision of its mighty war engines, would not be able to hold out for long. Already, the dragonspawn had begun to recover, overcoming their surprise and hesitation to hone in on that which threatened. In addition, the damage did not seem as extensive as Jarom had first believed. Catapults and ballistae—referred to by the Parthans as "slings" and "arrows"—were relatively effective, launching boulders and spears that crushed and pierced the enemy as though they were insects. Much like insects, however, the dragonspawn were displaying now a remarkable elusiveness, skittering off to one side or another with lightning reflexes. Rynar and his battalions had scored some early hits, and remained relentless in their barrage. But Jarom could see already that in the end, none of it would be enough.

Fortunately, it had never been planned that the Fifth Division do anything more than serve as yet another distraction, a safer means by which to occupy the attention of the pursuing hordes long enough to spring the remaining divisions from the slopes above. And in that regard, it was a masterful success. Having captured the full focus of the approaching enemy, Jarom watched with morbid anticipation as, under cover of Rynar's attack and that of the archers positioned atop the ridgelines, the forward divisions of the Parthan West Legion stormed into the fray, their gleaming weapons thirsting for dragon blood.

Having earned every inch of high ground with sweat and blood, cavalry and infantry alike slammed into the narrowed line of dragonspawn. The earth shuddered at the impact; the sky was rent with a cacophony of screams. But Jarom hardly noticed, swept up now in the pitch and sway of battle, having settled into its rhythm. He sat defiant before the storm, at the edge of the tornado. Lean much closer, it seemed, and he would be sucked in and devoured.

Unwilling to risk harm to friendly troops, Rynar cut off his long-range assault, shouting commands that would have his men focus instead on maintaining the southern front. The main battle was now in the hands of the forward divisions. The idea was for the tip of each wedge to drive through the horde while the lines farther back followed through, dicing the enemy line into segments and pulverizing the separated pockets of dragonspawn as they progressed. If each tooth of the trap held its shape and direction, then by the time the eastern divisions clamped tight against those from the west, there would be nothing left of their adversary save for the severed ends to the north and south. It was a straightforward tactic, executed now by soldiers made masters of war throughout years of engagement against their Menzo adversaries.

Then again, they were no longer fighting the Menzoes.

For a time, it seemed that all would proceed according to plan. The zest for battle displayed days ago before setting forth from the city of Leaven had carried over to this moment in which it mattered, horror and fear replaced with indignation. They also had the strategic advantage, both in their formations and weaponry. Lightweight swords, flails, and morning stars had been eschewed in favor of lances, maces, and axes—weapons heavy enough to cut and pierce a dragonspawn's scaled hide. Plate was the armor of choice, replacing the chain mail and leathers less apt to turn the enemy's claws. In almost all facets, mobility had been sacrificed for the sake of strength—a gamble that appeared to be paying off.

Those first few moments, however, proved misleading. Though devastated by the unexpected crush from either side, the dragonspawn recovered quickly. Sooner than anyone could have expected, the front lines of the wedges found themselves thinning beneath the frenetic counterassault, their overall formation blunted and turned aside. Those who were not slain were forced to stall and finally to retreat back to the strength of their main force. Within minutes, the momentum they had worked so hard to gain was lost.

Jarom watched it all from his position of relative safety as a member of the chief general's command units. Locked now in a vicious struggle, the dragonspawn had little choice but to forget about the Sword for now. Those that did break away to come after him were cut down from behind or blasted by Rynar's frontline engines, a wall of ballistae and the like through which there appeared to be no holes. Given this distance from the main conflict and his lack of battlefield experience, Jarom could not be certain of what was happening. But he read the truth in the gradual change that came over Corathel's features. At first flush with determined confidence, the legion commander was now pale with grim understanding.

The trap had been broken. Regardless of their superior numbers, the forward divisions had failed. Only Ledryk's ranks, at the northern edge of the draw, had attained the original objective, and alone in the heart of the wicked multitude, facing a surge of reinforcements from the city, they did not stand a chance. The other wedges had been shattered, cracked through with widening streams of dragonspawn. Here they were, mere moments into the battle, and already much of the fighting, so carefully orchestrated, had dissolved into chaotic melee.

"General!" Corathel barked at Rynar.

"Sir!"

"Cover fire only on my command. All troops, prepare to charge."

Jarom looked to the chief general as the man's orders were acknowledged and passed by mid-level commanders throughout the ranks. Weapons clanked and armor jostled as those around him prepared to join the fray.

"Time for that weapon of yours to make a difference," Corathel grumbled.

Jarom swallowed thickly, but felt strangely unafraid. The Sword would protect him as it had before. The Sword would protect them all. It was for this reason that he had unearthed it from its place of burial. It was for this moment that he had risked and overcome so much. With all that had happened, all that destiny had helped him to achieve, he could not possibly fail.

He watched Rynar prep his team of operators for a break in the assault, an open window through which Corathel's battalion could charge. The Fifth General was cursing and spitting as an entire company of war engines readied for shutdown, their triggers released from fully loaded barrels and nests. The man was obviously frustrated by his diminished role, almost the exact opposite of what Jarom himself was feeling. But it was too late for either of them to change matters.

A moment later, the command was given, and Jarom rode into battle once more. This time, there would be no chance for confusion. His orders were clear. Hack into the enemy lines, kill as many as possible, and rally those whose hearts by now would be beginning to waver. Bring them hope. Bring them strength. Bring them victory.

And so he did, gritting his teeth and charging ahead like a man possessed. Howls rose up around him, those of his men and those of the enemy, a crescendo of sound that ushered his entry into the draw. The dragonspawn rushed to welcome him, and in the back of his mind, where rational thoughts hid from the heat of his wrath, Jarom hoped that the shifting of their focus alone would provide Corathel's soldiers a chance. Let the creatures turn their backs on the forward divisions. Let them come to him. Let them die.

His horse went down almost immediately, torn out from underneath him. But this time, Jarom held tight to the Sword. He came up with the weapon in hand, sweeping out to clear his ground, spilling the blood of those beasts that had ventured too close. He did not stop there, but lunged ahead, hacking and stabbing, working his blade at all the right angles. A feverish intensity sustained him, fueled by the divine fires that roared through his veins. And yet, its fury did nothing to cloud his awareness. He sensed everything around him, visualizing attacks before they happened and reacting with the swiftness of thought to cut them off. Once again, the young Fason felt as if he were the instrument and the Sword his wielder. For the talisman guided his movements as though it sensed his objective and knew better than he how to accomplish it. It was the weapon, he now realized, more than his training, that had him sweeping through the enemy ranks with relentless precision, turning him this way and that, defending him from unseen attacks. At one point he slipped and fell, only to spin around without thought and impale a dragonspawn upon his ready blade. And so it continued. An extension of his will, the Sword helped him to carve through the enemy with an intelligence and efficiency that Jarom could not have imagined.

Almost as reassuring was Kylac's presence. Armed with

his supernatural dexterity and lethal blades, the inimitable youth was a blur of sharpened edges, whirring and slashing and mowing a path wherever he chose. He would engage three of the beasts at one time, slipping through their defenses to inflict wound upon wound while inevitably vaulting just out of reach of an ambitious enemy swipe. The only trouble was that each dragonspawn would shrug off seven or eight wounds—one or two of which would have slain a mortal man—before perishing, causing the youth's work to be long and arduous. Nevertheless, with the Sword in hand and Kylac as his shield, Jarom pressed onward without hesitation, without fear, silently daring any and all to come near.

Filling in behind his lead, helping to turn a cut into a gash, were Corathel and his men. Though not as fast as Kylac, the chief general never stopped moving. To pause for rest was to allow an unseen enemy to strike a man down from behind. To stop for even a breath could make it one's last. So the legion commander and his men were in constant motion, swinging and ducking, punching and spinning, slashing and dodging, always protecting themselves from harm. Utilizing courage and fitness, instinct and knowledge, they kept themselves alive and punished those who opposed them.

Still, theirs was an enemy that could not be driven off, but had to be annihilated. Jarom realized this and worried for his comrades, who could not raise their blades forever. After all, no man could.

Except for him. Jarom's arm was indefatigable, and he raised it pitilessly. Each swing bore the fury and determination of the first. His shoulders did not burn. His lungs never lacked breath. The weapon's divine strength was his strength, and with this endless reserve of stamina, he was able to concentrate solely on the skills at his disposal, to guide—and be guided by—the Sword, and thus eradicate his enemies with uncanny proficiency.

The thick scales of the dragonspawn did nothing to protect them from the Sword's flaming assaults. And with a blazing desire that matched the power of his sword arm, Jarom continued to fight like a whirlwind unleashed. The bodies of fallen foes began to heap up around him. Their black blood drenched his face and arms and darkened the ground at his feet. Each time it cleared a body, however, the Crimson Sword cleansed itself by virtue of the flames from within. Jarom hoped that for nearby soldiers, this would elicit faith amid the clouds of gloom, for whenever they sought it, they could find the divine symbol pure and powerful. He hoped that its spirit would hoist their hearts and exalt their souls, with the promise that they could prevail over any evil.

Midmorning arrived, the sun rising high along its arc to paint the draw and leave the larger shadows no place to hide. Dust and smoke filled the air with thick, choking clouds. Small fires burned, but the dragonspawn, Jarom had learned, were not apt to use their heated breath as a weapon. First of all, the spurts of flame were smaller than he had expected, and did little damage to those who wore heavy helms with visors and face shields. Second, the short time it took for a dragonspawn to rear back and draw breath was often enough time for the creature's opponent to deliver a killing blow. Given the damage he had seen to the land and its dwellings during his northward travels, Jarom had expected far worse. But as was often the case with marauders, it would seem their destructive forces were most effective when put to use unchallenged, after those they hunted had already fled.

Despite his lack of weariness, sweat stung Jarom's eyes. He had led Corathel's battalion far enough north to help rally the scattered Fourth Division, and had nearly carved his way to the Third. He had not yet come across either Lar or Maltyk, and wondered how the lieutenant generals fared. Of those to whom he had been introduced before the battle, how many would survive?

All he could do, he told himself, was to continue pressing forward. He could hear by the screams that those to the north were having a much harder time. He had to reach them, and quickly. But the friendly force that trailed him had begun to slow. Jarom might have gone ahead without them, but it made little sense to abandon one group for the other. He would remain patient and stay with his regiments. Together, they would continue north through the draw until the city was theirs and the dragonspawn were no more.

But his commitment to do both—to remain with those he had already rallied and to lead them onward—soon proved impossible. The dragonspawn continued to press, adamant on destroying him. While he managed to fend them off, those who followed began to be pushed back. Rather than leave them, Jarom eased back as well, in accordance with Corathel's commands. Best to hold the lines they had worked so hard to re-form, maintain an unbroken front, and pick their moments to advance.

As the army wearied, those moments became few and far between, until finally, they ceased altogether. Those with Jarom fell farther and farther back, forced into steady retreat. Although the soldiers of the West Legion fought valiantly beneath the rising sun, Jarom soon came to recognize their slim chances for survival, let alone victory. The enemy was simply too strong. They had come for a battle of attrition, thinking their nearly thirty thousand armored soldiers sufficient to stomp out six thousand or so dragonspawn. But in the time it took to slay even one of the foul beasts, ten men would fall. Without a major change, this battle would be a rout.

Jarom cast about for that advantage, seeking something, anything, that could shift the tides in their favor. But all he found was death and despair. The enemy's virulent press was unrelenting, and his own army's objectives had been reduced to the sole goal of self-preservation. Jarom could see it in their eyes. Each time a man tripped over his comrade's severed head or mangled torso, or slipped in a puddle of bloody entrails, his spirit would falter. Each time a soldier watched a dragonspawn chew into his friend's throat or separate limbs from body with its claws, he would recoil in horror. Fear chipped insidiously at the walls of these men's hearts, and thoughts of capitulation began to encumber their minds.

At the south end of the draw, still shielded from the more intense fighting, Fifth General Rynar recognized and understood the truth of his army's rapidly deteriorating morale. What they had to run to, and how they would ever regroup for another assault, he could not fathom. But he could not stand by and watch his countrymen be slaughtered within that frothing cauldron of death. He closed his eyes, trembling with denial, then gave way to good sense and put the horn to his lips.

Jarom heard the horn's mournful cry and knew at once the day was lost. They were to break away now or surrender their lives altogether.

But Jarom was not yet willing. Although the signal only confirmed what he himself had been feeling, and while he trusted the judgment of Corathel and his lieutenant generals, he could not believe that despite all their preparations, despite all their fury and desire, they had been thwarted in this endeavor. The day could not already be lost—could not be lost at all. They needed to win this struggle, to prove to themselves and to whoever it was who commanded these creatures that they would not be so easily driven from their lands. If they were to admit defeat now, then this war would be over before it had begun.

He cried out, breaking away from the others, ignoring the horn's wail and charging forward once more. Against all hope, many of those around him did the same, lashing out with renewed vigor. All of a sudden, it was the dragonspawn who were on their heels, pressed by a frantic surge.

For several moments, the conflict raged with fresh fury as the men of Partha tried to rally. The Sword flared with crimson radiance, and the soldiers who accompanied Jarom did their best to respond. But the dragonspawn yielded little ground, and with half of the Parthan force peeling away in anxious retreat, there were not enough men to sustain Jarom's rush.

They had lost.

Despite the warmth of the Sword, Jarom's blood went cold. His throat constricted, tears of rage came to his eyes, and the cavity of his chest became hollow. Had he been alone, he might have continued his charge until the darkness of death consumed him, for in that moment, he hardly cared.

But he knew that others would follow, and he could not in good conscience guide them to that same end. Bitter in defeat, he began to withdraw.

It was in that moment of ultimate despair that the thundering clamor of charging horses transcended the tumult. Jarom paused, wondering at the implications of the fresh uproar. When he heard the groans of dismay from those behind him, he actually turned to witness the approach of a third army as it gushed in from the lands south. Though he could not see who they were, he recognized quickly enough that they had come with hostile intent, riding hard with weapons leveled into the rear of the Fifth Division, an enemy force large enough to seal off any retreat.

Dread and disbelief obscured Jarom's thinking. He fell numb, and lowered his sword arm. He did not even see the hulking shadow that fell over him until he felt the blow that sent him reeling, the impact like that of a blacksmith's hammer slamming into his chest. He watched the Sword as it flew again from his grasp. It landed in the dirt, its red glow dimmed. Almost at once, a swarm of dragonspawn piled atop it like ants upon a discarded morsel. Powerless to thwart them, Jarom turned, his lungs still straining for breath, to find a boulder standing over him. No, not standing, but moving toward him. And not a boulder, but a giant creature that looked like one, craggy and pitted, chiseled, it would seem, from shiny black volcanic rock.

The obsidian creature reached for him, green eyes aglow, its height and bulk blotting out the sun. Jarom lay back, unable to divert its onslaught, unable to breathe. He saw and then felt a stone hand clamp about his face.

Then his lungs surrendered and his entire world disappeared.

CHAPTER THIRTY-ONE

A lone torch hung on the wall, crackling within its iron sconce. Smoke billowed forth, acrid and invasive, while its flames slapped defiantly against the encroaching darkness, the limbs of a creature not to be restrained. Its persistent gleam illuminated the hall—the walls of thick stone, the cracked and weathered floor—and cast a faint light through the iron bars of the cell in dust-filled streams.

Jarom stared at the source of that light, mesmerized by its flickering dance. Understanding escaped him. He lay upon his side on a floor of stone slabs, the air musty, his body caked with dried sweat. On three sides, the walls of his prison matched the floor, while the fourth consisted of those vertically fixed bars of thick iron, chipped and flaking with rust. The corridor beyond, draped in a darkness pierced only by the single torch, lay empty. He was alone.

He sensed no imminent peril, and so hauled himself into a sitting position. A savage pounding assaulted his head as he did so, an angry pulse that seemed to resonate throughout his body. A variety of aches and pains wrenched at the bones and muscles beneath his skin, which was marred by scores of cuts and scrapes, none of which he remembered receiving. He inspected himself gingerly, fearful of finding something twisted or broken. He found blood in his hair, beneath his nose, and at the corner of his mouth, and a massive bruise whose purple color stained nearly the whole of his chest. Nevertheless, despite his battered condition, he found no sign of long-term injury.

He regained his senses suddenly, and with them his last memory—the Sword! He had lost the Crimson Sword! As if the incident might have been a nightmare, he swept the grime-ridden floor for some sign of his weapon. A moment later, he closed his eyes, swallowing the truth like shards of glass. How could he have been so stupid? He had broken the first rule of combat and become distracted, turning his back to the life-and-death matter upon which he'd been focused. A hard lesson for which he had paid an unbearable price.

He and those who had depended on him. His family. His friends. Allion. Kylac. Marisha.

A fresh lump came to his throat as he wondered what had become of each. Were they all dead? Or had they managed to escape? If alive, were they going to rescue him, or did they believe him slain? Or did they know the truth but not care? Had they decided to punish him for his loss by leaving him in the clutches of the enemy?

A torrent of despair unleashed itself upon his hapless mind. There was no way of knowing how long he'd already spent in this cell, and he had no idea as to what his next move should be. It would be impossible to break free of his prison, especially when he could not be certain as to where his prison was. He assumed he'd been hauled into the dungeons of Kraagen Keep, but who knew? Regardless, if he could not escape, what could he do?

Jarom lowered his head into his filthy hands. *You've done enough,* he sneered derisively. Devastation dug at his chest like knives. He hoped that his friends *had* deserted him. It was the least he deserved. For the Sword was now in the hands of the dragonspawn. Not only had he squandered its power and failed those he sought to defend, but he had unwittingly given it over to the enemy.

He closed his mind to the thought. No need to imagine the worst. A better question was, why? Why was he here? That he had been taken captive was of small consolation unless it meant others had as well. This quickly became the one small hope he would permit himself, that all of the others they had feared dead were imprisoned as he was. Marisha might still be alive.

Not that it made any difference.

It was this realization, above all others, that burned him. Nothing he'd accomplished up till now meant anything. With but a single defeat, all of the success on which he prided himself had been stripped away. The retrieval of the Sword, though miraculous at the time, had turned out to be a hollow victory. Destiny, it would seem, was little more than a cruel prankster, lifting him to such heights only to desert him in the end.

Famished, thirsty, and already on the verge of madness, he decided at last to take advantage of the only luxury afforded him—sleep. Perhaps his dreams might reveal some sort of plan.

He lay back upon the unyielding stone floor, hands folded beneath his head, and closed his eyes. But the battle awaited him, memories of his pitched struggle against the dragon-spawn—relentless images of the enemy, his friends, his lost blade. It had all happened so fast that he'd not yet reflected on the horror of it. But now it was all there, the piercing shrieks of pain and terror, the pungent stench of sweat and blood, the ruthless press of those who sought his life, and the carnage—so much carnage! The Crimson Sword, he sensed, had dampened his emotional awareness, had shielded him from all but that which he had needed to know to remain alive. Or perhaps it had simply been the blood coursing through his veins. Whichever, it was not until now that he felt the full force of his virgin brush with war, that vortex of rage and horror set upon the earth like a window into the Abyss. It raked at him with lightning gusts, a thunderhead of pain and sadness, fury and denial, hope and despair—and ultimately, death. It scoured his mind and ravaged his soul, sucking off pieces of his humanity forever.

How did men like Corathel do it? How did they bring themselves to march into battle time after time while knowing what horror awaited them? It was a matter of necessity, Jarom supposed, of desperation, of doing what needed to be done. Eventually, they were strengthened by their trials, became hardened to the pain. Put to it enough times, he too might learn to cover up his scars, to bury them beneath a callus of indifference. But now those wounds were fresh, howling in confusion, screaming to be closed.

When he closed his eyes, there was no escape. He was thus unable to rest, even for a moment. At last he curtailed his efforts and stood up, grimacing at the stiffness plaguing his muscles. He stretched briefly and stepped over to the iron bars, his breath clouding in the dank chill of his prison.

What now? he wondered. What was to happen to him? He discovered that they hadn't bothered to take his dagger. What was he going to do, scrape his way from the cell, run outside, and fight off hordes of dragonspawn to his freedom? Or maybe the enemy forces had gone. Perhaps they had simply left him to rot. Surely it was presumptuous to suppose he had been locked away for interrogation or any other purpose. What could they possibly need to know from him? He was nothing more than an inept young man who had possessed an incredible weapon, and he had already given them the Sword. What further value might he hold?

He found himself thinking back on a lifetime removed. Back home, as the guardian of his community, he'd been blessed with an unmistakable sense of identity and worth, respected and even envied by those around him. But he was a fool to have believed that his status within that small village would equate to anything in the larger world. Out here, he was nothing, just a poor man's friend, and a poor friend at that.

All of a sudden, Jarom felt the sharp pangs of loneliness and despair. Self-incrimination aside, he was terrified by the thought that he had indeed been sentenced to death, and would perish without ever knowing what had become of his friends or his world. He shook his head. His thoughts had come full circle, back to those he had sought to avoid. It was best, he reminded himself, that he did not know. For with the combined power of the dragonspawn and the Sword of Asahiel, he might as easily ask himself: What world?

The sudden screech of iron against stone curbed his morbid musings. Jarom fell back from the wall of bars. A fit of what sounded to be hacking and coughing accompanied the rasp of clawed footsteps upon the floor of the corridor beyond his cell. In the unseen darkness, a door crashed shut.

A single dragonspawn stepped into view, greasy and scaled. Its six-foot frame appeared even more menacing given the tight walls and low ceiling of the narrow corridor, and its ghastly stench filled Jarom's nostrils. Stopping before his cell, the creature extended a finger in his direction while glaring back down the length of hall from which it had come. The beast snarled, as though pointing him out to someone.

It was then that Jarom caught the slow footsteps that followed. The chill he felt deepened from within.

"Leave," hissed a voice that pricked Jarom's spine.

The dragonspawn glared with murderous defiance, but scraped its way back down the corridor without wasting a glance in Jarom's direction, the oil of its body glimmering in the faint light. The door screeched open once again, then closed. Silence settled over the room like a shroud.

"Who's there?" Jarom dared to ask after a moment, more to relieve his own tension than anything else.

He received no response and, for a moment, decided that the stranger must have followed the dragonspawn from the chamber. Thinking it odd, he was just about to turn and reclaim his seat on the stone floor when a man drifted into view, wrapped in a cocoon of dark robes with the hood thrown back. His black hair hung in loose, gnarled strands about his face and shoulders, while yellow eyes, narrowed into slits, pierced the darkness. Without being told, Jarom knew at once who it was.

The wizard.

Before he could think to put up a strong front, Jarom fell back from the penetrating gaze. He had envisioned the wizard before now, of course, a presence both sinister and powerful, with a glare full of hatred and promised pain. His imagination had fallen well short of the truth. Nothing in his own mind could have prepared him to glimpse this shell of a man, ravaged and hollow, a shadow whose eyes might have been tunnels of fire leading straight from the Abyss. He stared at the creature in horror, mindful of the fact that it was this man, standing before him, who was at the root of his trials and pain. It was this man who had changed his life forever, whose invasion had driven him to undertake this accursed quest in the first place. A quest that could only end in death.

"Come closer," the voice rasped. "The lighting is poor."

But Jarom could not have moved had he wished to. Held fast by his terror, he could only stare, unblinking.

Without warning, the top of the wizard's serpent-head staff burst into flames. Jarom started, but managed to hold his ground. The staff's flames pushed back the darkness, filling the chamber with their unnatural radiance.

The wizard's lips drew wide and tight across his mouth, a menacing smile. "My brother."

Shadows thrashed upon the walls, black spirits searching for escape. At first, Jarom was only scarcely aware the wizard had spoken. Then he gaped in horror. He wanted to scream out in denial, but found he could not. For deep down, in some dark corner of his being, he recognized the truth.

"Who are you?" he managed to ask.

"I am your elder brother, Soric, firstborn of Sorl and Ellebe, crown prince and now king of Alson."

The wizard whispered the words as if in challenge. While confused by this, Jarom watched him with morbid fascination, as he might a great predator at feast. At the same time, he was struck by a halting realization, another truth, previously hidden, that seemed to undermine and make invalid all that he had been working to achieve.

"Then you *are* king." His eyes fell as he forced himself to speak the words aloud, to admit if only to himself that he had been misguided in his prior beliefs to the contrary.

"And you are Torin, favored son, born after my departure. Conceived for no other reason than to erase the memory of my existence. The young upstart who would have my throne."

Jarom looked up. The wizard's taut smirk remained, even as his anger radiated outward in waves.

"I don't want your throne," Jarom contended. "I want only to be left alone, to live in peace."

"Would that you had come to me before," the wizard said. "I might have spared you. I might have made you my family and offered you protection."

Unsure what to make of this, Jarom simply stared. Was this man his enemy, or wasn't he?

The wizard leveled his gaze until its fires burned into him once more. "Alas, that decision rests now with the Demon Queen. The decision to spare or destroy your life is hers alone, as it shall be for all henceforth."

Despite the tempest of his thoughts, Jarom caught and was confused by the reference. "Demon Queen?"

"An archdemon, my brother. A ruler of the Eternal Abyss. A creature of fire who has lived for ages untold."

Jarom blinked, struggling to make sense of the words.

"We await the divine grace of her presence even now. Upon her arrival, she will find me a loyal servant to be rewarded, while condemning those who oppose her inevitable reign."

Jarom's thoughts came whirring under control, the answers he had sought since stumbling across the ruins of Feverroot finally falling into place. It was not the wizard who commanded these armies of dragonspawn, but this so-called Demon Queen, a creature whose rumored powers had cowed even one as powerful as Soric without so much as a confrontation. It was the wizard's armies that had attacked from the south at Bane Draw, finishing off the soldiers of the West Legion and preventing their escape. He had done so in an effort to show allegiance to one who would not likely tolerate his existence.

"And you would serve such a creature?" Jarom snapped, absorbing his newfound understanding like a second wind.

"You have seen her armies. You have witnessed but a measure of their strength. These dragons are mere fodder for her private minions, demons all that serve her without question. You have failed to defeat her dragons. You are powerless to defeat her demons. And you cannot fathom her own powers, divine energies such as this world has not known in ages!"

Jarom cringed from the flaring head of the wizard's staff.

A sick feeling churned in his stomach. Could any of what he was being told be true? The horrifying possibility seemed fabricated and remote. A demon emerged suddenly from history to devour his world and its people like cattle? It sounded to him more like a nightmare designed to frighten children. Despite all he had witnessed over the past several weeks, he questioned whether or not such creatures could even exist. And yet, here he'd been able to recover one of the mythical Swords of Asahiel. What made this tale any less likely than his own?

The Sword, Jarom thought suddenly. The wizard had made no mention of the Crimson Sword! A sudden hope found life in the dark folds of his despair. Could it be that the weapon had somehow evaded the enemy's clutches? That might explain why he was still here. At once, however, Jarom ridiculed himself for his optimism. So what if it had? Thinking back, it was First General Ledryk who had proven the most insightful of them all: With a hundred Crimson Swords, they might have stood a chance against this enemy. At best, they had but one.

"If she's so powerful," Jarom challenged, unable to keep his voice from quivering, "why has she not conquered the world before now?"

The wizard chuckled. "Yes, my brother. Doubt the truth of her strength. But know this. You would be better off had her general chosen to slay you. For when the Queen arrives, you will learn the true measure of suffering, as our father taught me. You are dead, my brother. You need know no more."

Even then, Jarom might have continued to argue, if for no other reason than to learn what more the wizard might reveal. But his brother, it would seem, had finished with him.

"I must go," the wizard hissed. "I merely wanted to see you once, to assure you that your efforts have been in vain. We might have been brothers, had you not chosen like the rest—to judge me as vermin rather than the king I was born to be. For that I must despise you. You are a wasted seed. Had the Queen not done so, I would have destroyed you."

The flames upon the staff's head flickered and died, and

as unexpectedly as he had come, the wizard, his brother
Soric, strode quietly from the room.

Jarom thought to call after him, but did not. The man's
stinging words reinforced a truth he had already known. His
friends and the world in which they lived were dead, claimed
by a dark force of primordial evil. It made little difference who
led them, be it a man poisoned through the use of magic or a
queen of demons. All of his struggles, all of his triumphs, had
been rendered meaningless. What was left to worry about?

His eyes followed after the other's slow departure. Jarom
shook his head. Death would be but a small step for this
man, this spiteful creature who had once been his brother; he
lived in the Abyss even now. Despite his own fear, his anger
and frustration, Jarom pitied the man.

The wizard disappeared from view. A moment later, the
iron door opened and closed, and once again, the torch in the
corridor was Jarom's only companion in the darkness.

She could hear them, scraping about like rats, prowling the
darkness beyond her limited field of vision. She could smell
them, even over the sweat and rot and excrement of those
who shared her prison cell. In smelling them, she could taste
them, like carrion on her tongue. She could still feel their
greasy touch, the rake of their claws against her flesh. She
just couldn't see them.

In all ways but one, she sensed the presence of her captors, ever present and watchful—a cold and constant reminder that there could be no escape.

She and her fellow hostages had been locked away for a
little more than a day now with almost nothing to sustain
them. Once, buckets of food—a black, foul-smelling gruel
that tasted of bile—and water—stagnant and unpure—had
been poured down atop them. She had eaten and drunk that
which she could scrape off her body, the floor, and the bars
that formed the ceiling of their pit. She had done so in order
to stay alive, to fuel her ceaseless hope for survival. One or
two others had tried, but had retched and been unable to do
so. Most had not even bothered to make the attempt.

She was one of the few to have made it—the only to have lasted this long. Among the first to be taken, she had watched innocent people perish by the thousands, unable to survive the conditions of their northward march. They had been forced ahead almost without rest, young and old alike, stopping only as long as it took for the dragon-creatures to raze another city. They had been allowed to feed themselves only with what food and water they could forage along the way—often after the dragons had trampled the earth and left it scorched with their fires. Most simply could not bear the strain, giving way to starvation, exhaustion, and pain.

Those who died were fed upon by the dragons. The living as well, when they stumbled and could not get up, or when one of the beasts was struck with hunger. As best as she could tell, it was the only reason for which they were being kept alive. With each conquest, more were added to their ranks, replenishing those who had been consumed. And yet, their overall numbers continued to dwindle.

She looked about, peering into the faces of strangers. She had long since watched the last of those she knew fall and be devoured. Alone, she had continued on, watching others come and go. Parthans at first, then Menzoes. At last, they had been brought here, to Kraagen Keep, a city she recognized from the hearthside stories she had been told while growing up. Like a flock of sheep led by wolves, they had been herded into this near-lightless cavern and locked away in a collection of slave pits. A dozen per cell, where unused shackles revealed a design to hold three. Those for whom there had been no room had been slaughtered on the spot or hauled off to reaches unknown. Those who had been caged were no longer marching, but had been granted no relief. For all, she supposed, the end would be the same.

One met her gaze, a boy of perhaps twelve. He was filthy and ragged, devoid of hope, his eyes revealing a broken soul. The kind of injury for which there was no cure. She did her best to appear reassuring and felt foolish for doing so, imagining that she looked much the same. But if she did, then it was a lie, for a fire still burned in her heart. She was determined to survive, to somehow make it right, to do what she could to relieve the suffering—including her own—if only she could find a way to begin. Perhaps she would start with this boy. Perhaps she could find a way, somehow, to ease his hurt, to close if not heal his wounds, to—

The boy looked away, a lost and tattered thing.

Marisha Valour felt her heart break. Many, she knew, had become numb to it all, retreating into the smallest recesses of their own being in search of false comfort. She, however, remained haunted by the unforgettable images, atrocities for which she somehow felt responsible. As a healer, to witness so much pain and to be unable to help went against every fiber of her moral being. She had seen and treated, she thought, every form of physical harm and violence a man could endure, but nothing could have readied her for this. It was unconscionable. She had tried to convince herself over and over again that it wasn't happening. And yet, here she was.

She resisted the urge to reach down. Even now, she could not bring herself to reveal the source of her strength. Not even to people such as these, who considered themselves dead though their lungs still drew breath. People who would not even whisper among themselves for fear of attracting the dragons. They hoped to die first. They hoped that when the beasts tore into their bodies, those bodies would be cold. It was the best they *could* hope for, to avoid being eaten alive—to not feel every rake of claw, every tear of muscle, every crack of bone. They hoped the others would not have to listen to them scream.

So she sat in silence, huddled in a corner of her pit, wrapped in a blanket of resolve in order to ward off the chill misery that surrounded her. Her knees were drawn close to her chest, her arms wrapped about them in the manner of a frightened child. Many of the others sat the same way, their bodies pressed tight not for warmth, but for lack of room. All about was darkness and gloom.

Then came the subtle glow that pushed back the black edges surrounding their pit, followed by the sound of feet scrabbling near. Marisha looked up, squinting against the brightness, and watched as others among her did the same, tensing in fear.

A pair of dragon snouts thrust into view beyond the iron lattice. The people fell back, shrinking against one another, noses crinkling in disgust. The dragons paused. The light grew brighter as a man stepped forward. He bore a staff, whose tip glowed with smokeless radiance. Marisha gaped, surprised at his appearance. What was a human doing with the dragons?

The man considered them for a moment, his pallid face showing nothing.

"Take them."

The dragons slid free the locking bar and flung open the heavy floor gate. They then reached down for those who occupied the pit. The people cringed, whimpering softly, but one by one, allowed themselves to be hauled to their feet and marched up the short pair of steps set against the front wall, hewn from the earthen stone.

Marisha refused. She shied back, pressed into her corner, and ignored the hissing demands of her captors. Something in the manner with which the human bored into her with those yellow eyes told her that this was the end. And while the opportunity for escape may have passed, she would not be marched willingly to her own demise.

One of the dragons leapt into the pit. Marisha yelped a harsh denial as the beast seized her by the wrist and yanked her to her feet. Still she refused to cooperate, pulling against the creature that held her and dragging her blistered feet. The dragon spun on her, raising a single claw high.

"Wait!"

It was the man's voice, strong and certain, that stopped the beast. Had she not seen it for herself, she would not have believed it possible for any human to order these creatures around. Marisha saw fierce anger flashing in the dragon's intelligent eyes. And yet, its hand remained held high, hovering over her like an executioner's axe as the beast turned its head and snarled.

She looked past the dragon to the man who commanded

it. He was smiling at her struggles, amused by her recalcitrance. All of a sudden, she was no longer certain he was human.

"Leave her."

The dragon growled, hissing and spitting its displeasure.

"We are preparing a feast. Let us save her for dessert."

The dragon turned back and snarled in Marisha's face. Despite a brave effort, she recoiled from its jagged teeth and rancid breath. The beast released her, flinging her away, then bounded from the pit without use of the stairs. Marisha almost forgot to crouch as the ceiling of her prison slammed shut.

With the ringing of iron still in her ears, she gazed up at he who had spared her.

"What are you doing with them?" she asked. She hated that her voice sounded weak and timid, echoing within the hollow of the pit.

The man above only smirked, then turned slowly from view. Behind him, the locking bar slid shut, and his dragon escort moved to follow.

Marisha gazed after the retreating globe of brightness, trying not to think of those who had been taken, or the many she had loved who had gone before. But try as she might, she could not seem to shake a singular image, that of the eyes of a young boy, windows through which she had glimpsed a shattered soul.

Her determination died, and she crumpled to the floor. Tears washed her cheeks, tears of grief and despair and loss. She could not take any more. *Please,* she begged, *let it end.*

After a moment, she looked up. She listened for the presence of her jailors, those left behind to guard the cavern and its pits, and sensed nothing nearby. She was isolated in her prison, abandoned in the cavern gloom.

Slowly, carefully, she reached for the chain hung low about her neck. Choking back tears, she drew in its length, pulling forth that which granted her her courage, stamina, unnatural strength and endurance. She felt its warmth upon her chest, her throat, until finally, it came free of her bodice with its muted red glow.

She cupped that glow at once, wrapping the ruby pendant in the fingers of one hand, seeking the heat of the crimson fire that swirled within.

Alone in the darkness, she gripped the stone and continued to cry.

CHAPTER THIRTY-TWO

Spithaera smiled, eyes closed, as she arose from beneath the churning waters and felt the light upon her face. Not the light of magic, but that of a world from which she had been locked away for too long. She relished its touch, the caress of moon and stars, of a heavens agleam with possibility. Even after the waters went still, the portal sealed, she lay basking in their cool embrace, feeling their soft ripples lap about her naked form.

She opened her eyes, and her smile vanished. Gravlith stood at the edge of the pool as expected, along with a clutch of her dragonborn. She was surprised, however, to find a human standing beside her general, a male. His appearance, ghastly as it was, did not frighten her. She knew that Gravlith would not tolerate the presence of anyone threatening. Nonetheless, she did not care for surprises.

Spithaera leaned forward and placed her feet beneath her, to stand waist deep in the waters of a square-bound pool. Her new solar was clean and spacious. Natural light shone through ceiling and windows, soft and pleasant where it gleamed against the decorative marble. Far more comfortable than the cave to which she had confined herself for nearly a thousand years.

She exited the bath by way of the inlaid stairs behind her, turning her back to Gravlith and the others. Water dripped from her body, pooling upon the marble. A dragonborn approached, crouched obsequiously as it extended to her a silken robe. Spithaera ignored the creature, choosing instead to step around the edge of the pool and stand fully exposed before her minions. She fixed the human with a scowl.

"Who is this mortal?"

The man was doing his best not to look at her, but did so for a moment before glancing away again, no doubt surprised by the magical translation echoing in his thoughts that made her archaic words understandable.

One of their rulers, my queen. The magus, from the west.

Spithaera looked to her general, acknowledging his mental response. She might have known. Her demons had reported much on this one. A wizard, they had told her, whose powers and ambitions were not unlike her own. One of the few who posed a potential threat to her dominance.

"Mitzb made no mention."

He arrived just this morning, my queen. His armies assisted in routing a minor invasion force.

"Then he seeks to curry favor," Spithaera decided. She walked a tight circle around the stone-faced wizard, her breath upon his ear. "But does he do so as a true ally? Or does he seek to win my trust in order to betray me?"

Her soothing voice did little to mask the veiled threat, and it pleased her when the wizard stiffened in understanding.

She stopped pacing, coming to stand directly before him. "Speak, wizard."

The man did so, keeping his eyes averted. "I seek only to serve you."

"Are you not the one who calls himself king of Alson?"

"'Twas a title I was born to. I abdicate it now to you, my queen." He bowed his head to emphasize his subservience.

Spithaera smiled her most wicked smile. The man was saying all the right things, but one did not win her trust with words.

"And your conquest?"

"My birthright, nothing more. Or so I believed. But I realize now the truth. I was sent to pave the path of your coming, to provide this world but a taste of its future beneath your destined reign."

Spithaera's smile widened, revealing her sharpened teeth. This one was good. Too good, perhaps. The safest thing would be to dispose of him now, before he had a chance to prove how devious he might be. And yet, she did not want to act in haste. He was clearly a man of talents. She was more than a little impressed that he had managed to remain alive and secure for himself a place among her hordes. Gravlith had chosen to accept him, if only long enough for her to make her own decision concerning his fate. Perhaps she should show similar restraint.

After all, her first mission had been accomplished in but a matter of weeks. Almost the whole of the island east was hers. Locked away within this castle were the slaves gathered during the initial invasion. Those upon whom she and her children did not feed would serve her. With half the land secured and still no sign of capable resistance, the time was soon coming to make her presence known. For now, it was enough to bask in the light of this realm, free of the darkness within which she had cocooned herself for nearly a millennium. Should he prove faithful, having one such as the wizard to help carry out her work would be an unexpected asset, one she did not wish to dismiss out of hand.

My queen.

"Yes, Gravlith."

There is another human with whom you may wish to speak.

"And who might that be."

He came with the invaders.

"You said it was a minor force. A force that, for all we know, was employed by our wizard here as part of some master plan." She so enjoyed watching the man tense, sweating beneath her intense scrutiny. "Why should this other interest me?"

My queen, he wielded a Sword of Asahiel.

Spithaera's head whipped about, her gaze catching hold of her general. In an instant, the wizard and any machinations he might be harboring were forgotten. For a moment, she stared at her demon, allowing his message to take hold, wondering if it was possible that he was mistaken. Her jaw clenched, her teeth deadly razors that scraped together.

"Show me."

Jarom had no real way of knowing how long he'd been alone in his cell. He had tried again to sleep, hoping that by the time he awoke, his nightmare would have passed. Instead, he was left staring in the darkness, his legs and buttocks gone numb beneath him. He sat now fiddling with his dagger, having already dulled the tip of the blade chiseling at the mortar seams, scraping at the rusted iron, and trying to pick the lock of his prison. He had given up quickly, understanding full well that this time there was no secret passage waiting to be revealed, no sealed portal to be broken through, and that even if he made it from his cell, there was no escaping his captors. He was trapped.

The torch in the hall was still alive, though its flame had burned low. It must have been several hours, he decided, scarcely enough time to come to terms with the idea that the wizard was in fact his elder brother, heir to the throne of Alson through right of birth. Doubtless, the fact that he had been banished and stripped of such claims meant little to his brother's way of thinking. And in truth, it meant little to Jarom's as well. If Soric hadn't become so ruthless, then this entire conflict could have been avoided. Soric would remain king, and Jarom would be allowed to return home to his normal life. But that was wishful thinking, and foolish at that. He might as well wish that his brother had never been banished in the first place. And if he hadn't, then Jarom—or Torin—might never have gone to live in Diln at all. He might not have even been born. And while that thought held a very definite appeal to him at the moment, he recognized well enough the futility of trying to remake the past. Remove one thread, and the whole thing would unravel.

The squeal of the outer door chased away such thoughts. Jarom looked up, tucking his dagger beneath his legs. He held his breath, wondering who it could be, knowing that whoever had come to visit was not welcome. If they threatened, he decided, they would leave their share of blood on the floor.

A long shadow fell across the corridor. Jarom sat up, his back flat against the cool stone of the rear wall. His pulse quickened, and his hand fell closer to his leg and the weapon concealed beneath.

A moment later, the tension drained from his body, fear giving way to surprise. A woman had come before him, tall and shapely, with glowing eyes the color of emeralds. The Demon Queen, he thought, but not as he had envisioned. This was no monster of the Abyss, but a delicate creature of unrivaled beauty, dark and seductive, a forbidden fantasy in skintight leathers and satin cloak.

Jarom remained breathless as she gazed upon him.

"What a delicious-looking . . ." She paused, her lips parting in a sinful smile. ". . . mortal."

He registered the words as they escaped her mouth—that perfect mouth—and found that he understood them. How, he did not know, for the words themselves were indecipherable. Magic, he supposed. He blinked uncertainly. What did she just call him? A morsel?

"They tell me you had a sword, a very special sword. Is this true?"

Jarom tried to ignore the physical words and to focus on the translation that echoed in his mind. When the woman had finished, he repeated her message to himself, making certain this time to grasp its meaning.

"Speak."

That he understood. He gulped for air, and in the process, managed to dislodge his tongue from his throat. "I lost it."

"So it is true! A Sword of Asahiel!"

For a moment, Jarom wasn't sure whether she was enraged or excited by the fact. Then she stepped forward, draping herself against the bars of his cell.

"Give it to me."

She said it as if seeking to quench a dire thirst. Jarom was taken aback by her need, and just barely managed to stammer a response. "But I no longer have the blade."

"You will obtain it. You did so once. You shall do so again. I will have it, as I will have you."

Jarom wasn't entirely certain of her meaning. Nor did he think that he wanted to be. His eyes fell as he searched for a response, but snagged on her chest. How could such a being, not even human, be so utterly tempting? He swallowed hard, then forced himself to meet her unnatural gaze.

"No."

"No?"

"I will not serve you."

"Serve me? You have wielded a power not known for three thousand years, a power wielded by the Ha'Rasha to shape this very earth!" She leaned forward, pressing her breasts through the bars. "Share it with me. Tell me its secrets. Do so, and whatever you most desire shall be yours."

Jarom held his tongue, unsure what was happening, unsure what to feel. He found surprising strength in the knowledge that the Sword had in fact eluded the grasp of his enemies. How, he could only guess, although he had a sneaking suspicion that a certain warrior youth had something to do with it, assuming the boy was still alive. Or perhaps the Queen's own minions were keeping it from her. Regardless, he failed to see where he fit into any of it.

The Queen must have taken his silence as a continued refusal, for she pulled back, sighing softly. Her smile remained, warm and enticing, as she fixed him with an icy stare.

"To deny me is to deny yourself," she purred. "Think on it."

She twirled away and, in a swish of dark satin, left him to his thoughts. Even after she had gone, her gentle laughter echoed in his ears. It was an alluring sound, filled with unspoken promise. It almost made him wish she was still there, reminding him of the void left by her departure. That and her fragrance, sweet and aromatic, like a forest glen abloom with spring flowers. It filled his nose, pushing aside the dank of his prison, leaving him to feel comfortably light-headed. Mostly, he was amazed, amazed that she had not killed him on the spot, that she had instead offered him a choice of futures other than death.

Thinking no longer of his brother the wizard, and with a diminished sense of fear, Jarom retreated once more into the privacy of his mind and wondered, given this odd turn of events, what he might do.

When next he heard the shrill grating of the outer door on its rusted hinges, Jarom scrambled to his feet. In the handful of hours since the Demon Queen had left him, he had made his decision. Difficult as it had been, he now knew what he must do. He need only summon the courage to follow through.

After a moment, he began to question his own ears. He remained alone in the smothering darkness left after the torch in the hall had burned out. There were no lights, and no sounds of approach. He listened for the telltale thud of the door closing behind whoever had entered, but was left waiting.

He had about given up when a faint glow eased its way through the black folds. Jarom squinted, but held steady, raising one arm to help shield his eyes. A small firebrand appeared before the bars of his cell, clutched by a robed figure whose outline was nearly invisible.

Then the figure's hood lifted, and Jarom found himself gazing upon a familiar face.

"Kylac?" he gasped. His shock was such that he stumbled backwards, where he struck his head against the wall behind him.

"Ya didn't really thinks I was going to leave ya, did ya?" the youth asked, grinning.

For a moment, Jarom just stood there rubbing his head, beside himself with disbelief. Kylac glanced over his shoulder, then pulled forth a ring of keys. One by one, he began testing them against the lock of Jarom's cell door.

"What are you doing here?" Jarom finally managed to ask.

"Keeping my promise," the youth replied, his nimble fingers tossing aside one after another of the wrong keys.

"I thought you were dead."

Kylac scoffed. "Hardly. Although I have to say, finding ya was no easy task."

"What happened?"

The youth glanced at him with a measure of reproach. "We were separated. That horn was the signal for retreat, ya know."

Jarom recalled then those final moments of battle, when he had refused Rynar's call and continued on in a desperate rush. Once again, a predicament in which he found himself was through no one's fault but his own.

Kylac, however, did not dwell on the indiscretion. "When Stone Man showed up, I saw him attack ya. If'n he'd wanted ya dead, you'd have been so 'fore I gots a chance to save ya." Again, the youth's eyes met his, as though to make sure Jarom understood the gravity of his words. "So I went for the Sword instead, doing what I figured you'd want me to do, and hoping that without the Sword, they might keep ya alive."

"Then you have the Sword?" Jarom could hardly believe the luck.

"It's with Corathel and the others. I didn't dare tote it into this wolf's den."

Jarom nodded. It still felt as if everything happening right now was a dream, too wonderful to be true.

"So Corathel made it?"

"Allion too. They're waiting for us at the rendezvous. . . . Ah—there we goes."

The lock gave with a sharp click, and the grating of metal broke the stillness as Jarom's cell door swung open.

He shook his head as he came forward. "I thought you were the Demon Queen."

"Who?"

"The leader of the dragonspawn," Jarom explained, his movements helping to clear his head. "She—"

"Later," Kylac interrupted, waving him off. "It won't make any difference if'n we don't makes it out o' here." The youth ushered him from the cell and closed the door behind him. "Come, we must move quickly."

Jarom obeyed, following his young friend down the murky length of the dungeon corridor. As they came upon the outer door, Jarom saw that Kylac had used the body of a slain dragonspawn to prop it open.

"Any trouble with the guards?" Jarom whispered.

Spinning back to signal silence, the youth flashed him a fierce smile.

They slipped past the open door and scurried down a dimly lit tunnel beyond, Kylac moving silently and Jarom making every effort to do the same. Darting this way and that through a maze of corridors and side passages, ushered by the dragonspawn snarls that echoed through a network of ventilation ducts, they worked their way steadily from the dungeon levels to the floors above. At last they came upon a primary shaft through which fresh air flowed into the keep. The passage was barely large enough to crawl through, but Jarom did so at Kylac's urging. At the far end were the remains of an iron grillwork, skillfully removed from its seating by one who knew the business of stealth—that, and an impossibly strong blade.

Jarom didn't hesitate, poking his head into a brilliant night sky. The tunnel, he realized, emptied out along the wall of Dagger Canyon. They were at the edge of the plateau, somewhere beneath the city. Jarom breathed deeply of the refreshing coolness. He closed his eyes, letting go his concerns about the Demon Queen and the choice she had given him, about his brother the wizard, about all but his blessed freedom. He felt himself smile. Perhaps destiny had not deserted him after all.

"We have to climb down to the canyon floor, then back up the other side," Kylac whispered to him from behind.

Jarom nodded, scurrying cautiously from the ventilation shaft and onto a narrow, weed-choked precipice below.

"Keep moving," the youth said, having joined him a moment later. "We's only a few hours 'fore Corathel and the others go on without us."

But Jarom needed no prompting as he fell into step beside the youth. His aches and pains forgotten, he matched his friend stride for slippery stride down the narrow, pebble-strewn trail.

"Allion will be eager to see ya. He'd be here now if'n I'd have let him come."

"What of the army?" Jarom asked. "How many escaped?"

"We don't know, exactly," Kylac admitted. "The men were ordered to scatter into the hills and make their own way south. Most will find their way to Atharvan."

"How many are with the general?"

"Forty, at the time I left. Maybe more by now. Commanders mostly. They were the only ones who knew of the prearranged rendezvous point."

Forty? The number echoed ominously in Jarom's head. From more than twenty-seven thousand, his army's numbers had been reduced to *forty*. The rest had been driven off like a flock of birds, killed or captured or . . .

Jarom stumbled to a sudden halt. So obsessed had he been with his own escape that he had completely forgotten why he had come after the dragonspawn in the first place.

"What's wrong?" Kylac demanded.

"What about the captives? There must be others being held within the city."

The youth shook his head, his features twisting with guilt and frustration. "As we'd hoped. But there's nothing we can do for them right now."

"We can't abandon them! We came here to rescue them!"

"And ya thinks I don't realize that?" The youth came forward a step, fixing him with a hard glare. "But unless ya know how to make thousands o' people silent and invisible . . ." He trailed off, shaking his head. "Ya should be grateful I succeeded in finding yourself."

Jarom started to object further, but realized that Kylac was right. As it was, he could consider himself lucky if even the two of them escaped unscathed. Nevertheless, he felt the threat of tears as he thought of Marisha Valour and what would become of her—if it hadn't already.

"There's just no way, lad. If'n there was, I'd be leading the charge. I'm sorry."

Jarom glanced up toward the mesa and the hulking shadow of the fallen keep. A feeling of helplessness washed through him, followed by a growing rage.

"I won't stands here and tell ya ·everything will be all right. We're going to crawl through fire 'fore this is over, and may not make it out again. The best ya can do is mind those feelings ya gots right now and remember them for later, 'cause this is but the beginning, my friend."

Jarom refused to match the other's gaze, afraid that if he did so, he might lose control. An image of Marisha floated before his mind's eye, just beyond his reach. Strange that someone he had known for such a short time and hadn't seen in what seemed like ages had come to mean so much to him. Already, his mental picture of her was fading, losing color and definition. Only his anger kept him from weeping.

"Here, maybe this will make ya feel better."

The youth shrugged a wrapped bundle from his shoulder, out from under his cloak. Jarom had paid little attention to the protrusion, assuming it to be a quiver of arrows or some such. Now, however, just seeing the object in the youth's hands, he knew exactly what it was.

"I believe it's yours."

The folds of cloth fell away, revealing a familiar red glow. Jarom remained breathless as Kylac held forth the Sword, then gingerly wrapped his hands around the consoling warmth of its hilt.

"You said you left it behind."

"I lied. Didn't want you to go getting any crazy ideas."

"You keep it," Jarom decided suddenly, sick of himself, sick of everything in that moment. "I'll just lose it again."

"I would have," Kylac bantered, "but broadswords are the clumsiest things." When that failed to lighten Jarom's surly mood, the youth scowled. "You'd do better not to misjudge your own strength," he said seriously. "Or that o' those ya care about."

Something in Kylac's words caught Jarom's attention, and he fixed the other with a suspicious eye. The youth was on the verge of telling him something, but didn't know if he should.

"Marisha," Jarom said. His chest tightened in fear. She was dead. He knew it. But he had to ask. "What about Marisha?"

Kylac shook his head. "I only meant, if she has lasted this long, she can survive a while longer."

"She's alive?" He felt his heart flutter.

The youth hesitated, though his gaze remained steady and calculating. "If'n ya go back for her now, you're a dead man."

"You know where she is." His tone was accusing.

But Kylac refused to back down. "If'n she was alone, maybe. But she's locked away with several others. The cavern is well guarded. There's too many—"

"Show me."

Again, the youth shook his head. "Jarom, there's no . . ."

Jarom was through arguing. He heard the other pause as he spun around and charged back up the trail.

". . . time."

He stood before her, shimmering in the darkness, a ghost from her past. Sunken eyes gave an even greater sense of depth to his emotion and the matchless wisdom lying beneath. She reached up with a slender hand, running her fingers through his dark beard, tracing the strong set of his jawline.

She saw herself as she was then, a young girl of six, perched upon her father's lap with eyes bright and inquisitive. She watched herself as though through the eyes of another.

Why must I keep it secret, Father?

He answered at once, in that deep, soothing voice. *It is for you alone, child.*

But why?

Because, my child, it is more precious than a seashore made of gemstones. There are many in this world who would hurt you to possess it.

But it's so beautiful. May I show it to no one?

Under no circumstances. It is a sacred key that I am entrusting to you. I do so that you will always remember me. But for your own protection, and that of your mother, none but the two of you may ever know of its existence. Do you understand?

She nodded solemnly. A big responsibility for a little girl such as she. Her father smiled before placing the talisman in her hand. She cupped it reverently, gasping slightly at the warm rush that tingled through her veins. After a moment, he took up the loose edges of chain and clasped them together behind her neck. She continued to hold the flaming stone until he pulled it from her. He dropped it down the front of her bodice, where she gripped it through the soft fabric. She gazed up at him, soulful eyes full of longing. He reached for her, and she wrapped her arms about his neck in a desperate hug meant to last a lifetime. . . .

Marisha awoke, huddled in the darkness, curled into a ball on the floor of her pit. In one hand, she gripped tightly her pendant. The Pendant of Asahiel, her father had called it, passed down to her much as his father had passed it to him. A gift from the Finlorian elves, fashioned from a stone rumored to have come from one of the great Swords. A priceless heirloom of divine origin.

Marisha blinked the memory into the back of her mind. She did not care to count the number of times she had relived this moment since that day. Over the years, some of the details had faded, forcing her imagination to fill in the gaps. But the bulk remained unchanged. A nightmare, in many ways. For it was the last time she had lain eyes upon her beloved father, and marked the time from which, ever since, she had been burdened with questions whose answers she was not allowed to seek.

He had given it to her when she and her mother had left him. A charm to remember him by, a talisman to keep her safe. At six years of age, she had scarcely understood. A dozen years later, little had changed. She still knew nothing about how the Pendant had come into being, nor how her family had come to possess it. And she had only a vague understanding of its powers, of the comfort and strength it seemed to grant her. All she really knew were the stories her father had told her of the Swords and the promise she had given him, the promise she had kept all these years. To guard the secret of its existence as though her very life depended upon it.

Her mother might have been able to tell her more, but had always refused to discuss it. To this day, she knew not why her mother had left her father, only that she had discovered some frightening secret she couldn't face. Marisha sensed that the stone had something to do with it. If nothing else, the Pendant seemed to remind the elder woman of the pain she had suffered, a pain related to—if not caused by—Marisha's father. The most her mother had ever done was to remind her of the vow she'd made, and to caution against anything that might see that vow broken.

As if Marisha had ever truly considered doing so. Though it seemed at times that to keep her charge sacred would require her to live a confused and solitary life, she had sworn a solemn oath. She cherished her father like a saint, a man made perfect in her memory by the long years of separation. She would not dream of dishonoring that memory by going against his wishes, even if it meant a lifetime of unanswered questions.

It was not until a few weeks ago that her commitment had truly been challenged. When she'd met Jarom and learned of his quest, and glimpsed through their conversations the depths of his desire, she had very nearly broken down and shown him the stone. He seemed such a selfless and good-natured young man. And surely his was a noble cause—to help save the lives of his people. To drive a murderous tyrant from his lands. Her own mother had died two years ago, and while surrounded by friends in her tiny community, Marisha was more alone now than she'd ever been, causing her to question to a greater extent that which she had been raised to believe. In the case of Jarom, she had wondered whether her silence would do more harm than good. Had she shared with him the Pendant and what little she knew of its powers, if only to bolster the courage he would need to succeed in his expedition, would she not have been justified in doing so?

She wondered where he was now, the determined young man who had come so unexpectedly into her life, and who had disappeared as suddenly. She wondered if he could succeed where doubtless so many others had failed. She didn't believe so. And yet, he had seemed so confident in what he believed was his destiny. It was this, in part, that so fasci-

nated her, his willingness to sacrifice everything for a cause
in which he had such absolute faith, a cause much larger
than himself. Besides, she thought with a wry grin, she
wouldn't put anything past Kylac.

The smile felt strange upon her face and she could not
sustain it. Regardless of what had become of her friends,
there was little they could do for her. Her own fate, it
seemed, was indeed to die alone, haunted by thoughts of
what might have been.

She sat up, looking again to the soft glow of the Pendant
in her hand. What could she do with the stone? That she had
managed to keep it from being discovered before now was a
minor miracle. Surely there was no way to keep it hidden
when the enemy stripped and devoured her. The last thing
she wanted was for her father's trust to fall into the hands of
these unnatural brutes. There was no hope for her. But if she
could keep the stone safe, then perhaps she could go to her
grave with a measure of peace.

Her eyes searched the walls and floor of the small,
cramped pit. It was simply a hole dug in the mountain earth;
there were no bricks to loosen and hide the Pendant behind.
Nor were there any cracks or niches to be found. She could
try to bury the talisman in excrement. Or else she could
swallow it and hope the beasts would eat her stomach without tearing it apart and finding what lay inside. Neither
choice offered much hope of success. Nor did she think that
she could break the stone from the chain to which it was fastened, meaning she would have that extra length to dispose
of as well. Still, she thought in desperation, she had to try
something.

The sound of a scuffle came from somewhere above, followed by a muffled squeal from one of the dragons. Startled,
Marisha fumbled her pendant, instinctively shoving it back between her breasts, deep within the tied folds of her dress. She
strained her ears against a sudden silence, the only noise that
of her quick pulse and shallow breathing. Then she heard the
footsteps, swift and cautious. Not of scaled foot and claw, but
of hardened leather—the leather of boots a man might wear.
And not a company, but a single person, moving toward her.

For an instant, Marisha did not know what to feel. Fear? Hope?

A faint light appeared, closer than any of those that hung within the cavern above, and a steady glow that did not flicker. Though it might have been a trick of her mind after peering so long at her pendant, it appeared red in color. Thinking she heard whispers, she hunched deeper while keeping her eyes locked overhead.

A moment later, she gave a sharp gasp of surprise, quite certain that madness had finally taken her. For a face had come into view, staring down at her through the iron bars of her earthen cage. It was a face she had all but forgotten, despite a conscious effort to memorize it. A face she had never thought to see again. She told herself it couldn't be, but by all appearances, it was.

It was the man for whom she had nearly violated a life-long oath. A young man with dark hair and blue eyes, whom she had first met when he was on the verge of death, but whom she had helped nurse back to health. Some who heard his story might call him Torin, prince of Alson. She knew him simply as Jarom.

Soric strode with quiet purpose down the torchlit tunnel. His gait was neither hurried nor slow, but perfectly measured. A lot had happened in the last few weeks, much of it unexpected. He needed time to meditate, to think on all that had transpired and to reevaluate his course.

Thus far, he did not regret bringing his mercenary army east and giving them over to the Demon Queen. Whether or not he had done so, she would have wisely considered him a threat. Had he remained in Alson and tried to fend her off, surely he would have perished. By making this grand gesture of submission, the worst that could happen would be for her to think him insincere. And although she had been less than receptive upon her arrival, the fact that she had not destroyed him on the spot convinced him he had made the right choice. If nothing else, he had bought himself some time.

But he remained vulnerable. With no army to call his own, he was relying entirely now on his own powers. And formidable as those were, a mortal's learning would never surpass that of a being whose command of such forces was innate, practiced as easily as he drew breath. Especially one such as Spithaera, who had harnessed and consumed nature's energies into her own form. Should he be forced into a confrontation, he had no delusions but that his magic skills would fail to save him. No, the true test lay in his ability to please the Queen, to prove his value and thus secure for himself a place at her side. He was not yet concerned about the long run. He had waited for more than twenty years to reclaim what was his; if necessary, he could wait a while longer. If he managed to survive a week, he would be fine. But given their initial encounter, he was unsure his act of devotion would grant him even that.

That he had arrived in time to help rout the human resistance had been an unexpected bonus. Certainly, it had made it easier for him to ingratiate himself among the Queen's minions. His men, of course, were horrified, having had no prior knowledge of his true agenda. He had made a quick example of those who sought to question him on the road east as to their destination. By the time the rest found themselves partnered with dragons in the slaughter of humans, it was too late to desert. Now they were numbered among the Queen's playthings.

The wizard descended a flight of steps and turned down a branching corridor. Though he had helped to organize it, he had not been invited to the Queen's welcoming feast. Nor, in truth, had he been prepared to attend the festivities, except to demonstrate himself a loyal follower. Instead, he had kept to the shadows of a preparation chamber, out of sight and mind, knowing that to be the best way to remain alive this day—hoping that by tomorrow, he would have found another.

His presence, however, had not gone entirely unnoticed. When signaled to do so by the Queen's general—the obsidian demon she called Gravlith—he had sent for the human girl left behind earlier. The one who still had fight in her.

The one the Queen would enjoy killing herself. But the pair of dragons he had sent had failed to return promptly. Knowing that he alone would suffer for any delay and subsequent disappointment, he'd been swift to follow after, to learn what was taking so long. In all probability, the dim-witted brutes had simply forgotten in which pit the girl had been stored.

He was still reflecting on his precarious ground with the Demon Queen when he came upon one of the dragon sentries—or dragonborn, as the Queen called them. The beast sat against the wall, crouched on its haunches. Strangely enough, it did not bother to mark his approach. By now, Soric would have expected the usual growl and glare, or at the very least, that infernal hacking sound. This one, it appeared, was sleeping.

He pulled up alongside the beast, peering down at it from the deep shadow of his drawn cowl. Something was wrong. The creature was impossibly still. Not even its chest was moving. Besides, the wizard had seen no indication that the dragonborn ever slept, least of all one assigned to duty. If Gravlith or Spithaera herself were here to see this, the lazy beast would already be—

He saw it then, the fresh slit beneath its throat, from which a thick wash of black blood had poured forth to coat its chest.

Tightening his grip upon his staff, Soric gathered up his robes and hastened down the empty corridor.

As Jarom looked down into the slave pit, a rush of emotions surged through him. Disgust at the conditions in which Marisha had been kept, rage at the wounds that marred her soft flesh, but most of all, joy at having found her again. She was so filthy and ragged that he might not have recognized her. But he hadn't forgotten those soulful blue eyes and how they made him feel. It hardly seemed possible. He had told himself all along that she was alive, warning himself not to give up on her. Now, after all that had been endured, they were reunited at last.

Marisha continued to gaze up at him, blinking as though he were an apparition. Perhaps it was only the traumatic circumstances surrounding them, but Jarom was so overwhelmed that it took him a minute to find his voice.

"Hold on," he whispered finally, offering her a broad grin. "Kylac will have you out in a moment."

She continued to gape wordlessly until Kylac, coming up silently on his heels, slid into her view. "Kylac!"

"Quiet!" the youth hissed.

She came to her feet, hunched forward, the pit not quite deep enough to stand in. "I'd not expected to see you again."

Kylac dropped to a crouch. "Where are your cellmates?"

"They were taken. Your timing couldn't have been better. I don't think I would have been here much longer."

Jarom looked to the youth, who met his meaningful gaze. "Keep watch," Kylac told him.

Jarom did, casting about for sign of enemies while the youth worked to release the large pin that secured the door to Marisha's cell. The immense cavern was dimly lit by flaming cressets hammered into the ceiling. Scattered throughout were scores of pits like those before which he stood, hundreds perhaps, all covered with latched iron gates. He focused on the tunnels leading in, which remained empty. Kylac had completed a sweep of the perimeter before allowing him to enter, working his way around to dispatch half a dozen dragonspawn sentries. A third of the number, the youth had claimed, that had been posted mere hours before, though where the others might have been drawn to, he couldn't say. Regardless, the young assassin had made such swift and silent work of the guards that Jarom doubted all twenty would have posed a problem.

The locking bar came away with a rasp, and Kylac swung the gate upwards on a groaning hinge. Jarom moved forward at once, lowering a hand to help Marisha from the pit. She accepted it, and allowed him to pull her up to him, where she surprised him by throwing her arms around his neck, wrapping him close. Jarom held her with his free hand, uncertain if he should ever let go.

After a moment, she pulled away, leaving her hands upon the back of his neck. Her eyes fell upon the Sword.

"Is that . . . ?" She failed to finish, enraptured by the talisman's aura.

Jarom nodded. "If we manage to make it out of here, I'll tell you the story."

"Then the dragons still hold the city?"

"Yes," Jarom replied. "We haven't much time. Where are Master Nimbrus and the others?"

"Dead. I'm all that's left." Her eyes began to glimmer.

"Marisha, I'm so sorry." He pulled her close once more, where she remained for but a moment.

"Are you two alone?" she asked, glancing around as though to answer her own question.

Jarom nodded.

She let go to embrace Kylac. "Come," she sniffed. "We've many others to set free."

But the youth shook his head. "There's no time, Marisha. And no way to sneak them out o' the city. I'm sorry."

"But they're dying!"

"As will those who still have a chance to be saved if'n we stays here much longer."

Marisha looked as though the youth had slapped her. "I don't understand. You came back for me."

"His idea," Kylac admitted, indicating Jarom. "I tried to talk him out of it."

Jarom swallowed as Marisha turned to him, her question in her eyes.

"Why?"

"Because I owe you my life. You and your people."

"And you?" she demanded of Kylac. "Why are you here if you think you shouldn't be?"

"I owe him mine." The youth looked to Jarom. "Although I'd say this settles the score."

Marisha considered them both. "Then go on ahead," she determined finally. "I'm not leaving these innocents to die."

Kylac shook his head. "Marisha—"

"Go, Kylac," Jarom said. "She's right."

"No, she's not. And if'n ya thinks for a minute you're staying with her, I'm afraid I'll have to ask ya to give up the Sword."

Jarom hesitated, then turned the blade around, extending the hilt of the weapon to his friend.

"What are you doing?" Marisha gasped.

"I came too far to let you die here alone," Jarom told her. "But the Sword needs to be where it can do the most good."

Pain and indecision wrestled upon Marisha's face. Jarom recognized her dilemma. It was the same that plagued him—and, he imagined, despite the youth's strong stance, Kylac as well. If they tried to save the thousands who had been taken captive, they would all be seized and tossed right back into prison. And yet, how could they abandon so many to such suffering? Even though they were strangers, Marisha seemed wracked by guilt at the thought of leaving them. If she chose to die rather than live with that guilt, Jarom would understand, and was willing to do the same.

He worried privately that returning for Marisha was in many ways a selfish act. Even Kylac, a close friend, had been unwilling to risk the uproar to ensue over the extrication of a dozen prisoners—which, from what he had seen earlier, would have been required in order to save her. Jarom had been alone, else the youth might not have sprung him, either. As it had turned out, they were lucky in that Marisha was also alone. But the pragmatic youth had pressed their luck as far as he was willing. With Marisha beside them, Jarom was inclined to agree. That would seem to support, in his own mind, the fear that he had come to help himself more so than any other. He would therefore allow Marisha to make the final decision.

"Good luck, the both o' ya," Kylac said, taking the Sword from Jarom. "I'll come back for ya if'n I can."

"Wait," Marisha said softly. She glanced around at the many pits, then stared at the glowing talisman in Kylac's hands. She recognized, Jarom thought, the value of the Sword—why it was needed, and what it meant for him to give it up. She looked to him, eyes agleam. "I can't let you do this."

"Marisha," he assured her, "we'll do whatever you ask."

"Listen to me," Kylac urged, "both o' ya. Don't confuse foolishness with courage. Dying alongside these people won't help them."

Marisha rubbed at her tears with a dirty sleeve.

"This war ain't over. We can either waste time putting out flames, or we can takes aim at the heart of the beast. But unless we leaves now, we'll never have the chance."

The youth's lack of emotion was forgivable, Jarom thought, given his upbringing, but that didn't make it something to be admired.

Marisha glowered, then turned to Jarom for reassurance. "Then promise me we won't stop until the beast is dead."

Jarom nodded, a lump in his throat. Her dress was in tatters, her face painted with grime. And yet, in that moment, she appeared undeniably beautiful. "I promise."

"Another night," Kylac whispered, handing Jarom back the Sword. "Another night."

Marisha nodded. Already, Kylac was setting the pace of departure, heading on cat's paws toward the nearest exit tunnel. Marisha clung to Jarom's arm as they quietly followed. Jarom searched the darkness left and right, wary of any sign that they had been discovered. He felt as though they were being watched, but could not place the source of his discomfort. Marisha, he noticed, remained focused on the path ahead, refusing to let her gaze fall to either side, where she might catch a glimpse of the pits and the ravaged figures sleeping within. She leaned close, and he welcomed her warmth—and that of the Crimson Sword—as the phantom eyes continued after, cold and piercing.

The wizard slowed as he came around the corner, nearly tripping over the corpse of a second dragonborn, slumped in a dark pool of its own blood. With his breath rasping softly in his ears, he stepped over the creature and looked past the mouth of the tunnel, where it emptied into the cavern of slave pits beyond.

He was only mildly surprised by what he saw. A handful of dragonborn sentries lay bleeding about the cavern. Fewer than before, he noted, realizing that the rest had probably made their way to the Queen's feast. Halfway across the room stood a man wielding a sword sheathed in a scarlet glow. His back was turned so that Soric could not quite see his face. Then he shifted, glancing back and forth as if checking for enemies, and looked right in Soric's direction.

Torin! The wizard clenched. So, his brother had managed to free himself from his dungeon cell and sought now to . . . What? Why would he come here? Even as Soric watched, the door of the pit before which Torin stood swung open, at the hands of a second individual of whom the wizard could see little. With the barrier pulled away, Torin reached forth a hand to escort the prisoners from below.

A wide smile spread across the wizard's face as the very lass he had come to fetch stepped free and wrapped Torin in a warm embrace. How perfectly ironic, he thought, that the girl he had inadvertently spared should belong to his hated brother. Too bad their reunion was to be short-lived.

The wizard started forward, then hesitated, sensing an opportunity, waiting to see what more his brother had planned. For several moments, the three figures argued among themselves, knotted tightly in the near darkness. At one point, his brother handed the sword over to the other, only to accept it back a moment later. Immediately thereafter, they were off, speeding across the cavern and into a distant tunnel.

Soric watched them go and did nothing to stop them. A choice he might regret on the morrow. But his suspicions told him otherwise. He knew of the Queen's interest in Torin and the Sword of Asahiel, rumored to have been used in the attack on this keep. Handing them over to her was sure to win him fair graces. But he knew as well that if the Queen had everything she wanted, she would have no further use for him, and would likely destroy him. Better to keep her wanting. Better to make her believe that it was he who held the key to obtaining that which she desired. In so doing, he would make himself indispensable to her efforts, a champion to her cause.

And when the time was right, her usurper.

CHAPTER THIRTY-THREE

What was that, my dear?" Spithaera asked, stroking the dragonborn's cheek. Her painted nails brushed the creature's scaled flesh, gleaming like bloodied daggers.

The beast struggled to answer. Its entire body quivered, eyes wide and staring. Its tongue lolled within its mouth, numb with terror. At last, croaking and sputtering in its own language, it repeated the message it had been sent to deliver.

"Escaped," the Demon Queen echoed.

She continued to lean forward in her chair of plush felt, seated in her private audience chamber. She had awakened early, roused from her slumber by a pair of dragonborn sentries who gave word of an urgent message. She had only barely paused to don a silk robe before heading out to meet the messenger she had found whimpering at the foot of her throne.

Despite its stammering words and copious slaver, its report had been clear. So impossible was the news, however, that she had forced the trembling wretch to repeat it. Now that it had, she felt her fury rising.

"I see. And of what worth does that make you to me?"

Her low growl wracked the pitiable dragonborn's body until it seemed that it would shatter. Her nails, maintaining their reassuring stroke, fell from its cheek to its neck.

In an instant, those nails extended, stabbing clear through to the other side of her victim's throat. The creature grunted, its eyes rolling back in their sockets. It thrashed against her hold but could not begin to break free. A moment later, she retracted her switchblade nails from the twitching corpse, which slumped to the floor.

She leapt from her chair, teeth clenched, menace flashing in her emerald eyes. Her open robe billowed about her tall, slender frame as she paced the room on bare feet like a caged animal. She then whirled upon the pair of sentries standing guard at the main entrance to the chamber, where her venomous glance set them to trembling as vigorously as their comrade a moment before.

"Fetch me the wizard!" she shrieked.

Allion peered through the foliage, trying to catch a glimpse of those who approached. He could hear their passage through the underbrush, slow and stealthy, but they were yet too far off, screened away by a dense tangle of branches and leaves. He did not think they were dragonspawn, for the beasts would have offered no pretense as to their coming. More likely a party of those mercenaries who had joined the battle to cut off their retreat, sent now to search the woods for those who had escaped the slaughter at the draw.

Allion raised his bow from his lap, fitting an arrow to the string. Whoever it turned out to be, they would not make it back to alert any others as to their discovery.

The first rays of actual sunlight were finally breaking through the gray and misty morn. Their touch was welcomed by the cold hunter, who had long since gone stiff and numb beneath his woolens and leathers. He had been on the outer watch for half the night. He had volunteered for the position, wanting to be among the first to spy the return of Kylac or any others of the scattered West Legion. But the last to rejoin the group had arrived hours ago, with reports of what had happened to their respective companies and platoons. By now, he had received word from every division but that of the First, and could paint a fairly clear picture of the army's chaotic retreat. Although he wished otherwise, Allion knew in his heart that no more would rally here.

The sounds of approach drew closer, slow and cautious. Allion stood from where he sat crouched among a thick

stand of spruce and elm, his knees cracking with the effort.
Suddenly, as if alerted to his presence, the movement
stopped. The hunter held his breath, drawing back his bowstring and taking aim around the side of a mossy bole.

He nearly fell over backwards when he found himself
staring into the face of Kylac Kronus. The youth was leaned
up against one of the outer trees of his shelter, a pace away,
feigning boredom. Allion sputtered in surprise, and had to
catch himself from releasing his arrow toward the now grinning youth.

"Easy, my friend. It's me."

"I can see that," Allion stammered, regaining his balance
and composure. "I nearly shot you, you know."

Kylac shrugged the notion aside as he called back toward
the woods. "Come. It's one o' ours."

Allion could not yet see who the youth was talking to, but
heard the movement resume. He glanced at Kylac, whose
grin widened in smug delight, then watched as a pair of familiar figures came into view along the forest trail, a fair-
haired woman hanging on the arm of a dark-haired man.

"Jarom!" he hailed, stumbling down the rise.

There was a flurry of exclamations and embraces, followed by smiles and openmouthed stares.

"I'd feared the worst," Allion admitted.

"Then you were right," Jarom replied.

Allion frowned slightly, not sure what to make of his
friend's statement, but too relieved to care.

"Where's Corathel?" Kylac asked.

"They moved the main camp down by the river. Come, I'll
take you to him."

Jarom shook his head in denial as he gazed upon the huddled
forms of resting soldiers, all camouflaged with forest debris.
Fifty-three, at last count, according to Allion, up slightly
from when Kylac had left. Fifty-five including Marisha and
himself. At least the majority appeared to be uninjured. But
then, most of the wounded had probably been hewn down
during the harrowing flight.

He tried not to think of the many who had been slain or scattered, just as he had tried to put out of mind those they had left behind in the slave pits and other unknown holding pens at Kraagen Keep. Marisha, still close, had hardly spoken since her rescue, too busy wrestling demons of her own. He wondered what she thought, of him and of Kylac. Surely she recognized they had done what they could. To have attempted more would only have cost them their freedom as well. And selfish though it may seem, safeguarding their freedom would make the larger difference in this struggle. More than once he had almost spoken to her, but in each instance had thought better of it. He did not want to do anything that might drive her from him. She would share her feelings with him when she was ready.

They continued on through the forest encampment, following after Allion and offering grim nods to those who marked their approach. Jarom could not tell whether the soldiers he came across were happy to see him. He was still bearer of the Crimson Sword, but it was he, in great part, who had convinced them to undertake this battle in the first place. He recalled the rally that had taken place before setting forth from Leaven. By his very presence with the Sword, he had promised so much. Thus far, he had delivered only death and disappointment.

They arrived at a riverbank, whether the Kraagmal or the Llornel, Jarom wasn't certain. Nor did he care. A dozen horses were tethered to a line stretched between a pair of trees, with sacks of food supplies and ammunition stores piled up about them. Among these, Jarom was surprised to spy the familiar leather bag carrying the tome that he and Allion had discovered outside of Earthwyn. The hunter must have carried it from the battle, for Allion had last had it in his possession. But of all the things his friend could have snatched during the retreat—water, food, medical supplies, ammunition—he had chosen the book, probably in perceived loyalty to Jarom's wishes. Once again, Jarom shook his head. How had they come to place such importance in this cumbersome and ultimately useless artifact? With so many lives at stake, what had happened to their priorities?

They passed by the line of horses and followed Allion down the bank. Corathel and his lieutenant generals were seated below, conferring quietly among themselves. Second General Jasyn was there, his left shoulder immobilized by bandages that kept it strapped to his chest. As was Third General Maltyk, one of his knees grotesquely swollen. The Fourth and Fifth generals were also in attendance—the towering Lar, sporting an infinite number of cuts, scrapes, and bruises, and the scowling Rynar, who appeared mostly unscathed.

The discussion halted abruptly at the approach of the new arrivals, with the chief general rising swiftly to greet them.

"Glad you could join us," Corathel offered, clasping hands first with Kylac. "We'd just about given up on your return."

He moved on to Jarom, who saw in the general's gaze a fiery determination that brooked no despair.

"I see your choice in companions has improved," the chief general said to him, bowing to Marisha. Jarom did not miss the color that rose to her cheeks at the remark.

Before he could respond, the division commanders were upon him.

"Better late than never," Lar rumbled, clapping him on the back with a great hand.

Rynar agreed. "I was sorry not to see you earlier."

"Not as sorry as I," Jarom assured him, turning to Jasyn.

"Dislocation," the other said, glancing at his wrapped shoulder. "I'll be fine."

He looked to Maltyk, the only one of them not to rise. "How's the knee?"

"Painful. The long run here didn't help."

Jarom glanced about. "Ledryk?" he asked, recognizing the First General's absence.

Corathel shook his head. "No word. I suspect that if any of us make it out of this, we'll have some promotions to make."

Jarom nodded solemnly, gulping down a surprising pang of loss that settled like a thorn in his stomach.

"We have many to mourn," Corathel reminded him. "Now is not the time."

"I'd best be getting back to the watch," Allion announced. "We'll catch up later, my friend."

Jarom managed a weak nod as the other turned to head back up the bank.

"We leave within the hour," Corathel called after.

Allion acknowledged the order, then scurried off into the surrounding trees.

"The rest of you," Corathel beckoned, "sit with us."

The chief general retook his seat in the muddy grass. Jarom joined him, dropping with Kylac and Marisha into a cross-legged sitting position. He felt the woman slide in close and grasp his hand, which he squeezed reassuringly. Glancing over, his eyes found hers, and he gave silent thanks once again, despite all their losses, for the fortunes granted him.

"So," Corathel began, fixing the newcomers with a stern gaze, "what have we learned?"

Spithaera was still pacing back and forth across the floor of her private audience chamber when her sentries returned. She looked up upon their arrival to find the wizard in tow.

"Leave," she snarled to the pair of dragonborn, who skittered promptly from the room.

She had thought to slay the man who bowed before her hours earlier, at the conclusion of her feast, when he had promised Gravlith, for her delight, a mortal woman willing to fight for her life, but had instead delivered yet another in a long line of submissive slaves—a young maiden of moderate beauty who had barely summoned the courage to scream. Though disappointed, Spithaera had been of such merry humor, so thoroughly exultant in the celebration of her recent triumphs, that she had elected to spare the man. Now, having learned of the escape of the mortal she most coveted, the wielder of a Sword of Asahiel, her mood had changed.

She stalked forward to stand before him, ignoring the fact that her robe was still open.

"Have you anything further to say for yourself?"

He met her gaze without blinking, a loyal supplicant whose very posture trembled with adoration. "My queen?"

"I have dealt with men of your learning and ambition in the past," she said, spitting her distaste. "But for my coming, you would enslave the world entire as you did your own land."

She paused, allowing him the opportunity for denial. He made none.

"Therefore, wizard, I have decided to destroy you."

She snapped her fingers, and in came Gravlith, entering from a side passage that led back to her inner chambers. The massive demon headed for the wizard without breaking stride.

"But slowly, of course, that you may beseech my mercy."

To the wizard's credit, he did not snivel or recoil, but stood unwavering in the center of the room as Gravlith clamped a heavy hand about his neck, hoisted him from the chamber floor, and began to squeeze.

"My queen," he rasped, pushing the words through his steadily collapsing throat, "I live or die only to serve you."

Spithaera sat back in her throne, crossing one leg before her to show that she was unimpressed.

"I am brother to the one you seek."

That had her attention. She leaned forward, an elbow to her knee, chin resting lightly in her hand.

"I know how you might lure him . . ."

His words ended in a garbled squeak, his breath expired. She observed his throes with piqued interest. He was doing his best not to thrash, but his pallid skin had already gone purple.

Finally, she snapped her fingers once again. Without question, Gravlith dropped the fragile mortal to the floor, where he collapsed in a rumpled heap.

"Then I have ways in which to use talents such as yours."

"As you wish," the wizard gasped, rubbing at his injured throat. "I serve your every desire always, my queen."

Spithaera glared at him, then spun from the room in a swish of silk, her pet demon following hard upon her heels.

Time dragged by while they waited for Corathel's response. Jarom sat quiet, listening to the rushing of the river and the chirping of the woods. He could feel Marisha's pulse through her skin, her hand still holding his. Across the circle of generals, the legion commander's face twisted in consternation.

"We've already sent word to King Galdric," the chief general argued. "He'll be expecting us."

"Then send new word," Jarom replied.

It had taken some time to relate to Corathel and his lieutenants that which Jarom had learned while inside Kraagen Keep. Thereafter, the discussion had taken up where it had left off before his return—what to do next. To the chief general, it was clear that if they were to regroup, they must do so with the East Legion at Atharvan, his home city and Partha's capital to the southeast. Jarom, however, had devised another idea, and had been unable to keep it to himself.

"You're certain this 'Demon Queen' will come after you and bypass Atharvan?" Corathel asked, frowning.

Jarom nodded. "She wants the Sword. It has to be the one power she's seen thus far that frightens her. Unless I'm wrong, her armies will be crawling all over in search of us."

The chief general gave a mighty sigh. "You're asking me to abandon my people to fend for themselves." His tone was weary, his features sullen.

"I'm no general," Jarom admitted, "but I don't see how this group could reinforce Atharvan against a full-scale assault. Luring the dragonspawn away from your king's city is the best way to save it."

Corathel regarded him with a cautionary expression. "The emperor will not be pleased that we've brought this upon him."

Jarom shrugged the danger aside. "This fight would've made it his way soon enough. He should be grateful we're willing to make our final stand with him."

The chief general shook his head, then looked to his lieutenants, his questioning gaze sweeping their dirty faces.

"We have little choice now, do we?" Rynar snapped. "Alson has been overrun by this wizard, our lands have been devastated, Menzos eradicated. It would seem Kuuria is our last defense."

Jasyn agreed. "The emperor must know by now of the terror that threatens, and yet he refuses to send aid. The man can't hide behind his polished walls forever."

"I'd rather do battle in their lands than ours," said Maltyk. "Let them sweep up when this is over."

Lar simply nodded.

Corathel turned to Kylac, who had remained conspicuously silent. "What do you think?"

"Ya sure ya wants me to have a say in this? My last plan didn't turn out so well."

"I'd not have asked otherwise."

"With respect, General, I thinks you're once again letting emotion cloud judgment. Jarom's plan makes the most sense."

The chief general scowled, but gritted away his retort. "So be it," he declared finally. "We'll ford the river, then, and keep to the western bank, making straight for the Gaperon."

When no other voice presented itself, the conference ended.

"Ready the men. I want us gone before the next mark of the sun."

The council broke, its members dispersing in order to make ready the necessary preparations. Jarom remained where he was, exchanging handclasps and repeated greetings with each of the departing generals. He hadn't told anyone that the wizard was his elder brother. He wasn't sure why, only that he worried for the shadow it might cast upon himself. Besides, it hardly seemed relevant given their knowledge of the Demon Queen as their primary enemy. In all likelihood, Soric had been slain already.

"Come," Kylac said to Marisha when just the three of them were left standing there. "We'll find a place for ya to wash up."

Marisha nodded, letting go of Jarom's hand and allowing the youth to lead her away.

"You'd best do the same," Kylac suggested to him.

Jarom nodded, focusing on the lingering warmth of Marisha's touch. The ache left by her departure reminded him of the feeling he'd had upon leaving his village back when this adventure had begun. Strange. In the matter of a few short weeks, his life had come to seem so terribly complicated. And yet, he'd experienced so much, and changed so significantly, that he was no longer sure he would go back if he could. Though he yearned in many ways for the simplicity and serenity and certainty of his past, the future held the greater promise.

Unsure what to think of destiny's games, he strolled along the riverbank in the opposite direction. Finding a small cove that offered a measure of privacy, he stripped off the filthy garments he had worn since the battle at Kraagen Keep and waded into the river. The frigid waters stole his breath at first, but then their chill infused his bones and muscles, dulling the aches caused by wounds and lack of sleep. The Sword he kept with him. Though its pristine surface needed no cleaning, he was afraid to let it go for even a moment. He'd not forgotten the feeling of devastation upon realizing he had lost the blade, nor the depths of his despair. Even now, a measure of that hopelessness remained, a grim reminder that little had changed. Despite his improbable rescue and that of Marisha, the truth was that they had been utterly defeated, having failed in their grand attempt to win back their lands. How many more chances might they get?

A friendly shout drew him from his musings, that of a soldier happening by his pile of clothes left on the shoreline. Jarom nodded eagerly at the other's offer to find him a fresh set, if possible. Even had he time to clean the clothes, the stench of death and failure permeated them like smoke, and would never come free.

He had finished bathing by the time the soldier returned, a pair of breeches and tunic in hand. Standard issue, the other said, of a Parthan infantryman, mostly black in color. They were a tight fit, but not so much as to restrict his movements, and Jarom thanked the man profusely.

They set off together toward the main camp, where, among the miscellaneous stores, Jarom found a scabbard for the Sword. He felt immeasurably better after that, more so than he deserved. He helped to pack onto the horses supplies that the company would be carrying, and to drown in the river those that they would not. No sense in leaving an obvious trail for the Demon Queen's minions to follow.

By the time they were ready to leave, Marisha had rejoined him, clean and radiant and smelling of sweet fruit. She was outfitted in the lightweight layers of a Parthan archer, minus the leather armor. Though her hair remained unkempt and the clothes were baggy, Jarom could not have been more enchanted, and he stopped just short of telling her so.

They set forth moments later, rejoined by their close friends Allion and Kylac. Despite the circumstances—or perhaps because of them—it was a happy reunion.

The feeling did not last beyond the journey's start. Able to salvage little from the supply wagons in terms of foodstuffs, they made their meals primarily from whatever they could gather along the way. And with the land empty—torn and ravaged even miles from the swath of destruction that the Parthan army had followed northward—food in any form was a rare commodity. With hunger came weariness, especially given that they were forced to march afoot, and that many had scarcely slept since their desperate retreat from Bane Draw. Jarom took notice as, little by little, physical hardship began to strip away the layers of resolve in which the survivors had cloaked themselves, while grief and doubt weakened them from within.

He did his best to fight off the depression and lethargy that overwhelmed so many of the others, and with the perpetual reassurances of the Sword, was successful for a time. It wasn't long, however, before his misgivings caught up to him. After all, he could no longer trust the Sword. If it had failed him once, it might do so again. And if he could not place his faith in the Sword, then where was he to find his strength?

True to her nature, Marisha was the first to notice his discomfort. With reassurances both silent and spoken, she set about the task of restoring his confidence. In her kind words, soft touches, and imploring looks, Jarom found patience and understanding and a genuine interest in his well-being. Despite the cloud of sorrow hanging over his world, despite his fear that the enemy they faced would prove too powerful, one glimpse of Marisha's face would brighten his mood, adding warmth and hope to his day. It was because of her, Jarom realized, that the long road south to Kuuria seemed barely an inconvenience.

She spent a great amount of time asking him about the Sword—how he had found it, what it was like to wield it in battle, and so on. Not surprising, given her intense interest back in Feverroot. Her ongoing fascination reminded him of his own, and it pleased him greatly to be able to satisfy her curiosity. She held the talisman for a time, marveling at its perfect beauty and resonating strength. As she did so, he confided in her all that he knew, his entire history with the blade up until the moment he'd lost it in battle. He found that it helped his own understanding of the weapon to articulate its perceived powers. Neither she nor Kylac questioned his assertion that the Sword had guided his actions in the battle at Kraagen Keep. The youth was quick to point out what he had done right and where he had made mistakes, but even then had little to say, other than to suggest that as long as he wielded a divine blade and concentrated on what he knew, he would do fine.

"And it never grows heavy?" Marisha asked.

"Never," Jarom confirmed. "Even against the dragonspawn, I never lacked breath or strength. And yet . . ."

"Yes?"

He glanced about to make sure no one else was listening, lowering his voice to mask his shame. "The Sword failed me. At Bane Draw, we had the enemy outnumbered. We were decimated, and I was powerless to prevent it. What good is the Sword if it fails us when it matters most?"

Marisha regarded him with a warm, sad expression. "The Sword didn't fail you, Jarom. Only when you forgot your goal were you made vulnerable. The Sword acts as an extension of your will. It is your own focus and determination, your own passion and desire, that ultimately determine its power."

Jarom mulled the words over in his head. That did indeed seem to be the way he remembered it. And her assessment rang true. He looked to her with newfound admiration as she handed him the Sword, surprised by her insight.

"What did you mean, back at Feverroot, when you told me the Swords existed?"

The question seemed to catch her off guard. "I told you before. I merely meant that you must believe in what—"

"No," Jarom insisted. "That wasn't about what *I* believed. You were telling me what *you* believed. How is that?"

For a moment, the woman looked decidedly uncomfortable, casting about as though for a place to hide. "My father," she answered finally. "He used to tell me stories when I was very young. The Swords were always my favorite."

"This is the first time you've mentioned your father," Jarom noted.

"My mother left him when I was still a girl. I barely remember him."

"Oh," he grunted, feeling awkward. "I'm sorry."

Marisha flashed him that ready smile, assuring him that all was forgiven. "Just don't let me catch you doubting yourself again."

Jarom nodded, not sure what else he might say, puzzled and amazed by this young woman and her uncommon inner strength.

The day ground by. Although the threat of pursuit hung over them like a pall, they saw no sign of the dragonspawn, nor any of the private demons of which the wizard had spoken. Still, the members of the company tread softly and spoke with muted voices, spread out in long lines meant to hide their tracks. The border to Kuuria was at best a week away; it was far too early to start feeling safe. Four scouts had been sent out on horseback, one in each direction. The eastern rider was to speed word to King Galdric as to Corathel's course, so that the Parthan king could send reinforcements south if he so chose. The remaining riders were to return every hour on the hour with a report on enemy activity. Thus far, all was clear.

By midafternoon, the smear of clouds staining the sky finally turned volatile, dumping intermittent torrents of rain upon the men as they trudged onward through the thin woodland fringe that sprouted along either edge of the river. Soon the entire company was soaked through, and began shivering when a wind arose from the east. It was at this point that Jarom found himself near the rear of the procession, Marisha at his side, listening to Allion share with Kylac more of the intricacies of archery. The youth, who had all but mastered Allion's skill already, appeared to be paying attention until he halted suddenly, signaling for those around him to be still.

"What is it?"

Kylac said nothing, but stood frozen in concentration. Jarom watched him for a moment, straining to hear. But if something was out there, the sounds of its passing were drowned out by the roar of the river's waters, rushing southward to Llornel Lake, and the heavy patter of rain thrumming against the earth.

"There."

Jarom traced the youth's gaze across the rain-swollen shallows to the river's opposite bank. At first he saw nothing more than the wet foliage, a writhing mesh of branches and vines whitewashed in mist. Then, all of a sudden, he caught his breath, startled to find a pair of glowing green eyes peering at them from out of the gloom.

"By the gods," Marisha gasped.

Jarom blinked to be certain of what he saw. The eyes belonged to the shadow of what appeared to be a giant wolf, crouched on its hind legs. Its sleek black fur offered stark contrast to the backdrop of woodland greenery, with bony spikes that ran the length of its spine. While he watched, the beast kept perfectly still, its haunting orbs seeming to study him.

Then, without warning, it threw its nose to the heavens and unleashed a frightful howl. A sense of dread filled Jarom's heart as he recognized the demonic call.

"Kill it!" Kylac said sharply.

Jarom drew forth the Crimson Sword. The wolf creature sprang forward, lean and powerful, bounding from the far bank and into the shallows. The rushing waters swallowed the beast initially, until it stood, rising to where the river's surface reached only to the base of its chest. With feral hunger, it waded toward them, snarling its hatred, clawed limbs shredding the river into spray and foam.

An arrow flew to meet it, striking the creature square in the chest. A barrage followed, half a dozen bolts burying themselves in the wolf's muscular body. Still the beast came on, barking and thrashing, until finally it gave a sharp yelp and vanished beneath the churning waters.

The horrified onlookers caught their breath. Marisha looked to Jarom, eyes wide with fear. "Was that—?"

The creature reappeared at their feet, erupting from the water's edge and clawing its way up the near shore. Marisha squealed. Jarom stepped in front of her, the Sword raised in defense. But he could see that the wolf's rear legs no longer worked, and before the demon could drag more than its torso onto the muddy bank, the light retreated from its eyes, their color fading to a dull red. The beast stretched forth a clawed hand, then surrendered its struggle, little more than a twitching pincushion of arrow feathers and oozing black blood.

Its convulsions persisted for several long moments. Almost the whole of the company had gathered around now, alerted by the commotion. As the last of them came forward, Corathel among them, the death throes ended and the corpse began to decompose before their eyes. Skin and bones, teeth and claws melted into the sodden earth, while the waters about the monster's legs came to a sudden, feverish boil. Within seconds, the creature had vanished, and the waters about it grew still.

Jarom found Allion with bow in hand, and was unsurprised by the other's white-faced expression. "Did that look as familiar to you as it did to me?"

The hunter nodded. "Seems we've had dealings with the Demon Queen's minions before."

Kylac turned to Corathel. "There'll be more."

The chief general nodded. "I don't like our chances of concealing a group this large with scouring demons on the prowl. I was hoping to avoid this, but I think we should consider separating into smaller companies."

"What if we face an attack?" Allion asked. "Our numbers are hardly sufficient to defend ourselves as is."

A few among the men grumbled their assent.

"We'll have to risk it," Kylac said. "Our objective at the moment is flight, not fight."

"Five parties," Corathel determined, "no less than ten men each. We'll stagger them by half-hour intervals. Space enough to hide our movements, while still allowing us to mass together quickly if necessary."

"But don't we *want* the Queen to know of our whereabouts?" Allion questioned. "How else are we to make certain her forces follow us?"

Corathel shook his head. "We must reveal our general intent only. If they can track our specific location, we're finished."

"They'll be watching," Kylac assured them all. "No need for us to tip our hand."

"Each of my generals will organize a party to command. I'll take the last." The chief general turned to his lieutenants, huddled behind him. "Except Maltyk," he decided, noting the other's leg, which had continued to swell.

"I'm fine," the Third General grimaced.

"You've enough responsibility tending to that knee," Corathel insisted, his tone enough to finish the argument.

"You should let me look at that," Marisha offered. "I'd be happy to travel with you."

"I still need someone to guide the fifth party. Kylac, would you be willing?"

"Have Jarom do it," the youth suggested. "I'd like to remain free to do some scouting on my own."

Jarom met the gaze of the chief general and nodded without hesitation. "Consider it done."

"To it, then," the legion commander ordered his charges. As the men began to organize themselves into groups, he passed by Jarom, muttering under his breath. "Maybe this way, at least one of us will make it to Kuuria alive."

The great black beast lay sprawled across the cavern floor. For forgotten centuries he had slept there, unconcerned with the world beyond his mountain realm. In that time, he had grown to a height of more than sixty paces, with a wingspan nearly twice that length. Impenetrable scales armored the whole of his body, and a line of spines, each as tall as a man, ran from the nape of his neck to the tip of his tail. Coarse tufts of matted black fur crested his head, hung about his face, and clung to his limbs in lines and patches, irrefutable testimony as to his age and great wisdom.

He had a languid look about him, but Spithaera knew better. His rest was like that of a scorpion at hunt, a ruse meant to draw the unwary close. She need not study the sneer engraved upon his face to know what manner of creature he was, nor look at the carpet of bones that lay scattered among piles of loose rocks—the remains of those who once upon a time had been foolish enough to come here in search of glories unknown. She need only recall the first time she had looked into the eyes of the great beast, one of the very few to have done so, and found the truth of a heart much like her own. Make no mistake. He was as ancient as fear itself, and every bit as deadly. An awesome creature, even by the standards of his own kind.

Fitting, as he was the last.

She observed him silently for a moment longer before softly calling his name.

"Killangrathor."

The mighty dragon pricked his ears and raised a massive eyelid to reveal the flaming orb beneath. Onyx scales shimmered in the half-light given off by a radiant pool of molten rock that hissed and bubbled behind him, fed by a river that flowed sluggishly along the near wall of the mountain's core. The dragon considered her with a snort, and Spithaera grimaced as the stench of his breath washed over her.

"I need more."

Killangrathor snarled in response, a guttural sound that escaped through a curl in his lip. His mental retort slapped at her with undisguised annoyance, his cavernous lungs and throat incapable of forming the words that she or any lesser creature would understand.

"Don't take that tone with me, you filthy brute," Spithaera snapped. "They've found a Sword of Asahiel."

Despite her knowledge of the dragon's true vigilance, the Demon Queen was nonetheless startled when Killangrathor lifted his head like a cobra and swung it close. His eyes fixed upon her, a firestorm of hatred raging within. His nostrils flared; his lips quivered. The whole of his monstrous body began to tremble. All of a sudden, Spithaera found herself calculating her odds of defeating this creature, before turning instead to thoughts of escape.

"Forgive me, mighty Killangrathor. I felt you should know."

The immense cavern seemed to shrink as Killangrathor came to his feet, swelling his chest and beating his wings within the jagged confines. Hooks and spines bristled upon his iron flesh. He tossed back his huge head and let loose a roar that shook the mountain's foundations. A burst of flame sparked from his nostrils, chased by tendrils of smoke toward the cavern ceiling hundreds of feet above. Behind him, the molten pool roiled and spat, sloshing dangerously. Spithaera saw now the magical residue that swirled heavily within, like oil gathered in water.

The dragon's oaths resonated within her mind like caged thunder. The Swords of Asahiel. The cursed weapons that had butchered his kind and chased him into the bowels of this mountain more than seven thousand years ago. The hated talismans wielded by the Finlorian elves during the ancient Dragon Wars. The fires of Mount Krakken, he swore, would rage like never before. She would have her armies, and with them, she would lay waste this land and all who cowered behind the Sword of Asahiel.

Spithaera straightened, emboldened by his words, no longer cowed by the display. Already, Killangrathor was clawing at the cavern walls, tearing free the raw materials that would be used to add to her army of dragonborn. If his initial rage was any indication, she would soon have more than she needed. Enough to claim the Sword by force, if not by seduction. Enough to make the world safe, once and for all, for her and her children.

She permitted herself a small grin, unable to hide her fiendish elation. It lasted until a boulder crashed at her feet, flinging shattered bits of stone in every direction.

Turning from the cavern lair, she left the dragon to his work.

CHAPTER THIRTY-FOUR

Dusk arrived early, ushered in by a turbulent sky of black and gray as Jarom led his eleven-man party southward along the dark edge of Llornel Lake. The storm had intensified over the past two days, blotting out the sun's feeble rays with its thick clouds and pelting sheets of rain. Winds tore at the weary travelers with a lusty zeal, whipping through their tightly wrapped bodies like skeletal fingers, raking and clawing with bone-numbing chill. Fantasies of a fire, dry clothes, and a warm meal were shared by all.

But it had been predetermined by Chief General Corathel that the parties would march until they had attained the southern tip of the heaving lake, an estimated two-day journey from when they had first separated. There they would regroup and discuss whether or not to alter their strategy before turning west to cross the rugged plains. Not until then, all agreed, would they pause to rest—despite this hounding night.

It was only fitting, Jarom decided, that nature offer a constant reminder as to their plight. Like the earth around them, the world was disintegrating, being washed away in a muddy torrent of chaos. Like the storm clouds overhead, the future was a bleak and harrowing prospect rolling in upon them, black and inexorable. Lands had been ravaged; lives had been uprooted and destroyed. For their surroundings to be anything but a cheerless reflection of their hearts and souls would have seemed utterly incongruous.

Nevertheless, Jarom was sick of the cold and dreary darkness. He had been traveling for three days now since reuniting with Corathel and the others, two as the leader of this company. It was up to him to keep morale high and to prevent spirits from faltering—a task that seemed more and more difficult as they became more worn down.

He told himself there was no help for it but to keep plodding on. But he could not help but think that he was missing something, something he could be doing to affect matters in a positive manner. Despite Marisha's constant assurances—or perhaps because of them—he sensed that he was failing them all, and that if he did not figure out quickly what it was he was supposed to do, it would be too late.

With his head and will bent against the passion of the storm, he trudged blindly through the gloom. He nearly tripped over the object before spying it. A moment later, he saw it for what it was, a human carcass, mangled and twisted beyond recognition, wrapped in the familiar surcoat and partial plate armor of a Parthan soldier.

He called a halt, the horror in his stomach causing him to forget for a moment his dire hunger. He knelt beside the body, turning it over to find the man's face. Half of it had been caved inward, a ruined mash of flesh and bone and missing teeth. What remained was frozen in a mask of terror. Though no longer steaming, his blood was still warm.

Jarom spun away, fighting hard not to retch, grateful now that his stomach was empty. Before he could think to suggest it himself, Maltyk hobbled up and sent forth the members of their tiny company to scour the area. Nine more bodies were located, all crushed and mutilated like the first, discarded like midden. Weapons lay scattered about or clenched in unyielding fists, many of them broken. It was the party immediately in front of their own, led by Second General Jasyn. The general himself was unaccounted for, and Maltyk promptly ordered an expanded search that would focus on finding traces of the man, as well as any signs that might indicate the fate of those parties gone before.

"Look at these prints!" Jarom gasped, crouched in private conversation with Maltyk and Allion. The three men knelt

over a small crater in the earth, a footprint nearly twice as
long as a man's and almost as wide. Identical tracks had been
found all over the area, pools filled with water from the sopping heavens.

"This was no wolf," Allion observed grimly.

"We found a trail through the brush that leads to the
water's edge, sir," a young colonel reported. "It may have
belonged to General Jasyn."

"What about the others?" Jarom asked, blinking against
the rain, feeling it stream down the sides of his nose. "Those
that passed before?"

"There's no indication they fell under attack. It appears
whatever came through here found only General Jasyn's
party."

"But is in pursuit of the others," Jarom added.

Allion stared at him. "Or waiting for others to come by."

Jarom cast about nervously, probing the mist that had
rolled in off the lake. He listened silently to the steady drumming of rainfall and the restless churning of the lake's waves
against the shore, searching for the danger that lurked just
beyond his limited range of vision. He glanced at Marisha,
who was examining the fallen to make sure that none could
be saved, then turned to Maltyk.

"We'd best not stay here. I think we should try to catch up
with Lar and Rynar."

Maltyk rested a palm against his swollen and bandaged
knee, and winced. "You won't be able to make it with me.
I'll hang back and warn Corathel."

A couple of the men gasped as a silent figure materialized
out of the darkness. Jarom jumped to his feet, freeing the
Sword from its scabbard. He was approached by a hooded
wraith, a chameleon in a green-gray cloak.

"I'll take care o' that."

Jarom heaved a sigh of relief. "Kylac. It's good to see you."

"Lar and Rynar have already been warned," Kylac informed them, the rain dripping from his face and hood, "and
are waiting for ya'll to join 'em. I'll notify Corathel."

"Any sign of Jasyn?" Maltyk asked.

Kylac nodded. "He's with the others. Lad was lucky to get away. I'll spare ya the details. They're a shade gruesome."

"All right," Jarom said. "Let's gather—"

The remainder of his words stuck in his throat as a sudden shriek pierced the night. One and all whirled in the direction of the cry, weapons drawn. This time, there was no searching, no scouring of the mists. Before them stood a creature that Jarom recognized, a massive man chiseled from shiny black stone, all jagged and rough-edged. At eight feet, it towered easily over the tallest of them, with thick limbs and a squarish head. Its eyes blazed with what had become a familiar green glow. How anything that large and heavy could have stolen upon them, even in the mists, was incomprehensible. Yet there it stood, mere paces from where they had gathered, with a freshly broken body writhing in its huge, craggy hands.

While the rest of them stood agape, Kylac put himself before the demon, his cloak flung wide, his slender blades weaving slowly in the rain-swept air before him. For a moment, the stone giant ignored the youth, its blazing eyes making a sweep of the entire group. It paused when it spied Jarom and the glowing Sword, though its sculpted features gave not a hint as to its thoughts or feelings. Then it looked back to Kylac, and without so much as a grunt, crumpled the carcass in its hands before flinging it aside and lumbering forward to meet the young master's challenge.

With a speed and agility that belied its size, the stone demon launched a pulverizing fist toward the waiting youth. But Kylac remained the quicker, disappearing and then reappearing behind his assailant. His blades flew to their work, chipping away at the beast's legs, jointed pillars of gleaming obsidian. Sparks flew, winking in and out like fireflies around the point of contact. The living monolith, however, simply whirled about, unscarred by the youth's assault and undeterred from its goal.

Kylac didn't hesitate. Ducking a second blow, he slipped past beneath the demon's armpit, trailing with his lethal blades in a reversed grip, slashing mercilessly against the stone torso. But Jarom saw, with mounting horror, the same results as before. The youth's blades, the strength of which were unmatched by any weapon other than the Crimson Sword itself, had failed to mar the demon's gleaming skin.

"I can't scratch it!" Kylac howled in warning. If he was rattled by the discovery, his voice did not reflect it. "Go!" he shouted while sidestepping another punch. "Continue south! I'll holds him off!"

Jarom's thoughts raced. The youth's bravery was all well and good, but if he could not scratch the beast, then he could not kill it, and thereby posed no more than a nuisance to this creature from which he sought to save them all.

With a determined shout, Jarom charged to the aid of his young friend. He attacked the beast from behind, intent on smashing it to rubble. The Crimson Sword arced high overhead. But at the last possible moment, he was met by a wide-flung backhand that forced him to lower his strike. He did so in an instant. Sword and stone clashed, sheathing flames leaping forth as the blade sliced through a forearm as thick as a man's chest, severing the demon's hand and wrist. Blood poured from the wound, a spray of molten rock that splattered upon the wet grasses beneath and turned them to ash.

But the creature offered no indication of pain, audible or otherwise. Nor did the blow slow the windmill strike of its remaining hand. A closed fist crunched into Jarom and sent him hurtling through the air. He flew backwards, stars in his eyes, replaying in his mind his defeat at the hands of this same creature upon the battlefield at Kraagen Keep. The only difference was that this time, he somehow managed to cling to the Sword, landing with a splash in the rain-soaked mud at the lake's edge, where all the world spun out of control.

He rolled himself up onto an elbow, struggling to maintain focus. He could not let himself black out as he had against the serpentine lizard in the ruins of Thrak-Symbos and again at Bane Draw. Doing so would mean his end. He heard Marisha cry out in dismay. Through a haze of shifting lines, he watched her come for him, then looked past her, trying to find where it was that Kylac and the demon had gone to.

Undaunted, the youth was making his third pass at the giant, aiming his blades this time into the stump of its severed arm. His strike was true, one blade following the other to stab at the open wound. Again, though, his efforts proved futile, his swords unable to damage further the veins of molten rock that burned throughout the demon's adamantine flesh. That his weapons survived contact with the flaming blood was incredible, but even then, they could do little more than scrape harmlessly against the impenetrable layers of stone tissue.

As the youth dropped to a crouch, dancing clear of the lava stream crawling forward at the monster's feet, the remainder of the company took up the fight. A barrage of arrows pelted the beast, several striking about the head and eyes, drawing its attention from Kylac. But all bounced away, their sharp heads blunted or broken, collecting on the ground like the bones of wildfowl at a king's feast. A moment later, the shower ceased as the first trio of foot soldiers closed in.

With howls of madness they charged, bodies weaving in practiced formation, weapons cleaving the air. Two lunged at the demon's flanks, aiming high, while a third dove at its knees. Of the first pair, one man caught a flying fist in the face, crumpling instantly as his skull caved inward. The other actually struck the demon a glancing blow to the shoulder, only to catch an elbow that shattered his rib cage and sent him staggering backwards. The third man, aiming low, was knocked aside by a jagged knee, where he teetered momentarily before splashing to his back in a puddle of the demon's blood. His wail was cut short as the molten rock melted his spine and burned a gaping hole in his lungs.

As the first wave fell, a second, larger group rushed in. In defiance of what they had witnessed thus far, the soldiers thrust at the demon with their blades of iron and steel. Jarom was on his knees now, helped by Marisha, who was checking him for critical damage. He did his best to ignore her, but could not seem to find the strength to push her away. Instead, he watched as the majority of those maneuvering into striking distance were smashed by either a stone fist or flaming stump, while those few who actually struck the creature found their assaults to be as ineffectual as those that had gone before. Except to the Crimson Sword, gripped loosely in Jarom's hands, the demon was invincible.

Managing at last to breathe deeply and see clearly, Jarom pulled free and started back toward the battle. His friends were dying, and it seemed that he alone could save them. Nothing, he would have thought, could stop him from doing so.

He was wrong.

Marisha's scream stopped him in his tracks and spun him hard about. He found her flat on her back, a tentacle lined with barbs wrapped about her ankle. The serpentine arm belonged to a second demon, a hideous, shell-covered leech risen up from the lake's waters, half hidden in the rushes. It gave a yank. The line of barbs dug into Marisha's flesh, and then she was sliding toward the creature, her fingers raking up handfuls of mud.

Jarom rushed to save her. Following the tentacle to its roots, he spied the creature's mouth, with mandibles that parted to reveal a slime webbing stretched over a nest of tongues and teeth. He tried not to think of it as he charged ahead, coming up beside Marisha to chop through the arm that held her, halting her progress.

The water demon gave a terrible, stuttering squeal. Jarom glanced at it as he kicked away the severed appendage and helped Marisha to her feet. A pair of soldiers came skidding up to stand beside him. He could not even manage a warning before the creature exploded from the lake in a frenzy of movement.

A dozen tentacles whipped through the air, snapping about like banners caught in a strong wind. At the end of each was a tiny maw, ringed with needlelike teeth that clicked together hungrily. Jarom raised his blade in time to deflect the tentacles that lashed at him. The Parthan soldiers were not so lucky. Intercepting the brunt of the assault, they raised their heavy axes in a valiant effort to protect their comrades. They may as well have been chopping at roaches in the dark. The flailing arms were simply too fast, and too strong. One of the men scored a minor nick before his weapon was swatted away. The other managed not even that. Both were torn apart. In a horrific display, the leech beat them into submission with the sides of its tentacles, barbs tearing. It then began to devour their outer flesh—not like a lion, with its central mouth, but like a swarm of rats, with those at the ends of its arms. The men cried out, then vanished in a red spray that showered Jarom and Marisha as they scrambled away. By the time Jarom looked back, all that remained was a pair of bloody skeletons, ravaged and lacerated beyond recognition.

Something about the deaths struck Jarom as horridly familiar. He slipped and stumbled, and both he and Marisha went down. As the leech came for them, pulling its body from the rushes, Jarom realized what the corpses reminded him of—the Nieten! The creature that was to have devoured him during his swim across the bog in the jungles of Vosges. He recalled then how the Powaii had found it, as though it had been fed upon by a school of flesh-eating fish. If the signature of death was any indication, he now knew what had saved him.

There was no time to confirm his suspicions. All that mattered was that the same beast was here now to slay him.

"Move!" he hollered at Marisha. Blood was dripping from her lower leg where the demon had seized her. She rose to her feet, only to fall again, her soft leather boots slipping and sliding in the marshy earth. Jarom spun back to the lake as the writhing mass of saw-blade tentacles reached for them.

In the next instant, Kylac was there, leaping into the vortex of that whipping storm.

"No!" Jarom cried, then felt his eyes go wide and his jaw go slack. In all their shared encounters, he had never seen the youth move so fast. Left and right, he almost flew, then forward and back. Like a thrashing rag doll, every part of him seemed to move independently. But what appeared a reckless flailing of fear and desperation was in fact a whirlwind of movements both calculated and instinctive. Somehow, the youth was still alive, alone in the midst of those shredding arms. And, Jarom realized, gaining the upper hand.

Though armored with a shell-like coating, the leech's tentacles were no match for the honed edges of Kylac's blades. Chunks of severed flesh dropped to the earth, hissing angrily as they splashed into wet pools, and the amphibious demon screeched in pain. The creature intensified its attack, but the youth, as always, held his ground. Black blood flew through the air in gouts as the demon continued to squirm, flinging its severed appendages in all directions. One by one, its arms grew shorter, until finally, improbably, it began to back away.

Jarom scrambled to his feet.

"Behind us!" Kylac shouted.

Jarom whirled. The stone demon was lumbering toward them, the weight of its crushing footfalls absorbed by the spongy earth. Ignoring the pathetic attempts of those soldiers who sought to slow its advance, it was coming now for Jarom and the Sword.

Marisha was retreating behind him, a knife in hand, back toward the lake. He trusted that Kylac would continue to shield her from the water demon, but it was up to him to shield them all from the stone giant. Allion was bombarding the giant with a steady stream of arrows, but to no avail. Nothing could deter the beast. Nothing but him.

Tired of running, tired of hiding, tired of fear, Jarom coiled, bracing for the assault, the Sword warm in his hands.

A sudden, scintillating light caused him to squint and turn his head. The accompanying thunderclap nearly knocked him from his feet. When he looked up, he found the obsidian giant stopped in its tracks, a steady stream of lightning crackling down from the heavens to stun its massive frame. Blinded by the glare, Jarom cast about in bewilderment. Thin white bolts continued to pour down from the black clouds above, forcing the demon to its knees. Then he saw the old man, a towering frame cloaked in brown robes. He could not see a face, for the man's head was bowed in concentration. But he saw the gnarled, outstretched hands, cupped skyward, calling forth in steady summons to the brilliant, thundering streams.

The man fell to one knee.

"The Sword!" he snarled. "I can't keep this up forever."

Jarom rushed forward as commanded, his movements stiff and disjointed in the flashing light. He came up directly in front of the mostly paralyzed demon, which reached for him. Without hesitation, he plunged the blade, bursting with crimson flames, through the creature's chest. When he tore the weapon free, the demon's blood gushed forth in a wash of flaming heat, forcing him away. At the same time, the cascade of lightning ceased, freeing the demon from its prison. Jarom braced for a response, but the brute was already finished, falling forward to splash facedown in its own blood. It made no other sound, and gave not a single twitch. Its massive body simply melted into steam and was borne away by the wind.

The sounds of battle, however, remained. Jarom spun back to the lake, prepared now to help Kylac finish off the water demon. He should have known better. Despite the creature's unrestrained frenzy, the youth had found his rhythm, striking with increasing frequency and relentless precision. As Jarom and the others looked on, Kylac's blades bit into the demon's head, piercing its shell to expose the mushy flesh beneath. The weapons withdrew, ripping up and down, then went in again. Flogging tentacles swatted at him, only to be sent away in pieces. The beast had made it back to the water, but it was too late for retreat. At last, the whir of the youth's blades ceased as the green glow left the creature's eyes and its lifeless body sank from view beneath the roiling lake.

Kylac held ready at the water's edge a moment longer, his chest heaving from his sustained efforts. Jarom moved forward to put an arm around Marisha.

"I'm fine," she said. "Let me tend to the others."

Together, the three turned back toward the rest of their company, only to find a dark-bearded, thin-limbed giant of a man coming to meet them.

"We owe ya our lives," Kylac offered in greeting.

"Then I no longer owe you mine," the man huffed in reply. "Where is the book?"

Jarom glanced between the two, then found the older man glaring down upon him.

"How do you . . . ?" He stopped himself, putting it all together. "An Entient? An Entient of Whitlock?"

"As clever as you are fortunate," the aged man snapped. "Do you possess the book or not?"

"I have it here," piped Allion, striding forward with the muddy leather bag in tow. "It's an honor—"

The Entient growled irritably, snatching the bag from Allion and removing from it the hefty tome. He ran his fingers gently over the cover.

Jarom felt a rush of elation, a profound sense of justification in his and Allion's longtime efforts to retain the artifact. He glanced at his friend and found the other beaming with shared enthusiasm.

"You know," Allion told the old man, "you're lucky we still have that thing."

The Entient regarded the hunter with a withering scowl as he opened the book and began leafing through its pages. From his vantage, Jarom just barely caught a glimpse of the phantom writings as they began to reappear, coaxed forth by the old man's touch.

"How did you find us?" he dared ask.

"I've been looking," the other responded gruffly. He snapped the book shut with a measure of satisfaction. "Come."

Jarom frowned. "Where are we going?"

"The time has come to pay your respects to those who facilitated your recovery of the Sword."

Jarom shared with Allion another disbelieving glance. "Then it *was* you who was behind all of this."

"Cast not your blame upon me," came the bitter retort as the old man stuffed the tome back into its bag. "I and many others have been opposed to this scheme from the first."

"But someone you know. Another of your order—"

"Of course." The old man's glowing blue eyes glinted

with cruel amusement. "Surely you do not still prefer some ethereal notion of universal preordination to explain away all that has transpired."

Jarom could only stare, openmouthed and silent, no longer certain what he believed.

The other gave a derisive snort. "Keep to it, then. What you call destiny, I call the machinations of tired old men. Regardless, my associates expect now to see this Sword of Asahiel, and in return, will share with you how you might vanquish the Demon Queen—if it even be possible."

Jarom could think of no response, and so stood unmoving, lashed by wind and rain as the old man slung the leather bag over his shoulder and began marching toward his waiting steed. The moans of those who had been wounded in the fight against the demons echoed in the night and drew his attention. He looked around, taking in an array of injuries to which Marisha was dutifully attending.

"Some are hurt," he managed.

"Any of those who accompanied you in your retrieval of the Sword?"

"No. But—"

"But what? This is your war, not mine. If you wish to know how you might survive it, come with me. But do not ask me to wait. I have wasted too much time already."

Jarom found Marisha, who looked up from where she crouched beside the shattered arm of a nearby soldier.

"Go," she said. "These men need my attention."

"I won't leave you," he said stubbornly, childishly.

"Go," she repeated, more firmly this time. "Learn what you must. I'll be waiting for you in Kuuria."

"Looks like you've got no choice," Maltyk grunted, limping up beside Marisha. The Third General gave a nod toward the Entient, who had finished securing his leather bag to the saddle of his mount and was stretching his left foot for the stirrups.

Jarom looked back to Marisha and Maltyk. The right side of the lieutenant general's face was masked in blood. "We'll wait here for Corathel and then meet up with the others," the commander assured him. "She'll be safe."

"Wounded or not," the Entient offered brusquely, shifting uncomfortably in his saddle, "I'd recommend moving now. At the very least, get away from the water. If you've not yet figured it out, that is how the Queen's demons get from place to place."

With that, the old man gave a slap of his reins and started away into the night.

"This is happening too fast," Jarom protested, searching madly for another option.

"All the more reason to get moving," Kylac argued, his eyes tracing the departure of the Entient. Already the old man was fading away into the evening mists.

Jarom felt as though he were being drawn and quartered. He knew he must go with the Entient—not only to learn what he could of the Demon Queen, but to discover once and for all the unsettling truth of his own life. And yet, to leave Marisha when they had only so recently been re-united . . .

His mouth worked uselessly, ready to churn out any number of alternatives. But the facts of the situation were stacked against any argument he might raise. The protests he intended to summon sounded in his own mind flimsy and foolish. There was nothing more to be said, nothing left to be done.

He stared back at Marisha, whose eyes lifted to share with him a lingering glance. Something in her look suggested that she might actually be sharing his torment. But he saw also her determination. He had asked her to leave others behind before. She would not be asked to do so again.

He started to go to her when a low moan drew her back to her work. With no other choice, Jarom turned away, towed by Kylac and Allion after the steadily departing Entient.

CHAPTER THIRTY-FIVE

Jarom rode with head bowed along the deserted mountain slope. Muddy trails had long since given way to unbroken stone, high up within the Aspandel Mountains. The air was thin and cold and as brittle as fine porcelain. Overhead, the skies continued to churn, swirling black clouds dripping dark rain upon them. They had already gone higher and deeper into the range than he had with Allion when searching for the Entients' stronghold weeks ago. He knew not how much farther they had to go, but realized now just how foolish he'd been to think he might ever find the place himself.

He watched his breath cloud before him in the moonlight, keeping dolefully silent. Any excitement he might have felt at the prospect of entering Whitlock and meeting with the mystical Entients had long since deserted him. It had been a rough journey, taxing to both mind and body. Soon after Marisha and the remaining members of his company had been swallowed by the lakeside mists, their sounds drowned out by the plodding footfalls of the rider he and his companions followed, Jarom had found his thoughts flush with questions. He had mulled them over for a time, trying to place them in sequence, but they danced around like a flurry of snowflakes, and he thought of new ones with every step. At last, he had given up on any sensible arrangement and simply began asking them, only to have his hopes for resolution swiftly dashed.

"Many of your questions will never be answered," the Entient had grumbled. "Those that will, will be answered at Whitlock and not before."

He had thought the flat response unnecessarily rude, but was not foolish enough to express that sentiment. Instead, he had settled back with his friends, slogging along in their mounted guide's muddy wake. The petulant old man had time for nothing. He had already refused them a brief stop to the south to explain the situation to Lar and Rynar, who would have begun by then to worry over the late arrival of Jarom's company.

"Let them worry. The truth will be known soon enough. There is no need for you to waste everyone's time."

It was this that had caused Jarom to be wary of asking the Entient anything further. But there was so much he wished to know, and he had feared that by waiting, he would forget some of those questions and fail to ask them later. He had hoped that if careful in his approach, he might be able to coax the old codger from his shell. Alas, he may as well have tried talking a fish from the water or an owl into the light.

They had pressed onward until midnight before the Entient surprised them all by allowing them to stop for the evening. They had done so at an abandoned farmstead, whose fleeing owners had left behind a stable full of starving horses. The Entient himself, still nameless to those who followed, had seemed tireless. If he settled down to sleep, he had been the last to do so. And before sunrise the next morning he had roused them with a rough shake, not a word.

They had emptied the stables, keeping three of the animals as steeds and setting the rest free. They had eaten while they rode, partaking of roots and berries—provided by the Entient—that none of the friends had seen before. They had done so in silence. Not only did the old man refuse to speak, but he preferred that no one else did either. So they had respected his wishes, keeping their thoughts focused on what lay ahead. Although, if the rest of the Entients were even half as cantankerous as this one, Jarom wondered why they bothered.

With the entire company on horseback, they had made

good time across the sodden plains of southern Partha. To the south, the black shadow of the Kalmira Forest had flanked them, a mysterious labyrinth choked with mist. Ahead had loomed the Aspandels, a rugged mound of sloping peaks all folded one upon the other like an immense blanket dropped to the earth by some giant passerby. By sunset, marked only by a dimming of the faint glow within the western clouds, they had pulled themselves free of the sucking grasslands and worked their way into the drier, rockier terrain of the deep mountains.

Which was where they stood now. Jarom, for one, was cold and weary and sick of the entire affair. Not a moment had gone by in which he had not thought of Marisha and worried for her safety. Or that of the others, for that matter. Without him and Kylac, what chance did they stand if they faced another attack? He had deserted them, and the reasons for doing so, so clear and sound at the time, seemed now vague and insubstantial.

He was also afraid. Not of what he might learn about the Demon Queen, but of what he might learn of himself. So much of his courage and confidence had been wrapped up in what had become an unshakable belief that it was his destiny to find the Sword and use it to help the peoples of these lands. If what the Entient suggested was true, if his success had been driven not by fate but by the hidden goals of this secret order, what might that mean for his future endeavors?

Perhaps they were one and the same, fate and the Entients. Or if not, then surely one must dictate the other. Either way, he had been chosen, and he had to believe there was a reason for it. Until he learned otherwise, his faith would remain his shield. As the old man had suggested, the truth would be known soon enough.

They persisted on well into the night, walking their horses at a slow pace to save the beasts from slipping on the wet stone of the winding footpaths here above the tree line. It seemed to Jarom that if they were to take shelter, they should have done so long before in the forests below. But he was not about to start questioning the old man now, not after having held his tongue for so long. It would serve the other right if they all froze to death.

Then, as abruptly as he had appeared to them, the Entient stopped. They stood before a featureless wall of rock, its face covered over with twisting vines and clinging scrub. Jarom glanced at his friends uncertainly as the old man dismounted and marched up to the rock wall. A single hand reached forth from the cocoon of his sopping robes to touch the rugged stone, and he bowed his head in concentration. A moment later, he turned to them, keeping his hand upon the cliff face.

"It is open."

Jarom eyed the wall and then the man skeptically. He had not seen the slightest alteration in the stone's appearance.

"Well, go on! I'm not going to leave it wide to the world all day!"

The three friends glanced at one another with shared uncertainty. Kylac dismounted, with Allion following suit. Jarom met the Entient's glare before reluctantly doing the same.

The youth stepped forward, shoulders hunched with determination. Still he hesitated, looking to the Entient before passing through the wall and vanishing from sight.

Jarom watched Allion's eyes go as wide as his own, but the Entient gave them no time to marvel.

"Go," he growled, "or remain out here."

Together, the two men from Diln mustered enough faith to stride through the magical portal. Like a curtain of smoke, the stone offered no resistance to their passing. Within, they found themselves reunited with Kylac, standing in a narrow, torchlit corridor of mountain stone. Iron arches ran up from along the walls, ribs that helped to support the tall and craggy ceiling. At the far end, directly ahead of them, an immense pair of double doors, also wrought from iron, sealed off further passage. A handful of smaller doors lined the jagged walls, sealing various side tunnels from view. All was flat and unembellished, utilitarian, lacking any form of decoration. Even the air was stale and uninviting, although warmer and drier than the outdoors.

Despite the foyer's stark appearance, Jarom was over-whelmed with a sudden sense of awe. Whitlock, fabled home of the Entients. A place few believed to exist at all. And yet here he stood, he and his friends, welcomed into yet another inner sanctum of the forgotten world.

"What about the horses?" Kylac asked as their reluctant host appeared beside them.

"They will be tended to."

He offered no further explanation. Nor did he allow them additional time to appreciate their surroundings. In a rush of brown robes that swept the earthen floor, the towering man marched down the tunnel. Before reaching the vaulted dou-ble doors, he turned to his right and lay his palm upon one of the smaller ones embedded in the side wall. It swung open without a whisper of sound.

"Come."

The three young visitors obeyed, shaking the rain from their cloaks and shuffling forward. The Entient stood at the open door, pointing inward, herding them into the chamber beyond. His tall frame blocked all other passage. Jarom watched Kylac and Allion duck inside compliantly. But when his turn came, he couldn't help but crane his neck past the Entient and direct his gaze down the hall toward the double iron doors, wondering what secrets lay hidden beyond.

"You try my patience, young Sword-bearer."

Jarom glanced up, and with the old man's scowl like a yoke upon his shoulders, slipped inside after his friends.

He found them waiting for him within, where a dozen men draped in long white robes busied themselves at a table, upon which lay a scattered array of scrolls and tomes. Like the corridor through which they had passed, the room was otherwise empty, stark and windowless and musty with age.

"Ah, you've arrived," one of the men exclaimed.

Books were closed, scrolls tucked away. Jarom and his companions remained silent. For the most part, the Entients all looked the same, tall and robed, with hair and beards gone gray or white. Their faces were long and wizened and bore the scars of centuries. Their eyes, however, were of a crystalline blue so bright and sharp they almost seemed to glow.

"Greetings, friends," remarked a second of those gathered, seated at the table's head. While the others worked around him, this man sat calmly, a trace of a smirk upon his thin lips. "I trust Ranunculus did not ruin your trip entirely."

Jarom glanced back at the Entient who had led them here, who with his peppered black beard now appeared quite young when compared to the others. His only response to the elder's remark was a caustic glare.

"Relax, my friend. You are home again."

Ranunculus muttered to himself and turned away.

"Are you not going to view the Sword?" one called after him. It was the first who had greeted them, a gray-hair.

"I've seen it," Ranunculus grumbled in reply as he stalked from the room.

"But the rest of us have not."

Jarom turned to find the white-haired leader focusing upon him with those sapphire eyes.

"Come, young man. Let us glimpse this shard of divinity."

Behind Ranunculus, the iron door slammed shut.

Killangrathor worked feverishly, thrusting yet another boulder into the river of magma that churned its way through his mountain lair. He held it there for a moment as he worked his birthing magic, using his innate powers to channel Krakken's blood into the stone. When it was finished, he pulled the egg free and set it aside, his scaled hand unscarred by the terrible heat of the molten earth.

Almost at once, the outer layers crumbled away, revealing another of his dragonborn. The beast hissed and cried, flinging the crumbled bits of its shell into the lava river from which it had been bred. Killangrathor helped to brush away the excess stone, which melted into streaks of oily blue waste and was swept away by the river's flow toward the distant collection pool. The pool itself sputtered and boiled, the whole of its flaming surface turned blue with the magical residue.

The dragon scraped another fistful of rock from the cavern wall. As he did so, his most recent creation stumbled about the river's craggy bank. Though fully matured, its first steps were awkward. Before it could turn toward the chamber wherein its brethren waited, it lost its balance and splashed into the lava stream. Killangrathor glanced over, but made no effort to rescue the unworthy creature, sneering as it thrashed about and was carried downstream. While the molten earth did not harm it, the streaks of magical waste burned through its throat and torso like flaming spears. Killangrathor watched until its carcass floated into the collection pool, where it was devoured as if by acid.

When it was gone, the dragon plunged a fresh boulder into the lava, keeping clear of the destructive blue wastes, and gave birth to another seed.

"Forged at the dawn of time," the one called Maventhrowe recounted. "Blessed with all of the divine power and wisdom of the Ceilhigh for use in the creation of this earth."

Jarom returned the weapon to its sheath with a private sigh. He had been at this for close to an hour now, and had yet to learn anything that would justify abandoning Marisha and the others. One by one, the Entients in attendance had introduced themselves, a litany of names that Jarom had not even tried to remember. There were two exceptions: the welcoming gray-hair, Htomah, and the white-hair to whom the others seemed to defer, Maventhrowe. After that, they had made formal their request to view the Sword, bidding Jarom keep his questions in check. He had obliged them, having little choice, and watched them pass the talisman around the table. Each Entient handled it in turn, offering an exclamation of wonder and delight, remarking on its splendor in hushed and solemn tones.

While they did so, Jarom had been urged to share where and how, precisely, he had found the Sword. Feeling awkward and insignificant among beings who existed somewhere between the realms of god and man, Jarom had shared for what seemed the hundredth time the tale of his adventure through the ruins of Thrak-Symbos. He painted with his words a description of the fallen city. He betrayed with his voice the emotions with which he had grappled, the alternating feelings of awe, exhilaration, and fear. He told them of their guide, Cwingen U'uyen, of their search through the catacombs, of their battle with the strange and deadly serpentine lizard, of the Sword's resting place and appearance, and of the enchanted portals that had opened up once they had claimed the talisman as their own, enabling their escape.

The Entients had listened attentively throughout, allowing him to proceed at his own pace. They did not interrupt, did not ask questions, did not express emotion of any kind. They just sat there concentrating, seeming to memorize every detail of the oration—much of which, he sensed, they already knew. If what he told them shed light on any of the mysteries yet surrounding the blade or the fall of the ancient Finlorian city, they kept it to themselves.

When it was over, Maventhrowe had handed back the Sword and permitted him his first question. Had it happened earlier, Jarom would not have known where to begin. But the course of their meeting had turned his thoughts squarely to the Sword. He had not missed how brilliantly the talisman glowed at the touch of these men, its illumination engulfing the chamber at their unspoken desire. Thus, his most immediate craving was to know more of its true history and powers.

"They were never meant for mortal hands," Maventhrowe continued to explain. "But a little more than seven thousand years ago, when the children of the Dragon God unleashed at His command a campaign of conquest upon this earth, the elven avatars in possession of the Swords had little choice but to pass them on to the elves of the time, else risk watching the Finlorians and all other inhabitants be destroyed."

Jarom nodded patiently. He was not looking for a recitation of legends he already knew.

"Of course, the Finlorians prevailed, and were given to keep the Swords. Over time, they were stolen, purchased, and stolen again, obtained through murder and outright war, until eventually, all were lost. That which you now hold was passed down along the lines of Finlorian royalty since the close of the Dragon Wars, only to be buried with their greatest city an eon ago, claimed by the forces of nature. Despite the efforts of countless thieves, treasure hunters, and fools, it was not to be seen again."

"You have called it an instrument of peace and order," Jarom prompted. "How am I to unlock its power against this chaos that threatens us?"

"The secrets concerning its power disappeared even before the Finlorian elves," Maventhrowe replied sadly, "and have yet to be fully reclaimed. But understand what it means when I say that the Sword's power is divine. It is without limitation, except that which we as mortals would place upon it. The wielder, therefore, is the one who determines its strength."

Despite every effort to maintain a tone and posture of complete respect, Jarom was aghast. He had truly believed that once here among the Entients, he would learn all that he needed in order to unleash the full magnitude of the blade's power, as described in the fables and legends he had grown up with. It seemed impossible that these self-proclaimed avatars of the human race, men who professed dealings that could not be fully understood by mortals such as he, should know nothing more than that which he had already divined for himself. If so, then why had he come? Had he truly been summoned for no other reason than to help fill a void in their histories?

He leaned forward in his seat at the ironwood table, flanked by Allion and Kylac to either side. "Then why me? Why was I chosen?"

"Chosen?" the Entient echoed with a bemused expression. "So much time has passed that few even believe in the Swords of Asahiel, or in anything of the world as it was before the coming of man. In you we saw a person with the faith and desire and need to retrieve this weapon of legend. But it was you who elected this course, long ago. The recovery of the Sword was your doing. We merely did what we could to help you along."

"The book," Allion surmised. "You sent it with your friend to Earthwyn, to be delivered to us."

Maventhrowe nodded.

"But if it was intended for us," the hunter asked, "why was it warded against our touch?"

"Our tomes are warded against any but an Entient's hands," Maventhrowe clarified. "A general safeguard. Ranunculus was to meet you at the library, as a scholar who could show you what you needed to be on your way—chiefly, the location of Thrak-Symbos. As it happened," he added, glancing sidelong at Htomah, "things did not unfold exactly as we had planned. Nevertheless, it would seem our trust in your dedication was well placed."

"Why did you not come for us before?" Jarom asked. "Before we headed east, we searched for you here within these mountains. Surely you knew this at the time. If you truly wished for me to succeed, why did you not give me these answers to begin with?"

There was a bitter edge to his voice. Though much of this was as he'd suspected from the first, it bothered him to think that he had been so easily manipulated. As this conversation lengthened, he found himself feeling more and more defensive, less trusting of these meddlesome creatures who were perhaps partly responsible for all that he had endured.

Maventhrowe sighed. "We contemplated doing just that. But it was decided that you had as much information as we had to give you. The only thing more we could have provided was the sure knowledge that the Sword existed." He paused, fixing Jarom with a mischievous gleam in his eye. "But you knew, did you not? You already had a perfect faith in the Sword. Had you failed, had you surrendered to your despair, then you would have proven yourself unworthy, and we would have seen to it that another made the journey in your stead."

"What?" Jarom wheezed, the wind stolen from his lungs.

"There were others before you, in recent centuries. At this time, you were our first choice, our best choice, but not the only one to whom we thought we could turn. He may lack your strong sense of purpose, but young master Kronus here seemed a worthy alternative, which was why we led him to you."

Kylac shot the other a suspicious look. "Led? How was I led?"

"Subtle promptings," the Entient replied, waving the question aside. "Dreams, thoughts, the direction of the wind. You would not have noticed. You wander much of the time without regard for your ultimate destination. It is this that caused some to question your potential use, but it made for us an easy enough task to direct you down this path."

Jarom barely registered the old man's words. There it was, spelled out for him at last, the horrible truth he had sought to avoid. All this time, he had been acting under the false assumption that he was somehow preordained for this purpose. Shielded by his faith in the immutable power of destiny, he had embarked on an incredible—an impossible—quest. Worse, he had dragged others along with him, endangering their lives, because all along he had believed that nothing could reroute the waters of fate upon which his vessel ran. Now, suddenly, that vessel was wrecked upon a hidden reef, its hull shredded, its masts splintered by harsh waves of reality.

"And the Nieten?" he asked, already knowing the answer.

"Ironic, is it not?" Maventhrowe confirmed with a smile. "That one of Spithaera's scouts should inadvertently clear your way to the talisman she now covets?"

Irony, not destiny. Like the life he had been raised to believe was his, this entire journey had been a lie. He was a pawn. A plaything of the Ceilhigh and of beings who resided a step below. The Sword was his by mistake. A chance roll of the dice. Neither the weapon nor its power belonged to him. He knew nothing of either, and understood now, too late, that he never would. There was to be no sudden revelation, no euphoric moment of realization in which he would take command of the blade and fulfill his destiny. There was nothing in the stars to predict his eventual triumph over the forces of darkness. There was only the raw, stinging truth, set free at last. That the history of his race upon these lands was about to come to an end because he—a frightened

young man with a belief in a greater power that did not
exist—had assumed he could prevent it.

"I can't do this." A sickening feeling churned within the
pit of his stomach, wrenching at muscles and organs and
forcing bile into his throat. How had this happened? How
had he become so deluded? How, given the mercy of the
gods, could he have been so selfish and wrongheaded?

"The Sword is yours," Maventhrowe reminded him, seeing right through his fears. "You have already succeeded in
what you set out to do. Do not let our small influence belit-
tle what you have accomplished."

But Jarom found no solace in the other's reassurances. "I
only sought the Sword because—"

"Because you felt powerless to fulfill the duties assigned
to you. Because you wished to reclaim the peace of your
past."

"Yes. And I thought . . . It seemed destined that I—"

"Destiny is what you make of it. Your faith in its power
has granted you rare determination, but be warned, it cannot
shield you from the horrors you must now face. Like the
Sword, its strengths and weaknesses are yours to decide.
Knowing that, whose shoulders would you cast this burden
upon?"

Jarom slouched in his seat, worn and confused. A flame
flickered at the center of the table, thrashing against the
glass walls of its lamp casing: a fly caught in a spider's web.
He stared at it, feeling much the same, trapped by the silence
of the room around him. A victim of his own choices and, as
Ranunculus had put it, the machinations of tired old men.

And yet, Maventhrowe was right. He could not help what
had already been done. He didn't know how to proceed, with
his belief in destiny shattered and nothing more than his own
strength to rely upon. But if he was to run, who would assume the responsibility? He looked to his friends, those who
had risked so much on his behalf—first Kylac, then Allion.
Finally, his eyes fell to the hilt of the Sword. His fingers
played about the flaming heartstones encrusted within the
weblike patterns of silver, seeking comfort not to be found.

At last, he lifted his gaze in helpless resignation. "How

can I be expected to wield a weapon I know nothing about against one such as the Demon Queen?"

"The forces of magic once used to defeat the Queen no longer exist in today's world," Maventhrowe acknowledged. His tone remained slow and casual, as though nothing of which they spoke was of any real concern. "Spithaera has come to realize this. But as you have seen, the mere presence of the Crimson Sword will keep her at bay."

"She will not dare to directly challenge the Sword's power so long as she knows nothing of you, its wielder," the one called Htomah added.

Maventhrowe continued as if the other had not spoken. "During this time, she will rely on her armies to secure her position. It is this, her hesitation, that grants you what may be the only opportunity to weaken her before it is too late."

"You must defeat her armies," Htomah explained, "for until then, you cannot begin to challenge her. Succeed, and the Sword may be enough to deter her, perhaps send her into hiding for another thousand years."

"But how?" Jarom snapped, recalling their utter defeat at Kraagen Keep. "How are we to defeat them?"

Maventhrowe shook his head, his great white mane shifting from side to side. "You fight now a war of attrition against the dragonspawn—as you so aptly named them. It is a war you cannot win. Even as we speak, their numbers are increasing."

Jarom gawked. "Increasing?"

"The Queen's armies are not any natural offspring. They are the children of Killangrathor, the mighty black dragon who has lived within Mount Krakken since the days of the Dragon Wars."

"His wisdom and power are matched by no other creature upon this world," Htomah said, "and it is by his magic that the dragonspawn are born."

Maventhrowe regarded them with a grim smile. "As I said, your people chose an appropriate name. Killangrathor uses the fires of the mountain itself to spawn these beasts. Thus, scores become hundreds, which in turn become legions. The longer this war drags on, the more of this enemy you will face."

Jarom gaped. When he spoke, his voice was choked with disbelief. "So this dragon serves the Demon Queen as well?"

"A creature such as Killangrathor serves no one. But his hatred drives him to assist, however he can, in the destruction of humankind. That hatred will only grow more vehement when he learns that you possess a weapon once used to scatter and slay his mighty kin."

Jarom shook his head, reeling from all that he had been told. "So now we have to slay a dragon as well, just to stop our enemy from growing?"

Maventhrowe lifted a wrinkled hand into the air. "If you can slay Killangrathor, then the forces born of his magic cannot be sustained and will cease to exist."

A temporary hush fell over the room. Jarom locked eyes with Kylac, a mirror for his skepticism.

"And you're certain the Sword has the power to defeat him?" Jarom asked, seeking reassurance from any quarter.

Maventhrowe and Htomah glanced at each other while the remainder of the Entients continued to sit in stone-faced observation.

"After careful consideration," Maventhrowe confessed, "we would caution against hunting Killangrathor with the Sword of Asahiel."

Once again, Jarom was incredulous. "Why?"

"Spithaera will be watching for you, and the Sword. She will know your intent and may warn Killangrathor. Fear of the Sword may flush the dragon from his mountain."

"But—"

"To drive him from his self-imposed prison could only result in catastrophe. At best, he would flee and hide. He may not create more dragonspawn, but you will have lost the opportunity to destroy those he has given already to the Queen."

"And at worst?"

Maventhrowe merely shook his head.

"I don't understand," Allion admitted. "How can a creature so powerful fear even the Crimson Sword?"

"You do not command the whole of the Sword's power. Killangrathor does not know this. He has seen the weapon's full fury, and will not have forgotten it. It is what has kept him silent, hidden away all these years."

"What other choice do we have?" Jarom blurted in dismay. "If we cannot hunt him with the Sword, and if he can lay waste our entire armies, what hope do you offer us?"

The Entient's sapphire eyes sparkled. "Killangrathor will bleed if pricked with a weapon strong enough. The true challenge lies in getting close enough to strike."

Jarom wondered what the Entients were getting at, but could not seem to think the information through. He had been force-fed too much, none of it palatable. His question was answered a moment later, however, as the collective gaze of those who had summoned them here found its way to Kylac.

"Me?" the youth balked. For the first time since Jarom had known him, the boy sounded startled.

"Your weapons will be those that vanquish Killangrathor. We have seen this."

Kylac snorted, his surprise giving way to amusement. "Then I suggest ya looks again. Do I seem fool enough to provoke such a creature?"

"Can you think of another better suited to the task?"

"The kind o' man who would hang himself in his own barn," came the easy reply. "Which I ain't."

"But you must," Htomah insisted, rising halfway to his feet. "In this case, there is no one else."

Kylac locked stares with the old man and didn't flinch. The others watched in silence. Jarom shook his head. It wasn't fair of the Entients to ask this of the youth. If any man alive could get close enough to strike at a dragon, it was Kylac Kronus. And if there existed a weapon other than the Crimson Sword that could cleave the monster's flesh, then it would have to be the youth's unique blades. But to suggest that because he fit a need he was somehow responsible for such a burden was ludicrous. It made no more sense than his own calling as king simply because Ellebe, a mother he had never known, had been queen. If the Entients knew something as a result of a vision and could guarantee the results, that might be one thing. But had they not just exposed such predetermined destinies as myth?

When it seemed the air could not grow any more tense, Maventhrowe waved his comrade down. "The choice is yours," he told Jarom and his companions. "You may, of course, elect to leave Killangrathor be and continue fighting the dragonspawn forever. You have heard our counsel. That which you do with it is up to you."

There it was again, that infuriating calm, lackadaisical in its blunt analysis. Jarom could have ripped his own hair out by the roots.

"Why is that?" he demanded. "Why is everything up to us? This is your world, too. Why won't you do more to help?"

He waited for Maventhrowe's expression to tighten, for those great bushy brows to furrow in angry reprimand. But the Entient seemed untroubled by his outburst, regarding him with a look of pity. "We have already sacrificed more than you will ever be able to appreciate. You may trust in us or choose your own path. Whichever judgment you make, I suggest you be swift about it."

Jarom swallowed, staring at the other glumly.

"Have you any other questions?"

Even more than before, Jarom wanted to say. Instead, he made himself ask about the Demon Queen, of how she had come to this realm in the first place and what had caused her to return now—on the off chance that some of it might prove relevant. In response, he learned briefly of the world of men as it had been nearly a thousand years ago, ruled by warring sects of reckless magic-users in the distant land of Sekulon. It was a foolish council of magi that had summoned the Demon Queen to aid in their cause, only to quickly become slave to hers. The result was a vicious twenty-year war between the armies of those who resisted and those who were seduced by the dark queen. When the Entients became involved, as they were now, the tides had turned. Rather than risk being destroyed utterly, Spithaera had slipped away, abandoning her hordes of men and goblins, which were swiftly scattered. Most believed her vanquished, although Maventhrowe and his kin had been warned by their forefathers to anticipate her return.

Ironically, while it was forces of magic that had enabled mankind to survive, the close of this war marked the end of the age in which its practice was predominant. Turning his back to the arcane arts, man had set his sights instead on taming the seas and colonizing lands beyond his own. Not two decades following Spithaera's withdrawal, the first human settlers had staked claim to these wild shores, not knowing the Queen herself had done the same. So it was that now they were forced to contend anew with a demon's dreams of conquest—which, with the aid of Killangrathor and the lack of opposing magics, had seemingly become much easier to accomplish.

As to her revival, the Entients would only reveal that the Queen had been awakened by a pair of children whose curiosity had gotten the better of them. Jarom did not ask them to elaborate. He was no longer troubled by the vagaries of that which they chose to share and that which they chose to conceal. His disillusionment was complete. Once upon a time, he'd had such high expectations, of himself and of these legendary beings. But the coming together of the two had yielded nothing but disappointment.

The council ended soon thereafter, with Maventhrowe giving praise to the three of them for completing their quest and gratitude for sharing the Sword of Asahiel with him and his kind. Jarom did his best to appear gracious and appreciative. He and his companions were then excused and shown to a series of rooms directly across from the meeting chamber. The rooms were small and stark, but fitted with beds warm and soft and with tubs of steaming water. Food was brought to them, which they ate in shared silence, not yet ready to discuss even among themselves that which they had learned. Perhaps in the morning, after a few hours' rest, some of it would make better sense.

So Jarom ate and bathed and settled in under his blankets. For a time, he stared at the ceiling, a screen for shadows cast by a single candle set on the table beside him. He thought not of dragons or demons or swords, but of his loft back home, where for so many years he had lain in a bed much like this and dreamed of the future he might know.

At last he closed his eyes, not in any futile attempt at slumber, but in useless denial of what that future had brought him, thinking that if he wished hard enough, it might just all go away.

At dawn, Jarom stood with his friends in the entry tunnel, just inside the keep, waiting to pass again through the secret portal set in the mountain wall.

"Speed be with you," Htomah urged. "The fate of all depends on it."

"Bear in mind," Maventhrowe added, "you are better prepared for this than you know."

Jarom considered the pair with a doubtful expression, but nodded. The Entients remained an enigma, full of contradictions that defied reason. On the one hand, they seemed kind and caring, philanthropists of the highest order. On the other hand, what could be more important than this war that threatened all of mankind? They professed best wishes for his success, lending him help and guidance that few others could. Yet they refused to give him all the answers he needed. And while it seemed that the whole of his adventure had gone according to their designs, they claimed to have had little to do with anything beyond the initial impetus.

Perhaps he was not meant to understand. Perhaps they had been right in that he could not. He was attempting with a mortal's logic to unlock the minds and motives of beings whose composition he did not comprehend. They were in fact mortal, or so the attack on Ranunculus outside of Earthwyn would suggest. And yet, they possessed powers and concerns of a decidedly immortal nature. Another contradiction. It went on without end.

Maventhrowe reached forth to touch the rock wall. When prompted, the three companions bid their final farewells and stepped through.

The air outside was cold and crisp, sunrise little more than a hint of brightness amid the dark clouds massed to the east. They found their mounts waiting, three coursers fed and watered and rested, their coats groomed and sleek. The animals were already saddled, leather bags stuffed full of provisions.

Jarom glanced back and placed his hand against the very solid mountainside. A great weariness settled over him. Though brief, his slumber had been undisturbed by thirst, aches, or dreams. He had awakened neither stiff nor sore, and, after a morning meal and another bath, could not remember the last time he had felt so warm and comfortable.

All of that was gone now. Reality had come back to him like a bucket of ice water poured over his head. He shifted his gaze slightly, and thought that he could see—across more than fifty leagues of land, through heavy mists and distant rains—the reddish glow of Mount Krakken.

"Come," Kylac said after a moment of silence. "We're much to discuss and many miles to cover while doing so."

Jarom climbed into his saddle. The thought of catching up with Marisha was the only one that appealed to him now. If all had gone smoothly, Corathel's company would reach the Gaperon by tomorrow night. With a fast pace and long hours, Jarom and his companions could hope to arrive soon thereafter. Perhaps by then, they would have some idea as to what it was they intended to do.

Following Kylac's lead, he spurred his horse into a canter down the mountain trail, leaving the mysterious Entients and their hidden stronghold behind.

He did not look back.

As they marched down the length of the deserted foyer, heading back to their studies, Htomah could contain himself no longer.

"You might have mentioned to the Kronus youth the truth of his blades."

"It matters not," Maventhrowe replied. "Killangrathor will not oppose a token of his own god, regardless of His fallen state."

"And knowing this might have helped the youth's conviction to carry out his charge. If he decides not to go, or shies away too soon . . ."

As was his way, Maventhrowe dismissed the concern. "Young master Kronus has not shirked a fight in all his life. Let us trust that he will not do so now."

The double doors of wrought iron at the end of the hall swung open.

Htomah hesitated. "And Torin?"

Maventhrowe gave his familiar, tight-lipped smile. "We shall see."

CHAPTER THIRTY-SIX

The land was unnaturally quiet as Corathel marched his company of commanders into the northernmost reaches of the Gaperon. For the moment, it appeared they were safe. But after coming this far, he was not about to let his guard down now.

The survivors of those who had traveled south with him from Kraagen Keep had reunited at the southern tip of Llornel Lake as planned. Haggard and haunted by their run-ins with the Demon Queen's minions, they had then pressed across the plains to the southwest. Those who could not walk were given the packhorses to ride, with the most vital of the dislodged provisions being split among those able to carry them and the rest simply left behind. The chief general had tried not to show how dispirited he had been at the unexpected loss of Jarom, Kylac, and Allion, and could only hope that their meeting would prove worthwhile.

Three days of travel had brought them at last to this gateway into the lands of Kuuria—hard days of more than sixteen hours each, with little food or rest. They were now less than two score in number. One man had died of his injuries along the way and had been given a swift burial in a shallow grave. Meanwhile, Marisha's healing skills had helped to keep alive two or three others who should not have been. Given the severity of their wounds, there were times in which the general had wondered what she was keeping them alive for.

By luck or grace, they had come across no more demons.

They had kept clear of open waterways following the old man's suggestion, but what that had to do with their fortune was anyone's guess.

He looked again to the man they followed, a disheveled scout with a dented helm shifted to one side. His own outrider had not returned, but had gone ahead south to the Kuurian border with the latest news after being met by a sentry patrol stationed within the northern end of the pass. Or so this man they now followed had claimed, a rider sent forth by the northern patrol officer to greet them. He looked to Corathel more like a brigand than a soldier, perhaps with the intent of leading them into an ambush. The man professed fealty not to Kuuria, but to Drakmar, a barony of Alson. He had shared with them little else, seeming as wary of them as they were of him. If not, Corathel would have been even more suspicious.

A flash of movement caught the chief general's eye, and he turned to watch a squirrel race to the top of a gnarled tree and disappear from view. He was struck again by the ghostly silence that blanketed this normally bustling highway. Nevertheless, the fresh tracks of a large company marred the trail before him. Ordinarily dry and well trampled, the earth here was covered with a fresh crust as a result of the recent rains, a muddy layer found torn and littered. Somewhere in the rocks ahead, he smelled ash and fire and roasted meat. A sentry patrol, perhaps, as their escort claimed. But just as easily, a nest of highwaymen that had disposed of his outrider and lay in wait now for the rest of them.

He slowed his pace, allowing the distance between them and their escort to widen, then signaled to Second General Jasyn and Fourth General Lar to take up their flanks. The wounded, riding in the center of their column, fell back under implied order. Lines tightened into a semblance of formation, with stern gazes to match.

The rider they followed stopped. Corathel's hand went to the haft of his sword, with his men doing the same. All came to a halt as the Drakmar herald gave a shrill whistle.

A moment later, three men in dusty chain mail stepped from behind a boulder, coming forward to block Corathel's path. Their leader strode front and center, a man of short stature but muscular build. Dirt and grime clung to a beard in desperate need of a trim, and a large mace was strapped to his back. The two soldiers who flanked him brandished heavy broadswords, their scowls dangerous.

Corathel held his ground, his weapon in its sheath, as the trio approached. They came to within a dozen paces and stopped.

"You are Corathel?" the leader asked.

Though deep and sonorous, the voice gave the other away as a young man not fully comfortable in his own skin. Corathel said nothing at first, but watched the man's eyes as they shifted about. He almost smiled when he caught their reaction to the imposing Lar.

"Chief general of the Parthan West Legion," he acknowledged. "And you are?"

The other tried not to seem hesitant. "Nevik, baron of Drakmar. My men and I stand watch for those to the south."

"So your runner has told me. And mine?"

"Well, I assure you. He bears word of your troubles to the border guard."

Corathel frowned. "Then the border is still closed?"

"With an entire battalion now set guard," Nevik spat. His posture changed instantly, their shared distaste of the Kurian authority helping him to relax in his degree of mistrust.

"There should have been others, messengers from Leaven and Laulk."

The bearded man nodded, flashing a quick hand signal. Almost at once, his troops began appearing from behind the rocks and trees that served as their cover, spilling out of gullies and ravines by the dozens. They came ahead slowly to assemble guardedly behind their leader.

"All were granted passage south," Nevik assured him, then shook his head. "Whether or not they were allowed beyond the border, I cannot say."

Corathel nodded, distracted by the notion that the emperor might not even allow them into his lands, an error in judgment that would almost certainly prove fatal to them all.

"All bore word of a terrible razing to the east by an army of dragons," Nevik prompted. "Your rider said he had news of a failed siege and of a black force headed this way."

Corathel saw in the other's face a mask of hard emotions—fear and anger, weariness and sorrow, desperation and despair. He wished briefly that he had something with which to assuage the young man's concerns. Alas, all he had was the truth.

He glanced to the heavens, a murky wash of twilight, and dropped his hand from his sword hilt. "Come," he said. "My men need food and rest. Share with me your story, and you shall have mine. Together, let us find a way to convince the emperor's guard to save themselves and the rest of us from a great doom."

Leaving command of his patrol to a Captain Eames, the young baron led them a mile south to where his main army was encamped. There were a little more than three hundred men under allegiance to the Drakmar standard, Nevik disclosed. The rest, including his lord father, had been killed in an ill-advised siege against the usurping wizard at Krynwall, or had deserted upon retreat. Those who remained had come south to Kuuria with their families and neighbors, only to be hemmed up like sheep at the border while the Imperial Council debated whether to allow these masses to take shelter within their lands. While the civilians found homes within the makeshift refugee camps and prayed for a favorable resolution from the Council, Nevik had taken it upon himself to guard their backs, and so had led the remnants of his army here, to the north end of the pass.

Their own camp was a rather modest collection of tents and pavilions offering just enough protection from the elements to keep them alive. Corathel found it well organized. The army had been divided into thirds and duties broken down into shifts. Each man was assigned eight hours on frontline patrol, eight hours tending to the needs of the camp, and eight hours of rest. After three weeks, the men seemed to have adapted to the routine. Nevik explained that despite a plethora of ongoing difficulties made worse by short tempers and downcast spirits, they were doing the best they could.

Corathel understood all too well. Many among his own troops were so sick at heart that had the Demon Queen or her armies stormed upon them at that very moment, they would have been too tired to care.

They were provided a dinner of overripe fruit, sour mead, and meat that had been heavily seasoned to hide its taste. Neither Corathel nor any of those with him complained. They had been afforded perhaps their final chance to stretch and eat and attempt to enjoy one another's company, and they were not about to take that for granted. Despite the overwhelming outlook of misery and gloom, the sound of raucous laughter was prevalent among those who saw themselves living on stolen time. For a short while, that which they had endured was forgotten.

The same could not be said for Corathel himself, who spent the whole of his evening in harrowing reflection, divulging to Nevik all that he knew. Some of it, the baron had already pieced together from scattered reports. Much he had written off as embellished hearsay or even lunatic ravings. But the chief general was compelled to confirm the other's darkest fears and bring to life new ones, watching as little by little the young man's skepticism gave way to horrified disbelief.

Of particular interest to the baron and his advisors was the story of Jarom, he who had not only recovered a mythical Crimson Sword, but who also claimed to be none other than Torin, lost heir to the throne of Alson. With all that had transpired, Nevik had come to believe that he stood in line to inherit the crown, should there be one to wear when this was over. When Corathel learned this, he found himself treading softly around the topic, caring little for the matter of Alsonian royal ascension, but not wishing to be the cause of any internal strife. He did note, however, that while Nevik's advisors scoffed at the absurdity of the notion of the infant prince's return, the baron himself looked almost relieved.

Hours slipped by, drawing moon and stars high overhead, as the leaders shared with one another their respective plights. Of those at Laulk, Nevik had heard little. As far as he knew, the residents of that out-of-the-way city remained, and had not yet been accosted. Any citizens Corathel had sent there from Crylag, Leaven, and communities in between were to be assumed safe for now.

When all had been recounted, talk turned at last to the emperor of Kuuria and Corathel's plans for the morrow.

"Good luck getting that old codger to listen," Nevik remarked bitterly. "He has left our children out in the cold—to say nothing of his constant refusals to offer military aid."

Corathel sipped from a steaming cup of honey-flavored water. "He cannot ignore the danger now to his own lands."

The baron shrugged, unconvinced. "I suppose we'll find out soon enough."

Corathel could see that the other had already accepted the inevitable. He searched his thoughts for a word of consolation, but came up empty. Not even the Crimson Sword, at one time a ray of hope, could provide much solace. Considering its failure to bring them victory at Kraagen Keep, the talisman would seem to offer no more than a minor contribution to their struggle. And with but a few hundred men to represent the active strength of two once-powerful nations, Alson and Partha, the outcome to this war appeared obvious. How much difference could the armies of Kuuria make? Not enough, he decided privately. Not enough.

Jarom came upon them shortly after midnight. A runner had gone before him from the front line, so that by the time he and his companions were escorted into the main camp, Corathel and the others were waiting. They were greeted without enthusiasm, which was just as well, as Jarom hadn't the stomach for a festive reunion.

He and his friends dismounted, handing their weary steeds over to an attendant while introductions were made.

"I'm told you are the son of Sorl," said Nevik, baron of Drakmar, as he clasped Jarom's hand in greeting.

Jarom shook his head. "A rumor I yet hope will prove false."

The other smiled. "Perhaps while you're at it, you would be good enough to help me will away the rest of this chaos."

"The heavens are clouded over with my prayers," Jarom assured him with a sigh.

"Then hear me this," Nevik countered, his face serious. "Lead us to victory, and I shall place the crown upon your head myself."

Jarom wasn't sure how to respond. It seemed to him pointless to be discussing the issue of his alleged birthright. Granted, should that time ever come, the debate would have to begin here, with the highest-standing nobleman of Alson. But for now, he was just another soldier fighting for his future.

He started to tell the other that he was not seeking to draw support for a royal claim when he recognized the pleading look in Nevik's eyes. The young baron was, like the rest of them, in desperate search of an unexpected hope, a godsend, something or someone to come forth and deliver them from this threat. While Jarom pitied any who would put that faith in him, he could not bring himself to dash it out of hand. So he nodded instead, choking down another dose of expectations with a thin smile.

When he turned back to the others, he found Jasyn and Maltyk grinning at him. He realized why when he gave a half turn in time to catch Marisha in a warm hug.

"Delivered safely as promised," Maltyk said with a wave of his hand.

"Thank you for not leaving me alone with these rapscallions any longer," Marisha quipped. She pulled back and gave him her brightest smile. "How did your meeting go?"

And so they gathered once more around the warmth of a cooking fire, Jarom and Marisha, Allion and Kylac, Corathel and his surviving lieutenants—Jasyn, Maltyk, Lar, and Rynar—and Nevik and his advisors. When all had settled in, the new arrivals set to relating the words of the Entients. Kylac did most of the talking, for which Jarom was grateful. After a single glance at the distraught faces of those around him, the youth focused his account on that which would afford them a measure of hope. He told them of Killangrathor and the true nature of the dragonspawn, and of how they might be destroyed. His narrative was tight and matter-of-fact; his tone betrayed neither excitement nor fear. He concluded quickly, and when he did, Jarom saw that few, if any, seemed encouraged by the news. Some were despondent. Most were skeptical.

"You're sure about this?" Corathel asked. "A dragon?"

"I've lived most of my life in the shadow of Mount Krakken," Jasyn said. "I've never heard anything about a dragon."

Kylac shrugged. "We're as sure as we can be. We's only their word to go on."

"I'd rather fight armies of warriors, human or not, than a dragon," Nevik muttered.

"You do not yet realize just how powerful these dragonspawn are," Corathel argued. "And if they are multiplying . . ." He trailed off, shaking his head.

"It doesn't matter," Kylac said flatly. "He's going to see more than his fill o' dragonspawn 'fore this is done. We's already decided to heed the old men's advice."

Corathel frowned. "How do you mean?"

"Allion and I will tend to the dragon while the rest o' ya work to slow the army's advance."

Jarom felt Marisha's eyes upon him, but made no effort to answer her unspoken question. He had already done what he could to sway his friends from this course, debating the matter with them for two full days.

Corathel, however, balked at the notion. "Two of you? Two of you against the Skullmars and a living dragon?" He gave a condescending snort. "It could take months just to find your way to Krakken!"

Kylac brushed aside the rebuke and its underlying concern with a shake of his head. "We need but follow the trail o' dragonspawn back to its source. Once the dragon and its armies are dead, we can worry 'bout this Demon Queen together."

"And what will you do if another army of dragonspawn comes marching by? From what I know of the Skullmars, you'll find scant cover in which to hide."

"Precisely why no more than two should go. Allion and I mights be able to slither past. An army or even half a dozen soldiers could not."

The chief general bit back his next response, grinding it away between clenched teeth. "And what's your plan of attack?" he asked instead.

"To creep up as close as possible, then skewer the beast through the eyes."

The youth whipped out his gleaming blades and thrust them forward into the center of the flames, as though exercising the very motion he would use against Killangrathor. The speed and suddenness of his action startled Nevik and his advisors—who had not yet seen the youth in action—nearly from their seats. Beside him, Jarom felt Marisha jump.

"I don't like this at all," Corathel persisted, shaking his head in disapproval. He too glanced in Jarom's direction, as if measuring in his silence a hidden ally and seeking his assistance before it was too late.

But Kylac caught the look and moved quickly to quash any further objections. "It's the only way, and Jarom there knows it. It makes no sense to do as the old men suggest on the one hand, only to ignore their warnings on the other. Besides, you'll need Jarom and the Sword if'n there's to be any land left by the time we gets back."

Corathel sighed. He realized, Jarom saw, that the youth had decided this matter long before now.

"But hey," Kylac allowed, sheathing his blades with a whisper of rustled cloth, "you're the strategist. If'n ya gots an idea that doesn't call for me to go poking around a dragon's snout, I'd love to hear it."

The chief general scowled at his young friend, while the entire gathering went as silent as Jarom. For several moments, they listened to the crackle of the fire around which they had gathered—the snapping of charred cinders, the pop of escaping air. Snores and murmurs and harsh laughter were heard from the other groups of soldiers at home within the encampment. Jarom noticed that every now and then, a few of those closest by would glance in their direction, but that for the most part, the men seemed to be keeping to their own concerns, caring little for what their leaders were determining. He wondered if this was how it felt to be an Entient, playing games with men's fates.

"And if you don't succeed?" Nevik dared, breaking at last the uncomfortable silence.

Kylac grinned. "Then I'll be dead, and whatever happens afterward will be none o' my affair."

That ended the discussion, as far as Jarom was concerned. What remained were logistical matters better left to Corathel, Nevik, and those of military experience in terms of abandoning the northern position and heading south on the morrow. When Kylac and Allion excused themselves, Jarom was swift to follow.

Before they dispersed, Jarom granted Nevik's request with what had become a customary presentation of the Crimson Sword. Doing so improved the other's spirits, but not his own. When it was finished, Nevik clapped him on the shoulder and called for an attendant, making certain that accommodations were in order for Corathel and his troops, and commanding that Jarom and his closest friends be shown to the baron's own tent for the night. Jarom expressed his gratitude, then accompanied his companions from the halo of the fire's warmth in search of rest.

But sleep would not come. Long after the sounds of the camp had died into stillness and the last of its leaders gone to bed, Jarom tossed and turned or just lay motionless, staring up at the canvas ceiling and listening to the deep, rhythmic breathing of his slumbering companions. Try as he might, he could not put his mind at ease in regard to their new course. Every now and then, he would glance over to where Allion and Kylac lay in their bedrolls beside him, and wonder whether this was to be the last night he would ever spend in their company.

In an effort to ward off thoughts of the future, he forced himself to think of the past. He wondered how his father was doing, and his friends, and whether or not they missed him. He wished he had the opportunity to visit them one last time, to assure them he was all right, even though he wasn't. He made a mental note to ask Nevik to send a rider north to check on them, to send fresh warning of the danger facing them all and to flee the village before it was too late. The thought saddened him. Diln and its forest colors had always been spectacular in the fall.

"You should be trying to sleep."

Jarom glanced over as Marisha drew back the curtain of the baron's sleeping area, which had become hers for the night. She sat up within her cot under a heap of wool blankets, her head propped upon an elbow, her hair a delicate cascade of tresses.

"I didn't mean to wake you," he whispered.

"Tell me," she said, her voice hushed so as not to disturb the others, "why are you not yet using your given name?"

Jarom blinked, confused.

"Torin," she clarified, and Jarom tensed. "You all but denied it when you met with the baron this evening."

"I don't even know who that is."

"It's just a name."

He blew out a long, slow breath. "Perhaps. But it comes at the cost of my own, and with a responsibility I'm not ready for—and that doesn't interest me in any case."

"Your responsibilities remain, no matter what you call yourself." Her eyes glimmered in the faint light streaming in from the open tent flap. "You are who you are. You shouldn't be afraid of it."

"I'm not," he argued, and surprised himself with the realization that what he said was true. "Not anymore. I don't want it, but I no longer fear it."

"Then why not accept it?"

He looked away, focused on the canvas ceiling once more. "It's just . . . I haven't done anything to earn it. I doubt that I ever will."

"We don't always earn our blessings," she offered with a smile, "any more than we earn our sufferings. Some things just are. And just as we must cope with the hardships, it would be wrong of you to squander the fortunes."

"I don't see it as a blessing," he huffed.

"Then see it as a hardship. In either case, hiding from it isn't the answer. Embrace it. Learn from it. Make the most of it. There are illnesses we face but once, easily overcome as children, that can prove deadly to those who are grown. That which we endure now often shields us from greater trials later on."

Jarom nodded as though he understood, uncertain that he did.

"Go to sleep," she said, and closed the curtain between them. Suddenly weary, Jarom lay back and did as she asked.

The dawn was swift in its arrival, as if driven westward by an already impending night. Jarom awoke tired and miserable. He stepped from the tent, the last to do so, and glared with puffy eyes at the new day. To the east, beyond the jagged wall of the Aspandels, the sky looked like a volcanic mountainside, with the sun spewing flaming red lava streams over and through clouds of blackened stone. He marked the sight, then dismissed it, his mood as foul as the day that greeted him.

Already the Drakmar soldiers were striking camp. No sense in leaving behind a stationary patrol to be shredded by the dragonspawn. Mobile scouts would stand watch for the dark tide's coming, but the bulk of Nevik's army would move south with Corathel—hopefully into Kuuria and on to Morethil, where they would discuss with Emperor Derreg how best to defend their lands from the imminent onslaught.

He worked his way through the clusters of activity, searching for Kylac or Allion, who he knew would be departing early. Time was critical, and the pair had wasted enough already in escorting him here to the Gaperon while determining whether or not to do as the Entients advised. Had they headed due east from Whitlock, Jarom thought, they could have been more than halfway to the Skullmars by now.

He found Kylac first, engaged in last-minute conversation with Corathel. As he came upon them, Kylac turned to bid him farewell. The chief general offered a grim nod and set off in another direction.

"I hope you know what you're doing," he told the youth. "This all depends on you."

Kylac shook his head. "Oh no, you're not squirming out o' this that easily. I'll do my part, but only if'n ya promise to do yours."

Jarom grunted as he clasped the other's arm, noncommittal.

Kylac refused to let go, staring him in the eye. "I wants your oath."

"Very well. I promise."

He sought out Allion then, who Kylac said was prepping the horses. The hunter looked up at his approach and flashed a weak smile. In that moment, a terrible sensation struck Jarom, a sinking feeling in the hollow of his stomach that he could not fight off. Though his faith in such things had been shattered, he took it as a premonition, a harbinger of doom: Either he or Allion was certain to perish before these trials were over. In either case, this was it, the last time he would ever lay eyes on the man, he who had been his best friend since he could remember.

"Take the Sword," Jarom urged quietly, glancing over his shoulder to make certain that Kylac had not followed him. "I don't care what the Entients say. You'll need it."

Allion put his hands up as a wall between them. "We've been over this, my friend. Kylac would kill me if he discovered that I'd accepted the Sword from you."

"He would not."

"Well, that's what he told me," Allion said as he adjusted his saddle. "And I'd rather not take the chance."

Jarom turned again in search of the youth. "He knows me that well?"

"I guess so."

"You're not afraid of a mere boy, are you?"

Allion's incredulous look made them both laugh.

"I suppose you're right," he said, glancing down in defeat.

"Cheer up," Allion advised, his own enthusiasm a facade. "You've got a lot to live for when this is over. You're a king, remember? With a castle and a treasury and everything. And," he continued, lowering his voice and glancing about as if he were about to relay a great secret, "I think that Lewellyn girl likes you."

Jarom felt himself redden.

"Are we ready?"

Both looked up as Kylac approached.

"Waiting on you," Allion replied, then bent close to

Jarom. "Take care of her," the hunter said, clasping his fore-arm and drawing him in for a hug, "and yourself. Hold off those armies for us. I'll meet you back at Diln or at Kryn-wall when this is over."

Jarom nodded, but failed to squeeze any words past the lump in his throat.

Moments later, his friends were gone, riding north and then east on their way to the Skullmars, Mount Krakken, and a visit with Killangrathor. Within that same hour, Jarom found himself traveling in the opposite direction, south toward Morethil, the capital of Kuuria, where, as he had intended weeks ago before much of this had happened, he would rally the support of the Imperial Council against a dark force that threatened his lands. He would do as he had promised Kylac, wielding as best he could the divine fury of the Crimson Sword. For the sake of those who would follow him into battle against the dragonspawn, he would try to play out his charade as champion, hero, savior of mankind.

Of course, all the while, he would recognize that any real hope for the peoples of Pentania rested upon the shoulders of two young men heading east, who intended to kill a certain very powerful dragon.

CHAPTER THIRTY-SEVEN

The garish banners of Emperor Derreg whipped in the wind. Jarom studied them as he approached, shading his eyes against the afternoon sun. He wasn't sure which was more blinding, the cloudless sky or the patterns and colors of the many standards flapping high atop the shining towers and polished parapets. Among those he recognized were the blue and white of the land of Kuuria, the red and green of the city of Morethil, and the garnet and gold of the imperial house. These were set prominently amid dozens of others, flags and streamers embroidered with the insignias of what must have been every baron and liege lord sworn to the Kurian Empire. Together, they heralded the emperor and all his glory as surely as a choir full of trumpets.

There were no such horns set in place to proclaim his own arrival, just a contingent of grim-faced riders—the emperor's retinue—sent forth to receive him. It had seemed to Jarom a forced courtesy, more a sign of the emperor's frustration and curiosity than respect. Their captain, Lorron, High Guardian of Morethil, spoke graciously enough, but there was a stiffness in his voice that caused Jarom to suspect their presence was not entirely welcome. Nevertheless, the emperor had arranged for an audience straightaway.

They headed along the highway toward the city's main gate, a portal twice as large as any Jarom had seen before, with a double portcullis and iron gates flung wide. At Corathel's insistence, Jarom rode while most of those behind him marched. As the only royal among them, he was now the leader of this band, and a horse would help him to look the part. Jarom had refused at first, reminding the chief general of the many women and children and walking wounded that followed. But Corathel had been steadfast that where the emperor was concerned, one could not underestimate the importance of etiquette. For a supposed king to be seen kicking up the same dust as this band of commoners would hurt his standing in the emperor's eyes, and thus undermine all they hoped to accomplish here.

So far, it was working. Gaining entrance to these lands south of the border had been easier than expected. Jarom would never forget the look on the face of the border commander, now a full-fledged colonel, as he had ridden his mount forward at the head of his army, parting the sea of refugees flooding the southern reaches of the Gaperon. A lower-ranked officer had tried to stop him, of course, with the same proclamation of imperial decree that Jarom had heard when he had attempted to pass through before. This time, however, he would not be turned away. Instead, he had sent for the battalion commander, and when the other had come, unsheathed the Crimson Sword.

"If you men wish to outlive the week's end, you'll kindly gather your weapons and follow me."

He could only guess as to which held the greatest influence—his words, the Sword, or his stern appearance—for the colonel had surrendered without a fight. Perhaps it had more to do with the messages and whispers that had preceded him. Most of those assigned to the blockade lines seemed apprehensive enough after what they had heard in recent days, and with both Jarom and Corathel to confirm many of those rumors, were more than ready to give up their post and head home.

And so, just like that, the floodgates had opened and the beleaguered peoples of the north had poured through. Jarom had continued to lead the way, Corathel and Nevik and an escort of Kuurian soldiers at his sides. The rest of the border guard had remained behind to facilitate the entry of what Jarom estimated to be well over a hundred thousand refugees. The emperor would not be pleased, the colonel had warned, mimicking Corathel's earlier assessment. At this point, few cared.

Also left behind were the clouds and rains of the northern lands, trapped against the mountain peaks. Dry earth and warm skies greeted them, and for those who had been through the worst over the past weeks, it was like a sign from the heavens themselves—a fresh beginning and a re-birth of hope. Jarom wasn't so optimistic, but would do nothing to show it. Champions did not doubt or denigrate signs of fortune; they expected and welcomed them.

They had marched for a day and a half to reach Morethil, outdistancing many of those who followed but heralded as always by a line of couriers who made their intent known. By the time they had set out that morning, they had already received word from the emperor that he would see them. The emperor, it was said, would learn more of this bearer of the Crimson Sword and of the alleged threat to his own empire. As if the man had any choice, Jarom had thought dryly.

So it was that he and his ragtag armies had come at last to Morethil, capital of Kuuria, seat of power for the Imperial Council and the largest city in all the realms. The city was everything Jarom had heard it would be. Its towers and tur-rets spired to the sun, their scrubbed walls of marble and whitestone gleaming with the light of day. Kuuria was the preeminent kingdom of Pentania—the oldest, the largest, the most civilized—and Emperor Derreg had dedicated a lifetime to the development of a city that would serve as the jewel in his empire's crown. Efforts had begun a little more than fifty years ago and persisted even today, making it one of the newest cities of the modern age. It was said to flaunt splendors unrivaled in the five recognized realms, and was a marvel in which the citizens of Kuuria placed their greatest pride.

Lorron was kind enough to share with him these and other self-flattering insights while the emperor's troops made way for them to pass beneath the shadow of the monstrous gate-house. Overall, the city was not unlike an archer's target, di-vided by soaring stone battlements into four concentric rings. The Imperial Palace and Gardens lay at the very center, in what had been dubbed the Heart of the Empire. To get there, they would pass through the Ring of Defense, the Ring of Commerce, and the Ring of Dwellings. Lorron had promised him that, as a newcomer to their fair city, it was an experience he would not soon forget.

Jarom nodded, seeing nothing to be gained in telling the High Guardian that under the circumstances, he wouldn't trade his horse's hindquarters for what was to him just another city doomed to be reduced to rubble.

Which was not to say he wasn't impressed. As he entered the outermost ring, he craned his neck to view the tops of the walls, both inner and outer, that surrounded the whole of the city within. The Ring of Defense, Lorron claimed, was an unbreakable band, capable of withstanding any assault. The stone of the outer wall was more than twenty feet thick. Within was housed a garrison of forty thousand, at full strength, along with everything needed to sustain them. Barracks, armories, training grounds, guardhouses, stables—if military in nature, it was here. The prisons as well, Lorron noted, set within and beneath the outer wall, so as to keep criminals as far as possible from the general populace. The saying was that should the city ever face an attack, the guilty would die first.

When asked what contingencies the army had should the outer ring fall, Lorron had laughed. His forces could, he supposed, fall back and defend each inner ring, though none of these had been designed or equipped to repel a full-scale invasion. In that regard, the city depended upon the Ring of Defense—which, Lorron assured him, was perfectly suited to the task.

They veered quickly off the main thoroughfare, working their way around the outer ring. No one questioned Morethil's High Guardian until he brought them to an unexpected halt. When asked, Lorron shared with them the emperor's desire that they be fed and offered the opportunity to bathe before being granted their audience. Jarom declined the offer even before Corathel and Nevik turned to him in protest. He assured their escort that they had no such need, that time was of the essence and the sooner they reached the palace, the better. To this, the High Guardian expressed less cordially the emperor's concern that their presence here might cause undue hysteria among the people, and that he wasn't about to allow their entire force to go marching through his streets, let alone be admitted onto imperial grounds. If they desired, he would accompany those who would actually be meeting with the emperor now, but the rest were to remain behind.

Jarom reluctantly agreed, and followed Lorron into what turned out to be a cavernous mess hall. There, he bid a temporary farewell to Marisha, Corathel's lieutenants, and the other three hundred plus soldiers hailing from Drakmar and the decimated Parthan West Legion. Most seemed only too content to remain behind with a warm meal, and so Jarom felt marginally better as he, Corathel, and Nevik accompanied Lorron from the room.

They moved quickly after that. A pair of horses were provided for his two companions so that the rest would not be slowed by their pace. Passing underneath the arch of another massive gatehouse, they left the Ring of Defense and entered the Ring of Commerce. This, Lorron explained, was the largest ring overall, much wider than that which encircled it. Within its area sprawled the markets, taverns, foundries, silos, guild houses—any and all yards and structures pertaining to matters of private or imperial-owned enterprise. Jarom could not help but marvel at the order and cleanliness of paved streets, painted buildings, unbroken signs—even the fresh-scented air. All of Morethil, Lorron boasted, was scrupulously maintained by cleaning crews that worked day and night. Business practices and codes of honesty were strictly enforced. It was the safest, most unpolluted collection of markets in all the realms, with merchants and patrons who traveled regularly from the farthest reaches of Pentania to take advantage of a limitless wealth of opportunity.

Most of those who packed the walks and waysides appeared to be going about their normal affairs, which startled Jarom. Had the citizens of this fair city any true idea as to what was about to befall them, they would have fled by now—into the sea, if necessary. He wanted to scream at them, to shout out a warning before it was too late. But the men of Lorron's company had arranged themselves so as to shield him and his companions from any curious onlookers, as though to prevent him from doing just that. Jarom gritted his teeth. He understood the need to avoid a mass hysteria, but to purposefully shield an entire population from the calamity about to befall them seemed akin to murder.

As he looked closer, however, he realized that the word was out, it just wasn't being received. Doomsayers clogged nearly every corner, calling out to the masses with admonitions both general and specific. For the most part, these men and women were ignored by those with more practical business to conduct, and thus left alone by the scores of city watchmen on patrol. One, however, a withered old hunchback, became so agitated at their appearance that the emperor's own guardsmen were compelled to remove him. At this, Jarom looked to his companions for their reactions, but said nothing.

After nearly an hour of working their way straight through along a main road toward the city center, they came at last to the Ring of Dwellings. In addition to the one through which they rode, more than a dozen major gates offered passage between the city's commercial and residential rings. Once again, Jarom was duly impressed. The sanitary functionality of the Ring of Commerce was replaced here by a serene beauty like that enjoyed in his most romanticized visions of his own forest home. The only enterprises allowed by city ordinance within this section were those of small, quiet horticulture and the communal care of young ones. Jarom saw public parks and private homes, nestled down winding lanes, arranged in cloverlike clusters, or lined row upon row in delicate harmony. Trees and flowers of every variety grew along lawns and roadways. Their mixed fragrances permeated the air, reminding Jarom of better times and places. As he glimpsed the elderly pruning their gardens and the children at play, he too was made oblivious momentarily to the dark specter that threatened their peace and contentment.

It was with a measure of regret and a renewed sense of urgency that he arrived at last at the entrance to the Heart of the Empire. If the rest of the city could be considered extraordinary, then its center belonged only in a mummer's tale. It began with the gardens, a lush and dizzying array of leaves and branches and blossoms, all expertly arranged and dutifully tended. Among these were the fountains, whose basins and sculptures were carved with amazing detail, and whose plumes jetted in some instances dozens of feet into the air. Natural waterfalls poured here and there down the hillsides, keeping the fountains fed. Had he the time, Jarom would have liked to wander the full network of carriageways and footpaths that intersected this veritable forest of splendors. Instead, he had to settle for his view from the primary roadway, from which he glimpsed a mother bird feeding her young, a pair of young lovers sharing an outdoor luncheon, and a lone painter capturing a scene on his canvas.

At the center of it all, among the gardens and fountains and outbuildings, was a breathtaking castle. Jarom had glimpsed the palace of Krynwall perhaps half a dozen times while making deliveries to Alson's capital city. Once upon a time, he had thought it a grand achievement. No longer. The tower set aside for the emperor's kitchen staff was larger, cleaner, and more elaborate than the entire royal complex at Krynwall. Beyond that were the towers for visiting dignitaries, the Imperial Cathedral, and of course, the main palace, in which the emperor resided with his family and conducted the affairs of his empire. Altogether, it was a sweeping mass of walls and turrets and windows of painted glass that rose skyward without blemish. And as he did his best to take it all in, Jarom could not deny a pang of envy. Even if he managed to one day sit upon the throne for which he'd been born, his city would seem a pale and wretched thing compared to the grandeur found here.

They passed servants and work crews of every kind along the way—couriers, groundskeepers, stewards, and of course, patrols of the Imperial Guard. All made way for Lorron and company, saluting or bowing according to station. Jarom's head turned this way and that, trying to glimpse everyone

and everything at once, knowing that whenever he focused
his attention in one direction, he was missing something in
the other.

They came at last to a receiving courtyard fit for a king,
but which Lorron explained to him was a side entrance allowing swifter entry. Half a dozen guardsmen, wearing
robes of velvet over suits of glimmering mail, stood before
an elevated pair of doors emblazoned with the imperial sigil.
They stood as statues in perfect formation, staring straight
ahead. Not a stitch was loose, nor a seam off-center. The
heads of their halberds had been polished to a fine gloss, and
Jarom suspected that if he were to look closely, he would
find not a single fingerprint.

Lorron gave a nod, and the palace guardsmen snapped
into motion. One came forward to take the High Guardian's
steed, while two others set aside their halberds and reached
for the massive iron pull rings hanging one from each door.
A command was given for the company to dismount. Jarom
did so, and a moment later, was accompanied by his friends,
Lorron, and a third of the High Guardian's men as he
climbed the shining marble steps toward the Imperial
Palace. As he passed the guardsman holding the door on his
left, he nodded in greeting, but the young soldier refused to
look his way.

Within lay the most majestic foyer Jarom had ever seen.
Huge tapestries hung from the walls, lavishly embroidered
with silken trim. The walls themselves were of speckless
whitestone, and arced skyward toward a domed ceiling
whose height he could not begin to guess. All the while,
windows of stained glass split the sun's rays into myriad
streamers of color, which splayed upon the floor to form the
crest of Morethil's imperial family in exacting detail.

And this for a side entrance, Jarom recalled in breathless
amazement.

He kept silent as he followed Lorron across the length of
the floor, feeling as though he had entered a place of worship. Their footfalls echoed in eerie cadence, muted by the
vastness of the chamber and trapped, he assumed, within the
dome above. Imperial Guard lined the walls to either side,

and once again, with a gesture from the High Guardian, opened a set of doors to allow them passage.

The ancient Thrak-Symbos, in all its glory, could not have appeared more splendid, Jarom decided. From room to room they went, some filled with paintings and tapestries, others with ornamental weapons and armor, and still others with columns and sculptures and decorative engravings. A plush carpet covered these inner hallways, as thick and soft as sponge grass beneath his feet. They did not pause until they reached a lavish sitting chamber, complete with a flaming hearth and floor-length windows that offered magnificent views of the gardens below. Like every other, the room seemed to Jarom twice as large as it needed to be, but he held the comment in check. Here, Lorron took his leave of them in order to brief the emperor on their arrival, assigning six of his men to remain behind and see to any needs they might have. An attendant appeared, offering drinks, hot or cold, and bid them make themselves comfortable. Jarom asked for a flagon of ice water, and with a glance at the soldiers set to guard against his exit, sat down to wait.

An hour passed before Lorron came for them again. By then, both Corathel and Nevik were almost climbing the walls in aggravation, with Jarom at a loss for how to calm them. He was himself more than a little vexed by the inexcusable delay, but doubted that loosing his frustrations would help matters.

"The emperor will see you now."

That was it. No word of excuse or apology. Ignoring the smoldering looks aimed his way by Corathel and Nevik, Morethil's High Guardian turned on his heels and led them away.

They followed yet another series of corridors until they came upon a single door, arched high and wreathed in gold. Upon their approach, a sentry turned to knock twice upon its graven surface. The door swung wide, opened by another sentry within.

"All hail His Majesty, Father of Morethil, emperor of Kuria," announced the second sentry as they entered.

Jarom's eyes swept quickly around the room. This was

not the throne room, he decided at once, although it was
larger and grander than many of those he'd heard tell of. The
chamber was divided essentially into two halves, one raised,
one sunken. A pair of steps lowered them first into the
gallery area, where an array of kneeling pads were arranged
on the floor before the emperor's platform. Mirrors lined the
walls to either side, enhancing the apparent size of the room
and providing an infinite number of reflections as Jarom
glanced into their depths. The raised area was at the far end,
with broad steps leading up to it. Large fonts sat to either
side of a jeweled throne, the backdrop to which was a wall
of windows that overlooked a stunning expanse of the city.
Gazing out this window, his back turned to them, was the
emperor himself.

Even before he turned around, Jarom knew him to be the
oldest mortal he had ever seen. His hair was white and wispy
and had thinned until there was almost nothing left. His
hands, clasped behind him, were wrinkled and colorless save
for the swollen veins running through them. Silken robes
hung from stooped shoulders, one of which lifted higher than
the other in a gnarled hump.

A dozen members of the Imperial Guard lined the steps to
the emperor's platform. One of them gave a signal to the
ushering sentry, who closed the door and placed his back to
it. None met Jarom's gaze as he watched them execute their
duties.

When the door closed, the emperor turned from his window. As he did so, Lorron knelt before him. Grudgingly,
Corathel and Nevik did likewise. Jarom, in accordance with
the courtesies on which Corathel had briefed him, bowed in
acknowledgment, but kept his feet.

Wreathed in light from the tall windows, the emperor
seemed to Jarom an apparition already fading from the
world of men. His face was frightfully pale and grotesquely
hollow, with a luxuriant beard as pure as fresh-driven snow.
His gaunt body trembled uncontrollably as he moved toward
his throne, assisted at the arm by a young attendant. Though
surely he needed one, there was no sign of a cane.

When slouched in his seat of power, the aged man seized

the arms, molded to his grip, as if to prevent his decrepit bones from spilling onto the floor. His attendant moved to stand silent and motionless to one side. Sunken gray eyes peered at Jarom from beneath raked brows, squinting.

"Rise," the emperor bid them, his voice a choked whisper.

Lorron did so, followed by Corathel and Nevik. "Your Majesty, I present to you King Torin of Alson."

He gave the announcement with a slight bow and an outstretched arm, making no effort to introduce Jarom's companions.

"You may approach," the emperor rasped. The trembling of his body intensified as he spoke, causing Jarom an unexpected degree of discomfort.

Nevertheless, he did as he was asked, feeling the layers of carpet move like down beneath his feet. His movements were slow and steady, his hands at his sides and away from the hilt of the Sword, which was pushed back on his belt. The Imperial Guard did nothing to acknowledge him, though Jarom did not doubt that were he to make any sudden moves, he would find himself hacked into pieces and fed to the emperor's dogs.

He stopped at the base of the steps leading to the platform above, waiting while the emperor studied him.

"You bear the look of your grandfather," the other said, drawing breath between phrases. "An admirable man. Not like your father."

Jarom nodded, deferring to the other's judgment where it concerned a paternity he had never known.

"Of unnatural health, I should think, for a lad buried near twenty years ago."

Jarom remained silent while the emperor wheezed at his own jape. It would seem the man had heard the whole of his story, as relayed by messenger in the days before their arrival. He had anticipated having to explain it all again, filling in gaps lost in the translation. But it seemed the other was prepared to make up his mind using that which he'd already been told.

"I would see this Sword." The laughter was gone. The emperor's face was a stern, shriveled mask.

Jarom nodded. As he reached for his weapon, the Imperial Guard readied theirs. He tried not to let it bother him as he lay the Sword across his outstretched arms. With a nod from the emperor, he mounted the steps until he stood just beneath the other's throne.

The old man leaned forward, eyes widening. He made no effort to reach for the blade, but his pale face came near enough to reflect its glow. After a moment, he waved the talisman aside and gestured for his attendant.

As Jarom sheathed the Sword, the attendant helped the emperor to his feet. Together, they moved around the throne to the bank of windows, with the old man waving Jarom after.

"Your subjects have begun their descent upon my city," the emperor remarked.

Jarom missed neither the bitter tone nor the look of disgust as he gazed with the other toward Morethil's distant outer wall. Sure enough, the first of the refugees from northern Pentania had arrived, and were now being catalogued and received by soldiers of the Imperial Army.

"I fear their presence will bring panic to our streets."

"I dare say, Your Majesty, that such panic is warranted." Corathel had briefed him not only on how to conduct himself, but also on what to say. This was the first prearranged verbal response he'd been given the opportunity to use.

The emperor regarded him with what was either a nod or just another, more violent tremor. "Of this demon and her forces, is there anything you would add?"

Again, the emperor was referring to the account sent forth by courier. And again, without knowing the exact state of that message as it had been delivered, Jarom was not at full liberty to give answer. However, judging by the fact that both he and the countless refugees whose entreaties had been spurned for so long had been admitted inside Morethil's walls, the emperor knew and was willing to accept the truth.

There were only two items of interest his courier had not been given to relate, both of which Jarom still wished to remain hidden. The first was that concerning the wizard as his elder brother, an almost meaningless revelation that he still felt could only hurt his cause. The second was that which concerned Killangrathor. It had been decided early on that to try to explain the magical ties between the dragonspawn and this great monster of myth could only hamper the already questionable credibility of their tale, and that their quest to slay the beast might provide a target for ridicule and an excuse not to become involved in the conflict. His job was to convince the Imperial Council that only their combined military forces stood a chance of preserving their lands. Thus, he needed the situation to appear as dire as possible, and their plans beyond reproach.

"It is as Your Majesty has heard," he offered with a bow. "Either Kuuria withstands this evil, or we all succumb to it."

The emperor eyed him with a haunting, skeletal look. Somehow, Jarom met that gaze and kept his secrets to himself.

"And how do you propose we fight it?"

"We must assemble the whole of the empire's strength and march swiftly north to the Gaperon, where the narrowed terrain will help to shield us from the enemy's full force."

The emperor's reply was mocking. "I had a battalion set in place at the pass already. It is you who has relieved them of that duty, in violation of my personal order."

"Charge me, Your Majesty, with the insubordination of your commanders. To remain in such limited numbers would have cost them their lives. But we must regroup with an undivided force if we—"

"And abandon our cities?" the other rasped accusingly.

Jarom had to grope for his response. "By defending the Gaperon, Your Majesty, we protect all of your cities, and stand a better chance of—"

"We stand a better chance behind walls built for defense than out on the open range," the emperor replied flatly.

Jarom found himself fast running out of planned arguments. "In the case of Morethil, that may be. But yours would be a force divided from those at Souaris, Stralk, and others, and would leave the rest of your lands at the mercy of the Demon Queen."

The emperor was a long time in responding.

"Do you not love my city?" he asked, lifting a frail arm and waving it slowly across Morethil's panoramic sweep. "It is my dearest child, my legacy to this world. Over the course of my years, I have watched it bloom from the tiniest seedling into that which you bear witness to today. I will not forsake it." His tone turned cold, dangerous. "I would sooner return my body to the earth than abandon it without a fight."

He frowned anew at the weary masses straggling in through the distant gates of the outer wall, then faced Jarom squarely. "You will conceive another plan."

An openmouthed Jarom glanced back at Corathel. Their briefings had not provided for this, a complete dismissal of their entire argument. Had the old man listened to any of what he had just been told?

The emperor caught his look, and scowled at the Parthan chief general. "I will consult the Council," he allowed, "and shall send word of our deliberations."

"We could join you," Jarom tried.

"The Council does not lend ear to outside influences," the emperor snapped, with greater strength than Jarom had imagined possible. "We shall meet again before supper. For the sake of all, I suggest you ply your time wisely."

"Your Majesty—"

"You have your leave."

"But . . ."

He had taken but a single step after the emperor when the Imperial Guard had him about the arms, weapons bristling. He looked again to Corathel, and found the chief general shaking his head. Jarom forced himself to relax, and within moments, had been escorted from the audience chamber.

They were returned to the sitting room with four times the amount of guardsmen as before. Lorron seemed almost sympathetic when he left them, promising to do what he could in lending his voice to the Council.

When the High Guardian had gone, Jarom turned back to his companions. Nevik took a seat while Corathel clenched his fists in red-faced fury. Jarom's eyes then drifted to the

garden-view windows, where the afternoon light was beginning to darken.

"Good luck, Kylac," he muttered to himself. "It's all up to
you, my friend."

The creature peered out through the opening of its shelter, a
deep hollow in an old oak where once a gnarled branch had
been ripped from the trunk by lightning. A strafing rain
roosted in the skies overhead, tearing through the sievelike
forest canopy as it had all that day. It was the same storm
that had driven the creature to take shelter the evening before, confiscating this, the abandoned nest of some great
owl. Or at least, it had thought the nest abandoned. Earlier
that morning, the owl had returned from its nightly hunt and
had fought to take back its home.

It had made for a fine breakfast.

Mitzb blinked against the incessant showers. The demon
had wasted too much time here, but could not quite bring itself to brave the stinging weather. The Queen would understand. She loved her pet as it loved her. She would not want
it to be uncomfortable.

Its tiny ears pricked at the sound of movement. Not that
of a fluttering bird or skittering rodent, but thick and heavy,
passing through the brush below. As it neared, Mitzb leaned
out carefully for a better look.

Its beady eyes fixed upon a pair of riders working their
mounts at a canter through the heavy undergrowth. Both
were cocooned within the folds of their cloaks, huddled
against the cruel elements. They rode eastward, heading
deeper into the trees, where the land was cloaked in the
darkness of night in this, the midafternoon.

The trailing rider called forward to his companion. "Do
you suppose he knows we're coming?"

The other replied without looking back. "Killangrathor?
Let's hope not."

The imp nearly toppled from its perch. Its lavender skin
had gone brown and green, a camouflage for its presence.
Even so, it eased away now into the shadow of its hollow,

pushing back against the sharp bones and scattered feathers of the owl carcass.

"I pray it's not like this all the way to the Skullmars," the trailing rider spoke again, shivering from the cold. "We'll never make it on those paths in weather like this."

"We don't have a choice, my friend," the other said grimly.

They went silent after that, heads focused on the narrow trail before them. No matter. The little demon had heard enough. All of a sudden, the rain and its own discomfort was no longer a concern. The Queen would want to know of this.

Nevertheless, Mitzb waited for some time until after the duo had passed, having seen the longbow strapped to the back of the second rider and not wishing to take any chances. Even if it were to escape an attack, 'twould be best if its enemies remained unsuspecting.

When at last all had died away save the drumming of the rains, the imp stepped to the edge of its shelter. With a mischievous sneer and a click of its needlelike teeth, it spread its leathery wings and took flight.

The man was heralded as Prince Deven, eldest of Emperor Derreg's surviving sons and First Son of Morethil. To Jarom, he looked less like the heir to an empire than one set soon to pass it on—a man whose own advanced age could not be hidden by his stylish clothes, fake smile, or the dyes used to color his hair.

Corathel could not have cared if he was the Great Fiend himself. He practically lunged at the crown prince almost before the introduction had been made, forcing the accompanying Lorron to come between them and drawing more than just menacing looks from the Imperial Guard.

"Where in Krakken's blazes have you been?" Corathel growled, a dozen blades at his throat.

Once again, they had been left waiting, this time for hours, until the red glare of sunset lit their sitting chamber like the volcanic rivers to which the chief general referred. In that time, Jarom had expressed his hope that Lorron and the other members of the Imperial Council might convince Derreg of the necessity of their proposed course. But Corathel had relieved him of that notion at once, claiming that the Imperial Council, though it consisted of representatives from each of Kuuria's major cities, was nothing more than a puppet the emperor used to impose his will over the baronies and townships under his rule. Even if its members wished to do so, they would be unable to bend the old man's will. And since any other method of defense against the dragonspawn that they could think of seemed laughably absurd—and would require time they didn't have—Corathel had grown angrier by the minute.

"Careful, sir," Lorron said in an effort to calm the chief general. "We are all on the same side here."

"Are we?" Corathel snorted. "Then how do you explain this delay? We lose lives with every wasted moment."

"Beginning with your own," Lorron warned, "should you maintain this hostility."

Corathel glowered as he forced himself to relent. Blades fell away, but remained at the ready.

Prince Deven appeared quite taken aback by it all. "Forgive me my late arrival. There is much to be tended to. Which of you is King Torin?"

Heads turned as Jarom came forward a pace and nodded to the imperial prince. "I am, sir."

"I am sent to confer with you on your proposed course of attack," Deven replied in the tones of a man who had never known strife. He ignored the Parthan chief general as he moved toward Jarom.

But Corathel was beyond any pretense at protocol. "There is nothing more to debate."

Deven turned reluctantly toward the fuming general. "You have devised a new plan, then?"

Corathel glared at the prince. "I have. Declare your father unfit to rule on this matter. Persuade the Council to grant you his voice, and put an end to this madness without further hesitation."

The prince looked horrified. "I will not," he gasped. "My father is of keen mind. You will not find—"

"Then my armies make for Souaris," Corathel snapped, "in hopes that King Thelin is a man who listens better to reason."

Deven's features drew taut. "King Thelin is beholden to the will of the Imperial Council. Do not presume that you can so easily divide this empire against itself."

"But that is exactly what your father is doing! He would abandon each of your cities to its own defenses, leaving all to be annihilated!"

"Do not underestimate our chances," the prince remarked. "Morethil is well built to—"

"Morethil be damned!" Corathel roared, bringing a stunned silence to the room. When he proceeded, he did so through clenched teeth. "Suppose for a moment that Morethil, Souaris, and a handful of others manage to hold out a week, a month, even a year. Deprived of all trade and agriculture, how long can these individual bastions survive?"

Prince Deven stroked his gray-flecked beard. "My father the emperor has suggested that those of us who do nothing to provoke this demon and her minions may be left alone. Massing our strength against them can only lead to war."

Jarom was about to blurt out his own incredulity when Corathel shook his head.

"A romantic notion," the chief general sighed. "Act on it, and you shall meet with the same fate as the rest of us."

"It is the will of the Council," Deven repeated, as though incapable of thinking for himself.

"Then I must beg your leave," Corathel concluded with a mocking bow. He glanced back at Jarom and Nevik before heading toward the exit.

Jarom was about to follow when the Imperial Guard snapped into motion. A pair blocked the doorway while the others formed a tight circle about the chief general.

"I'm sorry," Deven said, turning to address Jarom, "but my father the emperor gave strict orders. Under no circumstances are you or the Crimson Sword to leave this city."

"Please, General," Lorron added, eyeing Corathel, "do not try anything foolish."

Corathel was rigid with understanding. "So that is why he sent his son. This is not a conference, but an arrest."

"What of the others?" Jarom asked.

"Your soldiers will be granted continued harbor. Your civilians as well. All will be safe within these walls, provided you help to make sure of that."

Jarom stared at the man and his airs, and felt his own anger stirring. Of what use was a prince as likely as not to lose his birthright before he inherited it? "And if I refuse?"

"Then you will be held on the charge of impersonating a king, and your peoples will find what shelter they can on the open range."

Jarom glanced between the prince of Morethil and the High Guardian, neither of whom seemed to delight in this task, but both of whom appeared determined to carry it out.

Corathel remained between the two, deathly still, ringed by Imperial Guard. "To the Abyss with the rest of the world as long as the majesty of Morethil lives on," he sneered. "I must have been mistaken about the mind of your emperor."

"Keep your scorn," Deven replied. "Riders have been deployed throughout the empire with word of your proposed strategy. The Council has granted permission to the other cities to respond as they see fit."

Corathel spat. "Even better. Send forth the others as a shield while hunkering in your cave. You cowardly—" He stopped short as his legs were knocked out from beneath him.

"Save it for the battle," Lorron urged him. At the High Guardian's signal, a pair of Imperial Guard worked to bind the chief general's hands. "See them to their quarters and post a guard."

Neither Jarom nor Nevik made any move to resist as additional guardsmen filed into the room and took up positions of escort to either side.

When Corathel had been safely bound, Lorron had him hauled to his feet. The chief general turned to him at once.

"I'll be looking forward to fighting at your side," he snarled as he was led from the room.

Lorron raised a questioning eyebrow.

"So that I'll be there to taste your blood when a dragon-spawn rips your throat out."

An ugly grimace flashed across Lorron's countenance, and for the first time in days, Jarom saw Corathel smile.

CHAPTER THIRTY-EIGHT

This task demanded something special. A force both swift and voracious. The talents of a creature that had never known failure. This task called for Raxxth.

She knew it at once. Still, Spithaera continued to circle her demon-ringed cavern, contemplating the strengths and weaknesses of each of her minions—alone and in combination. Once or twice she paused, thinking she had come upon a more desirable solution. But the harder she sought to avoid him, the clearer her need became. Finally, she surrendered to that need and came to stand reluctantly before him.

His sculpture was unremarkable compared to many of her brood, with a humanoid frame tall and lean and a tusked, dragon snout. Sleek and beautiful in his simplicity, she supposed. He squatted upright on a pair of haunches thin and powerful, slightly hunched, with broad shoulders and a tiny waist. His arms were long and sinewy and of deceptive strength, with claws that raked the ground. In form, he was something between an ape and a wolf. In savagery, he was without peer.

Spithaera reached out to touch his face, then hesitated yet again. She recognized the pair of mortals most recently spied upon by Mitzb, having matched the imp's description to those provided by Gravlith and Cheel, Rwom and Lobac. Cheel, like Rwom weeks ago, had been hacked into so many pieces by the boy swordsman it was a wonder she had managed to re-form in her inert state. And Lobac had been slain twice already by the archer.

Spithaera shook her head. There was no one else. Only Raxxth would do. He who was more lethal than any handful of her minions—which was just as well. For should she send others to assist in the hunt, Raxxth would destroy them long before these friends of the wizard's brother—the one called Torin—ever could. He would go alone. But he would be enough.

With a resolute sigh, she hoisted him from the ring of statues, wrapping her slender arms about his stone form. When she had placed him within the glowing waters of her summoning pool, she stepped back, taking one last moment to reconsider. Once upon a time, she had regarded him as her most prized possession, back when she had thought she might be able to control him. In the end, she had quit trying, deciding it was this, above all other traits, that made him so deadly. But it also made him practically worthless, of forbidden use except in matters of the most extreme urgency.

Reminding herself of what was at stake, she stepped forward once more.

"Hik lar rothe krine aldrayne . . ." she chanted, then paused. Fool that she was, she had nearly forgotten the wards for her own safety. While the statue before her began to radiate with the pool's greenish glow, she gathered her defenses in the form of a swirling light until her own hand glowed with readied power.

"Rathrok!"

A hand shot forward, the color of smoke, swifter than even she had anticipated. Spithaera recoiled, hurling her ball of light. When she turned back, she found her demon paralyzed in mid-lunge.

"Curse you, Raxxth!"

She looked to her forearm, where his claws had drawn blood. At once, however, her anger dissipated, and a cruel smile came to her lips.

"Raxxth, my sweet, my unfailing champion."

The demon remained frozen, his green-glowing eyes throbbing with fury.

"I have an errand for you. You shall emerge from the Emerald River, south of the Skullmar Mountains. There you will find two men on the trail to Mount Krakken. Destroy them, Raxxth."

She opened the portal, and her demon began to sink within the pool's suddenly churning waters. When all but his head had passed beneath the surface, she released her paralyzing dweomer. Raxxth barked in response, gnashing the water between his teeth.

When he was gone, and the pool's surface placid once more, Spithaera gave a weary sigh of relief. She hated to take such chances, but spared no doubt as to whether she had done the right thing. Unlikely as it was that an entire army of boy swordsmen and archers would prove even a temporary distraction for the mighty Killangrathor, Raxxth would ensure that this pair never made it far enough to find out. Chances were he would return within the hour, his teeth and claws stained with fresh blood and splintered bone.

Spithaera smirked at the thought, filled with sudden and certain relief. Troubled no more by the threat to her armies of dragonborn, she refocused her mental efforts on the greater threat—young Torin and the Crimson Sword.

Allion sat astride his horse on the muddy bank, staring dishearteningly at the surface of the river before him.

"Ready?" Kylac asked him.

The hunter swallowed. "After you."

They had resumed their trek through the Kalmira at dawn, and had been on the trail for a little more than half the day. Keeping to the shelter of the trees while avoiding the many tributaries of the Emerald River had helped to screen them thus far from demons on the prowl. To pick up the swath of devastation that would lead them to Krakken, however, they would have to cross the Emerald not once, but twice as it forked its way out of the mountains to the north. After putting it off for as long as possible, the time for the first of those crossings had come.

Kylac gave a slight shrug and urged his mount forward into the icy waters. They had searched long and hard for a section narrow and shallow enough to cross. The rain was still falling; the river swollen and dangerous. But Allion was less concerned with drowning than he was with coming upon an army of the Demon Queen's minions. And no amount of scouting could prepare them for that.

But his fears, it would seem, were unfounded. Though both horse and rider were being swept rapidly downstream, Kylac was more than halfway across already. All of a sudden, Allion faced the prospect of crossing by himself or being left behind on the western bank.

With his breath in his throat, he put bare heels to his steed's flanks. His cloak and boots were in a bundle before him in an effort to keep them dry. Why, he wasn't sure, since they were mostly soaked through already. But it had given him an excuse to stall that he had eagerly accepted.

His horse, it seemed, could sense his reluctance. Twice he had to kick the animal before it gave the slightest response. It took one step, then another, sinking into the mud of the river's bank. When its front hooves hit the water, it stopped and shook its head with a whinny of displeasure.

A third kick and a slap of the reins finally got the horse moving in earnest. Allion gritted his teeth as it surged into the chilling flow. It was too late in the season, he thought, to be braving such temperatures. Not to mention, they needed to be heading north, and with every moment spent within its current, the river drew them south. But at this point, there was nothing he could do about either. And so he closed his eyes, feeling the strain of the animal beneath him and trying hard not to be reminded of the time he had crossed a similar tributary en route to Feverroot, a wounded Jarom in tow. The time in which that nameless monster had surfaced from almost directly beneath them.

He opened his eyes when they reached the far shore, signaled by the lurching of his mount from the clinging waters. Gripping tight and leaning forward in the saddle, he searched at once for Kylac. He found the youth several strides upriver, and turned his steed toward the other. This time, the animal needed no urging, seemingly anxious to catch up to its companion. Moments later, they were headed east again, deep into the woods, where despite his fears, a bone-rattling chill, and the ground they had lost, Allion was much relieved.

They were a fair ways along before they stopped to wring some of the water from their clothes, after which they returned their boots to their feet and their cloaks to their shoulders. By then, Allion felt immeasurably better. One down, one to go.

They rode in silence, their ears pricked to the sounds of the forest, a sense dulled by the endless patter of rain. The archer found it soothing, as he often had back home while making his almost daily hunts to help feed the families of his village. He wondered again how those families were doing, especially his own. He missed them more than he would have cared to admit, his mother and father, even his annoying siblings. He missed wrestling with the village children and sharing with them stories, lending excitement to their mundane lives. He missed also the lazy afternoons stretched out along the banks of the stream that he and Jarom had made their own. It was sobering to realize that regardless of how this mess turned out, he was unlikely to ever know such quiet, innocent contentment again.

A short time later, they came across what Allion assumed to be demon tracks. They were not, Kylac told him, but rather bear tracks, of a species found almost exclusively on the island of Nivvia, in the gulf off the coast of Vosges. A man-eater nonetheless, and a hungry one at that to have wandered this far north in search of prey. Should it catch wind of them, Kylac said, they could expect its company.

Allion had to take the youth's word for it. The most dangerous predators in his own forest, the Kalgren, were wolves and some of the smaller varieties of hunting cats. Neither made a mark in the earth half as large or as deep as this one.

"These look fresh," he observed, trying to imagine the size of a beast whose claws alone were as long as his own fingers. "How close is it?"

"Too close," Kylac replied, gazing off into the trees through which the tracks disappeared. "I thinks I might have myself a look."

"And how is that a good idea?"

"The last thing we needs is for it to catch us unawares. A fight with one o' these things would draw the attention o' half the forest."

"It's that deadly?" Allion asked, unable to hide his skepticism. It wasn't that he disbelieved the youth or the many stories he had heard, but after their encounters with demons and lightning-spewing lizards, he found it unlikely that anything nature had to offer could cause them that much trouble.

Kylac merely nodded. "Take my horse and continue east. I'll catch up."

"You're not thinking of doing anything rash, I trust."

The youth grinned, a little too broadly. "It *would* make a fine dinner," he admitted. Then, off Allion's frown, "I just wants to get a better idea o' where it is and, if necessary, throws it off our scent. I'll be back within the hour."

But he wasn't. An hour went by, and then two. Allion did his best not to worry. This wasn't the first time he'd found himself alone in dangerous woods. Yet this was not his forest, and under the circumstances, he had a difficult time putting himself at ease. The woods were cold and quiet and black with rain. He could see nothing beyond a dozen paces, and so had to rely on his other senses. That which he could taste and touch, smell and hear, did nothing to threaten. But his stomach knotted with worry, the kind of intuition one learned to listen to when having spent as much time as he had out in the wild. He tried to convince himself that he was simply overreacting to Kylac's departure, but failed.

He came upon a scarred section of forest belonging to the path paved by the armies of dragonspawn heading north into Partha. The other would be found farther east, the southerly trail that he and Kylac would follow in reverse. Assuming, of course, that the youth ever returned.

He paused at the edge of the blasted clearing, peering both north and south as far as his eyesight would allow. The land remained deathly silent and still. A couple of weeks had done little to restore the greenery or return the animals to their burrows and nests. He saw a lone bird sitting on a blackened stump, overlooking the devastation with cruel eyes, no doubt feeding upon the worms as they emerged from the ashen earth. Due to the rains, there were scarcely even insects to be found.

He had never felt so forlorn.

He was about to move on when he heard the cry, so sudden and terrible that he nearly pitched from his saddle. It was difficult to tell from the echo how far away it was—a league, maybe. Farther, if the gods his parents had taught him to worship were kind and true. It was a roar unlike any he had ever heard, deep and yawning and filled with rage. For an instant, he thought it might be that of Killangrathor himself, the dragon come from his mountain to slay them. The very idea was enough to rake his spine with fear.

But then, just as quickly, the beast's cry changed to a yelp of pain. Allion's horse reared, while Kylac's tried to pull away from where its lead rope was affixed to the hunter's saddle. Somehow, Allion managed to control them both, though he could not say the same for himself. His heart raced. When his breathing resumed, it came in ragged gasps.

He remembered then the ruckus Kylac had said would ensue should they be forced to fight the beast whose tracks they had come across. Judging by the sounds, Kylac had been compelled to do just that. If there was any solace to be found, it was in that the youth had finished the job quickly.

For a moment, Allion was unsure whether or not to proceed. He searched for the bird and found that it had taken flight. Perhaps he should do the same.

He eased out from the shelter of the trees and into the swath of broken and blistered earth. The horses offered no complaint, pushing the pace without his command over the twisted branches and fallen trunks. He worried somewhat for their footing, but decided not to fight them. He only hoped that Kylac would find them soon.

When the youth did finally catch up to them, perhaps half an hour later, his face was the color of the mist, as close to fear as Allion had seen him come. Kylac uttered nary a word, but leapt into his saddle and bid Allion untie his lead rope.

"What's wrong?" the hunter asked, his sense of relief at

seeing his companion again fleeing like rats before the sun. "Didn't you kill it?"

Kylac shook his head. "No," he said, in a tone that lacked its customary swagger. "But I saw what did."

Allion did not ask what that was. He didn't need to. The youth's awestruck mask said it all.

They set forth again at a rapid pace, Kylac leading, Allion following close behind. Hanging limbs and wet leaves slapped at them and their mounts. It was clear that speed had become their priority, with the youth making no effort to hide the thrashing of their passage. Allion neither saw the demon nor heard its pursuit, but he knew it was there. He could feel it in the way his neck skin crawled. Whatever it was that had killed the great bear was coming now for them.

His anxiety continued to build, welling steadily toward acute terror. His eyes searched the shadowed foliage behind him and to the sides. He began seeing demons where there weren't any, with normal trees and brush taking on monstrous characteristics. His heart pounded at a rate his steed could not begin to match, and he felt his veins swelling with the pressure.

And then he heard it, faint and distant when compared to the thundering of his own passage, but discernible nonetheless. The cracking of branches, the tearing of brush, the squeaks and flutter of animals disturbed.

"It's gaining on us!" he shouted.

Kylac did not look back, but gave his horse another kick. They were already galloping as quickly as they could over the narrow, uneven animal trails. If they did not find a clearer path, and soon, whatever it was giving chase would have them.

A throaty roar arose ahead of them, long and unbroken. So intent was he on that which followed that Allion only recognized it when it was too late.

As he broke free of the entangling underbrush, he skidded to a halt. Before him, the river was a churning beast of spray and foam. The opposite bank lay naught but thirty paces across, but Allion's throat constricted as his gaze followed the raging waters south. Fifty paces downriver, they cascaded over a steep falls, their screams reverberating within the canyon below. Allion looked to Kylac with both dread and disbelief.

They were trapped.

Kylac dropped from his mount. "Your bow," he demanded, "and an arrow."

"What are you doing?" Allion managed to ask as he fumbled for the requested items.

"We have to cross."

"What?" the hunter cried. "Nothing can cross this!"

"I hope you're right," the youth replied as he secured the end of a fine, silken rope to the arrow Allion had handed him. He tied it off just behind the head, then nocked the arrow to the bowstring and drew it back.

"You'll have to adjust for . . ."

But the rest of what the archer had to say became pointless as Kylac released the bolt and sent it sailing across the river. It whistled through the rain-swept air, tugging after it the uncoiling rope. With a muffled thwack, the arrow buried itself deep in the trunk of a mossy hardwood lying fallen upon the far shore.

Allion frowned. "That's never going to hold us."

"It will," Kylac disagreed, taking up the loose end of the rope and handing it to him. "Grab tight."

"What about the horses?"

"We'll have to make do without 'em. We'll be afoot once we reach the mountains anyway."

A heavy crash echoed from within the forest behind them, as though a tree had been splintered and toppled. The brush nearby began to ripple and sway.

"Go," the youth commanded.

Allion glanced out across the river, steeling himself for what he knew they must do. "Wait," he said, turning back toward Kylac. "What are you—"

His words ended in a grunt as the youth's spinning kick caught him in the chest and sent him stumbling backwards. For a moment, he teetered on the edge of the bank, his arms flailing madly overhead in a desperate attempt to regain balance. Kylac, he noted, was facing the woods, the bow cast aside and his own weapons drawn. An instant later, Allion toppled over at the waist and plunged into the river.

All of a sudden, he was simply another bit of debris being swept downstream by the relentless current. Through sheer instinct, he managed to hang onto the rope, a frail thread wrapped about his wrist and clutched so tightly that his fingers hurt. There was a tug from the other end as the rope drew taut, holding him fast despite the river's push. As a result, he found himself thrown against the bank, separated now from his friend, his mount, and his weapons on the far side. He looked toward them just in time to spy the demon bound from the forest.

He had only barely caught a glimpse of its lean limbs and crooked tusks before it barreled into the waiting Kylac. He cried out as it happened, only to swallow a choking mouthful of river for his effort. The waters churned and sprayed, making it virtually impossible to follow his friend's struggle. It was all he could do just to hang on.

Then his anchor broke, some part giving way to the strain. His heart lurched and his eyes widened as he felt himself slipping away. Hanging roots exposed along the bank clawed at him as he swept past, and he managed to grab hold of one sturdy enough to catch him. It bent against the rush, but did not break, and for another moment, he was safe.

His attention turned back to the battle. The combatants were locked in a tight circle. Kylac was spinning, the demon snarling. Allion heard the youth's blades as they hacked into the creature, like axes splitting logs. But the demon did not seem to notice, ripping and snarling in an uncontrolled frenzy. Not a drop of blood oozed from its wounds, and the beast showed no signs of weakening.

Their precise movements were impossible to follow, like a pair of cats tearing at each other atop a midden heap. The hunter could not tell which had the upper hand, and strung out as he was, was helpless to intervene. He was about to turn back to his own struggle when the fight came to an abrupt halt.

Kylac had found an opening and gone for the kill. His slender longsword was buried in the creature's neck, clear to the collarbone. But once again, the bloodless wound did not faze the demon. Shrugging past the brutal assault, it slapped the youth's arms out wide and barreled forward. As Kylac's weapons dropped to the sodden earth, his body, with that of the demon, tumbled with a great splash into the river.

In an instant, both were tossed downstream. Allion held his breath—the youth would be over the falls in seconds if he did not act fast. Kylac seemed to realize this, focusing upon an aged oak that sprouted from the bank at the crest of the waterfall. It leaned out over the edge, as if peering through the rising mists to catch a glimpse of the maelstrom raging far below. Half of its roots dug deeply into the bank, while the other half extended out over the river. If only the youth could reach it . . .

He had just about grabbed onto it when the demon's hand seized his ankle, hauling him back from the lifesaving cage. There was no time to fight the creature off. But then a boulder in the river came between them, its jagged edge striking the demon's arm and breaking its grip. The creature spun away, reeling against the current, and was tossed over the falls. Kylac stretched out for all he was worth, reaching once more for the roots . . .

His fingers brushed a tiny tendril's slick surface before he too disappeared over the edge.

A short while later, Allion found himself knelt upon the eastern shore, shivering against an uncontrollable chill. He had no idea as to how long he'd hung there from his own root, staring out at the lip of the falls and waiting for Kylac to reemerge. All he knew was that it could not have happened the way he saw it. Kylac Kronus was not dead. Not after all they had endured. Not with so much that remained to be done.

Eventually, the river's incessant tug had reminded him of his own predicament. Though numbed through by the frigid waters, he'd managed to drag himself to safety, pulling his body through the mesh of roots and mud that dominated the riverbank. There, he had lain still, his breath coming in heavy gasps as he coughed the water from his lungs. For a time, he'd been aware of nothing beyond the soft ground beneath him. At last, he'd hauled himself to his knees, his head hung low, facing—but unable to make himself look at—the falls.

A whicker from his horse drew his attention to the western bank. The animals, along with all of his weapons and supplies, were unreachable and therefore useless. He had only a hunting knife and Kylac's rope, wrapped still around his wrist. That and the broken pieces of the arrow to which it had been affixed. Hardly enough with which to go hunting dragons.

And yet, what choice did he have? Until Killangrathor was slain, the dragonspawn destroyed, and the Demon Queen driven into exile, Kylac's sacrifice would have no meaning. The hunter was not about to let that happen.

He got to his feet, determined. He would continue upriver until he found a ford, swim across, and head south again to retrieve the discarded weapons. With any luck, his horse would not have wandered too far, and he would be able to reclaim his foodstuffs and his quiver of arrows as well. He shuddered to think of what unnatural minion he might come across in all of that time so near the water, but reminded himself yet again that he had no choice.

He turned to leave, only to be overcome by the pangs of his loss. He stopped, looking back one last time toward the falls.

Farewell, my friend. May your adventures continue in a better place.

All at once, he felt his anger boiling, heating him from within. Fighting back tears, he stormed northward along the shoreline, coiling his rope. He envisioned himself using it to hang Killangrathor from the ceiling of the monster's own cavern. It was a fool's notion, he knew, but that didn't stop him from fashioning a noose with one end of the slender line, making it large enough to encircle a dragon's neck.

Kylac awoke to a great thundering all around him. His eyes snapped open at once, searching for the answers to questions he had not expected to have the opportunity to ask. He found himself sprawled within a broad nest of tree roots that hung just beneath the lip of the waterfall, densely intertwined and filled with deadwood, loose stones, and other river debris. Like the net of a fisherman sifting for food, only he was the fish, and this net had saved his life.

He sat up, shaking his head against a nagging dizziness. His blood was on the surface of a stone that had served as his pillow after the tumble. Aside from that, he was remarkably unharmed.

Of the demon, there was no sign. Doubtless, its carcass lay somewhere below, pulverized by the jagged rocks and pounding sheets of water at the base of the falls. Kylac searched the misty spray, but saw only the flat, lifeless waters of the river as they continued downstream. More than likely, the beast had returned already to its mother, the Demon Queen. He found himself hoping that she would think twice before sending that one after them again.

His attention turned to more immediate concerns, such as climbing toward shore and seeing what had become of Allion. He held little hope that his companion had waited around after seeing him go over the falls. But the hunter would be hard-pressed to go it alone without weapons and supplies, whichever way he had decided to turn. Kylac had thought only to protect the other from the demon, which he had. But he would have to hurry now if he expected to catch up before some other ill befell the man.

After casting a final glance into the cauldron below, the youth scrambled to be on his way.

CHAPTER THIRTY-NINE

A brisk wind raked the battlement of Morethil's outer wall. Jarom steeled himself against its brush, refusing to shiver. His gaze was fixed to the north, narrowed but unblinking as he watched the enemy approach.

Beside him, Prince Deven droned on in his address to his soldiers. Jarom was paying scant attention, caring little for the other's patriotic rubbish, having joined the man only because he saw little point in refusing. A crush of imperial troops had gathered atop the battlement within the shadow of the gatehouse parapet, staring up at their city's First Son with anxious faces. Others did so from the floor of the Ring of Defense, having paused en route to their battle stations. It seemed to Jarom that all the world was looking at them, and he took the time to seek out familiar faces within the crowd, those he would miss the most should this day end in calamity.

He found first those of Corathel and his lieutenants— Jasyn and Maltyk, Lar and Rynar—huddled in private conference. Though frustrated by the emperor's narrow-minded foolishness, the chief general was determined to make the most of a difficult situation. Rather than waste time and energy plotting escape, it had been agreed that they would treat Morethil as their last bastion of defense. Since that moment, Corathel seemed to have forgotten that his forces were being held within the city against their will. Overcoming suspicions from both Lorron, the city's High Guardian, and Deven, its crown prince, the Parthan chief general had spearheaded a rigorous series of strategy sessions over the past three days, putting to use his knowledge of their enemy. The result was an improvement in the city's defenses that just might, he claimed, enable them to survive.

Nevik stood at the base of the steps leading down from the gatehouse parapet. Jarom had made fast friends with the young baron over the past few days. Nevik seemed the type who would lend himself readily to any noble cause. Like Jasyn and Maltyk, he possessed a rare sense of humor, with a knack for making Jarom laugh when he most needed it. Most importantly, Nevik, more than anyone, understood the demons with which Jarom wrestled, having grappled with many of them himself. Both had lost their fathers—one to war, the other to a long-hidden secret. As a result, both had been thrust into positions of leadership that neither had asked for, and had been watching men for whom they felt responsible die ever since. It hardly seemed fair, and there were few things that could unite men like the bitterness at having endured a common wrong.

Finally, and dearest of all, was Marisha. Jarom couldn't see her from where he stood, but could imagine her easily enough—her soft white skin, high cheeks full and round, bright eyes, and ready smile. He had been with her moments ago, drawn to a quiet corner of one of the pavilions set up within the Ring of Commerce as temporary housing for the many refugees come to Morethil. Day and night, she had taken it upon herself to help tend to the sick and wounded, a life's purpose from which she knew no rest. And yet, when he had come by this time to check on her, she had pulled him aside, a troubled look in her eyes.

"Are you all right?" he had asked at once. "You look as though you could use some sleep."

"No more than you," she replied, her smile faint.

He only nodded. It didn't require the skills of a Lewellyn healer to see that he'd not enjoyed a full night's rest in days.

"There's something I should share with you," she said, struggling, "something I need to show you. I swore not to, you see. But it may be important to our struggle."

Though confused, he gave her an encouraging smile.

"It probably doesn't matter, but, well . . . I was hoping you could help me with a mystery. I thought that you, more than anyone, might be able to do so."

"Well, what is it?" he asked, taking her hands in his. She was so enigmatic, so beautiful and enticing, a ray of light beneath a passing storm cloud.

She worked for several moments around whatever it was she wanted to say, her brow furrowed, her lips twisting. She had finally met his gaze when Prince Deven and his retainers interrupted them.

"King Torin," the prince hailed, his pampered face drained of color. "The enemy approaches. My lord father has asked me to address the troops. I should like you to accompany me."

"I'll be with you in a moment, Lord Prince," he offered in response, turning at once back to Marisha. "You were saying?"

But Marisha seemed almost relieved by the intrusion. "Later, when this is over. You've got enough to worry about."

Jarom stared at her, a look of concern fronting his puzzlement and fascination.

"King Torin . . ." Deven repeated, insistent.

"It's too late to be of any help to us now," Marisha assured him, mysterious, disarming.

"This may be our last chance."

"It won't be," she promised him, leaning in for a quick embrace. For a moment, his cares were forgotten. "Go."

And so he had, whisked away to participate in this final rally. All the while, as he threaded his way through the ranks of soldiers and climbed the city ramparts, he was left thinking of her. Strange that someone so open and caring could be so withdrawn when it came to matters of her own. It reminded him of how little he actually knew about her. She'd been raised in the village of Feverroot by her mother, who had passed away just a few short years ago. And, as he'd recently learned, her father had never really been a part of her life. Beyond that, she had claimed, there wasn't much to tell, just common stories of accidents caused and basic childhood mischief. Up until now, he'd not pressed her for more. Should he survive this day, he intended to do so.

A flurry of raindrops stung his eyes, caught in a gust of wind. It forced him to blink, drawing his attention back to the thunder of impending battle.

". . . and we shall stand victorious!" Deven was vowing. "For yourselves, for your families, for all of mankind, we shall defy this vile scourge and claim for ourselves once and for all our rightful place in this world!"

A chorus of cheers erupted from the soldiers below.

"See for yourselves the active role of the gods in this struggle. See for yourselves the glory of the Crimson Sword!"

Taking his cue, Jarom mechanically drew forth the divine talisman and lifted it overhead. A collective gasp shuddered through the crowd, growing into a frenzy of cries and cheers as he waved the blade slowly, back and forth, to heighten the effect. At the same time, his stomach churned at the notion that he was somehow supposed to lead this army to victory, that some five hundred thousand souls residing now within these walls were relying on him to save them. It was enough to make him wish that he had never found the Sword in the first place.

With most caught up in the emotion of the rally, and with Jarom's own gaze fixed to the north, no one noticed the shadow swooping down from the darkened heavens. By the time Jarom looked up, alerted by the Sword, it was too late. The Demon Queen was already on top of him, seated astride some sort of winged lion. Her lips parted in a fanged smile as a stream of lightning crackled forth from her outstretched hand.

Cries of alarm met Spithaera's shriek. Those around him scattered. But Jarom kept his feet, lifting the Sword in reflex. He cringed behind the glowing blade, closing his eyes and waiting for the images of his life to flash before them.

When the bolts struck, there was no pain, only a balmy sensation that flowed through him. He continued to hear the sounds around him, though they were muted—the cries of his men turning to gasps, the crackle of lightning, the roar of . . . *flames*?

He opened his eyes to find his body encompassed in crimson fire, a swirling shell fueled by the Sword. Its heat filled his veins, but did not touch his skin. Lightning crackled, lapping against its wall, but could not touch him.

Alone within the center of the conflagration, Jarom could scarcely believe it. Unbidden, the weapon had unleashed its power to confront that of the Demon Queen, a shield that protected both talisman and wielder. Not only that, but the flames raced outward along the trail of lightning as he watched, devouring it like a line of oil to its source. When Spithaera realized this, her eyes went wide and she ceased her assault. The magical energy burned away, the flames died, and Jarom's shield disintegrated into the ether. Jarom, unharmed, gaped at his assailant, who circled now at a safe distance overhead.

Her raucous laughter filled the brooding skies. "Behold your strength!" she shrieked. "Behold your power!"

Jarom settled into a defensive crouch, the Sword held ready before him.

"Look at the rabble you defend, the wretched creatures you have been made to serve."

He refused to do so, holding her captive within his gaze. But he could sense those around him rising to their feet.

"Do not limit yourself to their needs. Come to me, be one with me, and I shall teach you pleasures you have never known!" A silken cape billowed about her, while the straps of leather in which she was clothed clung tightly to her perfect skin. Even from this distance, her physical charms were evident. A creature of death, he reminded himself, and yet as beautiful to behold as life itself.

"Surrender now, before it is too late. Let the lives of those precious to you be spared. Else, defy me, and watch all for which you care be destroyed."

With that, her winged mount gave a yawning cry as it swerved higher and away to the north. Jarom watched her go, struck by the realization that he could hardly blame her. To a being such as she, humans must seem as insects, tolerated when serving a specific use, but most often destroyed.

Moments later, all that remained were the echoes of her laughter, borne upon the wind like retreating thunder.

"Afraid to fight her own battles, is she?"

Jarom turned to find Lorron, the city's High Guardian, at his shoulder.

"Let us pray so," he replied, and meant it. Despite the outcome of their brief encounter, he was more than a little unnerved by the boldness of her attack. So much for the counsel of the Entients. He seemed to recall one of them suggesting that Spithaera would not risk such a direct challenge. What else might they have been wrong about?

A cheer rose up, slowly at first, then strong and certain as it ushered the Demon Queen's departure. Once again, Jarom raised the Sword to thunderous applause. The emperor could not have asked for a more heartening display. To witness a fuller measure of the Sword's power and to see his adversary chased off like that would stir a warrior's heart, or nothing would.

His enthusiasm was short-lived. As the frenzy died and the troops took to their stations, the rumble of the approaching horde grew steadily louder, a foreshadowing of doom. They came without drums, without horns, without fanfare of any kind. There was not one standard or sigil among them. None was needed. Their stampede alone was enough to fill his heart with dread—the rending of the earth beneath their claws, the hiss and slaver of their cries. Forgetting his battle assignments, Jarom stood in place upon the rampart and watched them come.

"Are you all right?"

Nevik. The young baron was studying him carefully, his bearded face a mix of awe and concern.

Jarom blinked. "I'm fine."

"For a dead man, you mean."

Jarom nodded. Under any other circumstances, he might have managed a smile.

"You've learned how to unlock its fires," Nevik observed, eyeing the Sword with due caution. "Good for us, I suppose."

"I had nothing to do with it," Jarom admitted with a shake

of his head. Once again, he had been lucky, and nothing more.

"That's not how it looked from where I stood."

"It must have been protecting itself, as it did against the jailor at Leaven." He looked to the Sword in wonder. "I guess it decided to throw me in as part of the bargain."

"Thunderstorms and spellcasters beware."

Jarom gave another halfhearted nod, then turned back to the horizon. Nevik looked with him, as did nearly every other man perched upon one level or another of the battlement. For as far as the eye could see, the surrounding plains were covered with dragonspawn, sloshing ever nearer in eddying waves. And while the armorers and artillery squads and runners and reserve soldiers stationed on the floor of the ring below could not see the vile horde for themselves, they caught its reflection in the fear and disbelief that soured the faces of even the bravest of their comrades positioned above.

"There must be twenty thousand," gasped Nevik.

Jarom did not care to give an estimate of his own. If the baron was right, it was a force four times the strength of that which they had faced at Bane Draw. Granted, their own armies, spread around the city's circular outer wall, doubled these new numbers. But if a margin of four or five to one had been insufficient at Kraagen Keep, then what was a margin of two to one going to do for them here?

It was hard not to dwell on the fact that their forty thousand could have been a hundred thousand, huddled not within this single city but massed at the Gaperon in defense of all of Kuuria. Strategically, there was no reason for the dragonspawn not to pass them by as they had Leaven, leaving Derreg's armies to rot until forced from their cage. And if that happened . . .

"It appears they mean to attack, at least," Nevik noted, as if reading Jarom's thoughts.

Jarom nodded. There was a difference, he knew. Those at Leaven had posed no threat to the Demon Queen's supremacy, and thus had simply escaped her attention. Here, it was the Sword she wanted, the Sword she was determined to have. Sure enough, she meant to sack Morethil, and if he were to flee, she would hunt him wherever he went.

"The emperor would have done better to cast us out of his city altogether," he said with a grim smirk. Instead, Derreg had sent word throughout the land, as if news of the Sword's presence, when picked up by the Queen's spies, would dissuade her from laying siege, deflecting her assault elsewhere. Fool that he was, the old man had drawn her right to them.

"King Torin, your units are ready."

Had he not recognized the voice, Jarom would have expected to find a runner, not Jasyn, Second General of the Parthan West Legion, delivering the message and a smart salute.

"At ease, soldier," Jarom groaned. All of a sudden, among even his closer companions, his birth name had become the label of choice, feeding an already overwhelming sense of expectation. "I thought I asked you not to address me like that."

"Your pardon, milord," the other said with a crooked grin.

Jarom shook his head. "Lead on."

The rains began to fall more heavily as Jarom and Nevik followed the lieutenant general from the assembly parapet and down to the main rampart. Deven managed to wish them strength and courage as they passed, looking for all the world like a lad about to soil his breeches. Jarom simply glared at the man.

After that, everywhere was motion. Behind him, the High Guardian escorted the First Son to the turret of high command, with orders for the Imperial Guard to watch the skies for the Demon Queen's return. To either side, especially on the ground below, men-at-arms chased about like ants in apparent confusion. Ahead, General Jasyn pushed his way past throngs of grim-faced soldiers, an unnatural spring in his step.

"Anxious, are we?"

The lieutenant general chomped his teeth together in a broad grin. "Reckoning time. You have to love it."

Jarom nodded, trying not to reveal his belief that the other was fully mad. He remembered something the Second General had told him at Kraagen Keep, that a man was never so alive as in the moments before battle. He remembered also thinking that war was something a soldier simply had to dull himself to in order to carry out his duties. Since then, he'd learned this wasn't always the case. Some, like Jasyn, lived for every moment of it.

Somewhere to his right, Corathel barked commands. Jarom searched for the man, but the chief general's voice was soon drowned out by the scores of criers who carried his orders and dozens of others throughout the lines. The very air, cold and wet, sent chills down Jarom's spine that had nothing to do with the weather. If this was the thrill to which Jasyn referred, then he and those like him could damn well keep it.

He passed fewer than half a dozen familiar faces, while everyone seemed to know him—no doubt because of the Sword, which he held aloft so as to more easily part the agitated throng. He worked to acknowledge their nods and salutes until at last he reached his fighting position, a section of wall to the west of the northern gatehouse. Actual command of its units fell to a veteran officer of the Imperial Army who reported directly to Lorron or the prince himself. As usual, Jarom's involvement was to be largely ceremonial. He was a standard more than a soldier, a rally flag and little more. He only hoped it would remain that way.

"Head up," Jasyn cautioned him, "or have it served to you on a platter."

Jarom nodded, clasping the man's forearm in parting. He did the same with Nevik. "I'll see you both at supper."

"Don't forget to wash," the baron replied. "This looks to be messy work."

They left him then, making way toward their own regiments. At the emperor's behest, Lorron had assigned each of the visiting commanders to separate companies, as if fearing some kind of mutiny should they be left united—as if they were not all of them in this together. Corathel had not bothered to argue. Thus, Jasyn made his way now along the wall toward the city's eastern gate, while Nevik went down to join his three hundred from Drakmar, who were being held as reserves. To the west was Maltyk; to the south, the soft-spoken giant, Lar. At least Rynar was nearby, entrenched below with a bank of war machines set to guard the interior of the main portal. And Corathel, whom Jarom spotted now across the way, on the wall east of the gatehouse tower. For what it was worth, he and the chief general would share the same clear view of the slaughter.

The howls of the dragonspawn were deafening as they made their final rush. As the forward waves came within range, the first arrow volleys were unleashed. A great whistle signaled the release of thousands of arrows from longbow and crossbow. Joining them was the metallic twang of the ballistae mounted along the crenellated battlement, each of which launched a dozen spears with the pull of a single trigger. The result was an armor-piercing hailstorm the likes of which Jarom could never have imagined, and he found himself gritting his teeth as the enemy vanguard collapsed beneath the vicious counterassault.

But the dragonspawn came on, many with shafts protruding from their faces and chests. The ones killed or slowed by the wounds they had received were trampled by those that came behind them. Another volley was loosed, then another, with teams of men working to keep the more powerful ballistae loaded and firing. Great crushing stones were dropped through tubes built into the wall and launched by gravity outward, carving thin streams in the enemy lines as they went bouncing and rolling along. The defenders did their work well, but as Corathel had warned, it was a stalling tactic at best. Within moments, the beasts reached the outer wall, and their siege began.

They attacked as Corathel had said they would, in what seemed a mad and senseless panic. Lacking towers, ladders, or ropes, some leapt at the walls as if they might simply scrabble to the top by hand. Others hurled their bodies against the marble blocks as if nothing more were required to knock them to the ground. They hissed and snarled and spat quick bursts of flame, as if their fury alone might bring the city to ruin.

Ridiculous as it first seemed, the same strategy had razed
every fortress and holdfast they had come across during
their devastation of Corathel's lands to the east. Eventually,
flames had caught, walls had crumbled or been scaled, and
the cities had been overrun. They could expect the same to
happen here.

But in these early stages, Jarom had hope that Morethil
might indeed hold out where the others had not. The outer
wall was taller and thicker than any the dragonspawn had
yet faced. They would smash their bodies into pulp before
they brought it down from the base. Nor could they find purchase with their claws upon its polished face. If they were to
scale it, it would not be until they had built a mound with
their own dead. And with the rains washing down upon
them, their fires could do little more than blacken the previously unblemished whitestone.

Still, time stood not in Morethil's favor. The dragonspawn
were as thick and relentless as a swarm of locusts. They were
indeed crawling all over one another to gain the heights, crushing and killing those beneath without thought. Nor did the defenders have unlimited resources. Against this enemy, the city
could not manufacture weapons and supplies as quickly as
they were exhausted. Whether they held out for days, weeks,
or months, their endurance would inevitably fail them, as
would their ammunition, food, and already precarious morale.
Unless Kylac and Allion were able to carry out the Entients'
unfathomable charge, victory seemed already a fool's notion.

He remained silent in his assessment, of course, and if any
among the Imperial Army entertained similar thoughts of
despair, they kept it to themselves. Corathel had done an excellent job of preparing them for the horror they would face;
indeed, he had exaggerated the threat to the point that many
of those Jarom now observed seemed unimpressed by the
truth. Or perhaps they were simply too blind to recognize
defeat when it stared them in the face. In either case, they
fought back the assailants with a resolve to match the
enemy's fury, harrying them with their iron-tipped rains,
their pummeling stones, and with cauldrons of water in
place of flammable oils.

If *they* believed they could succeed, Jarom thought, then perhaps he should too.

But he could not seem to overcome a nagging sense that something was amiss. As the battle continued to unfold, he realized all at once what that might be. According to intelligences Corathel had pieced together at Leaven, the dragonspawn had in their victory at Crylag encircled the entire city, not only to create a choking press, but to cut off any escape. Here, they had not yet made any move to do so.

Because they had not the numbers required, Jarom decided quickly. So vast was the city's area that if they were to surround it, their lines would not be nearly deep enough to overrun the walls, leaving them as targets and nothing more. They could cut off outside supply routes, but would be unable to storm the city. He thought it through and over again. His reasoning was sound. So why did he not feel better about it?

A moment later, he knew.

He spied the demon first, the obsidian giant encountered at Bane Draw and then again on the misty shores of Llornel Lake. Thick as they were, the dragonspawn parted at its coming, dancing aside and hissing it on. Behind it, upon a black cloud in the shape of a nightmare steed, came the wizard.

Jarom gaped, then shoved his way forward to the edge of the rampart. Peering out between a pair of sharpened merlons, he gained an unmistakable look at the raven-colored hair and gimlet eyes of his elder brother. Somehow, Soric was still alive, dressed now for battle in studded leathers as black as hatred itself. Behind his demon escort, he was riding steadily toward the main gate. As he neared, the dragonspawn cleared away from the iron portal, affording the magic-user an unobstructed view.

"Wizard!" Jarom shouted, the only alarm he had time to share. "Wizard!"

Criers took up his call. Within moments, the battlement rang with warning shouts.

Alarms turned to commands. Commands became motion. A heavy concentration of forward artillery was trained upon the wizard's position. Jarom imagined the bolts tearing through his brother's frame and felt oddly impassive at the notion.

"Fire!"

The missiles flew. But to Jarom's surprise and dismay, they never reached their mark. Instead, they bounced away as if striking an invisible wall, skittering to one side or the other with dulled tips and broken shafts. The wizard came on.

Another volley was loosed, then another. To their credit, Morethil's soldiers refused to give up. But the wizard's spell showed no sign of weakening beneath their assault. When he had reached a point no more than thirty paces from the main gate, he came to a halt and dissolved his sorcerous steed.

And began to chant.

Jarom could not begin to make out the words, only that the man's lips were moving. There he stood beneath the shadow of the gatehouse, untouched by rain and arrows alike, the serpent staff clenched in his hands. After several anxious moments, he slammed the butt of that staff to the earth.

A great shudder rippled beneath Jarom's feet, causing him to clutch the wall for balance. It passed quickly, only to be followed by a terrible groan. For a moment, no one knew exactly what had happened. Then Jarom heard the shouts and positioned himself for a better look. A cold terror ripped through him.

The gates to the city were opening.

Both the primary and secondary portcullises had been locked in their closed positions. Interior and exterior doors had been barred and buttressed with wooden beams from within. No force, magical or otherwise, could possibly pry through that barrier. Jarom told himself this over and over, even as the rising gates snapped free of their moorings and the iron doors bent inward.

The archers above intensified their assault. Men below labored frantically to reinforce the barrier. Nothing worked. Bars and braces bent and twisted and fell aside in splintered ruin, until finally, the massive doors were flung wide.

For Jarom, time stood still. That was why the dragon-spawn hadn't surrounded them. They were simply waiting for the right opening. And here it was. Just like that, before the defenders had created a sizable dent in the enemy's ranks, the dragonspawn were free to ravage the city from within.

"Now!"

Jarom recognized Rynar's shrill voice as it peaked above the tumult. The Fifth General stood at ground level beside an instrument of death wheeled into place just inside the city. Loaded upon it were eight enormous logs, each as long and as thick as a man, sharpened to a point. With the area be-tween them cleared save for the ruin of the gates and the lines of schilltrons, Rynar had the wizard squarely in his sights.

The machine's operator pulled the ballista's trigger. Noth-ing happened. In an instant, the dragonspawn were through the breach, raking at one another in their haste. So great was the crush from behind that the first to enter were impaled upon the iron tips of the readied schilltrons. Those that came after swelled over and past them before they could die.

Jarom remained fixated on the giant ballista.

"The rain has swollen the anchor rope!" Rynar was shout-ing. "Cut it!"

"Where?" the operator cried helplessly.

Rynar lunged, dirk slashing. Corded strands frayed and snapped, and with a resounding whoosh, the logs were launched forward, annihilating the foremost wave of enemies.

The wizard, however, was still alive.

There was no time to reflect upon the missed opportunity. Scrabbling over the debris and the bodies of their wounded brethren came the dragonspawn, shrieking their cries. Al-ready, waiting units of pikemen were diving in upon the enemy's flanks, trying valiantly to force them back. Corathel and others were leading troops down from the battlement to assist, even as archers continued their attack from above. The soul-strafing clamor Jarom had first heard at Bane Draw had found its way now into Morethil's vaunted Ring of De-fense, and as it echoed within the towering walls, seemed al-ready to have surrounded him.

He waited no longer, but launched himself down the nearest flight of steps and into the fray, brandishing the Crimson Sword before him. They had but moments to overcome this disadvantage, else the city would be lost.

Rain and darkness created a haze through which movement seemed less than real. The dragonspawn were carving through the human blockades, leaving only blood and death behind them. Men shrieked, in pain and in horror. Jarom could almost feel their courage failing—helpless to withstand this unnatural scourge.

In moments, he found himself among them, adrift within a foaming sea. He gave little thought to caution or strategy, but let the Sword guide him. Its divine power ripped through him in flaming torrents, an endless rush of passion and strength, even as his outer senses remained calm and alert. One after another, the black-scaled bodies fell before him. Cheers went up, and a knot of soldiers gathered in his wake. With grim purpose, he led them in the direction of the shattered gatehouse, hoping to meet up with Corathel and battle at his friend's side.

He had expected to find the man locked in mortal combat, but he could not, this early in the fight, have envisioned the truth. In their rush to secure the breach, the imperial soldiers following the chief general had exposed their northern flank. Through cunning or instinct or sheer accident, a line of dragonspawn had stabbed through like a jouster's lance. The flank had crumpled, allowing the enemy to drive a wedge between Corathel's regiment and the battlement. With each passing instant, the gulf between the two widened, with one stream of dragonspawn forming a noose about the chief general, and the other carving a path to the heights above.

Jarom hacked and spun through the swelling hordes, leaving behind a swath of death. Dragonspawn from all sides moved to intercept him, drawn to the power of the Sword. No sooner did an enemy present itself, however, than it was hewn down, its soul cast back into whatever mystical fire had given it birth. All the while, Corathel's voice bellowed forth commands, a sound Jarom used as a beacon. Almost before he realized it, he had traced the sound to its source, and in a final flurry, cleared the ground of enemies between them.

He found no time for celebration.

"Colonel, hold this position!" Corathel bellowed. "Torin, the battlement!"

No one questioned the commands. With Corathel at his side, Jarom led his immediate followers into the river of dragonspawn that had crested the rampart and was working its way now toward the assembly parapet above. Lorron, he saw, was already engaged, directing Imperial Guard in the defense of Prince Deven, who was trapped in the command turret. The dragonspawn, he realized, had gone straight for their throat.

He surged up the steps, keeping close to the wall and away from the edge, where weapons and bodies rained down like hailstones. Bits and pieces of men littered the blood-slicked marble beneath his feet. Screams ushered his ascent. Although fully aware, he remained numb to all but the fires of the Sword, which demanded their release. He gave it to them time and again, tireless, unflinching, a capsule of divine strength and instinct. None could withstand his calculated fury.

Most were easy targets, grappling already with soldiers who sought to hold the battlement. Jarom reached the heights and continued on with single-minded purpose. Corathel and others remained at his heels. Dragonspawn squealed as he cut them down, their reptilian eyes narrowed against the radiance of his blade. Within moments, the path to the city's high commanders had been cleared.

From the elevated vantage of the assembly parapet, Jarom gazed down upon the slaughter. In more places than he cared to count, dragonspawn had pierced the defensive lines and gone over, around, or through the protective flanks. Already, the main courtyard was a frenzied mixture of friend and foe, with scattered teams of men defeating one enemy only to spin about and face another. The sheer number of imperial soldiers coming around from east and west was helping to contain the damage for now, like the banks of a river. But the river was flooding, threatening to drown all beneath its rush.

"Deven!" Corathel shouted, eschewing the other's title. "You can't force them back. The ring is going to fall!"

The prince looked to Lorron, who was waving away one of the men attempting to inspect a gash in his forehead. Jarom held his breath as he awaited the High Guardian's assessment.

"I fear he's right, my lord prince. Unless we can seal the gates, it is but a matter of time."

Jarom's eyes widened in surprise. A sheen of sweat coated his skin, though he felt not the slightest threat of exhaustion.

"Then we retreat into the Ring of Commerce," Deven decided, "and work better this time to hold the gates!"

Corathel shook his head. "You know the inner rings cannot hold. Withdraw into them, and we leave ourselves surrounded. Your people must evacuate now."

Deven was aghast. "My lord father would never allow it!"

"You would rather they be butchered? Order the evacuation. Send them west before the enemy surrounds us. You've no other choice."

Jarom cursed at the bitter truth. In his arrogance, Emperor Derreg had constructed a city without any emergency exit. There were no tunnels through which its citizens could escape should Morethil be overrun. An unnavigable maze of sewers, perhaps, barred at every turn against unlawful entry, but nothing through which five hundred thousand souls could make a hasty retreat. Corathel, in their strategy sessions over the past few days, had urged the city leaders to begin work immediately on such a route, or to allow those who wished to depart for lands west or south to do so. But Deven would have none of it. The safest place for all of them, he insisted, was right here behind Morethil's walls, with the Crimson Sword set to guard her gates.

For a moment, the prince seemed to consider the chief general's request. "No," he said at last, then snarled in anger. "These beasts will not take from me my home!"

"They will!" Corathel snapped. "Whether or not they take your life first!"

This time, both Deven and Corathel turned to Lorron. The

High Guardian ignored their stares, gazing out over the peaceful sweep of the inner city and its citizens, many of whom stood upon walls and rooftops, seeking to follow the ebb and flow of the yet distant battle. He then looked to one of his guardsmen.

"Carry word to the city watch. All citizens are to evacuate at once."

"You will not! Belay that order, Sergeant!"

"Forgive me, Lord Prince, but as High Guardian, my first duty is to the people of this city," Lorron insisted, obviously torn. He faced the bewildered guardsman squarely. "You have my order, Sergeant. Carry it out."

Deven turned purple with rage. "As crown prince and future emperor, I rescind that order and hereby strip the High Guardian of his command!"

"You may indeed bring such a motion before the Council. Until then, my commission stands. Sergeant, give the order."

The sergeant considered all that he had heard, then turned to leave. Steel rasped as Deven's dagger came free. Before the unfortunate soldier had taken two steps, he slumped to his knees, blood gushing from a hole in the side of his neck.

Imperial Guard rushed in to restrain the maddened prince. Before they reached him, he made a lunge for Lorron. The High Guardian drew no weapon, but did step aside, allowing Deven to barrel past. The prince's own momentum carried him right over the forward edge of the crenellated wall, where he plummeted with a ceaseless wail into the sea of dragonspawn below. By the time Jarom caught sight of him, the enemy had ripped the man's body to shreds.

He looked to Lorron, who after witnessing the First Son's demise, found his gaze.

"It will take some time to escort my people safely away."

"We'll hold the enemy for as long as it takes," Jarom promised. "Quickly now, before it's too late."

It was an easy vow to make, but another matter altogether to see it carried through. Lorron departed at once, his contingent in tow, to notify the emperor, oversee the exodus, and assemble a rear guard to protect them all on what was sure to be a harrowing flight. He left the battle in their hands, commanding his highest officers to follow Corathel's orders as if they were his own. After sending word to Nevik to lead his refugees away and take Marisha with them, Jarom turned his full attention back to the fray.

For the next few hours, he helped Corathel orchestrate a mostly losing effort, moving from one point to another, keeping to those areas in which combat was at its heaviest or most critical. At times, the chief general used him as a lure to draw lines of dragonspawn this way or that. At other times, he was sent to spearhead counterassaults or rescue maneuvers. It was the type of fighting to which Corathel was accustomed, toward which he had dedicated a lifetime of practice and study. Although the enemy strengthened its position little by little, Jarom knew that were it not for the chief general's tactical savvy, the city would have fallen—like so many others to the dragonspawn—with hardly a fight.

The wizard and demon golem were both curiously absent. When first they had disappeared, Jarom had feared they meant to circle the city and open its remaining gates. But the lookouts registered no such intent. The dragonspawn remained focused on storming the shattered north gate, and there was no further sign of their leaders. For a time, Jarom worried over what that might mean, believing the Queen and her minions too cunning not to press every advantage. Surely they were up to something, but for the lives of those he loved, he couldn't think of what that might be.

Reports came and went, messengers dispatched by Lorron to advise them of the High Guardian's progress and to inquire as to theirs. The evacuation was proceeding far more smoothly than Jarom would have believed. With three gates open to them—west, south, and east—Morethil's populace was pouring out in steady streams via foot, wagon, and horseback. Every soldier who could be spared was helping out—emptying homes, relieving people of unnecessary possessions, directing traffic, controlling panic, or standing ready should the enemy take notice. Although something about all of this also concerned him, Jarom was too busy to question their good fortune.

Inevitably, their luck ran out. It happened while defending

a gateway between the Ring of Defense and the Ring of Commerce. Thus far, the dragonspawn had proceeded from the main courtyard less than a half turn to the east, and only a quarter turn to the west—just a few miles in each direction—and had secured less than a third as much of the battlements above. In addition, city forces maintained a complete buffer around the inner wall. As if frustrated by their own lack of progress, the dragonspawn made a push for the inner ring, where the defenses were thinnest. Jarom and Corathel cut them off, but in doing so, found themselves severed from the main force, alone with perhaps fifty men. Sensing their vulnerability—and the magnitude of the kill—the dragonspawn closed in.

"We can't keep this up!" Corathel managed to shout.

"We finish it!" Jarom cried. He lopped the head from a foe with a tremendous swing and roared again, "We finish it!"

But no matter the direction he turned, he could not find a seam in the enemy's press. They were trapped, and their numbers were dwindling.

To the east, a chorus of human battle cries grew stronger. Before long, the dragonspawn's push slackened from that direction, with many of them turning to confront the new threat. Jarom understood why when an axe blade erupted from the breastbone of one of the beasts as it prepared to lunge at him. The blade wrenched free, the twitching carcass fell away, and Jarom found himself eye to chest with a grim-faced Lar, whose men worked even now to erect a human shield around them.

"Lar, my friend!" Jarom exclaimed. "You don't know how good it is to see you."

"Well done," Corathel agreed, catching his breath as he clasped the Fourth General's hand. Both men, Jarom noted, were drenched with rain and sweat and spattered with blood—both the black of dragonspawn and the red of men slain beside them. It was impossible to tell if either was wounded.

"We heard you were keeping the fight to yourselves," came another familiar voice. Second General Jasyn swaggered into view, grinning fiercely and twirling a dagger in his hand.

A frightful crash went up from the left flank. Jarom spun. The dragonspawn had managed to collapse a portion of the inner gateway and had begun to pour through into the Ring of Commerce. A reserve force charged to meet them, a force comprised mostly of men bearing the sigil of Drakmar. When the foray had ended, fewer than a handful of the enemy had escaped into the city, while for the moment, both the integrity of the portal and the shield of men around it had been restored.

As a company of soldiers gave chase to the runaway drag-onspawn, Jarom rushed to confront Nevik.

"What are you still doing here?"

"I tried to send word," the baron replied. "My folk have gone. But that lady of yours seems determined to be the last to leave. I argued, but she was very persuasive. My soldiers and I decided to stay with her."

Jarom was horrified. He should have known that Marisha would refuse to depart until all others were safely away.

"General, the city is near to being overwhelmed." It was a dire assessment, made more so in that it came from the usually silent, unflappable Lar.

Corathel nodded. "Time to organize our retreat."

"No!" Jarom protested. "It's too soon!"

"We've done all we can. Derreg created this mess. Let him live with it."

Jarom was adamant. "I can't allow that."

"We haven't a choice," the chief general insisted. "We make our escape now or never."

Jarom started to object, then noticed for the first time the truly ragged state of the defenders around him. They had been at this for nearly four hours now, an impossible stand by any means. He himself had tired neither physically nor mentally, but that was due to only one reason—a reason held clutched in his bloodstained hands. These men with whom he fought had but a small measure of the Sword's aura to fuel them. How could he ask them to give more than they already had?

He hadn't the right. And yet, he wasn't about to allow those such as Marisha and Nevik to fall victim to their own courage. There had to be a way.

"We need a distraction," he decided.

Corathel regarded him suspiciously. "How do you mean?"

"We draw them from the city. Like we've done all along. It worked to save Leaven, and Atharvan."

"It would seem a little late for that."

"Not if we give them what they want."

The chief general frowned with understanding. "Give them the Sword, and you may just give them the war."

"I don't intend to go down without a fight."

"You'll never make it. Not by yourself. And a man would have to be mad to join you."

Jarom gave the other a wry smirk. "Know where I can find such a man?"

Corathel pursed his lips, peering over Jarom's shoulder, where the sounds of battle were drawing closer once more. He then looked into Jarom's eyes and tightened his grip upon his sword.

"May the bards make us heroes, and not just fools," the chief general muttered, then shouted to his commanders. "We make for Souaris, my friends, by way of the north gate."

Even Jasyn blanched at the prospect before defying his fears with a grimace.

"Have the criers send word."

"Where's Maltyk?"

"Assisting Lorron with the civilian rear guard. Have him warn . . ."

Jarom turned to Nevik as plans were made and orders sent forth. "Take your soldiers and go now. Carry Marisha kicking and screaming if you have to. I'll catch up on the road to Souaris."

The young baron started to protest, then nodded instead. "It shall be done, my lord."

Moments later, it began. As ordered, the troops fell back against the inner wall, allowing the enemy to pour east and west in greater numbers around the outer portion of the Ring of Defense. It was a feint, of course, designed to lure as many of the dragonspawn as possible into the city, while keeping the inner rings secure. Driven by a feral instinct so strong it made them almost mindless with fury, the black beasts were only too willing to seize the offered opening. When the lands fronting the north gate had been all but cleared, Jarom led the charge.

It was a desperate maneuver that bore little chance of success. But Jarom forged ahead into the thick of the enemy horde, spinning and slashing in a dance of flaming splendor. Behind him came the others in wedge formation, those few he knew—Corathel, Jasyn, Lar—and roughly two thousand he didn't. They drove deep into the fallen courtyard and beyond, engaging only those who stood directly in their path. They coughed and blinked against soot and ash, dodging the flames of war machines and stockpiles that had been set ablaze and burned now despite the rains. Through the choking, stinging haze loomed the blasted outer gates, a mass of twisted iron and flaming cinders yawning like a dragon's maw. Surging past the rear waves of dragonspawn that sought to bar their path, Jarom led them through.

The highway beyond was a slough of blood and water. While deflecting an enemy blow, Jarom's feet went out from under him, a near fall that should have been the end of him. But Lar was there, catching him and shoving him forward, his axe sweeping outward in great whooshing arcs. Others were not so lucky. Jarom could hear them slipping and splashing and shrieking their final screams, even as their overall numbers continued to spill forth.

He looked back, fearful that the dragonspawn might simply clamp down on the north gate, trap those pouring after him, and continue their siege. But they were too busy giving chase. Picking and tearing at the edges of his flushing columns, they followed him and his allies through the gatehouse like a beacon. As more of the enemy realized what was happening, they too turned about to partake in the hunt. The city was forgotten. It was he who carried the treasure they sought.

Eventually, their reverse push through the north gate would indeed overcome that of Morethil's remaining armies. When that happened, the bulk of those armies would allow the dragonspawn to leave, then turn around and follow their civilians from the city through gates west, east, and south. It was precisely as Corathel had planned and Jarom had dared hope: one feint after another, pulling the enemy around by its collective snout. All in all, it looked to be a rousing success.

Except, of course, for Jarom and the roughly two thousand souls who followed him.

For them there was only the open rangelands and a nightmare chase from which Jarom harbored no delusions of escape. Even with the Sword to bestow upon him—and to a lesser extent, those around him—unnatural endurance, the dragonspawn were faster, stronger, and never seemed to tire. And there were far too many to turn around and confront. With mounts, they might have stood a chance—for all the good such thinking did them.

They ran as hard and as fast as they could, hoping to pull the enemy as far as possible from the city and its stragglers. Jarom steeled himself against the cries of those who stumbled or were ripped down from behind. Many, when they grew too tired, spun to face their deaths head-on, hoping to buy the vanguard a little more time. At one point, Jarom did the same. Not because his legs were heavy or his lungs leaden, for the Sword shielded him from such pains. But he was tired of men dying to protect him, tired of suffering brought about because he refused to relinquish the Sword. Surely, many who followed him would elect a life of slavery over no life at all. Who was he to deny them that choice?

But his friends would have none of it, seizing him by the arms and spinning him back around. Together, they ran on, although they knew they wouldn't make it—until suddenly, like an oasis risen from the desert dunes, there it was, a line of armored horse bearing toward them as they crested a ridgeline. For a moment, Jarom feared it to be a force under command of the wizard, like that which had thwarted their retreat at Bane Draw. But Corathel's exclamation of surprise told him otherwise. *"Souari!"* the chief general cried, pointing to their standards. *"Souari!"*

The columns of faceless soldiers thundered past, lances and visors lowered, iron-shod hooves tearing at the earth. A commander wearing no helmet, with hair so blond as to be almost white, reined in before them.

"King Torin," he greeted with a sly smile. "I've word you could use a little aid."

Jarom was too stunned to question how or why, or to balk at the use of that other name.

"Continue north. My men will ferry you across the river. You'll find horses and wagons beyond the vale that will carry you west."

The stranger gave a sharp salute, then charged down the hill in pursuit of his fellow soldiers. Already, their circling attacks were working to disengage the legions of dragon-spawn from Jarom's trailing forces.

Jarom remained where he was, but urged his followers past. The trio of Parthan generals stayed with him. To a man, they shook their heads in disbelief. Not only at their unexpected fortune, but at the trail of carnage left in their wake. In the distance, Morethil smoldered beneath a blackened sky.

"Time to go," Corathel urged him. Even with what looked to be a thousand horse, the dragonspawn would not be stalled for long. "You did well today."

Jarom frowned. As he saw it, they had failed twice now, first at Kraagen Keep, and now surrendering Morethil in less than a day. They would have to do much better to buy Kylac and Allion the time they needed to stop Killangrathor.

But they could do nothing more this day. With a stinging sense of shame, Jarom turned away.

From high atop the city, locked within a private tower, Emperor Derreg drew back from the mounted spyglass through which he had observed the desperate retreat of those who followed the Crimson Sword. He had cursed their cowardice, just as he had cursed his High Guardian and the others who had tried to remove him. And yet, fate seemed to favor the craven on this day, for while many had been hewn down, Torin himself had escaped—assisted, no less, by those treasonous dogs from Souaris. Never had he trusted that Culmaril clan, so proud and aloof, clinging to airs for which there was no place in his empire. He should have stripped them of their lands and titles and had them flogged in his streets long ago.

One day soon, he would have their heads. He would have all of their heads, and would mount them on spikes atop every merlon and crenel that lined his battlements.

He turned to his aide. "Help me to my bedchamber."

The boy came forward, dutiful as always, though his cheeks had gone pale with shock. Morethil was all but deserted. Just a few old souls like him remained, faithful to the end, they and the criminals trapped in their cells beneath his outer wall. He was surprised that Lorron had not freed them all, the traitor.

They were alone in his tower, he and the boy. A handful of Imperial Guard remained, securing his door from without, but the bulk had left with Lorron, who had proclaimed a duty to the city's rabble that outweighed even that to their emperor. Oath breakers all. On second thought, he would not mount their heads. He did not wish to stain his walls with their blood.

The boy helped him into his favorite sitting chair, then left to fetch a pitcher of ale. It was but a matter of time now. Eventually, they would return. Not his armies or his subjects, but the dragons, those filthy brutes that had set flame to his fair city. They would return to finish what they had begun, now that the Crimson Sword was beyond their reach, razing Morethil to the ground. He could see them now as they swept westward into the deeper lands of Kuuria, not around his city, but through each of its successive rings, laying waste to all he had ever achieved.

His chest tightened. The city would be his pyre. Perhaps, he thought, that was how it should be.

By the time his aide returned to him, Derreg, emperor of Kuuria, Father of Morethil, was already dead.

CHAPTER FORTY

*H*e entered the camp under cover of darkness, cloaked and hooded so that only his face was visible. Most were dressed the same, huddled under blankets around meager fires, seeking their own relief from the incessant rains. Few bothered to look his way, and none drew near. Just as he wanted it.

"Torin!"

He turned. The man who approached wore a brooch emblazoned with the boar's-head sigil of Drakmar.

"My scouts must have missed you," the young baron said, unable to contain his elation. "Are you all right? Where are the others?"

He accepted the other's arm, clasping it in greeting. "I came on ahead. Where is she? Is she safe?"

"Marisha? Yes, she's well. Tending to the wounded, of course."

"I need to see her."

The baron seemed bemused by his brusque manner, but waved him forward. "Of course. I'll take you to her."

"Quietly. I don't want to draw everyone's attention."

"I understand," the baron agreed. "Come. This way."

Together, they worked their way through the clusters of refugees fled that day from Morethil. Most were awake yet silent, no doubt stunned into quiet reflection as a result of their ordeal. Lovers held each other, mothers whispered to their young. Many worked to soothe the pain of blisters and saddle sores. It must have been a horrifying flight, with an untold number of days to go.

"What happened? Did Commander Troy find you?"

He shook his head. "Later, my friend."

The baron glanced back at him, solemn with concern, then fell into silence.

His guide made a handful of inquiries that led them deeper into the encampment. There were no tents or pavilions. Those with serious wounds had been gathered protectively in the center, many of them stashed away beneath crude lean-tos. It was from one of these shelters that she emerged, her face as bright and defiant as he remembered it.

The baron hailed her. "Marisha!"

She turned, glancing about, then rushed forward to embrace him.

"I'd dared not hope," she whispered, her head pressed tight against his shoulder. A moment later, she pulled back. "What's wrong? Are you hurt?"

"Marisha," he said, and smiled. "We need to speak. Alone."

She stared up at him, and nodded. "What is it?"

He took her by the hand, then glanced back at the baron. "Please see that we're not followed."

The other nodded. "I'll be on post to the southeast." His brow was lined with worry, but he kept it to himself. "The gods will see us through this," the young baron offered consolingly.

He gave no reply before leading Marisha away.

They proceeded back the way he had come, to the east beyond the fringe of the camp. No one troubled their progress, not even the outer watch, whose grim faces were set on the distant horizon in search of riders with word of enemy pursuit. Marisha held his hand tightly, but respected his wish for silence.

Past the sprawling clusters of refugees, he turned north, leading her up and over a series of small hills through a thickening number of trees. They had gone several hundred paces beyond the sight or sound of any other being before he brought them to a halt in a small, fir-ringed clearing.

"Jarom, you're frightening me," she said, taking a few steps past him into the center of the grove.

The surrounding brush began to rustle. A company of black-clad mercenaries emerged from the foliage, weapons drawn.

Marisha gave a gasp of surprise, then spun back on him. The wizard smiled at her horror as his guise melted away, his features morphing from those of his younger brother into his own.

A massive hand of gleaming obsidian clamped over her mouth, muffling her scream.

Nevik took his seat around the fire shared with his surviving commanders, accepting the portions of stale bread and burnt meat offered to him. His face wrinkled at the taste, but he ate them anyway. It was perhaps the best he could hope for until they arrived at Souaris—or whatever their next destination ended up being.

"Captain Eames is dead, sir."

Nevik glanced at his hawk-nosed lieutenant, Heman, who had himself lost three fingers on his left hand in the day's battle. Eames had lost more than that, taking a slash that had turned his thigh into a fountain. Tightly bandaged, the captain had survived long enough to flee the city with the rest of them, refusing even to be carted. But when Nevik had visited the man an hour ago, he had seen the truth.

"We'll build a cairn, for him and the others. I want no man of ours left to these Kuurian vultures."

"As you wish, Lord Baron. I'll see to it at once."

"Stay as you are, Lieutenant," Nevik countered, noting the other's grimace when he began to rise. "Mind those wounds. I'll see to it myself."

He had just finished the last of his meal when the scout appeared, riding up fast. The bowlegged youth dismounted and gave a hurried salute. "My lord, King Torin has arrived."

"Yes, Corporal. I've met with him already."

"My lord?"

"I took him to see his lady. He's with her now."

The scout stared at him, confused. "My lord, I met him beyond the east checkpoint. With his leave, I rode ahead to alert you of his coming."

Nevik stopped, giving the other his full attention. "He was on horse?"

"Yes, my lord. He and some two hundred others. They stopped to report with General Maltyk of the rear guard."

It was now Nevik's turn to show confusion. "But, if he is to the east . . ." He paused, a slow and certain dread building within. "You are certain he stayed back with the others?"

"Yes, my lord."

"Sound the alarm."

"My lord?"

"Sound the alarm!" he roared, and went racing through the camp.

Two hundred. Of his two thousand, that was all that remained. Everyone, it seemed, was in line to congratulate him on their success, to toast the daring maneuver that had enabled the city to complete its evacuation. All Jarom could think about was the eighteen hundred souls left unburied on the sodden rangelands of eastern Kuuria—that, and the countless wives and parents and children to whom he would somehow have to apologize.

Reckless. That's what it was. They all would have perished, and the Sword would now be in the hands of the enemy, had it not been for Troy and his Souari cavalry. The flaxen-haired commander had caught up with them some time ago, with word that the enemy hordes had turned south again toward Morethil. Whether they meant to occupy the city or simply raze it to the ground was unknown, but at least they would find it all but empty.

It was Nevik who had given the commander word of Jarom's predicament. Troy and his cavalry battalions had been patrolling the highway between Souaris and Morethil for several days now, ever since their king had received word from the Imperial Council as to the state of affairs. When they had come across the first of the citizens fleeing the besieged city, they had moved east to assist with the rear guard. Later, upon hearing from the baron of Drakmar about

Jarom's desperate ruse, Troy and his followers had peeled away from that group and come at once.

They could rest easy throughout the night, Troy had assured him. A relay of scouts would keep them apprised of any enemy movements, and they should know some time before daybreak as to the fate of Morethil. Come dawn, they were to continue west. All were welcome at Souaris—a two-day journey, given the number and condition of those who traveled. There, they need not fear the kind of tragedy with which they had met this day. In the five hundred years of its existence, not once had their city fallen to an invader. Once inside her walls, all would be safe.

Jarom had thanked the man, though he cringed at the thought of yet another city said to be impregnable. The commander had every right to take pride in his city, to assume it might stand as it always had. But by now, Jarom knew better.

Leaving Troy and his cavalry behind, Jarom had pressed on in pursuit of the others, survivors in tow. Well after nightfall, they had run across one of Nevik's scouts, just before catching up with Morethil's rear guard. To ease his friend's worry, Jarom had sent the scout on ahead while he and his men stopped to share all that they knew with Maltyk. The Third General, while pleased to see them, was understandably grave. It was estimated that the army had lost half its number in the day's battle, leaving them with something in the realm of twenty thousand. That number had grown even smaller when Lorron had taken a contingent of Imperial Guard and gone back for the emperor, leaving hours earlier along a southerly course. As of yet, they had not returned, and based upon Troy's news that the dragonspawn had also gone back to Morethil, it was unlikely the High Guardian or any of those who had gone with him had escaped. But of greatest concern to the Parthan commander was that Rynar was missing. And while it was possible the Fifth General was lost amid the throngs somewhere within the refugee camp, Maltyk had had runners searching for him all evening. Thus far, there had been no word.

It had been a lot to swallow all at once, but there was no other way to take it. When the reports had concluded,

Jarom had excused himself for the main camp, meaning to visit with Nevik and Marisha while leaving Corathel, his lieutenants, and the two hundred of two thousand to reintegrate themselves with Maltyk and the remnants of Morethil's army.

Those remnants, strung north and south in their rearguard formation, were stationed more than a mile to the east of the civilian encampment. Jarom had traveled perhaps two-thirds of that distance when he heard the clangor of weapons and the shouts of men. The commotion was coming down from the north, echoing across the pocket of empty range between soldiers and refugees. No sooner had he determined its location than he put heel to flank, urging his horse into a gallop.

His heart began to race. The closer he got, the more he knew something was terribly wrong. Could the enemy have found them? It did not sound like dragonspawn. Nor did he believe they could have gotten this close without being detected by either Commander Troy's scouts or their own. Whatever was happening was unexpected, and thus even more worrisome.

He thundered his way over slopes and ravines, heedless of the threat to his mount and himself as they tore through the darkness. Trees rose up about him, hardwoods stark and leafless and evergreens tall and proud. The clamor had grown louder. He was almost on top of it.

A soldier burst from the brush onto the path before him, wide-eyed and weaponless, clutching at a gash in his shoulder. He appeared so suddenly that Jarom had not the time to alter his steed's course, and promptly knocked the wounded man spinning to the ground. Looking back, he just barely caught a glimpse of the sprawled man's armored dress—black and silver, like that worn by the mercenaries from whom he had rescued Queen Ellebe all those weeks ago—before he and his horse barreled through the screen of trees from which the other had fled.

In the grove beyond, the fighting was mostly under control. More than two dozen bodies lay dead or wounded upon the woodland earth, several of them Drakmar assigned as watchmen to the main camp, but many more wearing the black and silver of mercenaries belonging to the wizard Soric. Jarom quickly spotted Nevik among the survivors, wielding his mace to devastating effect. The baron's opponent had blood in his eyes, making it difficult for him to parry the other's attacks. In desperation, the mercenary reached up with one hand to wipe clear his vision. Nevik promptly reversed his grip with a strike that followed the other's movement, smashing the soldier's hand deep into the fleshy matter of his own face.

"Marisha!" Nevik shouted, spying Jarom while moving already to engage another foe. "They took her east!"

Jarom did not have to ask who. Even amid the waning chaos and human debris, he recognized the deep, rain-filled prints of the Demon Queen's obsidian golem. With the demon, no doubt, was the wizard.

He spun about with an angry shout, the Crimson Sword still sheathed across his back. Leaving behind these fodder meant to cover their leaders' escape, he charged after the demon's departing trail.

"Torin, wait!"

The plea was lost to the thunder of his passage as his mount carried him north and east through the foothills of the Tenstrock Mountains. The rear guard would no doubt be astir by now, but Jarom held little hope that they could respond in time. His enemies would circle above the northern flank just as they must have done coming in. Or perhaps the demon, who had proven impervious to any iron- or steel-edged assault—and the wizard, shielded by his spells—would punch right through their ranks. In either case, he alone could save Marisha, assuming he could catch them.

Blinded by fear and denial, he might have lost the demon's trail as it broke free of the trees to cross an uneven stretch of open range. But revealed in the distance under the muted glow of cloud-choked moonlight was the demon itself. Slumped over its shoulder was a human form that bounced lifelessly with each of the golem's loping strides.

Before he could even verify that it was Marisha, or that she was still alive, the demon and its burden crested a ridgeline and were gone from view. Snarling with red-vision fury, Jarom kicked his horse onward.

It was then that he saw the wizard, riding well behind the golem on his steed of mist. Wisps of dark smoke curled in the wind where the animal's legs should have been, bearing the magic-user up the slope over which his demon companion had just disappeared.

But before the wizard could do the same, he glanced back and seemed to spy Jarom's approach. Instead of continuing on, the sorcerer came to a halt atop the ridgeline, looking back and forth to the low-level mountains that ringed this narrow valley on either side. There, he remained astride his sorcerous mount and waited for Jarom to come.

Jarom did not know what the other had planned; nor did he care. When he reached the base of the hill atop which his brother waited, he drew the Sword from the scabbard slung across his back. He gritted his teeth as the talisman's warmth worked to temper his rage, unwilling to be mollified. Ignoring the protests of his horse, he surged on up the slope.

They never reached the top. When they had come to within fifty lengths, Jarom could see that the wizard was chanting. At thirty, the sorcerer arced the head of his staff low to the ground in a wide, sweeping motion. The earth responded, heaving violently, then splitting wide. A dark crevasse formed across the breadth of the valley at the wizard's feet, stretching north and south to cut off Jarom's pursuit. The resulting quake unleashed a landslide of boulders and deadwood that sent Jarom and his mount skidding. The terrified animal screamed and reared but managed to keep its feet, even as slender fissures rent the hill's surface like lightning and showers of loose stone bounced and scrabbled down the slope.

When it was over, the earth gone still, Jarom was surprised to find that the wizard remained. Small wonder, he realized, as he calmed his steed and urged it ahead through a choking cloud of dust. For the gulf that the sorcerer had opened between them was near twenty paces across and probably twice as deep, with no way around except to circle the entire valley. Perched upon the lower lip of the chasm, Jarom glared up to find the wizard's loathsome smile.

"Surprised, my brother?" the creature hissed down at him. "The Queen knew you would escape Morethil, just as you escaped her at Kraagen Keep. But the maiden, the one you most desire, would likely have perished in the slaughter. Flushing her free was the best way to take her alive."

"No," Jarom said. "You could not have planned this." He shook his head vehemently, as if by the strength of his denial he might alter the truth.

"No?" the wizard echoed. "Why else would we have allowed this flock to escape? They are nothing, my brother. In time, the Queen will have them all, to do with as she pleases. But the maiden is special, is she not? She is the key, the key to you, my brother. Now that we have her, you will surrender the Sword without further struggle."

"Return her to me now," Jarom countered, "and I shall let you live out the remainder of your exile as decreed by your father."

The wizard laughed, though he seemed somehow less amused. "Threats, my brother? I fear not your stolen power. Were it not for the Queen, I would destroy you here and now."

Jarom did not believe it for a moment. If his brother truly thought he could destroy him and take the Sword for himself, surely he would have done so already.

"Then how about this?" Jarom tried, thinking back to their first meeting at Kraagen Keep. "If ever you thought to make me family, let us fight together and settle our differences later."

Soric scoffed. "Too late for that, my brother. You had your chance when you fled from me like a brigand. Helping you now would be like joining the mouse against the snake."

Jarom was frantic, but did not know how to respond. His survivalist brother wasn't prepared to defy the Demon Queen. And he, in turn, was not about to abandon Marisha. Trapped as he was on this side of the chasm, the matter seemed a stalemate.

"Your friends arrive."

Jarom turned, just for a moment, to see the emergence of

Nevik and a dozen or more Drakmar soldiers pouring from the woodland fringe a quarter-mile away.

"They think to save you," the wizard taunted. "Heed well the message they carry. The life you cherish most depends upon your choice."

The sorcerer waved his hand over the top of his steed's misty head, turning it about.

"Ride fast, my brother," Jarom called after him, "and your demon as well. I'm coming for you!"

The wizard ignored his taunt, cresting the shattered ridge-line to disappear to the east.

Jarom jerked hard the reins of his own mount, spinning back to the west. When he reached Nevik and his breathless troops at the base of the hill, he reared to a halt.

"He spoke of a message," he demanded tersely.

Nevik glanced at those around him, sweat dripping from his forehead.

"The wizard's men," Jarom insisted. "What did they say?"

The baron took a gulp of air. "The demon has taken Marisha to Morethil. She will be held there in exchange for the Sword." He hesitated, sucking in another breath. "They said the sooner you arrive, the more of her will remain."

"How did this happen?"

"Forgive me, my lord, the wizard—"

"Never mind," Jarom snorted. "Inform General Corathel. Tell him I've gone east in pursuit."

"My lord?"

"Do it, Lord Baron. Proceed west at sunrise, whether or not I've returned."

He went to snap the reins, but before he could, the burly young Nevik reached up and grabbed one side in his hand. The horse, lathered already almost beyond use, was only too happy to remain where it was.

"I'm sorry, my lord, but I can't let you do that."

Jarom looked at the other in shock. "Unhand my reins."

The baron shook his head.

"Nevik!"

"My friend, listen to me. You gain nothing by surrendering to their demands. Think on it."

But Jarom couldn't think, not where Marisha was concerned. He tried to recall their final moment together, her promise that it would not be their last. Yet all he could see was her prone form strung over the demon's shoulder. He loved her; that much was plain to him now. In all of this, the one possibility he couldn't bear was that he might be forced to live without her.

As he glared down at his friend, anger turned to pain.

"They'll not harm her," Nevik reassured him, "not as long as they believe in the advantage she gives them. But if we are to face them, it must be in a time and manner of our choosing, not theirs."

It made sense. But did that matter? Jarom wasn't sure. He did note, however, his friend's use of *we* instead of *you,* as if to say that whatever Jarom decided, he was not in this alone.

The tranquillity of the Sword's fire swept through him. It seemed to taste his hunger for vengeance, but now was not the time. Not like this, in a move that could at best be considered reckless and headstrong. He was reminded of the diversion he had led that day to help free Morethil's people—a false triumph that had cost them eighteen hundred lives. He would not, he vowed, make that same mistake again.

He looked to the western trees, where a swarm of riders from the rear guard were sweeping down to check on the uproar. In that moment, a change came over him, a chill as undulating and powerful as the Sword's warmth. It was a feeling of determination, born of acceptance. The time for denial and lack of confidence had long since passed. Like it or not, this was what his life had become. It mattered not what excuses he might muster. King, hero, savior—the bards could call it what they willed. But it was his mantle to wear, not because of some mysterious fate or predetermined calling, but because there was a need. And he would not let that need go unanswered for fear of the unknown.

"My lord?"

He turned his gaze back to Nevik, the courageous young baron who had managed to come to terms with the unwanted burdens of his own life weeks ago. If only the gods would now grant him similar strength.

"My lord?"

"We ride for Souaris," he agreed. "But know this. Today marks our final defeat. When next demons or dragons dare to confront us, it will be they who shriek to the heavens cries of injustice. Not you. And not I."

The baron's hand fell from his reins. Jarom sheathed the Crimson Sword and rode forward to meet his troops, leaving an astonished Nevik to stare after. The last thing he noted was the fierce pride shining in the man's eyes, and a resolve to match his own.

CHAPTER FORTY-ONE

Allion dropped his head back, refreshed by the chill water as it dribbled down his face. He closed his eyes against the brilliance of the late afternoon sun, basking in its welcome radiance. With the water to wash away the grime of his journey and the sun to warm his bones, he felt better than he had in days. But for the ache in his heart, he might have felt whole.

It had been three days now since the tragedy at the falls that had taken Kylac and left the hunter with nothing more than a knife, a length of rope, and his wits—the latter of which had been questionable for a time. Though determined at first to press onward in his hunt of Killangrathor, not a moment had passed in which he did not challenge his own decision. The Entients had said nothing about his involvement. He had come as a companion to Kylac and nothing more. With the youth gone, he really had no business being here. To think he might somehow manage to fulfill the other's charge—weary, half starved, and weaponless—was a discredit to the youth's memory.

Nevertheless, he had not turned back, resolved to at least reclaim his horse and possessions before he made a final decision. Small task *that* had turned out to be. Swollen by the ceaseless rains and made rapid by an increasingly steep and rugged ascent, the river had proven an unconquerable adversary. Although it would have taken him farther from Mount Krakken, he would have done better to search for a crossing downstream from where the demon had assaulted them. His horse might have been able to withstand the currents at these higher elevations, but he certainly could not. As a result, he had been forced to continue his exhausting march hour after hour through the northern Kalmira, harried by wind and rains, haunted by grief and fear, and without any real hope that his journey would ever end.

Around midmorning of this third day, the assailing storm had passed on to the west. Hours later he had come upon this site, deep within the Skullmar foothills, where the twin banks of the Emerald unexpectedly converged as the mighty river took its journey beneath the earth. Land east and west intersected behind an immense, horizontal fissure from which the thundering waters rushed, and which shrouded the actual source of the Emerald in subterranean mystery. At last, by crawling over the lip of this grotto, he had found his way across.

Finished washing at the river's edge, the hunter untucked his legs from beneath him and sat back on a coarse patch of scrub grass. The thought of another three days' march, this time south along the western shore, was too much to comprehend at the moment. Since setting out alone, he had slept only in fits and starts, and after three days, he had reached the end of his strength. He needed his rest, and he needed it now.

Which did not mean that he could abandon concerns for his own safety. Lying down out here in the open was an invitation for disaster. Nor would he be able to rest comfortably without rigging some form of sentry. As he considered his possessions, however, a minor plan took shape.

He headed downriver, seeking the cover of the forest. After a fair amount of searching, he found what looked to be a perfect resting place, buried within a copse of trees. The trunks were close, their branches tightly interlocked over a small bed of needles. The ground was elevated on three sides, leaving a single, obvious point of entry.

The laying of the trap took him close to an hour, but by the time he had finished, he was undeniably pleased with his efforts. He had managed both noose and trip wire from the single length of rope, and found a heavy log to serve as counterweight. All was carefully concealed, a snare like that used in his youth to catch small animals. That it might work to capture one of the Demon Queen's minions was more than he dared hope, but at the very least, it should give him fair warning should anything try to approach.

Satisfied, he slipped back through the wall of trees and into the center of their stand. He had scarcely settled down when a wave of nothingness fell over him, drawing him into a fast, dreamless sleep.

He awoke to the sound of a sharp thwack and a frightening crash. For a moment, he knew not where he was, nor even who he was. Then he remembered, as he lay listening to the crack and sway of something heavy within the trees. Leaves and needles fluttered down around him, ripped free by the sudden, whiplike motion.

His trap had been sprung.

With a start, Allion pulled free his hunting knife. He could scarcely see. Dusk had come and gone, taking with it the last of the day's light. In the pale wash of moon and stars, dimmed further by the screen of his woodland surroundings, he could just make out the opening that led down from his shelter.

His first thought was to flee, to clamber down the back wall of the shallow rise and to race as far and as fast as he could from whatever had happened upon him. But as the seconds passed without cry or commotion, he reconsidered. Perhaps it was not a demon, but some small animal that might serve as a meal. If it did not thrash or threaten, why should he run?

He crept forward, hardly daring to breathe as he stole through the brush. His heart thrummed frantically, but he could find no way to control it. The commotion of the trees settled. The only sounds were the rushing of the river and the creaking of the thick, low-hanging branch over which his quarry was now hung.

He edged down along the forward trail, crouched low, at one with the soft soil beneath his feet. Through a narrow

break in the foliage, he could see now his prey, a black silhouette against the murky night. It was a forest creature, as
he had hoped, about the size of a marten, although longer
and leaner than he would have expected. It continued to
swing softly, silently, back and forth, dangling by its feet.
Whatever it was, it could do him no harm.

Shaking his head at his own paranoia, he stepped from his
shelter, striding in for a closer look. When he reached the
trap, he hesitated, confused. Suspended within his snare was
nothing more than a gnarled, moss-covered branch. Before
he could so much as glance in either direction, a hand
gripped his forehead from behind, and he felt the cold edge
of a blade pressed against his throat.

"We meet again," a harsh voice hissed in his ear.

An image formed in his mind, the image of a face he had
hoped never to see again. He gulped, as surprised as he was
terrified that the wizard's assassin would have caught up to
him, here and now.

"What do you want, Talyzar?" he growled. He had not the
patience for this. If the assassin meant to kill him, then he
could damn well get on with it.

His captor laughed. "Come now, do I truly smell so foul?"

Allion frowned with recognition. "Kylac?"

The blade at his throat fell away, and Allion spun about,
unrestrained. Before him, a great, roguish grin splitting his
youthful features, was none other than Kylac Kronus.

The hunter blinked repeatedly, then clutched the other's
arm to make sure he had not gone mad. "Kylac! You're
alive!"

He threw his arms about the boy and embraced him
warmly. Kylac only laughed.

"But how? I watched you go over the falls."

The youth shrugged. "It seems not even the gods can resist my charm."

For a moment, Allion just stared at the lad, still worried
that he might disappear into the ether. Then he remembered
the youth's knavish prank.

"Is this your way of greeting all old friends?" he asked,
rubbing his throat while thinking back to their reunion at the

jailhouse in Leaven, in which he and Jarom had been introduced to General Corathel.

"You're the one who left me for dead. Besides, what sort
o' friend tries to string his companions up by their heels?"

Allion smirked at the thought of his trap until he remembered the purpose for it. "What about the demon?"

Kylac shook his head. "No sign. I do believe we's seen the
last o' that one."

The hunter responded with a hopeful smile.

Together, they went back to where the youth had left their
horses before stealing upon him. They would be setting the
animals free in the morning, Kylac explained. The mounts
would be of little use on the treacherous Skullmar trails, and
might actually work against their need for stealth. Better to
let them loose here in the forest than on the scarred, sun-
baked slopes beyond.

Allion nodded. Their few possessions were light enough
to carry. If the youth could manage it, so could he.

"I'll wager you're happy to have that back," Kylac said to
him as Allion inspected the pull of his longbow.

The hunter looked up, his expression serious. "Promise
me you won't ever do anything like that to me again."

"What? Save your life?"

"If that's what you call it."

The youth grinned. "Let it never be said I made a promise I couldn't keep."

They returned then to Allion's resting place, tethering the
horses to a sapling spruce in the shadow of the backside
ridge. No reason not to keep their steeds through the night,
in case they had to make a quick escape. If nothing else, the
animals made worthy sentinels.

With that in mind, they did not bother resetting Allion's
snare, agreeing instead to take turns sleeping. The youth offered to take first watch, to which Allion had no complaint.

But it was a long time before he could make himself lie
down to rest. Instead, he spent hours talking and laughing in
hushed tones with his newfound companion. So thrilled was
he by Kylac's return that Allion could not stop asking the
youth about this and other adventures, if for no other reason

than to hear his friend's voice. Kylac did not seem to mind, sharing readily tales of his wanderings over the past few years. For a time, Allion tried to focus on the youth's former life as a member of his father's assassins guild. But try as he might, he could learn nothing more about that part of the boy's background—while Kylac had a way of turning those same inquiries back on him. Before he knew it, he was the one sharing childhood stories, many of which included Jarom, whose name became an all-too-poignant reminder as to what he was doing here. No doubt by now his friend was fighting to hold back the Demon Queen and her forces as they marched across western Pentania—through Kuuria, perhaps even Alson. Sobered by the realization, Allion finally grew quiet and fell asleep.

When Kylac woke him, dawn was upon them. The hunter did not bother to scold the youth for allowing him to sleep through his turn at watch, knowing that it would do no good. He simply followed the other's lead in stripping his mount of its tack and arranging upon his own back those provisions he would carry with him. The rest could be reclaimed later, should they manage to survive this, or more likely left to rot. When ready to depart, he slapped his horse on the rump and set forth on foot.

They retraced his steps of the previous evening north and crossed over the mouth of the river to the east. They continued in that direction, zigzagging over the sharp and broken terrain. They had gone no more than two or three miles before they came upon the trail they sought, that which the dragonspawn had taken south from Krakken. There, they rested a moment, eyeing its twisted and rutted sweep. Neither Allion nor his companion mentioned the more recent tracks, of an army of dragonspawn much larger than that with which they had battled at Kraagen Keep. With a renewed sense of purpose, they headed north.

The trail was as narrow and treacherous as any other that wound its way through the jagged wasteland of the Skullmar Mountains. Travel was slow and arduous. There was no sign of further rain, but the heat almost made Allion wish otherwise.

All that day and the next, they worked their way forward with steady determination, stopping only to sleep and to forage when necessary. They ate sparingly, and always while on the move. Nightfall brought with it a biting wind and glacial temperatures. With daybreak came the return of a sweltering heat. It was not long before Allion began to doubt his chances of surviving the trek, let alone the ultimate encounter. He did his best not to think about either, but given the desolation of his surroundings, found that he had little choice.

Their march only became more grueling as the trail they followed brought them into the higher elevations. Clefts and fissures threatened to swallow them at every turn. In the distance, Mount Krakken quivered and bellowed, spewing ash and fire in an ominous display. The volcano's breath formed a smoky haze that consumed the northern sky and swept westward with the prevailing winds. Should those winds turn, they would be hard-pressed to even breathe.

It was in the early afternoon on their second day through the mountains when they crested a steep knoll and reached a dead end.

An immense valley stretched away below them, a cauldron of blackness in which thousands of dragonspawn rasped and snorted, like some foul, simmering brew. Corathel's fear had proven prophetic. The entire mass was moving south, advancing on their position. They could not remain where they were for long.

"What now?" Allion asked, his tongue thick in his throat.

He found Kylac eyeing their surroundings.

"We'll have to circle the cliffs."

Allion gawked at the sheer walls of stone that encircled the valley's upper rim. "Are you mad? There are no trails at all! You expect me to go dangling out there like some worm on a hook? What if they spot us? What if we fall?"

Kylac was frowning. Even he did not seem to like his suggestion. "Consider our options."

"What options?"

The youth winked at him, then shuffled down a side trail leading off along the valley's eastern slope.

Allion scowled, following reluctantly. A moment later, he was glad that he had. For as they scurried behind a tangle of boulders and scrub brush, a lone dragonspawn, sniffing about at the south edge of the valley, clawed its way into view over the abandoned ridgeline.

"Quiet!" Kylac hissed, pulling him low.

It was too late for that, Allion knew. The creature had their scent. They had only moments before it discovered where they had gone.

He was reaching for his bow when Kylac stopped him and pointed. The dragonspawn was intently focused, not on them, but on something coming up from the south along the main trail. The creature crouched, eyes narrowed. A snarl escaped its lips.

The demon bounded into view, the same gray-skinned brute that had been swept over the falls. Without slowing, it pounced upon the waiting dragonspawn, swallowing the other's head in its jaws. The momentum of its spring sent both tumbling over the ridgeline and into the valley below, where the weaker beast was ripped apart without so much as a scream.

Its brethren, however, were quick to respond to the threat. By the time Kylac and Allion leaned forward to get a look, the valley floor was churning with enraged dragonspawn. They attacked the invader in swarms, their claws and teeth raking its bloodless flesh. Still, the demon was like a wasp among honeybees. Its long arms slashed and tore while it bit off one after another of its assailants' heads. It plowed through their ranks, throwing them from its back, shaking them from its limbs.

"I can't believe that thing is alive," Allion gasped.

Alive, not vanquished and then somehow reborn like the demon wolf he had faced in the Aspandels and again on the banks of the Llornel River. For he had seen the open wounds upon this creature's skin as it lunged past—open, not scarred—including the telltale gash to its neck inflicted by Kylac's blade.

A cacophony of sounds rang from below, grunts and growls, shrieks and wails, all of which echoed against the ring of stone bluffs and pierced Allion's ears. Although the outcome seemed clear, the hunter continued to watch, mesmerized by the display. Sure enough, despite its mostly one-sided slaughter, the demon was soon buried beneath a black tide of dragonspawn.

"It's not," Kylac replied, and resumed his perilous crawl out along the valley rim.

The Great Hall within the Palace of Kings was not at all as Jarom had envisioned it. It was a cold, cavernous chamber that smelled of must and age. Lacking were the elaborate engravings and pedestals and statuary he had come to expect, along with the carpets and paintings and tapestries that might have given it warmth. There were no windows and thus no light, save for the numerous sconces and cressets and candelabrums that held their smoky candles and torches. All was of iron and granite and limestone, none of it polished or ornamented. Banners hung from the walls in celebration of the lines of human kings come and gone through the centuries. But even those colors were muted and drab, worn and faded and covered with the dust and soot of ages gone. Nowhere could Jarom find the gleam of gold or bronze or the sparkle of precious gems. All was sterile and rough-edged, of practical purpose or not to be found.

It was here, nearly four hundred years ago, that the League of Man had officially formed, dividing the lands of Tritos east and west into the first human nations of Partha and Kuuria and proclaiming this the Age of Man. Even before then, this city and this room in particular had long been viewed as the ruling seat of man, the chamber within which his race governed all of its affairs. Regardless of the exact moment, it was here that mankind had come to realize his supremacy over the wilderness that had claimed these lands since the fall of the Finlorian Empire some three thousand years ago. It was here that modern man had come of age. It was only fitting that they were here now to discuss his demise.

"How long do we have?"

"Days," Jarom replied. "Maybe hours."

Thelin Culmaril, king of Souaris, had been described to him by Commander Troy as a kind and patient man, with a strength of will forged of iron. Jarom saw none of that in the figure seated on the dais before him. The man he saw seemed a broken husk set to wither before his very eyes. His frame looked hardy enough, younger and stronger than that of one closing upon fifty years, and his gray hair had the look of stone, thick and timeless. But his eyes gave him away. The light had gone out of them, and without that, the rest seemed ready to crumble like the face of a mountain in a winter storm.

Troy had explained to Jarom before they ever reached the outer gates that the entire city was still in mourning over the deaths of its young heirs, Prince Garett and Princess El-wonyssa. The children had vanished while exploring as they always did the labyrinth of tunnels and caverns in the mountains behind their home—a family tradition. Although the pair always marked their trail, it had taken weeks for the search parties to discover and retrieve their remains from the subterranean chasm into which they had fallen. In truth, only Lyssa's body had been found. Rett was still missing, but had been presumed dead, his body lost to depths where none could follow. Just last week, Queen Loisse herself had begged her husband call off the hunt, no longer able to cope with the false promise of hope.

And yet, while understandably scarred by the tragedy, the king would have to be strong, Jarom knew, if his city and his people were to take up arms against the Demon Queen and her dragonspawn army. And that they must, as the fate of mankind now depended upon it.

For several moments, Thelin sat quiet in his throne, a rough-hewn pile of granite blocks worn smooth over time. Jarom waited patiently, as did the others left to suffer the man's silence. Corathel and Nevik were with him, as well as a representative of Morethil's armies who stood in place of the missing Lorron. Souari halberdiers lined the walls, and Troy, who had turned out to be high commander of the entire Souari army, stood post to the right of his king.

"Very well. You shall be placed within the highest levels of command. Commander Troy will advise you as to our defensive strategies."

The king's expression never changed. Whatever else he might be feeling was lost beneath the shroud of his private devastation.

Jarom bowed low. "To you and yours, we are grateful, Your Highness."

Protocol did not require that he treat the other with such deference. Souaris, like any other Kuurian city outside of Morethil, was considered a barony, with its ruler granted—and limited to—the rights and privileges thereof. When formed, the Imperial Council had continued to recognize the Culmaril line of kings out of respect for Souaris's famed history and traditions that dated back to the League of Man—and, Troy had boasted, because no one could take it from them had they wanted to. But as far as lordships were concerned, Thelin's was limited to a single city, more like Nevik's than Jarom's, with his greater title being largely ceremonial.

But to Jarom, it didn't feel that way. As long as he stood within this ancient court, and the man before him held the lives of so many in his hand, the young king of Alson felt it only fitting to pay full and proper respects.

"Commander, see to it that all of King Torin's needs are met."

As before, with both Nevik and Emperor Derreg, there had been almost no discussion as to whether or not his own claim to royalty was legitimate. Incredible as his story seemed, none cared to dispute as of yet the account shared with him by Ellebe concerning his born identity, accepting at face value the truth as Jarom understood it. Perhaps because he wielded the Sword of Asahiel. Perhaps because the only other claimant at this time was the wizard, whose ruthlessness was widely known. Or perhaps because it simply didn't matter in light of the overall circumstances. Jarom's sense in this case was that he could have claimed not just the throne of Alson, but the throne of Souaris as well, without drawing so much as a whimper from the ruler before him.

The rows of armed guard saluted as their king took to his feet. He did not acknowledge them, but glanced instead to the smaller, padded chair beside his own. It was said that Thelin himself had added it to the Great Hall, the one piece of furniture that showed a touch of warmth. He had done so that his wife the queen could attend with him such occasions of assembly and lend her voice to the proceedings from a place of honor. He apologized again for her absence, but the queen was ill.

Wearing his furs like a yoke upon his shoulders, he took his leave through a curtained archway behind his throne.

When he had gone, Commander Troy stepped forward, tall and proud. "King Torin, if you and your advisors would follow me?"

Jarom nodded. Even now, it made him cringe to have to answer to that name. But he was determined at this point to let others use or reject it as they willed, to do as Marisha had suggested by not denying it himself.

"We are yours, Commander. Lead on."

The moon was well into its arc by the time Allion and Kylac reached the threshold of Mount Krakken.

Amazingly enough, the youth's plan to lead them around the rim of the valley had worked. Bent on their own march to the south and further occupied with their fight against the demon, the dragonspawn had paid no notice to the tiny figures crawling along the slopes overhead. Thankfully, they had not been forced to keep to those slopes for long. Once they had worked their way around to the rear of the unsuspecting hordes, they had slipped down to the valley floor, leaving the dragonspawn well behind them.

With hands and shoulders aching and raw, Allion had followed his companion northward without fear of pursuit. The journey, however, had not been easy. The valley was immense, its cracked and pitted length stretching beyond the visible horizon, clear to the base of Mount Krakken itself. The upper reaches of the volcano were an angry cone of cinders and flames and sulfurous stench. Quakes rattled the blackened landscape, dislodging boulders from the heights, and even in the chill of night, the heat was unbearable.

Yet here they stood. Despite the torturous conditions, they had come at last upon a gateway to the inner mountain and the lair of Killangrathor. It rose before them to menacing heights, a dark and jagged fissure from which untold legions of dragonspawn had poured. A foul vapor drifted from the mouth of the ancient lava tube, causing the air to shimmer. Rumbling echoes escaped from within—the crack of stone, the hiss of steam, the splitting and grinding of earth. It struck Allion that if there truly existed an abyss into which all denizens of evil were cast, then surely its entrance lay within the mountain before him.

As ridiculous as it seemed, Kylac decided that they should try to sleep before entering the tunnel. Locating a nest of mostly smaller, smoother rocks aback of the forbidding cleft, the hunter and his companion unfurled their bedrolls upon the crunchy surface of glasslike stones and lay down for a few hours' rest.

"So, just how does one prepare himself for battle with a dragon?" Allion asked, then coughed, staring up at a shadowy night sky.

Kylac was slow to respond. "Well, I haven't fought any more o' the beasts than yourself, but first, try to envision the most awesome, horrifying creature you'll ever meet. Ya won't accomplish much if'n ya rush in there and become paralyzed with fear."

"Nothing can be so terrifying as to render me helpless to move," the hunter scoffed.

Kylac snickered, then eyed him sternly. "You'd best believe otherwise, my friend, 'cause I'm going to be too busy to collect your ashes."

Allion worked again to clear his throat. "Anything else?"

"Not that I can tells ya. All I can says is that we'll know if'n we're not prepared."

"How's that?"

"'Cause we'll be watching this world from some other plane of existence."

Allion did nothing to encourage conversation after that,

but focused instead on what could very well be his final
night's rest. The mountain's roar reverberated in his head,
and the heat broiled his flesh. Now and then, he actually
managed to fall asleep, only to face one nightmare after another. And yet, he prayed the dawn would never come. For
the countless terrors of his imagination could inflict no
harm, whereas with the rising of the sun, he would be forced
to confront a very real and deadly horror that knew no such
mercy.

Somewhere deep within that fiery corridor, Killangrathor
awaited.

Alone on the terrace of his assigned quarters, Jarom gazed
down upon the city below. In its own way, Souaris was every
bit as majestic as Morethil. Though rugged and unrefined,
its beauty could not be denied. It remained today as it always had, stark and immutable, the first great city of
mankind.

And perhaps the last.

It was the vanity of Emperor Derreg and the folly of the
Imperial Council that had reduced them to this: Lorron,
Rynar, and roughly twenty thousand imperial soldiers dead;
Marisha a captive of the Demon Queen; the rest of them running from one city to the next with families in tow. Only,
there would be no running from Souaris. It was here that
man had arisen to power. It would be here that he faced his
ultimate fall. If routed, the survivors would funnel into the
caves and mines and hollows beneath the mountains, chased
underground to live like rats. There was nowhere else for
them to go. For if Souaris could not stand, no fortress would.

After hours spent in study of the city's defenses, Jarom
had all but agreed with Commander Troy's assessment.
Souaris was impregnable. The bulk of the city lay cradled
within the arms of the Tenstrock Mountains. Its battlements
reached forth like ribs from this adamantine spine, dividing
the scattered clusters of homes and businesses into progres-
sive rungs that marched like a flight of steps up the mountainside. There were five battlements in all, each a wall some

twenty paces thick, built of great blocks harvested from the mountain quarries and fortified with iron. They were as much an eyesore as anything else, gray and craggy and scarred by the blades and fires of battles past. But they were the same walls that had held for half a millennium against the savagery of an untamed world. They could do so now.

Although Morethil and others had borrowed elements of its design, none could match Souaris's full defensive arsenal. Jarom was still awestruck by the volume and condition of the city's armaments, from its war engines and artillery stores to its oil vats and machicolations. Great boulders lay strewn upon the range below to impede an enemy's approach, while every step of land and roadway leading in was targeted from the towers and ramparts above, leaving no dead angles. But what amazed him most of all was the strategy and mechanism by which the defenders could take flight to a higher level of the city should one of the battlements be overrun. Jarom could scarcely fathom how the city architects had envisioned such a system, let alone how they had found the time and coin and men to engineer and build it. At this, Troy had only laughed. Art and splendor were all well and good, but of what value was a city as clean and beautiful as Morethil when razed to the ground?

Far below, Jarom could just make out the shadow of activity taking place within the lowermost tier, which had been cleared of all but military operations for the impending siege. The second and third and fourth tiers were more visible, awash in the light of moon and stars and a thousand thousand lamps and torches. It was at these levels that a Souari populace of some two hundred thousand souls braced for horrors unknown, sharing their suddenly crowded streets and dwellings with nearly half a million refugees from Morethil and lands beyond. Jarom's own quarters were located within the south wing of the Palace of Kings, built upon a plateau jutting forth over the highest tier. Thus far in history, he had been told, the fourth tier had seen battle only once, while the fifth bore not a single scar. If the latest reports on the enemy's movements were correct, come tomorrow they would see if history could remain unchanged.

A knock sounded, unexpectedly close. Jarom spun to find Nevik standing in the open doorway leading out to his private terrace.

"Your pardon, my lord. I didn't mean to disturb you."

Jarom shook his head.

"No one answered. The guardsman let me in. I can come back later—"

"It's all right, my friend. Please, have a seat."

The young baron declined, moving instead to join him at the balustrade.

"Magnificent," Nevik offered after a moment of silence. "It's as if you can see the world entire."

Jarom nodded, but did not respond.

"Are you well, my lord? Your summons sounded urgent."

"Did Corathel and Troy receive word?"

Nevik shook his head. "I couldn't say, my lord. I came straightaway."

"Please, Nevik, call me Jarom, or Torin if you must. You have sworn no oath to me."

"You are still my king."

"Then you have leave to call me familiar. Please."

"Shall I see to the whereabouts of the chief general and high commander?"

Jarom thought about it. His gaze was still locked upon the expansive sweep of the city falling sharply away at his feet. "No. I'll meet with them later. What I tell them then I shall tell you now."

"My lord?" At Jarom's glare, he corrected himself with a slight bow. "Forgive me. Torin, my friend. You have my ear."

Jarom hesitated, weighing the gravity of his decision yet again. He moved over to a bench and table fashioned from stone and set among an array of potted plants in a corner of the terrace. Upon the table was a pile of scrolls, outlines of the city's defenses that he had been given to study. Nevik sat down across from him.

"Tomorrow, against the Queen's armies, you stand alone. I will not be here."

Nevik gaped at him. "My lord, you cannot—"

"I mean to find Spithaera's lair."

The baron blinked, confused. "Her lair? How?"

"According to the Entients, she was unleashed by a pair of children."

"The king's children?"

"They didn't say, but after speaking with Paladius, I believe so."

"Who?"

"The children's escort. He accompanied the young prince and princess the day they disappeared. They ran off from him in order to explore a new series of tunnels. Always before, when they had done so, they returned unharmed. If I can follow their trail, I believe it will lead me to Spithaera."

Nevik scowled. "If her lair is down there, would the search parties not have already found it?"

"Perhaps," Jarom allowed. "But perhaps not. They weren't actually looking for anything more than remains."

The baron continued to frown.

"It was you who suggested I choose the time and manner of our confrontation."

Nevik's eyes narrowed with suspicion. "You mean to rescue Marisha."

Jarom did not bother to deny it. "She's everything worth living for. I did not come this far to sacrifice that."

"A king's responsibility is to his people. If Souaris falls, then Kuuria falls, Partha falls, Alson—"

Jarom slapped at the city drawings in exasperation. "You and Corathel, you're the tacticians. You will help Troy to command our forces against the dragonspawn. I will remain until the battle is under way. Hopefully, it will be some time before the enemy realizes I've gone."

The young baron mulled it over. "I shall go with you."

Jarom shook his head. "Your men look to you for strength and guidance. I would not deprive them of that."

"And yet, we all look to you for the same."

"And I am trying to give it," he sighed, "in the best way I know how. No matter what happens with Killangrathor, if Spithaera lives, all our struggles stand for naught."

"Chasing after the Demon Queen herself was not part of the Entients' plan," Nevik reminded him.

Jarom nodded. He had considered that, thinking long and hard upon the faith-shattering lesson handed him at Whitlock. But if what the Entients had taught him was true, no man was born for a specific purpose, but became what he willed of his own volition—by seizing the various opportunities presented by circumstance. So be it. He would do what he could, for himself and for those who followed him, reacting to the situation as Kylac had taught him. In the end, it would have to be enough.

"I am no longer their pawn," he replied with a grim smile. "Plans have changed."

CHAPTER FORTY-TWO

The dragonspawn came as before, a suffocating wave almost without end. The sky above them broiled, a fierce storm borne upon their shoulders, as if their unnatural presence had brought the heavens to tears. The city of Souaris awaited them like a general leading his troops into battle, jutting from its foundation, as immutable as the mountain stone upon which it had been erected. Peering out through a crenel upon the eastern rim of the lowermost battlement, Jarom swore to himself that this time, things would be different.

"I see no sign of the Queen," Corathel remarked, standing next to him. The chief general lowered his spyglass. "You should go now, if you mean to do this."

Jarom was no longer sure. It had seemed a fair notion last night, to hunt down and see what he might do to draw the Demon Queen back to her lair. To separate her from her armies and settle this matter between them once and for all. Corathel had supported the idea, thinking it a chance, at least, to turn the tables. Commander Troy had even offered to send a patrol to guide him. But now, with the dragonspawn upon them once again, it felt more like running than fighting. And the last thing he wanted was to desert this brave people in the moment of battle—a battle that he had brought upon them.

Corathel turned to him. "The sooner you leave, the sooner you can return to us."

Jarom nodded. He could feel the thunder of the enemy's

charge as it reverberated through earth and stone. It made
him want to fly down and meet them in open battle, to
avenge his earlier defeats and those individuals he had cared
for and lost. As before, his stomach churned with anticipation—only this time, the feeling did not make him sick. He
was beginning to understand, he thought, the eagerness with
which Second General Jasyn greeted these horrific conflicts.
A man *was* never so alive . . .

But the best he could do, he knew, was to be on his way.
Though considered a legion of the Imperial Army, the mili-
tia garrisoned here were defenders of Souaris, first and foremost. These were proud men who would not back down, a
force of thirty thousand—better than one-seventh of the
population—that was as much a part of the city's tradition as
its weaponry and battlements. Standing with them were the
twenty thousand from Morethil, as well as the dregs that had
followed him from lands north, desperate men with nowhere
left to go. All would fight to the death. If he truly wanted to
save as many lives as he could, he had no other choice.

"I'll be back before sunset," he assured the chief general,
clasping the man's arm. Neither had yet invited discussion
over what might happen should he fail, and neither did so
now. "May the Ceilhigh watch over you."

Corathel managed a tight-lipped smile, his face weary yet
ever determined. "Make haste."

Jarom turned his gaze back to the oncoming swarm, making one last sweep for any sign that the Queen intended anything out of the ordinary in her siege of Souaris, anything
that might demand his direct involvement. He spied none,
and at Corathel's urging, headed for the nearest steps leading down to the courtyard below. Even now, after it had already been decided, he wrestled with what it was he must
do. As before, at Kraagen Keep, he had come to the only
conclusion he could. It bothered him to have to hide the truth
from Corathel and the others, but he knew they would only
try to talk him out of it. He could not let that happen. If he
was to do this, he had to remain strong.

By the time he reached the courtyard, the fighting had
begun, with the Souari defenders launching their first volley

of range weapons. Beyond the sealed outer wall, the dragonspawn roared with fiendish delight.

He found his ready steed, that which would carry him back up through the levels of the city. With barely a nod to the stable boy, Jarom climbed into the saddle, kicked his heels, and started forward as the rains began to fall.

To the west, stationed alongside Commander Troy nearer the main gate, Nevik clutched the haft of his mace. He wished again that he had been permitted to accompany Torin on the trail of Garett and Elwonyssa. Better that than standing here upon the ramparts, waiting for the battle to claim him. Then again, so long as they were able to keep the dragonspawn on the other side of these massive walls, his weapon need not be called upon at all.

He knew well enough the likelihood of that.

Though he had been well briefed on the tactics that had felled Morethil, Commander Troy had asked that one among their command circle stand with him throughout the battle as personal advisor. With Torin's planned departure, that duty had fallen to Nevik. Corathel had been assigned to the east, along with his lieutenant generals. They were in charge of all defenses to that side of the central city gates, with Troy assuming control of the west. When asked to join him, the young baron had been unable to think of a good reason to refuse.

And so he stood, wet and cold beneath his chain mail, with the shriek of the enemy almost more than he could bear. Rain drummed against his iron helm, a sound that had always driven him to near madness. Like his father, he rarely wore the thing, and had the knots on his skull to prove it. But given the scale and intensity of this day's struggle, assigned as he was to the forward lines, he would have to be a fool not to.

"The brutes are determined," Troy acknowledged, showing Nevik that customary half smile that suggested he was hiding something. "I'll give them that."

Dragonspawn raked at the outer wall and the surrounding cliffs, climbing upon their own dead in an effort to crest the battlement. Others hammered at the city's iron portal, to no avail. Despite the fury of their assault, it was clear that theirs was a useless struggle. Nothing short of the gods would lay low these bulwarks, so thick and strong and well defended. Nor would they be scaled by such primitive means.

"Where is this wizard you spoke of?" Troy asked him.

"Devoured by the vermin he serves, if there is any justice," Nevik grumbled.

There wasn't. Soon thereafter, he appeared before them, almost as if called forth by their utterance. The baron's eyes narrowed with hatred as the armored villain parted the sea of dragonspawn, led by his demon cohort. Nevik had not forgotten that it was this man, not the Demon Queen, who had chased him from his lands and begun the war that had claimed the life of his father. And it was this man, more than the Demon Queen, whom he wished to see punished for these crimes. He clenched at the other's approach, tightening his grip upon his mace.

This time, he was able to see for himself that which until now he had only heard tell of—the phantom shield used to repel the strongest missile attack, followed by the earth-rumbling force used to pry open the city gates. The defenders of Souaris had done all they could on such short notice to thwart the magical assault, using stone and timbers and slabs of iron to buttress the main portal. But as before, their efforts were in vain. The more the materials resisted, the harder the wizard's spell pressed, until finally, inevitably, the opening caved.

When it did, the Souari ground forces, those upon whom the battle truly depended, were waiting. Knowing this time the inevitable outcome, they had dedicated only a small portion of their troops to the ramparts, just enough to keep the enemy from clambering over the walls. The vast majority stood ready within the courtyard. By the time the first of the dragonspawn forced their way through, Troy and Nevik had united with their regiment and were leading the counter-charge.

They stopped short at the edge of the pit, a trench wide and deep that stretched across the length of the roadway leading into the city. Sappers had worked throughout the night to make Corathel's design a reality, preparing for this moment. Though left uncovered and plainly visible, there was no way around the trap. With animalistic savagery, the initial enemy waves rushed in, only to plummet some thirty feet to the bedrock below, where they were skewered upon iron barbs and crushed by those falling after.

But the pit could only hold so many bodies. Within a stunningly brief amount of time, its depths had been filled, forming a bridge over which spilled the remaining hordes. Nevik braced himself as they came ahead heedlessly, racing through an opening that led directly to Troy and his personal regiment. But as the enemy reached them, the commander gave his signal. Companies of pikemen crashed down upon the bared flanks from both sides, raking and stabbing as the brutes advanced. Everywhere Nevik looked, dragonspawn were being lured down one lane or another, tempted by open ground, only to be buried beneath the heavy spears and lances and axes and cudgels that could do their armored flesh the most harm. Against a more wary opponent, the strategy never would have worked. Against the dragonspawn, it resulted in wholesale slaughter.

For hours, a steady rotation of troops helped to maintain this simple yet effective approach. At times of rest, Nevik sat back with the high commander to view the results. At times of duty, he found himself on the front lines, working with teams of men to bring down one after another of the foul beasts. Battle was fast and furious, with enemies continuing to pour in recklessly while the defenders hacked at them from all angles, decimating their ranks and doing what they could to quash the assault. While his shoulders ached and his chest heaved, Nevik drew upon every hatred, every love, every strength of human passion he could muster, resisting death alongside his companions like the cornered animals they were.

But they were in fact human, slow and frail compared to the horde that sought to swallow them. Their patience and cunning and superior numbers bought them time, but could not buy them victory. Once again, the unwavering strength of the dragonspawn eventually won over. First one, then ten, then scores of the creatures broke through the allied lines, creating seams that enabled those that followed to further split and divide the defenders. And without their formations, they were doomed.

For Nevik, fatigue settled in, followed hard upon by despair. With cramps in his legs and blood upon his face, he braced for yet another offensive foray, fearing it would be his last.

Then he heard the ringing of the bells.

Deafened by the clamor and attuned to the voice of his commander, Nevik was slow to recognize the sound for what it was. But then he was receiving new orders, and his heart surged with hope. The bells were hung in towers throughout the city, most notably upon each of the battlements. The central bell, mounted high atop the Palace of Kings, was rung by order of the king himself when a conflict appeared to be slipping out of control. It was ringing now, a great, resonating tone carried forth by each of the bells below. The signal to retreat.

It was happening all at once, remarkable to envision, and a miracle to behold. As one, the ground troops began working their way toward the ramp that would carry them to the second gate and city level. Overhead, soldiers atop the battlement raced along iron catwalks that sloped upward along a line of support pilings, granting direct access to the top of the next wall. As the last of them reached this new rampart, the soldiers knocked free the bolts and pins and cast the end segments of these sky bridges into the fray below, sending more than a few overanxious dragonspawn to their deaths and cutting off any pursuit. They then went to work immediately on shielding the withdrawal of the ground troops, using their arrows and war engines as cover from above.

Nevik worked his way along with this lower press, watching it all unfold. Before he knew it, he had climbed the iron ramp and passed beneath the gatehouse of the city's second tier, opened wide to receive them. He turned at once, as instructed, to help cover the escape of those who came after. The dragonspawn were on their heels, but only a handful would be able to follow. For when the last of the survivors had passed through, the bells rang again, and the final trap was sprung.

The young baron of Drakmar did not see those in charge of the winches and release levers, but he witnessed firsthand the impressive results. The supports were yanked free, and with a massive groan that raked his spine, the entire ramp slipped from the precipice upon which it rested. It fell away with an earth-jarring crash, dropping the wide-eyed hordes that stood upon it and crushing those that milled frenetically beneath.

Those dragonspawn that had managed to follow the defenders into the second tier were swiftly slaughtered. The portcullis descended, and the doors were closed. Moments later, Nevik found himself atop the second battlement, peering down upon the lost outer level. The retreat was a success. Without the ramp, the dragonspawn were left staring upward at a shelf of mountain stone and the rampart atop it. To even reach the doors of the second tier, the enemy would need to climb or fly.

The upper city was secure, granting the weary forces a much-needed reprieve. And yet, it was hard for Nevik to find solace. For the noonday sun was just now passing unseen behind the thick cover of storm clouds, and already the first tier of Souaris, the legendary City of Man, was flooded with dragonspawn.

Allion pitched to the earth, tripped up once again by the rugged terrain of the scabrous corridor. He cried out as the sharp stone bloodied his hands and knees, tearing holes in the spun wool of his breeches. He gasped for breath, only to choke on the suffocating heat.

Kylac reached down to help him.

"I can't do it," he rasped, resisting the other's pull.

He was ashamed of the words, but that didn't make them untrue. He'd gone as far as he could. All that morning, he had followed Kylac down the vast, lightless tunnel into which the trail of dragonspawn had led, wondering how many more of the ancient vents and tubes burrowed through the mountain's core. He had kept silent concerning his exhaustion, his fears, and the unbearable temperatures, determined to see this through. But hours had passed without any indication that this journey into the Abyss would ever come to an end, and he could take it no longer.

The youth hesitated, a hovering presence. Allion continued to heave, wilting beneath the weight of his friend's gaze. He wondered what the other might say that could possibly lend him strength.

"Fair enough."

The hunter looked up, surprised.

"Take this," the youth said, lighting a second torch from the one he carried. "Rest here. When ya can, makes your way back out to the valley."

Allion said nothing. Sweat dripped from his brow to fall upon the jagged floor. He rolled over, slumping to his seat.

"I'll come for ya as soon as I finish."

The hunter accepted the torch. Even Kylac was sweating, he saw, although his companion did not seem otherwise affected by the infernal conditions.

"Don't tarry," the youth warned him. "The air is poison."

"Kylac . . ." he began, but could not find the right words. "I'm sorry."

His friend's gaze was unaccusing. "We'll have a drink together when this business is over. 'Tis the least I owes ya for seeing me this far."

The youth gripped his shoulder in parting. Allion thought in that moment to try again to rise, but before he could, Kylac spun away and jogged off down the tunnel, disappearing into the dark void of the mountain's throat.

They leaned out over the chasm as if in flight, two weeping angels carved in alabaster. A gift, Troy had said, from one of the city's many grieving citizens, used to mark the spot from which it was believed the children had fallen. A more elaborate memorial was still being designed, but in the meantime, he was to look for the angels.

For a long time, Jarom studied them. In the crimson radiance of the Sword, their eyes were of fire, their tears of blood. One boy, one girl, holding hands as they soared from this pit of darkness toward Olirian fields.

At last he turned away to take stock of his surroundings. He had declined Troy's offer of a guide patrol, claiming that he wanted to travel as quickly and quietly as possible. The trail would be clear after all of the recent traffic, and a company of armored men would only alert the Demon Queen of his coming. The high commander had frowned, but had not argued the point—thankfully, since most of what Jarom had told him was a lie.

He'd had no trouble at all following the proper path as it wound along beyond the entrance of an abandoned gem mine. The signs and markings were clear. What surprised him was how far he'd had to go. He was impressed at first, and then later amazed that two so young had delved so deep into this lightless underground. It had taken him hours, marching mile after mile in stifling solitude, bathed in the red glow of his divine talisman. But at long last, here he was.

A walk of wooden planks had been built along the narrowest of ledges leading to the stone shelf upon which he now stood. Had it not been for the footprints found here, on the other side of that sheer stone face, it would have been easy enough for the search parties to assume that it was from the ledge the children had fallen. And in truth, it may have been. But their tracks *had* been found on this side. If Garett and Elwonyssa, with their smaller feet and lightweight bodies, had managed to traverse the precipice once, why not again?

Even more confusing were the tracks themselves. Once across the ledge, it was said, boot prints from both children led up to the rock wall opposite the chasm. A second set was found for Elwonyssa, leading away from the wall and straight into that gulf. Her remains had been discovered below, and it was there that the angel statues had been mounted. But Garett's prints had ended at the wall, and his body had yet to be found.

Of course, there had been so much activity upon this shelf

over the last few weeks that any trace of the children's movements had long since been erased from the thin layer of fine stone dust. Perhaps the searchers had been mistaken about the prints. But theirs was the only account Jarom had to go by. And since the cut of the chasm marked this shelf as a dead end, it would seem there were only so many places he could look.

He inspected briefly the harness and rigging that had been used to lower searchers and then to retrieve the girl's remains from the abyss below. So much commotion. Though absent now, it was easy enough to imagine the clamor of the work crews with their pounding hammers and squeaking pulleys and vociferous shouts. Surely, if the Queen were nearby, she would have heard them, and either killed them all or gone into hiding. But where could she hide?

For the briefest of moments, he considered strapping himself into the harness and rappelling into the chasm. But with no one to operate the whim, he dismissed the notion almost at once. Besides, the crews had already combed the depths in search of the boy and found nothing unusual.

Nevertheless, he found himself stepping up to the precipice and peering out over the edge. The crews had described it as bottomless. Although rife with crags and ledges like that upon which Elwonyssa had been found, the chasm floor remained shrouded in mystery. Perhaps they had simply not gone deep enough.

Jarom shook his head. He was going about this all wrong. Based upon the words of the Entients, the children had awakened the Demon Queen. In her sleeping state, Spithaera would not have come swooping out of the dark to claim them. Nor was it reasonable to suspect that the children had gone down into that chasm on purpose, without the proper equipment. Were they that foolish or irresponsible, they would have perished during their expeditions long ago. Garett and Elwonyssa were accomplished explorers. Despite their young age, they knew what they were doing. While Spithaera might have taken flight into the pit before him, it was not there that the king's children would have found her. There had to be something more, something he was missing. . . .

He turned back toward the rock wall where Garett's tracks had ended, and he wondered again, what had happened to the boy? He thought he knew. For whatever it was had caused his young sister to march straight off this ledge. Had they lost their light or become lost, they would have simply waited for help to arrive. Something terrible had happened, something so dark and frightening as to devour the boy and drive the girl away in a mad panic. If his suspicions were correct . . .

He reached the wall and began exploring its rugged surface for cracks or seams. His fingers moved quickly, trembling with excitement. He was right. He had to be. It was the only thing that made sense.

Come, demon, he thought with a determined grimace. *Where are you?*

From his position atop the second battlement, Nevik gazed down upon the swelling tide of dragonspawn. The rain was falling now in sheets, pummeling the besieged city. Between the two, the young baron felt as though he had been stranded on an island in the middle of a rising ocean, with nowhere left to run.

Once again, the black sea parted, making way for the wizard and demon. Nevik's eyes followed the pair, as did those of every other man who lined the rampart not engaged already in ranged combat. As one, the defenders held their breath, anxious to see what the leaders of this horde intended.

"Let them work through this puzzle," Troy scoffed in challenge.

Nevik was not so confident, but could not quite disagree. Even if the wizard were to work his magic and force open the gates, the dragonspawn could not reach the opening. And there was the faint hope, given by city scholars familiar with the history—if not the practice—of such things, that the magic might fail, since the plane of ground upon which the wizard stood was so far below that which he would try to affect. Of course, at this point, there was no way to escape the city, either. At best, the baron decided, it would come down to a battle of wills as to who could maintain this struggle the longest. Given that, he still did not like their chances.

He glanced back, looking beyond the courtyard to the many shops and homes sitting stark and ghostlike along the streets and alleys rising up behind the defense wall. The second tier belonged now to the military alone. Drilled much like the army on how to withdraw higher into the city, the Souari people had evacuated into the third and fourth levels, taking with them the many refugees come from cities and lands outside their own. Hopefully, they would not be forced to displace again.

A tremor, familiar now, captured his attention. Nevik spun, fearing the worst. Sure enough, the butt of the wizard's staff was held firmly against the earth, while the man's pallid flesh reddened with strain. The gates to the second battlement, however, scarcely groaned, this time resisting the sorcerer's will.

"Hah!" Troy exclaimed triumphantly. "It would seem the villain is mortal after all!"

A hopeful murmur ran across the battlement and down through the ground forces setting stage in the courtyard below. At long last, perhaps fate had smiled upon them.

When the wizard ceased his struggle, those murmurs became cheers, loud enough almost to drown out the snarls of the enemy and the whistle of arrows. While others celebrated, however, Nevik continued to study the wizard and demon. They appeared to be communicating, although the golem had no mouth with which to respond, and stood motionless the entire time. Nevik leaned forward upon the wall. Whatever it was they were discussing did not bode well for the defenders.

Troy turned away, giving orders to his runner for standing down part of the army in order to rest. Just then, the wizard and demon separated, with the magic-user lifting his arms out wide. Nevik clutched blindly for the high commander's shoulder, pulling the other back.

Troy frowned. "What's this?"

The wizard was once again chanting and gesturing, whipping his arms and staff about in an overhead motion. A black mist began swirling over the fallen ramp, gradually taking shape. Before their eyes, it thickened and solidified, until it had formed what appeared to be a bridge to the second gate.

The demon stepped forward. The black mist held beneath its feet. With strides sure and strong, it climbed the length of the sorcerous ramp to begin hammering upon the city portal with its massive fists. Almost at once, the iron doors began to bend inward, while the wooden beams set down to reinforce the barrier from within began to splinter and crack.

"Such strength is not possible!" Troy gasped.

An alarm rose up from those set to ward the gateway. Atop the battlement, soldiers began to focus upon the new threat. Stones and arrows rained down upon the demon golem. Molten iron and oils were spilled through the machicolations. Finally, even the cauldrons themselves were heaved over the edge. But nothing worked to dislodge the creature, or to weaken the integrity of the magical bridge upon which it stood. Its pounding did not relent, and within moments, the outcome of its attack became inevitable.

The dragonspawn, many of which had grown restless, surged up the ramp, abandoning both the squabbles taken up among themselves and the human carcasses upon which they fed. The mist remained solid beneath their weight, and all of a sudden, the enemy army was once again raking at the defenders' door.

"Come," Troy growled in disgust, making for the yard and his assembled ground forces. "Let us try this again."

Nevik looked once more at the wizard, standing all but forgotten amid the throngs of dragonspawn racing past, then picked up his mace and followed after.

Allion slipped and staggered, hurrying as best he could down the endless length of jagged tunnel. His throat was parched, his lungs raw. Sweat and smoke stung his eyes. Yet he refused to falter, resolved to overcome his pain and exhaustion, determined to go on.

When he had first regained his strength, he had intended

to head back out to the valley as Kylac had bade him. But while taking his feet, he had thought of the dragonspawn horde they had passed in that valley—a horde of thousands, rushing to join the countless others already at war with his friends and neighbors. If he did not do something about it, here and now, it would be left to Jarom to overcome them. He could not let that happen.

Nor could he let Kylac proceed alone. The youth had left him behind before, in the ruins of Thrak-Symbos, and were it not for his timely arrival, and that of Cwingen U'uyen, both Kylac and Jarom would have perished. Whether the youth could admit it or not, two were better than one, especially against a creature as powerful as Killangrathor.

And so the hunter had taken up his torch and a loping pace, no longer concerned with whether he made it out of this alive, only that his family and loved ones were not made to suffer for his weakness. Through the blistering heat of the volcanic vent he jogged, hoping to come upon Kylac before it was too late. After all, for all his daring, he did not want to face the dragon alone.

His trek seemed timeless. It might have been hours or minutes when at last he came across a beacon in the darkness. The light was that of a torch, still burning, but abandoned at the base of the wall before a crook in the tunnel. Allion's heart caught in his throat as he scurried forward.

When he reached the bend, he peered around the corner. A faint red glow revealed what appeared to be the end of the corridor through which he traveled, perhaps fifty paces ahead. Crouched in the circle of that opening, a vague shadow against the black wall, was Kylac Kronus.

Feeling something between relief and terror, Allion set down his torch beside that of the youth, so that its smoke and radiance, faint as they were within this vast tube of sulfurous darkness, would not give away their presence. He crept forward then, feeling his way along the sharp crags of the wall, keeping his eyes on the fiery half-light ahead. As he did, he was assaulted by a thick, oppressive stench, and he found himself holding his breath to keep from being nauseated. At the same time, a strange new rumble echoed from somewhere within the volcano's core just ahead, a soft thunder released in steady, almost rhythmic intervals that grew louder with each step.

When he had cut in half the distance between himself and the tunnel's end, his companion turned to greet him with a quieting motion. Allion nodded and slowed his pace, stealing ahead now with a snail's patience. Mountains had been born in less time than it took him to reach Kylac's position. When at last he did, the youth pulled him down behind a pile of loose stones and fixed him with a warning stare.

The hunter made no sound as he peered around the ragged edge of the cave's mouth. In doing so, his eyes widened, after which everything he knew and felt about himself and the world at large fell away. For what looked at first to be a great rise in the center of the cavern floor was in fact the most awesome, most horrifying creature he had ever seen, its giant nostrils flaring gently as they emitted a resonating snore.

Jarom slumped to his seat, his back scraping against the rock wall opposite the chasm. Once again, his hopes and efforts had met with defeat. He had searched and studied the rough face of the wall over and again. There was nothing to be found.

In all likelihood, he had been wrong about the entire thing. The death of the Culmaril children was an accident, and had nothing whatsoever to do with the revival of the Demon Queen. That the timing of the events so closely coincided was mere happenstance.

He preferred that explanation to the idea that he was simply too inept to uncover the mystery. He did not want to believe that the only thing separating him from the lair of the Queen was some secret door through which he could not pass, or some puzzle he was not wise enough to solve. For if a pair of children could find their way in, why couldn't he?

Because he was weak and cowardly, lacking in wits enough to realize the truth and too selfish to accept the responsibility in any case. Here he was, hiding underground, miles removed from a battle under way. Men were dying, in part because of decisions he had made. And rather than stand beside them, he had run away, deceiving himself and others into thinking that his objective was just as important as theirs, when all he really was doing was avoiding the task he'd been given.

He lifted the Crimson Sword before him, peering not into its swirling flames, but at the polish of the outer blade. In that crystalline mirror, he could see his reflection, that of a young man old before his time, one who had been somehow cheated even in victory. All for which he had ever dreamed—and more—seemed within reach, arrayed before him like a glittering mound of riches. Vanquish the Queen, and life might once again be his, not in the exact manner for which he had once hoped, but with joys and benefits that far outweighed the sorrows and obligations. He was so close, in a contest where being close accounted for nothing.

He bent nearer, trying to peer into his own eyes through the Sword's gleam. Perhaps there was something about him that invited misfortune and failure, some aspect of his body or soul that if isolated, could be removed, making way for—

His eyes shifted, making sure of what they were seeing. It was difficult to tell, given the flaming red background of the Sword's reflection. He adjusted the angle of the blade, shifting focus from his own stunned features to the wall behind him. There it was, in the middle of the stone face.

An opening.

He slapped back with his left hand, groping. The rock was rough and cold to the touch, as solid and unyielding as before. But when he looked at that hand through the reflection of his weapon, he saw his fingers playing not upon the stone surface, but upon a pocket of empty air marking the entrance to a tunnel in the cavern wall.

Jarom scrambled to his feet, turning to face the hidden opening. At once, his thoughts flashed back to the mountain bluff in which had lain the doorway to Whitlock. It was not altogether unlikely. Both the Entients and the Demon Queen were avatars of their respective kind. A dweomer such as this might be used by both. But could he counteract it?

He checked again, exploring with first his physical senses and then the Sword. Neither would agree on what existed before him. So which was the illusion? Clearly, the Sword was telling him the truth. The talisman had already shown an aversion to magic, and unlike his own mortal senses, it could not be deceived.

But would it penetrate a force that did not threaten? That was his only hope. For he had not the skill or knowledge of those beings who played with such powers. And he had already failed to trigger its lock or to shove his way past. If the Sword could not carve through this artifice, nothing would.

Knowing this, he held his breath as he raised the Sword overhead. At the top of his arc, he hesitated, closing his eyes and reminding himself that this was his one chance to save Marisha and bring an end to this struggle. He let his desire and that of the Sword build within him, mixing and swirling until they were one.

Then he struck.

The false door erupted in flames, its blockading magic consumed by the Sword's power. But the blade itself encountered only empty air, and swept through cleanly. Having anticipated *some* form of physical contact, Jarom was spun about by his own momentum.

By the time he recovered, the curtain of fire was gone, revealing that which the Sword had shown him: a rough-hewn tunnel that burrowed into darkness beyond the cavern wall. Jarom did not have to wonder what was down there. He knew.

Setting his jaw with renewed determination, he proceeded cautiously ahead.

CHAPTER FORTY-THREE

The retreat bells were ringing.

They had been for some time now. But unlike before, when the first tier had fallen, Nevik found himself not in a reserve segment of the rotation, but on the front lines—and thus in poor position to heed their call. Try as he might, he could not free himself from the fighting long enough to make his escape.

Pitched battle raged around him. It was all the baron could do not to simply spin about and flee toward the ramp. But to turn his back for even a moment would surely result in his death. And so he remained alongside the soldiers of his assigned company, backing slowly into the shadow of the third wall, relying on those using the catwalks and battlements above to help stall the dragonspawn advance, praying for the miracle that might save him.

Another of the beasts sprang at him. Engaged already with one to his left, Nevik had no chance to deflect its attack. But from his right, a Souari spearman stepped forward to intercept the creature, skewering it through the throat on the end of his pike. There it thrashed and squealed through shredded vocal cords, but continued to slide forward along the spear's shaft. Nevik shifted and spun, disengaging from his first opponent to help with the other. His mace crashed down atop its skull, and its struggles ceased.

He came back around to his previous assailant, which had slashed its way past a pair of pikemen and was at his throat once again. Nevik recoiled, just barely dodging a swipe that would have claimed his head, helm and all. As it was, the creature's claws raked his shoulder, tearing through chain links and drawing blood. The baron stumbled backwards, only to trip on the fallen body of a slain dragonspawn. He cried out as he fell, staring suddenly skyward at the stormy heavens.

But Troy was there. By the time Nevik's opponent came at him, it did so missing one arm, and with a sheen of black blood covering its chest. Another pair of Souari soldiers moved in to finish the beast, while the high commander helped a weary Nevik to his feet.

Then, suddenly, they were on the ramp. Nevik could barely control his own legs as Troy pushed and prodded him toward the gates above, killing rogue dragonspawn as he went. A wall of defenders followed, many of whom were swallowed up by the enemy. The bells rang again, sounding this time the signal to drop the ramp. Nevik felt his eyes widen in horror. They were not going to make it.

With their comrades at their flanks and the dragonspawn on their tail, they made their final dash. With a desperate lunge, they just barely found the flooring of the third tier as the supports were pulled and the ramp behind them fell away. Once again, those dragonspawn that had breached the gates behind or alongside them were met by a swarm of Souari they could not withstand. Their screams split the air like lightning, while with a thunderous clap, the iron gates slammed shut.

"Are you hurt?"

Nevik regarded the soldier slowly, strangely, wondering why the young man was yelling at him.

"Sir, are you hurt?"

Still Nevik did not answer. The soldier, a collector of the dead and wounded, waved for a stretcher crew.

"He's fine, Sergeant," Troy determined for him, waving the collector off and hoisting Nevik upright.

The young sergeant scowled. Nevik looked at him and gave a reassuring nod. The collector shook his head, then went about his business.

With his legs loose and wobbly beneath him, Nevik followed Troy once again in climbing to the top of the defense wall. The third, he recalled. Civilians were still scrambling from the streets and buildings beyond, making for the fourth tier. Their fight to hold the second had not lasted a quarter of an hour. Fatigued as they were, they would be lucky to hold the third for half that time.

"We've got to stop that wizard and his demon!" Troy snarled.

Nevik nodded. That did indeed seem the only hope they had of slowing this assault. But they had already tried everything at their disposal, both in armaments and stratagems. They could not begin to fight past the hordes of dragon-spawn to engage either wizard or demon in direct combat. And even if they could, it would seem from experience that each was impervious to attack. The situation was hopeless.

Their adversaries, too, must have realized this. For they came at once through the enemy swarm, wizard and demon, to enable the dragonspawn to storm the third tier. As before, the defenders used every weapon at their disposal to disrupt the sorcerer's spellcasting and the golem's assault on the city gates. And as before, their efforts were in vain.

As he listened to the pummeling of the demon's fists and the anxious shriek of dragonspawn crowded behind it upon the magical ramp, Nevik watched not the useless counterassault, but the startling look of resignation that crept across Commander Troy's face. Like a moon eclipsing the sun, it stole away all but the faintest aura of light, leaving behind only a black silhouette of the man's once radiant pride and determination. He dared not look to see how many others appeared the same.

The high commander shook his head. "Whatever it is Torin abandoned us to do," he muttered, "he had better finish soon."

With that, the brave man marched back into battle, shouting encouragement to all. A shame it was, Nevik thought, that there was little anyone could do at this point to encourage him.

Allion stood agape at the mouth of the dragon's lair, paralyzed with fear. Even in sleep, Killangrathor lay blanketed in seeming invulnerability. The monster sprawled not more than a hundred paces from where he crouched, resting comfortably upon a mound of crushed rock and splintered bones—bones, Allion realized, of creatures he did not quite recognize, creatures of a forgotten age. Its lips were drawn back in a grimace of perpetual hatred, revealing a jagged wall of teeth, the smallest of which appeared larger than his own forearm. Curled in slumber, its armored body looked to be greater than thirty horse lengths from head to tail— thirty lengths of sheer strength and power. It was the ugliest creature he had ever seen, and the most beautiful. A creature that could destroy him in the same manner that he might crush a bothersome flea. That such a beast could even exist—

A nudge from his companion broke the train of his marveling thoughts. But it was not until the youth wrenched his arm painfully that he was able to tear his gaze from the awesome beast—that which he had come to kill. If the idea had seemed ridiculous before, it was utterly preposterous now, and the look with which he faced his young friend said so.

But Kylac had already made up his mind. He pointed to a nearby ledge, off to the right of the cavern entrance. When Allion opened his mouth, the youth silenced him, then continued to gesture. The ledge was easily accessible, with a ramped formation leading up to it. It was from there that he wanted the hunter to cover his approach.

Again, Allion tried to voice his protest. And again, Kylac waved it aside. The youth was right, he supposed. They had come too far to back down now. They could take their chances, keeping faith in what the Entients had told them, or they could spend the next week retracing a path from these mountains, only to perish in the hopeless struggle against the ever increasing swarms of dragonspawn. He decided quickly. Better to be done with it here and now.

He nodded, unslinging his bow from across his shoulder and gripping it in one hand. With his other, he reached forward to clasp Kylac's arm. For the briefest of moments, the companions faced each other, bracing themselves for the task, taking proper account, and wishing silent hopes for fortune and success. Then, just as quickly, the youth was gone, a shadow slipping silently across the cavern floor.

Allion watched him for as long as it took to draw breath. He then set down his quiver amid the stones of his shelter and drew from it a dozen iron-tipped arrows. Gripping them tightly to prevent them from clattering, he stepped out into the vast opening of the dragon's hall, clinging to his weapons and his courage though his entire body was wracked with fear. One last time, he considered bolting back down the tunnel leading in. But then he saw Kylac, drifting toward the center of the cavern and the confrontation that awaited him there—a terror the youth meant to face, with or without his help.

The hunter closed his eyes, praying for mercy and a steady hand. As silently as possible, he moved into position.

The demon loomed over him, wolflike, only much larger, an emaciated frame standing upon its rear haunches. A row of spikes lined its back, while its clawed hands raked at the air. Teeth filled its open mouth like the natural rock formations of its cavern home, spires with which to pierce and shred. Around these, its lips were frozen in a terrible snarl.

Even in its inert form, it was a fearsome beast. Yet Jarom faced the statue with more wonder than concern, its smooth planes and sharp edges illuminated by the soft green light of the pool behind him. It was but one of many that lined the cavern's perimeter, facing that central pool and its stone rim. Yet this one he recognized, a nightmare tracked to its day-time lair.

He studied the many scars around its head and chest, then reached up to brush with his fingertips that which encircled its neck. The coarse stone felt cold to the touch.

He drew back, looking once more about the chamber. Like the cavern that housed them, the ring of statues was enormous. There were dozens, scores. A few looked to be missing, here and there, where a creature carved into the exterior face of the central well looked out onto an empty pedestal. A veritable army of demons, held in perpetual thrall.

Of the Queen herself there was no sign.

The Sword's warmth coursed through him. Jarom turned back to the statue of the demon wolf, and a grim smile spread slowly across his face.

With a mighty arc, he sliced through the creature's neck. Before its head could hit the floor, he split its torso with a diagonal swipe. One more cut, and the remainder of the beast toppled, its sculpted limbs reduced to rubble.

Jarom stepped away, euphoric as he watched the lifeless pieces crash to the ground. Without waiting for the dust to settle, he turned his attention to the next statue, tightening his grip upon the Sword.

Nevik winced at the pungent smell of concentrated garlic. His unseeing eyes snapped open, then focused on the one who held him, a woman in brown robes with a face pocked and scarred. For a moment, he heard nothing; then the clamor of battle rushed in upon him like the roar of a pounding surf.

"What happened?" he croaked.

The nurse put away her smelling agents and used a stinging cloth to dab at the wounds upon his face and forehead.

"The third tier is fallen. You were dragged to safety. Hold still."

Nevik sat up, pulling his head from the woman's lap. He lay surrounded by dead and wounded beneath the awning of a makeshift infirmary. Everywhere he looked, men lay writhing in pools of blood, with missing limbs or terrible gashes that exposed bones or internal organs. A flock of healers and surgeons and nurses scurried about, tending to those who moaned the loudest with poultices and tourniquets and pain-numbing brews. In most cases, they could do little more than ease the man's final suffering.

"That wound will fester if you don't lay back and let me clean it."

It all came back to him in a rush. Their battle within the third tier had been as fierce as any of which Nevik had ever heard tell. The dragonspawn had torn into their ranks with unbridled frenzy, driven by their sense of victory. The defenders had matched that fury with their own desperation, but once again, had been forced to fall back almost as soon as the portal was breached. That withdrawal left them now within the fourth tier of the city, just one beneath its apex. They had suffered staggering losses below, and were in danger of failing to survive the day.

The baron pressed a weary hand to his forehead, resisting both the nurse's efforts and the droves of pain working to extinguish the light of his world.

"Commander Troy? I saw him go down."

"A momentary inconvenience," came the commander's own reply.

Nevik turned to find a hobbled Troy limping into view on a bandaged leg. Despite the pallid hue of his flesh and the fresh blood seeping from his dressing, the commander was inspecting his heavy broadsword as he drew near.

"Commander," Nevik greeted with relief, then scowled. "What are you doing?"

"Come to see this through."

The baron opened his mouth to protest, but something in the other's eyes caused him to lose the words. He swallowed and nodded. "They'll have to kill me to get to you."

Troy touched the nurse on the shoulder, dismissing her.

"Milord, this man—"

"Will not die of fever, I promise you. Move along."

The woman bowed and gathered up her things. As she was leaving, a soldier came up to them, the bronze of his partial plate stained black with enemy blood.

"Ho there, is it time for our victory salute already? I was not aware the battle was won."

"General!" the baron welcomed as Corathel and Troy clasped hands.

The high commander grinned. "Glad to know you're still with us. What draws you from the front lines?"

"A scratch, nothing more," Corathel assured them. Upon inspection, Nevik saw that the chief general's left arm was slick with blood beneath a fresh and poorly stitched wound. "Is it time, then, to make for the mines?"

Troy's gaze drifted toward the upper city and the lines of women and children, elderly and infirm, that pushed in great swarming masses toward their final refuge. "None will set camp within the highest tier," he agreed. "But our armies have two battlements yet to defend."

"Well then, who commands them?"

Troy looked over their collective wounds. "As we're all but half-men at this point, what say you we do it together?"

The three soldiers exchanged glances.

"First one down buys eternal rounds when we reach Olirium," Corathel proposed.

"In that case, let's help the baron to his feet and have him lead the way."

The three shared smiles and forced laughter all around, using these to mask their dread concern. It ended when criers spread word of the wizard's advance, followed hard upon by a terrible pounding against the gatehouse doors. Dizzied and hobbled and one-armed, Nevik and his friends rushed to meet it.

In place upon his ledge, bow in hand and arrows laid out before him, Allion gazed out over Killangrathor's lair. The cavern itself was awe-inspiring, with its pitted walls, its bleeding lava fissures, and its river and pool of molten stone. It was the fiery streams that gave the chamber its light, for the pool, while larger than all of the other veins combined, was covered over by a mysterious blue sludge that hissed and boiled. The heat and fumes were all but unbearable, while oddly enough, the quakes seemed less forceful here, with the volcano's roar a distant echo and the earth's trembling only slight beneath his feet. Surely the chamber in which he crouched was just one of many such pockets existing deep within Krakken's core, but it felt like the exact center—like the eye of a great storm or the belly of the Great Fiend himself.

Across the way, Kylac drifted like a wraith toward the sleeping monster whose lair this was, his blades still in their sheaths. Allion watched the youth with streams of sweat pouring unchecked down his face. He wondered whether the boy was giving thought to the scattered bones over which he tread, the discards of victims from the past. Dragonhunters one and all who had sought fame and glory in Killangrathor's death. Goblins and giants, ogres and trolls, elves and dwarves, and perhaps even men. An army that had gathered over untold centuries only to be burned to ashes, smashed into splinters, ground into dust.

And together, he and Kylac had come to join them.

The youth stepped slowly, surely, over the slippery pile of loose stone, drawing near to the sleeping dragon's head. Seeing his friend in such close proximity to those massive jaws might have caused Allion to scream had he not been too terrified to do so. Instead, he held his breath and fought to control the drumming in his chest, certain that at any moment, the sound would give them away.

At last, when he was made all but deaf by the pounding of his pulse, he watched Kylac crest the mound and come to stand before the dragon's lidded eye. With trembling hands, Allion reached for an arrow and fingered its fletching, awaiting the youth's signal.

Kylac turned to him and nodded.

Allion blanched. The youth must have recognized the look of sudden horror that came across his face, or else realized that the snoring had stopped, for he spun back at once to discover that which the archer already had.

The open eye of Killangrathor, wide and unblinking, staring directly at him.

After that, everything happened at once. The dragon's head reared back, impossibly fast. Kylac might have been reaching for his blades, but Killangrathor's movement shook the pile of earth upon which he stood, forcing him to concentrate instead on his lost footing. A jawless skull skittered near Allion's position. He fired, but his arrow flew wide. By the time he had nocked another, the dragon was drawing breath as though it meant to suck all air from the cavern. With the beast no longer within striking distance, Kylac had given up on his weapons and was diving for cover behind a mound of boulders.

Killangrathor's great head chased after him like a bolt of lightning, spewing fire.

Alone within the lair of the Demon Queen, Jarom hacked and spun, charging about the cavern in a flaming fury. Nearly half of the demon statues lay in useless mounds of debris, their broken pieces scattered about the chamber floor. The dust of their passing filled the air, forming a choking haze that he did his best to ignore. For as he saw it, his work was only half finished.

He had not known what to expect once inside the Queen's den, but this wasn't it. Still, it seemed an opportunity too good to be true. Of course, to put a stop to the massacre against his people, he needed to face the Queen herself. Things might yet fail to work out. She might choose not even to show. But he felt better knowing that regardless of the final outcome, the Queen would leave her share of blood upon the floor.

And so Jarom moved from statue to statue, feeding on his own frenzy, trusting that once shattered, these foul minions would never again be given rein to wreak havoc upon his fellow man. At long last, he was making a difference.

A mighty slash split some nameless fiend right down the middle. As the two halves fell away, a bolt of scintillating light exploded against the wall just above his head. He ducked away from the rock fragments that showered over him, whirling at once to face the new threat.

He found Spithaera hovering ankle-deep within the center of her stone-rimmed pool. Marisha knelt low beside her, submerged to the waist in the suddenly foaming waters, a fistful of hair clutched in the Demon Queen's iron fist. The Queen's free hand flickered and sparked with crackling energy.

Spithaera's eyes flashed, and Jarom could feel the anger behind her forced smile. Even without the echoing translation that filled his thoughts, he might have guessed the meaning of her words as she grinned at him through clenched teeth.

"We've been expecting you."

CHAPTER FORTY-FOUR

The blare of trumpets was nearly lost amid the cacophony of sounds—the pounding upon the gatehouse portal, the anxious shriek of dragonspawn, the assaults of men upon the battlement, the preparation of ground troops, and underscoring all, the ceaseless thrumming of rain. Nevik felt the commotion more than he heard it, turning with Troy at the unexpected movement behind them. To his surprise, the rear lines were parting to make way for a mounted cadre of royal guard. In their midst rode King Thelin on the back of a white charger. With banners and fanfare, the entire procession was advancing steadily toward the main gate of the fourth tier, cheered on by those it passed.

Troy, however, seemed none too pleased.

"Your Majesty," he greeted with a bow. "Surely you do not mean to join this slaughter."

The king arched one heavy brow, dressed in a suit of mail without shine or polish and streaked with rain. "I beg your pardon, Commander, but I will not sit idle while the city of my forebears is snatched from our grasp!"

"But, Sire—"

"If anyone should not be fighting, it is a high commander who can scarcely stand." King Thelin stared at Troy's bandaged leg. "Must I relieve you of your duty, Commander?"

Troy started to protest, but seemed to change his mind. He bowed again. "We shall be honored to have you at our side."

The king nodded, then looked past them as the iron doors of the fourth gate exploded inward. "By the gods," he whispered.

Nevik turned. Dragonspawn surged through the opening and past the blockade to engage those within. The baron lifted his mace, standing ready to meet them. In the next moment, he was borne under by the crush.

The blast of flames that erupted from the dragon's maw turned red the rocks it touched, transforming them into livid coals. Even from his distant position, Allion felt its heat like that of a furnace, and recoiled against it. He could not bring himself to look for Kylac. Surely the youth was dead.

But the boy must have been quicker than he thought, for all of a sudden, there he was, rolling out from behind a pile of stones not far from the cavern entrance. Amazingly enough, he looked to be unharmed, without so much as a trailer of smoke to mar his clothes. He came to his feet, shaking his head.

Killangrathor swung about, his neck moving with serpentine swiftness. For an instant, the black dragon paused, snorting at the air. Allion followed the beast's gaze, which was directed not at Kylac, but off to one side, at the tunnel leading in. The youth, who looked to be waiting on the dragon so that he could dodge its next attack, remained in a crouch, his back turned to whatever approached.

From the mouth of the corridor burst the tusked, gray-skinned demon they had left behind in the valley, its hairless flesh tattered and smeared with dragonspawn blood. Allion gaped, too surprised to give warning, too slow for it to have made any difference. At the last possible moment, Kylac finally risked turning his attention from the dragon. He was too late. The demon barreled into him before the youth could draw a blade. Together, they went rolling across the floor in a tangled heap.

Killangrathor began to draw breath.

"No!" Allion screamed.

Up came his bow. As the dragon whirled upon him, two arrows bounced off the armored sides of its face. The third struck its eye like the harmless bite of some tiny insect.

Killangrathor roared. His tail came around like a whip,

missing Allion, but slamming into his ledge. The rock upon which he knelt crumbled, and the hunter felt himself tumbling amid a shower of crushing debris.

He remained alert, even as his flesh cried out against the sharp and pummeling assault. The dragon had already turned from him, looking back to where the others tussled. It spotted them at once and strode in furiously, rocking the chamber with its thunderous footfalls, kicking up a cloud of dust and bones. This time, there was no chance for Kylac to escape. It was more a matter of which would kill him first. For as the demon gained the upper hand and was about to chomp down on Kylac's head, Killangrathor lunged, engulfing them both with dragonfire.

Jarom stayed where he was, crouched defensively, the Crimson Sword held like a shield before him. Deathly beautiful in a gown of transparent silk, Spithaera considered the destruction that filled her chamber. She had to be furious, but hid it well beneath a tone smooth and alluring.

"I had thought you would return to us at Morethil. As a mortal, you continue to amaze me."

Marisha whimpered softly, her neck twisted awkwardly by the Demon Queen's merciless grasp.

"Let her go," Jarom demanded. It was an instinctive plea. Even to him, it sounded ridiculous.

Spithaera smiled, showing him her free hand, that which flickered with magical energy. Slowly, deliberately, she moved that hand, stretching forth her fingers so that they pointed down at Marisha's cheek. Marisha stiffened, her tear-streaked face defiant. The threads of lightning crackled hungrily.

"One last chance, Torin, my sweet. You may possess all the world, or you may possess nothing. The choice is yours."

He was surrounded by screams. They may have been cries of the living, or the keening of the dead. He no longer knew the difference, nor to which group he belonged. He lay among a pile of fresh corpses, trapped in a stupor from which he could not shake free.

King Thelin fought from atop his charger, swinging his broadsword and fighting to rally his men. Commander Troy, Chief General Corathel, and countless others struggled for their lives. But for Nevik, the struggle was over, ended the moment he had slipped and been knocked aside, striking his head against the cobblestones so hard that his mace had gone flying from his nerveless fingers. He had tried to stand, but could not. All that remained for him was the tear and pull of tooth and claw when it came time for the dragonspawn to feed.

It would not be long. The enemy fought with the same strength it had brought at the battle's inception, drawn by the promise of victory like sharks to blood in the water. And while the fifth tier remained to them, the Souari defenders seemed determined to hold the fourth as though it were the last, as if knowing what little difference one more battlement would make. They would stand, and they would die, many of them too weary to raise a blade, but using their bodies as a shield for those behind them. It was a senseless massacre, furious and final, from which only one army would emerge triumphant.

Still Nevik remained where he was, lost in his delirium, denied the release of death. Though his body would not respond, his eyes roved in their sockets, staring one way, then another. At last, his foggy gaze came to settle upon the yawning breach through which the enemy waves poured. Beyond, standing head and shoulders above the swelling dragonspawn, was a man of obsidian flesh, unmoved by the storm. Somewhere below, Nevik knew, stood the wizard. It was really the only regret the baron had, that he would not be there to witness the death of this villain, this creature whose hunger was such that he delighted in death, even when he did not directly profit from it. Had he the strength, he might yet take up his weapon and slay the sorcerer, avenge his father, and thereby die a happy man.

Instead he closed his eyes against the pelting rains and waited for his father's spirit to take him home.

Pain coursed through his broken leg in relentless waves, threatening to render him unconscious. Allion fought against it, biting back what would have been yet another wasted scream. There was no time to express his torment, no time for fury or grief. This time, there could be no doubt. Kylac was gone, borne away on a river of flame. And while he had no hope of killing the dragon from where he lay, battered and half buried in a mound of shattered stone, the hunter, like a thrashing fish with a hook in its mouth, was too desperate to realize it.

He was still groping for his bow amid the rubble as Killangrathor's conflagration burned itself out. When it did, the hunter froze in stunned disbelief. He must have taken a terrible blow to the head—it was the only way to explain that which he saw before him.

As before, a trail of melted and superheated rock revealed the path of the dragon's blast. Caught in the center of that swath, the demon had been incinerated, its flesh a scattering of ashes swept up in the residual gusts of Killangrathor's breath.

Kylac Kronus knelt among its remains, unscathed.

The youth stared at the demon's flaming skull as it crumbled into embers—which did not vanish, but remained on the cavern floor. All around him, trailers of smoke drifted from the now blackened stone. He looked about in confusion, wondering, no doubt, how it was he still lived.

His gaze found that of Killangrathor. The great dragon was blinking, by all appearances as bewildered as he.

But the ageless monster would not be taken by its surprise. It started forward with a sneer, claws twitching.

Kylac came to his feet, determined. This time, he did not run. Instead, a pair of blades flashed in his hands.

Killangrathor stopped. His eyes bulged, then squinted, and he began to recoil as if blinded by the sun. Allion glanced between the two, then settled on Kylac, trying to figure out what it was that had so startled the beast. The youth hadn't moved. Nothing had changed, nothing but—

The hunter stared at the blades in Kylac's hands, and a forgotten statement echoed in his head.

Your weapons will be those that vanquish Killangrathor.

A promise, given by the Entients.

Your weapons will be those . . .

The youth's weapons. But how?

Your weapons . . .

The dragon backed away, using its arms and wings to fend off the unseen glare of Kylac's blades. After witnessing the youth twice prove impervious to dragonfire, Allion would have thought nothing could surprise him. But this did. Kylac had taken not a single step in its direction, and yet the mighty dragon cowered like a whipped dog, groveling as it made its slow retreat.

Behind it, the sludge-filled lava pool hissed and boiled as though a living thing.

Allion glanced back at Kylac. The youth stood motionless, awestruck by the scene unfolding before them.

Convulsions wracked the dragon's body. Its eyes rolled back; its wings lifted skyward. With a sound that was both whimper and growl, it dipped itself into the molten pool.

Killangrathor screamed, a great wail that rocked the mountain to its foundations. Allion winced at a sudden stench and caught his breath as he realized what was happening. While the lava itself did the dragon no harm, the blue sludge that filled the pool was devouring its flesh like acid. And yet, Killangrathor continued to lower himself into its depths, to be eaten away rather than confront the mysterious power of the youth's swords.

The stench of burning dragon permeated the vast chamber. The cavern shook, dislodging great chunks of rock from a ceiling lost in darkness. They shattered as they fell, causing Allion to cringe, trapped within his cover of loose stone. For those brief, terrible moments, he was certain the mountain would crumble atop him, sealing his destiny along with that of Killangrathor.

But then the screams stopped. With most of its body lost

beneath the lava line, the dragon's great head slapped down
against the cavern floor, its lidded eyes gleaming lifelessly.
Its wings fell after, collapsing like the sails of a splintered
mast. The volcano shuddered in response, then grew still,
and the fires of Mount Krakken began to cool.

He had come to save Marisha from a fate she didn't deserve. He
had come to save his people by putting an end to the Demon
Queen's conquest. He had insisted on coming alone, for he
meant to achieve all of this in the only way he knew how.

He had come to surrender.

He did not see it as an act of cowardice. On the contrary,
it seemed the bravest choice he could make. If by his own
death he could change matters, he would gladly make that
sacrifice instead. But his death alone would not be enough
to win Marisha or his friends or the people of Pentania any
sort of peace. It was the Sword that the Queen truly desired.
And while submitting to her will might not earn the promised reprieve for humankind, it remained their best and
brightest hope.

Why, then, did he feel as though giving up the Sword
would be a betrayal of those he was fighting to save? It was
the only responsible decision, the one means by which he
could positively affect the outcome of this war. It was the
same determination he had made while imprisoned at Kraagen Keep. Perish in useless defiance, or do as the Queen
asked and give the peoples of these lands a chance, at least,
to stave off annihilation. It was his own selfish vanity that
had led him to believe he could defeat such a creature—a
misplaced faith in the importance of his own destiny. The
greatest leaders were those who knew when to fight and
when to lay down the sword. Even Kylac had shown him
that, when attacked by the A'awari in the jungles of Vosges.
If he meant to lead this people as he had determined he
must, now was the time to show he had learned that lesson.

Nevik would disagree. As would Corathel, Troy, and others. Even Marisha seemed to be pleading with him not to do
this, as if sensing his indecision. All had resisted. But what

had their resistance won them? Pain and death and sorrow—the only spoils to be claimed. Had they surrendered in the beginning, how many lives might they have saved?

He began to tremble as he lowered his weapon. Spithaera's eyes widened with delight. He looked to Marisha, beseeching her forgiveness. Her features were filthy, her clothes tattered. Angry tears streamed down her cheeks. She stared back at him and shook her head, causing him to waver.

"She is nothing to us, my Torin. Can you not see? We are higher creatures, you and I. It is a violation of nature for the hawk to live as a sparrow. Soar with me, and I shall show you glories she cannot imagine."

He did not want to believe that the Queen's temptation had anything to do with his decision. But perhaps she was right. He could not deny that he was drawn to her, enticed by her dark grace and beauty. Perhaps he *was* cheating himself. Perhaps he was in fact better than these others he was trying so hard to protect. Perhaps he should give less thought to their needs and more to his own.

He dismissed the notion at once. His worth was no greater than that of his fellow man. All he need do was think of Marisha—of her unswerving strength and compassion—to be reminded of that.

And yet, what was he to do? Let her die? Maintain this refusal and he would essentially be sacrificing her life for but a chance to save others—most of whom he didn't know. Undoubtedly, she would urge him to do just that. But even if he managed to deliver them all, were their lives worth more than hers?

As before, when she had first been abducted by the wizard and demon, Jarom could not seem to think straight. Despite all his careful reasoning on why he should capitulate, his sense now was that if he gave up the Sword, both he and Marisha were dead, with the others set soon to follow. But all he could see were those bolts as they came ever nearer to singeing her fair skin—

A sudden gleam caught his attention, a familiar red glow barely visible at the neck of Marisha's ripped bodice. Jarom blinked, averting his gaze from what was surely a trick of his imagination. He looked again to the Demon Queen, who mistook the cause of his hesitation. Her eyes flashed their emerald fire.

"Use her as you will, if that is your craving, but do not enslave yourself to such weakness!"

The Queen shook her fist in emphasis, rattling her captive. Marisha grimaced and squealed, a mouse underfoot, held trapped and waiting for the killing blow. But with that same motion, a ruby pendant fell free from its place of concealment to dangle below Marisha's chest. Jarom saw it clearly now, but still could not believe it. For within the polished surface of the perfect stone burned the fires of the Sword of Asahiel.

Jarom did well to hide his astonishment by focusing on his adversary. He had seen it, but the Queen had not. Marisha's kneeling form hid it from view, and the demon's attention was concentrated on him. Beneath his tightly guarded facade, his mind reeled. How? Where could such a stone have come from? Why would Marisha possess it? And if she did, why would she not have shown him long ago?

And yet, if it was real, it would explain much that had confused him before. Marisha's intense interest in the legends of the Swords, her guarantee that the talismans existed, her intimate sense of their mysterious workings, her unshared secrets, including that before the battle at Morethil . . .

A stinging sweat filled his eyes, yet he dared not move to wipe it away—to do anything that might draw the Queen's attention to this unexpected revelation. As he continued to hesitate, the lethal magic sparking upon her free hand danced ever nearer to Marisha's face, her throat . . .

A sudden idea entered his head, a desperate hope that gave his heart cheer—and just as quickly filled it with fear. What if he was wrong about the pendant? What if this was all a trick of the Demon Queen? His pulse raced. His instincts screamed. But what were they telling him? Was he to take the risk, or avoid it?

"Destiny separates the strong from the weak," Spithaera urged. "Do not resist that for which you were born."

Jarom cringed. There it was again, the idea that his fate was predetermined, the outcome to this struggle already decided. Except now Jarom knew better. He tensed even more, glancing back and forth between the lightning held in check upon the Queen's hand and the soft crimson glow emanating from Marisha's pendant.

"You have been given a choice. Choose now!"

Impossible. He could not make this decision. The potential consequences were more than he could endure.

For the first time while in possession of the Sword, Jarom's shoulders ached, the weight of the talisman too great to bear. Once again, his arms began to lower, and he looked to Marisha in apology.

But as their eyes met, a fresh strength coursed through him. Shining through her pain and fear was an unmistakable tenacity and calm. Even now, without any rational hope of escape, the woman refused to yield. All she asked was that he be the one to decide their fate, not the Demon Queen. Come what may, she would face this challenge with a spirit unbroken.

For an eternal moment, Jarom lost himself in that gaze. When the moment had passed, his veins were filled with a heat born not of the Sword's divine touch, but of the assurance that her faith was with him. He need not fear for her. He need only do what he believed he must.

A slow smile had begun to spread across Spithaera's features as she watched Jarom's defenses lower with the crumbling of his resolve. That smile vanished now as he swallowed hard, raised the weapon in his hands, and turned to stare at her from beneath the shelf of a determined brow.

"So be it," he agreed. "Then let destiny separate us."

He charged, lifting the Sword overhead. Spithaera's eyes widened, then narrowed in fury. Without pause, she unleashed the pent-up magic from her outspread fingertips, launching a stream of bolts directly into Marisha's face.

They never reached their mark. As Marisha closed her eyes against the blinding assault, a sheath of crimson flame burst forth from the heartstone pendant that dangled from her neck. Before the Demon Queen realized what was happening, those same guardian flames had engulfed her hand, tracing the magic back to its source, consuming it like oil.

Spithaera howled, releasing Marisha and staring at her hand in denial. Jarom leapt atop the wall surrounding the pool, but then halted. He had guessed correctly about the stone and the divine power within, but the flames had not stopped upon consuming the Queen's unleashed energies. At such close proximity, she had been unable to cut short her attack as she had above the ramparts of Morethil. As a result, the crimson fire had chased those energies into the flesh that housed them, filling whatever network of veins through which the demon's magic ran. Even now, as she turned upon him with a glare of both hatred and horror, Spithaera's eyes erupted from their sockets in twin spurts of red flame.

Marisha lunged toward the edge of the pool, splashing free of its churning center. Spithaera sprang after, arms extended, and Jarom dropped between them, a human schilltron as he intercepted her strike. It was the demon's own weight that drove the Crimson Sword squarely through the center of her torso.

The Demon Queen shrieked anew, burning from within, spitting a mouthful of fire from the center of her wracked visage. Her dark flesh turned red, then burst into flame, like parchment lit slowly from beneath. Jarom held fast to the Sword, even as he shied away from the radiance of her burning shell. The water about their feet hissed and boiled, but could not extinguish the divine fires that eclipsed her form. Almost at once, Spithaera was swallowed by a pillar of flames, and as quickly as they had begun, her cries ended in a garbled yelp.

The curtain of fire parted and died into ether. When it did, not a trace of the Demon Queen remained, save for her ring of broken statues, the stone rim of her pool, and the gentle swirling of the now ordinary waters where before she had stood.

Even as he gave himself up for dead, Nevik opened his eyes, drawn to a change in the tumult around him. He saw King

Thelin, not far from where he lay, being overwhelmed by a clutch of dragonspawn. Both Troy and Corathel fought at the king's side, along with dozens of soldiers and guardsmen, but could do little to help. Everywhere the baron looked, Souari defenders were falling back in defeat.

Then he noticed that the dragonspawn were no longer attacking, but doubling over as if sick. Entire swarms coughed and writhed and pitched to the earth. A delusion, perhaps, but it appeared to the dazed Nevik that the beasts were beginning to shrivel and transform into jagged boulders of volcanic rock.

"What in Krakken's blazes . . . ?"

He knew not who said it first, but the murmur spread like wildfire as the scene continued to unfold. Nevik's eyes shifted and caught. There, down below the fourth tier, at the base of his sorcerous ramp, stood the wizard. He too was observing the unnatural spectacle, and within moments had apparently seen enough. With an effortless summons, his steed of black mist took shape and rose up beneath him. The wizard turned its head and rode hurriedly toward the lower gates, surrounded by an avalanche of boulders that bounced and rained about him.

A tremendous cheer ushered his retreat, an uproar that gained in strength as more and more of the survivors put aside their shock and amazement and joined in the celebration. Before long, their cry of victory transcended even the echo of grinding boulders, and between the two, the entire city shook.

The furor had not yet begun to settle when a strong pair of hands pulled Nevik to his feet. And while he had not the strength to do so on his own, the baron found himself standing, propped between a pair of soldiers who were presenting him to Troy. The commander greeted him with a joyful cry and a hearty embrace.

All around them, soldiers did the same, clasping hands, hollering praises, and searching already to assist the wounded. Upon the ramparts, entire battalions danced and shouted, their weapons held high. Before he knew it, Nevik was surrounded by Chief General Corathel, King Thelin, and scores of their comrades, all of them gathering near the shattered portal to better view the sights below.

"The Ceilhigh are watching over us," King Thelin observed, his solemn words all but lost in the ongoing tumult.

At that moment, a fiery explosion drew their attention to a shadowed alcove of the fourth-level gatehouse. There stood the forgotten demon golem. Its head had erupted into a geyser of flames. Before any could respond, it too fell to the earth—not like the others, but engulfed in the swirling tendrils of a crimson fire.

"That they are," Corathel agreed, lowering his sword. He studied the demon with a private smile, watching it burn. "That they are."

Nevik said nothing, but tilted his head toward a break in the heavens, from which both the sun and the rains washed down upon his face.

CHAPTER FORTY-FIVE

*J*arom sat before the hearth in his overstuffed chair, staring into the flames and searching for steady ground amid a tossing sea of emotions. Although the War of the Demon Queen appeared to be over, there was much yet with which to come to terms. Quiet moments such as this had been hard to come by since leaving Souaris, and reflection thus far had offered little comfort. Just when he managed to accept and set aside one set of consequences, another presented itself, equally unpalatable. At this point, it seemed as though the deluge of hard truths would never end.

He had remained at Souaris for just three days following the demise of the dragonspawn—of which he had learned upon emerging with Marisha from the caves beneath the city. The cleanup and celebration were to last weeks, and Jarom had not wanted to abandon his fellow soldiers completely. He had agreed to stay a fortnight along with Nevik and their people, bidding farewell to Corathel, Jasyn, Maltyk, Lar, and the handful of others remaining from the Parthan West Legion who had set forth to the east with the coming of the very next dawn. He had hoped that would be enough time for Kylac and Allion to return from the Skull-mars, assuming both had survived their encounter with Killangrathor. It was also time needed to gather intelligence before setting forth with Commander Troy and an army of twenty thousand or more—whatever it would take—to reclaim his own lands from the wizard. Until that day should arrive, Jarom was asked not to burden himself, but to take his rest and accept the heartfelt gratitude of the Kuurian people.

Three days later, he had received word of Diln.

He had ridden forth at once, accompanied by Nevik, Marisha, and five hundred Souari cavalry. It had taken them four days to reach his village, with stays at Morethil, the Gaperon, and Earthwyn along the way. Once there, he had spent three long days sifting through the ashes and burying the remains of his friends and loved ones. Even with Marisha to comfort him, he found it to be the most difficult task he had ever undertaken. For the destruction of his home, though long feared, was far worse than he had imagined. The village center, the outlying homes, the forest itself—all had been ravaged if not utterly destroyed. What lives remained were those who had fled north to Glendon or to parts unknown, as his scouts were able to learn. Of life within the wasteland of the village proper, there was no sign.

The thought that its ruin might have been prevented had he acted differently tore at him. Had he done exactly as he'd been told and not been waylaid by his own stubborn quest for the Sword, Diln might have been saved. Despite the fact that he had found the Sword and used it to help vanquish a greater threat, he could not stop thinking about all of the rationalizations he'd made along the way, decisions that had kept him on the path of the Sword and away from his home and kin. That in turning back sooner he might still have failed to prevent their slaughter was to him a moot point. His people and his home had suffered the ultimate price because of him. Regardless of the excuses tendered on his behalf, he would bear those scars for the rest of his life.

On his third day among the remains, one of his outriders had returned from Glendon with a party of village survivors that included former Elders Olenn and Banon, and Allion's own father. By grace, the hunter's entire family had escaped the massacre. This revelation had assuaged some of Jarom's grief, and the company of friends had spent the evening catching up on all that had occurred in the months following his departure. Allion's father was made grave by the mystery of his son's current whereabouts, but shed tears of pride to learn of the young man's pivotal role in the conflict. The Ceilhigh were merciful, the older man claimed, and would see his son home safely. Jarom had only nodded, keeping his doubts to himself.

The next morning, he had set forth for Krynwall, having received word that the city was no longer occupied by the wizard or his forces. Already, the people who had taken to the nearby forests and hills were beginning to return, rejoining those who had been trapped in the city all along. Thus far, it was a mostly lawless rabble of looters and thieves, but according to his scout, the soldiers under his command would be more than enough to establish order. They could proceed without fear.

And so he had, feeling it his duty to make safe the capital for those tens of thousands who would eventually find their way home. In fact, he had been staggered by the numbers already doing just that. Once clear of the forest, he had found almost every step of highway lined with those making their return, all of whom hailed his arrival. Their unexpected adoration took him by surprise, but did little to alleviate a continued host of nagging concerns. For while those around him celebrated the wizard's withdrawal, Jarom understood that his brother would not have gone far. If anything, this defeat would make him that much more dangerous when next they met. Jarom, for one, would not be looking forward to that day.

And yet, upon witnessing the aftermath of the wizard's infestation, that feeling began to change. Trepidation gave way to anger as he saw for himself the damage wrought upon this once proud city, a city he had admired in his youth. Granted, the sparks for much of that damage had been struck by their blood father, Sorl. But what the old king had weakened through misuse and neglect, the wizard and his army had brought to ruin, pillaging and burning and poisoning all with barbaric trappings of death and despair. Among these, staked out upon the highest parapet of the royal palace, were the headless remains of one identified to him as Queen Ellebe. Another fear come to pass. His mother, slain by her own son, for what crime no one could guess. It was upon this discovery that a cold fire had burned away the last of Jarom's apprehension. Perhaps he would be looking forward to Soric's return after all.

That had been more than two weeks ago. Since that time, he had been troubled mostly with affairs for which he had no true knowledge or experience—those of restoring order to a city and kingdom. There was so much to be done that he had known not where to begin. Were it not for Nevik, he might have abandoned the entire undertaking and run screaming for the hills. But the baron of Drakmar stayed by his side, helping him to appoint city leaders, arrange meetings, and implement plans for everything from the renovation of homes and trade centers within the city to the distribution of aid to outlying communities. There were issues concerning a tax structure, the conscription of an army, and a thousand others in between—enough to give him constant headaches and make sleep itself a forgotten dream. But Nevik worked tirelessly, compelling Jarom to do the same.

In truth, he was grateful for the distraction. If not utterly engrossed with work at all times, his thoughts invariably wandered to the east, tracking two friends he could only pray were still alive. Obviously, Allion and Kylac had succeeded in their quest, but as to whether either had survived—or would survive the journey home—Jarom had no guarantee. As the passing days advanced in number, so too did his concerns. From the day of his arrival, he had sent forth scouts, posting lookouts at all the major crossroads. Thus far, there had been neither word nor sign, with winter stealing fast upon them. Should they fail to arrive before the first snows fell upon the grasslands, Jarom intended to go after them himself—all the way to the Skullmars if need be—so as to ensure their safe return.

Or at the very least, the recovery of their remains.

He rose from his chair and moved to a window overlooking the palace grounds. The palace itself was in better condition than he had hoped. Rumors were that the king's tower had been transformed by some fear-inducing magic, but if so, then it had reverted to its original form upon the wizard's departure. And while it indeed lacked the polish and beauty of Morethil, or even the stern majesty of Souaris, it provided ample room for himself and his friends, and more privileges than they required.

He let his gaze drift higher, taking in the rose-colored sweep of the late afternoon horizon as it broke over the distant trees. As he did, he reached idly to pet the one-eyed cat perched upon the sill—an animal he could not seem to banish from these chambers. Though it no longer hissed at him as it had in the beginning, the cat once again shied from his touch, so Jarom let it be.

No sooner had he withdrawn his hand than there was a rap at his door.

"Come," he said, keeping his gaze upon the forest.

He turned as the door opened, and was glad that he did. Marisha entered with a twirl, the trailing folds of an elegant gown spinning about her voluptuous figure.

She came to a stop before him. "Well, do you like it?"

The fabric was silk, delicate and formfitting. Its pale azure hue seemed to highlight the color of her sapphire eyes.

"It's lovely." The scent of her perfume was intoxicating, but it was the brightness of her smile that most captivated him. "Where did you get it?"

"An adorable young tailor fashioned it for me—a gift for the friend of his king."

And then there was that, looming over all—the specter of who he must become. Before his journey to Krynwall, he had held on to the hope that the people might choose not to accept him. After all, the story of Prince Torin's staged death and sudden reappearance was still incredible. However, most seemed to agree that in light of everything else that had happened, it was not altogether inconceivable. Besides, only Nevik perhaps held equal claim, and the young baron was more than happy to defer to Jarom, lending word and support that had gone a long way toward securing the people's acceptance and sealing Jarom's fate.

Of course, Jarom suspected that none of it really mattered—not his birthright, not the lack of worthy rivals, and not the backing of the highest-ranking nobleman to survive the wizard's invasion. He was the wielder of the fabled

Crimson Sword. As such, he was already a legend among the land's populace—a distinction with which he was decidedly uncomfortable. The people wanted him as their ruler because they viewed him as some kind of savior. That what he'd done had in no way prepared him for the daily tasks and responsibilities of ruling a kingdom was lost on them. He was not just a man, but a hero, an icon, a figurehead. That was what they needed of him. That was what they expected.

Nevertheless, Jarom had done all he could to put off any kind of coronation. The people of Alson were already pushing for it. Kings and governors from east to west encouraged it—at least openly. Doubtless, there were factions within and without the capital city who would like to use this opportunity to seize power for themselves, but none dared challenge him, given his popularity among the people. In the end, he suspected he would have to allow them their ceremony. He did not want it, but he was running short on reasons to avoid it. Other than Nevik, whom did he trust? And if he were to leave it all behind, where would he go? What else was he to do? His friends had all but convinced him that the most good he could do in rebuilding these lands was to be done from right here, as king. In any case, he could not put off his decision much longer.

As if sensing his discomfort, Marisha stepped forward and slipped her arms about his waist. Where would he be without her continued support? Jarom wondered. Despite talk of returning to Partha, she had agreed to remain with him at least until Kylac and Allion returned. Of course, he wished for her to stay longer, but he had yet to work up the courage to ask.

His gaze slipped down to her neck. He fingered the chains of her pendant, lying hidden beneath her dress, but she took hold of the stone before he could pull it free.

"How are you feeling?" she asked, drawing his attention away from the secret talisman. A secret she was yet unwilling to share with the world. A secret she had only barely discussed with him.

"I don't know," Jarom admitted.

Her golden brow raised in question.

He tried to explain, to put into words that which he did not understand in thought. "When this business started," he began, "I wanted nothing to do with it. I was as happy as I believed possible. But retrieving a Sword of Asahiel had been my lifelong dream. After finding it, and meeting you . . ."

He hesitated, suddenly unsure of himself.

Marisha smiled. "Go on."

Jarom considered his words carefully. "I've never been so mistaken as I was concerning my own potential happiness."

Marisha's smile broadened. "So what's wrong?"

Jarom's look became incredulous, and all with which he had been wrestling came gushing forth at once. "What's wrong? Marisha, our homes are destroyed, our friends and families butchered. My mother was slain trying to protect me, and her killer has vanished without a trace. It's been nearly a month now without a word from Allion or Kylac—"

"I worry for them also," Marisha said softly, pressing her fingers against his lips. "But I'm sure they are well and will come as quickly as they can."

Jarom removed her fingers from his mouth, taking them in his hand. "I was going to say," he offered with a sense of shame, "that despite it all, I'm not sure now that I would change things if I could."

The young woman's smile turned sad. "Do not feel guilty for finding the goodness in life. You are right to let go of the past."

"Marisha—"

"We have all suffered. We have all persevered. No matter the circumstances, one must learn to make the best of things."

Jarom shook his head, then looked away. "What I believed to be my destiny was nothing of the sort."

"But it is, here and now, made so by your own actions."

His gaze fell, but she continued, near exasperation. "You have liberated these lands with little more than your faith and determination. You have brought peace to an entire race. Just what will it take to make you happy?"

His eyes came up suddenly. "Marry me."

"What?"

"Be my queen, here at Krynwall. Rule Alson with me."

Marisha stared at him wordlessly, and for a moment, Jarom was afraid she meant to reject him out of hand. Then her smile returned, her radiant face beaming.

"Shall I dispatch a herald to announce the news, my lord?"

Jarom did not trust himself to speak. He merely stared into her eyes, and grinned for the first time in weeks.

He was about to embrace her when his peace was disturbed yet again, this time by a youthful herald who didn't bother to knock, but who banged into the room so loud and fast as to startle the cat from its ledge. Jarom and Marisha spun to face him, alarmed. The boy's wind scraped in and out of his lungs in heaving gasps.

"I beg . . . your pardon . . . my lady," he apologized with a bow.

"What is it?" Jarom asked, stepping forward with concern.

"My lord," the boy panted, "Masters Allion and Kylac have arrived . . . and request an audience."

Jarom gaped at the lad until understanding took hold. His heart fluttered as he glanced at Marisha. "Where did you leave them?"

"He didn't," said Allion as he hobbled through the doorway on a tattered leg splint. "He just outran us."

Jarom rushed forward with Marisha on his heels. Kylac entered upon Allion's. The four friends exchanged a flurry of clasps and embraces.

"What took you so long?" Jarom looked worriedly at the hunter's mending leg.

"Don't trouble over me. The dragon got much worse."

Jarom smiled. He scanned Kylac for any sign of injury, but saw none.

"We stopped through Diln," Allion added somberly. "Olenn was there. He told us you had, too."

Jarom nodded.

"Has my family arrived yet?"

"I'm expecting them any day. You don't know how happy they'll be to see you."

"And I them." Allion's smile was fleeting. "Our sorrow is shared, my friend."

"So, what happened?" Marisha asked.

"You won't believe it," the hunter claimed, glancing at Kylac. "We scarcely believe it ourselves."

Jarom and Marisha regarded the pair curiously.

"Let's just say the Entients owe us at least one more explanation."

"Well, let us hear all about it," Jarom said. "Tonight, we celebrate the return of the dragonslayers in regal fashion."

"And what of our betrothal?" Marisha reminded him with mock indignation. "Is there no cause to celebrate that?"

Kylac chuckled. "I'll be. I never saw *that* coming." The wry remark ended in a wink to Jarom and another hug for Marisha.

"I couldn't be happier for you," Allion offered, embracing each in turn. "For the both of you."

"Graces!" piped the forgotten herald. "I've got to tell the people!"

Before anyone could stop him, the boy raced from the room, crowing at the top of his lungs.

EPILOGUE

Deep within the halls of Whitlock, the Entient Htomah leaned toward the crystalline mirror in anticipation. For weeks he had been hard at work, trapped here in the scrying chamber, trying to retrace the path of Torin and his friends through the ruins of Thrak-Symbos. As difficult as it was to scry the aura of a living being, it was next to impossible to observe an area without one. Despite the detailed account he and his order had been given, he had at times during this task wondered whether it would not have been easier to simply walk the same trails in physical form.

Much of this was his own fault. After scrying upon them consistently throughout most of their journey, he had given up during the endless days in which they had wandered lost through the upper catacombs. By the time he had checked back with them, they were already free of the ruins, the Sword in hand. At that point, all efforts had turned toward measuring Torin's current progress, so that he might be returned to Whitlock to present the talisman and deliver his account. Only after listening to that account—and later, after witnessing Spithaera's surprising demise and the stunning revelation of the young healer-woman's pendant—had he decided that the mysterious antechamber in which the Sword had been housed merited a closer look. By then, some had feared it was too late.

But now, at last, he believed he was almost there. Through the ruined cathedral, following the exhale of their breath. Down to the lower level of the catacombs, marked by small, dried patches of Torin's blood. The residue of the party's presence was faint, but Htomah could just make it out. Sweat dripped from his brow, which knotted in concentration. He felt the strain throughout his body, but would not let go, not now, not when he was so close—

And then he had it. His focus was poor, the colors and lines bleeding together in a swirling fog. But there it was— the crypt with its broken ceiling and rotting basilisk carcass, the spacious antechamber behind the now missing slab of stone, the well inside . . .

Htomah smiled. Here it was that Torin had drawn the Sword of Asahiel. After much toil and frustration, here at last could the Entients see for themselves that which Torin had seen. The chamber of the Sword was as the young man had described leaving it, dark and silent, with its central dais, crumbled altar, and surrounding basilisk holes. Of the creatures themselves, there was still no sign, chased away by—

A sharp movement startled Htomah and caused him to fall back. Immediately, the image vanished, the crystalline mirror gone dark and empty. The Entient blinked several times before remembering to draw breath. He could not have seen what he thought he had. He was tired, was all. He had overextended his limits for one day. Although the presence of Torin and his companions would continue to fade, now that he had marked the proper trail, he should have an easier time finding it on the morrow.

Until then, until he was sure, he would keep it to himself. Maventhrowe and the others considered him fretful enough. Their gentle mockery he could tolerate. But he did not want to bring it to the point where they ignored his admonitions altogether.

In the meantime, he had plenty more with which to concern himself, not the least of which was this Marisha Valour, a common healer who no longer seemed so common.

And so Htomah stepped from the room, dismissing for now that which he could not have seen: in the center of the chamber from which the Sword had been drawn, within that empty pit, a black claw reaching forth to clutch the stone lip.

If you enjoyed reading
The Crimson Sword,
then read the following selection from

The Obsidian Key
Book Two of the Legend of Asahiel,

---

available in hardcover from Eos in June 2006.

CHAPTER ONE

*T*he winter storm tore across the land, ripping and snarling like a caged beast set free at last. Its howling breath wailed in his ears. Its frigid claws raked his skin. The darkness of its maw enveloped the earth, rendering deliberate progress a fool's dream.

Grum looked again to his battered compass, scraping at the layer of ice that shielded its surface. Its needle swung uselessly, spinning back and forth in random circles. He shook the instrument and bid it to the smelter of Achthium's Forge. To the west were the Skullmars, the treacherous peaks from which they'd been blown off course. To the east, the tempest of the sea. Or so he assumed. The world around him had disappeared, its planes and edges smudged together until all that remained was a hazy smear. Head bowed, eyes squinted against frenzied gusts of windblown earth, he could scarcely spy the ground beneath his feet, let alone even the largest of markers that might guide him home.

He risked a backwards glance to check on his companions. He could see but one, Raegak, tethered to him at the waist in their makeshift line. Beyond that, the rope stretched into the swirling void of pelting ice and strafing winds. He could only hope the others were still there, stumping after, knowing that to become separated now would mean dying alone in these frozen wastes.

Not that remaining together afforded great consolation. Truth was, they were hopelessly lost, miles from the safety and comfort of their subterranean home. And even if home

lay just around the bend, were they to stumble half a step to
the left or right, they might pass right on by without ever
knowing it.

Raegak glanced up, eyes hollow, cheeks lashed, snow
clinging to his beard. Grum looked quickly away, hiding his
compass within a gnarled fist, determined to mask his dismay from those who looked to him for solace. He was
toifeam, leader of his expedition, and by Achthium, he
would see them through.

To accentuate this silent oath, he crammed the worthless
compass deep into a leather pouch. At that same moment,
the earth fell away, and he found himself scrabbling against
a clutching blackness. Chunks of ice and gravel skittered beneath his feet, while a shower of snow cascaded about him.
Everything seemed to be sucking him down, down into
some depthless pit, like an insect into a fur-spider's lair . . .

A sharp tug caught him about the waist, folding him violently forward and snatching the wind from his lungs. For a
moment he slid downward again, before coming to a lurching halt. Curtains of snow slid past as his companions struggled with their footing above. He hung there, twisting in the
abyss, before reaching up for the lip of the pit, where Raegak, stout legs braced against the earth, bent down and offered a leather-wrapped hand.

Moments later, Grum huddled with his companions
around the rim of the breach, peering into its depths. Should
it prove to be the shelter that saved them, he would forgive
himself his fright from the fall. Nevertheless, he had lived in
these mountains long enough to know not to trust them.
Such clefts in the earth's hide might become fissures descending hundreds, even thousands of feet—or if not, might
open into the den of some surly creature in no mood to share
its home. Even the most foolish of his kin knew better than
to enter such an opening without knowing what lay within.

Producing with frozen hands a flint and steel, Grum
worked to light the pitch-coated head of a thornweed firebrand. He may as well have tried to do so beneath the black
waters of the sea. No sooner did the sparks flare to life than
they were borne away by shrieking flurries. Grum persisted,

ignoring the stiffness setting into his unmoving joints, lips pressed tight in a determined frown. At last, feeling the hopeless stares of his comrades upon him, he slipped his flint back into its pouch and motioned for Raegak to put the torch away.

He regarded each of his companions in turn—Raegak, Durin, Alfrigg, and Eitri. Friends for more than a generation, their faces held a shared understanding, hopes and fears mirroring his own. They would have to risk it. To prolong their exposure any longer would be fatal.

After a few quick signals, each began working loose the knot that bound him to his companions. Grum alone left his intact, for he would be lowered first. Only after assuring himself of the relative safety of this hidden cave would the others follow. With any luck, nature's wrath would expire by morning and allow them to begin the task of finding their way back from this wayward trek.

With the thickness of their gloves—and the fingers within numbed almost beyond use—even this simple task proved arduous. Doubled over, they picked at the iced ropes while quivering lips muttered private oaths. Grum watched them for a moment, until a flicker of motion drew his attention down into the hole. He leaned forward, peering intently, but saw only the void. He was about to shake it off as a trick of the storm when it came again, just a hint of movement, of something even darker than the ink in which it swam, shriveled and twisted, almost like—

He fell back as the thing shot forward, blinding in its swiftness. There was a flap of wings, a splash of blood, and a terrible cry that just barely resounded in the din of the gale. By the time Grum had regained his balance, Raegak knelt in the snow, his empty shoulder socket gushing. Already, the thing had moved on. An ebony claw seized Alfrigg by the face. He screamed as barbed nails gouged his flesh, tearing free chunks of skin and even an eyeball. Before he too had fallen to his knees, a silent Durin lay gasping, his throat flayed wide.

Grum brought his pick-axe up just in time to deflect a strike from the whirlwind that pressed him. It hit him like a

sack of gravel, and off he flew into the blizzard, the pick-axe
sailing from his grasp. He caught a glimpse of red-bearded
Eitri, battle-axe drawn, peering up at a shapeless mass of
whipping black tendrils—like a shredded pennant snapping
in the breeze. Raegak, the iron bear, was rising to his feet.
Then the battle-scene vanished, devoured by a roaring curtain of ice.

Down an invisible slope he flew, skidding headfirst on his
backside. His fingers clawed desperately, leather gauntlets
plowing the frozen earth. As before, however, he jerked to a
halt almost before he realized what was happening. This
time, the rope bit into his skin, wedged into a seam of his
woolen garments, pinching the organs beneath. He grimaced
sharply, then reached immediately for his own battle-axe,
his first and only thought that his companions needed him.

That changed when the rope about his waist gave a sharp
tug. He sat up, seeking to find his feet, when another yank
threw him back once more. He knew straightaway by the
strength of the force that it was not his companions who
were at the other end, hauling him back.

Panic seized him. Instinctively, he gave up trying to free
the unwieldy battle-axe and reached instead for his smaller
hand-axe. It slipped from his belt, and he clung to it like a
poisoned man to his only elixir.

Just then, the creature snatched his ankle with a crushing
grip. Grum felt his bones splinter, and he arched his back in
agony, letting loose an involuntary wail. His enemy pulled,
dragging him up toward the lip of the hole that moments before had tempted him with salvation. Summoning his
strength, Grum bucked at the waist and brought the blade of
his weapon down hard. A shriek rang out, and, as the creature recoiled, Grum aimed a second strike at the length of
rope that served as his tether. It split at once, curled up
against the edge of a stone and cleaved by the diamond-
edged sharpness of his blade. As his enemy leaned in, more
carefully this time, Grum gave a shout and hurled himself
out of harm's way.

The fire in his ankle erupted as he bounced and rolled
down the icy mountainside. The slope wasn't steep, but the

slippery conditions would not allow him to slow. Nor did he try. Using gravity as his ally, he clenched his jaw and rolled onward, as far and fast as his god would allow from the savage beast above. He gave no thought to where he was going. His only prayer was that whatever he had uncovered would not give chase.

He should have known better. The Skullmar Mountains, even at low elevation, comprised some of the most unforgiving terrain found above or below the earth. Though impossible to gauge, he doubted he had covered even a hundred paces before the ground beneath him once again gave way. This time, there was nothing to halt his descent as first the fall, and then frigid darkness claimed him.

It was the light that finally woke him, illuminating a world that was both foreign and familiar. It was a world without color, without sound, without taste or smell. And yet, it remained somehow a world of pain.

Numbed, yes, though not so fully that he was dead to its touch. It coursed through him in shallow waves, radiating from one area in particular. Drawn down the length of his body, his gaze fell upon the region of his lower left leg.

Understanding, creeping along a pace or two back, leapt forth like a thief from the bushes. Although packed loosely in fallen snow, his shattered ankle bone lay exposed enough to reveal the truth. His memory flashed back in an instant to the secret cave, the sudden struggle, his rolling flight from the creature that had ambushed them all.

And after? He opened his eyes, realizing only then that he had closed them against the onrush of mental imagery. His colorless prison he now recognized as a crevasse, a scar in the surface-earth whose floor was filled with a mattress of snow. It was this bedding that had saved him, unless he missed his guess, for the rift's opening stood at least two dozen feet above where he now lay. The breach itself had been plugged by a wedge of ice and boulders, sent skidding after him as part of the small avalanche that he himself had no doubt triggered. All in all, a fortunate turn, for the natu-

ral barrier had sheltered him from both beast and storm—the
only explanation as to why he still drew breath.

Any joy wrought by this discovery quickly faded, however, as he thought of his friends. He had to assume they had
perished, far from their homes in the shadow-earth, made to
face death out-of-doors like a pack of wild dogs. He shut his
eyes in pained remembrance: Raegak, *bairn* of Raethor;
Durin, bairn of Nethrim; Alfrigg, bairn of Adwan: Eitri,
bairn of Yarro.

And Tyrungrum, bairn of Garungum, he added harshly,
tacking his own name to the list. For if he did not haul himself from this hole quickly, it would become his cairn. Dwar-
ven flesh or no, he could not survive these elements forever.
If the cold did not claim him, his hunger would. As it was,
he ran the risk of being buried alive if he could not dig free
before the next layer of snow fell.

Tentatively, Grum lifted an arm from where it lay half-
buried in powdery snowfall. He reached first for his face and
then his head, feeling along its growths and protuberances,
tracing the signature collection of bone spurs that marked
him unique among his people. At least a handful of those
spurs—along with his nose—were frostbitten, he was sure.
But a little frostbite was the least of his concerns.

Somewhat encouraged, he shook free his other arm and
worked now to pat along his chest and each of his gnarled
limbs, making sure all was intact. It took more than a steep
fall to damage a Hrothgari, he thought heartily. His brightening mood, however, lasted only as long as it took to haul
himself into a sitting position, at which point, the pain in his
crushed ankle flared to agony. He gritted away the worst of
it, waiting for the body-stiffening waves to subside. Eventually they did, though he shuddered to think of how it would
feel once he had thawed.

First things first, he reminded himself, forcing his eyes
open and his head back. At least the storm had passed. The
sun shone brightly through cracks in the ceiling of his
shelter—and through those covered areas where the ice and
snow were thinnest. Water dripped here and there, mostly to
catch along cavern walls already wet with moisture. It oc-

curred to him that his roof might melt suddenly and dump upon him. But then, that would be almost too easy.

He cast about for his hand-axe, remembering belatedly that he had let it go early on after making his escape, so as not to carve his own hide during his frantic tumble down the mountain slope. His pick-axe was gone as well. All that remained to him was the hefty battle-axe strapped to his pack—that which he had been unable to free in the fight above. A poor climbing tool, but it would have to suffice.

As he reached around to grip the weapon's familiar haft, he recalled his final vision of Eitri, axe in hand to face certain death. In another time and place, the image might have brought tears to his eyes. But time now was his enemy. He would pay tribute to his comrades and beg their families' forgiveness later.

Biting down against the pain that any movement seemed to inflame, he shifted his pack from his knotted shoulders. When at last he had shrugged free, he paused to catch his breath. He then brought the pack around in front of him, careful to set it to the side and not on his lap. He paused momentarily to admire the bag's straps and buckles, not one of which had failed him.

Then he went to work.

Like it or not, he had to do something about his leg. He didn't need to see beneath his boot to know that his toes would be purple with blood loss. Judging by its mashed appearance, the limb was lost to him, if not now, then by the time he dragged it back to Ungarveld. But fresh wounds were often deceiving, and he preferred that a surgeon make the final determination—not to mention any amputation. Still, he could not have it flinging about, threatening his climb at every pull.

After some quick rummaging, he pulled free an unguent, then changed his mind and took three long draughts from his mead cask. Only then did he dip his fingers in the salve with grim intent. Rather than cut away his boot and leave his foot exposed, he reached carefully inside the padded interior . . .

A mere brush against the damaged area was like bathing it in molten metal. His resulting bellow echoed in the confines of the narrow cavern and within the canyons of his throbbing ears.

The noise, as much as the pain, gave him pause. He bit off his own scream—nearly taking his tongue off in the bargain—and shook his head, which clenched and boiled up like a blister. As the spasms wracked his body, he listened intently, fearful of what monsters the outburst might bring down upon him.

But as the moments passed, and the only sounds remained those muffled by the closeness of his icy tomb, he began to relax and think clearly once more. Had the creature from above wanted him, it would have sniffed him out the night before. His trek had taken him into the southern reaches of the Skullmars along the eastern coastline. His friends were dead. Just who did he suspect might hear him?

He'd spent just a short time alone, and already he was raving. He needed to get moving before madness set in.

He decided against further use of the unguent. As of this moment, he'd be lucky to die of infection. And its numbing properties wouldn't do much more than the snow already had.

Seeing no way around it, he doubled up a length of leather and placed it in his mouth to guard against further screams. He then unstoppered his scroll tube, set aside the rolled maps of tanned goatskin, and used a diamond-edged dirk to split the hard leather canister down its center. After carving out the base, he had himself the makings of an excellent splint.

Lashing the guard into place was another matter altogether. By his estimation, it took more than fifty drips from Achthium's Spear, though the great stalactite by which his kinsmen gauged the passing of time was far away from here. Still, he only lost consciousness once, and completed the task with no more than a dozen swallows of mead. When finished, he felt immeasurably better about his prospects.

He fastened his climbing spikes next, to the foot of his good leg. He sure as stone wouldn't be putting any weight on the damaged one. His hammer and anchors hung in a pouch about his waist. The rest of his belongings, those not needed for the actual climb, he left in his pack, to which he measured and tied a long length of rope. He secured the other end of a rear loop in his belt, making sure to leave plenty of slack. He could not have the pack weighing him down, and yet, he wanted to be sure he would be able to retrieve it once he'd reached the top.

As a final precaution, he gathered as much loose snow as possible into the center of the chamber, so as to more deeply cushion any fall. After that, he attached his hand spikes, mapped his desired path, and began to climb.

It seemed impossible at first. Just rolling over and levering himself from the floor was a test of will unlike any he could recall. As soon as he stood, the blood began returning to his feet, causing him to swoon with agony. But the mead helped, and the thought of having to start all over again kept him upright. Reaching up, he set his first anchor, buckled tight his safety rope, and with one leg, lunged for his first mark.

He made it, and clung there for some time, grimacing in pain, wondering how in the world he could make himself do this. It would be so much easier to simply lie down and let the ice take him. Yet he was determined that if Achthium were to come for him, here and now, He would not find him lying down.

It grew easier after that, though his pace was methodical at best. From shelf to shelf he hauled himself, doing most of the work with his hands, while using his good foot as his base. Where there wasn't a handhold, he used his axe to chip away at the earthen skin. He set his anchors dutifully, at least every third pull. Despite his best efforts to protect it, his wounded leg bounced and swayed, clipping the stone every now and then, causing him to grind his teeth into nubs. But the splint served its purpose, shielding him from the worst of it, allowing him to continue.

Hours passed. Hunger and thirst assailed him. Grum ignored these aches as he did all the others. He let nothing stand in his way as he drew himself ever higher, until at last, the doorway to his freedom came within reach.

Perched beneath the lip of the crevasse, he paused to gather his strength. Above the sound of his own labored breathing, he heard what he believed to be more than just the wind. There was that, to be sure, whistling through the cracks of his ceiling, but there was something else, deeper and angrier, the unmistakable restlessness of the sea. Had he and his team strayed so far?

When ready, he set a final anchor and pulled forth his axe. The daylight was fading, its red glow through the ice dimmed. The sooner he emerged, the better, especially if he wished to find new, suitable shelter before nightfall.

He stopped short, however, before making his first cut. Once again, fear gripped him, the dread possibility that that creature might still be out there, waiting for him. Hack through this blanket of packed snow, and he might bring his own death down upon him.

Grum growled the notion away as he had before. If that was his fate, so be it. He deserved no better than his friends.

The snow was thicker than it appeared, and more solid. Sun melt throughout the day had helped turn it to ice. Grum braced himself as well as he could and continued to chip away, forced to hit harder than he would have liked. After all, he had to be careful not to dislodge the entire pack, for if he were to do so, he might end up right back at the bottom.

As if made manifest by his concern, the wedge of ice and stone gave a shudder before cracking and shearing away. A jagged boulder struck his wrist, and his axe went spinning into the chasm below. Grum closed his eyes and clung to the rock face, doing his best to ride out the sudden storm. Had he glanced up, he might have seen the larger boulder that slipped in after, skidding down from somewhere higher up the escarpment. When it struck him, his world exploded, and amid the telltale song of snapping anchors, he felt himself bouncing, flailing, plummeting once again, down into darkness.

When consciousness next greeted him, Grum knew right away that he was in worse shape than before. His head rang, and his vision would not seem to clear. The snow around his head was colored pink with blood, and the pain in his crushed ankle reached now through both legs, clear to his waist.

He lay this time upon his stomach, his arms sprawled out in pinwheel fashion. When he brought them in and tried to push up, a piercing agony in his lower region dropped him back and left him whimpering. He tried again, having no other choice, and twisted his head around to survey the damage. A boulder had landed atop him, sandwiching both legs, and now held him pinned.

Turning back, he cast about for his axe. A couple of his teeth lay in the bloody snow before him, and a hand went to his swollen jaw. His weapon was nowhere to be seen, buried, in all likelihood, on the other side of the cavern. If only he might have fallen on its edge, so as to end his suffering quickly.

Instead, he kept himself alive for two more days. Foolish hope, perhaps, or sheer stubbornness. He had no right to expect a rescue, and there was no longer any way to set himself free. He ate the snow, though it chilled him from within, while his shelter continued to ward him from the storms that swept overhead. He became ill, and was set upon by delirium, to the point that he was not surprised when the voices of his slain comrades began to call down to him.

"Grum! Grum, are you alive?"

Grum moaned and stirred, but was unable to escape the haunting echoes.

"Grum, we're coming for you."

He dreamt then that they were there, surrounding him. Durin and Alfrigg, even Raegak, with his missing arm, lowered down in a leather sling. They inspected him, and let him sip mead. He mumbled his apologies, but still the wayward spirits would not let him be. They dismissed his concerns and whispered reassurances that all would be well.

The throbbing pain had for the most part died away, but it wracked him anew as the boulder was shifted aside. There was more discussion, and then he felt himself being hoisted skyward, no doubt lifting free of his mortal coil so as to join the bellows winds of the Great Smithy in His everlasting Earthforge.

The Forge itself was scintillating in its brightness. Grum squinted against its glare as he was brought from the fissure and hauled from the sling. There was much more jostling than he had imagined might be found in the afterlife. And still, the nagging pain. He felt himself being set down again in the snow, the way it crunched beneath his weight. But if he was now a spirit . . .

His eyes flickered open. The glare was gone, blocked by the shadows of his friends, who encircled him. They were all there now, even Eitri, who grinned broadly.

"Thought we might have smelled the last of you," the red-bearded dwarf said.

Only then, as he heard the other's voice crisp and clear in the brine-filled wind, did Grum realize the truth. He was not dead, but very much alive. More importantly, so were his friends, those who had granted him his salvation. Impossible, he knew, but he could no longer deny the physical evidence.

"You're—" he tried to say, but his voice cracked, lending further proof to his realization. "You're alive."

His companions glanced at one another, their smiles cold.

"And so shall you be, my *athair*," Raegak offered. "So shall you be."

The others laughed, grunting harshly. Grum's own mirth began to fade as his gaze shifted from face to face. Something wasn't right. It was clear his friends all bore the wounds from their final battle. What *wasn't* clear was how they had survived them. Raegak's bloody stump was unbound. Alfrigg's face remained a mangled mask of torn flesh. Durin's laugh hissed weirdly through shredded vocal cords.

He turned to Eitri, inspecting the other more closely. A great gash was revealed in his side. Grum saw a hint of internal organs. Like those of the others, the wound remained open, yet did not seem to trouble him in the least.

Grum felt his pulse quicken. Even so, he questioned anew whether he was awake or dreaming.

Then the dagger struck his chest, biting his lung, so that his scream was choked short by a mouthful of blood.

He looked over, gaping first at the familiar bone handle protruding from his chest, then at the gloved hand of he who held it. Raegak smiled and hissed in his ear, although Grum was no longer certain it was him his friend was speaking to.

"Taste, my athair. Taste this realm of flesh."

It was a world unglimpsed by man, a world of mystery and wonder, uninhabitable by his standards of life. Yet there it flourished in the lightless depths, a veritable jungle of strange and exotic plants, animals, and organisms—forms of life that were not troubled by the frigid cold and impossible pressures, or that needed sunlight to thrive. Creatures here milked the earth of its thermal energies, or fed upon those that did. They saw in ways that beings of light could not, and dwelled their entire lives in isolation from the world above—a world as separate and foreign to them as they to it.

Except for him.

He alone among his deep-sea brethren had seen that world and others, he who bore an awareness and experience unmatched by any mortal being. But this was his home now, and he had learned to cherish the isolation of his surroundings, the tranquility of his final resting spot. Untroubled by even the harshest elements of his environment, he had long ago come to terms with his fate, even learned to take comfort in it. It was as good a place as any in which to while away his eternity.

And yet, he could ignore the waking summons no more. After weeks of restlessness, he had at last stirred to life, allowing his barnacle-encrusted eyelid to slide slowly open. After so many centuries, so many mortal ages, it had taken him but a moment to orient himself, lying upon the bottom of the Oloron Sea, countless fathoms below the world above.

A world to which he must soon return.

He shifted his gargantuan body, and the millions of creatures that had made his coral-covered hide their home scattered. The tides themselves recoiled as he knew they would. For nothing so great had ever lived—or ever would again.

Still, even he could not resist the call, that which beckoned him to emerge, to make known his wrath upon the world. So be it. For despite the passing of centuries, it felt as though he had just barely settled down once again to rest, and his anger was indeed kindled. He would answer the call. He would resume his timeless hunt.

And he would feed.